Nick sprinted across the carp
not be far behind. Outside, h
that boldly displayed he and
parking garage he ran up to the second level where he had parked their car. He looked back and saw John run up the ramp. He was almost to the car but figured he had no time to unlock it, climb in, start the car and drive off before John would be on him. Instinctively, he walked in behind a van and hid next to a concrete wall. It wasn't but a few seconds when John ran by, but then stopped and looked in every direction. Taking out his radio he made a call. Nick listened intently, John's voice amplified due to the closed quarters. "Brad, it's John. I just chased Falco into the parking garage to the second floor. I'm not sure where he went. I think I'll go back down and watch the exit gate. He can't get out of here without passing by me. We've got him now."

Looking around the edge of the van, Nick watched John disappear around the corner. There was no way he could get past John, unless he acted now! Running to the rental he unlocked the door, hopped in and turned the ignition. He figured John, now on the lower level, might have heard the car start up. Backing out, he turned toward the exit ramp down to the first level. When he turned the corner, there stood John in the middle of the ramp. Without the slightest hesitation, Nick floored the accelerator, the car lurching forward. John had little time to react as Nick guided the car directly at him.

John jumped to the side and rolled on the hard concrete. Nick blasted past and smashed through the self-pay wood gate and out onto the street. Making an immediate right hand turn he sped up the street but had to stop for a red light at the next block. Looking in the rearview mirror he saw John running up the sidewalk. The light changed green just when John reached out and touched the trunk of the car. Nick glanced back and saw John standing in the middle of the street, out of breath, his hands on his hips out of frustration.

The next two lights were green and he found himself pulling up in front of the coffee shop. Shelby saw him and got up slowly. Nick jumped out and signaled for her to hurry. She no sooner jumped in the car than Nick hit the gas and turned at the next intersection. Out of breath, he gasped, "We have to get out of Pittsburgh...now!"

DELAYED EXPOSURE

GARY YEAGLE

Delayed Exposure

A Davis Studio Publication
P.O. Box 4714
Louisville, KY 40204

Printed in the United States of America

ISBN: 1535331283
ISBN-13: 978-1535331289

DEDICATION

This book is dedicated to one of my three best friends who recently passed away. Credit, one of my three beloved cats, always sat in the room where I write. Credit passed away before this book was complete. I will always remember him as a patient friend who was always ready to roll around on the floor with me when I got frustrated with my writing.

God, in the Bible, tells us that in the end the lion will lie down with the lamb. This gives me great comfort in knowing that pets do indeed go to heaven. Why wouldn't they? They know or do no evil. They simply love and want to be loved. I look forward to seeing my old friend, Credit, when I pass through The Golden Gates. Thank you for your animals Lord!

ACKNOWLEDGMENTS

A special thanks to Margaret and Marie of Davis Studio Publishers. I appreciate their expertise in editing and formatting, not to mention their valuable suggestions and comments. With their help, Lowcountry Burn, first in the series, and Delayed Exposure have come to fruition. It's nice to be surrounded with experts that know what they are doing.

CHAPTER ONE

IN TWO WEEKS THANKSGIVING WOULD BE DESCENDING ON the Lowcountry. It was early winter in Beaufort, South Carolina and there was what Carolinians considered a chill in the air, the temperature hanging in the low forties, ten degrees lower than normal for the time of year. A bright red Ford Mustang convertible sped across the Woods Memorial Bridge. The driver, Brad Schulte, made a left onto Bay Street and pointed at the large banner spanning the street: CONGRATULATIONS – BEAUFORT HIGH SCHOOL – 1989 STATE HIGH SCHOOL FOOTBALL CHAMPIONS!

Tim Durham, sitting in the passenger seat, waved and yelled at three girls who were walking up the street, "Go Beaufort!"

Miles Gaston, sprawled out in the backseat, stood up, waved his ball hat at the girls and shouted, "We kicked South Charleston's butt!"

Brad laughed, turned and looked at his close friend, suggesting, "You better sit down Miles before you fall into the street!"

Tim slapped Brad on the shoulder and joined in on the laughter.

Plopping back down in the seat, Miles shook his head and smiled. "I can't ever remember Beaufort being this excited about any of the school's athletic teams."

"That's because our school has never had a state champ before," said Brad. Pointing at a window sign congratulating the football team, he went on, "Every business on the street has a sign up. This is unbelievable!"

A car going in the opposite direction filled with students honked and sped up the street. People on the sidewalks cheered and waved.

"State champs!"

"Go Beaufort!"

"We're number one!"

Two blocks up the street, Brad made a left into the small downtown marina and pulled into the farthest spot available next to the Beaufort River. It was late Saturday evening and the shops lining Bay Street were closed for the day. The parking lot, which was normally crammed with tourists, was practically empty. To the left the Beaufort Marina dock jutted out into the river, boats of all shapes and sizes anchored to the slatted wood walkway. On the right the Beaufort River disappeared in the distance. The sun had set in the west and soon darkness would settle in over Beaufort.

Jumping out of the car, Brad reached for the edge of the folded convertible top and ordered Tim, "Give me a hand putting the top up. If we don't it's gonna be a cold ride out to Fripp." Miles sank down in the seat while his two longtime friends pulled the top forward and secured it to the front windshield. Climbing back in the driver's side, Brad reached beneath the seat, produced a full bottle of Kentucky bourbon, and held it up. "Considering this is our last year together, I think a drink is in line."

Miles leaned up in between the front seat in amazement and asked, "Where did you get that?"

Unscrewing the top, Brad smiled, "I got it out of my father's liquor cabinet. He's got that thing so stocked, he'll never know the difference."

Tim nervously looked across the parking lot and then toward the street. "You better keep that bottle out of sight. With the entire high school, not to mention everyone in town out celebrating our victory, the cops will be out in full force."

Lowering the bottle to his lap, Brad then raised it to his lips and took a long swig. Swallowing the bourbon, he pointed at the bottle and remarked, "Now that's some good stuff!"

Tim, still searching the surrounding area for the police, took the bottle and commented, "I've known you for what...seventeen years and I never knew you drank?"

"I don't drink as a general rule, but for the past two years or so, I've been stealing a drink now and then from my father's cabinet. I'm hardly what you would call a serious drinker. Hell, most kids we know spill more alcohol in a year's time than I drink! Go on, take a swig. We deserve to celebrate. After all, we're the state champs!"

Checking the street once again, Tim took a short drink, swallowed and made a sour face. "I guess you have to acquire a taste for this stuff." Taking another swallow, he smiled and commented, "But it does go down smooth." Handing the bottle to Miles, he remarked, "Bottoms up ol' pal!"

Miles reluctantly took the bottle, but hesitated in drinking any of the bourbon. "If my mother and father knew I was drinking with you guys, they'd beat me within an inch of my life. I've never seen them take a drink. We don't even have any sort of alcohol in our house."

Tim looked at Brad and spoke, "I think we might have a problem here. It seems ol' Miles might be just as afraid of drinking as he is of girls."

Embarrassed, Miles sat forward and braced himself, "The hell you say!" Following three long swigs, he handed the bottle back to Brad, coughed and gagged. "God, why do people drink? This stuff doesn't even taste good. It reminds me of the first *and last* time I tried to smoke a cigarette. One puff was enough for me. It was sickening. Why on earth anyone in their right mind would want to suck cigarette smoke down into their lungs is beyond me." Gesturing at the bottle, he elaborated, "Now that I've had a few swallows of alcohol, I can't understand why people drink either."

Taking a short drink from the bottle, Brad held up an index finger to make a point. "I can't begin to tell you why people drink, but I can tell you why we are." Holding up the bottle, he stated enthusiastically, "First of all, we're celebrating the fact that we are the South Carolina State High School Football Champions and that's something no one will ever be able to take away from us. We earned it. Secondly, we are drinking because this coming summer will be our last together. Come June we'll all be graduating and then next fall we'll be off to different colleges. I'll be off to Pennsylvania to attend Penn State, Tim here is going down to Texas to play football for the Aggies and you Miles will be gracing the campus of the University of South Carolina." Handing the bottle across the seat to Tim, he went on, "Tim and I have been friends since we were born, so to speak. We've known each other for almost eighteen years. Our parents lived, have continued to live on the same street, and knew each other before we even came into this world. We were born on the same day and actually raised as brothers. When we were younger we stayed at each other's house overnight more times than I can count. We went to summer camp together, went on vacation with our families together. We were, and still are, like brothers."

Reaching for the bottle, Tim took a snort and then held it up toasting his two best friends. "Around the neighborhood we were known as the Dynamic Duo." Looking at Miles, he explained, "And then we met ol' Miles here." He looked directly at Brad and asked, "Do you remember the day Miles moved into the neighborhood?"

"You bet I do. We were six years old. I remember it like it was yesterday. We were up the street throwing that old football we had back and forth. Miles was sitting in a chair in the front yard of his new home while the movers went about assisting his folks move in. I threw you a long pass, which sailed over your head and bounced in the street. Miles got up and tossed the ball back to us. I recall it was a horrible throw. We walked up the street, introduced ourselves, and learned you had just moved from Arkansas with your folks, Miles. When we found out you didn't play football, let alone any other sport, we laughed and told you how Tim and I had been practicing our football skills since we were three years old. I was always the quarterback and Tim was the tight end. We practiced every day rain or shine and by the time we were six, I could toss the ball better than a lot of ten year olds in the neighborhood. Tim was fast as lightning. We'd spend an entire day running plays and dreaming of the day when we would be able to be on a real football team."

"I remember that day," added Tim. "Miles just stood there listening to us go on and on about how much we liked football, when all of a sudden, he yells, 'Back in Arkansas I was the fastest runner in the town where I lived."

Miles scooted forward and took the bottle. Following a long drink, he made a strange face when the liquor ran down his throat. "That's right. I was the fastest kid back home in Arkansas. Then, Brad here speaks up and says there is no one faster than you Tim. We agreed to a footrace the next day between Tim and me. I showed up the next morning wearing red high top sneakers. I remember you both laughing at me. Brad walked up the street to the corner and held his hat in the air. When he lowered that hat, we both took off."

Tim reached in the backseat and grabbed the bottle. "I remember that day. You smoked me. It wasn't even close. I couldn't believe how fast you were."

Brad smiled and added, "And from that day on we were no longer the Dynamic Duo, but The Three Musketeers."

Tim gestured wildly. "All for one and one for all. You, Miles, became our running back. We practiced every day until we were like a machine. Between my catching skills, Brad's ability to throw and Miles running the football we were a force to be reckoned with. I remember the next year when we played Pee Wee Football. We tore the league up and went undefeated."

"I remember that," said Miles, reaching for the bottle again. "Remember how pissed off all the parents were on the opposing teams. They wanted the three of us to be split up the next year because they thought it was unfair we were on the same team."

"And the next year the league did try to split us up," said Tim.

Miles took another swig and agreed, "Yeah, they did, but we refused to play unless they kept us together. Do you recall how mad our parents were because we refused to play on different teams?"

Brad nodded and spoke, "I remember my parents talking with me about the situation. My Mom was really ticked off and told me in life I wasn't always going to get my way. But my Dad, he went along with my wishes, saying he understood what it was like to have true friends and that was far more important than playing football."

Miles offered the bottle to Tim, who raised his hand and refused, "I've had enough."

Brad did likewise, waving the bottle off.

Miles took yet another gulp, belched and sat back in the seat. "Your Dad was right, Brad. There is nothing like having true friends. I've known you two guys for twelve years now. I couldn't ask for better friends." Taking another short swallow, he went on, "God, we've had some great times growing up together. After we refused to play in the Pee Wee League, we practiced on our own for the next two years until we went to middle school where they couldn't split us up. We went undefeated for the next three years; me the running back, Brad the quarterback and Tim the tight end. That's when *everyone* started to call us The Three Musketeers."

Brad reached in the backseat for the bourbon. "I think we better put a cork in this bottle. I think you've had enough Miles."

Miles took one last drink and gave up the bourbon. Sitting back, he placed his hand on his forehead and stated, "You may be right. I feel sort of dizzy."

Jamming the bottle under the seat, Brad started the car and backed out. "We need to start down to Fripp for the party."

Miles lay down in the seat and curled up in a fetal position. "I think I'll take a short snooze."

Tim shook his head. "We shouldn't have let him drink so much."

"Don't worry, he'll be fine," remarked Brad.

Crossing the bridge they entered Lady's Island when Tim stuck his head out the open window. "That bourbon really has a kick. I think I'm getting a little tipsy myself."

Brad looked in the backseat at Miles who was either sleeping or had passed out. Tim's shoulder length hair blew in the breeze while he took a number of deep breaths. Brad shook his head and said to himself, "Lightweights!"

Tim, now completely back in the confines of the car, picked up on their previous conversation at the marina. "Yeah, we really beat the crap out of all the schools we played in middle school. We were undefeated for three years. Do you remember when Coach Lambert from the high school came to our final game? Later that week, he came to each of our homes and talked with us and our parents, telling us how excited he was and how he was looking forward to the three of us attending and playing football for the Beaufort Eagles."

Stopping for a red light, Brad recalled the good ol' days. "Yeah, I remember when all that happened. That was back four years ago and here we are…state champs! Our freshman year was rough. Remember how we lost our first three games? Our offensive and defensive line left a lot to be desired. I kept getting sacked and the linemen were not opening any holes for Miles to run through. By the time we got things straightened out, even though we won our last seven games that year, we came in second place in our district."

Tim kicked off his deck shoes and placed his feet on the dashboard. "Yeah, but the next three years we won every game we played, well, except for the state championship game during our sophomore and junior years. Those kids from South Charleston were tough." Drumming his fingers on the dash in a make believe drumroll, he announced with great pride, "But then this year, our senior year, we went undefeated, played the powerful South Charleston team and spanked them 33-0." Sitting up straight in the seat he puffed out his chest and yelled, "We are the state champs!" Slouching back down in the seat, he asked, "So what's the deal on this party we're supposed to go to?"

The light changed and Brad hit the gas and shifted into first gear. "It's over on Fripp Island at Abigail James' house." Correcting himself, he went on to explain, "Well, it's really not at her house. Her old man, the one and only Bernard P. James, has rented the Olympic Pool Village at John Fripp Villas and the tennis courts across the street. He's putting on a huge barbeque and there's going to be a rock band there. I guess everyone from the high school is going to show up. Bringing home the state championship is probably the biggest thing that has ever happened at Beaufort High."

Tim shook his head in wonder. "Abigail James. Now there's a girl that's hard to figure. She is, easily, the most attractive high school girl I've ever laid my eyes on. Intelligent, straight A student, popular. Her father, ol' Bernard, has more money than you can imagine. She'll be going to college next year at Cornell up in New York State. She's got everything going for her, and yet she is the most promiscuous girl in school."

Brad agreed. "That's an understatement to say the least. Abigail James has sat on more laps than a package of napkins. Her casual sexual encounters at school include just about every male except me, you, and ol' Miles there. Abby is definitely sexually indiscriminate. I can't imagine why she is going to college. Her old man has millions. He buys her whatever she wants. College education or not, she'll never have to work a day in her life. She'll probably bed half the male population up there at Cornell, then wind up marrying a wealthy kid who is destined to be a brain surgeon. Wealthy people like the James family live their lives at a different level than normal folks like us. Don't get me wrong. Abby's a nice kid. Pleasant to talk to, nice to be around…but dangerous to get involved with. Because she has access to an endless supply of money, her value system is skewed. She's with a different guy every week. I guess because she can get anything she desires, she must be hard to please."

Tim turned and looked at his sleeping friend. "Our ol' buddy, Miles, is the exact opposite of Abigail. She has practically been with every boy in school while Miles remains a virgin. It's hard to believe. The boy is almost eighteen and yet still has never experienced the pleasure of a good sexual relationship, be it a one-nighter or one of a serious nature."

Brad laughed. "You kill me, Tim. There you sit giving out advice on sexual activities when you yourself have only been with one girl in your life. Why, you were just like Miles until you met LuAnn. You started dating our freshman year and you've never even considered being with another girl."

Tim frowned. "I guess you're right about that, but LuAnn is the girl for me. After we both finish college we're going to get married. I consider myself lucky to have discovered the love of my life at such a young age. Miles here hasn't even gotten started yet and you, well, you always have a good looking girl on your arm."

"Well, I do have to admit being the quarterback of the high school football team does have its perks. Girls seem to be drawn to me like a magnet. But, here's the thing. My main focus has always been on football. I've dated a lot of girls and even had a good ol' roll in the hay with a couple of them. I've always been careful not to get too involved. Hell, I'm only eighteen. There's lots of time for me to find the right girl." Looking in the rearview mirror, Brad laughed and angled his thumb toward the backseat. "I guess Miles is getting a late start in life when it comes to girls, but in the end he could wind up having more children than you and I put together."

"Now that's hard to imagine," said Tim. "Look at all the times we tried to line him up with a date. He'd get so nervous, he couldn't even talk let alone make a move on a girl. He's just plain afraid of the opposite sex."

"You know there's talk around school," said Brad, "that besides the fact Miles is a hell of a football player, some kids think he's queer."

Tim objected, "Now you and I both know that's a lot of crap. We've talked about that very fact with Miles and he has always assured us he is straight. The plain fact of the matter is he's just nervous around girls." Snapping his fingers, he continued, "Ya know, all those times we tried to set him up with a date, we were stupid. I mean as shy as Miles is he needs a girl with some experience. We should have tried to line him up with Abigail James. If anyone could get him over his fear of girls and introduce him to the world of sex, it would be Abby."

"There's no way Miles Gaston could even begin to handle a girl like her. She's far too experienced for him. Why she'd chew him up and spit him out. No, he needs a girl that's shy…like he is."

Cruising down the Sea Island Parkway at nearly sixty miles an hour, Brad did a double take and slowed the Mustang down. "Did you see that sports car back there parked on the side of the road?"

"No, I was too busy listening to you."

Looking in the rearview mirror, Brad explained, "Speak of the devil, I swear that was Abigail James' little yellow Miata and the person lifting the hood is none other than Abby herself." Pulling to the side of the road, Brad downshifted and made a quick U-turn.

"Where the hell are you going?" probed Tim.

"I'm going back to see if it's her. She might need some assistance."

The quick U-turn caused Miles in the back to sit up, but then he lay back down without saying a word.

As they got closer to the tiny sports car, Tim pointed, "I'll be damned! It is Abigail James."

Making yet another U-turn, Brad crossed the road and pulled in behind the Miata. The girl who had been looking beneath the hood stepped around to the side of the car when Brad brought the Mustang to a complete stop. Noticing Brad's car, she walked to the back of the Miata, waved at the boys and shouted, "I was starting to think no one was going to stop and give me a hand."

Looking out the front windshield, Tim shook his head. "God, she is gorgeous."

Abby went into a sexy pose and gave the boys a provocative salute which was followed by Tim's description, "Just look at those long tan legs, short white skirt, yellow, low cut tank top, that blond hair, the lips; she's got the whole package. I'd say she's dressed to kill!"

Getting out of the Mustang, Brad gestured with his head, "C'mon let's see if we can lend a hand to a damsel in distress."

Tim, now out of the car, asked, "Should I get Miles up?"

"No, let him sleep it off."

"Well, well," said Abby. "If it isn't two of The Three Musketeers come to rescue me. I see you have your football jerseys on. Number 6 and number 23. Where's number 17?"

Brad approached and nodded back toward the Mustang. "He's passed out in the backseat." Looking around Abby he pointed at the hood. "Car troubles?"

Abby, who could curse with the best, answered, "Damn right. Stupid assed car has only got two thousand miles on it and the son of a bitch still broke down!"

Brad walked past her and offered, "Let's have a look under the hood."

Tim followed as Abby brushed long locks of hair from her face and winked at him, "Hey Tim, what's up?"

"Nothing much. We were just heading out to Fripp for the party. We'll see if we can get your car started."

At the front of the car, Tim shot her a look and she responded by licking her moist red lips followed by a wide smile.

Leaning down into the engine beneath the hood, Tim thumped Brad on his arm. "What the hell are we doing? You don't know the first thing about cars and I sure as hell don't."

"I know, I know," mumbled Brad, "but we don't want to look like idiots. It's a man thing. Listen, we'll pull on a few wires and bang around some, ask her to try and start the car, which it more than likely won't, then we'll drop her off wherever she's going."

"I sure hope so. She just gave me a look like she wanted to eat me alive! I can't afford to get involved with the likes of Abigail James. LuAnn, well, she just wouldn't understand. I say we get out of here before she gets any ideas."

Giving Tim an odd look, Brad gave a meaningless tug on a set of wires and responded, "Look, we can't leave her out here on the side of the road. It's gonna get dark in a half hour. We'll do the right thing and drop her wherever she wants to go. Now, what's wrong with that? Surely LuAnn wouldn't be pissed off at you for helping someone out...would she?"

"I guess not."

"Good, now act like a mechanic and bang around over on your side. In a minute or so, we'll ask her to give it a try."

Seconds later, Brad and Tim stepped around the side of the car and confronted Abby. Placing his hands on his hips, Brad tried to speak in a professional manner, "I made a slight adjustment on your distributor cap. Climb in and give it a try."

Giving him the once over from head to toe, Abby opened the car door, climbed in and turned the ignition key. Not a sound came from the engine. Brad leaned in the window and suggested, "Try again." She turned the key with the same result, nothing.

Pointing at the gas gauge, Brad spoke, "Are you sure you're not out of gas?"

Without even looking at the gauge she signaled him to back up, got back out and flipped her long hair. "I may be blond, but I'm not that stupid. I just filled up earlier tonight."

Tim joined in on the conversation. "Where were you going when you broke down?"

"Out to Fripp. Isn't that where everyone's going?"

Tim, feeling stupid, answered, "I guess so."

Brad gestured at the Mustang and then pointed down the Sea Island Parkway. "Of course, we're going to the party. Tell ya what. What say we give you a lift over there? You can always call and get your car towed tomorrow."

Kicking the front tire viciously with her foot, she cursed, "Damn car. I hope somebody steals this piece of crap. I need to talk to my father about getting me a more dependable car." Without waiting for a response from either Brad or Tim she strutted back to the Mustang and waited for one of them to open the door. Tim was the first to react as he ran back, opened the passenger side door and flipped up the backseat so she could climb in. Seeing Miles sprawled out across the seat, she hesitated.

Brad, now on the other side of the car, reached in and shook Miles. "Miles, get up, we have a guest!"

Miles, not quite awake, sat up quickly, looked at Brad, then at Abby who was sliding in next to him. Looking her up and down, his eyes fell on the skirt that had risen dangerously high on her legs. Looking into the angelic face, he moved his head in amazement and asked, "Did I die and go to heaven?"

Abby let out a loud laugh. Placing her left hand on his knee, she answered, "You're not in heaven and I sure as hell ain't no angel!" Winking at Brad who was behind the wheel, she pointed up the road, "Fripp Island, here we come!"

Miles, still confused, asked, "What's going on?"

Tim, now in the passenger seat, spoke to Miles when Brad pulled onto the road. "Abby here had some car problems and we're taking her to the party."

Miles, feeling uncomfortable, slid across the seat so he could get away from Abby. "Oh, I see."

Abby slid across the seat, put her arm around Miles, and looked deep into his eyes. "Why so nervous, Miles? Most boys would give their eyeteeth to be in the backseat of a car with me."

Brad and Tim broke into hysterical laughter when the car crossed the St. Helena Sound.

Following a few seconds of awkwardness, Abby broke the silence, "So, I guess we're all off to college next year?"

Surprisingly, Miles was the first to answer. "That's right. I'm taking my football talents just up the road a couple of hours to Columbia where I'll be playing for the Gamecocks. Brad is heading for the cold north up to Pennsylvania where he will be playing for the Penn State Nittany Lions and Tim is going down to the Lone Star State to College Station where he will be catching passes for Texas A&M." Turning, so he was facing Abby, he elaborated, "And the word around school is you will be attending Cornell University up in New York."

Giving Miles a wide grin, Abby responded, "Cornell it is, for me."

Without looking in the backseat, Brad inquired, "Why Cornell? New York State is so far away."

"I really didn't have a choice in the matter," explained Abby. "Cornell is where my mother and father met when they attended there. Despite my father's vast wealth, he and my mother are quite adamant about me getting a college education. At this point I don't have the slightest idea what I'll major in. Perhaps, alcohol consumption and dating boys not from South Carolina. Actually, I have no interest in attending an institution of higher learning, but since my parents are obviously my meal ticket, I'll have to suck it up for the next four years." Reaching over she pinched Miles on his cheek and laughed, "I can tell you this, I'm going to make sure I have abundant fun while away at school."

"Speaking of abundant," said Brad, "this party your father is throwing I realize, and so does everyone else in the area, this wing ding is to celebrate our high school as state football champs, but it just seems over the top. This party tonight has got to cost him a small fortune."

Waving off the notion that the upcoming party was expensive, Abby smirked, "To the average person, the cost of putting on the type of party my father has arranged would be considered expensive, but Bernard P. James doesn't do anything less than extravagant. When you take into consideration my father's financial position in life, the amount of money, even though large, he'll sink into tonight's festivities would be like spitting in the river and expecting it to overflow. You have to understand how my father operates. He is a longtime Beaufort County resident. Born and raised right here in Beaufort, graduated from Beaufort High, member of the Beaufort Country Club and the Toastmasters, not to mention varied other respectable clubs and organizations around the area. My father is very well connected. I've heard it said the school system is planning a major remodeling and updating of all the local schools. My father doesn't do anything without expecting something in return. When the bidding starts I'm sure my father's construction company will get the job. So, don't get to thinking he's in love with the Beaufort High School football team and the fact that you are now state champions. Any money he spends tonight, he'll get back ten-fold in the form of business. In short, he loves money, not high school football."

Brad reached under the seat and passed the bottle to Tim and commented, "Maybe our guest would like a drink?"

Before Tim could even offer the bottle to Abby, she reached up and grabbed the bourbon. "I'd love a drink. This could be the first of many for me this evening." Unscrewing the top, she tilted the bottle to her lips and took two deep swallows. Wiping her mouth with the back of her hand she handed the bottle across the seat to Miles. "Have a drink with me, Miles."

"I don't know," said Miles. "I'm already half tanked."

"Well this could wind up being a first. I've yet to be with a boy who refused to drink with me. You wouldn't want to disappoint me now, would you Miles? I mean, I feel so honored to be here in the presence of the three reasons why our high school is the state champs. Without The Three Musketeers, our team would be crap!"

Suddenly, Miles' attitude changed. He took the bottle and held it up. "One for all and all for one!" Taking a long swallow, he handed the bottle back to Abby who blew him a kiss and then took another drink.

Crossing Hunting Island, Abby pointed the bottle at the entrance to the Hunting Island State Park. "You guys ever go out to the lighthouse?"

"Yes," replied Brad. "My folks have a yearly pass for the island. When I was younger my parents took me, Tim and Miles over there all the time to spend the day swimming and hiking back in the woods. You ever been?"

"Sure, lots of times," replied Abby. "My mother used to take me there for summer picnics back when I was in grade school. It's been quite a few years since I've been back."

Breaking out of the dense tree line, the Fripp Island Inlet spread out to the right and curved around the northern edge of the private island. To the left the Atlantic disappeared in the distance. There was a backup of cars on the Fripp Island Bridge filled with high school students waiting in line to get on the island and attend the James' party.

Tim looked out toward the ocean in the distance and asked Abby, "Were you born and raised out here on Fripp?"

"No," said Abby. "We lived in old Historic Beaufort in a mansion on Prince Street until I was five. My parents always wanted to live on Fripp. They were considering building a large house down at the end of the island, but then when the largest house on Fripp came up for sale my father snagged it up. It's the first house on the left after you pass the guard shack, the last house on River Club Drive. It's much larger than the house we had in Beaufort: six bedrooms, four and a half baths, and a four-car garage. We also have a beachfront home down in Key West, Florida and a lavish Swiss chalet in Switzerland. This coming summer before I head up to Cornell, we'll be flying over there for a two-week vacation. When I was there last year I learned how to ski. My ski instructor was a thirty-year-old man. God, he was good looking. Ya know, people in that part of the world are not so uptight about sex. Yeah, ol' Hans taught me a lot and I've got to tell you it was not all ski related. I guess that's one of the reasons I'll enjoy my time at Cornell. I can meet boys from all over the country, maybe some from other countries." Smiling mischievously, she held out her hands and wiggled her fingers at Miles. "It'll be like a sexual smorgasbord!"

Tim looked across the seat at Brad and gave him a look that silently stated, *What have we gotten ourselves into?*

The long line of cars was on the move again and soon they found themselves pulling up to the guard shack. A young man carrying a clipboard approached when Brad rolled down the window. Smiling pleasantly, the guard asked, "You here for the Beaufort football party?"

Brad nodded, "Yes, as a matter of fact the three of us are actually players on the team."

The guard then asked, "Could I please have your names? We have been supplied with a list of those expected."

Brad was about to speak but was interrupted when Abby leaned up between the seats. "Hey Neil, it's me Abby James. They're with me. It's all right."

The boy didn't even look at the list, but smiled and signaled them on through. "Have a nice time tonight, Miss James."

As they pulled out, Tim commented, "Well that was rather amazing. They didn't even check us out."

"Everyone knows my father," remarked Abby. "He is a powerful man in this county. Why, if I so much as complained about that guard back there, he'd be out of his job before morning."

The posted speed limit on the island of 25 mph had been reduced to 5 mph as the long line of cars made their way slowly up the two-lane paved road. In November the peaceful island was devoid of a lot of tourists, anyone out walking or riding bikes along the paved sidewalk that ran parallel to the street were more than likely locals who lived on Fripp.

Finally arriving at the entrance to the John Fripp Villas, Brad pulled to the side of the road, turned and spoke to Abby, "Do you want to be dropped here, at the tennis courts or by the pool?"

"The pool I guess," said Abby. "I'm meeting a couple of my gal pals there. I'm late. They're probably wondering where I'm at. So, I guess I'll see you guys later on tonight."

"Not for a couple of hours. Tim, Miles and I have to make a stop before we bless everyone with our presence at the party."

Settling back in the seat, Abby inquired, "I can't imagine anything being more exciting on this island than the party."

"I didn't say is was more exciting, it's just a place where the three of us have been going for years."

Looking suspiciously at all three boys, Abby took a sip of bourbon, licked her lips then said, "This sounds like some sort of secret place. Is it?"

Tim jumped in, "It's not really a secret place, just a place a lot of folks don't know about. For years, my folks have owned a rental place here on the island. Every summer me, Brad and Miles would come over here to Fripp and spend a few days now and then. We discovered what we have always thought was a special place at the end of Tarpon. I doubt if any of the tourists who come here know of it. We've never seen anyone else there."

Taking another drink, Abby gave Tim a strange look. "And you say this place is at the end of Tarpon?" Without waiting for a response, she went on, "I've been up at the end of Tarpon hundreds of times. I don't recall any special place. It's nothing more than a dead end dirt turnaround where many people go in the evening to watch the sunset. There really is no beach area, just a salt marsh on the right and a bunch of large rocks on the left. Out from that, you've got Skull Inlet and then on the other side, Pritchards Island. What's so special about that part of the island?"

"That's just it," pointed out Brad. "The small area we are talking about is behind those large rocks. There is no path leading beyond or through the rocks, so most people stop at the rocks. It's a little hard to get to, but on the other side of the rocks there is a small sandy area right next to the water, backed up by a wall of rocks that must be at least twenty feet high. The other side of the small beach is protected by yet another wall of rocks. In all the years we've been going there we've never seen any footprints other than our own. I know it must be hard to imagine that on a six square mile island there is an area where folks don't go, but we managed to find it. The truth is, the three of us have been going there for years. We've hashed out and talked over more problems than you can fathom on our beach. It's so quiet and peaceful there. It's like our own private paradise."

"And you take girls there…to this private paradise?" probed Abby.

"Oh no," said Brad. "We've never taken anyone else there."

"Well then, it looks like I'm the first girl you're going to take out there."

Frowning, Brad asked, "And what makes you think you're going to tag along with us tonight?"

"Hey, you already gave me the location. If I don't go along with you now, later on tonight, I could grab some of my friends and we could head on up to your private paradise. So, what's it going to be? Me, or a bunch of my crazy ass friends? If I take them up there your special place won't be so special anymore."

"What's the big deal?" chimed in Miles. Grabbing the bottle from Abby he took a long drink. "After this coming summer our little hidden unknown beach will be nothing more than a childhood memory. We'll all be off to college, all of us going in different directions. Between now and when we leave for college I bet we won't come over here but a few more times. I can't see any harm in letting Abby go along with us."

Brad gave Tim a strange look and then pulled back out onto the road and continued past the tennis courts and on down Tarpon. Tim bumped Brad on the shoulder and held up his hands like he hadn't understood what the strange look meant. Brad waved him off as if it was insignificant.

Passing Bonito Road they continued all the way down Tarpon, the island canal on their right. The sun had completely gone down and it was dark when they pulled into the large dirt turn around. Brad pulled the car to the right of the parking area and they all stepped out. Turning on a flashlight he had taken from the console, he shined the beam of light toward the rocks that ended at a path. Taking Abby by her arm, he suggested, "Careful, there are a lot of broken shells and loose rocks along the path."

Abby, who had grabbed the bourbon when she got out, held up the bottle and joked, "Yeah, we wouldn't want to drop this now, would we?"

When they arrived at the rocks, Brad climbed up and shined the light back down so she could follow. Miles and Tim were directly behind her while they climbed the rocks. Slipping, she fell back but Miles reached out and accidentally grabbed her by the buttocks. Embarrassed, Miles apologized, "I'm so sorry. I didn't mean to grab you there!"

Abby turned and smiled. "Believe me Miles. You're not the first Beaufort football player to touch my ass! Here, take this bottle before I drop it."

With everyone finally over the rocks, Brad shined the light out toward the water where there was a ten foot opening, the sand running right to the edge of the inlet. The beach area itself was only 10 x 15, three sides walled in by the rocks. The moon was shining brightly and there was a pale glow that fell over the area. Abby walked to the water's edge, kicked off her sandals and ventured into the cool water until it came to her knees. Turning she spoke to the boys, "This is incredible. I can't believe none of you have ever brought a girl out here." Walking back onto the sand, she took the bottle from Miles and drank deeply. "This place is perfect for casual sex or maybe some nude sunbathing or just some serious drinking. You're right, this is a private paradise." Handing the bottle back to Miles, she stretched, turned in a circle and held out her hands. "So now what do we do?"

Brad sat on a rock by the water and motioned toward the inlet. "We normally just sit and talk about whatever comes to mind."

Miles and Tim walked to the back of the small beach and sat when Miles took another drink and remarked, "I think I'm well on my way to being wasted."

Joining Brad on the rock, Abby dangled her bare feet in the water, looked directly at Brad and asked, "Let me ask you a question?"

"Go right ahead," said Brad. "If you've got something on your mind…speak your piece."

"Well, I was just wondering? They say you're the best quarterback we've had at Beaufort High…ever. My question is this. You can pass a football with the best of them and yet, you've never made a pass at me. Why is that? Do you not find me attractive?"

"You asked me two questions. I'll answer the second one first. I find you very attractive and any man, or I guess I should say male, would be crazy not to want to jump in the sack with you. That being said, you and I are cut from a different bolt of cloth. Your parents are wealthy beyond what my parents can even imagine. You get everything you want. I, on the other hand, have had to work my ass off to get what I want in life. You're on a much different socio-economic level than I am. Now, you might ask yourself, what does any of that have to do with you and I enjoying each other sexually. Here's the thing. I've only been with three girls when it comes to sex. Actually, looking back, I had feelings for each one of them. I dated each one of those girls for months before sex came into play. Now, don't take this personal, but you could be with someone for a few minutes and make the decision to climb in the sack with them. I'm not saying that's wrong; it's just a different way of looking at things. Let's face it. It's no secret you have a bit of a reputation around school for your ability to sleep around. I'm afraid if I got involved with you I'd suffer from comparison. That being said, I'm sure someday in the future you'll make someone a great wife. You and I are like oil and water. It would never work between us."

Abby laughed. "A lot of girls might be insulted by your candid comments but I find you to be very honest. It's true, I do have a reputation. It doesn't bother me in the least a lot of girls at school talk behind my back. The point is, I enjoy sex and I suppose I always will. At this point in my life I can't imagine being married and trying to remain faithful to a husband." Leaning over, she kissed Brad on the cheek. "I appreciate your honesty." Looking at Miles and Tim on the other side of the beach, she asked, "What about those two? Neither one of them made a move on me."

"That's easy to explain. Tim hooked up with LuAnn early in his freshman year. Here it is four years down the road and still to this day, she's the only girl he's ever been with. It's not that he wouldn't consider being with you, it's *any* other girl than LuAnn. He's planning to give her an engagement ring this summer. That's the way Tim is. I've known him all his life so far. When he makes a commitment to something, he sticks to it." Getting up, Brad walked to the edge of the water. "And then there's Miles. He's never been with a girl. He's still a virgin."

Opening her purse, Abby took out a pack of cigarettes and placed one between her lips. She flicked her lighter but was apparently out of fluid. Throwing the useless lighter back inside her purse, she held up the cigarette. "I don't suppose you have a light?"

"No, I don't. None of us do. We don't smoke."

Crumbling the cigarette in her hand, she dropped the remains to the sand and looked up at the star dotted sky, got up and joined Brad by the water. Looking back at the other two boys, she stated, "And you say Miles is a virgin? That's hard to believe. He must be the only player on the football team that's never been with a girl. I guess, in a way he and I have something in common. He's never been with a girl and I've never been with a virgin. I've always been with boys that have...at least some experience."

Brad looked at Tim and Miles, placed his arm around Abby and walked her to the rock wall. "I'm about to ask you something. You've given me an idea." Reaching in his pocket he pulled out his wallet and extracted a number of bills. "I have sixty-two dollars on me. If I were to give you this money do you think you could show Miles what to do...I mean sexually?"

Abby shook her head in amazement. "I've always heard you three are really close. To think you would pay someone to introduce your friend to sex is touching, but it's not going to happen...at least not that way. I don't need your sixty-two dollars." Holding up her purse, she went on, "Hell, right now I have a little over five hundred dollars on me. In short, I don't need money. I'm not a prostitute. I just enjoy good sex. Tell you what I'll do. I'll have sex with Miles for free. It'll be interesting to be with a virgin. Now, you're sure he's not queer...right?"

"He's not queer...he's just extremely shy when it comes to being around girls. You saw how he was in the backseat with you. The only reason he didn't completely freak out is because he's had way too much to drink." Looking in Miles direction, Brad turned back to Abby. "I think he might cooperate. If he doesn't...so what. We can't say we didn't try. Are you up for this?"

Laying her purse down on a rock, she confidently placed her hands on her slender hips and looked Brad square in his eyes. Displaying herself in a provocative manner, she explained, "I've not met the boy yet I couldn't seduce, well, except for you. Why don't you and Tim go for a walk on the other side of the rocks? Leave Miles to me. A half hour from now, he'll no longer be a virgin…guaranteed!"

Walking toward Tim and Miles, Abby smiled at Brad. "I don't think I'll need any alcohol to perform this little duty, but I might as well have a few drinks with Miles. When we get over there, I'll start talking to him while you and Tim disappear. In about thirty minutes or so, Miles will become a man."

Approaching Miles, Abby bent down and picked up the bottle, took Miles by the hand and spoke, "Let's go over by the rocks and have a drink or two. I want to ask you something about football."

Surprisingly, Miles got up and followed. He never even noticed his two friends when they disappeared over the rock wall. At the top of the wall, Tim stopped and asked Brad. "What are we doing? Where are we going?"

On the other side of the wall, Brad explained, "Remember the look I gave you back at the car?"

"Yeah, that was weird. What was that all about?"

"I had an idea maybe Abby would be willing to show Miles the ropes."

"You don't mean sex…with Miles…do you?"

"That's exactly what I'm talking about. Abby is up for the task. According to her she's never been with a virgin."

Looking back at the rock wall, Tim remarked, "Do you think Miles will go along?"

"I'm not sure, but he's had just about enough alcohol to the point where he might do it."

Brad started up the path. "C'mon let's go back to the car. Abby said she'd need about thirty minutes."

Tim grabbed Brad by his arm. "I'm sort of jealous. Miles is going to lose his virginity to the gorgeous Abigail James. I suspect if everything goes well, when we next see him, he'll be smiling from ear to ear."

Arriving at the car, Brad gave a thumbs up. "Let's hope so!"

CHAPTER TWO

TIM WALKED TO THE EDGE OF THE PARKING AREA, BENT down and tossed a small stone out into the water of Skull Inlet, while Brad wandered down the dirt turnaround where he sat on an old log that overlooked the tidal marsh to the north. Brad no more than sat down when a car, followed by a trail of dust, pulled up near the end of the lot. The unseen driver turned off the lights and stepped out. The driver, noticing Brad beneath the lone dim streetlight at the turnaround, approached and waved, "Hey Brad, how's come you're not back up the road at the party?"

Brad stood and answered, "I didn't expect to see you out here on Fripp tonight, Chester. If I recall, you've never been much on parties."

Holding up a camera suspended by a heavy leather strap around his neck, Chester responded with a broad smile, "You know me. Wherever the action is, I'll be close by with one of my cameras. I just left the pool. Just about everybody from school is there. A lot of the kids were asking if you were coming. I took quite a few great shots. I decided to come up here to the tidal marsh and get some night shots for a Fripp Island project I'm working on. What are you doing out here? Being the quarterback of the state football championship team I'd think you'd want to be in the thick of the festivities."

Nodding back toward his Mustang, Brad explained, "Well, me, Tim and Miles decided to drive down here and relax before we go to the party."

Pointing out at the dark marsh, Chester started down the side of a grass-covered abutment, "Don't let me interrupt your solitude. I'm going to go down in there and shoot some photos." Waving at Brad, Chester stepped onto a muddy path and continued speaking, "I'll see you at school on Monday."

Brad watched until Chester disappeared in the darkness. Seconds later, he could see a number of flashes from the camera while Chester went about his business. Walking back to the Mustang he joined Tim who was still tossing stones into the dark water below. Bending down to pick up more stones, Tim asked, "Who were you talking to?"

"Oh, Chester Finch." Pointing down into the tidal marsh, Brad went on, "You know how weird he is with that camera of his. He's down in there getting some photographic shots."

Seeing a number of flashes, Tim walked to the edge of the abutment. "Ol' Chester isn't as weird like most of us think. He might be a bit of a nerd, but the guy is really smart. I ran into him one time after football practice during our junior year. He was taking some shots of the practice field. We get to talking and he explains to me how when he finds a topic of interest he takes a number of shots of the area without even looking. Later on, after he develops the film, he then creates a framed collage of the photographs. It seems wherever he goes he always has a camera with him. He told me he has sold hundreds of Lowcountry collages to local gift shops. He also told me during his freshman year he made over ten thousand dollars selling collages. When you think about it, he's really not a nerd but a rather intelligent young man. He's got his own photography business, does a lot of local weddings, while most of the kids we know at school, if they work at all are probably flipping burgers or working over at the cinema. Just the other day some of the students in the cafeteria were saying that Chester was going to college at either Harvard or Yale. I guess he hasn't decided yet. In short, he strikes me as a genius. I mean, let's face it. You don't walk into Harvard or Yale without having something on the ball."

Looking across the tidal marsh at the lights from the Cabana Club Complex, Brad asked, "You ever been over to the Cabana Club?"

Chucking the last stone held in his hand, Tim responded, "Yeah, but only once. My parents were invited to a dinner party held there. They took me along. If you ask me it was kind of on the swanky side. The food was good, but some of the dinner guests there were, well, let's say, rather stuck on themselves. I recall one woman who was walking around. She had her nose so high up in the air if it would have rained, she'd have drown right then and there."

Brad laughed at Tim's description of his past dinner engagement at the Cabana. Looking at his watch, he turned and looked back toward the rocks at the end of the path. "It's been almost twenty-five minutes. Do you think Miles has got his oil changed by now or not?"

Tim shrugged. "Why don't we just start back and we'll play it by ear."

On the edge of the lot, Brad stopped and grabbed Tim by his shoulder. "Did you hear that? I thought I heard a muffled scream or something."

Tim looked at Brad like he was nuts. "I didn't hear anything." Then suddenly, there was yet another scream. "No, wait, now I hear it!"

Running toward the rocks, Brad joked, "C'mon, we need to get over there before Abby kills ol' Miles!"

Clamoring over the rocks, Brad jumped down onto the sand, Tim right behind him.

In the pale moonlight they could vaguely see Miles, completely naked, kneeling in the sand next to Abby who was lying prone on the ground. Running to the rock where he had left the flashlight, Brad returned and shined the beam of light on the couple. Tim, scanning the scene in front of him, backed up and placed his hand over his mouth mumbling, "Oh, my God!"

Brad ventured closer, not sure what to make of what he was seeing. Abby was sprawled on the sand, wearing nothing but a bra and panties. Her face was covered in blood and her body was contorted in a twisted position. Brad angled the light at Miles who pushed himself to his feet by means of a three-foot section of an old two by four that had obviously washed up on the small beach. The first few inches of the section of lumber, as well as Miles' arms, chest, hands, legs and face were splattered with blood.

Tim, standing by the rock wall, with a tone of great fear in his voice, whispered, "Abby looks dead. Don't tell me she's dead!"

Brad looked at Miles who remained silent while he stared blankly out at the water. Kneeling down next to Abby, Brad placed his finger on her neck, waited a few seconds then answered Tim's question. "She is dead. There's no pulse."

Miles tossed the bloodied piece of wood to the side and fell back to his knees. "I didn't mean to hurt her. But she wouldn't stop. She pissed me off. She could have just left, but no, she just kept calling me horrible names and hitting me."

Brad shined the light on Miles' face and noticed his bleeding nose. "You say she hit you?"

Miles remained silent but slowly nodded, yes.

Brad motioned to Tim. "Get over here and hold this light. We need to figure out what happened."

Tim refused. "I'm not going anywhere near her body. My God, Brad...she's dead! What are we going to do now?"

Brad walked over to Tim and grabbed him by the shoulder. "I don't know what we're going to do, but I can tell you what we're not going to do. We're not going to panic. We need to stay calm and ask Miles what happened. Then, and only then, can we decide what needs to be done."

Tim took the light from Brad and winced when he looked at Abby's bloody face. "We need to call the police. That's the logical and the right thing to do."

Miles stood and walked to Tim, pointing his finger directly at his face. "No police! The truth is...I killed Abigail James. I didn't mean to. It happened so fast I didn't even have time to think about what I was doing."

Brad picked up the bourbon and offered it to Miles. "Take a drink, calm down and tell us what happened after we left."

Miles grabbed the bottle and threw it violently against the rocks, the bottle shattering to pieces. "No more liquor. I'll never take another drink in my life as long as I live. That bourbon is the reason why Abby's dead!"

Brad placed his arm around Miles and tried to calm his friend. "Calm down, Miles. Let's sit down and talk about this."

Tim objected, "There's nothing to talk about. Abigail James is dead and that's it! We can't sit down and talk about this like it's the weather or something. This is serious! Why in the hell did we bring her along? We should have never stopped to help her out. This night is turning out to be a nightmare!"

Brad grabbed the light from Tim, shined it directly in his face, and shook him. "Tim, get hold of yourself. It may not be that cut and dried. We don't have all the facts. Now, let's calm down and see what we can find out."

Knocking Brad's hand away, Tim stood his ground. "Look Brad, this isn't the football field where you are the quarterback; where you tell everyone else what to do, what play we're going to run. There's a dead girl lying over there…and Miles killed her. What possible reason could there be for killing her?"

"That's what we're trying to find out! Now, if you want to stay over here by the rocks…fine! Miles and I are going to sit down and talk this thing out. In short, if you don't want to be involved, stay out of the way and be quiet so I can think!"

Miles walked to the edge of the water when Brad placed his arm around him and spoke calmly, "Why don't you get your clothes back on and then you can start from when Tim and I left you and Abby alone."

Miles bent down and cleaned his face with seawater, picked up his pants, underwear and football jersey, slipping them on. Looking back at Tim he asked, "What the hell's wrong with Tim? If he were in my shoes right now, I wouldn't abandon him!"

"Look," said Brad. "We're all a little stressed right now. Just calm down and explain to me what happened."

Suddenly, Tim joined them and apologized, "I'm sorry guys. I just wasn't expecting something like this to happen tonight. I've never seen a dead body before, especially someone I know."

Brad reached out and put his hand on Tim's shoulder. "We can talk about all that later. Right now we need to find out what happened."

Miles sat on a large rock and buried his face in his hands, then looked at his two friends and explained, "Abby took me over there by those rocks and we started to have a conversation about football. She asked me a lot of questions about how long I had been playing and what my plans for the future were. We must have talked for ten minutes before I even realized you two were gone. I remember standing up and looking for you. She told me not to worry and that we were going to spend some time alone. She kissed me full on the lips and told me everything was going to be all right. I guess, at that point I kind of figured out what was going to happen. Maybe it was the bourbon, I don't know. It was the strangest feeling. I wasn't afraid or nervous like I always am when I get around females. We lay down in the sand and she continued to kiss me, all the while leading my hands. After a few minutes, she stood up and removed all her clothes. I remember thinking how beautiful she looked, standing there in the moonlight. She told me to stand up, which I did. She removed my pants and there I stood. I've got to tell you guys, I was excited. It was finally going to happen for me. I was ready...if you know what I mean. She lay down on the sand and held her hands out for me. I knew there was no turning back. When I was on top of her I wasn't sure exactly what to do. She seemed so patient while she instructed me. But then, something happened. I wasn't doing it right. She told me to try again. I was getting nervous *and then,* suddenly, I didn't want to be there on the beach with her. I was out of my comfort zone. I went limp as a deflated water hose. I got up and she told me to get back on top of her. I told her I couldn't and that this was a bad idea. Then, her attitude changed and she became upset, saying this was the first time she had ever been with a boy who could not perform. She jumped up, put on her bra and panties and displayed herself, saying she couldn't believe I didn't want her. She said she had never been this far with a boy who had backed out of sex with her. I didn't say a word at that point. I just walked over to get my pants. I was embarrassed."

Miles got up, walked to the edge of the water, and looked out across Skull Inlet. "Then it happened! She pushed me from behind and called me a queer. I tried to ignore her but she just kept it up, saying what the kids said at school about me being queer must be true. She called me a joke and said she couldn't wait to spread it around school about how I had failed to perform. I did my best to not pay attention to what she was saying, but she wouldn't let it go. Finally, I had enough and I called her the Beaufort County Whore. She slapped me hard across my face. I guess I had enough. Maybe it was the bourbon. I slapped her back and she fell to the ground. I tried to help her up and I apologized. She got up on her own. I turned to get my pants and she kicked me square in the groin area. It was a direct hit and the pain was excruciating. I bent over in pain and then she hit me in the face with her purse." Reaching up, Miles wiped blood from his nose. "I think she may have broken my nose. She kicked me three times and told me I was nothing but a little faggot. She turned to get her clothes and that's when I lost control. I picked up that piece of lumber and hit her across her back. She rolled over and I just kept hitting her with that wood. I must have hit her six or seven times." Falling to his knees, Miles sobbed, "God, I killed her…I killed her!"

"Great, this is just great," said Tim. "What are we supposed to tell the police? That it was a case of self-defense and you feared for your life. That'll never fly. You outweigh her by a good seventy pounds. They'll never buy a story like that."

"Now, just hold on a second," pointed out Brad. "Miles has admitted he killed her, but it was not intentional…it was an accident."

Tim, who was getting upset once again walked over and shined the light down on the body. "Yeah, well try telling that to some judge. This isn't just anybody you killed, Miles. This happens to be Bernard P. James' daughter. The man probably has more money than anyone in the State of South Carolina. This was his only child and despite the fact he may be aware of her promiscuity, he isn't just going to walk away from this and neither are you Miles. When the truth of what happened tonight hits Beaufort County, Abby's father will be merciless and he won't spare any expense to make sure you suffer the consequences of killing his daughter."

"We can't allow that to happen," stated Brad. "Miles may have killed her, but Abby's father will go after all three of us. When they find out we arranged to have Abby have sex with Miles here on the beach and that we were all drinking, we'll all go down the tubes. Whether you realize it or not Tim, Miles might have struck the blow that killed Abby, but we, all three of us are responsible. I don't know about you, Tim, but I'm not ready to throw my life away because Abigail James has to screw every male from here down to Savannah. It's her own fault she's dead. If she would have been more sympathetic to Miles and hadn't lipped off, Miles would have had no provocation for killing her. I for one, say we make this entire thing go away."

Tim handed the flashlight to Brad, looked at Miles and asked smartly, "And how do you propose to accomplish that little feat?"

Brad sat on the rock and turned off the light. "First of all, we need to calm down and think this thing through. Second, we need to take a vote on what should be done, like we have always done whenever one of us has a problem." Pointing the flashlight at Tim, Brad asked, "You believe in democracy don't you?"

"Of course I do," snapped Tim.

"Good. Then we'll take a vote on whether we should go to the police and take our chances or make this go away." Brad stood and stepped toward Tim. "If the majority votes to go to the police, then I'll go along with that, but on the other hand if we vote to erase this night from our lives, then so be it. I'll stick to whatever the vote is...and you will too, Tim!"

Without hesitating, Brad raised his right hand. "I'm in favor of taking care of this ourselves and not involving the police in any way. Does anyone agree with me?"

Tim raised his hand and objected, "Not going to the police is a bad and dangerous idea. I say we go to the police immediately."

Brad turned to Miles. "Looks like we've got two different opinions of what has to be done. It's all up to you, Miles. Police or no police. What's it going to be?"

Miles walked over and looked down at the body, buried his face in his hands and fell to his knees. "I didn't mean to kill her. It was an accident." Picking up the section of bloodied wood, he pointed it at Tim and Brad. "I've been listening to what you have been saying and the truth is, the police will never buy into this being an accident. Bernard James will push for the maximum penalty for all three of us. There might be a slight possibility the police might cut us some slack, but not Bernard James. He'll go for the throat. We're no match for him." Raising his right hand, he confirmed, "I'm with Brad on this. We have to make this go away."

Brad walked over and helped Miles to his feet. "Well that's it then! This situation goes away."

Tim walked to the edge of the beach and looked out across Skull Inlet. "I don't like this. I think all we're going to do is get ourselves in even more trouble."

Miles walked over and placed his hand on Tim's shoulder. "Tim, tell me. Are you on board with this...or not?"

Looking defiantly at Brad, Tim agreed, "Yeah, I'm on board. I don't like it, but I'll go along. I don't know what the rest of this night has in store for us, but whatever we decide to do with Abby's body, well we're going to have to live with that for the rest of our lives!"

"I've thought of that," said Miles. "I guess I'd rather live with this being a free man. I sure as hell don't want to spend the rest of my life behind bars. We have our entire lives in front of us. Let's put this behind us." He turned to Brad and asked, "Okay, Mr. Quarterback, what's the call?"

Brad looked at his wristwatch. "It's just after eight o'clock. We have to get this mess cleaned up and then get to the party. I don't know how this is all going to turn out, but we have to think ahead…just in case. We need to get to the party soon and establish an alibi of our whereabouts tonight. Tim, you need to help me pull the body over near the water."

Tim backed up. "Oh no! I already told you I'm not going near that body. I'm going along with this, but I won't touch her."

Brad turned to Miles. "All right then. Miles and I will pull her to the edge of the beach. Tim, you need to open her purse. She told me she had over five hundred dollars with her. Spread the money around on the sand and scatter her clothes about. We'll make this look like a combination robbery and murder."

Tim agreed, but then asked, "Why are you taking her near the water?"

Brad bent over, grabbed her left arm, and motioned for Miles to take the right. "Simple. We're going to let Mother Nature take care of most of the work for us." Dragging the body across the sand, he elaborated, "The tide will be in about three hours from now. It'll wash everything on this beach away, our footprints, the money, her purse and clothes, even the body. If she drifts out into the inlet, or even into the ocean it could be days or weeks before she's discovered."

Tim, opening the purse, asked, "And what if she doesn't get washed out to sea? Then what? What if the tide forces her and all her belongings back against the rock wall and they remain here on the beach?"

"Like I said, it'll look like a robbery-murder. The main thing is any evidence of our presence here tonight will be washed away with the tide."

Placing the body near the water, Miles asked, "What about fingerprints on her clothing, the purse, the money?"

"I'm pretty sure the saltwater will dissolve any fingerprint evidence," said Brad.

Removing a small wallet from the purse, Tim commented, "God, she does have a lot of money in here." Throwing the money up in the air, the ocean breeze blew the bills in every direction. Tossing her skirt and tank top in opposite directions, Tim had a thought, "What about the broken glass from the bottle of bourbon. That might not all wash away."

"Good thinking," remarked Brad. "We need to locate all of the broken glass we can find and toss it down in between the rocks. These rocks are far too large to move. Between the tides running in and out of the rocks the glass should be hidden. If we locate the label, we need to take that with us along with the section of wood. We'll dispose of those later on tomorrow over on Lady's Island somewhere out in the marsh."

Joining Brad and Tim who were standing next to the body, Miles raised the section of wood and pointed it toward the dark sky and spoke softly, "God. Forgive us for what we have done!"

Just then, there was a series of bright flashes on the top of the rock wall behind them. Tim and Miles looked at each other in confusion, but Brad, realizing what had happened yelled, "Son of a bitch. Chester Finch just took pictures of us. C'mon we've got to catch him before he gets back to his car!"

Leading the way, Brad was up and over the wall in seconds. He could barely see Chester running at the end of the path near the lot twenty yards in the distance. Without waiting for Miles and Tim, Brad sprinted up the path, but tripped over a protruding rock. Falling hard, he yelled to Tim who had stopped to help him up, "Don't worry about me! You've got to catch Chester before he gets away!"

Miles, who was the fastest of the three, tore up the path after Chester. Slowly getting to his feet Brad ordered Tim, "Go with Miles. We can't afford to allow Chester to escape with that camera!"

Once around the corner of the path, Miles saw Chester when he arrived at his car and opened the door. Sprinting across the dirt lot, he heard the motor start up, but then sputter. Miles was running faster than he ever had before in his life. Chester turned the ignition key a second time and the car started. Backing the car up, he ran into the log Brad had been sitting on beforehand. The car went up and over the log and stalled. Chester got out of the car and started to run up Tarpon, but Miles tackled him before he got three feet. They went down hard and rolled on the pavement. Chester got to his feet quickly and started up the road again, but when body-slammed by Tim, they rolled in the grass on the side of the road.

Chester tried desperately to get to his feet as he yelled, "Let me be! I didn't do anything wrong!"

Tim pinned Chester to the ground when Brad arrived. Kneeling down, Brad turned Chester's head roughly and searched the surrounding area for the camera. "Where's that damn camera you had, Chester?"

Chester, now beginning to panic, stuttered, "It's…it's…in the front…seat…of my…car."

Brad turned and ordered Miles, "Go and get the camera...now! We have to destroy it."

Chester was getting hysterical. Reaching up, he hit Tim in the face. Tim tried to keep him at bay, but Chester hit him a second time, knocking him to the side. Chester got to his feet but was quickly wrestled to the ground by Brad. "Stop fighting, Chester. We just want the camera!"

Chester was yelling, "Why are you chasing me? Why do you have to destroy my camera? I haven't done anything to you guys!"

Miles returned with the camera and held it up. "Just like he said. It was right there in the front seat. What do we do now?"

Motioning to Miles, Brad ordered, "Get down here and help to restrain Chester. Give me the camera. That film is never going to be developed!" Fumbling with the camera, Brad tried to get to the film. "Damn, how in the hell do you get inside this contraption?" Frustrated, he threw the camera violently to the pavement, the expensive piece of equipment braking into a number of sections. Bending down, Brad carefully inspected the pieces. "It's broken to pieces and the damn film is still inside somewhere. We've got to destroy it!"

Seeing his camera smashed to bits, Chester struggled to get to get up, kicking his feet wildly his right knee connecting with Miles' groin. Miles, who was growing impatient with Chester, rolled to the side as he held his groin area and mumbled, "God, that's the second time I've been kicked in the nuts tonight!"

Tim, trying his best to keep Chester on the ground, yelled at Miles, "Can you give me a hand here? He's thrashing around like a maniac!"

Miles slapped Chester hard across his face and pointed a finger at him. "Settle down, Chester! We just want to know what you saw back there on that rock wall when you took those shots with your camera."

Chester, realizing his efforts to escape were futile started to calm down. "I didn't see anything. When I pick out an area to photograph, I just start shooting. I never know what I've taken pictures of until the film is developed. You didn't have to destroy my camera. It's very expensive. If you would have asked, I would have given you the film."

Brad was now standing over Chester, holding up the smashed camera. "And you think by just giving us the film that solves everything you saw tonight."

"I don't know what you're talking about. I didn't see anything. After I finished up shooting down in the marsh I walked over to the rocks. I heard some voices, so I climbed the rocks and started taking photos. I thought it might be you guys. I thought you might like some photos of yourselves. That's all!"

Tim shook Chester and asked, "And you didn't see anyone else with us?"

"What are you talking about? I didn't even know anyone else was with you."

"So, let me get this straight," said Miles. "If we let you go you're not going to say anything about what happened here tonight; about how we ran you down and broke your camera?"

"That's right. I'm not going to say anything. I don't understand why you broke my camera and why you're upset, but I promise I won't say anything. It'll be like it never happened. I swear!"

Brad ran his hand across his face, and then motioned to Tim. "Get Chester to his feet. Let's take him back and put him in his car so we can decide what we need to do."

Chester, on his feet spoke softly, "Look, guys. I can walk away from here. I don't need to go back to the car."

Grabbing Chester by his shoulder and leading him back to the dirt lot, Brad said firmly, "Yeah you do need to go back to the car. Tim, Miles and I need to talk about this."

Chester, sensing danger, yelled and tried to break free from Brad's grasp. "I don't want to go to the car. Let me go!"

Tim reached out and slapped Chester across the face. "Look, you need to settle down. You hit me twice and kicked Miles here in the nuts. You're gonna keep your mouth shut and do what we say…understand?"

Chester, with tears in his eyes answered meekly, "Yes, I understand."

Back at the car in seconds, Brad ordered, "Put Chester in the front seat and take the keys from the ignition."

Once Chester was planted in the seat, Brad leaned in the open window. "You sit tight, Chester. You try running and we'll beat the living crap out of you. Got it?"

Chester nodded slowly and stared out across the dark marsh at the Cabana Club lights.

Brad motioned Tim and Miles to the back of the car. "We need to keep an eye on Chester. If he bolts, we need to stop him." Leaning on the trunk of the car, he looked up into the star dotted sky. "Well tonight certainly turned out differently than we planned."

"That's for sure," said Tim sarcastically. "We should have gone directly to the party instead of stopping to see if we could give Abigail James a hand. We should have left her there on the side of the road. Someone else would have stopped to help her out."

Walking out into the lot, Miles turned and addressed his two friends. "We can stand around here all night and talk about what we should have done, but it's too late for that now. The horrible situation we find ourselves in has just elevated itself to a second level." Nodding back toward the rocks, he shook his head in disbelief. "Back over there lies the body of one of our high school friends; a girl we have all known for years. I killed her and there's no way the three of us are going to get away from that unless we make it go away, which we were in the process of doing before the arrival of Chester on the scene."

"I agree," added Brad. "We were indeed in the process of getting rid of any evidence that would implicate us. The untimely arrival of Chester means now we have more evidence that needs to be disposed of." Holding up the broken camera, he went on, "We don't know what's on the film inside this camera and no one is ever going to find out. We're going to smash it into tiny pieces, and scatter it in different areas. If anyone finds any of the pieces they won't even be able to detect that it was at one time part of a camera." Turning, he glanced at Chester who was sitting quietly. "And you're right, Miles. The situation has risen to another level. We are now faced with an even more serious problem than what we already had. Before Chester arrived on the scene it was relatively simple. We let the tide wash everything out to sea or at least cover up any evidence we were even on the beach with Abigail. As far as I'm concerned we were well on our way to making that situation go away and we were going to be off the hook." Gesturing with the camera again, he explained, "Chester has stated he didn't see anything. I for one am not ready to simply let him go with his word that he's not going to say anything about his confrontation with us out here tonight. I'll bet you a dime to a dollar as soon as we let him go and he runs into the police, he'll squeal like a pig. Without Chester in the picture things would have no doubt worked to our advantage. His presence here tonight has mucked up the works. What I'm saying is if we elect to let him go, I can guarantee you the police will be out here later tonight and eventually Chester will lead them over to the rocks. Depending on how soon they get back out here, they'll find Abigail's body. They'll start putting the pieces of the puzzle together and we'll wind up being implicated with her murder."

"We don't have any other choice other than to let Chester go," said Tim. "I mean, what else can we do? We can't just make Chester Finch disappear."

Brad signaled for Tim and Miles to walk a few paces away from the car. "Look, we've been playing football together for what…twelve years now. As the quarterback of the team you guys have always trusted my judgment. Remember the last game of our junior year when we played Port Royal? We were losing the game by a score of 9-6. We were on their 42 yard line with three seconds left on the clock. Our only chance was to kick a long field goal and hopefully tie the game. The chance of us making a fifty plus yard field goal was next to impossible. I could tell by just looking at the opposing players that they felt the game was in the bag. I suggested we go for a flea flicker play. I would take the hike, fall back like I was going to pass, but then flip the ball to Miles in the backfield who would start around the right end. I would fade off to the side, acting nonchalant like the game was over. Tim would break downfield and run to the end zone and as soon as the defenders saw

Miles running the ball, they'd give up on Tim. Miles would stop, reverse himself and toss the ball across the field back to me and then I would launch a long pass to Tim who was standing in the end zone by himself. We pulled it off and won the game 13-9. Trust me now! This situation is a game, believe it or not. It's the game of life and we can't just try to kick a field goal. We need to win this one. What I'm saying is we need a touchdown…right now! The situation with Chester is the same as with Abigail. He has to go away just like she has to."

Tim took a step forward. "Now wait a second here. When you say Chester has to go away just like Abigail, what are you actually saying? Abigail was already dead when we decided on how to make that situation, *go away*. Chester is still alive. It's a little bit different situation. We can't make him disappear." Turning so he was facing both Brad and Miles, he held out his hands. "If we don't put a stop to this right now, we're only digging a deeper hole for us to try and crawl out of. I think I have a solution to both problems: Abigail *and Chester*. Now, hear me out. I think we should get Chester out of the car, apologize to him, and explain he happened to show up at the wrong time, and *we panicked* when he started taking those photos unannounced. We can walk Chester over to where Abigail is and explain to him exactly what happened. I have no doubt he is aware of how she slept around. Let's face it, compared to Abigail James the three of us are squeaky clean *and* so is Chester. If we can convince him it was an accident then the four of us can go to the police and tell them what happened. It's not exactly a way out of this dilemma, but if we come forward before she is discovered, things might go a lot easier for us."

"That's sounds logical, but it will never work. Are you forgetting who that dead girl over there is? That's Abigail James. Her father is not going to be interested in things going easier on the three boys who are, accidently or not, responsible for his daughter's death. He'll want, no, he'll demand justice! And with the money and connections he has, we won't stand a snowball's chance in hell of walking away from her death."

"All right," said Tim. "I agree with what you say about Abigail's father, but that still doesn't solve our problem with Chester back there sitting in his car. What are we going to do about him? If we don't go to the police…he will!"

Laying the broken camera on the trunk, Brad looked at his two friends. "When I realized Chester was taking photographs of us *and Abigail,* I knew what had to be done. Before we even caught up to him, I knew what we had to do. I didn't have any time to think about it until the last couple of minutes. We can't let him go and we can't make him disappear. You guys are not going to like what I'm about to say." Brad lowered his head, took a deep breath then spoke softly, but firmly, "He has to go away like Abigail. He has to die!"

Tim stared back at Brad in amazement and emphasized, "Are you insane? I've known you for almost eighteen years now. Growing up as kids, you at times said some pretty stupid things…we all did, but this, this is, well, I can't believe you would even think that, let alone say it! This is the most insane thing I've ever heard you say." Looking at Miles, Tim continued, "Surely, you don't go along with this insanity?"

Miles lowered his head and thought, then looked out across the tidal marsh at the Cabana lights. "Tim, I've got to go with Brad on this. I agree with you we've all done some stupid things as kids growing up and we always stuck together and supported one another. We've already voted on what has to be done as far as Abigail is concerned. I know in your mind you must look at this situation with Chester as a separate issue, but it's not. It's another ugly piece of this puzzle we've gotten ourselves into tonight. If we don't *eliminate* Chester, the situation with Abigail will come back and bite us all right in the ass!"

"Look," said Tim, "I went along with what had to be done to Abigail, but I cannot and *will not* go along with this!"

Miles stepped close to Tim and put his index finger in his face. "Yeah you will go along with this. I am well aware you and Brad were friends for six years before I ever came on the scene. I've always felt like the least important of the three of us, but right now because I was the one who killed Abigail, I should have the final say on what takes place here tonight. If we eliminate Chester we can still walk away from this. It won't be easy to live with, but at least we'll be free men. Tell me, Tim. Do you want to spend the rest of your life in prison?"

Tim pushed Miles back and looked up at the sky. "You guys keep using the word eliminate like it's nothing. You can't sugarcoat what you're suggesting with fancy words. We're not talking about eliminating someone…we're talking about murdering someone!"

Throwing his hands up in a movement of hopelessness, Brad asked, "We have no other choice, Tim. It's either Chester or us! The moment we let him go, we'd be doing nothing but signing our own death warrant! Now, I'll admit Chester is getting the raw end of the stick here, but if we let him go, we'll spend the rest of our lives in jail, or worse. With Bernard James' involvement in his daughter's death, we could even be facing a death sentence. Tell me, Tim. Would you rather rot in prison for the rest of your life, die a horrible death in the electric chair or by a lethal dose, all the while Chester lives out the rest of his life? We've been dealt a bad hand tonight. We have to play the cards we hold in our hands. We don't have any choice."

Brad's short speech hit home and Tim finally realized there was no other option to what they were facing. His head sank and he buried his face in his hands. "I can't believe this is happening to us. A few hours ago we were sitting back in Beaufort taking a few sips of bourbon celebrating our longtime friendship and the fact that we are the South Carolina State High School Football Champs and now we are about to kill one of our high school friends!"

Miles interrupted, "Cut the crap, Tim. Brad's right. We need to get this thing over with and get to the party so if anything happens later on, we can say we were there." Miles turned to Brad and asked with sadness in his voice, "How do we *eliminate* Chester?"

Tim stepped in between Miles and Brad and got directly in Miles's face. "You're not going to get off that easy, Miles. You're the one who got us into this mess and you're the one who is going to have to do all the dirty work. You already killed one of our friends tonight. Why should Brad and I get our hands dirty? If there is to be any more killing done here tonight...you're going to have to do it!"

Miles agreed, "I did kill Abigail...you're right. But the one thing you're wrong about is your hands not getting dirty. They already are! If you and Brad wouldn't have come up with the insane idea of getting Abigail to try and get me to have sex with her we wouldn't be in the fix we find ourselves in right now. In the eyes of the law you and Brad are as guilty of Abigail's murder as I am."

"You're stretching things a bit, don't you think, Miles?" Pointing in the direction of Skull Inlet, Tim went on, "The fact of the matter is there is a girl laying over there that's dead because you, not Brad or myself, but you, beat her to death with a piece of wood. Now you can slice it any way you want, but the truth is...you killed her! And something else. You were the one after Brad and I voted who tilted the vote toward not involving the police and furthermore to go ahead and as you say, eliminate Chester. So, if Chester has to die it is to be by your hands...not mine and not Brad's."

The reality of what they were about to do was sinking in as Miles bent down and puked. Walking over to Miles, Brad placed his hand on Miles' back and asked, "Are you sure you're all right with this?"

Wiping his mouth, Miles stood erect and stated firmly, "Hell, we've come too far to turn back now. If we have to kill Chester in order to prevent spending the rest of our lives in prison, then so be it." Placing his hands on his hips, he looked up at the stars above. "The question is, how do we kill Chester?"

Brad snapped his fingers and stated, "Something Tim said earlier gives me an idea."

Gesturing at Tim, he elaborated, "Do you remember when you suggested we get Chester out of the car and apologize to him for the way we've acted? I say we take him down to where Abigail's body is and explain everything that happened, that her death was an accident. At some point when I get him out near the water's edge, then using the same piece of wood Abigail was killed with, you come up from behind him Miles, and hit him…hard. It's the perfect solution to our problem. When and if the two bodies are discovered it will appear both Abigail and Chester were killed by the same person, which they actually will be, but the police won't be able to figure out who the killer is." Holding out his hands for their approval, Brad asked, "Sound good?"

"How can you be so nonchalant about killing someone?" said Tim. "You make it sound like we're getting ready to order a pizza. No, it doesn't sound good, but what choice do we have? Look, as long as Miles does the deed and I don't have to be any more involved than talking to Chester about what happened to Abigail, I'm in. I can't believe I'm agreeing to this, but it's better than going to prison."

Brad rubbed his hands together, took a deep breath and stated calmly. "All right, let's get Chester out of the car. I'll do the talking. Just follow my lead. Come on."

Miles opened the driver's side door while Brad spoke, "Come on Chester, get out of the car."

Reluctantly, Chester stepped out and before he could say a word, Brad placed his arm around his shoulder. "Look, we need to apologize to you for what happened here tonight. We're sorry we ran you down and roughed you up. We're also sorry for breaking your camera. We'll pay for the camera. It's just that when you started to take those photos unannounced, well we panicked! You happened to show up at the wrong time. We have a problem maybe you can help us with. You, by far are the smartest kid in school. We need your advice." Turning, Brad started to lead Chester across the dirt lot. "Let's walk back down to where you took those photos. When we get there I'm sure you'll understand why we had to destroy your camera."

Chester seemed skeptical, but became more relaxed when Tim and Miles spoke up.

"I'm sorry I slapped you, Chester."

"Yeah, we really could use your help right now. "

Brad reached into his pocket and flipped the car keys to Chester. "You can leave after we show you our problem."

The fact Brad no longer was holding onto his arm, coupled with the handing over of the car keys relaxed Chester as he walked along, asking,

"So, what's this problem you guys have?"

Brad didn't answer right away, so Miles jumped in on the conversation. "It's kind of hard to explain. You'll understand when we get on the other side of the rocks. We don't know what to do."

Jokingly, Tim added, "Yeah, here we are state football champs and we don't know how to solve our little dilemma."

Brad started up the rock wall. "On the other side, you'll see what we're faced with."

Chester followed Brad up the rocks, Miles and Tim following. At the top of the rock wall, Brad pointed down at the dark beach below. "Be careful going down. It's kind of steep. When we get down there, stay put. I'll get the flashlight I left by the water and then we'll be able to see better."

Standing on the sand covered beach, Chester strained his eyes, but he could only make out the dark shadows of the high rocks on the opposite side and hear the gentle slapping of the small waves rolling up on the beach. Seconds passed when Brad picked up the flashlight and turned it on. Signaling to Chester, Brad spoke, "Come on over here where you can see what we've been trying to tell you about."

Chester walked across the sand and when the beam of light fell on Abigail's partially naked body, he stepped back and asked in a frightened tone, "Who is that girl? Is she dead?"

Brad answered both questions instantly and ran the light down her back and over her bare legs. "It's Abigail James and yes, *she's dead!"*

Leaning slightly toward the body, Chester looked closer, shook his head in disbelief and inquired, "I can't believe its Abby. She's in three of my classes. When did you guys find her out here?"

Brad cleared his throat and explained, "We didn't find her. Actually we brought her out here with us earlier this evening. Things kind of got out of hand." Placing his arm around Chester's shoulders Brad walked him to the edge of the water. "Chester, I know you're not exactly the most popular guy in school, but you've got to know that Abby slept around quite a bit."

Chester agreed, "I'm well aware of her sexual activities. I'm no doubt one of the few she probably hasn't had sex with."

"That's our problem," stated Brad. Lying, he went on, "Abby tried to have sex with Miles when things went bad."

Miles jumped in on the conversation. "I've never been with a girl before and wasn't sure what to do. When I realized I was not going to be able to go through with having sex with her here on this beach, she went off on me and started calling me all sorts of names and hitting me. I simply tried to defend myself, but wound up killing her. It was an accident. I didn't mean to."

Tim remained silent while Brad walked Chester a few feet to the left where the rocks jutted out into the inlet. Summing up what they were faced with, Brad explained, "You can imagine how Miles must have felt; how embarrassed he was when he couldn't perform. She even called Miles a queer and kicked him in his private parts."

Wiping dried blood from beneath his nose, Miles gestured, "She hit me with her purse. She was acting like a raving maniac. I think she may have busted my nose. I'm sorry she's dead, but what choice did I have, I couldn't stand there and let her beat on me…could I?"

Chester looked back at the opaque shape of Abby's body on the semi-dark sand. "To be honest with you I really don't know what I would have down in your situation, Miles. The obvious thing to do is go to the police and explain what happened. You can't just walk away and leave her out here."

"We've considered that," said Brad, "but I don't think the police will look at it the same way we are. Why should we suffer because Abby slept around? It's not fair."

Turning back to Brad, Chester pointed out, "I don't see where you have any choice. It's important you tell the truth." Chester looked out across the dark inlet when Brad held the flashlight up to his face and gave a chilling nod to Miles to strike the killing blow with the section of wood, but Miles hesitated. Brad leaned slightly toward Miles, gave him a hard look, and nodded once again at the wood in Miles' hand. Miles look a deep breath, raised the piece of blood-covered wood and brought it down on the back of Chester's head. Chester stumbled forward but kept his footing, shaking his head, confused about what had just happened.

Disparagingly, Brad, using his right foot, pushed Chester to his knees and ordered Miles, "Hit him again!"

Miles backed up, shook his head no, and refused.

Brad grabbed him by his arm and stated, "You have to finish the job we agreed on. Now, finish the job. Do it…now!"

Reluctantly, Miles stepped forward and holding the section of wood like a bat swung it, the lumber smashing into the side of Chester's head. There was a sickening crunching sound and Chester fell sideways down on the sand, the right side of his body in the water. Miles backed away, tossed the wood to the side, and stated clearly, "I won't hit him again, I can't do this anymore!"

"Look," argued Brad, "if we're going to pull this thing off we have to stick to our plan. Finish him!"

Miles backed away from the water. "No, I'm done with this. If you want Chester dead, then you'll have to do it."

Brad bent down and shined the light in Chester's face. Chester moaned in pain and his eyes were glazed over. Brad stood and approached Miles. "Damn it, Miles. He's still breathing...probably suffering. You need to finish the job and put him out of his misery."

Backing away from the water even farther, Miles pointed down at Chester and looked at Brad. "No Brad. You can't just pass the ball to me like we're in a football game. It's up to you. Now...you have to run the ball! You just can't stand by and watch. *You* have to finish what we started."

Tim spoke up, "I agree with Miles. You can't expect us to do everything you suggest or order. If you want Chester to die then you have to do it." Walking over to Miles, Tim placed his arm around his friend and commented sympathetically, "I think Miles has been through enough tonight."

Bending down, Brad spoke in a disgusting tone, "God, you guys are so weak." Tossing the flashlight to Tim, he then started to drag Chester completely out into the water. Forcing Chester's head down into the dark water was easy at first but then Chester started to struggle. Brad looked up at his friends and ordered sternly. "If you two don't get over here and give me a hand I swear to God I'll drown both of you along with Chester."

Tim, watching Chester's arms and feet slapping and kicking at the water, stepped quickly forward and remarked sadly, "I can't stand this any longer. We have to end this nightmare and then get the hell out of here! Miles, get down here and give us a hand."

Miles refused. "No, I've done my part. You two have to finish it!"

Holding Chester's arms down into the shallow water Tim started to tear up and he pleaded softly to Brad. "Make it quick, Brad. We need to get away from this place."

Nearly two minutes passed when Chester's arms and legs went limp. Tim let up the pressure on Chester's arms and sadly commented, "I think that's enough."

Brad, still holding Chester's head beneath the surface, shined the light in the water. "You may be right. There are no more air bubbles." Handing the light to Tim, he suggested, "Tim! You and Miles need to pick up the wood, including any broken pieces, then gather up all the broken glass from the bourbon bottle and don't forget the label. I'm going to keep Chester down for another minute or so to make sure. If we leave and he's not completely dead, all of our efforts will have been for nothing. Our escape from the events of this night depends on Chester's death. Make sure you check nothing is left behind that could incriminate any of us."

Using the flashlight, Tim located the section of wood while Miles started to pick up the broken pieces. Tim walked to the rear of the small beach and shined the light on the sand by the rocks where the bottle had been smashed. Miles joined him and carefully started to gather the broken pieces of glass.

Finally, after what Brad thought was a minute, he let up on Chester's head, then dragged him back onto the beach and positioned him next to Abigail. "There, that should do it." Looking in the direction of his two longtime friends, he asked, "Did you gather up everything we talked about?"

"I think so," said Tim.

"Think so doesn't cut it. We have to make sure any evidence that would implicate the three of us is not found. Check again, because once we leave we'll never return to this beach."

Tim scanned the beach area with the light and Miles walked around searching the sand. Seconds passed when Miles spoke. "We've got everything. Let's get out of here!"

The three boys climbed the rock wall and Tim turned one last time and shined the flashlight back down on the beach, the circle of light illuminating the ghastly sight of Chester and Abigail's bodies next to one another.

"Let's get back to the car," said Brad, "and let the tide do its work. Soon, within a couple of hours, both bodies, Abigail's clothing, her purse and the money we spread around will wash out to sea or back against the rocks. Either way, we're off the hook. C'mon let's go!"

Back in the car, out of breath from running up the path, Brad sat back in the driver's seat. Breathing heavily, Tim, in the passenger seat remarked, "What are we waiting for? I hope I never see this end of the island again as long as I live!"

Holding on to the steering wheel, Brad calmly stated, "We're not done yet."

Miles, in the back seat sat up and asked, "What could there possibly be left to do? We removed all of the evidence that would point to us. What else could there be?"

Looking in the rearview mirror, Brad confirmed, "We have to wipe any fingerprints we left in or on Chester's car away. When, and they will, find his car there can be no evidence we were even near that car." Holding up his beach towel, he explained very clearly what had to be done. "Miles, you and Tim walk over there and dust down the car…inside and out. Don't overlook anything. I'm going to use some broken Palmetto branches I saw laying on the side of the road to sweep the lot so any trace of our footprints or tire tracks will be erased. It'll be hard to sweep all of our tracks away but by the time the bodies are discovered there will have been a great number of cars and people driving and walking across this lot."

Ten minutes later, the three met back at Brad's Mustang. Standing near the edge of the rocks that led down to the inlet, he addressed his two friends, "Okay, I think we've got everything covered. I think we'll be all right."

"Good," said Tim. "I can't wait to get off this island. I've always loved it here on Fripp, but I'll never look at this island in the same way…ever!"

"I imagine we'd all like to just go home and try to forget about what happened tonight, but our work is not quite finished yet."

Miles leaned up between the seats and in a voice that carried incredulous doubt, asked, "What else could there possibly be left to do?"

Brad rolled down his window and took a deep breath of ocean air, then answered, "We have to go to the party. We need to show up in our swimsuits and football jerseys. We need to be seen together…The Three Musketeers, just like always. We need to eat hotdogs and burgers and drink sodas. We need to swim in the pool and talk with everyone we come in contact with, so that later on, depending on what happens we'll, all three of us, have solid alibis about our whereabouts at the time of the deaths of Chester and Abigail."

"I don't think I'll be able to act normal," said Miles. "LuAnn knows me like a book. She'll know I'm not myself."

Brad started the car and backed out. "Just tell her you're not feeling well. All we have to do is mingle with the crowd for a couple of hours then we can leave and put this behind us forever."

Tim opened the passenger door and ordered Brad, "Stop the car!"

Brad stopped the Mustang when Tim hopped out and walked to the edge of the lot and looked out across Skull Inlet. "What the hell's he doing?" asked Miles.

"I don't know," said Brad, "but whatever it is we don't have time for it."

Getting out of the car, Brad walked over and stood beside Tim. "Tim, what the hell are you doing? We have to get out of here…now!"

Tim turned to Brad, his face covered in tears. Looking in the direction of the beach, Tim spoke sadly, "This was always a special place for the three of us…our own little paradise right here on the island…a slice of heaven. It's so strange that in just an hour or so, our wonderful beach has turned into hell, a place I'll always remember, but never return to. It's seems like my childhood has been ripped away from me."

Miles joined his two companions and asked, "What the hell is going on?"

Placing his arm around Miles, Brad smiled sadly, "I guess we were just saying good bye to Fripp Island. Tim and I were just saying we'll never come back to this place…ever."

Miles looked out across the dark water and agreed. "I know I never will."

CHAPTER THREE

BRAD FOLDED HIS HANDS IN AN ACT OF RELIGIOUS RESPECT and slowly walked down the side aisle of the Carteret Street Methodist Church in Beaufort. Swallowing the small round coriander seed wafer he received during the Celebration of Communion, he stepped to the side allowing his mother and father to move silently into the third aisle on the left, where his family sat each and every Sunday morning since he had been born. Following his parents, he sat on the padded pew and began the process of thanking the Lord through prayer for the gift of the Body and Blood of Jesus Christ.

Finding it hard to pray, he sat back on the wooden oak pew and took a deep, relaxed breath. He had been attending church with his parents on a weekly basis for nearly eighteen years, but yet didn't consider himself nearly all that reverent. As a small baby and young boy he had simply gone to church because his parents always brought him along. In his heart, he believed there was a God, but at the moment the limited faith he did have seemed shaken. Normally, while in church, he always tried to pay attention to what the pastor said and on occasion even tried to apply the wisdom imparted on Sunday mornings to his life. This Sunday, however, had been the most difficult time he had ever spent in church. It seemed to him there was a very distinct difference between what mankind knew and what God knew. He was confident he, Tim and Miles had done everything possible to avoid being discovered as those who had murdered Abby and Chester in the eyes of the world, but was also aware that God knew the absolute truth and someday he and his two best friends were going to have to answer for what they had done.

Following the horrid night out on Fripp Island, he hadn't slept well. He had been up most of the night wondering if they had overlooked anything that might tie them in with the soon to be discovered bodies of Abby and Chester. He was confident they had been careful not to leave any clues behind that would implicate them, but he had seen enough movies and television shows to know even the most intelligent murderer always overlooked something. He was also concerned about how well Tim and Miles would hold up if there were an upcoming investigation into the double murder. Ever since they had been small boys he had been their appointed leader, deciding what they should do or where they should go. It had been his decision to cover up Abigail's death, and that Chester had to die. They had gone along with his decision, but would they hold up when the pressure of an intense investigation invaded the town of Beaufort? Would they stick to the story? Would they change the story or their alibi? He had to meet with his two friends again before school on Monday and go over what they agreed on. It was imperative their three stories were in alignment. Noticing his younger sister staring at him due to his lack of attention to what the pastor was saying, he gave her a look of *mind your own business!*

The service finally ended and Brad followed his parents to the back of the church where the preacher greeted each family when they exited. Shaking Brad's hand, Pastor Jonathan Phelps smiled and addressed Brad's parents, "Am I to understand Brad is going to be attending Penn State next year?"

Mrs. Schulte patted her son's shoulder and confirmed, "That's correct and we couldn't be more proud. He's receiving a full athletic scholarship for football."

Brad's sister added, "My brother is not only a jock, but he is quite smart. He carries a 3.8 grade point average. Even if he didn't play ball, he'd still be able to go to college."

Brad gave his sister a friendly shove and spoke to the pastor, "Sisters. You've got to love 'em."

Once, out in the parking lot, Mr. Schulte suggested, "How about breakfast at the Golden Corral?"

Brad's mother put her arm around her son and answered, "That sounds nice. I don't have to cook and someone else does the dishes."

Brad's sister thumped him on his arm with a challenge. "Bet I can eat more pancakes than you!"

Guiding her toward the family car, Brad commented, "We'll see."

Seated at a corner window table at the restaurant, Brad's sister went to gather up plates for the entire family. Mr. Schulte was about to suggest they head up to the buffet when they were approached by some neighbors who lived up the street from them. The man, loosening his necktie leaned across the table and shook Brad's father's hand. "Don, haven't seen you for what, almost two months now."

Mr. Schulte apologized, "I've been out of town quite a bit on business. We've got a big project going on in Atlanta. Come the first of the year, I should have everything wrapped up."

"That's good," said Mr. Latham. "The last time we played tennis you beat me hands down. I've been practicing my backhand. The next time we play you're going to have your hands full."

Gesturing at a nearby table, Mr. Schulte offered, "Why don't you pull that table over here and join us for breakfast. We can catch up."

Mrs. Latham nodded her approval when Brad's father got up and assisted Mr. Latham in moving the table next to theirs. After everyone was seated, Brad's mother stood and spoke, "I'm going to the buffet. Anyone care to join me?"

Minutes later, everyone was back at the table, their plates full of food. Mr. Schulte blessed the food and Brad no sooner stabbed a strip of bacon when Mr. Latham looked around the restaurant to see if anyone was listening, then leaned forward and spoke softly, "Did you hear the news this morning…about the two high school kids found murdered out on Fripp?"

The words Mr. Latham had spoken cut through Brad like a knife and he laid his fork back down and tried to compose himself.

Brad's mother was the first to respond. "No, we haven't heard a thing about any murders. When did this happen?"

Sylvia, Mr. Latham's wife, jumped in and explained, "According to the news, the bodies were found early this morning. The police know the identity of the victims but so far are not releasing that information. We do know it was a male and a female, the male's car was found near where the bodies were discovered. The only other thing they said was, at this point it appears the two were murdered."

"You say they were thought to be murdered?" said Mr. Schulte. "Why…that's just horrible." Looking across the table at his son, he asked, "Brad, you were over there at Fripp last night. You didn't say anything about any trouble at the party when you got home."

Brad, trying to divert the attention suddenly focused on him, blew the question off, "As far as I know, there wasn't any trouble at the party. Practically everyone from school was there. If anything, it was the opposite of trouble. Everyone was celebrating our state championship. Tim, Miles and I left just before midnight. Now, if something happened after that, well, I don't know."

Mrs. Schulte gave her son a stern look. "Don't tell me they had alcohol at that party?"

Brad, trying to downplay the activities at the party held his hands in the air in a display of who cares, and stated, "Look, it was just a bunch of high school kids having a good time. I'm sure someone probably brought liquor to the party. I certainly didn't drink any and I didn't notice anyone who was drunk or out of control. If these two kids were murdered out there it must have happened after we left the island." Desiring to get away from the table, Brad stood. "I'm going to get some juice. Anyone care for anything?"

No one responded when Brad stood and walked to the buffet area. Pouring himself a glass of juice, he took a drink, turned and looked back at his family. No one was paying him any attention. Keeping his eye on their table he walked slowly past the salad buffet and turned the corner into a short enclosed area that housed the restrooms. Checking one last time, he placed his juice on a ledge beneath a wall-mounted telephone and reached into his pocket for the correct change. Peering around the corner he quickly deposited the coins and dialed the number. Following two rings a pleasant voice answered, "Durham residence, whom am I speaking with?"

Brad recognized Tim's mother's voice and answered, "Mrs. Durham…hi, this is Brad. Is Tim around there somewhere?"

"He just went up to his room. He slept in this morning. He just finished his breakfast. Hold on, I'll fetch him."

It seemed like the silence on the opposite end of the phone would never end when finally, after a few seconds Tim answered, "Brad, what's up?"

Brad became serious. "Look, I can't talk long. I'm with my parents. In case you haven't heard, they found the bodies early this morning. I don't have time to talk about this right now. Call Miles and then meet me at the Waterfront Park in Beaufort at two this afternoon."

Tim looked down the hallway for his mother but she was not in the immediate area. Shielding his voice, he asked, "What do you mean they found the bodies?"

Brad looked around the corner at his table and noticed his father walking in his direction. "Gotta go!" said Brad. "We'll talk at the park."

He no sooner hung up the phone when his father turned the corner. Surprised, his father asked, "I thought you were going for juice?"

Holding up the glass, Brad gestured, "I did, but then I realized I needed to go to the restroom." Finishing off the remainder of juice, Brad walked backwards, still talking to his father, "Think I'll get a refill."

Much to Brad's dismay, when he returned to the table the main topic being discussed was still the recent murders.

"Has anyone been reported as missing?"

"I don't know. Surely the police must have contacted the parents of the victims."

"Well, if you ask me, when you get that many teenagers together in one place there's bound to be trouble."

"Yes, but who would have thought someone, in this case, two of our local students would be murdered at a celebration party."

Brad's mother and Mrs. Latham continued to banter back and forth while they ate scrambled eggs, sausage and French toast. Sitting quietly in his seat Brad looked across the table at his sister, who, not being able to get a word in, shook her head. Mr. Latham remained silent during the question and answer marathon between the two women. Brad's father returned to the table and following another minute of the constant barrage of comments, remarks and questions, Mr. Schulte suggested in a friendly tone, "Maybe we should talk about something else."

Mr. Latham agreed and changed the subject. "When do you think they'll be getting started on the new sewer system they've been talking about putting in?"

"They've been hashing it over for going on two years now," remarked Brad's father. "If they don't get on the stick and get the job started this year, well, with the election coming up we could have a new mayor here in Beaufort, not to mention a new city council. If that happens there's no telling when the proposed new sewers will come in."

The sewer conversation led to other topics in regard to local politics and when the city needed to make improvements. Even though the topic of the murders was no longer being discussed around the two tables, Brad's mind was totally focused on what he was going to say to Tim and Miles. Things were happening faster than he thought they would. He knew he'd be able to keep his cool, but he was still concerned how his two friends would react.

At 1:45 that afternoon, Brad pulled his Mustang into a parking spot next to the playground at the park, got out and walked across the brick paved walkway which led to the peaceful waterfront that ran next to the Beaufort River. Tim and Miles were already seated on a low stone wall next to a large grass-covered area adjacent to the river. Miles stood when Brad approached and commented in an impatient manner, "God, I thought you were never going to get here. I don't know about you, but I didn't get any sleep last night. I just kept lying there in bed thinking about what we did. I kept seeing Abby and Chester laying there on the beach."

"Take it easy," said Brad. "Calm down. We knew eventually the bodies would be discovered. It just happened sooner than we thought."

Tim joined them and spoke, "Right after you called me I turned on the news. It was on every station. They still haven't released the names. What are they waiting for?"

Miles sat back down on the wall and looked around to see if anyone was nearby, then suggested, "Maybe the bodies haven't been identified yet."

Brad joined Miles on the wall. "No, I'm sure they know who they are. Chester probably had some I.D. on him and Abby's purse was floating around there somewhere. They're just not saying much of anything yet until they have more to go on."

Tim walked to another wall that bordered the river, turned and nervously remarked, "I keep thinking we forgot something…something that's going to nail us in the end."

Brad stood and walked over to Tim and addressed his friends. "I was up all night thinking the same thing. Then, about three in the morning, it hit me. We did forget something!"

Miles stared at Brad in disbelief and asked as if he didn't want to hear the answer, "What…what did we forget?"

"Fingerprints…that's what!"

Miles objected, "How can that be? We completely dusted off every part of Chester's car we touched, inside and out."

"That's right," said Tim, "and we agreed the tide would dissolve any prints on Abby's purse, clothes or on the beach. We even dragged the lot to erase our footprints and tire tracks. How could there be any fingerprints left behind we overlooked?"

Brad leaned on the stone wall, held up his hands and wiggled his fingers. "Abby's bright Yellow Miata…that's how."

Tim, with a look of panic on his face added, "Oh my God, Brad's right. My fingerprints are all over that engine and so are Brad's!" Tim sat down on the wall and buried his face in his hands. "I knew something would go wrong. The very fact we tried to help Abby get her car started is the reason why we are going to be implicated. I knew we shouldn't have stopped. None of this would have even happened if we would have kept going."

Miles walked back and forth across the walk, then as if he had a revelation, spoke up, "Maybe…maybe they haven't found her car yet. We could drive over there and see if the Miata is still on the side of the road. If it is, we could dust the prints off the engine."

"Two things," said Brad, holding up his middle and index fingers. "You're not giving the local police much credit. They're not a bunch of bumbling idiots. They found Chester's car not far from the crime scene. It would only make sense they'd be on the lookout for Abby's car. Besides that, it's not like her car is well hidden. I mean, come on, a bright yellow sports car with the hood up sitting along the parkway. I think it's safe to say her car has not only been found but also towed to police headquarters. They'll go over not only Chester's car, but her car with a fine tooth comb."

"Damn it," said Tim. "Why didn't we think to dust off Abby's car? We could have done that in a few seconds on our way home. We drove right by her car. We just weren't thinking straight. When they find our prints on the car…we're sunk!"

"I don't think so," said Brad. "My second point is this. The very fact our prints are on the engine of the Miata could be one of the things in our favor."

Tim spoke up in amazement, "You've got to be kidding. How do you figure that?"

Brad sat on the wall. "Now, hear me out. If, and I say if, because we don't know if we'll even be questioned. But, if we are and we all say we didn't see Abby prior to the party, we'll be caught in a lie that could hang us out to dry. Remember when we pulled up to the guard shack at Fripp and the guard came out and asked who we were? Abby leaned up between the seats and told the guard not to worry because we were with her? We drove right on through. All the guard knows is what we told him; we were players on the football team. The one thing he will recall is that we were in a red Mustang, and so was Abigail James. When and if they question us the police may have already talked with that guard and therefore be aware Abby was with us on the island. What we need to do is be honest and tell the police up front that we did stop and try to help Abby get her car started. When we couldn't get it started we agreed to run her out to Fripp to the party. This will explain why our fingerprints are on her car, and then the guard's testimony about us being with her will be no surprise. On the other hand, if we say we hadn't seen her or were not with her, those prints will definitely bring us down. So, yes we did forget something, but if we play our cards right it could wind up being in our favor."

"This is getting out of hand," remarked Tim. "We're not professional killers. We're high school kids. I've got a bad feeling about the eventual outcome of an all-out investigation; a feeling that we are going to suffer greatly for what we've done. If we forgot about our prints on the Miata what else have we overlooked?"

"Believe me," said Brad. "Our prints on the Miata are the only thing we forgot. I was up all night going over and over what happened last night. I've considered every possible thing we may have forgotten. There is nothing else we forgot but there are a few loose ends we need to tie up and they need to be done today. We can't hesitate."

Tim looked at Brad in confusion. "What else is there? You've indicated that we covered all the bases. What loose ends could there be?"

Giving both of his friends a stern look, Brad commented, "You guys need to get your heads on straight. You can't expect me to come up with all the answers. Now, all three of us agreed to put last night behind us, but we have to see this through to the end and it's not completely over…just yet."

Confused, Miles asked, "What the hell are you talking about?"

Brad sat down on the wall and crossed his legs as if he had everything under control. "The loose ends I'm referring to, at this moment are laying in the trunk of my Mustang." Before the others could react, he explained, "The murder weapon, the broken glass from the bottle of bourbon, and the camera, still has to be destroyed like we agreed."

In frustration, Miles stood and raised his hands in frustration. "Brad's right. I forgot all about those items. I feel so stupid!"

Tim remained calm. "I also forgot about the wood, the glass and the camera. So, how do we go about disposing of these items?"

Brad pointed out, "While I was up last night I came up with the perfect plan for getting rid of them. First, we need to drive over to Lowes and purchase a cheap hammer and handsaw and some trash bags. Then, we drive over to Cat Island to a secluded place I know of. It's way back in the woods off an old road. We'll beat the camera and the glass to smithereens and cut the wood into small sections that we also pulverize into tiny pieces. We bag up the remains, then taking backroads toward Savannah, over the course of an hour we'll throw small portions of the remains out the windows every mile or so. No one…I mean no one will ever be able to determine there ever was a piece of wood, a bottle or the camera."

"What about the film?" asked Miles.

"We'll burn it and once again, spread the ashes over a couple of miles."

Tim started walking toward the parking lot. "Let's get it done. The sooner this is all over the better."

Brad stood at the end of an old dirt road at the end of Cat Island and kept watch for any unwelcome visitors while Tim and Miles went about the business of destroying the wood, glass and camera. Laying the camera on a flat rock Tim, used the hammer they had purchased, and pounded what was left of the square black photographic instrument repeatedly until it was reduced to a pile of small plastic pieces, while Miles went to work sawing the wood into small sections. Following ten minutes of destruction, Brad walked back into the small clearing to inspect their handy work. Nodding his approval, he threw each of his friends a trash bag and ordered, "Put the remains in these two bags then we'll head out and spread it along the road all the way from here over to the Savannah River where we'll toss the hammer and saw. Give me the film. I'll burn it before we leave."

Sitting at a remote window table of a restaurant in Savannah overlooking the Savannah River, Brad announced, "Lunch is on me."

After they ordered, Brad looked around the eating establishment and feeling comfortable that no one was sitting in hearing range; he summed up their afternoon. "The camera, the murder weapon, the broken bottle, the film, the hammer and saw will never be located by the police. I am confident everything tying us to the murders has been destroyed."

"Not correct," said Tim. "We really didn't destroy the saw and the hammer. Even though they are at the bottom of the river at some point someone might find one or both of them. Then what?"

Miles jumped in and commented, "Do you have any idea what's on the bottom of a river? Mud...that's what. Those tools will sink down in the mud and never be discovered and besides that, even if they are, we wiped them clean before we tossed them in. I agree with Brad. We're done covering our tracks."

"Not just yet," corrected Brad. "There's still one more thing I have to do when we get back to Beaufort. I have to wash the Mustang inside and out and I have to vacuum out the trunk and clean it with bleach in case any traces of blood were left behind. After I get that done, we can breathe easy. There is no way the police will be able to link us with the deaths of Abby and Chester."

After their meals were brought to their table, Brad hoisted his glass of iced tea in a toasting fashion. "Here's to The Three Musketeers and our futures of being free men." Following the clinking of glasses, Brad took a long refreshing drink, then spoke again, "There is one more thing we need to discuss and that's what we are going to say if questioned."

Tim bit into his sandwich. "Do you really think we'll be questioned?"

"I can't say for sure but we have to think ahead and prepare ourselves if that happens. The police could wind up questioning everyone who attended the party on Fripp the night of the murders."

"I see what you're saying," said Miles. "When and if they get around to questioning us we need to make sure our stories match."

"That's exactly right," remarked Brad. "Now, I spent a lot of time last night in the darkness of my room thinking about what we should say. Let me run through it and if you agree, then okay. If we need to change anything we're going to say now is the time to decide."

Sitting back in his chair he stared out the window while a large container ship slowly drifted by in the river. "Okay, here's what I'm thinking. We need to stick to the absolute truth, but only to a point. If we are questioned it will be done by an individual who is used to questioning people. Someone who has been trained to question people can tell if the person they are questioning is lying or telling the truth. If we stick as close to the truth as possible, we will not appear nervous or guarded. There are only a couple of areas we need to fabricate. I think we should start out by telling them the three of us drove over to Beaufort in the Mustang. We drove up and down Bay Street celebrating the state championship like everyone else in town was doing. We then inform them we pulled over into the marina parking lot for about thirty minutes because it was too early to head out to the party on Fripp. We explain that we sat there for a while and talked about our football careers as youngsters all the way up until the current time, including our futures as college football players…"

Miles interrupted, "What about the drinking? Do we tell them we had a few nips?"

Surprised, Brad answered, "No, that's one of the things we need to leave out of our story. First of all, we're all under age and secondly we don't want to give the police any reason to suspect us. We don't mention the bourbon…understand!"

Both Miles and Tim nodded while Brad continued, "The next thing we tell the police is we decided to head to Fripp. On the way we noticed Abby's yellow Miata parked on the side of the road with the hood up and we saw Abby herself looking under the hood." Leaning forward, Brad pointed out, "It's important that we refer to her as Abby and not Abigail. We want the police to realize she was a friend of ours."

Taking a bite of coleslaw, Brad went on, "If by the time they talk to us, they have discovered our fingerprints, the admission we stopped to help her will erase that fact as anything they could use against us. We simply explain we tried to get her car started, failed and then offered to take her to the party. We mention how strange it was when we approached the guard shack how the guard let us in due to the fact Abby said it was all right because we were with her. We then tell them we dropped her off by the pool by Captain John Fripp Villas since she said she was meeting some of her girlfriends. The last thing we say is we drove farther up Tarpon, parked the car then went to the tennis court area, had some dogs, burgers and sodas, mingled with the crowd, did some swimming at the pool, then headed back to Beaufort around midnight."

"I have a question," said Tim. "What if we are asked if we saw Abby later that night at the party?"

Brad smiled and answered, "Good question. I think we should say that we *did not* see Abby again. It's the perfect answer and the only answer we can give. No one is going to say they saw her there because she never made it to the party. We have to say the same thing which is good because that puts us at the party when she was not, which means she disappeared sometime after we dropped her off."

"That's good," said Miles, "that's really good."

Brad sat back and held out his hands. "Any other questions?"

Miles shook his head, no, but Tim spoke up, "Our story sounds simple enough but are we all going to remember what we discussed here today?"

"Oh, we'll remember it all right," stated Brad, "because we are going to spend the rest of the day going over the story until we've got it down...pat!"

Tim got up from the table and finished his drink. "I say we head back to Beaufort and help Brad clean up the Mustang. We can go over our story on the way."

Beaufort Police Chief, Trevor Green, yawned and looked at the clock above the cluttered file cabinet in the corner of his office: 7:15 Sunday evening. Pouring himself a cup of black coffee, he walked to the window and gazed out at the streetlight that shined on an adjacent parking lot. The sound of his office door being opened caused him to turn when he saw Detectives Jim Silk and Melvin Barrett enter, Barrett being the first to speak, "Evenin' Chief."

Motioning at two chairs across from his desk, Green offered, "Take a load off."

After the two detectives were seated, Trevor asked while holding his cup, "Coffee?"

"No thanks," said Silk. "Too late in the day for me. I have one cup on the way into work and one after I get here. After that, it just starts running through me."

"I'm gonna pass too," answered Barrett, making an unpleasant face. "How old is that stuff. I've had your late afternoon coffee before. It's like drinking hot mud, so no thanks."

The Chief smiled, sat down behind his desk and propped his feet up on the corner. "Anything new turn up yet?"

Silk shook his head in a negative manner and stated, "We're treading water right now. We're going through the standard procedures and getting nowhere."

Barrett looked at his watch and asked, "Anything in from the Medical Examiner?"

Green nodded at the corner of the desk at a manila folder. "The M.E. dropped off a preliminary report about an hour ago. Estimates the time of death at around eighteen to twenty-four hours ago. That puts the time of death somewhere between seven o'clock last night and as late as one in the morning. According to the report both victims were killed with the same murder weapon, which so far we haven't been able to locate. He found small splinters of wood imbedded in both victims' skulls. It was strange. The traces of wood that were discovered were not from a typical log or branch you can find washed up on the beach, but it was yellow pine. The M.E. thinks it's consistent with lumber that can be purchased at a lumber store, like a 2x4 or something like that. The wood fibers were really old and waterlogged indicating it had been in the water for a long time, so I guess it could have washed up on the beach at some point."

Picking up the folder, Silk looked up at the ceiling as he calculated time. "Eighteen to twenty-four hours would place the deaths about an hour or so before the party on Fripp started or about an hour before it ended at two a.m."

"Or anytime in between," added Barrett. "There were hundreds of high school kids on the island. It was one of the largest parties they've ever held out there." Motioning at the folder, Melvin inquired, "So I guess we can assume from the report the deaths were due to being struck with this piece of so called lumber?"

"As far as the James' girl is concerned, yes. The M.E. said she has a severe laceration on her back from being struck from behind. This blow could have knocked her to the ground or maybe she was already on the sand. There were six other blows the M.E. discovered. They were all head wounds, two on the back and four direct hits to her face. So, I guess we can deduce that during the attack, she at some point rolled over, therefore facing the killer. In short, she was beat to death. She suffered severe damage to the brain that caused internal bleeding."

Silk spoke up, "Correct me if I heard you wrong, but you said as far as the girl was concerned. Are you saying the Finch kid's death was not due to being struck with this lumber?"

"It's not what I'm saying. It's the prognosis of the Medical Examiner. He said the boy was only struck twice; once on the back and then on the side of the head. His wounds were less severe and more than likely did not kill Finch." Sadly, Green lowered his head and went on to explain. "Chester Finch died from drowning, probably after he was struck."

"With the tide coming in wouldn't both victims' lungs be filled with sea water? How can the examiner conclude Finch was drowned and the James girl was not?"

"It's all in the report. An unconscious person or a dead body lying on the beach when the tide rolls in will take water into their lungs, but because the body floats and the person cannot breath, the amount of water in the lungs is very limited. The James girl was consistent with that theory; some water in the lungs, but the Finch boy's lungs were filled to capacity. He was definitely drown, the girl was not."

Barrett thought for a moment, then went in a different direction, "The girl was only clothed in a bra and panties and the Finch boy was fully clothed. When we first came on the scene we were positive it was a sex crime."

"That's what I also thought. I guess that's what we all thought, but the report disproves any sexual activity. There were no traces of semen or penetration on the girl's body and there was no evidence of sexual activity on the Finch kid either. What was discovered were traces of bourbon in the girl's system but none in the Finch kid."

"That doesn't add up," remarked Silk skeptically. "The girl is practically naked and was drinking but the boy is fully clothed and has no trace of bourbon inside him. What the hell happened out there?"

Barrett gestured at the report. "Was nothing discovered from the evidence that was found?"

"There were no fingerprints whatsoever on the girl's sandals, her clothing or her purse. The money that was found floating around indicates an attempted robbery that may have gone wrong. The one thing we did find that could turn out to be a lead is the neck of a bottle that was broken. It was lying about halfway up the rock wall. The examiner found saliva traces from the James girl but not the Finch boy. Once again she was drinking, he was not. They did discover saliva traces from another person inside the neck of the bottle, which indicates someone else might have been at the crime scene. It could be our killer."

"And then there's Finch's car parked on the lot at the end of Tarpon," said Barrett. "No more than fifty yards from where the bodies were found. The more I sit here and think about these murders the more confusing it gets. The Finch vehicle was parked over the top of a log at an odd angle. The Finch kid had to have realized he backed over it. He would have had to be an idiot to park that way. It appeared he might have been trying to get away quickly when you look closely at the way the sand was disturbed from the tire marks. You would think, with Finch being the owner of the car that his prints would be everywhere, inside and out. That in itself seems odd and when you add the fact the girl's prints were nowhere to be found on the car…it's strange."

"Then there's her car," added Silk. "Parked on the side of the road nearly ten miles from Fripp. Her prints were on her car but no prints of the Finch boy were found. There were two sets of prints all over the engine and the hood was raised. This could get interesting if one of the set of prints matches up with the unknown saliva on the neck of that bottle of bourbon."

"This whole thing stinks," said Green. "But it's the early innings of the game. I guarantee you, our killer or killers made a mistake or a number of mistakes. We just have to find them. I want you two to go back out to Fripp tomorrow and start asking questions around the island. Someone may have seen or heard something that might be important. As for now, we all need to go home and get some rest. Myself, I'm bushed. After talking with Mr. and Mrs. James and the Finch boy's grandmother over at the morgue, not to mention the press who were quite upset because we told them we were not giving out any further information until tomorrow morning, I'm talked out. So, aside from you two going out to Fripp tomorrow and me dealing with the press, I'm going over to the high school and set up a schedule where we will interview every single teacher and student at the school, whether they attended the party or not. Somebody, somewhere has to know something."

Brad hung the long corrugated black vacuum hose back on its hook at the Beaufort carwash and looked in the backseat at Miles who was busy cleaning off the seats and the rear doors. Looking up at Brad, he remarked. "The perfume Abby was wearing still lingers, especially here in the backseat."

Tim, who looked in the opposite window suggested, "Maybe on the way home you could pick up one of those hanging pine scented air fresheners they make for cars. I hate the way those things smell, but they do the job. My dad puts a new one every month in his car."

"That's a good idea," said Brad. "I'll also leave the windows down tonight and let the night air freshen up the Mustang."

Tim, finishing up the front seat, crawled out of the car. Brad held his right hand out in a sign of friendship. When their right hands were joined, Brad announced like he always did since they were young boys, "The Three Musketeers…one for all and all for one!" Leaning up against the Mustang, he reaffirmed, "We're going to get through this. I have a feeling this investigation will lead them nowhere and eventually this whole thing will go way, just like we planned. Don't forget! When you get home before you turn in for the night, go over in your head the plan we discussed earlier. We must be prepared if the police decide to talk with us. I'll see you guys tomorrow morning at school." Sadly, Brad's head sunk and he remarked, "That's what Chester said to me when I first ran into him over on Fripp. He was a good kid. I'm sorry things worked out the way they did for Abby and him, but we can't give up on ourselves. Months from now, no, years from now this will be nothing more than a sad memory, but at least we won't be in prison."

CHAPTER FOUR

BRAD HATED MONDAY MORNINGS AT SCHOOL. TAKING HIS seat in the back row of his homeroom class, he thought about how he only had six months left before graduating as a senior. He had arrived at school early and was the first in the room. Within the next half hour, the room would be filled with his classmates, many that he had known since elementary school. Looking around the familiar room he wished it was a year down the road and he was sitting in a college classroom up north at Penn State. At the moment he wanted to get on with his life and leave Beaufort and the recent horrible night on Fripp Island behind. He found it hard to get the bloodied face of Abigail James out of his mind. He shook his head in disbelief while he relived the moments where he held Chester beneath the water until he drowned. His thoughts were interrupted when two girls walked into the room and said, "Good morning."

He returned their greeting with a nod of his head. He didn't feel like speaking to anyone. Nate Reynolds, an offensive lineman on the football team took his seat next to Brad, leaned over and whispered, "Did you hear about the murders at the party the other night?"

Not really wanting to respond, but realizing he had to act normal, Brad answered, "Yeah, I did hear about that." Acting like he didn't know anything about the murders, he asked, "Did they release the names of the students yet?"

"Yep, it was on the news a few minutes ago. They had a press conference down at police headquarters. I caught the news on the way in. Can you believe it? It was Abby James and Chester Finch; the two smartest kids in school."

Brad gave Nate a questioning look and asked another question, "Didn't you date Abby earlier in the year?"

"Yes, but that was back just after we started our senior year. It only lasted about three weeks and then she moved on to that new kid who transferred in here. She was only with him for about a month and then there was a long list of guys she dated." Staring out the windows of the room, Nate smiled sadly, "She was really something. She was only the second girl I had ever been with. Don't get me wrong, I don't want to say anything disgraceful about Abby, seeing as how she's gone, but that girl really knew the ropes when it came to sex."

"I wouldn't know," said Brad. "I never messed around with her as far as dating goes. I danced with her a few times at school dances and we joked around, but we never dated…even for one night. She was a good kid and so was Chester. I can't imagine who would want to kill a kid like that. He never bothered anyone. All he wanted to do was take photographs of everything in sight. They say he was going to go to Harvard or Yale."

"I heard he settled on Harvard," remarked Nate while nodding at three students who entered the room.

Brad, interested in what was said at the press conference, probed, "Did they say anything on the news about what was said at police headquarters?"

"Not much. After identifying the names of the victims, they said both victims' cars had been located and impounded. They said so far they didn't have much to go on. Currently they have no motive and there are no suspects at this time. The public will be updated as the investigation continues."

At precisely eight o'clock, Mr. Tison, the homeroom teacher shut the classroom door and stood in front of his large desk. Clearing his throat loudly he got the attention of the twenty-seven students in the room. "Class! We find ourselves faced again with yet another Monday morning. As you are all aware, we always start Monday off with a round robin discussion about how our weekend went." Thinking to himself and doing some silent math, he went on, "That has been my method of teaching for the past seventeen years. You, and all the students I have had in the past, have always enjoyed starting the week off in this fashion."

Walking to the large bank of windows, he stared out into the parking lot, turned and leaned on the windowsill. "Winning the state football championship has been without a doubt the most exciting thing that has happened to Beaufort High I can recall. I can't remember the faculty, the students, our alumni and the people of Beaufort more excited about a high school event. Sadly, a weekend that was to be filled with celebration and happiness ended tragically Saturday night out on Fripp Island." Walking back to his desk, Mr. Tison looked up at the ceiling. "Is there anyone in this room who does not know what I am referring to?"

The entire class remained silent and Tison continued, "Well, then since everyone is aware of what happened, I don't have to be concerned with shocking anyone this morning. There is no way to sugarcoat what I'm about to say." Tison hesitated, wiped a tear from his eye and composed himself. "Abigail James and Chester Finch were found murdered Saturday night. They were two of the most brilliant students I have ever had the privilege of teaching. Abby was slated to attend Cornell University and Chester had been accepted at Harvard. That being said we will not be discussing how our weekend went, because there is nothing joyful I can imagine anyone could say that would change the way we all must feel. I know you must have questions about this horrible incident and to be honest with you, I feel we should talk about this. But, before we get into any discussions I have a short announcement. This is directly from the school principal."

Unfolding an 8 x 10 sheet of white paper he read the typed message. "All students, teachers and faculty members will report to the assembly hall at nine o'clock this morning. No one will be excused. This is a mandatory assembly."

Folding the paper he tucked it inside his jacket pocket, and asked, "Any questions?"

Everyone remained silent until a girl in the front row raised her hand and not waiting for an acknowledgement, spoke up boldly, "What is this mandatory meeting about?"

Mr. Tison looked directly at the girl, then at the class and explained, "I am not at liberty to give you the details of the called assembly, however, it does not take any great feat of detective work for one to figure that it no doubt has to do with what happened at Fripp this past weekend. I realize everyone wants to know exactly what happened and why it happened, but that is for the police to figure out. Perhaps we should spend the next forty-five minutes trying to be positive rather than focusing on the negative. The healing process for all of us can only begin if we talk about Abby and Chester as we remember them. I'm sure between all of us there are numerous stories we can share about Abigail and Chester." Tison hesitated and waited for the first student to respond, but no one spoke up.

Leaning on the front of his desk, Tison crossed his arms and forced a smile. "Well, I can think of one very specific thing I remember about Abby. It's a side of her that few, if any of you may have encountered. Do you recall when a young girl by the name of Jeanie Schroeder came to our school? She moved here from Arkansas. Her folks, as it turned out were dirt poor. Jeanie didn't have anything remotely resembling new school clothing. If anything, the clothes she wore were shabby to say the least. She never had money for lunch at the cafeteria. She brought her lunch in a brown bag. Now, there's nothing wrong with electing to pack your lunch, but Jeanie's lunch always consisted of a single sandwich with one slice of meat or maybe a slice of cheese. Many times she had to eat tomato sandwiches. She never enjoyed a soda or a glass of cold milk. She always had to drink plain water. There's nothing wrong with drinking water either, but in her case she didn't have any other option. She had no confidence in herself, always walked around with her head down. From my observations, it didn't take long to discover most of the students here at Beaufort High didn't pay her any attention."

Walking to the left side of the room he started down the wall and continued talking while all of the students turned their heads in his direction. "Life can at times be very strange and sometimes help for someone in need can come from the person we least expect. In this case the help came from Abby James." Smiling as if he were remembering the moment like it was just yesterday, he went on, "I guess it was somewhere around a month after Jeanie came to Beaufort, when after a science class, Abby approached me and asked to speak with me privately. She asked me if my wife and I would drive her over to Savannah where no one knew her. She wanted my wife and I to help shop for clothing for Jeanie. In short, that day Abby spent over a thousand dollars, purchasing blouses, jeans, shoes and accessories for Jeanie. On the way back to Beaufort I asked her if this act of kindness was coming from her father and if the money she was spending was his. She told me the money she spent was from her own savings account and I was never to tell anyone she was the one who had purchased the clothes. She asked me to give Jeanie the clothing but not tell her where they came from. On top of that, Abby prepaid for Jeanie's lunch for the remainder of the year. As you probably all know, just last week Jeanie moved back to Arkansas. She came to see me on her final day at Beaufort High to thank me for whoever brought her those clothes and purchased her daily lunch. She told me to thank whoever it was because she now could hold her head high. She was leaving Beaufort a better person than when she arrived. I was going to tell Abby this week what Jeanie had said, but now it's too late. Who knows what Abigail James could have accomplished in life? We'll never know."

A girl, inspired by Tison's story, stood and spoke, "I have a story to share about Chester. It was last year just prior to our annual school Christmas play. I had worked hard and received the leading female role, but was nervous the first night of the play, what with all the parents and folks from town being in attendance. Something came over me and I started crying in my dressing room. There was a knock on the door, it slowly opened, and there stood Chester. He said he heard someone crying. He asked me what was wrong and I told him I didn't think I was going to be able to perform. Chester pulled up a chair and sat with me, explaining he didn't have all that important part in the play. He was in charge of the cameras and the lighting, but well, I was the leading lady. People were coming to see me perform and without me the play would be a flop. He helped me to my feet and told me to walk out there and give the performance of a lifetime and that it was impossible for me to make a mistake. That night, I remember everything going so smoothly when I went out onto the stage. After the play our instructor told me I had given one of the best performances she had ever seen at one of our plays. I looked for Chester to thank him but he was nowhere to be found. I guess life got in the way and after that I never got around to thanking him. The point is, Chester always had a kind word for whomever he was speaking with. He always had a smile on his face. I never found the time to thank him. And for that, well it saddens me."

For the next thirty minutes one student after another rose to their feet and shared a story about either Abby or Chester. Brad sat there and listened, each and every story tearing at his feelings. He wondered if those seated in the classroom could see the guilt on his face. He wanted to get up and say something about Abby or Chester, but his mind kept going back to the beach on Fripp as he pictured Abby and Chester lying there, Abby beat to death and Chester drowned.

While the minutes ticked by he tried to think of something nice he could stand up and say. Practically everyone in class had gotten up and made a comment or shared a short story. He found himself sweating profusely. Removing a handkerchief from his pants pocket, he wiped his brow. Pamela Baxter, who was sitting next to him, leaned over and asked, "Are you all right?"

Brad, taken off guard, mumbled an answer, "Yeah…sure…it's just, well this is so horrible. I'll be fine." Pamela gave him an odd look and then went back to paying attention to another student who was now talking about Chester. Sweat was running down the inside of Brad's shirt; he felt so clammy. Looking around the room everyone else seemed to be at ease. Pamela had noticed he was uneasy. Was his nervousness that noticeable? He had to get out of the room, away from the others. Standing, he signaled to Mr. Tison and walked toward the classroom door, "Excuse me, but I have to use the restroom." Tison nodded in approval when Brad exited the room.

Once in the restroom down the hall, he immediately went to the sink and splashed cold water over his face and wiped the back of his neck with a soaked paper towel. Leaning against one of the stall doors, he took a number of deep breaths and wondered if Tim and Miles were experiencing the same thing. He felt sick to his stomach, like he was going to throw up. Controlling himself, he realized it was nothing more than guilt. Looking at his watch he figured the class, in the next few minutes, would be heading down to the assembly hall. If he timed things right he might not even have to return to class. He could join them while they walked down the hall. Outside in the hallway he leaned up against a row of lockers and waited.

Suddenly around the corner, walked Mrs. Trent, the school guidance counselor. Seeing Brad standing next to the lockers, she stopped and spoke in a concerned tone, "Brad, you don't look well. Are you ill? Why are you not in your class?"

Brad, trying his best to be upbeat, answered, "I had to use the restroom and actually, I'm not feeling well at the moment. The news about the murders is, well, it's hard to believe."

Mrs. Trent, always the caring person, inquired, "Is there anything I can do for you at the moment?"

"No," said Brad. "I was getting ready to go back to class. I'll be fine. See ya at the assembly."

Brad watched Mrs. Trent walk down the hall. Returning to the restroom, he splashed more water on his face and realized he was going to have to get it together. He was bringing too much attention on himself; the last thing he needed.

Finally, ready to go back to class he stepped out into the hall, which was packed with students making their way to assembly. Forcing a smile, he nodded at Mr. Tison and melted into the hoard of noisy students.

Entering the large assembly hall, he immediately looked for Tim and Miles. A member of the teaching staff noticed Brad standing in the middle of the aisle, approached and gently ordered, "Mr. Schulte…please have a seat. The sooner we are all seated the sooner we can get the assembly started." Once again, Brad found that he was the center of attention, even if it was just for a few seconds. Complying, he took a seat on the end of a row, still craning his neck, searching for his friends.

Sitting back in the seat he once again wiped his forehead with the soaked handkerchief. It was then he noticed seated next to the school principal on the elevated stage, a uniformed police officer. Looking once again for Miles and Tim he thought, *The police are here. This can't be good!* Wringing his hands together he tried to relax when he had a second thought, *Relax, act normal like you don't know what's going on. There's no way they can single you out. The police have no way of knowing about your involvement in the murders.*

Following five minutes of loud talking and moving about by the large number of students, the principal stood and walked to the microphone and began to give direction, "If everyone would please find a seat and quiet down we can get started." Another minute or so passed when the noise was reduced to a sporadic cough here and there. All eyes were on the principal while she scanned the large room from side to side, and finally spoke softly, "Good morning students. It is with great sadness that I hold an assembly this morning. As you are all aware by now, via the news on the radio and television this morning or from talking with your homeroom teachers, two of your fellow students were found murdered on Fripp Island this past weekend. The names of the students are Abigail James and Chester Finch."

Gesturing at the seated officer behind her, she continued, "We have with us this morning, Captain Trevor Green, Beaufort's Police Chief. At this time he would like to address the school."

Chief Green stood and approached the microphone, looked out over the waiting students, then began, "Good morning. I wish I could be here under more pleasant circumstances, but unfortunately, that is not the case. The bodies of Miss James and Mr. Finch were discovered early Sunday morning on Fripp Island. The Beaufort Police are currently conducting an investigation into the murders. For the next few days we will be interviewing every teacher, faculty member and student of the school, regardless of whether you attended the party Saturday night out on Fripp or not. Someone, possibly someone right here in this room may have knowledge that may be vital to solving this horrible crime. Someone may have heard or witnessed something that to you may seem unimportant, but in fact may be very important in this case. Individual interviews will probably take no longer than a few minutes, depending on what you have to say. During the interviews we will not be divulging any information we now have. So, when you are called come prepared to answer questions…not ask questions. I will tell you this. So far, we have no motive, no clues to speak of and no suspects, so we're looking for answers. The interviews will start tomorrow morning. At this time I'm going to turn the assembly back over to your principal, Mrs. Lane. Thank you."

Principal Lane stepped back to the microphone, thanked Chief Green and addressed the students. "As we speak, schedules for when each one of you are to report to a specific room to be interviewed are being posted in the hallways and will be handed out to you by your homeroom teacher." Holding up a form, she explained, "There will also be a second form which you will be given today. This form is to be given to your parent or parents. The police are not allowed to interview anyone underage, which most of you are, so your parents are invited to sit with you during your interview. If your parent or parents do not elect to attend these meetings, then they are to sign the consent form, and you must bring it to school tomorrow. If no parent will be at your interview, a member of the faculty will sit in. As for now, you need to return to your respective classroom where your homeroom teacher will hand out schedules and parent consent forms. After that, you are excused for the day. Tomorrow it will be back to business as usual except for your individual interviews. Thank you. You may return to your homeroom."

During the mass exodus, Brad caught a brief glimpse of Miles, who signaled him by pointing toward the parking lot. Walking back to his room, he wondered how his two friends had reacted to the news of the police interviews. He had always considered himself the strongest emotionally, but with the way he felt at the moment, his two friends must be nervous wrecks.

Leaning on the Mustang he folded both forms and placed them in his pocket when he saw Miles and Tim approaching. Miles was the first to speak while he carefully looked around to make sure no one was within earshot. "You hit the nail right on the head, Brad, when you said we might be questioned."

Tim agreed, "Yeah, and this is happening way too fast for me."

"I agree," said Brad, "but if we don't panic and we think things through we're going to be fine."

Tim held up his paper. "I'm scheduled for tomorrow at eleven o'clock. How about you, Brad?"

Brad's answer came instantly, "Tomorrow morning…ten thirty, a half hour before you go in."

Miles shrugged. "They don't want to talk to me until Thursday…three days from now. I guess in a way I lucked out. By that time you guys can tell me what type of questions the police are asking. I can better prepare myself."

"I was hoping for the same thing," said Tim, "but Brad will no sooner finish up when they'll be calling me in. I won't know what to expect."

"None of us will know what to expect," said Brad. "They may not even ask us the same questions. Remember what I said about when and if we are questioned? The interviewers will be experts on the way people react to certain questions. If we stick to the story we agreed on, we'll come out of this on the other end with nothing to worry about."

Tim joined Brad next to the Mustang and commented nervously, "I hope I can remember everything we talked about."

"Look," remarked Brad. "You guys are acting like they already suspect us. You heard what they said. They have no current suspects, no motive, and no solid clues. What we have to be careful of is not to give them any reason whatsoever to suspect us and if we stay with our story, I guarantee you…we'll walk away from this. Here's what we're going to do. We need to stay a step ahead of the police. You two need to park your cars over at Publix. I'll meet you there in a few minutes. We'll grab a bucket of chicken and some drinks and head on over to Hunting Island. There won't be many people over there this time of year. We can go over our story again. We'll each go over the story and the other two will correct anything that is not correct. It's important we look like all the other students…clueless. Now, I'll see you guys in Publix's parking lot in a few."

Brad parked the Mustang in the first parking spot just off the large grass covered area that housed the lighthouse on Hunting Island. Walking across the grass Tim looked up at the towering black and white lighthouse and asked the others, "You guys ever been up to the top?"

Miles, carrying the fried chicken motioned at the tall structure and shook his head. "Nope…never will either. Don't like heights. Makes me dizzy."

Brad laughed. "My mother took me up there was I was a kid. I thought it was really interesting. You can see a long way from up top. Last year when I was dating Cathy Long, I took her up. We weren't up there very long. She was scared to death."

Taking on a more serious tone, Miles pointed at a small pavilion that housed two long rows of picnic tables. "There doesn't seem to be anyone around. What say we sit over there?"

Brad turned and started for the tables. "Guess that'll do."

Seated at the end of the first row, Miles opened the bucket of chicken while Tim put their three large sodas down on the old wooden slatted table. Grabbing a chicken leg Brad was about to speak when they were interrupted by a deep voice, "Good morning gentlemen!"

Turning, all three noticed the uniformed National Park Ranger who placed his foot on one of the table benches and smiled. "How's come you boys aren't in school today?"

Tim and Miles looked at one another, not quite sure how to answer, while Brad responded, "We were in school earlier this morning but we were all excused, the whole school. We received the announcement about those murders out on Fripp. Then we were told to go home for the rest of the day. School resumes tomorrow."

The officer, accepting the answer as logical, removed his hat and looked up into the late morning sun penetrating the tall trees by the pavilion. "It's warmer today than it was yesterday. I was raised in Ohio. This time of the year up there can be quite cold."

Holding up the bucket, Tim offered, "Piece of chicken?"

"No thanks," said the officer. Nodding at Brad, the man continued speaking, "I graduated from Beaufort High with your father. Neither one of us played football. We played baseball together. Your dad was pretty good. He was our second baseman. We've stayed friends over the years. I belong to the tennis club your father does. We play doubles about once a month. I have always been very supportive of Beaufort High, my wife and I attending the football games every year. We've been watching you three boys play ever since you were in the Pee Wee League. This year, winning the state championship, well that's pretty special."

Placing his hat back on his head he smiled sadly at the three boys. "But, with these recent murders, the celebrating has been cut short." Changing the subject, he angled his thumb back over his shoulder. "Noticed the red Mustang parked over there just after you pulled in. I figured it belonged to one of you three. I remember it from those fancy chrome rims."

Miles shot Tim a look of confusion. The officer seeing the look of wonder cleared things up and verified what he had previously stated. "I only recall the rims on the Mustang because I saw the car Saturday night when you guys pulled up along the Island Parkway to give the James' girl a helping hand. I was up the road on the opposite side of the highway getting gas. When I first pulled into the station I could see a young girl standing next to a bright yellow sports car. She looked like she was having car troubles so I figured when I was gassed up, if no one had stopped to help her out, I'd go over myself and see if I could lend a hand. After I paid for my gas I started to clean off my windshield when your Red Mustang made a U-turn, came back, and parked behind her. You guys got out, looked under the hood and apparently couldn't get the car started. When the girl got in your car and you headed up the road, there wasn't any reason for me to drive over. I never even knew it was the girl's car until they talked about it on the news this morning. It must be a shock to you boys to have actually seen her a few hours before she was murdered."

Brad answered without even hesitating, "Yeah, it is. We were just talking about that earlier at school this morning. We all knew Abby and the Finch kid. It's a shame. I can't imagine why someone would want to kill them."

The officer put his hands on his hips and shook his head. "I can't either. I never met the James girl but I have met Chester Finch on many an occasion. I can't tell you how many times he came out here to Hunting Island to take photos. I talked with him many a day. He was really an interesting character. Last week he was over here. Told me he was going to go to Harvard." Shaking his head once again in wonder, he stated, "It's a shame to lose two young people like that. They had their entire lives ahead of them…and now look." Nodding at the bucket of chicken, he smiled and started to walk toward the sidewalk down to the beach. "You boys enjoy your chicken and the day off. Tell your father, Brad, Officer Dalton said hello."

"Sure thing," said Brad.

When the officer was far enough away that they couldn't be heard, Miles pushed the bucket of chicken to the side and gestured in the direction of the officer. "I'm beginning to get the distinct feeling things are starting to pile up and not necessarily in our favor. First, the police showing up at school this morning and the fact we are going to be personally interviewed. Secondly, a park ranger, a man who represents authority, actually sees us not only near Abby's car but also with her hours before she's murdered. In the next few days what the hell else is going to pop up?"

Brad bit into his chicken, took a drink and calmly answered, "You need to calm down. It's that kind of an attitude that could very well sink us. Stop trying to poke holes in our story. The fact the park ranger saw us in the presence of Abby is not going to be anything the police will not already know. Remember, in our story we agreed to tell the police we stopped to give Abby a hand, and then we drove her over to Fripp. And, just because some park ranger saw us with her doesn't mean he's going to say anything to the police. He didn't act suspicious when he was discussing it with us. Like I have said all along. If we stick to our story, we'll be fine." Taking another bite of chicken, he went on, "Speaking of our story, that's the reason we came out here today so we could go over it and make sure we're on the same page. Tim, why don't you start off and tell us the story. We have to be as familiar with the story as we have always been with our football playbook. We knew all the plays by heart and for the most part they normally worked in our favor. We have to know this story by heart. Now, let's get started."

Brad looked at the clock in the corner of the room in his ten o'clock history class. It was ten-fifteen and he hadn't heard or paid attention to a single word the teacher had spoken. He was tired. He had been up most of the night running over the story he would tell the police. History class was the last opportunity he was going to have to go over the story in his mind. For the past two days he had driven into the heads of Miles and Tim the importance of a consistent story between the three of them. He had remained calm over the last forty-eight hours but now that his interview time was approaching, he couldn't help but feel nervous. He tried to relax and calm his nerves. He knew if he walked into the interview, the police chief or a detective would pick up on his nervousness immediately. He was snapped out his daydreaming by the teacher's voice, "Brad Schulte...Brad!"

Startled, Brad looked up when the teacher repeated, "Brad, it's now ten twenty-five. You need to head down to room 23, the guidance counselor's office, for your interview. When you are finished you are to report to whatever class you are scheduled to be in next."

Without saying a word, Brad stood and exited the room. Room 23 was a short walk down the hall. He would be there is less than two minutes. There was no sense in going over any part of the story at this point. If he didn't know it by now, well, it was too late.

He hesitated outside the door, took a deep breath and entered. Mrs. Trent sat at her desk in the rear of the office. A well-dressed man in a beige suit sat comfortably next to the desk in a cushioned chair. Mrs. Trent stood when Brad entered and held out her right hand, welcoming him, "Brad...right on time. Please have a seat."

The only other seat available was a stiff-backed wooden chair in front of the desk that was positioned so whoever sat there was facing both Mrs. Trent and her visitor. The well-dressed man stood and offered his hand. "Good Morning son. I'm Detective Melvin Barrett. I'm going to be asking you a few simple questions. You should be back to class in about ten minutes or so."

As Barrett sat back down, Mrs. Trent asked, "Are you feeling better today, Brad?"

Brad smiled and answered, "Yes, I am."

Picking up on what was said, Barrett seemed concerned and asked, "Have you not been feeling well, son?"

Brad did some quick thinking. The questioning had no doubt started. "Yesterday morning after the announcement about the murders, I was upset. I felt sick to my stomach. I suppose most of the students probably felt that way. I mean, it's not every day you receive news that one, or in this case, two of your schoolmates has been murdered."

Motioning at a pitcher of water and three glasses, Barrett offered, "Would you care for a glass of water?"

Brad tried his best to read the detective and wondered if the man was trying to relax him to the point where he might catch him off-guard. "No thank you," said Brad.

Crossing his legs, Barrett opened a manila file folder and removed a sheet of paper. "Well then, let's get started. First, I want to verify some basic information. Your name is Brad Schulte. You're a senior here at Beaufort High, quarterback of the football team, member of the student council and you sing in the school choir. Mrs. Trent was telling me before you came in that you are going to be attending South Carolina

University on a football scholarship."

Brad gave Mrs. Trent an odd look and wondered if the detective had thrown him a curve. Politely, Brad corrected Barrett, "The information you have about my future at college is incorrect. I'll be attending Penn State…not South Carolina University."

Confused, Barrett looked down at the paper and responded, "I'm sorry. I could have sworn Mrs. Trent told me it was South Carolina."

Mrs. Trent jumped in. "No, I'm rather sure I said it was Penn State. You must be confusing Brad with one of our other students. We have a number of students who will be going to South Carolina."

Barrett questioned Mrs. Trent. "But not as football players…right?"

Thinking, Mrs. Trent, snapped her fingers. "The only other football player we have that will be attending South Carolina is Miles Gaston. Miles and Brad are the best of friends. Maybe I did say South Carolina."

Picking up another folder that contained the list of students, Barrett ran his finger down the list, "Yes, here it is. Miles Gaston, South Carolina University. Miles was the tight end on the team this past year."

Brad corrected Barrett a second time. "No, that's wrong. Miles was our running back. Tim Durham was the tight end."

Clicking open an ink pen, Barrett made the corrections on the paper. "I don't know how I could have messed the information up, but with a stroke of the pen we'll just correct that."

Brad tried to relax but the misinformation the detective was giving was throwing him off. Was the wrong information actually a mistake or were they trick questions designed to unnerve him?

Barrett closed the folder, reached over to the desk, turned on a small recording device, and explained, "From here on out our conversation will be recorded."

Mrs. Trent interrupted when she realized. "Brad, since your parents are not present, did you bring along the signed consent form?"

Brad nodded and removed the form from his shirt pocket and laid it on the corner of the desk. Mrs. Trent picked up the signed document, read Mrs. Schulte's signature and nodded her head in approval.

Barrett picked up a legal pad and smiled at Brad. "Some of the questions I ask you may seem insignificant in relation to the murders, but it's important that we first get the feel of the students and the community on Saturday. We'll combine all the gathered information and see if anything raises a red flag. In short, we have to start somewhere. Now, let's start out with what you did on Saturday before you went to the party on Fripp. You did go to the party…right?"

"Yes, we did."

"And by *we,* who are you referring to?"

"The three of us: Tim, Miles and myself. I drove that night."

Holding up his index finger for Brad to stop talking, Barrett got a strange look on his face, picked up yet another folder and opened it. Scanning the paper slowly, he flipped to a second page and then a third, made a short note on his legal pad, stared at Brad for a moment, then continued, "Let's back up to earlier Saturday morning and into the afternoon. What did you do prior to going to the party?"

The odd actions of Detective Barrett were unnerving but Brad remained calm and asked, "Starting when on Saturday?"

"Well, let's see," said Barrett. "How about when you got up and we'll go from there until you decided to drive over to Fripp."

Brad shifted uncomfortably in the wooden chair. He had been talking to the detective for five minutes and the story he had rehearsed over and over the past two days hadn't even come into play yet. Taking a deep breath, which he thought would go undetected, he began, "I woke up just after nine o'clock. Had a light breakfast, and then I headed outside to do some yard work. We have a large amount of tree debris around our house that means this time of year our front and backyard can at times be covered with pine needles and moss. I raked and bagged until around eleven when I went back inside to grab some lunch. After lunch I went back, mowed the grass, and mulched the debris that was left behind. I guess I finished up around one o'clock. Later, I helped my mother carry a bunch of stuff into the garage for a yard sale she was planning to have in the next week or so. When my chores for the day were done, I relaxed on our front porch swing and read a book until it must have been close to three o'clock."

Surprisingly, Barrett interrupted Brad. "What type of reading do you enjoy?"

Brad felt like asking what that had to do with the murders, but remembered what he had been told previously, *When you come to your interview, you answer questions, you don't ask questions.*

Not wanting to seem uncooperative, he answered, "It was a political book. For some reason the past couple of years I've become very interested in politics. I find it quite fascinating. Who knows? Someday I may run for some sort of political office."

Barrett was taking some short notes so Brad just kept right on talking, which gave him an inner sense of being in control of the conversation. "I must have read for an hour or so, then I took a shower, got dressed and drove over to a car wash, washed and vacuumed out my Mustang."

Smiling, Barrett looked up from his notes and commented, "Politics, you say? Whether you become a politician or not in the future, you'll still find yourself immersed in politics. Politics unfortunately seem to be in every aspect of life."

Brad happened to be looking in Mrs. Trent's direction when she nodded in agreement with what Barrett had said. Once again, Brad found Barrett talking about something that had nothing to do with the murders.

Getting back to their previous topic, Barrett recapped what Brad had said. "So you washed and cleaned your car. Then what?"

Without missing a beat, Brad spoke with confidence, "Then I drove over to Miles and Tim's homes and picked them up for the party." Anticipating Barrett's next question, Brad kept right on talking. "We drove to downtown Beaufort, cruised up and down Bay Street, and joined in on the celebration of being state football champs. Eventually, we decided to park at the marina downtown because it was a little too early to head to Fripp."

Gaining control of the interview once again, Barrett interrupted, "And how long did you boys remain at the marina?"

"I guess it was somewhere around a half hour or so. We talked about how this summer was going to be our last together. We also talked about how we had been friends for almost twelve years and how we had played football together since Pee Wee League. We were all in a great mood because we were now state champs. I can't remember the exact time, but we finally pulled out and started for Fripp."

Doing some quick math in his head, Barrett stated, "It's about a half hour drive over there so I can only assume you arrived on the island before dark."

Brad, sensing the detective was searching, answered, "It took us nearly an hour to drive out to Fripp. We got sidetracked on the way."

Barrett gave Brad a look that warranted further explanation, which Brad picked up on as he explained, "When I say sidetracked what I mean is we made an unplanned stop. We noticed a sports car parked on the side of the parkway. It was a yellow Miata. The only person I know of in all of Beaufort County that drives a yellow Miata is Abby James. When we passed by we saw a female looking beneath the hood, so we decided to turn around and see if we could give her a hand."

Taking on a more serious tone, Barrett leaned forward and asked, "Did you notice if the girl was Abigail James?"

"At first, no. But like I said, I've never seen another yellow Miata around these parts. Everyone knew she drove a Miata...a yellow Miata. After we pulled in behind the car, the female stepped out to greet us. It was in fact, Abby James."

Moving his hands in a rotating motion, Barrett indicated for Brad to continue. "And then?"

Brad could see he had aroused Barrett's interest. Sitting back and trying to relax, he remarked with confidence, "We got out of my car, approached her, and asked if she was having car problems. She told us she was. We then told her we'd take a look at the engine and see if we could get the car started."

Nodding his head in approval, Barrett inquired, "And did you?"

"No, we did not succeed in getting her car running. Tim and I know very little if anything about car repairs. We looked under the hood, acted like we knew what we were doing and after a couple of minutes, we told her it was useless."

Barrett held up his ink pen and with a confused look, asked, "You said you and Tim were unfamiliar with car repairs. You did not mention your other friend…I believe his name is Miles. What was he doing while you and Tim were fumbling around with the engine?"

Brad shrugged. "I guess he was just talking with Abby." Wanting to get off the subject of Miles, he changed the immediate subject. "Abby asked us if we were going to the party. We told her we were and that we would be glad to give her a lift to Fripp."

Barrett was busy making a notation on his pad while talking at the same time. "Did you make any other stops on the way down to Fripp?"

"No, we drove straight through."

Trying to keep ahead of the detective, Brad snapped his fingers. "It was kind of strange when we arrived at the guard shack on the island."

Barrett stopped writing and asked, "How so?"

"It was like the guard was expecting us…well, not just us but a large number of students that were going to be attending the party. He said he had a list of those expected. When he asked us if we were going to the party we told him we were players on the Beaufort football team. He asked for our names, but then something quite odd happened. Abby leans up between the seats and calls him by name. I believe his name was Neil. She proceeds to let him know that it's okay because we are with her. He never did ask our names…he just signaled us through. I thought it was strange…that's all."

Barrett pursed his lips. You say Miss James called the guard by his first name?"

"That's correct…Neil."

"Did she see the guard's nametag or did she act like they knew one another?"

"She definitely knew him, but then again she lives on the island. I'm sure the guard is used to seeing her come and go all the time."

Nodding in agreement, Barrett moved on, "I assume your next stop was the actual party."

Brad confirmed, "Yes, it was. We dropped Abby off on Tarpon Boulevard by the swimming pool. She said that was good because she was meeting some of her girlfriends there. She jumped out and we had to drive further up the road where we could find a parking spot. We parked on the side of the road just past the tennis courts, got out and joined the party."

Holding his hands out, Barrett stated, "Explain, 'joined the party"?

"Well, we already had our swimsuits on, and of course our football jerseys. We ate some dogs and burgers and drank a couple of sodas. They had a band there so we did some dancing. We had our pictures taken quite often, then we walked down to the pool and swam some. I remember the water being quite cold despite the fact the pool is heated. We just hung out with everyone who was there. I think we started for home just before midnight."

Sitting back in his chair, Barrett removed his glasses, rubbed his tired eyes, and asked, "Did you happen to notice if there was anyone drinking alcohol at the party?"

Brad hesitated but then answered, "I'm sure there was some of that going on, however, I didn't run into anyone who was drunk or that even seemed to be drinking."

"Was there any disagreements or fighting during the party?"

Brad shrugged. "If there was, I wasn't aware of it."

"When you saw Abigail James later that night what did you talk about?"

Brad corrected Barrett. "I never saw her again for the rest of the night."

"Did anyone mention her name or talk to you about her?"

"No. After we dropped her off, I never saw her again."

"What about Miles and Tim? Did they see her again during the party?"

"I have no idea," said Brad. "You'll have to ask them that question. The three of us were together most of the evening. If they did see her again they never mentioned it to me."

"How about Chester Finch. Did you happen to see him at the party?"

"No, but that doesn't mean he wasn't there. He is really into photography. I'm sure he was there somewhere taking photos. He could have taken a picture of me without my even being aware of it. There were cameras going off all the time…everywhere. I'm only guessing he was there. I never saw him though."

Barrett remained silent while he read over the notes he had made, looked up at Brad and then back to his notes. The detective's stare sent a shiver down Brad's back.

After what seemed like an unending silence. Barrett asked, "Earlier you referred to Abigail James and Chester Finch as schoolmates. Were you close to either one of them?"

"No, I wouldn't say close. I mean not like the friendship I have with Miles and Tim."

"Did you ever date the James girl?"

"No, never!"

Barrett gave Brad another long stare and then stated. "That was an odd response. If you would have just said, no, well then, I would have just moved on, but you emphasized your answer by saying, 'No, never!"

Brad realized he had overemphasized his answer and remained silent when Mrs. Trent spoke up, "Excuse me, detective. What you perceive as an odd response is nothing more than Brad trying to be polite. How can I say this without being disrespectful to the James family? Let me put it this way. As the school guidance counselor I am aware of the goings on of the school; student habits, problems, you name it. Abigail James, even though one of our brightest students, wore what I can only describe as tarnished armor. In short, she liked to spend time with the boys. She had a reputation as a young lady that liked…no, enjoyed sleeping around. Brad here, is a gentlemen. He would never consider saying anything bad about anyone. He doesn't fit into the typical mold of a lot of high schools where you see the most gorgeous girl in school dating the school quarterback. That is the reason why he emphasized the word…never!"

Barrett, with respect made some short notes and answered, "Thank you, Mrs. Trent. That clears up that little matter. Now, let's discuss Chester Finch, a young boy who I have found out in the few interviews we have already conducted, was looked upon as a bit of a nerd. Brad, do you have any reason to think that Chester and Abigail were dating. I mean, why would these two students, who were about as different as day and night be on the beach together?"

Brad answered instantly, "I have no idea, sir."

Closing the folder, Barrett stood and extended his hand to Brad. "That will be all Mr. Schulte. You may return to your class." Handing Brad a business card, the detective explained, "If you happen to think of anything we may have overlooked, please feel free to give me a call. Depending on the information gathered over the next few days, we might interview some students a second time, so you may or may not be called in again. Have a good day and thank you for dropping by this morning."

Outside in the hallway, Brad leaned up against a row of lockers and thought, *I'm glad that's over. I wonder how Tim made out?*

CHAPTER FIVE

NICK FALCO LOOKED OUT THE SMALL SQUARE WINDOW AS the B-757 made its scheduled approach to the Toronto Pearson International Airport. Checking his seatbelt to make sure it was secure, he braced himself and sat back clenching both armrests. Taking a deep breath he looked up at the ceiling and closed his eyes, trying to relax. An older woman who was seated next to him ever since she had boarded in Pittsburgh, reached over and gently tapped his right hand and spoke softly, "Don't worry dear. We'll be down in a few seconds."

Nick smiled but refused to open his eyes. It wasn't even ten seconds when his eyes were jerked open when the plane's landing gear hit the Canadian tarmac. Placing his arms tightly around his throbbing chest, he lowered his head and winced when the pilot reversed the powerful engines, the large plane beginning its braking process. A few more seconds passed when the elderly lady tapped him on his arm. "You can relax. We're down now."

He chanced a look out the window, surprised to see a light mixture of snow and sleet. Feeling safe now that the plane had landed, Nick looked at the woman who had tried her best to comfort him during the flight. Patting her on the arm, he apologized, "I'm sorry you had to babysit me on the way up here, but this is the first time I've ever flown. I'm already dreading the flight back home and I just got here."

Looking out the window again, he shook his head in wonder and exclaimed, "I should have worn something a little warmer than this sweater. I wasn't expecting this type of weather. When I left Charleston, South Carolina this morning it was in the low fifties. What do you think the temperature is here?"

Opening her large purse, the woman answered, "Let's find out, young man." Removing an expensive looking cell phone from the purse she ran her fingers across the screen and commented, "My granddaughter got me this phone a few months ago. I never thought in all my life I'd ever use one of these gadgets, but now that I own one, why I just can't seem to get along without it." Moving her index finger sideways on the screen, she hesitated and then announced, "Here it is…the local weather. Looks like right now its twenty-one degrees with a wind chill of seventeen." Putting the cell back into the purse, she smiled pleasantly, "Is this your final stop for the day?"

"Yes, it is. I'm going to rent a car and then drive up to a place called Stony Lake. They tell me it's about two hours north of Toronto."

"I've never heard of it," said the woman. "Of course, I'm not familiar with anything in the Toronto area. I have an hour and a half layover here before my next flight which will take me to Vancouver where my daughter and her family live."

The flight attendant's voice over the intercom system interrupted the conversation, "*Please remain in your seats until taxi procedures are complete. At that time you may gather your bags and exit the plane*."

The woman sat back in her seat and spoke calmly, "You might as well relax. By the time they get to their assigned position at the terminal it could take ten to fifteen minutes. This Stony Lake you're going to. Is it a vacation area? I mean it sounds like a vacation spot."

"No, I'm not on vacation," said Nick. "It's just a little time away. I'm going to be visiting a friend. She has a house on the lake. This is my first time up here."

The woman smiled across the seat at Nick while she adjusted a scarf around her neck. "You look entirely too young to be retired. What do you do for a living?"

"Well, I was a painter."

The woman gave him an admiring stare. "You mean like an artist?"

"No. I paint houses; I used to paint houses. I had my own painting business in Cincinnati, but after a few years I found myself floundering on the edge of poverty. Then, on top of everything else, my grandmother died and left me a beachfront property and quite a bit of money. So, a few months ago I moved down to South Carolina to a private island called Fripp."

"So, I take it from what you've said your painting days have come to an end?"

"I'm not sure yet. Since I've lived on the island I've painted one house. Having enough money where you will never have to work again has its advantages, but there is also a downside. I can't swim in the ocean and walk on the beach every day. A person has to have a purpose for living. I don't know. I may start up my painting business again. I haven't really decided what I want to do with the rest of my life."

Looking down at Nick's left hand she inquired, "I assume from the lack of a wedding band on your hand you're not married."

"Never have been and there was a point when I thought I never would."

The woman gently patted his hand and remarked, "You seem like a nice young man. I'm sure there's a young lady out there somewhere in this world who will change your mind."

Nick glanced out the window when the plane came to a stop. Looking back at the woman, he nodded and thought about Shelby. "You might just be right."

Getting up from the seat she reached up for the overhead luggage compartment and complained, "I've been flying ever since I was a little girl but I can never get used to getting your bag from up top. It's always so difficult for me, especially since I'm older these days."

Joining her in the aisle, Nick offered, "Here, let me get your bag down for you."

Handing her the bag, he took down his own travelling bag and sat back down since the aisle toward the front of the plane was crowded with passengers jockeying for their exit from the aircraft.

The woman reached out and shook his hand. "I'm going to forge my way through. Being old has its perks. Everyone seems to just get out of my way. Enjoy your time up at that lake."

Nick watched as the old woman disappeared in the mass of flesh at the front of the plane. Settling back in the seat he decided to wait for the aisle to clear while he watched snowflakes melt on the window glass.

Fifteen minutes later, Nick found himself standing inside the large terminal. Since he hadn't spent much time in airports, he wasn't sure what he was supposed to do or where he was supposed to go. He saw a large sign indicating the direction to baggage pickup and another for departing passengers. What he was really looking for was car rentals. After wondering around aimlessly for a few minutes he stopped a passing flight attendant and asked, "Which way to car rentals?"

The young female attendant smiled pleasantly and answered, "Go down to the very end of the terminal and take a left down the escalator. You'll see all of the rental companies lined up against the north wall."

Thanking the young woman, Nick turned and almost ran smack dab into the woman he had sat next to on the plane. "Excuse me," blurted Nick. "I thought we already said our goodbyes!"

The woman gave him a wink and laughed. "We have to stop meeting like this!"

Nick watched the woman disappeared around a corner. Searching for the north wall he had been informed about, he spotted a number of bright car rental signs. Hertz, Alamo, National and on and on. Forcing his way through the ever-growing crowd, he stopped and stood in line at the first rental agency. He looked at his watch, 1:17 in the afternoon. He had planned on arriving at Stony Lake around five o'clock. He was right on schedule, but the line for rental cars was moving painfully slow.

The fact he had not pre-ordered a vehicle slowed the process down and the only reason he actually did finally get a car was due to a cancellation. He glanced at his watch and pulled out of the airport rental parking at 2:05. He was told it was approximately 120 miles to Stony Lake. He was still on schedule.

After making two wrong turns in Toronto, he finally arrived at Route 401, which ran parallel to Lake Ontario. Flipping on the car heater, it seemed like it took an eternity for a slight resemblance of heat to trickle out of the dash vents. He turned the heater on high but it did nothing to make him feel any warmer. If he wasn't so far out of the city he had half a mind to return the car for one with an adequate heating system. He erased the thought from his mind, realizing he was lucky to even get a car.

Looking out through the light snow at the vast lake reminded him of the Atlantic Ocean on Fripp. There were no buildings that could be seen in the distance, but unlike the ocean, there were no waves and the water appeared to be calm. After driving for half an hour, he could tell he was leaving the Toronto City limits and soon found himself passing an occasional development or small business. Another ten minutes passed when he came to Route 115 North that he was to follow up to Peterborough.

Soon, he found himself in farm country, dazzling white barns and herds of grazing cattle scattered across the Canadian countryside. Everything looked so pristine and clean; there were no cans, bottles or trash lying on the side of the highway. He figured either the Canadian motorist was overt to littering or the county and local government were quite adamant about keeping the roadways clean.

His admiration of the clean landscape of the country was interrupted when he placed his hand over the dashboard vent. There was no longer any trace of heat whatsoever, but a stream of cool air spilling out into the interior of the car. Realizing he still had over an hour's drive ahead of him he knew he required some warmth. Pulling over at a small general store on the outskirts of Peterborough, he got out, stretched and walked into the one story, cedar sided structure. The front porch was crammed with boxes and barrels filled with fruits and vegetables, nuts and local crafts.

Inside the store, Nick stood and stared at the walls lined with shelves containing canned goods, household items and cleaning supplies. In the center of the store there were three large tables piled high with clothing items. An older man, dressed in what Nick thought was authentic Indian attire nodded at him from behind an old wooden counter. Nick returned a nod of his own and began to look over the clothing items. A few minutes later he made his selections: a long sleeved white sweat shirt with Canada emblazoned on the front, a pair of cheap brown work gloves and a grey knit hat he could pull down over his ears. Taking his purchases to the counter, the old man smiled and spoke in a very odd accent, "Will that be all today, sir?"

From the way the man was dressed combined with his accent, Nick asked, "You wouldn't happen to be Native American...would you?"

The man returned a toothless smile and answered, "Nope...Native Canadian." Gesturing at three little girls and a woman who were standing at the end of the counter, the man went on to explain, "That's my family and we are direct descendants of the Haudenosaunee Tribe. There are only a few hundred of us left here in Ontario." The man looked Nick up and down and stated, "You're not from around here, are you?"

Nick, reaching for his wallet, confirmed, "No, I'm not from these parts. I was born and raised in Ohio and currently I live in South Carolina. Didn't expect it to be quite so cold up this way, so I need some warm clothes."

Giving Nick the total, the man took his credit card and ran it through an old fashioned imprinter and spoke, "Where're you heading?"

"Stony Lake. I guess I've got about another hour or so to go yet."

The woman approached Nick, placed a large Styrofoam cup in front of him and explained in broken English, "Special tea. Keep you warm and safe from evil spirits. Drink...it's free."

Nick politely objected, "You don't have to do that for me...I'll be fine once I get back on the road."

The man reached out, shoved the cup closer to Nick, and looked out over the top of his eyeglasses. "Everyone who comes in here gets a cup of that special tea. It is considered rude to turn it down according to our tribal laws. It will keep evil spirits away."

Nick, not wishing to offend the man or his wife smiled, picked up the cup and took a short swig. Nodding at the woman, he complimented her, "This is really good. I've never tasted tea this good. What's in here?"

The woman shuffled her three children toward a back room and spoke over her shoulder. "Secret...you just enjoy! Have good trip up at lake."

Nick turned back to the man but he had his back turned while he counted packs of cigarettes on a shelf. "See ya around," said Nick. "Thanks for the tea."

The man gestured without turning around. Nick shrugged, picked up his articles and headed for the door.

Outside, he placed the tea on top of an old barrel, slipped into the sweatshirt, put the knit hat on his head, slid his hands into the warm gloves, picked up the tea and went back to the car. Sitting in the car he noticed the snow had stopped and was now a light misty rain. He no sooner pulled out of the general store than he found himself crossing a bridge that spanned the Otonabee River. Twenty minutes later he was once again surrounded by the Canadian countryside.

Sipping at the tea, he turned the ineffective heater completely off. It was doing nothing but pushing cold air into the car. The additional clothing he had purchased would have to suffice. Daydreaming, he thought about the conversation he had on the plane with the woman about the fact he was not married. His thoughts once again were centered on Shelby Lee. He had only known her for five months and before that hadn't dated for five years. He recalled the day he met her on the beach. Smiling to himself, he shook his head and remembered the awkward conversation they had and how it turned out to be a dinner date. He had to admit to himself they had shared what could only be described as an incredible summer together. He had met some strange people over the summer months; people who had made his life difficult, but they were all gone from his life now.

Driving along for the next forty minutes he marveled at the scenic view that bordered the highway. To the north in the distance he could see low snow-covered mountains. On either side of the road there were forests of tall evergreens mixed with trees that had lost their leaves. He turned off the windshield wipers since the light rain had stopped.

Breaking out of a thick forest, he came to what appeared to be a small conglomeration of buildings. Slowing down, Nick noticed a small standard green sign indicating the name of the small community: YOUNGS POINT. Amelia had told him this was going to be the last town he came to before arriving at Stony Lake. Pulling over at a combination gas station and grocery store, he saw a lake on the left that disappeared in the distant forest.

Entering the store, the warmth from the inside of the building was a welcoming feeling. Spotting three coffee pots on a counter above a display of assorted donuts, Nick removed his gloves and hat. Pouring a large cup of decaf, he dumped in sugar and creamer. He selected a chocolate covered donut and walked to another counter where he saw a cash register. Directly behind the counter, he could see the lake through a large window.

A man emerged from behind a paneled wall and greeted Nick, "Howdy there." Nodding at the cup in Nick's hand, the man commented, "Good day for a cup of hot coffee."

Laying the donut and the coffee on the counter, Nick responded, "Boy, I'll say. I just drove up from Toronto. It was seventeen with the wind chill."

Angling his thumb toward the lake, the man added, "I was just outside checking the temperature. It's nineteen degrees out there. Pretty normal for this time of year."

Looking around the building, Nick gestured, "Seems rather slow around these parts. Nobody getting gas, not many cars on the road."

"You must not be from around here," said the man. "This is a big tourist area. When the leaves fall from the trees, which is normally around the end of October it gets slower than molasses running uphill in the winter until around the middle of April. Where're you from?"

"Down south. I'm driving up to Stony Lake to visit a friend."

"And who might your friend be? Hell, I know everyone around for miles."

"Amel..." Nick quickly corrected himself, "Emily Pike."

The man flashed a wide grin. "You know Em! She's about the most exciting person that's moved up here this past year. Everyone around here knows Em. She's involved with our local animal protection committee, she's in a local quilting group, volunteers down at the library, helps to keep the lake trails cleaned up and is a member of our book club and that's just the stuff I know of. Yeah, Em comes down here to the store every few days to gas up or grab some supplies." The man gave Nick a sideways look and continued, "You said you're from down south. I'll bet you a dime to a dollar you're from the Beaufort, Savannah, Charleston area. I say that because if you know Em, then you surely must know her brother, Carson."

Nick smiled, but knew he had to be careful when talking about anything that had to do with his grandmother. "Yes, I know Carson Pike well. He's a pretty nice fellow."

The man nodded out the window in the direction of the road out front. "Carson was up here about two weeks back. Came up to visit Em. He comes up about once a month. He told me he owns the house Em lives in. From the way he talks he must be quite the fisherman down there in South Carolina. He always says he's going to get some fishing in when he comes up, but by the time he gets the things that need to be done out at the lake house finished, it's time for him to head back south. He's quite the character."

Nick took a swig of coffee and thought to himself, *If you only knew!* Reaching for his wallet, he spoke, "Just let me pay for the coffee and the donut and I'll be on my way."

"Nonsense," replied the man. "Coffee and the donut are on the house. Em's done me a lot of favors over the past months. Why just last month she knitted a pair of baby booties for my daughters' newborn son. Since you're a friend of Em's, you don't owe me a cent."

Sipping at the hot coffee, Nick stated, "Emily gave me directions to her house, but I'm running a little late. I don't want to get turned around up here and wind up getting lost. It's going to be getting dark soon. Maybe you could give me some simple directions."

"Be glad to, son." Guiding Nick out onto the front porch of the building he pointed at the road that ran in front of them and explained, "Just keep following 115 for another mile or so. You'll come to a fork in the road. What you do is bear to the left. That'll put you on route 28 that runs parallel to Clear Lake. About twenty miles up the road you'll cross a covered bridge and then you'll be at the next lake, which is Stony Lake. Third dirt road on the right is Lakeview. Turn in there and you'll pass an old abandoned barn. Keep going for about a quarter mile and you'll break out into a small clearing next to the lake where you'll see a log cabin A-frame. That's Em's place. One of the nicest places on Stony Lake. From here, I'd say you'd arrive in about twenty minutes give or take."

Nick stepped off the porch and waved at the man, "Thank you for the coffee, donut and directions."

The man responded with a wave of his own. "Make sure you tell Em Hank said hello."

Climbing in the car, Nick held up the coffee and gestured, "Will do!"

Not even a mile up the road the snow started to fall again, large white fluffy flakes.

Both sides of the two lane paved road were flanked with tall pines, the lake occasionally coming into view. The sun was going down in the west and darkness would soon settle in over the vast forest he was driving through. Increasing his speed from 55 mph to 60, he drank the last of the coffee. The last thing he needed was to get lost in the Canadian wilderness. Arriving at the covered bridge, he let out a sigh of relief. According to Hank, when he got across the bridge he would be in the Stony Lake Region.

The snow was coming down heavier when he spotted Lakeview on the right. Turning down the dirt road, the tall pines completely blocked out what little sunlight that was left of the day. Turning on the headlights, he had to slow down considerably as the road was filled with ruts. Passing the old dilapidated barn Hank had mentioned, he rounded a long curve and there nestled in a stand of pines stood Em's large cabin. Pulling up in front of the house, Nick sat back and stretched. It had been a long day. Stepping out of the car he looked up at a second floor porch railing in front of a huge glass pyramid shaped window where he saw his grandmother standing. Smiling, he held out his gloved hands, indicating he had finally arrived.

Amelia pointed down at a three car attached garage and when the garage door opened she yelled down, "Park the car in there and then come in through the kitchen door."

Parking the rental car next to a Land Rover, Nick noticed a snowmobile and a heavy-duty snow blower in the far corner of the spacious garage. Getting out, he opened the house entrance door and found himself standing in a mudroom. From the next room, he heard Amelia's voice, "In here in the kitchen, Nick."

Passing a washer and dryer, he stepped into the rustic kitchen: whiskey barrel designed cabinets, cherry hardwood flooring, logged walls, wooden table and chairs and a wooden island topped with a stainless steel top. Amelia stood at the stove, stirring a large pot. Motioning at Nick with a large spoon, she smiled, "Welcome to Stony Lake." Walking across the kitchen, she gave him a hug and then held him at arms' length. "You look frozen." Removing the hat from his head she gestured at an adjoining room. "Why don't you go into the main room and sit by the fire and get warmed up. I've got a pot of my famous chicken noodle soup on the stove. We've got so much to talk about."

Nick was about to say something but she gently pushed him toward the main room. "Go on…get in front of that fire. I'll be in with soup, ham sandwiches and hot chocolate in a minute or so. I've almost got everything ready."

Taking off the gloves, Nick remarked, "A warm fire does sound good."

Entering the large great room, Nick marveled at the two-story vaulted beamed ceiling, the eight-foot creek stone fireplace, all of the furnishings created out of custom fashioned, walnut stained logs. The hardwood floors continued on from the kitchen, partially covered in three areas with large decorative throw rugs. A wooden railing ran across a large upper loft on three sides of the room, the fourth wall was covered with a two-story, log framed eight-foot wide window. Walking to the window, Nick gazed out at the peaceful lake that would soon be covered in darkness. Throwing his hat and gloves on an end table, he spoke to his unseen grandmother in the kitchen, "So, I take it this is the beautiful Stony Lake you've been telling me about?"

Entering the room with a tray that held two large bowls of soup and a plate of sandwiches, Amelia answered, "Yep, that's Stony Lake. The first lake you passed after leaving Young's Point was Clear Lake and the lake above Stony is called Upper Stony. The three lakes make up the eastern edge of the Kawartha Lakes Region."

Looking to the opposite side of the lake, in the distance Nick could barely make out five homes, only one with lights. "Not many people around right now?"

Setting the tray on a log coffee table, Amelia joined him at the large window. "That house with the lights is my closest neighbor, Pete Spivey. He's a few years older than me. His wife died a few years back. He heads up the lake clean up committee. The rest of those homes are summer cottages. With winter coming on, it's kind of dead around here, but come summer this place really hops with tourists." Walking back toward the kitchen, she went on, "Grab a bowl of soup and plant yourself over there if front of the fire. I'll be right back with some hot chocolate."

Sitting on a comfortable looking couch, Nick placed a bowl of soup on his lap and took a bite out of a ham sandwich. The heat from the blazing fire felt good on his hands and face.

Back in the great room, Amelia helped herself to a sandwich and some soup as she sat on a matching chair by the fireplace. Kicking off her slippers she asked, "So, how was the trip up?"

Slapping some spicy mustard on his sandwich, Nick shook his head. "I've taken better journeys. I thought I was going to throw up when we landed in Pittsburgh, but I managed to keep my breakfast down. When we landed in Toronto, I got a little queasy, but once again, didn't embarrass myself by upchucking in one of those puke bags they have on the back of the seats. Then, when I went to get a rental, they were out of cars. I did manage to get one because of a cancellation. Froze my ass off on the way up here to the lake. Turns out the heater was on the fritz. Oh, by the way I stopped in that gas station at Young's Point. Some fella by the name of Hank told me to say hello to you."

Amelia smiled. "Hank knows just about everyone around the lake area." Making herself comfortable, she crossed her legs and took a drink of hot chocolate. "How are things down on ol' Fripp? I can only assume things are back to normal."

Nick gave her a blank stare and answered, "Well, from all the years I visited you and Edward down on Fripp, I thought I knew what a normal life on the island was like. That being said, this past summer was anything but normal. Going down to Fripp to empty your ashes for your *so-called death,* turned out to be the beginning of an ongoing catastrophe. What with Carnahan's goons, Sparks and Simons, tailing me like two dogs in heat, Shelby Lee's ex-boyfriend wanting to beat the crap out of me and the RPS Killer on the loose, my new life living on Fripp didn't exactly get off to a good start."

Holding up her cup in a toasting fashion, Amelia spoke, "Here's to better days ahead. All those people and the situations they caused are behind us now." Getting up, she walked to the massive fireplace and tossed two logs on the flames, set her cup on the mantle, turned and commented, "Carson was up here about two weeks ago. I didn't know if you knew that or not. He told me he hadn't seen you much since the incident that evening at the house on Fripp."

"I've run into him a couple of times over at the Bonito Boathouse," said Nick, "but it seems like he doesn't have much time to talk with me. I mean it's been nearly four months since we got rid of the Carnahan's, Charley Sparks and Derek Simons. It's almost like Carson is avoiding me."

"We talked about that very thing when Carson was here. Even though it's been four months since we conned the Carnahan's, that particular situation still lingers. Carson received a call form Joseph Carnahan a couple of days before he was last up. Just like Carson figured, the Carnahan's are conducting a massive search for their two past employees, Charley and Derek. You and Carson did a good job of convincing them that Sparks and Simons took off with their 5.8 million. You, Carson and myself are the only ones who know the truth. Sparks and Simons are twenty miles out at the bottom of the Atlantic Ocean off Fripp. They have long since become fish food. They will never be found nor will their millions. I've got that money stashed in banks all over Canada. It's safe and so are we if we play it smart. Remember, the Carnahan's, along with everyone else down on Fripp think I'm dead and that's the way it must remain. Amelia Falco no longer exists. Up here in Canada I'm known, as you well know as Emily Pike, Carson's younger sister. Carson is an amazing person. He arranged to get me a social security card, birth certificate and driver's license all in the name of Emily Pike."

With a look of amazement, Nick asked, "How is that possible?"

"Carson knows people, who for the right price, can get about anything done, legal or illegal. Like I said, Carson is amazing. He was always there for Edward and me and whether you realize it or not, despite the fact he hasn't talked with you much since that night at the house, he has been keeping an eye on you. In the coming months the Carnahan's will eventually give up on ever locating Sparks and Simons and then they'll move on to other things, but in the meantime we still need to be careful. The Carnahan's are not stupid. If they get the slightest inkling we conned them, well, I'd hate to think about what would happen."

Nick got up, and taking his drink walked over and stood by the window overlooking the lake. "Speaking of the Carnahan's. There has been many a night over the past few months when I have woken up in a cold sweat. I start thinking and remembering about what happened that night at the house and quite frankly, it gives me the willies! Before we got there that night I remember Carson telling me once things got started they would go quick and things might not go the way I thought they should. He also told me everything is not as it appears. I had no idea Carson was going to shoot Simons in the leg and then seconds later, kill him by shooting him in the head. Then, on top of that, you walk in…my grandmother who I thought was dead. But there you stood…alive and well. If that wasn't enough of a shock, you turn around and shoot Charley in the head…killing him. We talked about what happened later that night, and I know you did it to revenge the death of Edward, but still, it's just hard to deal with. I didn't pull the trigger on either one of those men, but yet, from time to time, that night comes back to me and it's hard to believe it even happened. I guess it's hard for me to understand how both you and Carson can just go on with your lives like nothing happened!"

Walking back over to her chair, Amelia sat and held out her hands. "Acting like nothing happened is just a façade, at least for me. Before that night at the house I never so much as fired a gun. It was just a matter of revenge due to Edward's death that drove me to kill Charley Sparks. I have my moments when I think back on that night, but then I remind myself it was a form of justice, and that I can live with. Now Carson is a different matter. Killing Simons was not the first time he has killed."

With a look of astonishment, Nick returned to the couch. "What are you saying?"

"I'm saying Carson Pike has, let's just say, eliminated some people in the past that deserved to die. So, to him, killing Simons was necessary. You should be glad he was with you this summer. If it wouldn't have been for his help, I really would be dead. Who knows how things would have turned out if Carson hadn't been around? You have him to thank for your life. The Carnahan's would have killed you too." Taking a spoonful of soup to her lips, Amelia went on, "I'm sure you didn't come to Canada to talk about the Carnahan's." Changing the subject, she took a bite of her sandwich. "What ever happened to that Ike Miller character, the one who wanted to beat the crap out of you?"

"The last we heard, he lit out for Florida. I don't think either Shelby Lee or myself will ever hear from him again."

Going in a different direction again, Amelia stated, "I guess the folks on Fripp or for that matter, all of Beaufort County are glad the RPS Killer has met his demise. Did they ever find out who killed that monster?"

Nick, not wanting to get into a conversation about the RPS Killer, due to Shelby Lee's involvement, went about ending the topic. "No, they never did find out who killed him. I don't even think there was that much of an investigation. If they ever do find out who it was, they'll probably give them a medal."

Now it was Nick who changed the subject. "I didn't come up here to talk about last summer, but I do want to talk about the future. For the reminder of my life, even though you are my grandmother, Amelia Falco, I'll always have to refer to you as Emily Pike. Here's the thing. When I moved down to Fripp marriage was the last thing on my mind. I'm not quite sure just yet, but if I was to marry, Shelby Lee would be the type of woman I'd consider."

Amelia smiled. "Have you discussed this little tidbit with her?"

"No, I haven't. It's just that we seem to get along rather well. Her daughter, who is about to turn ten, just loves me and I think quite a bit of her too. What I'm trying to say is if I do get married in the future and have children, you would be their great grandmother."

"That's right, I would. I'd never be able to tell them that, but I still would be Kirby's great-grandmother."

"I know that's the way things have to be, but it doesn't seem right. Hell, I've already had to lie to Shelby Lee about your death and that fabrication of the truth will continue as long as I know her. In the future I'd have to lie to my own children whenever they are around you."

"I've thought about that many times since the night at the house. We had no other choice but to do what we did. Carson is all right with the way things panned out and as time rolls on, I'll be okay. What you have to do is figure out a way to deal with the past and live with it. My advice is that you enjoy the rest of your life. Think about it. You're living on a private island in a nice house right on the beach; you've got plenty of money and from what you just said a few moments ago, a nice girl you might consider marrying. The Carnahan's, Sparks and Simons, Ike Miller and the RPS Killer are all gone from your life. You need to move on and we're going to start tomorrow by hopping in a little runabout boat I own. There's a great little restaurant on the other side of the lake. We'll head on over there bright and early for breakfast where you can meet some of my new friends. Then we'll head on up to Upper Stony Lake and do some antique shopping at a couple of quaint lake shops I know of. If we get back before it gets too dark, maybe we can take a short hike by the lake. I'll fix us some pork chops for dinner tomorrow evening."

Walking back to the couch, Nick stopped in front of the fire and extended his hands, feeling the warmth. "I guess you're right. When you think about it…what do I have to worry about?"

Sipping his third beer of the evening, Nick realized it was almost nine o'clock. He and his grandmother had sat in front of the fire and had talked for almost four solid hours. Yawning, he got up and placed another log on the fire. Going back to the couch he noticed Amelia sorting through a stack of older looking newspapers. Sitting down, he asked, "Do you always read the paper before you place it the fire?"

Amelia looked up and answered, "Oh these? No, I would never think of burning these. Well, let me rephrase that. I might burn these; I haven't made a decision yet. Your grandfather, Edward, collected these newspapers. He collected a lot of different things. For instance, he collected matchbook covers from different places he visited over the years: restaurants, bars, businesses. He also collected beer cans or bottles from little known brewing companies." Holding up a newspaper, she elaborated, "He also collected newspaper articles, mostly pertaining to important things that happened on Fripp Island. Like this one right here about when the Ocean Creek Golf Course was completed back in 1994." Putting the paper on the floor she picked up the next and commented, "Or this one about when the new fire station was constructed in 1999." Throwing the paper to the floor she picked up the next, took a swig of beer, and remarked with great interest, "Now here's one I've forgotten about. Back in the fall of 1989 there were two high school students found murdered on Fripp."

Making a strange face, Nick stated, "I never heard anything about that."

Amelia gave her grandson an odd look and explained, "You were only one year old when that happened. Of course you didn't know about it. If I remember correctly, it was a male and a female who were the victims."

Interested, Nick asked, "Did they ever catch the killer…were the murders ever solved?"

Picking up four more papers she flipped through them. Edward kept all the articles for weeks after the murders. They're all here. That was twenty-seven years ago. I can't recall how it all turned out. It was a cold case for years. So, to tell you the truth I don't know if they ever did figure out who killed those two kids. If I remember correctly, I think they had three other students who they thought might be involved, but they never really could put things together, so the case remained unsolved. I can't remember the name of the male that was killed but I do recall the female's name. It was Abigail James. Her father still lives on Fripp. I never liked Bernard James. I do remember during the original investigation he was at odds with the police. As far as I know the case has never been solved to this day."

Tossing the papers down to the floor she picked up another, "Here's an article on when they decided to refurbish the lighthouse over on Hunting Island."

It was just before midnight when Nick climbed the spiral wooden staircase up to the second floor loft where he was to spend the night. The large king size oak bed faced the upper section of the two-story window that looked down over the lake. Placing the afghan Amelia had given him for additional warmth at the bottom of the bed, he sat on a rocker next to the window and gazed out at the dim light that was positioned next to a small wooden dock connected to the rear of the house. A matching log, boathouse sat next to the dock. Despite the fact he was tired, he couldn't bring himself to the point where he felt he could sleep in peace. It bothered him that even though things seemed to have returned to normal back on Fripp Island, he didn't feel normal, or for that matter honest.

Kicking off his shoes, he slipped the sweatshirt over his head and pitched it on top of an old wooden chest at the foot of the bed. He sat in silence and listened to the tick, tick, tick of a mantle clock on the nightstand. He thought about the fact that even though things were what most folks considered normal on Fripp, he to some extent, was living a lie. Even though the events of the past summer were behind him, those very events still were somehow controlling what the actual truth was.

His grandmother, who he loved dearly, was thought to be dead by everyone she knew on Fripp Island or in Beaufort County. There were only four people who knew her death was staged: himself, Carson, and then there was the county coroner who had been paid off and another close friend, a mortician in Beaufort who owed his grandmother a favor. He really didn't realize how her staged death was going to affect his life until he had flown up to Canada. He had told the woman who had sat next to him on the plane that his grandmother had died. It hadn't been necessary to mention the fact she died, but it had become second nature to do so. Then, at the gas station in Young's Point he had almost slipped up and mentioned his grandmother's first name, her real name. As long as he was in Canada he was to refer to her as Emily Pike, Carson's younger sister.

Crawling beneath the cool sheets and the warm wool blanket, he thought about his relationship with Shelby Lee Pickett. He had to lie to her about his grandmother's staged death and if he was going to have any chance of a future with her he wanted it to be based on honesty. Of course, Shelby and he had their own secret, and the mystery of who killed the RPS Killer still remained a rather large question mark for the rest of Beaufort County. He was the only person aside from Shelby Lee that knew Shelby had killed the man responsible for the deaths of a number of young girls in the Lowcountry over the past two years.

Shelby Lee had made him promise that her daughter, Kirby was never to know the RPS Killer turned out to be her father; a man she had never met. Laying his head on the soft pillow, Nick realized that Kirby, at ten years of age, or for that matter any age, would find it hard to deal with the fact that her mother actually killed her father. Staring up into the dark beamed ceiling, he felt as if he were in the middle of Amelia's secret and also that of Shelby's. If either one of these secrets ever reared their ugly heads and came out, it could be devastating.

CHAPTER SIX

FOR THE FOURTH TIME OVER THE PAST WEEK, NICK HAD survived the dreadful experience, at least for him, of landing in an airplane. Emerging from the long cubical corridor leading from the plane into the spacious interior of the Charleston Airport, he thought about the week spent at Stony Lake with his grandmother. The one comforting thought he was bringing back to the Lowcountry with him was that Amelia was safe and had plenty of new friends. It was apparent she was moving on with her life, putting the fact she had killed Charley Sparks behind her. It had been difficult for him, while meeting people in the Stony Lake area to remember that Amelia was to be referred to as Emily Pike, Carson's younger sister. Placing the strap of his carry-on bag over his shoulder, he searched the crowded reception area up ahead and looked for Shelby Lee. At the edge of the reception area there was a bottleneck of people hugging and shaking hands. Looking at his watch, he realized his flight had landed nearly five minutes early. Maybe she hadn't arrived yet.

Forcing his way through the crowd, he caught a brief glimpse of her sitting at the end of a long row of connected seats. Spotting him at the same time, she stood and waved. Weaving in and out of passengers and those waiting for loved ones, Nick kept being brushed and shoved to the side. Frustrated, he pointed at Shelby and then to a row of vending machines against a far wall. Seconds later, they met, Shelby giving him a hug and a peck on the lips as she commented, "Welcome home, sailor!"

Looking for Shelby's daughter, Nick asked, "Where's Kirby?"

"She's with my parents. She always gets so excited during the holiday season. Most children her age always look forward to Christmas, but Kirby has always been partial to Thanksgiving. By the way…don't forget. You're invited to my parents' house this Thursday for Thanksgiving. Kirby just called me on my cell a few minutes ago. As we speak she and my mother are at the market selecting the turkey and all the fixin's."

Nick apologized, "I almost forgot. I guess spending a week in the Canadian wilderness, which believe me, is a totally different environment, took my mind off what I had to do when I returned. I can't remember the last time I had a home cooked Thanksgiving meal." Moving slowly past the crowd, Nick continued, "When I was young and still living at home my mother always fixed our family a nice meal. But that all ended when she and my father divorced. That was back when I was ten years old. After my folks split up, my mother lost interest in most holidays. After I graduated from high school and started college, I'd always eat out for Thanksgiving. I was alone and didn't have anyone to share the holidays with."

"Well that's all changed now. You just show up at my parents' house this Thursday and make sure you come hungry. My mother, as they say, really puts on the dog when it comes to Thanksgiving. Oh, by the way, she wanted me to ask you what your favorite kind of pie is?"

"If you're trying to tell me your mother is going to bake a special pie for me, tell her it's not necessary."

"It's not a matter of a pie being special or necessary. It's a tradition at our house. Everyone gets their own pie, their favorite. Every year since I can recall she has baked me a cherry, my dad gets lemon meringue and Kirby goes for pumpkin. If there is not a pie setting on the table that represents your favorite, my mother will be offended, so that being said...what's your favorite?"

"Well, since you put it that way, let's go with blueberry."

Walking through a doorway that led to the parking garage, Nick asked, "What am I required to bring for this feast?"

"Just a big appetite and I suppose if you want...a bottle of that spiked eggnog you get at the liquor store. My father is the only one who'll drink it, but he loves the stuff."

"Spiked eggnog it is then!" said Nick, stopping next to Shelby's red Jeep.

Pulling out of the parking garage, Shelby paid the parking attendant and asked Nick, "So, tell me all about your trip up to Canada."

"Well I don't think I'd like to live there, especially in the winter. It was cold and it snowed some every day. Carson's sister said during the summer it's really nice around the lake. The worst part of the trip was the flying. If I go again, I might drive next time."

Twenty minutes later, they were on the outskirts of Charleston, heading for Beaufort while Nick finished telling Shelby about the weeklong trip. "I left early this morning, drove to Toronto, nervously boarded a flight to Pittsburgh, had a short layover, got on another flight, and here I am! It was nice up there but I'm glad to be back."

Shelby flipped on her turn signal and sped around a slow moving truck. "Did you know Carson's sister before this trip?"

Nick was afraid this was going to happen, that Shelby would start asking questions about Emily Pike. He had to make sure while answering he didn't say anything that would reveal that Emily was really his grandmother, Amelia. "No, I didn't. He never even talked about her. After what happened this past summer, he suggested that I could use some quiet time away from Fripp Island and I should spend a week at his sister's lake house." Casually changing the subject, Nick inquired, "Enough of my Canadian adventure. What went on down here while I was away, anything exciting?"

"Actually, I had two different things happen to me. I wouldn't call them exciting…but strange. I got two odd phone calls. You'll never guess who they were from?"

"You're right, I won't, so you might as well go ahead and just tell me."

The first call I got was right after you left for Canada. Franklin Schrock, my boss, called me and told me he received a call from those people responsible for Ike Miller leaving town. Supposedly, Ike was spotted in downtown Savannah by someone who works for the people who beat the hell out of him last summer…"

Interrupting Shelby, Nick blurted out, "You mean to tell me that son of a bitch is back! I thought we'd seen the last of him."

"It didn't turn out to be any big deal. Apparently, they tailed him to the car dealership he still happens to own. He was there for about an hour, then he drove back to the airport, and they found out he took a flight back to Tampa, where he is currently living. I asked Franklin if this was anything I needed to be concerned about and he told me he was assured by the people he knows, if Ike Miller so much as looks at me the wrong way, it'll be the last thing he ever does."

"That may be," said Nick, "but the fact still remains, he was in Savannah. Remember those two goons he sent to your apartment. If they still work for him, he could arrange for them to pay you a visit while he is in Florida. He doesn't have to be here to cause you harm."

"I know, but I don't intend to spend the rest of my life looking over my shoulder, expecting Ike Miller or one of his cronies to jump out from behind a dumpster or tree and give me the what for. That was one of the issues we had to face last summer. I just want to move on and live a normal life."

"I agree," said Nick, "but that doesn't mean you shouldn't be careful."

Passing another vehicle, Shelby looked in the rearview mirror and continued their conversation. "The second call I got was from Harold's mother, Mrs. Benjamin."

Nick turned sideways in the seat and stared over at Shelby. "Whoa, whoa, whoa! Are you telling me Mrs. Benjamin, the mother of Harold, the former RPS Killer, called you?"

"That's exactly what I'm saying," said Shelby. "I told you the two calls I got were odd."

Looking out the front windshield, Nick responded in a state of disbelief, "I'll be the first to admit the call about Ike Miller was odd, but a call from the mother of the RPS Killer. That's just plain weird. Why in the hell would she call you? What did she want?"

"When I answered the phone and discovered the caller was Mrs. Benjamin, that's the same thing I thought. The long and short of the call was she and her husband, Harold Theodore Benjamin IV, Harold's father, invited me to their home in Charleston."

In amazement, Nick probed, "The same home you and your parents went to after you discovered Harold was the father of your baby, Kirby?"

"Yep, the same house, their mansion in Charleston. Mrs. Benjamin insisted I bring Kirby along, but I explained that was going to be impossible. I told her Kirby never knew and still does not to this day know who her father is. I explained that being only ten years of age, the shock of finding out her father was the RPS Killer was something I was not going to expose her to. I told Mrs. Benjamin as far as I was concerned, Kirby was never to know Harold was her father. Surprisingly, Harold's mother seemed to understand and said she and her husband still wanted to meet with me at their house. I responded and told her as long as I didn't have to bring Kirby along, I'd come."

In amazement, Nick asked, "And you went?"

"Yes, I couldn't see any harm in going to see them."

"You have…to be…kidding me," stammered Nick. "How could you possibly go to the Benjamin's home and sit in front of them, all the while knowing you killed their son? Don't get me wrong. Harold deserved being killed when you consider all the young girls he killed, but still, that had to be one awkward meeting to sit through."

"It was awkward. I sat in the same chair I sat in when I was there ten years ago. To tell you the truth both Mr. and Mrs. Benjamin were quite pleasant. At first, Harold's mother did most of the talking while she explained how shocked she and her husband were when informed that Harold, their only son, was the RPS Killer. Mrs. Benjamin actually started to tear up, saying she just couldn't figure out what she had done wrong in raising Harold that caused him to turn him into such a monster. No mother wants to admit her child is a psycho. As I sat there listening to her go on, I kept thinking to myself what Harold told me about Dennis, his father's brother who molested him, and how he never told his parents about what happened. I suppose I could have told them what I knew, but that would have led to awkward questions about how I knew these things. Besides that, what difference would it make now?

"After a few minutes of conversation between Mrs. Benjamin and myself, Mr. Benjamin spoke up. He said it was really hard on the family when Harold was expelled from the academy. It was the end of the Benjamin family legacy of attending the school. A legacy that had been in existence for decades. The embarrassment of Harold's untimely departure from the prestigious military academy took quite a toll on the family. The rich and powerful in Charleston, of whom the Benjamin family had always been a part, holds a rather high standard for its elite members and the demise of Harold at the academy left a stain on their family. As the years passed, the Benjamin's slowly regained their status in Charleston society, but then when it was discovered their son was the RPS Killer, the bottom fell out. They are planning on moving out of state to save face, possibly Georgia or North Carolina.

"Following a long dissertation by Mr. Benjamin, I finally broke in and asked them why they really asked me to their home. Mrs. Benjamin answered my question by saying they realized beyond any doubt they would more than likely never get to meet Kirby, their granddaughter. But, seeing how they were her grandparents, they wanted to help with her future education. They explained to me that when and if I decided Kirby was going to college, they wanted to foot the bill, regardless of what it cost. Mr. Benjamin said it was the least they could do. We talked for about an hour about my work and my plans for the future and if I was going to continue to live in the Beaufort area. I left, telling them I appreciated their college funding offer and would consider it in the future. They told me they would be in touch about Kirby's future and then we said good bye."

Nick, looking out at the passing countryside, probed, "Are you going to actually consider the Benjamin's paying for Kirby's future college education?"

"At first, when I was driving home from the meeting, I really didn't want to get them involved in any way in Kirby's life, but the more I thought about it, the more I realized how sincere they seemed to be. All in all I think they are genuine in wanting to help their only granddaughter to succeed in life. Besides that, I don't have to make a decision right now. Kirby won't be attending college until nine years from now. Depending on what happens in the future I may not even need the Benjamin's financial assistance, but it's nice to know it's there."

As they turned onto route 21 South, Nick asked, "So, I take it from what you've said you never intend to tell Kirby about her father?"

"That's exactly right and as long as you and I are seeing one another you have to promise me you will honor my wishes."

Running his index finger and thumb over his lips, Nick responded, "Rebel, my lips are sealed. You're secret is safe with me."

Shaking her head in wonder, Shelby Lee remarked, "It's been months since last summer and yet two out of the three situations we were involved with have loomed their ugly heads; first, the call about Ike Miller and now my recent conversation with the RPS Killer's parents. I'm starting to think these things will never completely leave us."

Nick laughed at her statement and made an observation of his own. "Some folks would say two out of three isn't bad, but in this case they would be wrong."

Shelby Lee, in confusion looked across the seat, asking, "What on earth are you talking about?"

"What I'm saying is all three past situations are still out there lingering. When I was up at Carson's sister's place she told me Carson had been up two weeks prior and told her the Carnahans had contacted him. Apparently, they are still searching for Charley Sparks and Derek Simons, who they are still convinced, left for parts unknown with their millions. Personally, I don't think it's anything to worry about. Like everything else in life, time has a way of placing things that, at the moment, seem insurmountable on the back burner of our mind. Months from now, this Ike Miller business will be long forgotten, along with Harold, the Carnahans and everything else that was unpleasant this past summer."

"I suppose you're right," said Shelby, "but at times it's seems like what we went through a few months ago just keeps popping up in my thought process. I'm really looking forward to Thanksgiving and having you over to my folk's place. I look at it like a new chapter in the book of my life and right now you're one of the main characters."

Poking fun at Shelby, Nick laughed, "Why Shelby Lee Pickett. Are you saying you like me?"

Stopping for a red light in Beaufort just before crossing the Woods Memorial Bridge, Shelby looked at a crew of men busy putting up the downtown Christmas decorations. Looking at Nick, she smiled and returned the humor, "Yeah, I do kind of like you. I might let you stick around for a while."

The remainder of the drive out to Fripp Island was filled with various topics ranging from how Kirby was doing in school, the unusual warm temperature for the time of year, how her job in Savannah was going and how the scenery along the Sea Island Parkway never seemed to change.

Pulling into the driveway of his seaside home on Fripp Island, Nick sat back in the seat and suggested, "Maybe we could grab some lunch over at the Boathouse. I'm starving. I was leery of eating anything on the flight down from Canada. I didn't want to get sick on the plane, but now that I'm back home I've got a hankering for some good 'ol local seafood."

"That sounds great," said Shelby, "but I really do have to get back to Beaufort. There's so much to do to get my parents' house ready for the holidays. My father is anal about the house being completely decorated by Thanksgiving. We have to haul all of our Christmas decorations down from the overhead storage area above the garage, sort everything out, purchase a tree, and put out all of the yard ornaments. It takes two days to get everything set up. I always dread decorating the house but once we get started it's a lot of fun. Non-stop Christmas music playing throughout the house, plenty of homemade cookies, my father always complaining about how some of the lights never work, followed by trips to Lowes for replacements. By the time you show up, we'll have everything ready. Except for the absence of snow, you're liable to think you're back in Cincinnati."

"I've had my share of snow and ice during Christmas seasons up north," said Nick. "I'll take palm trees and warm temperatures any time. I'd rather walk down the beach in the sand than plow my way through a foot of snow." Climbing out of the Jeep, he waved, "See you Thursday."

Standing in the front yard he watched Shelby back out and head up Tarpon Boulevard. He no sooner turned to walk around to the back when he was approached by Genevieve, her black puppy at her side. "Nick, you're finally back from the cold north. Welcome home!"

Bending down and petting the pup, Nick remarked, "She's really getting big. How's she doing on the beach?"

Nodding toward the beach, Genevieve responded with great enthusiasm, "She loves the beach. She likes to run up and down the dunes and run through the low brush. This past week, she's started to venture into the water." Placing her hand on Nick's shoulder, she went on, "Thank you so much for getting her for me. She makes walking on the beach an adventure."

Before Nick could say a word, she explained, "I kept a close eye on your house. I vacuumed yesterday morning. Everything is shipshape. Listen, are you planning on attending the annual Thanksgiving dinner at the community center this Thursday?"

"I'd love to, said Nick, "but I promised Shelby Lee I'd spend the day with her at her parents' house in Beaufort."

"I understand. She seems like such a nice girl and her daughter is a cute little thing. I guess we'll let you skip the party, but you have to bring Shelby Lee to our Christmas party, also held at the community center. We always celebrate it the weekend prior to Christmas. There'll be dancing, lots of food and games. Everyone on the island always looks forward to the evening. I do hope you'll come."

"Count on it! I'll ask Shelby if she'd like to come along."

"Great then," said Genevieve. Turning back toward her house, she continued, "I've got to get Ruth here fed. She knows when we finish up our walk she gets to eat. See you later in the week."

Catching a brief glimpse of the ocean, Nick hesitated before opening the screen door on the porch and thought about how much he missed the Atlantic. He really wanted to take a walk down to the water's edge but his hunger at the moment overrode a short walk on the beach. Entering the house, he stood and looked around the large home. Everything looked in order. Genevieve had done a good job in taking care of his home while he was away. It wasn't even five minutes before he had changed into what he considered comfortable island attire: white polo shirt, khaki cargo pants and flip-flops. Walking out to the garage he uncovered the '49 Buick, let the antique car warm up for a few minutes then backed out and headed for the Bonito Boathouse.

Crossing the canal bridge, he turned onto Wahoo Drive and passed the house he had painted for Mr. Parker. A van was parked in the drive and two small children chased a dog across the yard. Apparently, Parker had rented out the place. He smiled to himself, feeling the paint job he had performed on the house was one of the reasons it was now being rented.

Arriving at the Boathouse he had to park across the street at the marina store because the lot was full. Bounding up the wooden stairs he entered the popular island restaurant and was greeted by the hostess. "Why, hello there Mr. Falco. Will you be dining with us this afternoon?"

Looking at the lunch special on a chalkboard behind the reception desk, he responded, "Most definitely."

Grabbing a menu, the hostess asked, "Dining area or bar?"

Following the young girl, Nick answered, "The bar sounds good."

Seating him at a window table, the girl informed him a waitress would be by soon. Gazing out the window, he noticed the Fripp Island Rescue boat tied up at the end of the long pier. He recalled the afternoon last summer when he, Travis and Chief Lysinger made the trip out beyond Pritchards Island where he discovered the skeletal hand of what was thought to belong to Susan Dunn, one of the RPS Killer's victims. *Shelby was right,* he thought. *The events of last summer seemed like they would never go away.*

After ordering the special and a draft beer, he looked out across the vast salt marsh to the north and wondered if they had discovered all the girls the RPS Killer had victimized. His thoughts were interrupted by a gruff voice, "I see you're back!"

Carson took a seat at the table, removed his hat and placed it on the back of a chair by the window. "Your grandmother called me this morning right after you left the house up at Stony Lake. She told me she really enjoyed the time you spent with her."

Nick, skipped the formality of saying hello, but immediately asked, "Why didn't you tell me the Carnahan's recently contacted you?"

Carson waved off Nick's concern. "It wasn't important. I told you they'd stay in touch for a period of time. There's nothing to worry about. They have no idea their money is tucked away safe and sound in Canada. They'll continue to go on the wild goose chase we sent them on. Don't worry. If it was anything to be concerned over don't you think I would have come to you?"

Nick had always trusted Carson, ever since he came to the island and he didn't have a reason not to trust him now. "I guess so." Signaling the waitress at the bar, Nick spoke across the room, "A beer for my friend here!"

Leaning forward, Carson spoke in a low tone, "Are you satisfied with Amelia's decision to live out the rest of her life in Canada?"

"Well, I really don't have much of a choice, now do I?" smirked Nick. "I understand she has to live a life of being Emily Pike and not my grandmother, Amelia Falco. I don't like it, but I understand it."

Sitting back, Carson folded his hands across his chest. "It's the way things are. Ya know, she thinks the world of you. It really was painful for her to get you involved in all this Carnahan business, but it will soon be over. Eventually they'll tire of looking for Sparks and Simons, who they'll never find if they continue to search for the next one hundred years. We just have to be careful until the time comes when they throw in the towel…and they will. Eventually, they'll move onto other business which will in no way be connected to you, Amelia or myself."

The waitress delivered Nick's lunch at which point Carson spoke up, "I think I'd like to have one of those…and another round of beer."

Realizing the topic of the Carnahan's had ended, Nick changed the subject. "Anything exciting happen around here during my absence?"

"Actually, something very exciting happened earlier this week. Grady Phillips moved back to Fripp."

Confused, Nick inquired, "Who is Grady Phillips and why is the fact that he, as you say, has moved back to Fripp exciting?"

Looking at Nick in amazement, Carson stated, "I take it you must not be a race fan?"

Holding his hands up in confusion, Nick answered, "What are you talking about? Horse racing, auto racing, foot races…what?"

"Auto racing," announced Carson. "Grady Phillips, up until I guess it must be about eight years ago was one of the top drivers in the Nascar Series. He was just released from prison and now he's moving back to Fripp."

About to take a drink of beer, Nick hesitated and gave Carson an odd look. "Prison! I thought you said this Grady Phillips was a race car driver."

"He was a driver; one of the most popular to come along in years. To date he has led one of the most interesting lives I think I've ever heard of. He is a colorful character, to say the least. Grady was born in the backwoods down around Beckley, West Virginia. According to Grady his family for decades has made moonshine of the highest quality. His family lived deep in the West Virginia Mountains. When Grady turned fifteen, his twin brothers were seventeen. He also had two sisters, one about seven years old and then his baby sister, just a few months old. At fifteen he started to run shine for this father. His brothers, had already been driving and delivering homemade hooch to customers in and around the state. It's how they and many other West Virginia families survived. Grady told me he drove this hopped up, '56 Chevy, 427 cubic inch, high performance engine, high speed transition with a police radio. Grady took to driving right away and that boy could do things with an automobile that were unbelievable. The local police were always out to nab moonshiners and from time to time, but not often, they were successful. Grady learned how to drive by observing his two brothers. He took driving to the next level. At sixteen he was the talk of local moonshiners, the police and the citizens in the Beckley area. Grady told me he loved to drive. His father would load that ol' Chevy up with gallons of shine for deliveries and then Grady would take off as early as one in the morning, speeding down country roads always on the lookout for the law. He was never caught. He told me he outran the police more times than he could remember. Then, after a year of running shine for his father, the bottom fell out. One of these brothers was killed in a flaming crash while being pursued by the police. Right after that the authorities really cracked down on the local moonshining business. Grady's surviving brother and his father were given prison sentences and their stills were smashed..."

Nick politely interrupted Carson, "How on earth do you know all this stuff?"

Taking a drink, Carson smiled. "When Grady lived here on Fripp, we'd go out fishing from time to time and he shared his past with me. Like I said he had a very interesting life. Anyway, after they arrested his father and his brother, the moonshining business came to a grinding halt around Beckley. Grady, even though capable of making shine himself didn't have the needed capital to start up again and besides, the authorities were constantly monitoring the mountains so it was just too difficult to start up the business again. Grady, now sixteen, with his father and brother in prison, became the man of the family and had to support his mother and two sisters. He had no other skills other than driving and he was quite the mechanic so he got a job at a local filling station in Beckley pumping gas and doing some minor mechanical work. The gas station where he worked sponsored a race car, a stock car to be exact. Stock car racing, was at that time very big in West Virginia. Following two years of working at the station, Grady found himself at a dead end. His father died in prison and when his brother was released he lit out for the west coast, leaving Grady to fend for his family. Then, an opportunity popped up. The driver of the stock car the station sponsored got married and moved up north. The station needed a driver and since Grady was now eighteen, they gave him a shot at driving at a local stock car race. Even then, he had a lot of fans; his past reputation as a former moonshine driver adding a touch of excitement to the already dangerous world of stock car racing in West Virginia. Grady Phillips turned the stock car racing circuit upside down. He wasn't anything like any of the other seasoned drivers. He drove with reckless abandon. If he didn't win a race it was because he would crash. He was constantly taking out other cars and running them off the track. Needless to say, all the other drivers hated him. He was constantly getting into fights out on the track. Despite his racetrack shenanigans and his lack of racing etiquette, he received the Rookie of the Year Award and continued to raise havoc at racetracks around the West Virginia race circuit for the next three years. Whenever Grady Phillips was on the racing card fans would show up in droves, because they knew they were in for more than just an ordinary stock car race..."

Interrupting Carson again, Nick gestured, "Wait a minute. I thought you said this Grady character just got out of prison."

Carson pointed his beer bottle at Nick and answered, "He was just released, but that part of the story comes along later. You have to hear his entire story prior to going to prison to appreciate how unique Grady really is."

Nick raised his hand and signaled a passing waitress. "Two more beers." Looking at Carson, he laughed and commented, "I think this might be a long afternoon."

Finishing his beer, Carson smiled and shrugged. "Well, what else do you have planned for the day?"

Nick smiled when Carson's food was delivered to the table. "Nothing special. As long as I've got some good seafood in front of me and an occasional beer, I guess I could sit here all afternoon and listen to you."

Salting his cod dinner, Carson continued with the Grady Phillips story. "Grady really started to make pretty good money and things went a lot easier for his family. One evening, after he had won a major race in Northern West Virginia, a businessman from Pittsburgh approached him. He had a number of drivers and race cars in the lower ranks of Nascar. He said he was looking for a new, exciting driver and Grady fit the bill. Grady accepted his proposal and graduated from stock car racing to Nascar. The cars were different, faster, better built, the drivers were more experienced but that didn't make any difference to Grady. He still ran drivers off the course and got into many a fight. The fans looked him at as more than just another driver. He was an entertainer. Four years later at the age of twenty-six he made the move to the highest level of Nascar. He travelled from one end of the country to the other. He was just so different from all the other drivers. Every time he stepped onto a track it was like he was back on those country roads as a youngster running moonshine. His brutality and lack of courtesy on the track ticked off the other drivers to no end. He was a hated man by the drivers but loved by racing fans everywhere he went. For the next eight years he tore up tracks across the country, amassed a fortune from winning races and from doing commercials. He won two racing titles in his first six years but then in his eighth year of racing he was involved in a five-car crash up at Watkins Glenn, New York and was seriously injured. It took him a year before he could return to racing. The drivers were pissed because Grady Phillips was back; the fans were excited about his return. But, it was never the same. The drivers blackballed him. They ganged up on him and it became difficult for him to even finish a race. His injuries had taken a lot out of him and he wasn't quite as feisty as he had been in the past. He lasted another three years after his return, but then decided to retire and that's when he moved here to Fripp. He bought that big stone house out by the golf course. Shortly after he moved in, I met him at Johnson's Creek one night when I was out with some friends for dinner. Back then, he was the most famous person to ever live here on the island. He was such a likeable person. I can't tell you how many times Grady, myself and two of my other fishing buddies went out for days fishing. At night, we'd sit around and swap stories. It got to the point where no one wanted to talk about anything they did in their past life, because everything we did seemed to pale in relation to the life Grady led."

"So, when did he go to prison? It doesn't sound like he lived the life of a criminal."

"The reason he went to prison came a few years after he made what I always thought was a bad decision. After Grady lived here for going on two years he started to date an older woman. No one knew who she was or where she was from but it was always thought she lived right here on Fripp. We just couldn't figure it. It was said this woman was twenty years his elder, but that's just the way Grady was. He didn't do anything considered normal."

"Was this woman the reason why he eventually wound up in prison?"

"No, as far as we know she had nothing to do with that part of his life. Grady was used to the flamboyant lifestyle of being a race car driver. He was used to hobnobbing with movie stars and high rollers, so he soon became bored with life here on Fripp. As you well know when you cross the Fripp Island Bridge you're entering a six square mile island that's rather laid back; a place where you can come to get away from it all."

Swallowing a bite of coleslaw, Nick disagreed. "When I used to come here as a young boy I was always amazed at how peaceful it was here. When I moved here earlier this year, *as you know,* things were anything but peaceful. It's only been the past couple of months things have calmed down around here."

Buttering a roll, Carson nodded in agreement, and then went on with the story of Grady Phillips. "I guess Grady just got tired of being away from it all. I'll never forget the day he called me and said he wanted to discuss something. We met at the marina in downtown Beaufort and headed out in my boat. You see, Grady was well aware that I had dealings with some pretty unusual people in the past; your grandfather, for instance, who had ties with organized crime, not to mention all the connections I had with folks in the underworld. He wanted my take on an offer he had been made. He had been contacted by a man who represented a *crew,* a crew from Philadelphia."

"Now, I'm confused," said Nick. "The way you said *crew* doesn't sound like a group that's on the up and up."

Winking at Nick, Carson confirmed, "You're right on the money. A crew is a term used to identify a group of men who make their living stealing things that don't belong to them. A crew is normally very professional and is only interested in making what is referred to as big heists. Diamonds, jewelry, valuable paintings or large sums of cash. They usually consist of four or five men. One man, normally the leader, is the brains of the group. He chooses what, when and where the heists are to be made. He organizes everything. He makes all the needed phone calls and contacts and acquires everything the crew will need during a specific heist; vehicles, clothing, equipment and so on. The other members of the crew consist of an expert safecracker, an explosive man, a man who is a weapons expert and finally a driver. In Grady's case, this Philadelphia crew was in need of a driver, which he was more than qualified for."

Nick cut into his fish and asked, "You said Grady wanted to get your take on the offer. So, what did you tell him?"

"I was honest with him and told him even though he would not have to take part in an actual heist itself, it was still quite dangerous. He would still be a member of the crew and if caught would be just as guilty as the others."

"And how can you be so sure of that? I mean, how would you know the ins and outs of one of these crews?"

Leaning forward and lowering his voice, Carson whispered, "Because I used to run with a crew out of New York. Long before I knew or met your grandparents, I served four years in the army as special ops. After I was discharged with honor from the army I went back to a civilian life. I was young and dumb back then, full of piss and vinegar. I got hooked up with a crew, not a very experienced one, but nonetheless, a crew. I was their weapons expert. We pulled two jobs, made some good money but then we disbanded and I'm glad. That was a long time ago. A time in my life I'd just as soon forget."

Sitting back in his chair Nick took a drink and shook his head in wonder. "And the hits just keep on coming. You amaze me, Carson. I guess I haven't quite figured out if you're one of the good guys or one of the bad. After this past summer I'm inclined to believe you tend to lean toward the good side of things. If it wouldn't have been for you looking out for me, I might not be sitting here right now talking with you." Getting back to the conversation about Grady, Nick asked, "So, did Grady accept this crew's offer?"

"He never told me if he did. Then, a few days later the word around the island was he had closed up his house and took off. Turns out, he did go with the crew's offer. He now had become a professional thief, even though his part was driving the getaway car. Four years passed and I thought I'd never hear anything about Grady Phillips ever again. It was strange though. He never sold his house here on Fripp. Apparently, the older woman he had been seeing made sure the place was kept up. Then, suddenly, at the age of forty-five Grady shows up and starts living here on Fripp like nothing ever happened."

"Did he contact you?"

"Yeah, he did. It was a few days after he moved back here when I ran into him right here at the Boathouse. He was sitting right over there at the bar nursing a beer. He saw me when I came in and signaled me to join him. He shared a very interesting story with me. He told me he had four very successful years with the Philadelphia crew, and had amassed quite a fortune from pulling just two heists a year with the crew. Then, his fifth year, things went awry. They were on a big heist up in Boston. Turned out it was a set-up. The Feds were waiting for them. They lifted four million dollars in diamonds from an exclusive jewelry store. Everything went down when they exited the building. The authorities were waiting outside. According to Grady there was a lot of gunfire that lasted for about a minute or so. Two of the crew members were shot and killed. One of the crew members, while still firing at the police, threw the diamonds in the getaway car, but then he was shot as well. Grady, realizing things were not going well, hightailed it out of there…with the diamonds. He is the only one who managed to escape. Aside from the two crew members who were killed, the other two members were captured and eventually sent off to prison."

Caught up in the story, Nick quickly asked, "And Grady was never caught?"

"Not right away," said Carson. "Grady drove the getaway car up into the State of Maine where he dumped the car and bought another vehicle. Remember, Grady was a wealthy man before he joined the crew, so he had plenty of money to assist him in avoiding the police. He travelled around the country for a few months until he felt it was safe to return to his house here on Fripp."

Pushing his plate to the side, Nick spoke with great excitement, "I have two questions. First, what happened to the diamonds?"

"That's what everyone wants to know and doesn't know. I know what happened to them because Grady told me. Right after he returned to Fripp he hid the gems somewhere on the island."

Holding up his hands, Nick remarked, "Please don't tell me this is another case of money, or in this instance, diamonds being hid in a house. We just went through all that last summer!"

"He didn't tell me where he hid the diamonds and I'm glad he didn't. The last thing I needed was the Feds snooping around my business. I guess Grady figured it was over but I knew the Feds were not going to just give up. I knew they'd show up here sooner or later."

Nick asked his second question. "I can only assume they must have caught up with him because you said he was just released from prison."

"Things went pretty normal around here for the next few months, and Grady kept to himself. I'd see him on occasion around the island, but we never went fishing again or had lunch together. It seemed to me he was just waiting for the authorities to come for him. And they did. At first, after they discovered he lived here on the island, they simply observed him; where he went, what he did. Then, they started to put the pressure on. I have to tell you that was one of the most intense times on Fripp.

The Feds were always around watching and asking questions. There was a sense of excitement in the air. Four million dollars of diamonds hidden somewhere on the island, a famous race car slash getaway driver for a professional theft ring living right here. It became a nightmare. Folks driving around in their golf carts with picks and shovels digging up the ground all over the place looking for the missing diamonds. Finally the police had to start fining people for defacing island property. People were even digging up their own yards. It was nuts! To answer your second question; yes, they did eventually nail Grady. The diamonds to this day have never been located. The Feds were so pissed. People here on the island were not interested in cooperating with them. We all looked at Grady Phillips like some sort of hero. They finally sent him off to prison on some trumped up tax evasion charge, but told Grady if he would reveal where the diamonds were hidden, he could walk away. Grady told them he didn't know anything about any diamonds and in doing so, he served time, which was only four years. He got out in two and like I said just returned to his house here on Fripp."

"Let me get this straight. Grady has returned and the diamonds are still here on the island someplace."

"That's about it, but it's not that simple. The Feds have to figure at some point Grady will try to recover the diamonds. I ran into Grady at Bill's Liquor Store on Lady's Island right after he moved back. We grabbed some lunch over at Steamers and he told me it would probably be years before the Feds would finally give up on recovering those diamonds. So, for the time being he was just going to leave the gems where they were. We parted ways and he told me he'd give me a call sometime and we could go out fishing. That was early last week. I haven't seen him around in the past few days. I guess he's busy getting his life back together."

"You mentioned that folks around here are excited about him moving back. Why do you suppose that is?"

"Look, anytime someone famous lives down the street from you or in the same general area it's always exciting. Grady is not only famous but he is looked at by many of the folks here on Fripp as an outlaw of sorts. Think about it. Many outlaws in our past history have been viewed as heroes, not villains. Jesse James, Robin Hood, Bonnie and Clyde and on and on. I guess a lot of folks fantasize living the type of flamboyant lives some criminals live."

"So then you are of the opinion Grady Phillips is a criminal?"

"Correction! Former criminal. He served his time. Besides that, when I think of my past who am I to point fingers. The only reason I never wound up in prison is due to the fact I never got caught."

“Do you think my grandfather was a criminal?”

“No, I do not. Actually, he was one of the most honest men I think I’ve ever met. Now, between him, your grandmother, and you and me, we all wound up conning the Carnahans. Simply put, we all, each and every one of us, have somewhat of a criminal side to ourselves.” Standing, Carson grabbed his hat and laid three twenties on the table. “Lunch is on me. Oh, yeah, there is something else I want to talk to you about, but that can wait until after Thanksgiving. Welcome back to Fripp!”

CHAPTER SEVEN

THE EARLY MORNING SUN FORMED A ZEBRA EFFECT ON the far wall of the semi-dark bedroom, shining through the partially open Venetian blinds. Nick sat up slowly and adjusted his eyes, kicked off the sheets and sat on the side of the bed. Digging his toes into the thick beige carpet he felt like crawling back in the sack. Running his hands through his hair, he thought about what a long day yesterday had been The flight from Canada, the drive from Charleston, the long lunch with Carson. He had returned to his house at two in the afternoon, drank two beers while sitting out on the sun porch, dozed off and then woke up at five o'clock and climbed the stairs to the bedroom where he had intentions of lying down for just a few minutes. Looking at the clock on the nightstand he realized that those few minutes had turned into fourteen hours of straight sleep. It was now 7:10 Monday morning. Getting up he considered a shower but then opted for a refreshing swim in the Atlantic.

Slipping on a pair of cutoff jeans, a T-shirt and an old pair of deck shoes, he went downstairs where he grabbed a small bottle of orange juice from the fridge, which he downed quickly. Out the backdoor he went, across the small yard and gravel road and up the three steps that led to the small bridge, crossing over the dunes. Stopping on the bridge he placed sunglasses over his eyes since the sun was blazing down on the beach. There wasn't a cloud to be seen in the sky. Walking down the steps on the opposite side of the bridge, he surveyed the beach. Not a soul in sight. It was late November and most of the people that could be found on the beach were locals. The tourist season, for the most part, was over and would not pick up until next April.

Crossing the sand he looked up and down the beach. He had it all to himself for the moment. In the distance he saw a small flock of Pelicans and closer in, the usual seagulls in their ever-searching quest for food. Stopping at the edge of the water, he kicked off his shoes and slipped out of his shirt. Placing his sunglasses in one of the shoes he ventured into the Atlantic. Just like he thought, the water was cold…refreshing, but cold. Walking out until the low waves licked at his waist, he dove under a small wave and surfaced seconds later. If he wasn't awake he was now! He swam out past two more waves then turned right and swam up the shoreline for two minutes, stood, then turned and headed back.

Floating on his back he smiled while the warm sun caressed his face.

After a few more short laps up and down the shoreline, he walked back to the beach, put his sunglasses on and stared directly up into the ball of sun over the ocean. He hadn't brought a towel with him so he would have to depend on the light breeze coming from the ocean to dry his body. Slipping into his deck shoes, he draped the T-shirt around his neck and started to walk up the beach. He hadn't walked up to the end of the island that bordered Skull Inlet for some time. From where he was he knew from past walking experience it would be about thirty-five minutes until he reached the end of the island.

Five minutes up the deserted beach he noticed the tide was just beginning it's twice daily process of going back out, the sea at the very edge of the high rock embankment that protected the homes lining the ocean side of Tarpon Blvd. Passing one of his favorite homes he admired the flat yellow-sided structure, the entire back of the home covered with high glass windows that offered a spectacular view of the Atlantic. A man seated on the spacious porch, read the newspaper and waved at Nick when he passed by.

Walking around slated wood steps in ankle deep water, he remained close to the rock wall. As he got further up the beach he knew eventually the tide would be out far enough where he would be walking on wet sand rather than in the receding ocean itself. The sun felt good on his back and it hadn't taken long to dry his skin. Since he hadn't thought to bring along suntan lotion he slipped his shirt back on and walked around yet another set of wooden steps leading down from one of the homes on Tarpon.

Daydreaming while he walked up the long beach he thought about Shelby Lee and the fact this coming Thursday he was going to be spending the day in Beaufort at her parents' house celebrating Thanksgiving. He was finally going to meet Shelby's parents. He had no doubt she and her daughter, Kirby, had told her parents he had recently moved to Fripp Island from Cincinnati, had inherited his grandmother's home and at one time had his own painting business. The relationship he had with Shelby Lee this past summer went much farther than her parents could ever imagine. What would they think if they knew the truth about their dealings with Ike Miller, Charley Sparks, Derek Simons, the Carnahans and last but certainly not least, the RPS Killer? What would they think of him if they knew he had sat by and watched his grandmother and close friend, Carson, kill two men right in his own home? More than that, what would they think of Shelby Lee if they knew she had been the mysterious person who had killed the RPS Killer, who was actually Kirby's father. Looking up the beach he pondered, *Sometimes the truth is better left untold!*

Coming to the first of two low wooden barricades that ran from the stone wall halfway out to the water, Nick stepped over the two-foot high wall of weather beaten wood, the sides in areas covered with barnacles and seaweed. This is where the beach made a sweeping turn to the right and started to curve around to Skull Inlet just a short distance up ahead. The beach at this point was extremely wide and the sand he was now walking across was completely dry since the earlier incoming water hadn't reached that far. He was now on a section of the beach often deserted, even during the height of the tourist season. As far as he knew Fripp Island Security didn't even come up this far. Perhaps, the wooden barricades had something to do with it. Not many people walked all the way to Skull Inlet. Occasionally, in the past, he had seen someone walking their dog or riding a bike, but all in all, it was the most secluded part of the beach on Fripp.

When he approached the second barrier, which was a combination of a low wooden wall and piles of large rocks, he noticed a faded red plastic bucket and a tiny blue shovel some child must have left behind following a day at the beach. Passing between two large rocks he was now on the final stretch of beach bordering Skull Inlet. There was not a single footprint to be seen. There were a number of shells scattered across the sand, many of them broken. To the left, situated out on a sand bar, there were a large flock of gulls, hundreds he estimated.

Directly across the inlet he could see Pritchards Island. Stopping for a moment he stared across at the deserted island and recalled the night not long ago where he had escaped the Carnahans and especially Derek Simons who had tried to drown him. Suddenly, the relaxation of his casual morning walk was invaded with thoughts of that horrible night. His long swim from Carnahan's yacht, and how he had stumbled blindly across the island. Maybe Shelby Lee was right? The events of the past summer might haunt them forever.

Still walking, he found himself at the farthest part of the island. There was a stone wall marking the end of the beach, but on the other side there was another sandy area, where he had never, not once seen a footprint. Climbing over the wall, he was now standing on a section of the beach he had never been on before. Crossing the warm sand he came to yet another wall of rocks that were much higher preventing him from seeing what was on the other side. He imagined if he kept going he would soon come to the turnaround at the end of Tarpon Blvd. *What the hell!* he thought. He was in an adventurous mood. He was going over the rock wall and would continue on until he came to Tarpon.

Climbing the rock wall was not as simple as it appeared and while he continued toward the top he realized the reason why people turned around rather than going on farther. At the top of the wall, he gazed out across to yet another high wall of huge rocks a few yards across the sand. Turning around, it seemed easier to climb down facing the wall.

Jumping the last two feet he landed solidly in the sand. Turning to face the water on the small enclosed beach he noticed a man sitting on a large rock near the water's edge. The man was staring out across the inlet and apparently hadn't noticed his descent from the rocks. Tired from his climb, Nick approached the man and offered an enthusiastic greeting, "Good Morning!"

The man, not expecting anyone turned quickly, hesitated, but then responded, "Morning to you."

Approaching the man, Nick went on to explain, "I've never been up the beach this far. Didn't even know this tiny section was tucked back in here."

The man removed a ball hat from his head and wiped his brow with a white handkerchief from his pocket. Giving Nick a weak smile, he responded, "No one ever comes this far down the beach. Most of the locals don't even know about this place."

Nick motioned toward an adjacent rock. "Mind if a sit for a spell?"

"No, not at all…it's a free ocean."

Looking across at the other side of the inlet, Nick asked, "Ever been over to Pritchards Island."

The man followed Nick's gaze and answered, "If you're referring to the land on the other side of the inlet…no, I've never been over there."

Nick turned back to the man. "Do you live here on the island or are you just visiting?"

"I live here. I have one of those tree houses out on the edge of Fiddlers Ridge. It's pretty secluded. I like it that way. Actually, I'm not here on Fripp that much. My work requires I do a lot of travelling around the country."

"What do you do for a living?"

"I own a chain of restaurants. Pattersons…have you ever heard of it?"

"No, can't say I have. Do you have any locations here in the Lowcountry?"

"I have two restaurants in the area but they are not under the Patterson name. I have one in Savannah, ironically called The Savannah. The other establishment I own is over in Charleston. It's called the Upper Deck. The closest Pattersons is down in Atlanta. I bought the chain from a man who retired quite a few years back and retained the name Pattersons because it was so well known. At the time he only had fourteen locations, mostly on the east coast. Currently, I have forty-three locations. Kansas City, Denver, Detroit, Dallas, L.A., just to mention a few. Travelling around to the various locations keeps me on the move. I also have a house in Sacramento and one down in Palm Beach." Gesturing at Nick, the man probed, "What is it that you do."

"Right now, not much at all. I just moved to Fripp earlier this year. After my grandmother died, I inherited a home she has down the road on Tarpon. At one time I was a house painter, but that's kind of gone by the wayside, although I did paint one house here on Fripp. My grandmother left me quite a bit of money, so it's not like I have to seek employment anytime soon." Changing the subject, Nick inquired, "Do you come here to this hidden beach often?"

"When I was a kid, which believe me was a long time ago, I used to come here quite often. After I graduated from high school I went off to college and never returned to Beaufort. It was a few years later that I purchased the restaurant chain. I didn't move back until I guess it was about two years ago. I'm only here for a couple of months during the year. The rest of my time is spent out on the west coast or down in Florida, in between when I'm travelling on business."

Looking back toward the other side of the rocks, the man asked, "I'm surprised you climbed those rocks. It's not an easy climb. I suppose that's the reason a lot of folks don't know about this spot." Taking a prolonged gander at Nick's face, the man asked, "Haven't I seen you here on the island somewhere? You look familiar."

"Well, like I said, I moved here earlier in the year. I don't play golf or tennis so you couldn't have seen me on the course or the links. I eat at the Bonito Boathouse quite often. Maybe you saw me there. Other than that, I walk quite a bit on the beach."

The man waved off what Nick said and commented, "No, that's not it. I don't do golf or tennis myself and I haven't dined at the Boathouse since I was a kid. I don't walk on the beach, but I'm sure I've seen you before."

Nick looked out across the inlet, "They say at times you can actually walk over to Pritchards Island when the tide is out."

Suddenly, it hit the man. Pointing at Nick, the man seemed to light up as he mentioned, "Now I remember where I saw you. I've seen you twice, both times last summer. The first time I saw you was at the Dockside in Port Royal. I was just leaving the restaurant when I saw you get into somewhat of a tussle, with what I recall as a rather big fellow. He was getting the best of you when all of a sudden this other man, a rather large hulking man himself jumped in and saved your skin. I was standing right there. You were with a girl who was driving a red Jeep. Am I right?"

"Yeah, that was me. I lucked out that evening. I had to get some stitches but other than that I was okay."

Continuing his observation, the man went on, "The other time I saw you was when you were interviewed on television outside of the Bonito Boathouse during all that RPS Killer business. If I remember correctly the reporter claimed you were the one who found the remains of what was her name…yeah, Susan Dunn, that's it. Right after that you sort of clammed up. It really seemed like it was a short and awkward interview."

"Yeah, that was me also *and you're right!* It was awkward."

"Let me ask you," said the man. "Did they ever prove the hand you found was that of the Dunn girl?"

"No, that turned out to be a dead end. The hand was nothing more than skeletal bones. They were not able to lift any prints, so even though the RPS Killer is dead and gone, the identity of the hand still remains a mystery."

Looking off to the north of Pritchards Island the man stated, "So what you're saying is that the rest of that particular girl's remains are still out there somewhere in those salt marshes."

"I suppose so. Even though the case is closed, there could still be remains of other girls out there we'll never discover."

The man shook his head in wonder. "I had no sooner moved back to Beaufort when the first girl was found and it just went from there…bad to worse! Well, I'm glad that's all over now. Did they ever find out who killed that monster?"

Nick, knowing Shelby Lee killed Harold Benjamin was ready to change the subject but went ahead and responded, "No, they never did find out who the person was. I really don't think they went to all that much effort to discover who it was. I can tell you this. Whoever it was, they did us all a big favor by taking that maniac out."

The man stood and walked to the edge of the water, bent down, picked up a broken shell and tossed it back into the sea. "Ya know, it's strange, all this business about the RPS Killer. It's strange because the actions of one man affected practically everyone and everyplace from Charleston to Savannah. From my own experience I can tell you it changed the business at both of my restaurants here in the Lowcountry."

Interested, Nick asked, "In what way?"

"Like I said, it's very strange. Before the RPS Killer was brought down, his actions changed my restaurant in Savannah. If you'll recall, all of the girls he killed or abducted were from the Savannah area. It got to the point where folks were leery of going out, especially in the evenings. My lunch business wasn't hurt that much but the dinner crowd was reduced dramatically because of all the killings. Now, during the same time, it was business as usual over in Charleston. I suppose because none of the victims were abducted or found in the Charleston area, it wasn't as much of a threat to people. Here's the thing. The RPS Killer is gone and business has returned to normal in Savannah while in Charleston it has spiked up even higher than normal. People are amazed the RPS Killer, Harold Benjamin, was from Charleston. According to what the news media said, this Harold came from a very prestigious family, a family quite popular with the high rollers in Charleston…those with money. This just wasn't any old normal person. This was the son of an extremely wealthy family. I guess it's something for people to gossip about." Turning back, facing Nick, the man gestured toward the opposite rock wall. "I've got to get back home and pack. Tomorrow I fly out for the west coast and then it's down to Florida for a few days. I won't be back here to Fripp for close to two weeks. Listen…I can give you a lift back to your place if you'd like."

"Appreciate it," said Nick, "But I think I'll walk back. I might even take another swim."

"All right then," said the man. Handing one of his business cards to Nick, he remarked, "Stop by one of my restaurants and if you'll present this card it will entitle you and your guest to a free drink and complimentary dessert."

Looking at the card, Nick smiled, "Thank you…thank you very much."

When Nick turned to climb back up the rock wall he was stopped by the man when he spoke, "Well, like I said I'm glad the RPS Killings have ended. One thing we all seem to forget. There is always a reason why a man kills and no one but that man really understands his motive, however bizarre it may be. Maybe I'll see you at one of my restaurants."

Nick, halfway up the rocks stopped, turned and watched the man approach the opposite wall. Yelling across the sand, Nick introduced himself, "By the way…my name is Nick."

The man turned and waved, "Nice to have met you. My name is Miles."

By the time Nick crossed the first barrier on his walk back to the house he noticed a man walking three chocolate labs. The dogs, spotting Nick, immediately bolted in his direction. The man chased after the trio of brown dogs and yelled a friendly greeting, "Don't worry...they're harmless! They won't bite." The dogs approached and circled Nick, the largest of the group then ran out and crashed into an incoming wave. The other two remaining canines sat at Nick's feet, one raising his paw for some attention. The owner was now at Nick's side, apologizing,

"I'm so sorry they interrupted your walk. I always try to bring them out to the beach early before people start to show up. I hope you don't mind."

Reaching down to pet the two dogs, Nick laughed when the third dog returned from the ocean. "I love dogs. I think they're great. Earlier this year I gave my neighbor a stray I bought from a man up on Lady's Island. She walks the dog every day on the beach."

The man looked back up at the closest house and waved at a woman who stood on the massive porch. "Looks like my breakfast is ready. We better get back to the house. Nice to meet you." Nick stood and watched while the three friendly animals trailed their master across the sand and up the long wooden steps to the house.

Crossing the second barrier, in the distance Nick could see the beach coming alive, images of people walking from the houses down to the beach, carrying beach chairs and umbrellas. Walking out next to the water's edge he came upon a large group of sandpipers, their thin legs moving them rapidly up the beach while they pecked at some sort of food as the waves rushed back out to sea. Farther up the beach, close to his house, the beach was no longer deserted. People with suntan lotion smeared on their noses, and sunglasses covering their eyes, sat in beach chairs and read their novels or listened to small radios. A father sat with his daughter at the edge of the water while the young girl piled wet sand in a bucket and turned it over in her effort to construct a crude sand castle. A woman took a photograph of her two small children posing in the low waves. He was glad he was almost back to the house. He really didn't like being on the beach when people started to show up. People for some reason, at least in his mind, had a way of erasing the beauty and pristine atmosphere of the beach. Cutting across the sand he made his way up and over the bridge back to his house.

Opening the refrigerator, he grabbed a bottle of water and started up the stairs for a quick shower when the doorbell rang. Looking at the grandfather clock in the large living room he noted the time at just after nine in the morning. He couldn't imagine who was at the door. Walking down the hall he saw the opaque image of someone standing on the other side. The doorbell rang again as he opened the door only to see Carson Pike standing there holding two steaming cups of coffee and a brown paper sack. Holding up the sack, Carson smiled and announced, "How about some breakfast?" Pushing himself past Nick he spoke without looking back, "I've got fresh brewed coffee and bacon, egg and cheese biscuits. I hope you haven't eaten yet."

Closing the door, Nick trailed Carson down the hall back to the kitchen. "No, I haven't eaten yet. I just got back from a walk on the beach. I was just about to take a shower, but it can wait."

Placing the coffee cups and the sack on the kitchen table, Carson walked over and looked out the kitchen window facing the beach. "I've got to hand it to you. They say it's good exercise to walk on the beach. Never done much beach walking myself. In all the years I've lived here, I've never walked the full distance of the beach. I know a lot of people enjoy that sort of thing but I think I would quickly get bored. My passion, as you well know, is being out *on the water* in my fishing boat, not walking *next to the water*."

Joining Carson at the large double window, Nick inquired, "So, what's up? I'm sure you didn't drop by this morning to compliment me on my ability to walk on the beach or even to bring me breakfast. What's on your mind?"

"If you'll recall, when we parted ways yesterday after lunch, I told you I had something I wanted to talk with you about. I thought it could wait until after Thanksgiving, but I just got a call from a lady I know. She needs a favor and I figure you might be the person who could help her out."

Before Nick could respond, Carson grabbed one of the coffees and the sack and headed for the back porch. "I'd rather have our breakfast outside. The inside of your house makes me a little nervous."

Grabbing the remaining coffee, Nick followed Carson out to the screened-in porch and remarked. "Why would my house make you nervous?"

Seating himself on a wicker chair, Carson took a sip of coffee. "Think about it. This is the first time since the night your grandmother and I shot Charley and Derek right inside there in your living room that I've been back to your house. I guess it's like returning to the scene of the crime."

Sitting down himself, Nick put his coffee on a small side table. "I know exactly what you mean. It took me weeks before I could even walk into the living room without looking at the chair Charley sat in when Amelia blew him away. Hell, there's still faded bloodstains on that chair. You can barely see them, but I know they're still there. That night after you carted Sparks and Simons out to sea, Amelia and I had quite a talk. One of the things she suggested was that I have the chair reupholstered, but I just haven't gotten around to it. That night still haunts me. I guess it always will." Getting off the subject of the past evening last summer at the house, Nick asked, "This lady that needs a favor. What's that all about?"

Unwrapping one of the sandwiches, Carson took a large bite, wiped the side of his mouth and then answered, "The lady's name is Mrs.

Yeats. She lives here on Fripp over in the Deer Lake area. I've known her for years. She knew your grandparents. She was never really that fond of Edward but she liked Amelia. They did a lot of things together. They belonged to the Preservation of Loggerhead Turtles, played some tennis together and helped to clean the beach. Gretchen...Mrs. Yeats... lost her husband a year before I moved here to Fripp. That was nearly thirty-some years back. The reason for my coming to you is I ran into Mrs. Yeats last week at Barefoot Farms picking up some produce. She told me she was thinking about selling her place and moving to Beaufort to a senior citizen living facility. She's around eighty and can still get around pretty well, but she said the house was too much for her anymore what with all the housework and lawn maintenance. She asked me if I knew of anyone who could give the house, inside and out...a good coat of paint. Of course, I thought of you right away, especially after the great job you did on Parker Sim's place. I told her I'd get in touch with you and see if you're interested and she said there was no hurry, but then she called me last night and explained there was an opening at the facility she was looking at and she needed to start getting the house ready to sell as soon as possible. So, what do you think?"

"If you're asking me if I'd be interested in painting another house here on Fripp, sure I guess so. How big is this house?"

"I've only been in the place one time and that was years ago at a Christmas party Gretchen threw. It has four bedrooms, three and a half baths, dining and living room, kitchen, small office area and of course a laundry room. It is one of those elevated homes where you can park underneath the actual house. It's two stories and there is a pool in the neighborhood. A lot of the homes at Deer Lake are rentals. I asked her when she got the house painted if she wanted to rent the place out, but she said no. That would be too much of a hassle for her. She said she'd rather sell the place, which brings me to the second thing I wanted to talk over with you. I thought maybe you might be interested in buying her property."

About to take a bite out of his breakfast sandwich, Nick looked at Carson in wonder. "Why on earth would I want to purchase a property?" Gesturing toward the large window at the back of the porch, he exclaimed, "In case you haven't noticed I already have a house. Why would I need a second house? You can only live in one at a time."

"I didn't mention buying the property with the thought in mind of you actually living there. I was thinking more along the lines of an investment...you could rent the place out for probably nine months out of the year. Rental properties in this part of the Lowcountry are always a good investment."

"Look, I've painted many a house over the past few years, but that's all I know about taking care of a property. I don't know how to repair a broken water heater or anything about plumbing or electrical and besides, what about all the paperwork involved in renting out a property?"

"You don't have to know all that stuff. You have money. You pay people who are experts in those fields when and if you have a need for them. You know Khelen Ridley. I'm sure he'd help you out and guide you to the proper people who could handle those particular situations. Aside from painting the house, you just sit back and allow the house to appreciate over the years, then later on, when and if you decide to sell the house you make a handsome profit."

Giving Carson a confused stare, Nick asked, "How can you be so sure it all works that way?"

"Because I just happen to own three rental properties. Two over on Harbor Island and another over on Cat Island. I purchased the one on Cat twenty years ago. I just sold it and made a net profit of seventy-nine thousand dollars. I'm planning on selling the two on Harbor within the next two years. I'll probably clear close to two hundred thousand combined on both properties. You see, that's the way it works. A lot of folks come down this way and purchase a rental property thinking they are going to get rich quick, but they soon discover with the overhead of maintaining a property, any cash flow they have is rapidly dissolved each year with repairs and upkeep. The secret is to borrow the money from the bank to initially purchase the property, then when you rent it out for let's say twelve hundred to fifteen hundred a month, most of that goes toward paying off the monthly mortgage. So, in short the people who rent from you are actually, over the years paying for the house. Then, down the road twenty years or so, you sell and since the property increases in value, you realize a large profit. I wish I had invested in even more properties when I was younger. It's just a method of insuring later on in life you'll have some money coming in."

"This all sounds very interesting;" said Nick, "even logical. Let's say, that I would consider purchasing this property. What is this lady…this Mrs. Yeats asking?"

The property was just recently appraised at $625,000. Fortunately, Gretchen has quite a bit of money so she is not concerned with actually making any money on this deal. She told me she wanted to move the property quickly and was going to put it on the market for $475,000. The way I see it…that's one hell of a deal. When she gets around to listing the property it won't last but a few days before some savvy investor snaps it up. I mean, you'd be picking up $150,000 in equity right out of the starting gates." Taking another bite of his sandwich followed by a swallow of coffee, Carson shrugged. "Do what you will, I just thought I'd mention it to you."

Nick got up and walked to the back screen and looked out at the ocean. "And you think I could get a loan?"

"Piece of cake," commented Carson. "You're the type of buyer banks love. You already own a house worth over a million dollars and you also have a fat bank account. They'll bend over backwards to help you buy that house."

Leaning on the windowsill, Nick nodded his head, "Tell ya what. Do you have this Gretchen's phone number and address?"

Carson patted his pants pocket. "Got it right here in my wallet."

"All right, give it to me. I'll give her a call later today and set up an appointment to give her an estimate on painting the house. While I'm there, I'll have a look around. Who knows? Maybe I will buy this property."

It was close to eleven o'clock when Nick stepped out of the shower and wrapped himself in a large terrycloth towel. Earlier, after Carson left and during the time he took his shower, Nick rolled the possibility of buying the Yeats property around in his mind. Carson made it sound easy enough, now all he needed to decide was if he wanted to be a Lowcountry landlord. Picking up the small piece of paper with Mrs. Yeats contact info on it he thought about what his grandmother was always saying. *A turtle doesn't get anywhere unless it sticks its neck out!* Picking up the phone on the nightstand, he dialed the number and waited while he continued to dry his wet hair.

After three rings a pleasant voice answered, "Yeats residence."

Nick cleared his throat and then identified himself, "Hello...Mrs. Yeats, my name is Nick Falco. I'm the person Carson Pike spoke to you about in regard to painting your house on Deer Lake. I have some free time today and if you'd like I could drop by, give your house the onceover and then give you an estimate."

"That would be wonderful. What time is good for you?"

"You name it. Actually, I'm free all day."

"If you could be here within the next hour that would be great because I have to drive into Beaufort by three o'clock because I have an appointment in town."

Nick picked up the small alarm clock and noted the time, 11:15. "Just give me about an hour. Let's say I drop by around 12:30. How's that sound?"

"Fine...just fine. I'll be waiting...Mr. Falco."

Hanging up the phone, Nick went to the large walk-in closet and selected a light blue polo shirt, white slacks and slip on dress shoes. It was important he look professional or at least like someone who was capable of purchasing the house. Downstairs, he rummaged through the fridge for something to eat. Carson's breakfast sandwich had done little to curb his appetite. Removing a package of sliced Swiss cheese and some deli ham, he slapped a slice of each on a piece of week old bread, slathered on some mustard and then added another slice of bread, grabbed a can of soda and went out onto the back porch. Surprisingly, in the last hour the sun had become hidden behind cloud cover and it began to appear that rain might be on the way for the South Carolina coastline.

Reclining in a wicker rocker he thought about the three modes of transportation he had and which he should take. His motorcycle was his favorite way to get around, but with the prospect of upcoming rain, combined with the way he was dressed, he thought he might appear stupid. There was also the possibility an older person may look at someone riding a motorcycle as rebellious. *The bike was out.* Next, he considered driving the 49' Buick, but thought better of it. It might seem too flamboyant. He would take the Lexus. What was it he had seen on television just the other day during an advertisement for Lexus? Their tag line was, *The pursuit of perfection.* It bespoke of prosperity and he was sure if Mrs. Yeats saw the car she would most likely be impressed. Finished with his sandwich, he stepped back inside and went to a roll top desk where he found a small black leather carrying case he assumed, at one time, had been owned by his grandfather. Tossing an 8 X 11 legal size notepad and two ink pens in the empty case, he inspected himself in the hallway mirror, and satisfied, headed out the back door to the garage.

Unlocking the garage door, Nick entered but then stopped when the door slammed shut behind him. Suddenly, he recalled the night last summer when he had been knocked out in the garage, only to wind up out at sea on the Carnahan's yacht. Staring at the door, Nick frowned in wonder. *Is there any place on this island where I won't be reminded of last summer?*

Shaking off the negative thought he opened the overhead door, climbed in the Lexus and said aloud, "I have got to get past last summer."

After a few minutes of the car warming up, he backed out, closed the garage and headed up Tarpon. Checking the gas gauge, he noticed he was at a quarter of a tank. He didn't like to get below a half tank. Tomorrow, he'd head into Lady's Island and gas up. Besides, he still had to pick up the spiked eggnog Shelby had requested.

It wasn't even three minutes when he turned onto Deer Lake Drive. He didn't know much about this part of the island. The most recent time he had been here was when he had first moved to Fripp and he had driven the golf cart up and down every possible road on the island. The only other time he had been to the Deer Lake area was when Amelia had driven him through the neighborhood as a small boy. All of the homes on either side of the paved road were tucked back into old live oaks, palm trees and large palmetto bushes. Each home, even though positioned next to one another, offered at least some level of privacy.

Pulling up to 311, he drove up a short gravel driveway and stopped in front of the two-story stucco structure. Parking in front of a wide, centered stairway, Nick got out and noticed right off, the blue colored paint that had, at some time, been applied had faded. It was easy to see the house was indeed in need of a new facelift. He would have never chosen the shade of blue the house was painted, but if it turned out that is what Mrs. Yeats wanted that's what he'd do if he got the job. *The customer was always right!*

Ascending the long stairway, he crossed the covered porch and rang the doorbell. Looking in one of the sidelights flanking the door he could see the image of someone approaching the door. When the door opened there stood a short, grandmother type woman; flowered dress, conservative shoes, eyeglasses perched on a pug nose, hair up in a bun. Offering Nick a tall glass of iced tea she held in her right hand, she spoke, "Mr. Falco, I presume. Please come in. I just finished making a batch of sun tea. It's sweet. I hope that will be all right?"

Taking the tea, Nick smiled. "Is there anything other than sweet tea in the south?"

Sitting down on a flowered love seat in the large foyer, she gestured at a matching chair. "Please have a seat while I give you the rundown on this place, then I'll give you the grand tour."

Setting his small briefcase at his feet, Nick took a swig of tea and made himself comfortable while Mrs. Yeats went on, "My name is Gretchen and I've lived in this house for thirty-seven years. My husband, Clark passed away a few years after we moved here. It's gotten to the point where I am just getting too old to care for the place so I've decided to sell the property and move to a senior living center in Beaufort. I hate to sell the place, because I've got so many memories here, but for future health reasons I must make this decision. The house needs a lot of attention and updating. All of the rooms and the exterior need a fresh coat of paint."

Standing, she gestured at an open door on the left. "Let's begin with the tour. Please follow me if you will."

Getting up, carrying his tea and briefcase, Nick followed her into a large bedroom while she explained, "This is the master bedroom. It has a large walk-in closet with an attached full bath." Crossing the hall she pointed at the hardwood flooring. "The house has wood flooring throughout. In some places it has seen better days. The floors will probably have to be replaced or carpeted over. Now, over here we have a spare bedroom for guests or it could be a bedroom for a child." Moving down the hall they entered a combination kitchen and living room that spanned the entire width of the home. On the back of the room there was a wall of sliding glass doors that, at the moment were open, leading out to an expansive screened-in back porch, overlooking a small pond surrounded by thick foliage and trees. Walking out onto the porch, Gretchen went on explaining, "This has always been my favorite part of the house."

Ten minutes later, back down in the kitchen, the tour of the entire house was complete. Sitting at the kitchen table, Gretchen placed a plate of peanut butter cookies in front of Nick, took one herself and sat. "Now, let's talk business, Nick. Is it all right if I refer to you by your first name?"

Nick bit into a cookie and answered. "Please do."

Looking around the kitchen, she remarked, "Carson Pike is a dear friend of mine. He always has been. I know for a fact he would never lead me wrong. He told me when it came to painting a house you're top notch. That's good enough for me. He also told me he was going to suggest to you that you consider buying my property. Did he have that conversation with you?"

Swallowing, Nick answered, "Yes, he did…earlier today we talked about that very thing. Carson told me you knew my grandparents, Edward and Amelia?"

"Yes, I knew them quite well, especially Amelia. We did a lot of things together. I'm really sorry you lost her earlier this year. I think we all lost her. She was indeed a great lady and everyone on the island who knew her will miss her." Looking at the oven in the kitchen she shook her head in sadness. "I can't tell you how many times Amelia came to my home during the Christmas holidays and together how many dozens of cookies we'd bake right here in this kitchen." Bringing herself back to the moment, she waved her wrinkled hand, "I'm getting off the reason why you're here. Now, about the house. Let's not beat around the bush, because I don't have a lot of time for that. So, Mr. Nick Falco, are you interested in painting this house or buying it?"

Nick finished his cookie, took a swallow of tea and smiled, "I'm considering both, because if I do buy your house, I'll probably be the one who winds up doing all the painting. Carson told me you were offering the home for $475,000. Is that correct?"

"Yes, that's correct. They tell me the house is worth $625,000. I just want to get the place sold and move on with my new life in Beaufort."

"Carson tells me this is a deal I can't pass up. I would like to buy your house, Mrs. Yeats...Gretchen, but I have to see if I can be approved for a loan before I can commit. Will you give me a day or so to contact a banker?"

"Of course. That will not be a problem. I've always been a good judge of character, Nick. You strike me as not only honest, but a good person. I think you would take care of my old house here and that's important to me. Let's say I give you a week. That should be plenty of time for you to set financial matters in place. Will an old fashioned handshake do or do you want something in writing?"

Sticking out his hand, Nick confidently answered, "A handshake will be just fine!"

CHAPTER EIGHT

NICK WALKED OUT OF THE MAGNOLIA BAKERY AND CAFÉ AT precisely eight-thirty, a half-hour prior to his scheduled meeting with Khelen Ridley. Wiping a few remaining crumbs of his breakfast off the front of his suit, the only one he owned, he climbed into the Lexus, sat back and relaxed and thought about what he hoped to accomplish. Following his meeting with Mrs. Yeats the previous day, he had called Ridley and set up a meeting to discuss what had to be done in order for him to purchase the house on Deer Lake Drive. He hadn't given Khelen all the details, but told the lawyer he would fill him in when they met.

Pulling onto Congress Street, he made a right onto Boundary and continued until he reached Bay. It was early Tuesday morning and most of the shops in downtown Beaufort were not open yet. A woman swept the sidewalk in front of her small jewelry store, while another man washed the windows of a gift shop. Passing the marina, he gazed out at the Beaufort River. There was one boat pulling out and two people boarding another watercraft tied to the dock. At the end of the downtown parking area, three people who worked for the buggy ride company were tending two different draft horses, while another employee wiped down the seats of one of the bright red buggies. Turning onto Prince Street, he made a quick left into one of five parking spaces on the side of the large white mansion that served as Khelen Ridley's office. Khelen's BMW convertible was parked in the first spot. Nick looked at his watch. He was ten minutes early but he decided to go in.

Khelen's secretary-receptionist was busy at her neat desk getting ready for the day while she arranged papers, a stapler, notepad and ink pens. Looking up from her tasks, she noticed Nick when he entered and smiled genuinely. "Good morning Mr. Falco. It's been what…almost five months since you were last here."

Nick walked to the desk and responded, "That sounds about right. I guess it was last July when I was here. You probably already know this but I have a nine o'clock appointment with Khelen."

"Yes, when he first got in this morning he informed me to be expecting you. He told me when you arrived to send you back. Would you care for coffee or maybe some water?"

Walking down the hall to Khelen's office, Nick politely declined, "No thank you. I just had breakfast."

Entering the attorney's office, he found the lawyer seated at his desk reading the morning paper. "Good morning, Khelen. Catching up on the latest news...are we?"

Tossing the paper to the side, Khelen stood and extended his right hand. "I never read the news. It's too depressing. A fire here, a robbery there, someone arrested on drug charges. The only thing I read are the funny pages and the stock market report. The funnies always make me smile and the stock report depending on the goings on of the previous day normally cause me to start the day with a good attitude. Yesterday was an especially good day. The Dow Jones Industrial was up 150 points, GE up 1.2 percent, Boeing 4 and quite a few other stocks I own a portion of are doing well. Stocks are always, over the long run a great investment. I made over three thousand dollars before I even crawled out of the sack today."

Pulling up a chair in front of the desk, Nick inquired, "Do you always make money? I've never followed the market. I've seen occasional reports on TV about how the market is up or down. Wasn't it just a couple of weeks ago when it was reported down over four hundred points?"

"Yep, that was a bad day for investors, but I'm in it for the long haul. I lost my ass that day, but since then the market had rebounded and I recouped everything I lost and have seen some substantial gains. If you'd like I can put you in touch with my broker. With all the money you now have you may want to consider investing in some selected stocks." Snapping his fingers, he suddenly remembered. "The money your grandmother left you. Didn't that include some stocks and bonds?"

"Yeah it did. I've never really paid much attention to those investments. I figure she and Edward had them for some time and I didn't need to mess around with them."

"That's precisely the wrong thing to do. You need to keep an eye on your investments on a daily basis. It only takes a few minutes. The market is susceptible to sudden up or downswings. It's all based on emotions, on how things are going in the world. All it takes is for one catastrophic moment or announcement and if you wait too long to react you can find yourself without a pot to you know what in." Opening his top desk drawer, he removed a file folder, produced a card and flipped it across the desktop in Nick's direction. "That card represents the broker here in Beaufort I have used for years. His name is Jim Strong and he's been in the business as far back as I can remember. He's made me a lot of money. What you need to do is give him a call and set up an appointment. When you go to see him take along the stock information

Amelia left you. You may need to make some changes…maybe not. Jim will steer you in the right direction."

Getting up, Khelen removed his suit coat and went on, "Now, let's get down to the reason for your visit today. You said on the phone yesterday you were considering purchasing a property down on Fripp…correct?"

Placing the business card in his jacket pocket, Nick responded, "Yes, that is correct. It's in the Deer Lake area. Are you familiar with that part of Fripp?"

"No, I'm not. Despite the fact I've been on Fripp Island hundreds of times over the years, there are some neighborhoods I've never been to, but without even seeing this house, the fact it's on Fripp itself tends to lead me to think it's a nice home."

"It is a nice home. It needs a serious coat of paint and quite a bit of updating, but it's situated in a great location in a secluded spot on Fripp. I'm thinking of fixing it up and renting it out."

"Smart move," commented Khelen. "Most people don't know this but ninety percent of the wealthiest people in America at one time or another are or were invested in real estate and the stock market. The market will always go up and property values will always appreciate. I own three apartment complexes. Two here in Beaufort and one over in Savannah." Walking to a small office refrigerator, he removed a bottle of cold water and offered, "Thirsty?"

Nick waved off the water, "No thanks."

Taking a drink, Khelen walked back and sat at his desk. "Give me the details on this property. First of all, why is the current owner selling?"

"I met with her at the home yesterday," said Nick. "The owner's name is Mrs. Yeats…Gretchen. She's a sweet old widowed lady, around eighty, who has lived in the house for over three decades. She is planning on moving to Beaufort to a senior living center. She told me the house appraised at $625,000. She has decided to sell the property for $475,000. Carson Pike told me that's a great deal and the property will sell fast, so I had better jump on it before someone else does. We sat in her kitchen, had iced tea and peanut butter cookies, and then shook hands. I told her I wanted to buy her house, but I needed a few days to see if I could actually get a loan. She agreed to give me a week, so I need to get moving on this. What do I need to do?"

"Does this Mrs. Yeats have a realtor?"

"I don't know. We never discussed that. I guess that's important…right?"

"Not necessarily. If she does not have a realtor, everything can be handled by an attorney who is qualified to conduct a closing meeting." Khelen smiled and held up his hands. "Just so happens…I'm a qualified real estate lawyer. What you need to do is give Mrs. Yeats a call and see if she has or is going to get a realtor. If she hasn't you can suggest having the closing right here in my office. It will save you both some real estate fees. We can have everything wrapped up in about an hour when all three of us get together. But first, before we do any of that we need to get the ball rolling and get you preapproved for a $475,000 loan at the bank. We can take care of that later on this morning. We'll just walk up the street and see ol' Albert Zellman, the president of the bank where Edward and Amelia dealt for years. Then we need to get a title search on the house started. If I were you I would request a property and insect inspection. It normally takes around thirty days to close on a real estate sale, but if we go with an immediate possession deal we can wrap this entire process up in a few days." Snapping his manicured fingers, Khelen remembered. "That's right…it's going to be Thanksgiving this Thursday. That throws a cog in the wheels. We only have today and Wednesday to get this underway. After that things will come to a grinding halt with the holiday looming over us. We might not be able to get you approved until next Monday or Tuesday. All of this depends on what Mrs. Yeats wants to do. Do you have her home number?"

"Yes, I do. Right here in my wallet."

"Why don't you give her a jingle and see how she feels about not utilizing a realtor and see when she can get together with you and me here at the office after the holiday." Getting up, Khelen gestured at the phone on the corner of the desk. "You can sit right here and make the call if you'd like. I can step out of the office if you need some privacy."

Walking around to the opposite side of the desk, Nick remarked, "No need for that. There is nothing I need to keep from you or that you do not need to hear."

"Nonetheless, I have to use the restroom. You go ahead and make your call. I'll just be a minute."

Khelen left the room while Nick dug out the slip of paper that had the required info he needed. Laying the small section of paper next to the phone, Nick dialed the number. Three rings later, the familiar voice of Gretchen Yeats answered, "Yeats residence!"

Nick was just hanging up the phone when Khelen returned to the office. Nick smiled and confirmed, "I just finished talking with Mrs. Yeats. She has no current realtor and would just as soon close on the house as soon as possible. Her place at the senior living center is ready for her to move in. When I told her you had been Amelia's lawyer for years, she said that was good enough for her. She told me if it's all right she could meet with us here at the office anytime next week. So, all we have to do is decide on a time, I'll give her a call and we're good to go."

Khelen clapped his hands. "Sounds good! Is ten o'clock next Tuesday morning good for you?"

"Yeah, ten's good for me. I'll just call her back and set things up."

"Good!" said Khelen, "I'm just going to step out and let Gwen know we're going to walk up the street to the bank."

Two minutes later, Nick walked out into the reception area where Khelen was talking with his secretary. Khelen stopped talking and shrugged his shoulders, waiting for the results of the phone call.

Nick responded by announcing. "She said she'd be here next Tuesday with the house keys at ten o'clock sharp."

"Excellent!" beamed Khelen. "Just let me grab my suit coat and we'll walk up to the bank."

Seconds later, Khelen returned and headed for the front door. "Next stop…Mr. Zellman's office!"

Outside, standing on the front sidewalk directly in front of the mansion, Nick asked, "How far is the bank?"

Khelen started walking toward the downtown section of Beaufort and nodded up the street. "It's only about four blocks. It's especially warm for this time of the year. It's a good day for a walk. C'mon."

Stepping out of the way of a man walking two dogs, Nick asked, "Didn't you tell me on the phone there was something you wanted to talk to me about?"

"Yes, I did. What with all this real estate talk, I forgot all about that."

Joking, Nick walked on the curbside of the street next to Khelen. "The last time someone said they wanted to talk with me about something happened to be yesterday when Carson Pike talked to me about buying the home on Deer Lake. That little conversation is going to cost me about a half million dollars. I hope whatever it is you want to discuss with me won't cost me any more money."

"What I want to discuss with you is rather unclear to me…and odd. Last evening I was coming in off the golf course with three of my friends at the country club. Since it was getting late, we decided to dine at the club. We had steak dinners and decided to relax in the lounge enjoying an expensive bottle of old brandy and some good cigars. An hour or so passed, when who walks in…Chic Brumly!"

Ridley hesitated as if Nick should know the name. Nick gestured, holding out his hands. "So, who is Chic Brumly?"

Stopping at an intersection while three vehicles passed, Khelen explained, "Chic Brumly is the sleaziest lawyer in Beaufort, maybe in the state of South Carolina. Now, I'll be the first one to admit that lawyers, in general, get a bad rap as far as the public is concerned. It seems like the minute you pass the bar exam, people start viewing you as dishonest. That may be true in some instances, but I think there are more honest lawyers than not. Chic Brumly is at the top of the list of dishonest lawyers. He is a bottom feeder, ambulance chasing sleaze." Crossing the street Khelen continued with his story, "Anyway, Brumly walks up to where we were sitting, leans over and whispers to me if he can speak to me alone. Needless to say when I got up and we walked off together I got some strange looks. Brumly is not that popular at the club and most people don't want to associate themselves with his kind. But, he is a member, so for the moment I gave him the benefit of the doubt…"

Interrupting Khelen, Nick inquired, "If this Chic Brumly is such a sleaze how did he get a membership to the club in the first place?"

"Easy…he has money. It is not a requirement to have a great attitude or be liked by everyone at the club in order to join. All it really takes is having more money than the average citizen, which Brumly has. Money can cover a lot of faults or blemishes. Aside from being a lawyer who, as far as I'm concerned, gives the legal profession a bad name he is also a private detective. He took a course over the internet and received a degree of sorts, stating he can function as a private detective and that includes carrying a firearm, which he always has strapped to his side beneath his suit coat. He handles a lot of what I call lowlife cases. Things like following a wife around and taking photos of her because her husband thinks she may be cheating. Despite the fact he himself is a lowlife, he has this uncanny ability to dig up dirt on just about anyone. Believe me, you don't want Chic Brumly investigating you in any way, shape or form. Once he hones in on you, he gets dug in deeper than a West Virginia Tick. I've had some dealings with him in the past. He knows how to work the system and runs right on the very edge, balancing his behavior between legal and illegal procedures. He's extremely difficult to insult and it seems he can talk his way out of most anything. In short, you don't want Chic Brumly involved in any aspect of your life."

Moving to the side to allow a mother and three children to pass, Khelen nodded at the women and then started up again, "I led Brumly to a corner of the club where we seated ourselves. Looking around to see if anyone was close enough to hear us, he leans forward in this evil way he has about himself and asked me if I know a Nick Falco."

Nick stopped dead on the sidewalk. "Wait a minute! Why would this, as you put it, unsavory lawyer, private detective want with me?"

"That's exactly the first thought that entered my mind. So I was quite careful with my answers to his questions. Knowing Chic as well as I do I figured he already was aware I knew you, so I simply answered, yes.

Believe me, I wasn't about to tell him anything about you, because at that point I had no idea in what direction he was headed. Going on the offensive I asked a question of my own, which was, what interest did he have in you." In his smug sort of way he made himself comfortable and proceeded to tell me he had a female client from Staten Island, New York…right outside the city. This woman's name is Maria Sparks."

The mention of the woman's last name caused Nick to almost stop walking, which Khelen noticed. Stopping himself, he asked, "You know this woman?"

"No, I don't know her."

Rubbing his right hand across his chin, Khelen hesitated, but then spoke up, "I can tell from your reaction something about this woman bothers you. Let me finish explaining what Brumly told me about this Maria Sparks and then you can fill in any holes, if there are any."

On the move again, Khelen gave Nick a rundown on what Brumly said. "This Sparks woman, Maria, has an older brother by the name of Charles, who apparently goes by Charley. According to her she and Charley are very close. They contact each other at least twice a week. There is nothing that goes on in either one's lives the other does not know of. Brumly explained that last July Charley and another man by the name of Simons began to follow you in Cincinnati and eventually followed you down here to Beaufort and then over to Fripp Island. Maria's brother works for a group of businessmen in New York City. Charley and this Simons person were given the assignment of recovering some money that Edward, your grandfather, had supposedly embezzled from their company. Earlier, prior to your coming down here to Beaufort, this Charley and his partner contacted Edward and tried to get the money back for the company, but Edward claimed he knew nothing of what they were referring to. Later on, after your grandfather passed away, the two men focused in on Amelia. Supposedly, this missing money was either hidden in your grandmother's house or on the property. Amelia was uncooperative and would not allow them to search the house or the property. After she died and left the house to you, I guess the company decided to send this Charley and Simons down here to see you about this money. Like your grandmother, you refused to allow them access to the house, saying you knew nothing about any money, but then the company, at some point, later received a call from Carson Pike who said he had located the money and desiring that the company stop bothering you, agreed to hand the money over to them at your house on Fripp. Mrs. Sparks said she got a call from Charley the night before they were to receive the money. The company claims Charley and this Simons received the money, called their superiors and that was that. But, here's where it gets even stranger. She said Charley and this Simons character disappeared. She hasn't received a call from her brother in months. The company thinks Charley and Simons left for parts unknown with the cash. But, this woman does not believe that. Even if her brother had taken the money, which she doesn't believe for a second, he would have still remained in touch with her. She is of the opinion Charley and maybe even this Simons were killed down here somewhere. She feels you may be a person who was the last to see her brother alive. So, that's why she wants to talk with you. Brumly has been paid a fee to locate you." Stopping and bending down to tie his left shoe, Khelen looked up at Nick. "Does any of this sound familiar or hold any truth?"

Nick sat on a nearby bench and buried his face in his hands. "I thought this mess was over…I guess it isn't!"

Khelen sat on the opposite end of the metal bench and calmly crossed his legs. "Well this is turning out to be quite an interesting morning *and* based on your reaction to what I just told you, it would seem there are some holes that need to be filled in. First of all I find it hard to believe your grandfather would embezzle money from anyone, let alone the people he worked for. Speaking of that, I never really knew the name of the company he was employed by. I was always under the impression he was a financial advisor for these folks. I know he made excellent money and he travelled a lot. So, let's start out by filling in that large hole first."

Nick's head was spinning. He was going to have to explain the past summer at least as far as the Carnahans were concerned to Ridley, but he was going to have to leave certain things out. This Maria Sparks might not even be Charley's sister. She might be a plant sent by the Carnahan family *and if* she reported back to them any story other than what he and Carson had convinced them of then there was going to be hell to pay. He wished Carson were here at the moment. He would know what to do, what to say. He always did.

Nick looked up and down the street, took a deep breath and then started his explanation of his strange reaction to the mention of not only Maria Sparks but to what Brumly had told Khelen. "I have to start way back at the beginning if you're going to understand any of this. It actually started before I even came down to Fripp for Amelia's funeral. I had an unpleasant run-in with this Sparks and Simons in Cincinnati the day before you called me about Amelia's death. They said they would probably be in touch with me later, but for the moment I didn't need to tell anyone about them. Actually, you met or at least have seen these two men before."

Khelen gave Nick an odd stare as if he didn't understand.

"They attended Amelia's funeral over on Fripp. You probably saw them there and were not aware of who they were. At that time I had no idea about this hidden, so-called embezzled money. Carson Pike, who has been a dear friend to me this past summer, had a confrontation with them at the funeral. Apparently he has had some dealings with these men in the past. I don't know exactly what that means but Carson told me if they bothered me I was to get in touch with him. It was Carson who told me about the money. My grandfather wanted to leave the employ of this company he worked for, but they were not in agreement with his request. My grandfather was a financial advisor for these people and it ticked him off that they would not release him from their employment, so he made some investments over the next few years using some of their capital, which benefited him greatly. Not being familiar with the financial world I really can't say myself if he really embezzled the money or not. Carson told me Edward informed him the money was hidden either in the house or on the property. I never saw this money, at least at first, but then it got to the point where Sparks and Simons began to pressure me. It was then Carson came to me and told me he had the money. It all became very confusing. I really don't know if Carson found the money or had it all along. He contacted the people the money supposedly belonged to and agreed to meet with Sparks and Simons at Amelia's house where we would hand the money over to them. They came to the house at the scheduled time and Carson showed up with two suitcases packed with stacks of bills. The amount was 5.8 million. We gave them the money; they called their boss who, at the time, was in Charleston. Sparks and Simons left the house and said the money would be back in the hands of the owners of the company within two hours. The next day Carson found another $600,000 he had overlooked. Wanting to clear the air completely Carson and I delivered this cash over to Charleston to the owner of the company, but he was far from satisfied because Sparks and Simons never showed up with the 5.8 mil. The last we heard was the company was conducting a massive search for Sparks and his pal. They were convinced they had taken off for parts unknown with their millions. That was the last time I heard from them until you mentioned this Sparks woman."

Khelen sat forward and shook his head. "This is a lot to absorb. Your story, from what you've told me, pretty much lines up with what Brumly said about what the Sparks woman claimed. However, there are still some questions I have about this whole thing. Edward's death. Remember when we first met? I told you I thought his death was very mysterious and there may have been foul play involved. Look, I always have and always will admire your grandfather. He was as honest as the day is long, so I really don't know what to make about this embezzlement business. Based on what you told me, I'm thinking I was right all along. Edward's death was not accidental. He could have been killed by the very people he worked for."

Nick broke in on Khelen's line of thought and added, "That's the same thing Carson told me. He was convinced not only the company Edward worked for had him killed but Sparks and Simons were the ones who carried out the deed."

Khelen looked directly at Nick and asked, "You don't think these two men actually killed Amelia as well, do you?"

"No, I've discussed that with Carson." Lying, Nick went on, "Carson said my grandmother died of natural causes. Now, I will say this. If Carson had not handed the money over to them, I don't think I would be sitting here today talking with you."

"Are you saying they would have killed you?"

"Let's just say they came pretty close. But, that's all over now. We handed over all the money to Sparks and Simons. What happened after that is anybody's guess."

Becoming serious, Khelen warned, "Just be careful. Brumly already knows you live out on Fripp. It won't take him long to locate your address. I'd say within the next few days, maybe after the Thanksgiving holiday, it wouldn't surprise me one bit if you find Chic Brumly knocking on your front door. He may even bring this Sparks woman along. The one thing you don't want to do is to give him a reason to start digging crap up on you. He may be a sleaze, but unfortunately, he is very good at what he does, as underhanded as it may seem. Listen, if you need any legal assistance in regard to this Sparks woman, don't hesitate to give me a call."

"I'll consider your offer. I think the first thing I'll do is let Carson in on what has or is about to happen. He's lived in this area for a long time. He may know who this Brumly character is. If anyone can handle the likes of this sleazy lawyer it would be Carson. Charley Sparks and Derek Simons were not very nice people...believe me! Carson handled them without getting me injured. He saved my ass last summer. Who knows? He may have to do the same thing this coming winter." Nick stood and looked up the street. "Look, if there is nothing else about this Sparks woman to discuss I say we move on to the bank and get the loan process started."

An hour and a half later, Nick and Khelen stood on the front porch of the attorney's mansion. "All right," said Khelen. "Albert said he'd make every effort to make sure you're approved by Monday so we can go ahead with our planned meeting with Mrs. Yeats on Tuesday. If things go according to plan, late Tuesday morning Mrs. Yeats will walk out of my office with a cashier's check for $475,000 and you'll have the keys to the Deer Lake property. Before you head out I want to warn you one more time about Chic Brumly. If you're going to contact Carson Pike you better get on the stick and get with him *today!* Brumly will not waste any time in tracking your whereabouts down. For all we know he could be on Fripp right now. Maybe he has already been to your house. Just be warned. Soon you'll be meeting him and you need to be prepared to deal with that. Remember, when you are approached he's slick and will ask you a series of complicated questions meant to confuse and frustrate you. Just stay calm, and remember, don't give him a reason to start digging into your past."

Walking down the wide Savannah style steps at the front of the mansion, Nick waved and remarked, "I'm going to give Carson a call before I pull out of your parking lot. With any luck, I should be meeting him later on this afternoon. Thanks for all your advice and help today, Khelen. See ya Tuesday morning!"

Sitting back in the comfortable leather seat of the Lexus, Nick went to the selection mode on his cell phone and hit enter when Carson's name popped up. Following a number of rings, Nick was just about to give up when Carson answered, "Carson Pike."

Relieved, Nick tried to remain calm, "Carson, I'm glad I got hold of you. I am just about to pull away from Khelen Ridley's office in Beaufort.

"Great," exclaimed Carson. "How'd everything go?"

"Everything as far as purchasing Mrs. Yeats property went fine. We should have everything wrapped up next Tuesday. But that's not the reason I'm calling. I think the Carnahans might be stirring the pot. Ridley told me he ran into some sleazy lawyer from Beaufort by the name of Chic Brumly. He is representing a woman by the name of Maria Sparks who claims she is Charley's sister. Did you know he had a sister?"

"No, I'm not aware of him having a sister, but that doesn't mean he doesn't. I know who Brumly is. He's just the type of person we do not need snooping around."

Ridley told me to be careful because Brumly is trying to track me down to discuss her brother's sudden disappearance. We need to get together, so I can prepare myself when he discovers where I live."

"You're absolutely right. I just happen to be on my way into Beaufort to do some work on my boat at the marina. What say we meet at Steamers on Lady's Island for lunch? We can set up a plan for this

Brumly. See ya in a few."

Carson was already seated at a corner table in the back of Steamers when Nick arrived. Pulling out a wooden chair Nick nodded at Carson and remarked, "My grandparents used to bring me here when I was a youngster when I would come down here on vacation. It's always been one of my favorite spots to eat here in the Lowcountry. I think I'll order their seafood chowder and maybe a crab cake."

Looking at the menu, Carson commented, "I'm going with the Frogmore Stew. I'm starved for some reason today."

After they ordered their lunch and a couple of beers, Carson surveyed the restaurant. "Not many people are seated close to us so we can talk freely, but if folks get too close we'll have to keep it down. No one else, other than you and me need to know about the conversation we're about to have. Now, what about this Maria Sparks?"

"Like I said, Khelen said she has hired a local lawyer by the name of Chic Brumly to track me down so she can talk to me about Charley Sparks' disappearance. I'm thinking she might not even be Charley's sister, but a plant sent here by the Carnahans in order to find out what may have really happened to Sparks and Simons."

Reaching for his beer, Carson affirmed, "You might be right, but then again she could also be employed by the Carnahans. If, as you say, she is simply down here to find out what happened to her brother, Charley, it's still a problem. This is something we want to eventually go away. With her being here in the area it does nothing but throw a lot of attention on you and eventually, me as well. Now, tell me everything Khelen told you about his conversation with Brumly and then tell me what you told Khelen about last summer."

Twenty minutes later, after hearing the events of the morning in regard to Maria Sparks and Chic Brumly, Carson sat back in amazement, thought for a moment and then commented, "You've learned well. You were honest with Ridley but only to a point. When we leave here later on I'm going to call some of my contacts in New York and see if I can get some info on this Maria Sparks. If it turns out she does not exist or is not in fact Charley's sister, then we know this is a move by the Carnahans to get us to slip up. If this Maria is on the up and up then we'll just have to deal with her and Brumly. I really don't think you'll hear from him until after Thanksgiving, but you never know. When you leave here today you have to be prepared to be confronted by him and possibly this woman. I know Brumly. He can read people like a book. If you are unsure of your answers or appear to be nervous in any way he'll pick up on it. You need to stick to the identical story we told the

Carnahans. If, this Brumly calls you and wants to meet with you, call me and I'll be at this meeting with you. After all, Brumly no doubt already knows I was there at the house with you when we handed the money over to Sparks and Simons. The reason Brumly wants to talk with you is that between the two of us you are the easier prey. If he comes to you and I am not around just remember, don't change our story one bit. The last time you saw Charley Sparks and Derek Simons they were walking out the back door of your house with two suitcases that contained 5.8 million dollars and as far as you know were headed to Charleston to meet with Joseph Carnahan. Don't add anything to our story, don't leave anything out. If Brumly asks you something you can't answer, just simply answer by saying you don't know. And remember, as far as you're concerned you had nothing to do with any of this money. You just happened to inherit your grandmother's home. You will not be able to overpower Brumly. He is not easily intimidated. Just remain humble and do not, I repeat, *do not* get upset. If he gets the slightest idea you are not telling him the truth, he'll be all over you like green on grass. Now, tomorrow is Wednesday, the day before Thanksgiving. You already know he is going to approach you at some point. This man is really a sleaze. He may observe you before he comes to you, so keeping that in mind just go ahead and do what you would normally do. You must appear normal. And, don't worry. This will all work out. Besides that, if things get too out of hand we can always ship you back up to Canada to Amelia's place. One more thing. If this Brumly gets too far out of line, then he'll have to deal with me."

Sitting back in his chair, Nick suddenly became very serious when he looked directly across the table at Carson. "Please assure me that doesn't mean you intend to deal with him like you did with Charley and Derek. Tell me Brumly is not going to become fish food?"

"It won't come to that, because that would only make matters worse. We have to con Brumly just like we did the Carnahans and if we stick to our story that's exactly what will happen. Now, let's finish up our lunch and try to enjoy the upcoming holiday."

CHAPTER NINE

IT WAS 10:05 WEDNESDAY MORNING AS NICK SPED ACROSS the Fripp Island bridge. He was determined to stay away from his house as long as possible throughout the day in order to avoid a confrontation with Chic Brumly. Both Carson and Khelen said the slimy lawyer wouldn't waste any time in tracking him down. If he could just get through the day, then tomorrow would be Thanksgiving and he was sure Brumly wouldn't be working. Besides, he was spending Thursday in Beaufort with Shelby's family. If he had to deal with this lawyer and the Sparks woman he'd rather wait until Friday or the coming weekend. If Brumly held off until the next week that was all right with him except for the fact he was going to be quite busy on Tuesday at Khelen's office going through the process of purchasing Mrs. Yeats' home.

Crossing Hunting Island, he reduced the speed of his motorcycle. He was always leery of deer running out of the woods that bordered both sides of the parkway. He thought about how his morning had gone so far and was pleased he had not run into Brumly. He had gotten up early, just before seven o'clock, enjoyed a long swim in the ocean then walked up the beach toward Skull Inlet, just like he had done earlier in the week. When he got to the high stone wall that hid the secluded small beach where he had met the man who owned the restaurant chain, he had considered climbing over to see if he was there again, but then remembered the man said he was going home to pack because he was flying to the coast and he wouldn't be back for two weeks. The fact the man was not going to be sitting on the beach plus he didn't feel like climbing over the high wall, Nick turned around and headed back for the house. He took his time walking back, didn't arrive until 9:30, at which point he took a quick shower, changed, jumped on his bike, and was now headed for Lady's Island. What with everything that had transpired on Tuesday he had forgotten to pick up the spiked eggnog Shelby had requested. After he picked up the nog he wasn't quite sure what he was going to do. As long as he wasn't at home, Brumly could not contact him. Maybe he'd drive around some, have lunch in Beaufort and take in a movie or he could just go to Hunting Island and relax. He was determined to avoid the unpopular lawyer.

It was just past ten-thirty when he pulled up at the far end of Bill's.

For the time of day the store was bustling with customers, no doubt stocking up on their favorite alcoholic beverages for the upcoming holiday. Getting off his bike he released the kickstand and started up the walk in front of the popular liquor store, when he noticed the pile of cardboard boxes employees always put out for customers to take. Staring at the boxes he remembered months ago when he had run into Charley and Derek in front of the store and how Derek had shoved him down onto the boxes. Shelby was right. It seemed wherever he or she seemed to go there were going to be bad memories of the past summer. Putting that day out of his mind he entered the store and asked an employee standing just inside where he could locate the eggnog. The employee walked him past the counter to a far wall in the corner where there was one bottle left. The employee snagged the bottle and handed it to Nick, commenting, "At this time of year this stuff flies off the shelf. Will there be anything else I can help you with today."

Reading the label on the front of the white bottle, Nick answered, "No thank you…this is all I'll be needing."

Falling in line behind three other customers, Nick waited patiently to pay for his purchase. The woman standing in line in front of him was dressed in what he thought was unusual for the area. She looked rather out of place. Long, jet-black hair, topped with what appeared to be a very expensive black velour ball hat studded with various gemstones. Her tight black leather pants were stuffed neatly into high spiked fashionable black boots with silver metal tips. The woman placed a bottle on the counter and inquired about the total. The counter service person gave her the total and then asked to see her I.D. The woman opened her purse and produced a driver's license. The woman behind the counter after examining the photo and the information on the plastic protected card smiled and remarked, "Thank you very much, Ms. Sparks. All the way from New York. Are you down here for the holidays?"

The woman replaced the card into her purse and answered in a thick New York accent, "No...I'm down here on a little business I have to take care of."

At the mention of the woman's last name, Nick froze, *Unless there are two different women from New York with the last name of Sparks down here in the Lowcountry, then I'm standing within inches of the woman who is looking for me!"*

Before Nick could even think or react the woman turned around to leave and ran smack dab into his chest. The woman, embarrassed, immediately apologized, "I'm so sorry, sir. Are you okay?"

Nick was speechless while he stared back at the woman's face; diamond studded earrings, heavy eye makeup, fire engine red lipstick.

He did manage to mutter, "Yeah...sure...I'm okay!"

The woman patted him on his shoulder and brushed by. "Have a nice Thanksgiving."

Nick was brought out of his complete amazement by a voice, "Next...please!"

He thought quickly, *If that was Maria Sparks, then there is a possibility Chic Brumly might be nearby, maybe waiting for her outside in the parking lot.* Placing his eggnog to the side on the counter, he spoke to the counter person, "I'll be right back. I just need to get something else." Gesturing to the man behind him to move up, Nick hurried toward the door to see where the woman went. Looking out the glass of the front door he didn't see her. He stepped out and then noticed her when she stepped into a dark blue Lincoln with South Carolina plates. It had to be Brumly's car. Forgetting about his purchase, Nick thought, *This is perfect! What better way to avoid the Sparks woman and Brumly than to follow them.* Climbing on his bike he fired up the motor and waited until the Lincoln pulled out, turning down the Sea Island Parkway in the direction of Fripp. Nick pulled out onto the street and was two cars behind the Lincoln. He just barely made the red light at the first intersection they came to but he was determined not to lose sight of the car.

Five miles down the road, now just one car separating him from the Lincoln, Nick thought, *This is bizarre! If that is Brumly up there driving that car and he is heading for Fripp, it's just too comical that I'm actually tailing him!*

By the time they reached Harbor Island, he was convinced the car was headed for Fripp. The car that was between he and the Lincoln turned off and now Nick was directly behind Brumly. He backed off so as not to be too obvious. There were not many places to turn off before they arrived at Fripp. He was more confident than ever they were headed for not only Fripp Island but also his house on Tarpon Blvd.

When he arrived at the Fripp Island Bridge, he pulled over into the Ross Point Boat landing and waited for the Lincoln to get completely across. When the car was almost across the span, Nick guided his bike back onto the road. By the time he arrived at the island guard shack, the Lincoln was pulling away and slowly making its way up Tarpon. Nick, out of curiosity, slowed down at the shack when a guard ventured out of the small stone structure. Recognizing Nick, the guard, rather than normally signaling him on through, motioned for him to completely stop. Looking in the direction the Lincoln had taken, the guard inquired, "You expecting guests this morning?"

Nick, not sure what the guard was suggesting, replied, "No, I'm not expecting anyone. Why do you ask?"

Nodding up the road the guard skeptically answered, "The car that was just here before you arrived. Well, there was a man and a woman who were looking for you. They already had your address and complete name. They were not property owners or island guests and normally I wouldn't let people like that come on the island, but then the man flashed some official ID, saying he was a private detective and was working on a case and needed to ask you some questions. He said you were not in any trouble but you might have some information that may be vital to the case. I hesitated and was not sure what to do. He then told me If I did not let him come onto the island I would be interfering with police business and if he had to go all the way back to Beaufort and get a warrant someone's head was going to roll. He then presented me with a card indicating he was not only a private detective but also a Beaufort County Attorney. He explained he was only going to be on the island for an hour or so, so I let them go on in. But, now that you tell me you are not expecting anyone, I don't think I should have signaled them on through."

"Don't worry about it," said Nick. "I don't know who these people are and I have no intentions of talking to them today, but do me a favor."

"Sure, what do you need?"

"Later, when they leave, if they stop by the station don't let them know you saw me."

The guard gave a sloppy salute and said, "Sure, I can do that. Have a good day, Mr. Falco."

The speed limit on the island was twenty-five mph and strictly enforced, but Nick, who always obeyed the island rules, pushed the bike to thirty so he could catch the Lincoln. He never did catch the car but by the time he passed his home further up Tarpon he saw the Lincoln parked in his driveway. He knew the Sparks woman was in the car and the driver had to be none other than Chic Brumly. Pulling into the unoccupied house on the opposite side of the street, he parked the bike on the side of the house, dismounted and ran through the trees until he was directly across from his house. Peering through the dense trees and foliage, he noticed a man step out of the driver's side. He reminded Nick of a used car salesman; slick dark hair, bright yellow sports coat, black slacks and shiny brown shoes with black tips. The man leaned in the window, said something to the woman, looked at his watch then bounded up the steps to the front door. He rang the doorbell and waited.

Nick smiled and thought, *You've got a long wait, pal! You can ring that bell until the cows come home and you're still not going to get to talk with me today!*

The man rang the bell a second time and walked to the end of the porch, looking down the side of the large home. Walking back to the front door he rang the bell a third time and waited. Removing what Nick thought was a business card from his wallet, the man took a pen from the inside of his jacket and wrote something down, stuck the card in between the door casing and walked back down the stairs. He went back to the car, leaned in the passenger side window, and conversed with the woman. Next, he walked past the garage and disappeared around the back of the house. Nick was concerned because he could not see what the man was up to, but was in no position to confront him without having to talk with him. *Surely, he won't break in the house,* thought Nick. Then, he recalled what Khelen Ridley had told him about Chic Brumly. About how he ran right on the edge of what's legal and what is not. He felt like walking around the side of the house and asking this pain in the ass lawyer, what in the hell he wanted, but knew he had to keep his cool. Ridley had informed him he didn't need to give Brumly a reason to start digging into his life. A minute or so passed when the man appeared on the other side of the house. He then walked back up onto the porch and tried to look in the curtained windows. If the man was indeed Chic Brumly, from the way he was acting, even though Nick had never met the man, based on his brazen action, he already didn't care for him.

Bounding down the steps, the man signaled the woman by raising his hands, indicating no one was home. The man was just about to get back in the Lincoln when Genevieve crossed her lawn and yelled, "Good morning!"

"Great, that's all I need," mumbled Nick. Genevieve, who was without a doubt the friendliest person on the island would tell this strange man everything she knew about her neighbor; Nick Falco.

After a five-minute conversation of which he could not hear a word, Nick saw the man hand Genevieve something, maybe a business card. The man then got in the Lincoln, backed out and headed back up Tarpon. Running back through the trees, Nick decided to continue following the couple. He was still not sure the man was indeed Chic Brumly but from what the guard had said to him and what he had witnessed, he was pretty sure he was. By the time he returned to his bike and was headed up Tarpon the Lincoln was out of sight. Blasting up Tarpon at forty mph, Nick slowed down when he passed the guard shack but then after he was across the bridge opened the bike up hitting nearly sixty mph. He hoped he could catch up with them so he could find out where they were going next.

Passing the Shrimp Shack on the Sea Island Parkway at close to seventy, he spotted the Lincoln parked in the dirt lot of the small eatery.

They had stopped for lunch. Nick pulled over into the first spot where he could turn around and drove back toward the popular tiny outdoor restaurant.

Parking at the edge of the lot, he got an idea and wondered if Brumly or the Sparks woman knew what he looked like. The Sparks woman who he had been nose to nose with back at the liquor store had no idea what he looked like or they wouldn't have left the lot. She would have gone to Brumly and he would have either entered the store or waited for him outside. The question was, did Brumly know what he looked like? How could this attorney possibly know that? The only way possible would be if the attorney had seen his driver's license. The only time he could recall when he had to show the license since he had been living on Fripp was when he had shown it to that officer back at Bill's earlier in the year when he had that scuffle with Derek Simons. He had also given his license to Albert Zellman at the bank so he could make a copy for the loan papers. *Screw it!* Thought Nick. *I'm going to chance it! Sooner or later, I'll have to face Brumly. If he recognizes me...then, so be it. It's not like the man is out to kill me. He just wants to talk.*

Getting off his bike, he walked past the Lincoln, looked in the windows and seeing nothing of interest walked up the elevated dock lined with old weathered dock posts and thick rope. The man wearing the bright yellow blazer was seated with the Sparks woman at a circular wooden table on the right. Nick walked across the large screened-in porch eating area and up to the order window. Keeping his eye on the couple he ordered a shrimp burger and a coke, took his order number and brazenly walked right past Brumly and the woman and sat at a table facing the screened wall. With his back to the couple he was only three feet away. He was no more than seated when he heard a number called, "Number 17...your order is ready."

Turing slightly, Nick observed the man get up, walk to the pickup window and return with a tray containing their lunch. Leaning back slightly, he was able to hear what was said. The Sparks woman removed the top bun on her sandwich and salted her burger and fries as she spoke, "So, what is our next move, Chic?"

Nick smiled to himself when she identified the man as Brumly.

The attorney took a drink and responded, "I'm planning on returning to Fripp around two o'clock this afternoon, but this time if our Mr. Falco is not at home we'll just hang around on the island and wait for him to arrive."

The sparks woman bit into her sandwich and spoke at the same time, "Fripp is a private island...right?"

"That's correct."

"How long will you, or I guess I should say we, be able to continue to gain access to the island before we're questioned or denied entry?"

"You just let me worry about that. The guards at their security shack are simply employees…they are not actual police. I don't think we'll have any problem getting back on the island this afternoon. Now, if we are not successful at making contact with Falco today, we'll back off tomorrow on Thanksgiving, but then we'll pick things up again on Friday. Don't worry, within the next few days, probably before the weekend is over we should have an opportunity to speak with Mr. Falco."

"I certainly hope so. I am confident my brother did not run off with the Carnahan's money. And, even if he did, he would still contact me. I haven't heard from him in months. I fear something happened to him while he was down here. The Carnahans told me there is a good possibility this Nick Falco, and a man by the name of Carson Pike, may have been the last two people to see my brother before he left the island. I don't care what it costs. I want to get to the bottom of this."

"Not to worry, Ms. Sparks. If Falco or even Carson Pike are hiding anything, believe me, with me on the case, eventually I'll get to the truth…guaranteed!"

Nick's number was called, "Number 18…your order is up!"

When Nick stood and turned, Brumly and the woman were both looking directly at him. Nick smiled at the couple and started to walk by, but was stopped by the woman. "Excuse me, but aren't you the young man I ran into at the liquor store this morning?"

"Nick, even though taken completely off-guard gathered himself and answered calmly, "Yes, that was me." Not wanting to appear nervous, Nick added, "We have to stop meeting like this. Excuse me, but my order is ready."

When he got to the pickup window, he took a deep breath of relief. It was obvious Brumly was not aware of what he looked like or he would have said something. Still, the man's stare made him nervous. Changing his mind at the window, Nick requested, "Do you think I could get my order to go?"

"Of course," answered the girl. "Just let me bag that up for you."

Glad he was no longer in the presence of the lawyer and Ms. Sparks, he walked across the dirt lot to his bike. Sitting on a large rock at the edge of the lot he unwrapped his sandwich. He had to decide what his next move was going to be. He already knew where they were going to be at two o'clock and that was back at his house. There didn't seem to be much of a reason to continue following the couple. No, he was going to finish his lunch then drive back to Fripp and talk with Genevieve. He had to find out what she told the lawyer about him. This was important; because when he finally did speak with this man he had to know what the man knew about him. It was close to twelve-thirty. Within the hour they would be heading back out to Fripp. He needed to get moving.

Crossing the Fripp Island Bridge, he got an idea when he pulled up next to the guard shack. The guard from his previous entry onto the island was still on duty. Emerging from the small building, the guard looked back at the bridge and then at Nick, "How did you make out with your detective friend?"

Nick laughed and commented, "I didn't talk with him and he's not what I would call my friend. I've never personally met the man. He's known around this area as kind of a shyster and that detective ID he showed you might be official and all, but the truth is he got his private detective license over the internet. That doesn't mean he's not a detective, but the internet…come on! What kind of training could the man have? You can get almost anything done over the net. I've heard it said you could even become an ordained minister on the internet. You take a course, answer a few questions, and presto, suddenly you're a man of the cloth! I certainly don't think I'd want that caliber of a minister conducting my marriage ceremony. Would you?"

The guard shrugged, "I guess not."

"That's my point," said Nick. "I can't take this guy serious as a private detective either. I didn't talk with him before and I'm not interested in talking to him when he comes back, which I just happen to know is going to be around two o'clock, about an hour from now. Now, I can't tell you and I wouldn't even attempt to tell you how to do your job, but the truth is that man and the woman who is with him should not be allowed on the island. As far as I know he is not a property owner and is not a guest of anyone here on the island. As a resident of this island, I along with all the other folks who live here, depend on island security to adhere to security policies of allowing those who are allowed on the island and preventing those who are not. If someone, like this so-called private detective, can simply flash a business card at security and then be allowed on the island than what good is it to even have security?"

The guard shook his head and confirmed, "I agree with you, but the man said if he had to go back to Beaufort and get a warrant someone's head was going to roll. He was referring to me and I don't want to get into any trouble with the law."

"Look," said Nick. "He is not here on any official police business. He's just snooping around and being a pain in the ass. The way I see it is, the *only* way you're going to get in trouble is by allowing people access to the island who, in fact are not permitted access. Maybe you should call the security office and explain what happened this morning and that the man is returning. If they condone him being here on the island, then I'll be all right with that, if not...that's okay also. The man's name is Chic Brumly and the woman is known as Ms. Sparks. You need to write those names down and call security. If you want to mention my name, I'm okay with that. I'm not trying to hide anything and I haven't done anything wrong. But, like everyone else on Fripp, I enjoy my privacy and when you think about it that's why we are a gated, secure community."

The guard looked back at the bridge, stepped back inside the shack and returned with a pen and a pad. "Give me those names again. I am going to call security. You're right. I shouldn't have let them in earlier and the only way I'll permit them access when they return is if security gives me the go ahead."

Climbing back on his bike, Nick nodded at the guard. "Thank you. You're doing the right thing."

Slowly passing the Community Center on his right, Nick smiled and thought he had done an excellent job of convincing the guard to deny Brumly access when he returned. The seedy lawyer would be pissed beyond belief, but his fast talking and ID flashing would be to no avail. Nick couldn't concern himself with any of that for the moment. He now had to get back to the house and contact Genevieve.

Pulling into the driveway of his house, ironically he saw his eighty-year-old neighbor digging in the dirt flowerbed that bordered the left side of her home. Parking his bike in front of the garage, he jumped off and started across the yard. Hearing his bike, Genevieve stood and waved at her next-door neighbor, "Good afternoon, Nick!"

Nick returned the wave. "Afternoon, Genevieve!"

Motioning toward the ground with a pointed metal garden trowel, Genevieve explained, "I was just digging up some of my plants that for some reason have died. It happens every year. I put the plants in the dirt, surround them with organic dirt and water them on a daily basis, and yet many of them do not survive. But, that being said, it gives me something to do. Lowes is now having their annual 50% off on plants sale. Later today, I'm going to drive into Beaufort and pick me up some new perennials and get them planted." Looking across the yard at the side of Nick's home, she mentioned, "I notice you have three small bushes that have seen their better days. Would you like me to pick up some new plants for you as well?"

Wanting to move on to the reason why he wanted to speak with Genevieve, he responded, "Sure, that would be fine. You pick out whatever you think and I'll pay you back, but there's something else I need to discuss with you."

Noticing the sense of urgency in Nick's voice she tossed the trowel to the ground, the pointed end sticking in the loose dirt at her feet. "Why so serious?"

"It's not all that serious. I just happen to know you talked with a man who visited my house earlier this morning."

Snapping her fingers, she remembered, "That's right…I did. I almost forgot. I was going to say something to you when you got home, but then we got to talking about all of our dead plants." Suddenly, as if she had a revelation, she gave Nick an odd look. "How do you know the man came to your house?"

"Because I was hiding in the trees across the street."

"Why would you do such a thing?"

"Because I didn't want to talk with the man. He's a sleazy lawyer from Beaufort and he's sticking his nose into my life and I don't like it…that's why! I saw him give you a business card. Do you have it?"

Reaching into an old garden apron she was wearing, she pulled out the square white card. "I have it right here in my apron."

Taking the card, Nick read the black lettering: *Charles "Chic" Brumly, Attorney at Law.* There was also a phone number, address and email address beneath the lawyer's name. At the very bottom of the card there was another short printed message: *Private Detective Services Available.*

Placing the card in his pocket, Nick probed, "This Brumly talked with you for nearly five minutes. What did you discuss with him?"

"Come to think of it, it really wasn't much of a discussion. He asked me one question after another and I answered them as best I could. I can see why you wouldn't want to talk with this man. He was pushy and impatient. I would no sooner answer one of his questions than he was asking the next. All of his questions were about you. How long have you lived next door, when were you usually at home, what type of vehicles you drove, have I ever been in your house, did I know Carson Pike, what was the name of the girl you're seeing and on and on. It was like I was being cross-examined. There was a woman with him but she never got out of the car. Did I do something wrong by talking to this man? If I did, it wasn't intentional. He was just so forceful. After he left, I felt like I had been mentally raped. Oh, and one other thing. He told me to tell you that you needed to give him a call because he needed to discuss something with you."

"You didn't do anything wrong, Genevieve. This lawyer, so I've been told is a legal parasite! I think he's planning on returning here to the house around two this afternoon. I've informed security to not allow him on the island. I don't know if that is going to happen or not. This Brumly may be able to sweet talk his way back on the island again. If he does return and he approaches you, you haven't seen me and you have no idea when I'll return home."

"Got it," said Genevieve. "I'm not planning to be here. I've got one more plant to dig up and then I'm off to Lowes and their plant sale."

Opening his wallet, Nick handed Genevieve a fifty and smiled, "Pick me out some nice plants. I'll probably see you later this evening. Have a nice trip to Beaufort."

Looking at his watch he noted the time, 1:15 in the afternoon. Even if Brumly did get back on the island, he still had at least forty-five minutes before he would evacuate the house. Walking up the porch stairs he removed an identical business card from in between the door and the jamb. One the back of the card was a handwritten note. *Please give me a call. It is a matter of great importance.*

Inside the house he climbed the stairs and changed into warmer clothing as the temperature had steadily dropped. Throwing on a sweatshirt and a pair of heavy painter's pants, he ran back down the stairs, grabbed a beer out of the fridge, sat on the back porch, and made plans for the next two hours. At around 1:45 he'd hop on his bike and drive down to the Mango Gift Shop parking lot across from the guard shack where he could watch and see what happened when Brumly returned. Then, at some point he was going to have to drive again into Bill's to pick up that spiked eggnog.

Parking his bike in the lot next to three different golf carts, Nick walked up the wide wooden incline that led to the Spring Tide Convenience Store, The Mango Gift Shop and Fripp Island Real Estate Office to another secluded parking lot concealed by a number of tall palmetto trees and low bushes. From this vantage point, Nick, peering out between two bushes, had a perfect view of the guard shack. Depending on how loud the people at the shack spoke, he may or may not be able to hear what was being said. Sitting on a nearby rock, Nick looked at his watch, 1:48. Brumly and his female client should be showing up in the next ten to fifteen minutes.

Getting up, he walked to the opposite side of the lot and popped a stick of gum in his mouth. Staring out at the vast salt marsh, he was reminded of the past summer and the RPS Killings. Once again, he had to remind himself that those events were last summer. This was a different season in the Lowcountry and the way things were headed it looked like he was going to be facing a new event in his life. A sleazebag lawyer who was dogging him. He knew eventually he was going to have to talk with Brumly. He wasn't looking forward to that conversation, as it would no doubt lead to some of the unpleasant events of the past summer.

Walking back to the rock he peered out between the bushes and thought to himself how stupid it all was. He had thought after last summer his life would hopefully return to one of normalcy, but at the moment that was not happening. He was hiding behind bushes in a parking lot waiting to see if Brumly and his companion would gain access to Fripp or not. He thought about Shelby Lee and her family. They were no doubt in the middle of preparing their home for tomorrow's Thanksgiving dinner and here he was playing a cat and mouse game with a man he didn't even know.

His daydreaming was interrupted when he saw the dark blue Lincoln pull up to the guard shack. Looking down at his watch he saw the time: two o'clock on the nose. If nothing else, Brumly was punctual. He tried his best to hear what was being said but was just too far out of range.

Brumly rolled down the car window, smiled, flashed his business card and remarked, "I'm back again to see Mr. Nick Falco. He was not at home when I was here earlier. I'm just going to pull on through. I may be here longer than before if he is still not home. We'll just have to camp out until he does return."

He started to roll the window back up but was prevented from doing so when the guard signaled he wanted to talk with him. "I'm sorry, Mr. Brumly. But I cannot allow you access to the island."

Surprised, Brumly shot the guard a look of confusion. "Why not…you let me come onto the island before and that was just three hours ago. Nothing has changed. I'm still on official police business. I've shown you all of my ID. Like I said before, if I am denied access to Fripp someone is going to be in trouble and it just might be you, young man!"

The guard shook his head and responded, "Official police business…really? If you were an actual detective with the Beaufort Police I'd agree with you. Just because you are a private detective does not give you the same authority as the police. I'm afraid you'll have to turn this car around and exit the island."

Brumly opened the car door and stepped out. "Now listen son! Do you know who you're talking to? I am a respected lawyer in this county and I am currently conducting an investigation into the disappearance of a man who may have breathed his last or at least was last seen right here on Fripp. Believe me, the last thing you want to do is interfere with this case." Angling his thumb back to the car, he remarked, "My client came all the way from New York City to find out what happened to her brother. She has gone to great expense to come down here not to mention the fee she has agreed to pay me to find the underlying cause of her brother's disappearance. I have an agreement with her that I will do everything in my power to solve her dilemma. If you think for one moment I'm going to stand here and have some young, wet behind the ears security guard stop me from doing my job you've got another thing coming. Now, that being said, I'm going to get back in my car and Ms. Sparks and myself will proceed to Mr. Falco's residence!"

Politely, the guard suggested, "I wouldn't do that if I were you, sir. I have been in contact with my superior and have been informed that if you run this gate, you will be arrested, fined and escorted off the island...period!"

Brumly placed his hands on his hips and looked up Tarpon Boulevard and commented sarcastically, "This whole situation borders on ridiculous. You say you've been in contact with your superior. Well, I for one would like the opportunity to speak to this *superior of yours!* Can you please get him on the phone?"

The guard remained calm and polite. "I can do better than that. I can call him and have him drive down here. He could be here in less than five minutes if you'd care to wait?"

"I'd like nothing better," snapped Brumly. "Call your boss. I'm sure I'll be able to reason with him. I should have known better than to try and reason with some part-time gate guard."

When the guard stepped into the shack to make the call, Brumly walked around the front of the Lincoln to the passenger window and spoke to the woman. "I apologize for this minor setback. When the head of security gets down here we'll clear this matter up and we'll be allowed on the island. Just sit tight."

It wasn't even three minutes when a Fripp Island Security Jeep pulled up next to the shack, a uniformed officer stepping out. When he approached the Lincoln, Brumly was the first to speak, "I assume you're the head of security here on the island?"

"That I am," said the officer. "Chief Lysinger, head of security here on Fripp. I understand you do not have a bona fide reason for being here on the island."

Brumly laughed. "Well, I don't know how they do things out this way, but I'd say that a missing person is definitely as you put it, a bona fide reason." Turning, he gestured at Ms. Sparks and went on to explain, "That woman in the front seat of my car is a client of mine. She is down here from New York. This past summer her brother, a Charley Sparks had some business dealings with two of your residents. A Nick Falco and one Carson Pike. These two gentlemen are reported as the last two to see Mr. Sparks while he was here on Fripp. I just want to ask Mr. Falco some questions."

Lysinger leaned casually against the wall of the shack and asked, "This so-called investigation you are conducting. Is it sanctioned by the Beaufort Police Department?"

"No, but that shouldn't make a difference. I am a licensed private detective in the State of South Carolina."

Mimicking Brumly's emphasis on the words *private detective,* Lysinger replied, "And this is a *private island.* If you think carrying a private detective's license allows you access anyplace, anytime or anywhere you, my dear friend, are sadly mistaken. Now, this conversation is concluded. You need to get back in your vehicle, make a U-turn around the guard shack and head back across the bridge. Understand?"

Brumly, not the least bit intimidated was bound and determined to get in the last word as he climbed back in the Lincoln. "You haven't heard the last of me Chief! I'll be back and I will, I repeat, *I will* speak with this Mr. Falco. I know people who live here on Fripp. I can arrange for one of them to invite me here to your little private island as a guest and then you won't be able to say or do squat!"

"If you return as a verified guest you will have no problem from me or any of the guards. You will be allowed on the island just like any other guest, but after you're on the island if you so much as bother one of our residents, I'll kick you off Fripp faster than you can sneeze. Now, move it!"

Crossing the bridge, Ms. Sparks turned and looked back at the guard shack and remarked, "I can't believe as a local detective you are being denied entry to the island. This would never happen up in New York. What in the hell is wrong with these people?"

"You're right," said Chic. "This is not New York. This is the extreme southern tip of Beaufort County, South Carolina. Fripp is the last island south of Beaufort. After Fripp Island there is nothing but the Atlantic Ocean. When you get out this far you're in the middle of nowhere. Fripp is surrounded by water dotted in many places by vast salt marsh areas. We can only push so hard and for so long. I know you may be thinking the Fripp Island Police are a bunch of small time swamp hicks, but believe me, they hold the same authority as any police force in the state. But, don't worry. If we can't go through them we'll go around them. Tomorrow is Thanksgiving. I'm driving over to Savannah to my mother's house for the day. It'll just be my parents, my two brothers, their families, and myself. If you'd like you are welcome to come along. I'd hate to see you spend the holiday by yourself."

"I'll pass if it's all the same," said Maria. "I'm not that much on all this holiday hubbub. Just drop me off at my hotel. They told me when I checked in they're having a Thanksgiving buffet for their guests. I think I'll hit that tomorrow and then maybe just hang around their indoor pool and relax."

"Okay, then," said Chic. "I'll give you a call Friday morning, let's say around seven. We can grab some breakfast and then we'll proceed in our efforts to contact this Mr. Falco. We'll get to talk with him before the weekend is out...guaranteed!"

Nick slathered his legs, arms and face with suntan lotion and sat in his beach chair. It was mid-afternoon and the sun was high in the clear blue sky. The temperature was in the low fifties and there wasn't the slightest hint of a breeze coming in off the ocean. Opening his small cooler, he removed an ice-cold beer and opened a novel he had taken down from the shelves of hundreds of books Amelia had collected over the years. Adjusting the sunglasses on his face he was going to just relax for the remainder of the day. Chic Brumly was no longer a threat, at least until Friday rolled around. But that was two days down the line. Opening the book to the first page, he smiled when he thought about the upcoming day at Shelby Lee's house with her parents. He was really looking forward to meeting her folks and celebrating the holiday with them. It was sort of like belonging to a family, and aside from his relationship with Amelia it was something he hadn't experienced in quite some time. Closing the book, he shut his eyes and lay back allowing the sun to caress his face as he thought, *Life is good!*

CHAPTER TEN

INSPECTING HIMSELF IN THE FLOOR-LENGTH MIRROR HE WAS satisfied; grey, pleated slacks, light blue button down oxford shirt, off-white cardigan sweater, cordovan loafers, brown and blue argyle socks and beige sports jacket. Within the next two hours or so he would be in Beaufort to meet Shelby Lee's parents. He thought he would be more nervous but surprisingly, he felt at ease. Running a comb though his short hair he slapped a small portion of English Leather cologne on his face and down the stairs he went.

Grabbing the spiked eggnog from the fridge, he walked out onto the screened-in back porch, locked the house and went into the garage. Opening the garage door he half expected to see Brumly and the Sparks woman standing in his driveway. Shaking the negative thought off, he was determined to enjoy Thanksgiving with Shelby and her family. Backing the Lexus out of the garage, he turned left and headed up Tarpon.

Pulling his cell phone from his jacket, he went to his contact list and hit Carson's number. Within seconds, Carson's familiar deep voice answered, "Carson Pike."

"Good morning, Carson! I thought I'd give you a call and let you know how yesterday went with Brumly and the Sparks woman."

Concerned, Carson asked, "Did they get in touch with you? Did you talk with them?"

"I really don't want to get into that now, but I'll just say I spent the day avoiding them. I'll call you tomorrow and fill you in on all the details." Changing gears, Nick went on, "I'm on my way to Beaufort right now to spend the day with Shelby's family. Are you spending the holiday somewhere?"

"As a matter of fact, I am. Parker Sims invited me over to his house. He's having a buffet and I guess we'll watch some football and maybe play some cards. He asked me to invite you along but I told him you had other plans. Grady Phillips will be there. You could have met him, but there'll be plenty of time for that later on. How did you make out with Khelen Ridley about purchasing Gretchen's house?"

"Just fine. Right now it looks like we'll be closing on the property this coming Tuesday. Listen, I've got another call to make. I'll call you tomorrow."

His second call of the morning was his grandmother, Amelia. At one time he had her number saved on his contact list, but Carson told him that was a bad idea. If the wrong person got hold of his phone and saw he had his dead grandmother's number saved, it could lead to some awkward questions. He now kept her number in his wallet. He had clipped her number to the sun visor before leaving the house earlier.

Punching in the Canadian number, Amelia, who had caller ID, answered almost immediately, "Nick! I was wondering if I'd hear from you today. How is the weather down there in South Carolina?"

"Mid-fifties. They say it might rain this evening. What's the temp up there in the cold north?"

"When I got up this morning it was twelve degrees. I don't think it'll get above freezing."

"I called you for two reason; the first, to wish you a happy Thanksgiving."

Amelia laughed. "In Canada Thanksgiving is celebrated the second week of October rather than the last week of November. Up here Thanksgiving has nothing to do with the Pilgrims or the New World. It's a very low key day. Some folks don't even celebrate it as a holiday. According to what I have learned, back in 1578 an English explorer by the name of Martin Frobisher was searching for a northern route to the Orient. He got as far as what we now call Newfoundland. He settled there and was glad he was safe, hence the first Canadian Thanksgiving."

"So, I guess that means you won't be celebrating today."

"Are you kidding me? I wouldn't think of missing Thanksgiving. I'm having about fourteen local people over to the house for a huge meal. They are all like me, Americans now living in Canada. I wish you were here. I miss you."

"I miss you too, but we both know how things are and that leads to the second reason I'm calling. Do you remember when I was up there last week and we talked about how the Carnahans had recently been in touch with Carson? It turns out Charley Sparks has a sister by the name of Maria. She's from Staten Island and apparently has been in touch with the Carnahans. For all we know she may be employed by them. She never has, and still does not to this day believe Charley and Derek took off with the Carnahan's millions. She is aware Charley and Derek received the money from Carson at the house. She feels they never left the island and something happened to them on Fripp. She has hired some lawyer down here by the name of Chic Brumly to track me down. She wants to ask me some questions since I may have been the last person to see her brother here on Fripp. Carson has told me this Brumly is a low-life and I need to be leery of him. So far, I've managed to avoid talking with him, but I think that's short lived. I'll probably have to confront both of them this coming weekend."

There was a moment of silence on the other end of the conversation and then Amelia commented, "Chic Brumly; the scrum of not only Beaufort County, but of South Carolina. Edward and I had some dealings with him in the past. He is not a man of integrity and is far from what I would consider an honest man. Does Carson know about this?"

"Yes, he does. He told me when I am confronted by Brumly and the Sparks woman to stick to the identical story we told the Carnahans."

"That's exactly right. You cannot add anything or take anything away from what we have led them to believe. If they even suspect we conned them it could mean our lives, all three of us; you, Carson and myself."

"I'm a little nervous about talking with this Brumly and the woman, because what she thinks may have happened, actually did. You and I both know Charley Sparks never left Fripp Island alive. When I talk with her and this lawyer, I must be able to convince them Charley and Derek left the house with the money. For all we know this woman may be a Carnahan plant. Listen, I've got to go. I'm getting close to Beaufort. I thought you should be updated on what's going on. I love you and I miss you. I'll try to get back up there to see you soon."

"You be careful. I'm going to give Carson a call when we hang up. I want to be sure he's on top of this. Now, you have a nice day over at Shelby's house. Happy Thanksgiving."

Placing his cell on the console of the Lexus, he noticed he was passing Bill's Liquor Store, another reminder of not only Brumly but also the Sparks woman. He wondered if he should have continued to follow them and find out where the woman was staying. Maybe he should have gone there and talked with her privately without the presence of Brumly. It was too late for that now. Friday would come soon enough and Brumly and the woman would be back on the prowl.

Crossing the Woods Memorial Bridge, he looked left down Bay Street. It was like a ghost town, not a single person walking the normally crammed streets. Continuing up Carteret Street three blocks he made a left on North Street, drove four blocks and turned right on Newcastle. Looking at the address he had clipped to the sun visor, he verified Shelby's address: 714. He was now in the three hundred block so he had a ways to go. Four cross streets later, he was in the seven hundred block.

Driving slowly up the street lined with old oaks he admired the neighborhood. It was one of those neighborhoods you rarely see; each and every house had a design of its own. It wasn't anything like the housing developments that seemed to be popping up everywhere. Row after row of identical cubicles; houses that had no character. Newcastle Street was lined with homes that bespoke of a great deal of character: some made of brick, others sided, some were ranch while others were two story, some with attached garages, others had none. Some had picket fences while others were fronted with neatly trimmed hedges, some had bow windows and others had stained glass doors. Pulling into the driveway of 714, Nick felt at home. It seemed like such a peaceful place to live.

He no more than stepped out of the car when Kirby came racing out of the house, across the porch and down the paved walkway where she gave him a hug. "Nick, I'm so glad you've come to my house for turkey day! I haven't seen you for weeks. I have so much to tell you. I got a part in our school Thanksgiving play. I'm going to be one of the pilgrims and I even get to speak. I hope you're hungry."

Leading him up the walk, Kirby kept right on talking, "My grandmother put the turkey in the oven early this morning. I've been helping her baste it. She says when it's golden brown, it will be time for us to eat. When she mashes up the potatoes I get to lick the beaters. You can have one if you like."

Finally able to get a word in, Nick placed his hand on her shoulder. "I haven't licked a beater since I was a young boy about your age. I'll be glad to help you out."

Shoving open the oak front door, Kirby yelled, "Nick is here!"

She led him through the living room and then the dining room where she opened a back porch door and pointed at the corner. "That's our Christmas tree. Grandpa and I went out last night and bought it. I got to pick it out. It's a six-footer. Grandpa says it's a Frazier Fir. Later today, we'll bring in the tree and set it up so we can decorate it. I have a special angel for the top and I also made an ornament at school for you to put on the tree."

Leading him back into the dining room, they came face to face with Shelby Lee and her parents. Shelby apologized, "I'm so sorry. She is so excited because you're here." Stepping forward she took Nick's hand and made the introductions, "Nick, this is my mother Peg and my father Ralph. Mom…dad, this is Nick Falco, the man Kirby and I have been telling you about for the past few months."

Ralph stepped forward and offered his right hand followed by an exceptionally strong handshake. Peg likewise stepped forward and gently touched Nick on his arm and suggested, "Why don't we go into the front room. You and Ralph can get acquainted while Shelby, Kirby and I continue with dinner preparations."

Nick suddenly remembered the eggnog. "Handing the white bottle to

Mr. Pickett, he explained, "Shelby said you really like spiked eggnog so I picked up a bottle. I hope it's the kind you like."

Taking the bottle, Ralph read the label out loud, "Evan Williams. This is the good stuff, the top of the line. I've had some other brands that claim they are spiked but this stuff here is really quite good, I think I'll get a glass with some ice and have some right now. How about you, Nick. Will you join me?"

"I think I will," said Nick. "Spiked eggnog sounds really good."

Peg rounded up her daughter and granddaughter and explained, "Why don't we let these two get acquainted. We have work to do in the kitchen." Walking toward the kitchen she spoke back over her shoulder, "I'll send Kirby right back with those nogs."

Kirby tugged on Peg's apron and asked, "Can I have some egg nog?"

"Yes you may, but not from this bottle. If you drink this you'll be asleep before dinner is even served. I have a carton of regular eggnog in the fridge you can have. You can drink as much of that as you'd like. Myself, I'm going to have a glass of red wine. How about you, Shel?"

"No, I think I'll hold off until we eat."

Sitting in a comfortable looking recliner, that was no doubt, *his chair,* Mr. Pickett reached over and took a pipe from a glass ashtray. "You don't mind if I smoke, do you?"

"Not at all. Go right ahead. You won't be bothering me a bit."

Opening a pouch of what Nick thought was leaf tobacco, Ralph took a small wad and with his thumb forced it down into the bowl of the pipe, then added yet another pinch. Lighting the pipe, Ralph asked. "Do you smoke, Nick?"

"No, I never have. Now, if you ask me if I take an occasional drink the answer would be yes. I enjoy a cold beer once in a while and I'm really looking forward to our eggnog."

Following four puffs, a small whiff of aromatic smoke began to rise from the pipe. Nick, smelling the pleasant aroma, asked, "What flavor or brand do you smoke?"

"Apple Brandy. I like the way it smells plus it doesn't leave an aftertaste in my mouth like some brands." Taking three more puffs, the pipe was now in full working order while Ralph explained, "In all my life, to date, I've never had a cigarette or a cigar, but I do love a good pipe."

Their conversation was interrupted when Kirby entered the room carrying two tall glasses of nog when she announced, "Here are your drinks." Handing one to Nick and the other to her grandfather, she retreated back to the kitchen explaining that she was needed.

Taking a sip of nog, Ralph stated, "Shelby tells me you're a house painter."

"That's true," answered Nick. "However the jury is still out whether I am a house painter or I used to be. You see, before I moved here to Fripp, I had my own painting business in Cincinnati. I started right out of college and for the first two years I danced around between losing money and breaking even. Then, the last two years things started to turn around. I had more business than I could handle, but at the beginning of this past year the bottom fell out in the Cincinnati market. It got to the point where I was barely making ends meet. Then, I get this call from a lawyer down here notifying me my grandmother had died. I came down for her funeral and was informed she had left me everything she owned: big house on the beach, brand new car, and quite a bit of money. I guess you could say I kind of went from rags to riches."

Taking a swig of the nog, he went on, "I'm not sure if I'm going to start my painting business down here up or not. I did paint one house on Fripp as a favor for a friend of mine. I'm not sure what I'm going to do with my life right now as far as working goes. My grandmother left me sitting pretty good. It's not like I have to find employment tomorrow. I might get into real estate. I am in the process of purchasing a second home on Fripp. It needs a good face lift as far as painting is concerned, inside and out and the place needs quite a bit of updating." Changing gears, Nick remarked, "Shelby told me you're a plumber."

Pointing the pipe at Nick, Ralph nodded. "That I am. Been in the plumbing racket for close to thirty-five years. I started in the business right out of high school, worked for three different companies for a number of years and then right before I got hitched up with Peg I decided to go out on my own. Over the years I've fixed more leaks and installed more toilets and water heaters than you can shake a stick at."

"Maybe I can throw some business your way. I may need some plumbing updates in the home I'm buying. After I get the place fixed up I'm planning to rent it out. I can do all the painting myself but I'll have to hire out most of the other work. Who knows? If things work out I may wind up buying another house later on."

Puffing on his pipe, Ralph asked, "You a sports fan, Nick?"

"I don't play any sports; golf, tennis, bowling…anything like that. But, I do enjoy baseball. Growing up and living in Cincinnati, you either wind up rooting for the Bengals or the Reds. I used to go to every Red's home game I could."

"Football is the game I like to watch. Not just professional, but high school and college as well. When I was a freshman at Beaufort High I had a choice: football or baseball. I opted for football, but it turned out I was too small. So, for the next four years I played shortstop for Beaufort

High. Despite the fact I couldn't play football didn't hamper my interest in the sport. Most folks in this area who follow professional football root for the Atlanta Falcons, which happens to be the closest professional team to Beaufort County. I've always gone against the grain. As a matter of fact I really don't care for the Falcons. I have always been, even since back in high school, a Pittsburgh Steelers fan."

Shelby entered the room and offered up the bottle of spiked nog. "Anyone care for a refill?"

Ralph held up his glass. "I'll take just a smidgeon."

Nick declined and stated, "I'm good."

Shelby poured a small measure into her father's glass and then spoke, "Mom told me to remind you to get the tree set up prior to dinner, so later on we can get it decorated." Setting the bottle on an end table, she smiled at Nick. "I'll just leave the nog here with you two…enjoy!"

Watching his daughter walk from the room to the kitchen, Mr. Pickett remarked," Well, I guess I've got my marching orders. I sure could use an extra hand, if you're up to it."

"I'd love to help. I haven't set up a Christmas tree, in well, I can't remember the last time. What do we do first?"

Standing, Ralph pointed at the chair Nick was seated in. "First, we have to move that chair. The tree goes right in front of the window you're sitting in front of. After we move the chair to the dining room, then we go out to the porch and drag the thing in here and set it up."

Setting his drink down on an end table Nick grabbed one side of the chair while Ralph lifted the other. Setting the chair next to a piano in the living room, Nick asked, "Who plays?"

"That would be Peg," admitted Ralph. "She's been tickling the ivories since she was six years old. When we met in high school our sophomore year, we were both in the school orchestra. I played the clarinet, not very good, but I still managed to acquire a seat. A few weeks after we met we started dating. By the time I graduated two years later, I lost interest in having a career as a musician. That's when I got into plumbing. Peg has never stopped playing the piano. She's really quite good. She plays not only the piano but the organ at our church and she does a lot of weddings and funerals." Gesturing toward the back porch door, Ralph suggested, "Let's grab the tree."

Out on the porch, Ralph lifted the tree and pointed at an old green tree stand lying on a plastic chair. "If you'll grab that stand and hold the door open I'll drag the tree in."

Once in the front room, Ralph stood the tree against the end of the couch and took the stand from Nick. Backing out the three turning screws, he remarked comically. "I hope we don't have as much trouble as I did last year when we set the tree up. I bought a tree with a thick trunk, thinking I wouldn't have as much trouble getting the thing to stand up straight. The trunk would not fit down into the stand so I had to cut on it. After an hour and a half I got the thing to stand straight. This year I was careful to get a tree with a slender base. Hopefully it will just drop right in." Finished with the third and final screw, Ralph handed the stand to Nick and directed him. "If you'll get down on the floor and center the stand about three feet out from the window, I'll lower the tree down and you can guide it into place."

Going down on one knee and then laying on his side, Nick gave the go ahead. "Okay…drop her down!"

With a grunt, Ralph hoisted the tree a foot off the ground and stepped forward while Nick gave him directions, "A few inches to the right…no, too far, back to the left just a little. Right there! Let her down." The tree passed through the circular opening when Nick spoke again. "Just hold it straight while I adjust these screws."

From beneath the tree, Nick asked, "I take it from what you said earlier high school football around these parts is a big deal."

"There's no question about that. It's always been that way here in Beaufort and the surrounding counties, actually all across the state. I suppose it'll always be that way. If you attend a high school baseball game or a soccer match, the amount of spectators, including parents, students or just local folks is always somewhat sporadic. Now, a football game…that's entirely different. The stands are packed, people standing on the sidelines and beyond the end zones. People down this way really like their football."

Finished with the last screw, Nick crawled out from under the tree and said, "I think you can let go. It should be fine."

Ralph let go of the tree, stood back and admired their handy work. Walking over and picking up his nog, he examined the tree again. "I think it needs to be moved slightly to the right, but we can do that later." Sitting back down in his chair, he continued with their previous topic of football, "I remember when I was a sophomore at Beaufort High. We had three kids on the team that were beyond good. In fact, they were excellent players, the best to come along in years. That was back in '89 and still to this day there has never been a trio quite like those boys. I grew up with them. When I was younger I lived farther down Newcastle. Brad Schulte and Tim Durham, that's two of the three boys, lived just up the street from my house. Those two kids were obsessed with football. We played a lot of street ball back then, but even in the off-season they would stand out in the street for hours on end and toss a football back and forth. Didn't make any difference what the weather was like; rain, cold, hot…they were always out there practicing. Brad was the quarterback and man could that kid throw. Tim, his best friend was fast…I mean lightning fast, and he could catch. Whenever we played street ball if they were on the same team you would get annihilated."

Relighting the pipe, Ralph continued with the story, "Then, a new kid moved here, his last name was Gaston. He turned out, believe it or not to be even faster than ol' Tim. He was just as obsessed as Brad and Tim and soon became the third member of their daily, year in year out practice sessions out in the street. Around the neighborhood they were called The Three Musketeers: Brad the quarterback, Tim the tight end and now, Gaston, their running back. To make a long story short they played Pop Warner football and then they all went to the same middle school. As a trio they never lost a game, not one, until they came to Beaufort High. Watching these kids grow up and play together, the whole town was excited when they entered high school. We were all so confident that a future state championship was in the cards for Beaufort…"

Politely interrupting Ralph, Nick inquired, "You said these boys were referred to as The Three Musketeers…right? I've heard of other names given to groups of players on certain teams; like The Four Horseman of Notre Dame or Pittsburgh's Steel Curtain. I've got to be honest with you. The name, The Three Musketeers, doesn't sound all that tough."

Clearing the question up, Ralph answered, "Their nickname didn't have to do with just their football skills. If you'll recall, the original Three Musketeers had a saying: One for all and all for one. They always had each other's backs and so did these three boys. They went everywhere and did everything together. If you so much as tangled with one the other two would be at his side. They were inseparable."

Laying his pipe to the side, Ralph emphasized, "When they got to high school, they got a wakeup call. Much to the amazement of everyone, Beaufort lost their first three games their freshman year. But after that, for the next three years we only lost two more games and that was the championship where Charleston South beat us two years running. But, all that changed in 1989 when The Three Musketeers were seniors. We played Charleston for the third straight year for the state championship and we took them down 33-0. Looking back over the past twenty-seven years I don't think there has ever been a more exciting time here in Beaufort. I mean…we were the state champions!"

Getting caught up in Mr. Pickett's enthusiasm for a season and *a game* that was nearly three decades in the past, Nick finished off his eggnog and asked, "So, what happened to these three Beaufort football stars?"

"Now, there is a sad story, a sad story indeed. Those three boys all went off to college on athletic scholarships to play football. Here in Beaufort we thought they were all destined to become professional ballplayers, but then the bottom fell out!"

"I can only assume from the way you answered, they never went to the pros."

"Worse than that. Two of the boys never even completed college. Brad quit after quarterbacking for Penn State following his junior year. He did finish college but never played football again. Tim, not only quit playing football, but left college after just two years and the Gaston kid left school after just his first year in college."

"That really seems odd. What happened to these kids?"

"Well, I have my own opinion. That being said it kind of lines up with what a lot of people here in Beaufort felt...and still feel today. To understand the tragedy of why these boys quit football, the game they all loved so much, you have to go back to the year we won the state championship…1989. I remember those times like it was yesterday. We won the game at Charleston Friday night and the next night, Saturday, we were to have a gigantic celebration party on Fripp Island, down where you now live. It was, and still is to this day, the biggest wingding ever thrown in these parts. A local businessman by the name of Bernard P. James paid for the entire thing. There was a band and a large barbecue; he rented the pool area and the tennis courts. All of the players on the team as well as all the students and faculty members of the school were invited. Anyone who was anybody in Beaufort was scheduled to attend."

Nick reached for the bottle and refilled his glass while he asked, "Did you and Peg go to the party?"

"No, we didn't. I had my learner's permit, but I wasn't allowed to drive after midnight. We figured the party would last much later into the night, so my driving us down to Fripp was out. Peg and I went to an early dinner and then to a movie. To tell you the truth…I'm glad we were not there that night. You see, something horrible happened…something so horrible it took away any enthusiasm anyone could have had about our victory. Two students were found murdered down at the end of the island over near Skull Inlet. Abigail James and Chester Finch; two of the brightest students at Beaufort High. The James girl was going to be attending Cornell University and the Finch kid had been accepted to Harvard. It was a devastating blow to not only the school and the community but the county as well. What's even more sad is Abigail James was the daughter of Bernard James, who sponsored the festivities."

Nick held up his hands. “Okay, I might be getting ahead of the story here, but I don’t seem to understand what any of this has to do with these three outstanding football players not finishing their schooling or going on to the pros.”

“I’m not sure any of this has anything to do with the way they turned out, but there are a lot of folks who would tend to disagree with me on that. There was a massive investigation following the double murders. The police came to the school and interviewed everyone, students, faculty…it didn’t matter. The police didn’t have a motive, a murder weapon, no suspects…nothing. Nothing added up. I remember Peg and I talking after we were interviewed at the school. The police were searching desperately for anything; maybe someone heard something or knew something, but after weeks of investigating, they came up empty handed.”

Suddenly, as if light bulb came on in his head, Nick remembered, “Wait a minute! I have heard about this case…and just recently. I was up in Canada last week visiting a friend of mine. The first night I was there we were going through some old newspaper clippings about things that happened on Fripp Island in the past. While going through the clippings my friend mentioned in passing about two high school students who had been found murdered on Fripp. If I remember correctly, the case was never solved and is now a cold case.”

“Your friend is right. That’s exactly the way things turned out. To this day no one really knows who killed those two students. Now, I have my own idea about who killed them and that very idea is shared with a lot of people in this area, including Bernard P. James. As the weeks went by and the investigation became more and more complicated, eventually the police came up with some rather vague clues…clues that pointed the fickle finger of fate at The Three Musketeers.”

“Do you mean to tell me they killed the two students?”

“Well let’s just say if they didn’t kill them they were somehow involved, which the police were never able to actually prove. The three boys were brought in for additional questioning on four different occasions: as a group and individually. The police knew they were involved, but they couldn’t connect the few dots of info they had together. That June the three boys graduated and the following fall they all went off to college, *Scott free,* according to Mr. James, Abigail’s father. He was convinced beyond any doubt those three boys not only killed his daughter, but the Finch kid as well. After all these years, no one knows for sure what happened that night twenty seven years ago out on Fripp.”

“So, what happened to the three boys?”

"Brad, the quarterback, like I said quit after three years of playing ball for Penn State. He finished up his senior year, got involved in politics and today, so I've been told, is the Mayor of Pittsburgh, the home of my Steelers. Supposedly, he is quite connected, wealthy and is being groomed for the next Governor of Pennsylvania. Tim, who left school after his first two years, transferred to a seminary and studied for the priesthood, became a Catholic priest and is now up in St. Louis. Just last year I heard he is in line to be the next archbishop in that diocese. The Gaston kid, who left after just one year of school, became a very successful businessman."

"Did these kids ever come back here to Beaufort?"

"They were all here a couple of years back for a class reunion, but besides that, they never came back. No, wait…I stand corrected. A couple of months back an electrician friend of mine heard the Gaston kid had a home somewhere here in Beaufort County."

"Do you think these three boys killed those two students?"

"I don't know. I guess I'm like a lot of folks around these parts. I want to see all the evidence before I condemn someone. The problem is the complete truth or the evidence will never be found, so all we can do, each one of us is have our own opinion."

Shelby entered the room and announced, "Dinner will be served in fifteen minutes. Dad, you need to get the electric carving knife out of the bottom of the hutch."

"What do I need to do," offered Nick.

"Not a thing. You've done enough already helping dad put up the tree." Walking over, she looked at the tree and jokingly commented, "And I for one am glad you were here to help with the tree. This is the first time in years we've had one that's relatively straight."

Ralph, rummaging through the hutch drawer countered with his own dose of comedy, "Hey, we men don't try to tell you ladies how to cook a meal, so don't go trying to inform us how to put up a Christmas tree."

Turning to Nick, Shelby gestured toward the long maple table in the living room and spoke, "You'll be seated right next to me on the other side. If you'd like to wash up there is a bathroom right down the hallway."

Looking at the smudges from the tree trunk that were on his hands, he agreed. "I think I will wash up a bit."

Minutes later, seated at the table Nick watched Shelby, her mother and Kirby carry in one bowl or plate of food after another: mashed potatoes with three large pads of butter stuck in the top of the fluffy white vegetables, a bowl each of peas and then corn. Hot buttered rolls, bacon wrapped asparagus, a cheese and relish tray, sweet potatoes slathered with a marshmallow sauce, a large bowl of homemade dressing and last but not least, Ralph carried in the golden brown turkey centered on a silver platter."

Peg, finished, placed her hands on her hips and inspected the feast. "I think we're good to go." Snapping her fingers, she remembered, "The cranberries! I always forget to bring those out."

Ralph, removing the cord from around the carver, noted, "She forgets those dang cranberries every year. We never eat them. It's almost like they're a decoration…not a food. As far as I'm concerned we can do without the cranberries, but what do I know. We can't get started until those cranberries are on the table."

Within the next minute Kirby carried a small silver dish on which was centered a sliced can of the jiggling fruit. After everyone was seated, Peg and Ralph directly across from Shelby and Nick, Kirby at the head of the table, Peg nodded at her granddaughter and suggested, "Would you like to say grace, Kirby?"

Reaching for Nick's hand she replied in her sweet southern draw accent. "I would love to."

Holding Shelby's hand, Nick smiled while he listened to Kirby bless the meal, "Dear Father in heaven. We thank you for not only this meal you have set before us, but also for the hands that prepared it. May we never forget those who have no food to eat today. And, oh yeah, thank you for our friend Nick coming to our home today. Amen!"

Ralph stood and began to carve the turkey as Shelby picked up the mashed potatoes and passed them to Nick.

It was close to seven o'clock, when Ralph stood and looked out the front room window. "Looks like the rain they predicted is finally hitting. I think I'm going to have another slice of pie and some more coffee. Anyone else?"

Nick declined, "Not for me. I've already had two pieces of blueberry, one with ice cream and a piece of that delicious chocolate cake you baked, Mrs. Pickett. I couldn't eat another thing if my life depended on it."

Shelby stood and looked at Nick while announcing, "I think Nick and I are going to sit out on the porch for a while."

Kirby jumped up, "Oh that sounds nice. We can just sit out there and have hot chocolate…"

Peg interrupted her and explained, "You can have your hot chocolate but you're not going out onto the porch with Nick and your mother."

"But why," objected Kirby.

"Because your mother and Nick need to spend some time together. In a few years you'll understand what I'm talking about, but for now we have some kitchen duties to attend to."

Ralph agreed, "Yeah sure, you young folks go right ahead. I'm fine. I've got me a full glass of nog and besides that another football game is just starting."

Nick politely excused himself from the front room while Shelby took him by the hand and led him to the front door.

Sitting on a suspended wooden swing, Shelby snuggled close to Nick and asked, "What do you think of my family?"

"Your mother reminds me of my grandmother, Amelia. Attentive, loving, always concerned about the needs of others. Of course, Kirby is as cute as always. Your father and I talked for over an hour in the front room before dinner."

Shelby nodded. "Yeah, he is a talker. Did you two solve any world problems?"

Nick grinned, "I did find out he really likes his football."

"When I was in the kitchen with my mother, she told me she thought you were a nice young man."

"Well, you know what they say, Rebel. If you can win the mother over then you've got your foot in the door."

Looking out at the rain, Shelby took Nick's hand and commented, "I really like the rain. Seems like I never tire of it. Sometimes at night I come out here and just sit and listen to the sound of the rain beating on the porch roof."

Nick listened to the rain for a moment and then spoke, "Listen, I want to thank you for inviting me to your home today. I think it was the nicest Thanksgiving I've ever had. I really enjoyed sitting in the front room and talking with your father. The meal your mother prepared was delicious. Then, only a few hours later we had turkey sandwiches and more dessert. I especially enjoyed decorating the tree."

Shelby smiled and continued to stare out at the rain pelting the street in front of the house.

Nick squeezed her hand and spoke up. "There's a couple of things I need to tell you. One is important and the other, not so much. Since you dropped me off on Fripp Monday a lot has happened. First of all, I'm buying a house out on Fripp. Carson told me about this woman who was interested in selling and he said it would be a great investment property. It needs a lot of work, but time is something I have plenty of these days. I'm closing on the house this coming Tuesday. Maybe I could pick you up Tuesday evening after you get home from work and I could run you over so you can tell me what you think."

"That sounds like a good idea. My boss, Mr. Schrock, owns a number of rental properties down on Tybee Island. I don't have to return to work until Wednesday, so if you want we can head over to Fripp earlier if you want."

"Okay, I'll buy you lunch at the Bonito Boathouse."

Shelby looked at Nick and inquired, "Was that the important thing or the not so much one?"

"That was the not so much issue. The other thing I wanted to tell you about really doesn't affect you, but depending on how things work out…it could."

"You've peaked my interest. What's up?"

"You know we discussed that the Carnahans are still hanging out there somewhere until they are convinced beyond doubt Charley Sparks and his goon partner took off with the money. Khelen Ridley, an attorney in Beaufort, told me a lady by the name of Maria Sparks, who just happens to be none other than Charley's sister, does not believe he and Simons took the money. She feels something happened to them on Fripp and that they never left the island. She is down here in Beaufort and has hired a local attorney, who by the way is a real pain in the ass! She wants him to track me down so she can ask me some questions about her brother. I don't think they'll try to contact you. Hell, they might not even know you exist. I hope that's the case, because this lawyer is a real sleaze. You or I don't need him snooping around our lives. It looks like I'll be talking with him in the next few days and then if everything goes the way I think it will, that should be it. This Ms. Sparks will go back to her home in Staten Island and this local lawyer will leave me be. I just wanted to let you know in case they contact you. I don't want you to be blindsided."

"Look, after what we went through this past summer I think I can just about handle anything. Just promise me when you talk with these people you'll be careful. We know, both of us, how things can get out of hand. Hopefully this will just blow over. I hope it does because I'm not ready for another adventure."

CHAPTER ELEVEN

THE WAVES WASHED UP AND OVER HIS BARE FEET WHILE Nick sat in an old beach chair at the edge of the water. The tide was coming in and soon he would either have to move back or if he waited long enough be knocked out of the chair when the waves grew stronger. Looking down at his waterproof watch, the glowing glass face read, 6:37 a.m. The sun would be up in the next fifteen minutes. Turning, he looked back at his house and could see the light from the back porch. A small beacon on the vast dark beach. An especially large wave smacked into his feet and splashed up into his chest and face. Getting up, he picked up the chair and moved back a few yards. Sitting back down his thoughts were centered on his plan for the day. He was confident Brumly and the Sparks woman would try to contact him. How and when, he couldn't be sure. He had beaten the low-life lawyer on Wednesday, and realized he accomplished nothing more than pissing the man off, which is what both Khelen Ridley and Carson had told him to avoid.

His thoughts were interrupted by the voice of his neighbor, Genevieve, "Good morning, Nick. What brings you out to the beach this early?"

"Just have some thinking to do," said Nick. "I do some of my best thinking out here on the beach. Just finishing up your walk?"

Reaching down, she pet her new, soaked walking partner on the head, "She just loves the beach…and waves. She's like an alarm clock. When five o'clock rolls around she's ready to go. I can't thank you enough for her. I thought I'd never have another dog, but now I realize I can't live without one."

Sitting in the sand, she asked, "How was your day in Beaufort with Shelby's family?"

"It was great! I met her parents, we had a nice meal. I really felt comfortable there. How about you? Did you have anyone over or did you go somewhere?"

"I went over to Parker Sims' house. He had some folks from around the island over. Carson was there and Grady Phillips too. I told Grady all about you. He said he'd like to meet you sometime." Changing her attitude, she became quite serious, "Someone broke into my garage during the night and stole my golf cart."

"You're kidding me! Here on Fripp. Why would anyone steal a golf cart? I mean…everyone already has one."

"That's the same thing I thought, but nonetheless, it's gone. They kicked in the garage entry door, opened the garage door from the inside and obviously drove off with the cart."

"Maybe it was just some kids. They probably took it for a joy ride and we'll find it on the side of one of the island roads. I wouldn't worry about it. Besides that, a golf cart can only be driven four miles from your residence. That's South Carolina law. Now, in a gated community like Fripp, four miles from any house can get you anyplace on the island. I've never checked it out but I don't think they'd allow you to drive a cart off Fripp. That cart will show up someplace on the island. What other reason than just riding around would someone have? It can't be sold, it really can't be hidden, unless someone dumps it out in the salt marsh and how would they get the thing out there. It just doesn't make any sense."

Nick stood and walked into the water allowing the low waves to wash the sand from his feet. Folding up his chair, he looked east and watched the very edge of the sun while it rose above the distant horizon. "I've got to head back up to the house. I think I may go and see this Brumly character this morning. The sooner I contact him the sooner he'll stop trailing me. Listen, do me a favor. I'm going to give this man a call. If I don't get to speak with him, I'll leave a message. For all I know he might head back out this way before I even get a chance to talk with him. So, later on this morning, if he shows up here again and you happen to see him let him know that I'm looking *for him!"* Starting back toward the house, he pet Ruth and once again assured Genevieve, "I'm sure your cart will show up."

Back at the house he made himself two eggs and fried up some bacon. Sitting at the kitchen table, he looked at the card Brumly had left in his door on Wednesday. He figured he had already ticked the lawyer off. Maybe by calling him and setting up an appointment to speak with Brumly he could defuse the situation. Maybe it wouldn't be as bad as he thought. It was close to seven-thirty. Maybe the lawyer wasn't even up yet. *The hell with it,* thought Nick. *I might as well get this over with.*

Picking the card up off the table, he walked to the wall mounted kitchen phone, dialed the Beaufort number and waited. Following eight ringtones, a recorded male voice sounded, *You have reached the office of Chic Brumly, attorney at law and private detective services. I am unable to answer your call at the moment, but if you will at the sound of the tone please leave your full name, number and reason for calling, I will return your call at the next convenient moment. Thank you for your call.*

Hanging up the phone Nick leaned against the wall and finished his orange juice. He had set the ball in motion. He had made the dreaded call. The only thing worse was if Brumly would have actually answered. *Soon enough,* thought Nick. *Soon enough!*

Deciding to watch the late edition of the morning news, he went into the sprawling living room, opened the large walnut console and hit the ON button on the remote. Pressing the channel button he came to the news. An attractive woman seated behind the familiar glass and laminate newscast desk was speaking, "*Early this morning the skeletal remains of what has been identified as a female body was discovered North of Pritchards Island, near the area where last summer a skeleton of a hand was found. Presently, authorities have stated the hand may belong to the remains found this morning, since there is only one hand on the remains. This latest discovery may be the rest of the remains of what is thought to be that of Susan Dunn, one of the possible victims of the now deceased RPS Killer. In other news…*"

Nick turned the television off. He'd heard enough. It wasn't even eight o'clock yet and he had already received his daily reminder of the past stressful summer. Khelen Ridley had been right when he said he didn't like to read much of the newspaper that was filled with rapes, murders and fires. Was it any wonder why the typical American was often negative? People got up in the morning and before or on the way to work caught the morning news to start their day off being informed of all the local and many of the world's problems. Then at lunch they might listen to or watch the noonday news report filled with yet more negativity. If this is not enough, when they got home following a hard day's work of whatever they did for a living, they receive another shot in the arm of catastrophic or depressing events that have recently happened in the world while they watch the evening news and finally just before they turn in for the night, they get their final dose of negativity by watching the late night news. The next day, it's simply starts over with a different buffet of bad news.

Sitting in his grandmother's rocking chair next to the stone fireplace he tried to convince himself he had done the right thing by calling Brumly. The ringing of the phone brought him back to the moment as he stared at the black phone hanging on the kitchen wall. The chance it was Brumly calling him back already was surprising. But then again, it could be someone else calling. The number of people who would call him was a small group: Carson, Genevieve, Ridley, Shelby or even Amelia. On the third ring he got up and crossed the living room and thought, *I hope it's not Brumly!*

Picking up the receiver, Nick answered in a calm voice, "Hello."

"A masculine voice on the other end, responded, "Is this Mr. Falco…Mr. Nick Falco?"

"Yes, this is Mr. Falco. And who am I speaking with?"

"My name is Mr. Brumly…I believe you just tried to call me a few minutes ago."

"Yes I did. You were at my home down here on Fripp Island, I believe on Wednesday and left one of your business cards stuck in my front door. It had a handwritten note on the back saying I was to call you and that it was a matter of great importance. The address on the front of your card read that your office is in Port Royal. I'm afraid you've got me at a disadvantage. I can't imagine why a lawyer or, I guess a private detective, would want to talk with me. What is this in regard to?"

"It is a matter of great importance and I'd rather not discuss it over the phone. Would it be possible for us to meet later on this morning or sometime today?"

Nick was already aware of what the lawyer wanted to talk with him about, but Brumly probably didn't know that. If Nick seemed too cooperative, it might put the lawyer on the alert. Trying to act like any normal person that had just been contacted by a strange lawyer, Nick probed, "I'd really like to know what this is all about. I just moved to this area earlier this year and I don't know who you are. I can't imagine why some local lawyer would want to meet with me."

"I am aware of the fact you just moved down here to Beaufort County last summer. There is nothing for you to be concerned over. I am a very well-known lawyer in these parts. You inherited your grandmother's home…correct?"

"Yes, I did."

"I have a few questions in regard to your grandmother. If we could just meet, we could get this cleared up in about an hour or so."

Nick could tell Brumly was becoming impatient by the slight change in the tone of voice and thought better of it to push any further. "Yeah, I guess I could meet you later on today."

"Good," said Brumly. "Would you rather I come out to the island on do you want to meet me in Port Royal at my office?"

Not having any desire to have this man in his home, Nick answered, "I can drive up later this morning. I could probably be there in thirty minutes."

Just like Nick figured the lawyer gently objected, "No, I'll need an hour before I can be at my office. Can you be here at ten?"

"Ten it is," responded Nick. "Where is your office located?"

"Are you familiar with the Port Royal area?"

"Yes, I am."

"Okay, what you do is come straight down Rebaut Road which eventually runs right into Port Royal. The first red light you encounter in Port Royal is Paris. On the right hand corner you'll see a large two story white stucco structure, the CBC Building. I'm on the first floor facing the street down at the end just past the Carolina Tavern. There is a parking area on the side, just come on in. See you at ten."

Brumly didn't even have enough courtesy to say goodbye; he just hung up. Nick smiled and put the kitchen phone back on the wall. From where he stood he figured he was still in control of the situation. He had deliberately suggested thirty minutes, having a pretty good idea Brumly would need more time because he probably had to pick up the Sparks woman, who he was quite sure would want to attend the meeting.

Crossing the Harbor Island Bridge, it was just starting to spit rain. He turned the wipers on low, sat back and tried to mentally prepare himself for the upcoming meeting with Brumly and Sparks. He had decided to wear the same clothing he worn to Shelby's on Thanksgiving. Thursday evening, after returning from Beaufort, he had tossed the clothing on a chair next to the bed. It was just easier to put them back on than digging through the closet for something else. It was just as well. He wanted to make a good first impression on the lawyer and the woman. They didn't know it, but they had already met him, at the Shrimp Shack, and the woman had bumped into him at Bills, even spoke to him. He wondered if they would remember him. He felt like he was still holding the upper hand. He had a rather good idea, based on what Khelen told him, as to why they wanted to meet with him. What he didn't know was if they knew what he knew. Would Brumly assume after telling Ridley he wanted to talk with a Mr. Nick Falco, that Khelen would make contact with the individual he was looking for?

Arriving at the intersection in Port Royal Brumly had described, after waiting for the light to change, Nick made a right into the lot and parked at the far end. He checked his watch: 9:45 a.m. He didn't want to walk in too early. He wondered if the lawyer and the woman were even there yet. Then, he noticed, parked at the rear of the building the dark blue Lincoln he had followed down the Sea Island Parkway on Wednesday. He and the woman were most likely inside waiting for his arrival. *I'll give it ten more minutes,* he thought, *and then I'll go in.*

Despite the fact it was in the low forties, he was sweating profusely. Pushing the electric window button on the door, the window slowly lowered, the cool air invading the interior of the Lexus. He didn't think he was nervous, but why else would he be sweating? Taking a swig from a water bottle he'd brought along, he then dumped a small portion of water on a napkin he took out of the glove box and gently wiped his forehead and took a deep breath. Trying to think of something else other than the soon to be meeting, he thought about the news he'd seen earlier and shook his head in wonder. When that newsperson elaborated about how last summer they had discovered a skeletal hand, the news media, even though they didn't mention his name were indirectly talking about him. Looking back, it really was amazing how he had noticed the hand sticking up out of the black marsh mud out past Pritchards Island. Harold T. Benjamin V, the former RPS Killer was dead and buried, and yet the after effects of his killing spree were still haunting the Lowcountry. Would it ever end? He decided to give Carson a quick call and update him on how he was dealing with Brumly.

Carson, his fishing boat parked in the middle of the Old Harbor River, just north of Fripp, checked on three of his four fishing lines, sat back and popped a can of ice cold beer when his cell phone rang. Sitting the beer down, he picked up the phone and answered, "Carson Pike."

"Carson," it's Nick. "I told you back on Thanksgiving I'd keep you updated on the Brumly situation. I decided to give the creep a call this morning. I'm in Port Royal right now sitting in the parking lot right outside his office. I've got about five minutes before I go in."

"Are you sure you can handle this lawyer by yourself? This guy has been around the blocks a few times. You really need to be careful what you say and *how* you say it. Amelia called me right after you talked with her Thursday morning. She is quite concerned about this Sparks woman coming down there and hiring Brumly to track you down. I assured her you and I have, and will continue to touch base on the situation. Just remember; do not deviate from our story. We did a great job of pulling off a con on the Carnahans, but that's not good enough. The best con is one that is never uncovered. Charley's sister is down here sniffing around. It's important we send her back to New York with the same story the Carnahans bought into. By this time I would have thought things would have started to settle down, but while this Sparks woman is down here, we have to continue the con. Understand?"

"I understand," said Nick. "Stick to our story."

"All right…good luck in there! Call me when you get out of the meeting. If we need to talk I can meet you later today."

Putting his cell in his jacket pocket, Nick checked the time, 9:57. *Close enough!*

Approaching a glass front door there was gold lettering that matched the info on Brumly's business card. *Charles "Chic" Brumly Attorney at Law.*

Pushing open the door, he entered what appeared to be a reception office, minus a receptionist. The room was small: 10 x 12 feet, thick light green shag carpet, knotty pine paneled walls, a computer centered on a small desk on one of those square green desk pads. The desk itself, looked old, not an antique, just old. The walls were bare of any pictures or framed certificates of accomplishments. The only other articles in the room were a woven wooden trashcan and a plain circular clock on the left hand wall. The time was 9:59. *Right on time!*

A matching knotty pine door on the right was slightly ajar. Crossing the outdated, worn carpet, Nick slowly pushed open the door. Standing there unnoticed, he saw a man and a woman with their backs to him in front of a small coffeemaker. Clearing his throat to get their attention, he adjusted his sports coat and tried to appear relaxed. Both the woman and the man turned. Nick quickly identified the couple as the man and woman he had sat next to at the Shrimp Shack. The man, holding a ceramic cup of coffee smiled and inquired, "You must be Mr. Falco."

Wanting to appear at ease, Nick answered, "Unless there is another Nick Falco in the area, I'm your man."

The woman, also holding coffee, gave Nick a strange look and placed her fingers to her lips as if she were thinking.

"Come in, come in," gestured Brumly. Holding up the cup he offered, "Would you care for a cup of morning life. I never seem to be able to function until after I've had my third cup...which this is."

Nick declined, "No thank you. I had breakfast earlier."

Brumly walked behind a desk that was in much better condition than the one in the lobby and took his seat. The woman sat in one of two matching green leather chairs on either side of the room. Crossing her legs, she took a drink of coffee and continued to stare at Nick in what he thought was an odd fashion. Brumly opened a desk drawer and commented, "Just let me get my folder and we can get started."

Nick took in the room. It was nothing like Khelen's mansion office, where the walls were painted in a pleasant, but professional deep grape color, the wall behind his expensive desk lined with shelves of thick, brown and green, numbered law books. Khelen's office was also decorated with numerous framed certificates of accomplishment. The only thing that hung on the light blue walls was a single certificate that stated *The South Carolina Board of...*It was too far away and the printing was too small for him to completely make it out.

His attention switched to the woman, who was still, at the moment, staring knives through him. He didn't stare back at her for very long, but just long enough to form an impression. Before, when she had bumped into him at Bill's Liquor Store and then when they had been face to face at the Shrimp Shack, he really didn't have time to get that good of a look at her. But now, she was seated directly across the room from him. She was definitely *big city,* dressed far too elaborately for Beaufort, especially little ol' laid back Port Royal. Nick gave her a quick once over from head to toe. The long black dyed hair beneath a fashionable grey designer jockey hat, her makeup, as far as he was concerned was over the top, but she did have an attractive face. A long grey and black striped jacket hid for the most part, what appeared to be a light beige silk blouse, covered with three strands of expensive looking jewelry. Her tight slacks matched the jacket and her tiny feet were encased in yellow stilettos. She tapped her bright red nails on the wooden armrest of the chair and continued to stare. Shifting his attention back to Brumly, he noticed the man was wearing a bright red coat versus the yellow he had been wearing on Wednesday.

Placing a brown folder on the top of the uncluttered desk, Brumly nodded at Nick and confirmed, "By now, I can only assume you know who I am." Standing, he reached across the desk and extended his hand. "Chic Brumly!"

Nick stood and returned the handshake and answered, "You already know who I am."

Sitting down, Brumly went about introducing the woman. Removing his sports coat he hung it on a cheap metal coatrack and gestured at the woman. "This is my client…Ms. Maria Sparks. She's down here from New York."

The woman leaned slightly forward and pointed at Nick. "Are you not the young man I nearly ran over at the liquor store last Wednesday?"

"Yes, I believe that was me," admitted Nick.

"And then later, we met briefly at that shrimp place."

"Right again!" said Nick. "At the time, on both occasions I had no idea you and Mr. Brumly were trying to get in touch with me. I guess it's a small world after all."

"Not quite small enough," snapped Ms. Sparks as she shot Brumly and unpleasant look. "I can understand my not recognizing Mr. Falco here when we bumped into one another at the liquor store and then again when we crossed paths at the island restaurant. What I can't seem to get my head around is that you, a competent attorney and *private detective,* did not know ahead of time what our friend here looked like. I'm paying you good money and quite a bit of it to get to the bottom of my brother's disappearance."

Brumly, not the least bit affected by Ms. Sparks' sudden outburst, calmly rolled up the sleeves of his pink shirt and loosened his grey necktie. "Calm down, Maria. What difference does any of that make? You hired me for two reasons. First, to track down one Mr. Nick Falco, which we no longer need to be concerned over because, in case you haven't noticed, is sitting directly across from you. So, as far as I'm concerned, to date, I've done my job. The second reason you hired me is to discover what really happened to your brother. Now, if you'll just sit back and let me do what I happen to be quite good at, maybe, just maybe we can get to the bottom of this."

The woman, obviously not used to being told what to do, sat back, took a swig of coffee and tried to compose her emotions. "Very well, Chic…let's move on."

Giving Nick somewhat of an apologetic smile, Brumly asked, "Mr. Falco or, should I refer to you as Nick?"

Nick smiled at the woman and answered, "Nick will be fine." Maria Sparks did not return his smile, but remained tense.

Opening the folder Brumly clicked an ink pen. "Okay, *Nick.* Does the last name…Sparks mean anything to you?"

Acting confused, Nick responded, "No…should it?"

Maria interrupted, "Look, Mr. Falco, if you are not going to be honest with myself or my attorney, this could get quite ugly!"

Continuing the charade, Nick remained calm and responded, "Whatever do you mean? I already told you. The last name, Sparks, your last name so I've been told, does not mean anything to me. But, apparently, you think it should. Would you care to fill me in?"

Brumly interrupted and held up his hand. "Maria, please let me take it from here." Addressing Nick, he explained, "We've already mentioned that Ms. Sparks is down here to find out what happened to her brother who seems to have disappeared."

Nick, still way ahead of the couple, bantered back, "I'm sorry your brother is missing, but what does any of that have to do with me?"

Maria, not comfortable with the way things were going spoke up despite Brumly's efforts to control the meeting. "Do you mean to tell me you're going to sit there and tell me you've never heard of my brother…Charley Sparks?"

Nick knew he was eventually going to have to admit he knew Charley or the story he planned on sticking to would not make any sense. Acting stupid, he tapped his forehead with the right hand and apologized, "Of course…Charley Sparks. Now I remember. I do know of him. We bumped heads a few times over the past summer."

Now it was Brumly who was concerned. "Bumped heads is not a phrase that bespeaks of two individuals getting along all that well. Can you expand on what you mean?"

"Sure, but I don't think Ms. Sparks is going to like what I have to say. If I recall, you did say you intended to get to the bottom of her brother's disappearance. Now, I can't tell you why he disappeared. I can only tell you what happened between the two of us."

Maria spoke up and set her cup down. "Look, I know my brother was no angel…who is? I already know he was down here on an assignment in Beaufort. Charley and I are very close. Since we graduated from high school, which was quite a ways back, we've been in touch with each other two to three times a week. There is nothing that goes on in his life or mine the other is not aware of. He called me every day when he was down here. I know where he went and what he did. So, Mr. Falco, let's hear your story. But, be warned before you begin. My brother was always up front with me. In some circles he was not the most well-liked person you'd want to meet, but he was always honest."

Nick looked at Brumly who had his hands folded on the desk. Chic smiled and gestured for him to begin. The match had begun and Brumly was in the middle. Nick was sure from what Maria said she knew far more than she was letting on *and* he knew far more about her brother than he was willing to reveal. Scratching his head, he thought, *This should be interesting!*

Moving to the front of his chair, he looked directly at Ms. Sparks and began, "The first time I laid eyes on your brother was before I even moved here. I was painting a house when I noticed a blue sedan sitting on the other side of the street. A man, who later on turned out to be Charley Sparks was watching me. At first I just blew it off as my imagination. But then after a few minutes, it was obvious. They, and I mean they, because there was another man in the car with your brother. I decided to cross the street and see what they wanted but they sped off before I could talk to them. I remember the car having an out of state license plate. Later on, while at a local bank, I'm walking out and I see the same car your brother had been driving. Out of curiosity I walked over to the unoccupied car and checked the plate, New York tags. I thought it was very strange for the same car your brother had been watching me from to be at the bank where I was. I had the strangest feeling I was being followed for some reason."

Chic broke in on Nicks' rundown. "And you had never seen the car or Charley before that day?"

"No…never!" Continuing with his version of what happened next, Nick explained, "While looking inside the car, I noticed my name and address on a slip of paper attached to the sun visor. Now, *I knew* I was being followed. Suddenly I'm attacked from behind. I was lifted off my feet and thrown to the ground face first. I got a pretty bad cut on my arm which later on resulted in my going to a medical center for stitches."

Maria held up her hand and asked, "Was Charley the one who attacked you?"

"Well, at the time I didn't know who Charley was, but it turned out that shortly after I was tossed around like a rag doll, your brother arrived on the scene and ordered this other man, who reminded me of a hulking, ugly giant, to let me be. It was at this point things became very strange. Your brother was concerned about my arm and suggested I should get it looked at. I then asked him why they were following me and why my name and address was on their sun visor. Your brother was quite vague and told me it was not important how they knew of me. He told me I would find out soon enough and in the next few days I would have to make some decisions. He strongly advised me not to go to the police in regard to our encounter. He made it clear I was in no danger and they would probably see me during the upcoming week. Then they got in the car and drove off. I had no idea who these men were or what they wanted and certainly didn't understand what future decisions they had been talking about."

Brumly spoke up while he wrote something in the folder, "This incident was the first time, as you say, you *bumped heads* with Charley Sparks? I assume later on you ran into him again?"

"That I did, but before I get into my next encounter with Charley and his monster friend, I want to ask Maria if my story so far lines up with what she knows." Nick figured as long as he was asking questions he was still in control.

Maria smiled across the room at Nick while she fiddled with the crease on her right pant leg. "All right, that sounds fair. I knew my brother was in Cincinnati keeping an eye on someone. The company he works for had sent him there. I had no idea who the person was he had been assigned to, but based on what you've told me, it's apparent it was indeed you. The evening after he had made contact with you for the first time, he phoned me and told me he and Derek, that's the man who works with him, were heading on to Beaufort, South Carolina. He really didn't divulge any of the details about when you first met, but I believe what you have told me so far is the truth. Mainly because your description of what Derek looked like and how he reacted sounds exactly the way he is. I've only met him once before in New York. You're right! He is a hulking, ugly monster as you put it earlier. He and my brother have gone on many assignments for their employer. Derek is a rather out of control person, but Charley usually keeps him under control. I can see where Charley would have told him to let you go and the fact you said my brother was concerned about your injured arm makes sense. Charley would much rather talk things over than get physical. So far, your story seems to be right on the money."

There was a brief moment of silence, but then Brumly still writing with the pen, spoke up, "Okay, back to what we were discussing before Maria verified your story. When was the next time you met Charley?"

"In Beaufort," answered Nick. "Later on that evening in Cincinnati after meeting your brother for the first time, I decided to take in a ballgame. During the game I get this call from a lawyer from Beaufort. Khelen Ridley, do you know him?"

Brumly smirked and answered, "Yes, I know Khelen quite well. His office is located on Church Street close to downtown. We are both members of the Beaufort County Club."

Nick, thinking it best not to mention Khelen had warned him about Brumly, moved on. "Ridley explained to me my grandmother had passed away and I was to be one of the pall bearers at her funeral which was being held out on Fripp Island. So, the next day I drove down to Beaufort, which turned out to be my second encounter with Charley Sparks. Let me rephrase that. It really wasn't much of an encounter at all. I didn't even get to see him, but I knew he had followed me. I arrived in Beaufort the evening prior to the funeral so I stayed at a hotel in town. The next morning when I woke up, whose car do I discover parked in the lot…"

Brumly interrupted and finished the statement, "Charley's car!"

"That's correct," verified Nick. "It was the same color and had the same New York tags. I knew Charley and probably that Derek character had followed me. Why, I still had no idea. At this point I still didn't know their names."

Brumly was about to say something but Nick kept on talking, "Later the same morning I went out to Fripp to the funeral and who do I run into? Charley and his goon partner. I was sitting off to the side trying to sort out why I was being followed plus the fact I was at my grandmother's funeral. It was a stressful morning. When Charley and Derek walked in the front door they spot me and come over to speak with me. They were all pissed off because they had gotten a flat tire back at the hotel and asked me if I knew anything about it…which I didn't. I guess I wasn't in the best of moods and I asked him why they were following me and what did they want. Charley, for some reason suddenly got pissed and told me to do what I was told and I snapped back saying I didn't understand any of this and what was I supposed to do? He told me I was supposed to do what I was told and nothing else. Derek, all the while is standing off to the side giving me the evil eye.

That guy gave me the creeps!"

Feeling a little more comfortable, Nick sat back and continued, "All of a sudden, a friend of my grandparents walks up and has, I guess you could say, a heated conversation with Charley. After a few moments Charley and his pal walk off into the main room."

Interested, Brumly inquired, "This friend of your grandparents. What's his name?"

"Carson Pike...do you know him?"

"Pike...of course I know him. Most people around here do. I haven't had any dealings with the man but I've heard he's a bit of an oddball." Laying his pen down, Chic thought for a moment and then asked, "It sounds to me like Pike already knew Charley."

"That's what I thought too," said Nick. "I asked him who these two men were. He didn't offer me their names, but their first names had been mentioned. Carson said they worked for the same company my grandfather had. He really didn't give me much information on them, but told me if they bothered me again to give him a call."

Maria spoke up, "Why would this Pike person, this odd ball everyone seems to know be interested in coming to your rescue which is what it sounds like? You say he worked for your grandparents. What did he do for them?"

Nick looked directly into her eyes and answered, "Well, that really isn't any of your business, *Ms. Sparks!*"

"It most certainly is! I'm paying Brumly here a hefty fee to discover what happened to my brother, and anything, I mean anything even remotely connected to his disappearance is my business. Do you understand?"

"Yeah, I understand and you have to understand I'm here of my own choosing. I didn't have to come here today...but I did! And as I came I can just as easily walk out of here. Do you understand?"

Maria didn't like being put in her place. Turning to Brumly she calmly asked, "Are you, as my attorney, going to sit there and allow him to talk to me in this fashion?"

Chic stood, walked to the front window and looked out at the street. Maria and Nick stared at the attorney's back and waited for his response. Finally, he turned back facing them and spoke firmly, "Look, boys and girls, I have sat through many a meeting, maybe not exactly like this one, but nonetheless, I have had many a client and person sit here in my office and talk over or debate issues. It has been my experience that arguing never solves anything. Now, do you think we could return to a normal exchange of words here? Because if we cannot, it's going to make for a long and nonproductive morning."

Maria and Nick remained quiet, when Brumly finally spoke to Nick, "So, did Charley or this Derek character ever bother you again?"

Nick folded his hands on his lap and sat back. "Yes they did. I guess it was about three days later. I stopped at Bill's Liquor Store to pick up a few items." Looking at Maria he stated, "You know, the place where you bumped into me."

Maria nodded but said nothing, so Nick continued, "Anyway, I'm walking out of the place when who do I run into? Charley and his friend. Derek grabs me roughly by the arm and leads me down the sidewalk to the end of the building where Charley is waiting. They had obviously been watching me throughout the day because they asked me what I had been talking to Khelen Ridley about. I told them it was none of their business and Derek said something about how he should wring my neck. He pushed me down on some cardboard boxes. Your brother, seeing things were getting out of hand, ordered Derek to ease off stating they couldn't talk to me there. He said they knew where I was going and there would be plenty of time to talk later. So, once again your brother saved me from the wrath of Derek."

Not giving either one of his opponents time to ask a question, Nick went on to his next brush with Charley Sparks. "It didn't take Charley long to approach me again. Actually, it was right here in Port Royal over at the Dockside over on 11th Street. I was having dinner with a lady friend. While she was using the ladies room, I just happen to notice Charley and Derek tucked away at a corner table. That was it for me. I was tired of them dogging me wherever I went. I got up and went to their table. I told them I was tired of them following me everywhere I went and I didn't want any trouble. Charley told me to relax; they were simply having dinner. I didn't believe that for a second. Charley told me to mind my own business and go back to my table. I told them to mind *their own business* and told them Carson Pike said if they bothered me again he would take care of them. As usual, Derek lost it, jumped up and said he wasn't the least bit scared of Pike. Charley strongly ordered Derek to sit and suggested I return to my table, which I did."

Thinking back, Nick estimated, "It must have been around forty minutes or so right after we finished dinner when Charley comes to our table and explains to the girl I was with, if I remember correctly, I was a *good egg,* then he drops a fifty on the table and says dinner is on him! This is where things really started to get weird. When we exited the restaurant, the girl I was with had an unexpected visitor, her soon to be ex-boyfriend. He gave her a pretty hard time and started to shove her around. What could I do? I just had dinner with this girl. I couldn't just stand there. I had to try and do something. This was a big man and I knew right off the bat I had made a mistake by getting involved. After we exchanged some heated words he shoved me and I went down. I got up and managed to get him down but he was up in no time. I knew I was toast; no match for this man. Just about the time he is standing over me ready to crush me to pieces, he is jerked from behind by none other than Derek, who manhandled the guy with little effort. Charley told him I was their friend and they did not appreciate him giving me a hard time. The last thing Charley said that evening was the girl and I had better get out of there before the police showed up. I wound up going to a medical care center for the second time in less than two weeks. I was really confused now. Your brother and Derek had been anything but nice to me and now they bought my dinner and saved my ass in the parking lot. I still had no idea what they wanted of me or what decisions I was going to, according to them, have to make."

Maria smiled in surprising approval. "Everything you have said so far seems to be the truth. I say *seems* because when Charley would call me he always just covered the basics of the day. I knew he and Derek followed you to the liquor store and the Dockside. He never gave me many details, just that he was following you. I just happen to know the next location when you, *bumped heads* with my brother." Looking at Brumly she gestured with her hand as if she were holding the pen. "Make sure you get all this down because we'll soon be at the end. Mr. Falco here was painting a house on Fripp Island, the next time he saw Charley. And it was after this meeting that Nick finally understood why Charley and Derek had been following him day after day." She looked across the room at Nick and smiled. "Tell me if I miss anything!"

Standing up, she removed her long coat, hung it on the back of the chair and sat back down. "Nick was informed his grandfather, Edward Falco, who happened to work for the same people Charley works for, embezzled around seven million dollars from the company over a number of years. When Edward's superiors caught on, they approached him and told him he must return the money. Edward pleaded ignorance and then died accidentally a few months later. The money was supposedly hidden either in the Falco home on Fripp or maybe even on the property. Next, the company decided to talk things over with Amelia Falco, your grandmother. She also refused to cooperate and later on died as well. So, the company had no other recourse than to approach you, Nick. It only made sense. You now owned the property. After hearing the truth about your grandparents you said you didn't believe a word and refused the company as well. You didn't believe, or maybe you just acted like you didn't believe, but just like your grandparents you refused the company what was rightfully theirs. When they left you that day they gave you a week to cooperate."

Nick smiled. "You are well informed, but not completely. They may have told me I had a week but that turned out to be a lie. Later that night I was knocked unconscious in my garage and carried off. I happen to know it was Charley and Derek because they were seen when they drove up to my house by my neighbor. She remembered them from when they had attended my grandmother's funeral. The next thing I know I wake up on a yacht parked nearly ten miles out in the ocean in front of Fripp. I was taken up top where I met a gentleman, excuse me, so-called *businessman* by the name of Joseph Carnahan. I remember them telling me it was sometime after two in the morning. Carnahan basically reviewed what Charley had told me the previous day: about the money and my grandparents' involvement. In short, I was given the option of cooperating with them before the sun came up or I would be killed; according to Carnahan, shackled with cinderblocks and tossed over the side…"

Maria interrupted, "But that never happened…did it? You managed to escape by jumping over the side, which no one expected out in the middle of the ocean. When Charley called me later the next day and said he was amazed you were able to swim away from the yacht…and survive. Well, at that point he wasn't sure you had, but they couldn't take any chances. They would wait and see if your body was discovered."

Nick held out both hands. "As you can plainly see…I did make it!"

Brumly became slightly upset. "Hold on here for a minute. Do you mean to tell me this Carnahan individual would have killed you if you hadn't escaped?"

"That's exactly what I'm saying and despite the fact I made it to shore, they still almost took me out. When I finally made it to Pritchards Island I was exhausted, but that was not the end of that night. Who do I run into shortly after I'm on land? Derek. He tried to drown me but for some reason, that still confuses me, I managed to get away."

Brumly looked down at his desk and then at Maria. "The more we talk the more complicated this seems to get. I need to ask you, Maria. Were you aware your brother and his associates had intentions of killing Mr. Falco?"

"No, my brother, over the years has gone on many assignments for the Carnahans. He only told me they wanted to recover the millions; he never mentioned Nick's life was in danger."

Sarcastically, Chic remarked, "Well, that's good to know, because If I thought for a moment you were involved in plotting Mr. Falco's demise, I may not be able to represent you any longer."

"Look Chic, I'm paying you to find out what happened to my brother. That's all! Don't try to make this into something it's not! I didn't make the trip down here to be questioned. I want answers to *my* questions. That's what I'm paying for. I want to know what happened to my brother!"

Brumly looked at Nick like it was his turn to speak.

Nick responded and looked across the room at Maria. "So, after I managed to escape I gave Carson Pike a call. He told me it was not safe to go to my home so he hid me. By that time the day was too far gone and Carson came up with a plan to put an end to all of this. He told me he had the money all along. He had found it in the house before I ever moved in. Carson Pike was a dear friend to both my grandparents and said my grandmother, Amelia, would have never wanted it to go this far. Carson said he was going to contact the Carnahans and make arrangements to hand the money over to them, but in return they were never to bother me again. The Carnahans agreed to this and the plan was set in motion. Carson requested your brother and Derek were to be the ones who picked up the money. They were to meet Carson and I at the house at midnight. They showed up right on time. There were two suitcases containing the money. I know it was in there because I saw it. It was unbelievable. Your brother was only at the house for maybe ten minutes. According to the plan we agreed on, after they received the money they were to call Carnahan in Charleston and verify they had the money. After this was done your brother and Derek left the house *and that* is the last time I ever saw them."

Maria was about to speak up but Nick cut her off and finished his story. "The next morning Carson called me and informed me he had located another six hundred thousand that belonged to the Carnahans. They had been expecting somewhere in the vicinity of seven million. We gave Charley and Derek 5.8 million. Carson explained that we needed to completely clear the air with the Carnahans so he said we were going over to Charleston and give Joseph the remaining six hundred thousand. This would mean the Carnahans would recoup 6.4 million and I would be off the hook."

Brumly spoke up, "I was led to believe the amount of money taken was somewhere around seven million. So, what you're telling us is the Carnahans were willing to accept 5.8 million."

"That's correct," verified Nick. "According to Carson the seven million dollar figure was just an estimate. I mean when you add the additional six hundred thousand to what we gave to your brother it comes out to 6.4 million. But, here's the thing. When we sat down with Joseph Carnahan over in Charleston and handed him the six hundred thousand, he goes on to explain that Charley and Derek never showed with the 5.8 mil. Carson and I couldn't understand what could have possibly happened. We were right there in my living room when Charley made the call to Carnahan saying they had the money and were going to leave immediately for Charleston…but they never showed!"

"What do you think happened to the money?" asked Brumly.

"I'll tell you the same thing Carson and I told Carnahan. There could be a possibility Charley and Derek took off with the money. Looking back, I don't think he liked that possibility. We talked for a while and then Carson and I left in the good graces of Carnahan. Since all of this happened I personally haven't heard a peep from the Carnahans. Now, Carson on the other hand has received a number of calls from Joseph as he and the others he works with are still searching the country for your brother and Derek. Carson told me their search went as far as overseas. Joseph told us before we left his presence after we gave him the additional money his organization would leave no stone unturned. As a matter of fact, Carson just recently informed me Carnahan called him just prior to Thanksgiving. So, in short, Ms. Sparks, I don't have any idea what happened to your brother, or Derek for that matter. If I had to make a choice I'd say he and Derek are living high off the hog somewhere on this planet."

"Now, just a minute here," said Maria as she sat forward. "I've sat here and listened to your story and for the most part it lines up with what Charley did tell me….except for the ending. I know for a fact Charley, after receiving the money, never left Fripp Island. The night before he was to pick up the money at your house he phoned me and told me he was going to wrap up his assignment. He told me after he had the money in his possession he was going to give me a call before he left the island. I never got the call! I don't think my brother ever left Fripp Island alive. When he didn't call me I began to worry so I called his cell. It was dead…I mean dead! It was like he didn't exist."

Giving Nick anything but a friendly smile, she stood and pointed down at him. "This is far from over. If I have to I'll stay down here until next summer in order to find out what happened to Charley…I will."

Nick, sensing and hoping the awkward meeting was about to end, moved things along when he stood and pointed back at her and explained, "Myself, I really don't give a crap in regard to what you may or may not do." Moving slightly toward Maria, hoping he could exude some sort of authority, Nick went on, "You said earlier your brother was no angel. If he would have so much as gotten close to me after I jumped ship out there in the ocean, I have no doubt he wouldn't have hesitated for one second to kill me. Despite the fact he seemed to be the type of person who would rather talk things out and avoid violence, I say your brother, Charley Sparks is a cold blooded killer. I know my grandfather's death was not the result of an accident. I have it from a quite reliable source that *your brother* and Derek Simons killed my grandfather. Fortunately, my grandmother passed away from natural causes before they could get to her or they would have killed her as well. Just like they would have killed me. You also said, if nothing else, your brother was honest. What a joke! He gave me a week to make a decision on cooperating with the Carnahans and then that very night knocks me out and kidnaps my ass! You say your brother was supposed to call you from Fripp after receiving the money. Well, he didn't! Why? Because he was on the run with 5.8 million dollars of Joseph Carnahan's money."

Nick was finished and turned to leave, but was stopped when Ms. Sparks spoke one last time. "If I have to I'll rent a house out of Fripp for weeks or possibly months. That will give Mr. Brumly complete access to your little gated community."

Nick, reaching for the doorknob turned and fired back his final comment. "You can do whatever you want, but be warned! If you so much as step foot on my property I'll have you tossed off the island in no time." Opening the door, he gave Brumly a salute. "Maybe I'll see you and Maria on the beach. Try to have a nice day!"

CHAPTER TWELVE

TUESDAY MORNING, NICK PARKED THE LEXUS IN BETWEEN Khelen's BMW and a brand new maroon Corvette. Getting out of the Lexus, he admired the sporty Chevrolet convertible: grey interior, six-speed transmission, stylish wheel covers. Either Khelen had bought a new car, or he had a well to do client. Nick ruled the latter out since he had a ten o'clock appointment with the lawyer that was to begin in just five minutes.

Walking around the side of the mansion to the massive front stairs, he bounded up the steps, crossed the large front porch and pushed open the huge oak door. Inside, he greeted Gwen, positioned at her desk, running a file across her manicured nails. Looking up, she noticed Nick, and then looked at the grandfather clock in the corner of the room. "Right on time, Mr. Falco. Mrs. Yeats is already here. Just go on back to Khelen's office. They're waiting for you."

Grabbing a peppermint from a glass dish at the corner of her desk, he popped it in his mouth and politely responded, "Yes Ma'am!"

Entering the office, Gretchen sat on the left of a small conference table. Khelen, on the end, motioned at Nick, "Coffee's over there by the window. Help yourself."

Nick walked to the coffeemaker and nodded at Mrs. Yeats. "Good morning, Gretchen. Are you ready to sell your house to me this morning?"

"I believe I am." Holding up the house keys, she waved them. "Mr. Ridley here tells me it's going to be quite simple. We both have to sign some papers, I get a big fat check and you get the keys. This is the first time I have ever sold a house. It's a lot easier than I thought it would be."

Khelen took a drink of coffee and smiled. "That's right and with any luck we should have all this wrapped up in about a half hour, I'd say."

Pouring himself a cup of coffee, Nick looked out the front window toward the Beaufort River and asked, "So Khelen, I see you've purchased a new Corvette."

Khelen shot Nick a strange look and answered, "Pardon?"

Motioning with his cup toward the outside parking lot, Nick explained, "That new Corvette parked next to your BMW. From what I can tell, it's quite an automobile."

Shrugging in confusion, Mrs. Yeats cleared up the mysterious car. "That's my car and it's not brand new. It's last year's model. It was a yearend clearance. I just traded in my previous Vet for it last month. It is a beauty…isn't it?"

Khelen looked at first Mrs. Yeats and then at Nick in amazement. Getting up and walking to a corner window he glanced out at the side lot. Turning back he pointed his cup at Mrs. Yeats and confirmed, "That new Corvette out there is yours?"

"Yes," said Gretchen proudly. "My husband, Clark always wanted a new Corvette. But, we could never afford one until a few years after we were married. Well, after that each year he would trade the car in and get a new model at the end of the year. So, we always had a relatively new Corvette. After he died, I just simply continued the tradition. I guess I've had a new one every year for the past thirty years or so."

Nick sat down at the conference table. "I was to understand you're in your eighties…right?"

"That's correct, actually eighty-three."

"And you drive a Corvette. Isn't that dangerous!"

Waving his statement off as unimportant, Gretchen smiled and remarked, "The car only goes as fast as you drive it. The speedometer in the Vet goes all the way up to 160 miles per hour. I've only driven this Corvette or any I've ever owned around fifty-five miles an hour and that's if I'm in a hurry!"

Khelen, now seated once again at the end of the table chimed in, "Only fifty-five…you're kidding?"

"I don't drive the car that much," said Gretchen. "If I have to go anywhere on the island, I usually take my golf cart. I do drive the Vet about once a week into Beaufort to pick up groceries and then there are my monthly trips to Charleston to visit my sister. Why, just two weeks ago I was on Rt. 17. A patrolman pulled me over and explained I was only going thirty-five in a sixty-five mile an hour zone. He pulled me over because it seemed so strange for a Corvette to be travelling so slowly. He suggested I need to go at least forty or I would be breaking the law. He didn't give me a ticket and we had quite a laugh when he informed me this was the first time he had ever told someone driving a Corvette they had to drive faster. I promised him I'd try to keep my foot down and he let me go. Next year about this time I'll be getting a newer model. I might go for a red one next time."

Khelen and Nick were sitting in silence staring at one another, not believing what they were hearing. Seeing they were at a loss for words, she continued, "Hey, I'm not dead, I'm just old! Well, anyway we didn't meet here this morning to discuss my choice of vehicles so I suggest we get on with this house selling business."

Opening a folder, Khelen removed a stack of papers and stated, "Most of these papers you'll be signing are government or state required. Now, I am not going to read every word on these documents because that would take us into the afternoon. Trust me…I'll go over everything you need to know."

It was 10:45 when Nick signed his final document and handed an ink pen to Mrs. Yeats, who signed as well. "Well, that's it then," announced Khelen. Pushing a cashier's check across the table in front of Gretchen, he smiled at Nick. "You now own the property at 311 Deer Lake Drive."

Gretchen smiled, looked over the check, folded it and placed it in her purse then slid the house keys across the table to Nick. "I trust you will take care of my home, Mr. Falco. I've had a lot of good memories living there. I have already removed the things I want to take with me. The rest is yours." Getting up from the table she reached over and shook both Khelen and Nick's hands. "It has been a pleasure dealing with both of you gentlemen. Now, if you'll excuse me I have a number of errands to run…mainly the bank." Walking toward the office door, she stopped and remembered. Turning back, she addressed Nick, "Two things I forgot to mention. There is small attic room just above the large bedroom upstairs. You'll need a stepladder to get up there. There's one outside hanging on the wall. I've got a bunch of old stuff stored up there…nothing important. When you go through it if you find anything you think I may have overlooked as important just give me a call at my new residence or you can just drop by and see me. The other thing is a couple dropped by the house early this morning. They were an odd pair. The woman was way overdressed and the man looked like a carnival barker: bright green sports coat, white slacks and tan fedora. They said they were friends of yours and they were thinking of renting the house when you have it ready. They asked me if it was all right to come inside and look around. I couldn't see any harm in it so I let them in and they walked through the house. Like I said, they were an odd pair. The woman was rather snoopy, opening closet doors and the like. The man asked most of the questions. How long have I known you? Did I know your grandparents? Was I friends with Carson Pike?" Smiling, Gretchen opened the office door and commented, "Things are looking up for you, Nick. You've only owned the house for a few minutes and it looks like you already have some potential renters. Good day."

Nick waited until she left the office. Getting up from the table, he went to the front window and watched Gretchen descend the front steps.

Turning back to Khelen, he swore softly, "Son of a bitch! Do you have any idea who those people were she was talking about?"

Khelen, a bit surprised at Nick's reaction, answered, "No, should I?"

"Think about it," emphasized Nick. "Remember our recent conversation about Ms. Sparks and Chic Brumly and how I needed to be careful if this lawyer and part-time detective approached me? I'm pretty sure the so-called couple Mrs. Yeats was referring to was them. I can't believe they were in the house."

"Calm down," said Khelen. "It's quite obvious you have run into Chic and his female client since we last talked. Sit down and tell me exactly what happened."

Pouring himself another cup of coffee, Nick walked back to the table and sat. "I don't suppose you still have that bottle of ol' scotch here in the office?"

Khelen smiled. "As a matter of fact…I do! Let's have a good snort while you tell me about what Chic's been up to."

Seconds later, Nick downed his alcohol in three swallows and then started, "You were right about Brumly. He is a slime bag."

Khelen sat back and sipped at his drink while Nick explained what had transpired since they had talked. Thirty minutes passed when Nick finished up, talking about the last time he had seen the Sparks woman and the lawyer. "The last thing Maria Sparks said was, if necessary, she was going to rent a place out on Fripp, therefore allowing her attorney, Brumly access anytime he pleased. She said she was determined to get to the bottom of her brother's disappearance. She probably already rented a place. How else could she be on the island? I can't believe Gretchen let them in the house."

"You can't place any blame on her, Nick," pointed out Khelen. "She's just a sweet old lady who probably thought she was doing you a favor. She's no match for the likes of Brumly. I warned you about him. He's like a bad cold you can't get rid of. The thing that really concerns me about him being in the house is he may have planted a bug."

Nick, pouring another small portion of scotch into his cup, asked, "A bug?"

"Yeah, ya know…a listening devise. He could have easily placed it anywhere in the house without Gretchen noticing."

"Is that legal?"

"Maybe…maybe not. It depends. Remember what I told you about Brumly. He runs right on the edge of what is legal and what is not. Now, if I were you I'd go over every inch of the house until I was satisfied you are not being listened in on *and* the sooner you get on it the better."

Finishing his drink, Nick inquired, “Is there anything we can do about Brumly and this woman following me around?”

“Not really...unless they break the law *and* you have to remember Brumly is a bona fide detective, which does give him a certain amount of leeway. He’s slick as they come. Like I told you before. Be careful what you do and say around him. As long as this Sparks woman is willing to pay him, he’ll keep digging into your life. You have one of my business cards…right?”

“Yes, I do. It’s on my refrigerator at home.”

“If you have any questions about anything he or this Sparks woman does, feel free to contact me. Congratulations on your new property. I have some family members who live in Wyoming. They love to come to Beaufort. I don’t think they’ve ever been out to Fripp. They won’t be coming until next summer. They always stay at a different beach location. Last year they spent a week over on Tybee Island. If you have your new place ready by next summer maybe I could drum you up some business. Excuse me, but I have to run. I have a luncheon engagement with some businessmen from the country club. Stay in touch.”

Nick pitched his empty cup in a trash container, stood and shook the lawyer’s hand. “Thanks for everything Khelen. I’m going to head back to Fripp and get to work on my new rental property.”

Heading down Sea Island Parkway, Nick gave Shelby a call. Surprisingly, she answered after just the first ring. “Hey, Nick! I’ve been expecting your call. How did the closing go?”

“Everything went fine. I’m on my way back to Fripp right now. Are you still planning to help me get the place straightened around?”

“Yes, I am. I’m way ahead of you. I’m already here on Fripp. I’m sitting on the beach just down from your house, catching up on some reading. I brought along some rags and cleaning supplies and I also stopped by Publix and got us some deli meats and cheese, baked beans, potato salad, rolls and drinks for lunch. I thought maybe we could eat at your new place.”

“That’s sounds good. I should be showing up in about twenty minutes or so. All I’ll have to do is jump into some work duds and we can be on our way. We can take the golf cart over to Deer Lake. We have a lot to talk about. See ya in a few!”

When Nick pulled into his driveway he saw Shelby Lee talking to Genevieve in the front yard. Getting out, he approached the two women and commented, “Well, what do you know. Two of my best friends talking to each other. What’s the latest girls?”

Concerned, Shelby pointed at Genevieve's house and explained, "Did you know someone stole Genevieve's golf cart?"

"Yes, I do know. We talked about it a few days ago." Looking at Genevieve, he asked, "So, they never found your cart?"

Genevieve held up her hands. "Not hide nor hair! I reported it to Chief Lysinger and he told me three other residents are also missing carts. He also informed me two expensive gas grills have been stolen. Later on in the day he phoned me and told me he had contacted the Beaufort Police to see if anyplace other than Fripp was being hit. Turns out, quite a few grills have been stolen from Lady's Island all the way down here to Fripp. The only golf carts reported missing are from right here on our island."

"Well, when you think about it, that makes sense," said Nick. "Practically everyone on Fripp owns a cart, because it's a confined area. When you get off the island, there are not many people who own carts. They use their vehicles for transportation. It's still puzzling though. How on earth are they getting the carts off the island without being noticed?"

Shelby jumped in on the conversation. "How much do these carts cost?"

"I'm not sure," answered Genevieve. "In the thirty some years I have lived here on Fripp I think I've had four or five different carts. This last one, the one taken, costs if I recall, around seven thousand dollars."

Nick added, "They are rather expensive when you consider how small they are. It could be that whoever is stealing these carts and the grills may be taking them across the state line and selling them elsewhere. I mean hell, they could sell a cart that's worth, let's say seven thousand for a couple of grand and make a nice profit."

"Well nonetheless," said Genevieve. "Someone stole mine and it pisses me off to no end. This is supposed to be a private island where crime does not exist. If I were you Nick, I'd keep an eye on your cart. By the way, that reminds me. That lawyer and his girlfriend were by again."

Nick couldn't believe what he had just heard. "Do you mean to tell me they were here on my property again?"

"No, they pulled up in my driveway. They were nice, just like the first time they were here. Nosy…but nice! The man, Chic, asked me if I had seen you around lately. I answered him just like you told me to. I told him you were looking for him. He went on to tell me you had already met with him, but he still had some questions he needed answered. The whole time he was talking with me the woman stood at the edge of my drive and took a number of pictures of your house. I've got to tell you,

Those folks have never done anything to me, but just from the way they conduct themselves, I don't think I care for either one of them."

Nick apologized, "I'm sorry they bothered you. If they come on your property or mine again, please let me know. I don't need them hanging around here and neither do you."

Genevieve patted Shelby on her shoulder, turned and headed back to her house. "I've got to go, I have a cherry pie in the oven. I'll make sure you both get a slice."

Watching the old woman walk across the grass, Shelby commented, "She certainly is a nice lady…isn't she?"

"The best," said Nick. "It really pisses me off Brumly is trying to get information on me through her."

Nick walked down the drive a few paces as if he were trying to clear his mind. "This should be a good day for me. I just bought a house." Walking back to Shelby, he suggested, "I refuse to allow this lawyer and this woman from New York to control my emotions." Smiling, he went on, "Speaking of golf carts. I'm going to go in the house and get changed. Why don't you gather up the lunch you got us and your cleaning supplies and start loading them in *my golf cart* which is in the garage. I should be down in a jif and then we can head out for Deer Lake."

Upstairs, Nick looked out the bedroom window down into the front drive where he watched Shelby Lee loading the cart. Slipping into his old painter's pants he smiled and thought about her. She was such a good person. He was going to have to make sure Brumly didn't get his claws into her life, like he was attempting to do his. He needed to fill her in on how things had gone so far with Brumly and the woman.

Racing down the steps, he grabbed two beers from the fridge and locked the house, then went into the garage where he grabbed two rolls of painters tape and a utility knife. Locking the garage, he crossed the drive and handed Shelby one of the beers. Flopping down in the driver's seat, he opened the beer and raised the can in a toasting fashion. "Rebel, here's to the remainder of this day turning out okay!"

Shelby opened her beer when Nick pulled out onto Tarpon. Passing John Fripp Condos, Nick spoke up. "There is something I need to discuss with you before we get to the house. I need to tell you everything that went on with Brumly and the Sparks woman since we talked about them on Thanksgiving. I met with them the next day, on Friday…"

Pulling up to 311 Deer Lake Drive, Nick finished the rundown on Brumly and the Sparks woman. "…And since they were already here at my new house this morning, Khelen feels there may be a possibility Brumly planted a bug in the house, so we have to be careful what we say. Just in case, we need to keep away from discussing anything that happened last summer. And when we get inside we need to look for this bug…this possible listening device. I have no idea what to look for. It will probably be small, about the size of a quarter or less."

"So let me get this straight. When we get inside we can't say anything about last summer and the entire time we're going to be searching for this *device?"*

"That about sums it up." Getting out of the cart, Nick held out his hands and presented the house. "What do you think?"

"It's much larger than I thought it would be. It definitely does need painting. This seems to be a cozy little neighborhood. It's secluded and close to the beach. When you get it fixed up I don't think you'll have problems renting it."

Pulling in the garage beneath the elevated home, Nick got out and grabbed two buckets with the cleaning supplies, while Shelby picked up the cooler and drinks. Heading for the front steps, Nick announced, "After I give you the grand tour, we can get to work looking for the, you know what."

Inside the front door, Nick pointed at the kitchen near the back of the house. "Mrs. Yeats told me the electricity is still on and will be switched over to my name later this week. You can put our lunch and drinks in the fridge." Placing the cleaning supplies on the kitchen counter, he motioned toward the stairs leading up to the top floor. "Feel free to look around." Opening the utensil cabinet drawer, he ran his hands through spoons, forks and knives looking for anything that might resemble a listening device."

Closing the refrigerator, Shelby started up the stairs to the second floor. "Think I'll just head up here and have a look see."

Nick continued to search each and every cabinet, looking inside closed containers, moving pots and pans and running his fingers along the inside edges and corners of each cabinet. Next, he went to the kitchen table and chairs and inspected every inch of the oak breakfast set. Running his hand under the edge of the countertop, he then stepped up on one of the kitchen chairs and looked at the top and then the back and sides of the refrigerator.

Satisfied the device was not hidden in the kitchen, he moved to the living room where he flipped up all the cushions on the couch and chairs, looked under a large circular throw rug and closely inspected a glass-fronted hutch. A half hour passed when Shelby descended the stairs and entered the front room where Nick was busy looking behind the television. Silently signaling to Nick to step outside, she made her way down the hallway connecting the front and rear of the home.

Out on the front porch, she sat on the top step next to Nick. "I searched everything…I mean everything upstairs. Both bedrooms, the bath and a small office and walk-in closet. I didn't find anything that looked unusual."

"Same thing downstairs," said Nick. "The more I think about this the more I think we could be wasting our time. So what if Brumly may have planted a bug. If we don't say anything that incriminates us in any way then there's nothing to worry about. I say we go back in, have our lunch and then get to work on this place. If Brumly did hide a bug it's not going to be easy to find. Remember this sort of thing is what he does for living. He might be a scumbag, but he still knows more about this kind of stuff than we do."

"I agree and besides, if we are inside the house and we are not talking to one another, it might send up a red flag. I think we should just act normally like two people cleaning up a house."

Nick stood. "Let's eat!"

Sitting at an eat-in bar top, Nick placed a slice of cheese and two slices of ham on a piece of bread, then squeezed mustard from a plastic packet on the sandwich. Spooning some baked beans onto a plastic plate, Shelby asked, "So I understand from my father you two had quite the conversation before dinner on Thanksgiving Day?"

"Yes we did," said Nick. "He's quite the football fan so I discovered. He told me he wanted to play at the high school level but wound up playing baseball instead."

Shelby finished making her own sandwich, took a bite and responded, "During football season, he watches every game on Sunday and then there's Monday Night Football and occasionally a game on Thursday. We have attended every Beaufort High game since I can remember. He told me he talked with you about the year Beaufort High won the state championship and about those two high school kids killed out here on Fripp."

"Yeah, we did discuss that. Listening to him talk about it, I came away with the feeling he thinks those three football players who, according to him, were persons of interest, got away with murder. He said, after all these years the case still remains unsolved."

"I know. He feels very strongly about how things turned out. You would think after all this time folks would have forgotten about that, and I think most people have. There has to be a great number of people who have moved down here to the Lowcountry after that horrible event who may not even be aware it ever happened. I think one of the main reasons why my father has never put that particular topic to rest is because he spoke with Mr. James about the murders."

Biting into his sandwich, Nick inquired, "Mr. James?"

"Yes, Bernard P James, the father of one of the students killed that night. I think, if I remember correctly, her name was Abigail. Anyway, a few years after the murders my father got a call from Mr. James. He had some plumbing work he needed done at his home right here on Fripp. I think ol' man James still lives here on the island...in the same house. My father had only been in the business for a few years but had already established a reputation as an honest and fair man. Mr. James, when talking with my father said he came highly recommended. My dad, so I'm told, drives out here and does some work for James. While he was writing out a bill my father tells Bernard he went to school with Abby, that's what they called her according to my father. Well, the next thing you know, Mr. James invites my dad to sit down with him to discuss his daughter's death. If my dad has told my mother and me this story once he's told it to us fifty times over the years. He said Mr. James was convinced beyond any doubt those three high school football players not only killed his daughter, but the other student as well. According to my father, Mr. James got quite emotional, telling my dad the police had those three kids dead to rights, but for some reason they couldn't seem to lock the case down. The three boys walked, but still, Mr. James felt they had gotten away with murder. He told my dad as long as he lived if he ever came up with something other than what the police already had he would go to any expense to bring those three boys to justice. My dad said Mr. James was very convincing and my father left his home that day convinced himself those boys were guilty as sin. It was over twenty some years ago my father talked with Mr. James and the case is still cold."

Chewing his last bite of baked beans, Nick stood and patted his stomach. "That hit the spot. I say we get back to work. I'm going to go out and grab my utility knife and painter's tape so we can get these interior walls taped off. Maybe tomorrow we can start to paint."

Crossing the front porch, Nick stared in amazement at the street in front of the house. Leaning up against the side of the blue Lincoln stood none other than Chic Brumly and his female counterpart. Looking at his watch, Chic gave a half-hearted wave, "Good afternoon, Mr. Falco. I was hoping I'd run into you over here."

Ms. Sparks stood at his side, a look of great accomplishment plastered on her face.

Brumly went on to explain, "Maria here wasn't exactly impressed with the outcome of our meeting last Friday. If you'll recall she told you she just might rent a place on the island, which as her ongoing guest, gives me access anytime I please. In short, you might be seeing quite a bit of Ms. Sparks and myself." Walking to the very edge of the front lawn, Chic held up his index finger to make a point. "Maria and I were talking this morning over breakfast and we both agreed criminals or people who have something to hide always make a mistake no matter how careful they are. They always overlook some minor detail that in the end winds up bringing them down. We're going to be spending a lot of time here on Fripp, asking a lot of people a lot of questions. It has been my experience if you dig long enough and deep enough, eventually you'll uncover something." Smiling smartly, he remarked, "By the way, we just love your new I house. I think you've made a good investment."

Nick walked down the steps and crossed the grass, stopping directly in front of Brumly. Standing his ground, Nick explained. "You take one step on my property and I'll have the police over here in less than five minutes. You already trespassed on this property earlier this morning."

"Ah…that's where you're wrong, son," pointed out Chic. "When we were here this morning the house was still owned by Mrs. Yeats. She was more than glad to show us around. You may own this property now, but this morning you did not. I've forgotten more about the law and the way the legal world works than you'll ever learn, Nick. Don't try to match wits with me."

Realizing Brumly was not going to back down, Nick made his next point. "And furthermore I don't want you bothering my neighbor, Genevieve. She's a nice lady and you don't need to be visiting her anymore."

Maria held up her camera. "Got some nice photos of your house today. I have to admit you're staying at a much more elaborate spot than I am."

At that moment two things happened. Shelby, hearing the loud voices stepped out onto the front porch and a golf cart pulled into the driveway and parked. Carson stepped out along with a strange man who was driving. Walking up to Nick, Carson smiled and introduced the stranger. "Nick Falco, this is Grady Phillips…Grady, this is Nick, the young man I've been telling you about."

Grady reached out and shook Nick's hand. The weak handshake equaled the way the man appeared. Extremely thin, no muscle tone whatsoever. His bare, pale white boney arms and legs stuck out beneath a pair of white cargo shorts and a cut-off T-shirt. Smiling broadly, Phillips grinned, "Nice to meet you, Nick."

Before Nick could say a word, Carson walked over and stood in front of Brumly. "Well, Chic Brumly. I guess the security on this island is not what I thought it was. It appears they'll let anyone on Fripp!"

Chic, still in control of himself laughed and turned to Ms. Sparks. "Maria, this is Carson Pike, the man Nick mentioned the other day at our meeting."

Maria held out her hand, but Carson refused it. Giving a shrug, she stated sarcastically, "My, my, so this is the Carson Pike everyone around here knows. Like you said Chic, he is a bit of an oddball!"

Carson gave her the onceover, realizing he was standing directly in front of Charley Sparks' sister, the man Nick's grandmother had shot in the head, the same man he himself had dumped out in the Atlantic. Charley's sister was a lot closer to the truth than she probably realized."

Grady stepped up, looked Brumly over and laughed, "Still dressing like a dandy, Brumly. You always did look and act shady." Turning to Nick, Grady explained, "Ol' Chic here was quite instrumental a few years ago in assisting the Feds to send my ass off to prison."

Chic spoke up instantly in his defense. "You deserved prison, Phillips. I know there are a lot of people who view you as some sort of celebrity. At one time you may have been a big deal race car driver on the Nascar circuit, but it turns out you're no more than a common thief..."

Maria interrupted the conversation and addressed Carson. "Am I to understand you were with Nick at his house when you turned the money over to my brother, Charley?"

Carson nodded, "That's right, I was. He and his partner, Derek Simons took the money and left the house. That was the last time I saw either one of those two. Nick here tells me you feel something happened to your brother and you feel he never left the island and you've hired Chic to get to the bottom of what you think may have happened. You're wasting your money. You've been told the truth...you just can't accept it. Your brother and his cohort took off with 5.8 million dollars. So, if I were you I'd head back to New York and forget this nonsense. And, another thing. I never cared for your brother. Charley Sparks was a low life murderer. I know for a fact he and Simons killed Nick's grandfather. I have no idea where your brother is or what's happened to him. To be honest with you...I simply don't care. If he is in fact dead, well then I say the world is better off!"

In an instant, Maria stepped forward and slapped Carson hard across the face. Raising her hand to slap him a second time, Carson reached out, grabbed her by the lapels of her jacket, and lifted her off her feet. Chic stepped forward and grabbed Carson by the arm and shouted, "Maria...this is not the way!"

Grady moved in front of Carson, swung Chic around and hit him with a hard right directly on the lawyer's nose. Falling back against the Lincoln, Chic raised his hand to his bleeding face. Shelby ran to join Nick and whispered, "Oh…my God!"

Carson gave Maria a rough shove. She stumbled but managed to keep her footing. Chic removed a handkerchief from his jacket pocket and held it to this bleeding nose. Through watery eyes, he pointed the blood-soaked hanky at Grady and forced a smile. "You're just as stupid as you've ever been. I'm going to report this to the local authorities. You're an ex-con. You've only been out of the joint for what…a couple of weeks. With any luck I can at least get your ass tossed in jail for a few days on an aggravated assault charge."

"Good luck with that," said Cason. "Your New York friend here struck the first blow and then you laid a hand on me. The way I see things is Mr. Phillips here was just looking out for my best interest. I think this whole thing borders on self-defense."

Nick stepped forward. "Yes, that's the way I see it."

Standing at Nick's side, Shelby added, "Me too…self-defense!"

Looking at Maria, Chic wiped his nose again and suggested, "Come on, there's nothing else we can accomplish right now." Getting in the front seat of the Lincoln, he rolled down the window and pointed the bloody hanky at the foursome. "You haven't heard the last of me…I guarantee you!"

Nick and Shelby stood and watched while the Lincoln sped off up the street. Carson turned and holding out his large hands, stated, "Well, I think I've had enough excitement for the day."

Grady placed his hands on his slim hips and agreed, "You and me both!"

Carson gestured at the house. "The real reason we stopped by was to see your new house. We thought, depending on what needs to be done, we could give you a hand."

Nick laughed. "I think you've already given us a helping hand." Walking toward the steps, he waved his hand. "Come on, I'll give you the nickel tour."

It was just after three o'clock when Nick and Shelby Lee stood on the front porch and watched Carson and Grady pull away in their golf cart. Shelby reached over and gently punched Nick on his right arm. "Well, you've still got it!"

Confused, Nick awkwardly asked, "Got…what?"

"Your ability to turn an average day or evening into a day of unusual events. Like last summer when we went on our first date at the Dockside. First, we run into Charley Sparks and Derek Simons who at the time, I had no idea were following you, then you get into a fight in the parking lot with Ike Miller and then wind up going to emergency care to get your arm patched up. If that wasn't enough, later in the middle of the night we find Amanda Schrock, half naked laying in your front yard. It seems like it was just one thing after another. Despite the fact I wound up killing Harold, it was a rather exciting summer. Here it is winter in the Lowcountry and I get the strangest feeling we are on the verge of another set of events most normal people will never get to experience. We drive over here to clean your house, wind up looking for a listening device that may or may not have been planted and in the process are witness to Carson getting slapped and Grady punching Brumly on the kisser." Laughing, she explained, "You seem to have this ability to show a girl, not necessarily a good time, but an unusual time. I can't wait to find out what's next."

"Well right now, I have to get this house taped out so I can paint tomorrow."

"While you're busy doing that I think I'm going to crawl up in the attic and see what's up there."

Chic was bent over the sink at the condo Maria had rented at John Fripp, just under a mile from Nick's house on Tarpon. Looking at the wet, pinkish stained washcloth in his hand, the lawyer commented, "I think I've finally got the bleeding stopped."

"Maria sipped at a mixed drink and asked, "Are you going to report this to the local police like you said."

"No, because that won't amount to anything. Pike was right. You made the first move when you slapped him. They could easily state self-defense and win. Besides that, when you consider everything else the police have to deal with this will be looked at as a minor altercation."

"But the man who was with Pike hit you in the face!"

"After you slapped Carson Pike in the face! Look, I know the law and the police are not going to try and figure out who was right or who was wrong. They will look at the situation…not those involved. And another thing. You have to stop not only speaking up when I'm talking but you must refrain from lashing out. You have to control your emotions and let me do my job. You're not being paid to find out what happened to your brother…I am!"

"But it's just so frustrating. I know Falco and Pike know more than what they're letting on."

"I agree, but we have to let things play out. Believe me, they'll make a mistake. Someone will do or say something that will bust this thing wide open. We have to remain patient and keep the pressure on. Now,

I'm going to head back to my office. Why don't you just relax for the rest of the day? I'll pick you up tomorrow morning. One of the things we're going to do is check out the girl who was with Falco today. One thing you can do. I found out Falco's neighbor, Genevieve walks on the beach every morning. It might be a good idea if you start walking on the beach in the mornings. Over the course of a few days or maybe even weeks you might be able to become friends with this old woman. At some point she may reveal something to us that might be important."

Nick was just finishing taping the frame of a doorway that led from the kitchen to the first floor bedroom when Shelby's voice got his attention. "Smile!"

On his knees, Nick turned and saw her standing in the kitchen, holding what looked like an old camera. Shelby moved her index finger like she was snapping off a shot, and then explained. "I found this camera up in the attic. It was in an old trunk filled with photographs and albums of pictures. This camera was just lying off to the side on top of everything. The only other stuff up there was an old lopsided rocker, two mismatched lamps and three boxes of old clothing. I brought the camera down because it is quite interesting. It's probably twenty-five to thirty years old. This type of camera was used back in the days when you actually took your roll of film to the drugstore and had it developed. Nowadays, it seems everyone uses their phone to take pictures." Walking down the hall she held out the black, marred camera and stated, "See here on the side in this small window. It indicates the number five, which means there are nineteen photos stored inside the camera that have not been developed. Didn't you say Mrs. Yeats told you everything in the house was yours?"

Getting to his feet, Nick reached for the camera and answered, "Yes, that's what she said, unless I came across something she may have overlooked."

Taking the camera back, Shelby gave Nick a grin. "When I was in junior high I was somewhat of a camera bug. I mean I snapped off pictures everywhere my parents took me. It was kind of a hobby for me. It got to the point where my dad said jokingly it was costing him a small fortune getting all the rolls of film I constantly took developed, so he built me a small darkroom in our basement. I haven't used the room in years, but I still have all the chemicals: hypo, fixer and what not, to develop film. I'm not sure I'll be able to develop the film inside this camera because it may be too old. I'm not even sure the chemicals I have in the basement are still good, but it's worth a try. Some of the pictures on this film might be valuable to Mrs. Yeats. When I get home tonight if everything works out I may have these developed by tomorrow. If nothing else it'll be fun. I haven't messed around with developing film in years. It'll be interesting to see if the film is still good."

Shelby had long since left for Beaufort. Nick sat in the living room of his Tarpon Blvd home, drank a beer, and stared out into the darkness behind his house. The grandfather clock in the corner chimed the time. On the tenth and final chime, Nick yawned and thought what a long day it had been. He had bought Gretchen's house, had witnessed what could only be described as an awkward tiff at the rental house with Ms. Sparks and Brumly pitted against Carson and Grady Phillips. He sat back and thought about Shelby and how excited she had been about finding that old camera and the prospect of developing the film. Deciding he was going to turn in for the night, he walked by the two matching chairs and noticed the outlined faded red bloodstains on the material. They were not that obvious but still, they were there. He had noticed those stains every day for the past few months and it always brought back the memory of what happened the night when Carson and Amelia had shot and killed Derek Simons and Charley Sparks right there in his own home. That very night Amelia had suggested he have both chairs reupholstered. He was going to have to get that done as soon as possible based on what Chic Brumly had said over at the Deer Lake house about how people who are criminals or have something to hide always overlook something. What if Brumly somehow got inside the house and saw the bloodstains? He should have taken care of this right after the incident. Now, it might be difficult. He couldn't have anyone come and pick up the chairs because Brumly may be watching his every move. He might have to call someone to come to the house and do the work right there. Grabbing another beer out of the fridge, he walked out of the house and down to the beach. It's where he did his best thinking.

CHAPTER THIRTEEN

STANDING ON THE LARGE ROCKS AT OCEAN POINT, NICK looked across Fripp Inlet at Hunting Island when his cell phone rang. Digging the phone from his jeans pocket, he knew it was Shelby calling. Stepping down on the wet sand he started back up the beach and answered, "Good morning. I assume you must be on your way to work."

"I am," said Shelby. "It's just past seven. I took a chance. I didn't know if you'd be up yet or not."

"Yep…got up at five and walked down to Ocean Point. What's up?"

"I was up until two this morning working on developing the film in the camera we found. Surprisingly the chemicals were still potent and the interior of the camera itself preserved the old film. I developed all nineteen photos. It appears there were three different locations where the pictures were taken. The last three photos are quite disturbing."

"What do you mean by disturbing? This is an eighty-three year old woman we're talking about."

"I could be wrong, but I don't think the pictures have anything to do with Mrs. Yeats."

"What do the pictures show? Why are the last three disturbing?"

"I can't explain why, but they are. You'll have to look at them yourself and decide. I really can't explain them over the phone. Besides that, I don't have the time right now. I'm almost at work. I have a short day today. I get off at two. If I drive directly to Fripp I can be at your place by three-thirty. I'll bring the photos with me. We can look at them together and possibly come up with a reasonable answer. Are you going over to your rental today?"

"Yeah, I thought I'd get the rest of the house taped off and maybe get a room or two painted."

"Okay, I'll see you around three-thirty. Keep an eye out for Brumly and the Sparks woman."

"You do the same. I'll see you this afternoon."

Coming out of the long curve of the Eastern end of the beach he stared up the long straight stretch and saw the Fripp Island water tower over a mile away in the early morning sunlight. Walking next to the edge of the outgoing tide he noticed a sand dollar wedged down in the wet sand.

Bending down, he picked up the treasure. Over the past few months since he moved to Fripp he had walked the beach at least two to three times a week and had only found seven sand dollars to date. It seemed anymore they were a rare find. He remembered as a youngster, whenever he came down to visit his grandparents and he walked the beach with Amelia, it would be a common practice to find seven or eight each time out. Cupping the treasure in his hand, he allowed the water to wash away the sand and continued up the beach.

He thought about Shelby Lee and hoped his advice about keeping an eye out for Brumly and the woman had been taken seriously. Maybe he was worried about nothing. After all, Shelby had no idea Charley Sparks and Derek Simons had been killed by Carson and his grandmother. Hell, she along with everyone else on Fripp thought Amelia was dead and buried. If Shelby was questioned about Maria's brother, she could only tell him what she knew and that her brother and Derek left the house with the money. When it came to Charley and Derek, Shelby had nothing *to hide*.

Ten minutes up the deserted beach, he noticed a woman standing at the edge of the water, looking out at the vast Atlantic. The woman, wearing a grey sweat suit, straw sun hat and yellow flip flops, held a cup of coffee and a cigarette in her right hand and brown beach bag in her left. Turning, she looked up the beach in his direction. Noticing the woman was Maria Sparks; he nonchalantly turned to the side, hoping she hadn't recognized him. Seconds later, he chanced a quick look back in her direction. She was lighting up another cigarette. Apparently she thought he was just someone out on the lonely beach. Thinking she must be staying close by, he walked at an angle toward the low dunes peppered with high stalks of Sea Oats.

Gazing through the tall beach plants, he continued to watch. She just stood there looking out at the gently rolling waves. Looking back in the direction toward Tarpon Blvd, he tried to get his bearings. There was a large three story yellow house that had been there for years next to a sand covered access road that led down to the beach and then there was a long, treated wood deck walk also leading to the beach. The deck walk was owned by John Fripp Condos and led directly from the grassy courtyard area that housed a swimming pool. Maybe she was renting one of the Fripp Condos or possibly she was staying across the street at the tennis court apartments. He didn't have any pressing appointments; he would wait and see where she went. If he had to he could follow her up the beach at a distance.

In the next few minutes the wind started to pick up blowing sand up the beach, making walking or standing on the flat sand unpleasant. He was just about to sit down on a small dune when he saw Maria turn and head for the deck walk. Staying hidden in the Sea Oats and the assorted bushes and small trees he walked perpendicular to the wooden walkway fifty yards to her right, crouching down while he moved toward the condos.

Once she was at the end of the deck and stepped down onto the paved walkway, he climbed a few larger rocks and stepped up onto the grassy area of three ocean front condos. Staying close to the three buildings, he walked swiftly toward the courtyard. Peering around the edge of the last building he saw Maria washing her feet off by means of an attached water hose at the edge of the courtyard.

Satisfied her feet were free of sand she slipped back into her flip flops and continued down a sandy path leading to a large circular grass area, a covered pool centered toward the back of the grass. Following, but staying behind a group of tall palm trees and low bushes, he watched her walk up onto the patio of an end unit. Setting the designer bag and her coffee cup on a round, wrought iron table, she slid open the patio door and disappeared behind a beige, floor length curtain. Running quickly to the patio of what appeared to be an unoccupied unit, he leaned up against the wall and peered around the corner. Since she left her bag outside he was confident she would return.

He didn't have to wait long. Two minutes passed, when she reappeared on the patio with a mixed drink and a book in her hand. She then walked to one of the plastic white lounge chairs surrounding the pool, spread a towel, set her drink on a small table, opened the book and then reclined with her back to him. Waiting for a few minutes to see what she would do, he realized she was no doubt relaxing with a good book. He got an idea. It would be risky, but only if she turned around. Stepping out from behind the wall he slowly made his way along the patios of six different units until he was standing just ten feet from where her bag was laying on the table. *The hell with it,* he thought. *I'm going to chance it!*

It only took him a few seconds to walk to the table while he checked the area for anyone who might be watching. The courtyard and the surrounding patios were empty of tourists. It was the slowest time of the year on Fripp. No one seemed to be around. Grabbing the bag he walked back to the connecting unit to where Maria was staying and keeping an eye on the woman, he sat at a table and searched the bag: pack of cigarettes, bottle of water, suntan lotion, note pad with attached ink pen and small purse. Nick smiled, *Perfect!*

Clicking the pen, he opened the notepad to a blank page and wrote down the information on her driver's license. Maria P. Sparks – 927

Carlton Avenue – Apt. #16 – Staten Island, New York. He jotted down her license number along with the information on three credit cards including expiration dates. He found a small folded piece of paper with a handwritten phone number. It was a strange area code. He wrote down the number. He noted other cards in the purse: membership card to a health spa, gift card to a chain of restaurants. Patterson's! *Where had he heard that name before?* There were seven one hundred dollar bills and some other assorted ones and fives in the billfold section of the purse. There was a small makeup pouch, a sewing kit and a cell phone. Placing everything back where he found it, he folded the slip of paper with the information he collected and placed it in his pocket. Keeping an eye on Maria and the surrounding area he walked casually back to her patio and placed the bag back where he had taken it from. The sound of the patio door being opened caused him to dive into some nearby bushes when Chic pulled back the curtain and emerged from the unit. Kneeling behind the bushes, Nick thought, *God...that was close!*

Looking around, he realized he was trapped, an eight foot grey fence at his back. Chic, noticing Maria, walked toward the lounger and spoke, "Maria! Are you about ready to go? We've a got a lot to do today!"

Maria got up and stretched. "Yeah, sure. Just let me get changed. Should only take me about ten minutes." Walking back to the patio she finished the remainder of what looked like a bloody Mary. "Where are we headed?"

"We're going to check out Pike. I know for a fact he has lived here on Fripp for years. He knows everyone on the island. We're going to snoop around and ask some questions. It seems like the logical move to make since he was at the house the night the money was given to your brother. We also need to find out if anyone around here knows this Shelby Lee Pickett. She may be involved somehow...maybe not."

Approaching the table, Maria noticed the beach bag lying on its side. Looking around the courtyard, she commented, "That's strange. When I left my bag on the table it was upright."

Chic laughed. "Stop being so paranoid! If you're insinuating someone tampered with your bag, well, that's not possible. I've checked it out. Aside from you there are only two other couples currently staying here at the condos and they are at the other end. Your purse probably just fell over. C'mon and get dressed so we can get to work."

Nick waited for a few seconds before he crawled out from behind the bush and carefully made his way down the fence line where there was a gate leading out to the front of the condos. Once out front, he looked to the right where he saw the familiar blue Lincoln parked, *Brumly's car!*

He thought about hanging around but that made no sense. He knew where they were going. Well, not exactly. He knew they were going to spend the day on Fripp asking questions about Carson and possibly Shelby Lee. There didn't seem to be any point in going back to the beach. He could make better time and get back to his house quicker by walking down Tarpon. Maria had said she needed ten minutes to get ready. If he hurried he could be back to his house before they left. Walking across the grass in front of the condos he pulled his cell phone out. He had to get in touch with Carson.

Following three rings and no answer, Nick decided to leave a message. "Carson…it's Nick! Listen, I just discovered where the Sparks woman is staying here on the island. I also got some personal info on her that might be of help to us. I'm not sure. Just a heads up! I overheard Drumly tell Ms. Sparks they were going to spend some time on the island today and see what, if anything, they could find out about you. Give me a call later. I'll be at the rental until around three o'clock, and then I'm heading home to meet Shelby at my place at three-thirty. Call me or drop by."

At nine thirty-five Nick pulled into the house on Deer Lake Drive, only to find Chief Lysinger and his deputy, Travis standing underneath the house in the garage. Getting out of his golf cart, Nick waved at the two local lawmen, "Chief, Travis…what's up?"

"Nothing special, Nick. I suppose you've heard about the recent rash of missing carts here on the island?" said Lysinger.

"I have," answered Nick. "My neighbor, Genevieve had hers stolen a few days back. Have you figured any of this out yet?"

"No, we haven't."

"Why the visit, Chief?"

Pointing at Mrs. Yeats' cart, Lysinger asked, "This cart yours?"

"Yes, it is. Mrs. Yeats had no use for it in Beaufort so she just left it here."

"Well if I were you I'd either chain it up or take it over to your place and stick it in the garage."

Travis spoke up, "Not that it'll make any difference. These thieves are bold. They cut chains and break into garages. Hell, they've even taken some gas grills right out of people's backyards. This morning we had reports of two more carts and another grill being lifted. It baffles me. I don't know how they're getting the stuff off the island."

Changing the subject, Lysinger looked up at the house they were standing under. "I understand you just bought this place from Gretchen Yeats."

Removing a five-gallon bucket of paint from the back of his cart, Nick nodded, "Yes, I did. I was going to try and get some painting done today. Is there another reason you dropped by other than to tell me about the missing carts?"

"Actually, there is. Carson Pike dropped by the office early this morning and told me all about what happened here yesterday between Chic Brumly and Grady Phillips."

"I stood right there in the front yard and witnessed the whole thing," confirmed Nick. "Brumly said he was going to press charges. Is that what this is all about?"

"I did talk with Brumly this morning right after I talked with Carson. Brumly never even mentioned the incident, so I just let it be. Brumly did ask me quite a few questions about you. He told me he was working for a Ms. Sparks from up New York way. Apparently she is concerned about what happened to her brother…a Charley Sparks. He's come up missing. This Sparks woman thinks you may know what happened to her brother. Brumly said he was going to be spending quite a bit of time on the island until he got to the bottom of the matter. Personally, I don't like Chic Brumly, but as long as he doesn't break any laws around here there is little I can do to prevent him from asking questions. That being said. If he gets out of line in any way, shape or form, make sure you let me know." Gesturing at the cart, Lysinger reminded Nick, "Make sure you get that cart secured or it could wind up missing. Have a nice day and good luck with the house."

Nick stood and watched as they drove off up the street. Grabbing the paint and three brushes he started up the front steps.

By eleven o'clock he had the rest of the rooms taped off. Getting a bottle of cold water out of a small cooler he had brought along he decided to walk the entire house to make sure he hadn't missed taping any of the walls. Satisfied with the downstairs he climbed the steps to the second floor. Entering the large upstairs bedroom he saw the stepladder Shelby had used to get up to the attic. Curious, Nick climbed the ladder and opened a ceiling trap door. Once up in the confined, low, eight by ten foot space he pulled a hanging cord, a dim light from the dust covered bulb filtering across the six-foot high area.

Allowing his eyes to become accustomed to the dim light, he was looking at exactly what Shelby told him she had found: a broken rocker, two odd looking lamps, boxes of disheveled clothing and an old trunk. This is where she found the camera. Opening the trunk, he discovered piles of photographs held together with rubber bands, a number of old dusty photo albums and some rag tag photographs. What was it Shelby had said about the film she had developed? *The last three developed pictures were disturbing! What on earth could she possibly be talking about?* Hearing a scratching noise he turned and saw a raccoon disappear into the rafters. *Great! I may have to get an exterminator over here.*

Having no desire to share the small attic with any of the local wildlife, he descended the ladder while closing the trap door. He looked at his watch. He'd paint for another two hours and then head home, grab a shower and wait for Shelby.

The grandfather clock in the living room chimed the time at four o'clock. Finishing his second beer since he had showered, he got up and looked out the picture window at the beach, thinking about how Shelby Lee was a half hour late. Thinking she might be hungry *when she did finally arrive,* he went about setting up a small buffet of deli meats and cheese, baked beans and potato salad from the previous day. Arranging the containers on the kitchen table, he went to one of the cabinets to collect some paper plates and napkins when Shelby burst in the back porch door, "I'm so sorry I'm late. The traffic was brutal until I got to Beaufort." Placing a briefcase on the kitchen counter, she inspected the table and smiled, "For me?"

Nick shrugged. "Well, I thought you might be hungry. I know I am. How about a brew?"

"That's the best idea I've heard today. Love one!"

Opening the fridge, Nick extracted a bottle and held it up. "Glass or bottle?"

"Bottle."

Sitting at the table she opened the beer, took a drink and then asked, "So how was your day so far?"

"To tell you the truth I thought it was going to be rather boring, but not so! I found out where Maria Sparks is staying here on Fripp. She's right up the road at John Fripps. I went thought her purse and got some information on her."

Shelby stopped from squirting mustard on a slice of bread as she asked in amazement. "Whoa, whoa…you looked through her purse. How did you manage that? After the way she talked to you over at the rental house, I can't imagine her allowing you to search her purse. I mean, she didn't exactly leave me with the impression she thought that much of you."

Making a sandwich for himself, Nick explained about Maria's purse and then commented, "I called Carson and left a message for him to call me. Hopefully he will. I plan to invite him over here later, that is, if he calls. I'll go over everything I discovered then. By the way, when I was at the house today I went up into the attic where you found the camera.

Speaking of the camera, you said at least three of the photos were disturbing. What on God's green earth are you talking about?"

Picking up the briefcase, she explained, "I've got all the pictures with me. I enlarged some of the photos so we can better determine what was going on at the time they were taken. If we could move the food over to the kitchen counter I can spread all the pictures out on the table because there is a pattern to them."

Moving the baked beans and the potato salad, Nick remarked, "Now you've really got me thinking. Why would there be disturbing photos in a camera of an eighty-three year old woman's home?" Moving the dishes containing the meat and cheese, he wiped off the table with a cloth and then joked, "Okay I'm ready for your presentation."

Taking a bite out of a ham and cheese sandwich, Shelby unzipped the briefcase and removed three manila folders numbered 1, 2 and 3. Laying the folders on the table she held up the first folder and explained, "Folder number one contains nine pictures that were taken, I feel, at a particular location. I also took the liberty of enlarging three of the pictures for clarification. The second folder has seven photos, once again at a certain location. I only enlarged two pictures in this folder. That brings us to number three, the disturbing pictures. Once again, these three were taken at yet another location and I enlarged all three." Taking a deep breath, she asked, "Ready?"

"After and intro like that how could I be anything but ready."

Opening the first folder she dumped the pictures on the table and had them numbered on the back from 1-9. The three enlargements she set off to the side. Moving around to the other side of the table so he could see the photos, he examined them and then stated, "Looks like someone was having a party."

"And that's not all," pointed out Shelby. Tapping one of the pictures she went on, "Look closely at number 3. In the background it looks like part of a sign in the picture."

Looking at the photo closely Nick saw what she was referring to. *FRIPP ISL…* Picking up the picture he agreed, "I think you're right. Someone was not only having a party but it appears to be right here on Fripp."

Pointing at number 6, Shelby mentioned, "In this picture, in the background we can see part of what might be a banner: *989 STATE HIGH SCHOOL FOOTB…*"

Nick was about to say something but Shelby reached for number 7 which pictured four men standing around a charcoal grill. In the background there was what appeared to be high, green see-through fencing in front of a building. Shelby then picked up the three enlargements of numbers 3, 6 and 7. So, what do you think so far?"

"Well, I don't think any of these are disturbing…"

Shelby cut him off, "They're not supposed to be. Only the last three in the third folder are disturbing but you must see all the others first."

Looking at the enlargements, Nick commented, "These pictures tell us not only where the party was held but when it was held. It was held right here on Fripp and it took place back in 1989. I'm pretty sure this photo with the grill was shot on the tennis courts across from John Fripp Condos." Picking up two more of the small photos, Nick pointed out, "There are a number of people wearing blue sports jerseys with gold numbers on the back. They kind of remind me of football jerseys. That combined with the photo of the partial banner is a pretty good indication of the reason for this party. Now, I might be putting the cart before the horse, but we just recently talked about this party."

Shelby agreed. "On the way to work this morning I was thinking the same thing. You and my father talked about how in 1989 Beaufort won the State High School Football Championship. This could have every well been the party when those two students were killed."

Opening the second folder she placed seven more pictures and two that were enlarged on the table. "Whoever took these pictures moved on to another location away from the party, that is if they were taken the same day. They appear to have been taken at some remote area. It's kind of hard to make out much because it was dark out when they were taken and the flash from the camera only partially lit up the area photographed." Picking up the two enlargements, she went on, "In the background we can see a number of lights, not especially from homes but it looks like stringed lights. Now, onto the third and final set of pictures!"

Opening the third folder she removed three smaller and three matching enlargements and laid them near the edge of the table. Nick picked up one of the enlargements, but remained silent while he picked up the other two and tried to compare the three. "This is insane! I can now see what you meant when you said these three were disturbing. Three individuals, all wearing football jerseys, like some of the people at the party. But these three are standing by what looks like someone laying on the sand…a girl, if I'm correct. In the smaller photos it's hard to make out but the enlargements clearly indicate it's a female. You can tell from the long hair."

Shelby picked up her sandwich and took a healthy bite. "Look at this person closest to the girl. In his hand he is holding a section of what looks like lumber. The wood appears to be stained, just like the girl's face."

Nick picked up the third enlargement and commented, "In this photo the three, what appears to be football players are slightly turned toward the camera as if they knew they were being photographed. What does it all mean?"

"I could be way out in left field here, but I think what we are looking at are the three boys who were thought to be the ones who killed Abigail James and Chester Finch."

"That's precisely what I'm starting to think." Pushing his sandwich to the side, he took a drink and then looked at all the photos in general. "If these pictures were all taken the same night then they tell a story…a story we cannot understand without more information. If the girl in the last three pictures is, in fact, Abigail James and the boys turn out to be the three boys your father mentioned to me, then the unsolved murders of the two students that happened twenty seven years ago could be solved."

Raising her finger, Shelby added, "But at this point there are too many loose ends. Is the girl in the last three pictures actually the James girl *and* are the three youths pictured the three that were thought to have murdered her? Then there's the question of the other student...the male student that was murdered. How does he fit into any of this?"

"And here's the weirdest thing of all," said Nick. "Why was the camera found in the attic of Gretchen Yeat's home? It's hard to imagine her being the killer. She's eighty-three years old."

"That may be, but remember this happened twenty-seven years ago. That would have made her what…fifty-six years old at the time of the murders. What connection could she possibly have with the three football players and the two students that were killed?"

Getting up, Nick went to the fridge and removed a beer, leaned up against the kitchen counter and took a swig. "We may have stumbled onto some clues that could bust these unsolved murders wide open. But we have to make absolutely sure we know what we are looking at and what we have. Here's what I think we should do first. We need to meet with Mrs. Yeats, the sooner the better. Maybe we could take her to lunch or dinner and take the camera with us. We explain we found it up in the attic. We don't mention anything about the developed film, just that we found the camera. We then ask her who the camera belongs to; if it is important to her."

"Okay, that's sound logical. Lunch is out for me. I'll be in Savannah at that time of the day at work. I could make supper though."

"Supper it is then. "I'll call Mrs. Yeats and set up a dinner engagement. It'll be perfect. She already told me at the closing if I discovered anything she may have overlooked that may be considered important I should contact her. I'll just let her know we found something she may want. I'll try to set it up for tomorrow night in Beaufort. And another thing: while you're at work in Savannah, I'm going to make a visit to the Beaufort High School Library. I'm going to take a gander at their 1989 school yearbook. I'll take these last three photos with me and see if the girl in the pictures matches that of the James girl. I'll also try to find out who wore the numbers on the jerseys in the pictures. Depending on what Mrs. Yeats can tell us about the camera and what I find out at the high school this could be quite interesting."

The conversation was interrupted when Nick's cell phone buzzed. Nick answered, "Hello?"

"Nick…Carson. I was out fishing all day. I was pretty far out. That's why I didn't get your call earlier. I'm just docking my boat. Let me get home and get cleaned up and then I'll drop by so we can discuss the Sparks woman and what you discovered."

Nick no sooner laid his phone down when it buzzed again. "Hello?"

"Nick…this is Emily calling from up north."

Realizing it was his grandmother, Amelia, he had to be careful what he said in the presence of Shelby. Playing along with the charade. Nick responded, "Emily Pike. Nice to hear from you. How was your Thanksgiving?"

"My Thanksgiving was fine…and yours?"

"I had a great time at Shelby Lee's house. She's here with me right now."

Amelia, realizing it was not a good time to talk, played along. "I'll call you back tonight when you can talk."

"All right…thanks for calling."

Shelby, gathering up the photos, inquired, "Was that Carson's sister…the one who lives in Canada?"

"Yeah that was her. She just wanted to know how Thanksgiving went. I told her I spent the day with you and your family."

Shelby gave him a strange look. "That was a quick conversation."

"Well, I guess once I told her you were here, she told me she'd call back later." Switching gears, Nick suggested, "We need to hide all these photos. Carson will be dropping by later. I don't want to involve him in any of this…at least not just yet. Carson is a no nonsense sort of creature. Remember last summer when he found out I was getting involved with Ike Miller and then we told him we were both involved with the RPS Killer? He wasn't so hot on us getting involved in either of those situations. Don't get me wrong. We came out on the good end of both of those dilemmas all right, but when you think about it, things could have been different. Ike Miller could have got the better of both of us, but fortunately that all backfired on him. The RPS Killer, ol' Harold, could have just as easily killed you, but *you* wound up killing *him.* Depending on what we find out in the next few days about this Abigail James business, I'd just as soon keep this between you and I."

Placing the last three pictures in folder number three, Shelby nodded, "Agreed!"

Gesturing toward the living room, Nick suggested, "Let's go on in and relax. I'm sure when Carson gets here and I share with him the latest on Maria Sparks, it'll be quite an interesting conversation."

CHAPTER FOURTEEN

NICK UNFOLDED THE WEBBED CHAIR AND LOOKED UP THE long deserted beach at the slender wedge of morning sun slowly rising above the distant horizon. Within the next ten minutes the entire beach would be flooded with the South Carolina sun. Walking into the water until he was ankle deep, he pulled the collar of his windbreaker up around his neck. In less than a month Christmas would be upon the Lowcountry. For early December, the temperature, at least according to the weatherman, was ten degrees below normal. The low waves licking at his feet felt freezing when he stepped back out of the cold Atlantic.

Sitting in the low chair, he lifted the pair of suspended binoculars hanging from his neck and removed the protective leather case. Looking through the long distance eyeglasses, he realized it was still too dark to see that far up the beach. Relaxing, he thought about the previous evening after Carson had finally dropped by. He, Shelby and Pike had talked about a number of things. The information he had collected on Maria Sparks, the fact Chic Brumly had not filed charges, and the lawyer and ever-persistent client had spent the day on the island, supposedly asking questions about Carson. Carson was not the least bit concerned over Brumly's interest in him. Carson did say the info Nick managed to extract from the woman's beach bag might come in handy later on. He was also glad they now knew where the Sparks woman was staying. Shelby Lee didn't seem to be overly concerned about any interest they had in her. Just as they had agreed, they did not share the information with Carson in relation to the photos Shelby had developed. The last thing they discussed just before nine-thirty when Carson and Shelby called it a night was the mystery of the missing golf carts. As soon as they left Nick phoned Gretchen Yeats and set up an early dinner with her. He drank a beer, watched the late night news, and turned in at 11:45.

Looking through the binoculars again, he noticed the beach had begun to accept the sunshine but was still murky looking. *Another five minutes,* thought Nick and then he should be able to see if Charley's sister would venture out to the beach again. Gazing out across the vast ocean in front of where he was seated, he wondered how long Maria Sparks would insist on Brumly pursuing the idea that he, Nick Falco, had something to do with her missing sibling. He thought about the handwritten phone number he found in her beach bag. Carson, upon reviewing the number confirmed it was a New York area code. Carson wrote down the number and said he would check it out.

He thought about the rental property and how he had only gotten one room painted. Considering the day ahead, he realized he wasn't going to get any painting done today. He planned on being at the high school library around ten o'clock to see if anything in the photographs matched something in the 1989 yearbook. He figured he would probably be done at the library by eleven, then he would probably get back to Fripp by noon at the latest. He and Shelby were not scheduled to meet with Gretchen until four-thirty, so he had about three hours of free time before he had to get ready to go back to Beaufort. Maybe he would have time to get at least one room painted.

He was just about to raise the binoculars again when his cell phone buzzed. Answering, he smiled, "Good morning Reb."

Her pleasant voice responded, "How did you know it was me calling?"

Nick chuckled, "Who else would be calling me this early in the day?"

"Did you manage to get in touch with Mrs. Yeats after I left last night?"

"Yes, I did. The dinner is set for four-thirty at the Dockside on Lady's Island. Gretchen is going to meet us there."

"Did she ask you any questions about the camera?"

"No, I didn't have to even mention the camera. After I told her we found something that might be of value to her, she suggested we meet and that's when I suggested dinner."

"Are you still planning on going to the library this morning?"

"Yep, my plan is to get there around ten."

"Slight change of plans," said Shelby. "Want some company?"

"Sure, but I thought you had to work today."

"I did, but I got a call last night from Franklin Schrock, my boss. He was pissed to say the least; not at me, but because of what happened at the office."

"What happened?"

"For some unknown reason the sprinkler system engaged and two of the office rooms got flooded. He told me to take the next two days off, but come this weekend I'd have to work to help gets things back in order after the cleanup. So, it looks like I'm free to tag along with you to the high school. It'll be fun. I haven't stepped back inside Beaufort High since I graduated."

"Sounds good. I've never been in the place so it'll be nice to have a guide with me. Do you want me to pick you up?"

"Okay, let's say 9:45."

"I'll be parked in front of your house at quarter of. Maybe we can grab some lunch after we're finished at the school. Bring along a notepad and a pen."

Shelby ended the call. "I'm excited about what we might discover. It's a date!"

Placing the phone back in his pants pocket, he raised the binoculars and scanned the beach directly in front of John Fripp. He could make out a man leading a dog down to the water's edge. Maybe it was too cold for Maria Sparks to walk out to the beach. He erased the thought from his mind and remembered she was from New York, where this time of year, it was always cold, even freezing. He doubted if the low forties on a windswept beach would have little effect on someone from up north.

Looking at his watch he noted the time, 7:36. He had time before he had to leave for Beaufort. Folding the chair, he walked it back to the small wooden bridge near the back of his house and laid the chair at the bottom of the steps. Putting the binoculars back into their case, he dropped them to his chest and started up the beach. He had enough time to check out what, if anything, Maria was up to this morning.

It wasn't even five minutes until he was at the wooden deck walk. He decided to walk over to the access road and approach the Condos from the side rather than going up the wooden walkway. He didn't want to place himself in the position of being in the middle, if Maria happened to cross the walk. That would be awkward. He only wanted to keep an eye on the woman, not necessarily run into her. He wasn't the least bit interested in having a conversation with the woman.

Exiting from the access road he walked to the front of the condos where he once again saw Brumly's car parked in front of her unit. Walking to the opposite side of the complex he passed through a fenced gateway on the opposite end of the courtyard. Standing in a small grove of trees, he brought the binoculars up and focused on her unit. The curtain was open and he could see Maria standing in the kitchen, Brumly seated at a bar by the counter taking a drink from a cup. *Probably making plans for the day,* thought Nick.

He watched the couple for the next ten minutes. Brumly drank his coffee and gestured with his hands while Maria chewed on what appeared to be some sort of breakfast sandwich. Nick wondered if they were going to spend yet another day on the island, snooping around. There were not that many places where one could go to ask questions: the marina, both golf courses, a real estate office, the community center, the police station, fire house and a few other locales. The island wasn't that big. Brumly had to be running out of options.

Placing the binoculars back inside the case, Nick walked back through the gate out to Tarpon Blvd and then made the ten-minute journey back to his house. He checked the time. He had time for a light breakfast and a shower, then he was off to Beaufort to pick up Shelby. Walking up Tarpon he had two thoughts that occupied his thought process. One golf cart after another passed by while he walked up the road. If someone was going to steal carts Fripp Island had to be considered a gold mine. It was the main mode of transportation on the island. Then, he recalled what Chief Lysinger said about getting the cart at Deer Lake secured. His other line of thinking was centered on what he and Shelby might discover at the high school.

It was exactly 9:45 when Nick pulled up in front of Shelby Lee's parents' house. He didn't even get a chance to turn the car off. She was waiting on the front porch. The briefcase at her side, she ran down the walk and hopped into the Lexus, smiled and asked, "Do you have any idea where the high school is?"

Nick shrugged. "Not the slightest. Which way?"

Making a rotating motion with her right index finger, she laughed and ordered, "Turn this rig around and head back down Newcastle until you come to Bay Street. Make a left on Bay, cross the bridge and then I'll let you know where to turn."

Making a U-turn, Nick confirmed, "Next stop…Lady's Island!"

Once across the bridge, it was only a minute when Shelby spoke and pointed, "Take the next right."

Making a right hand turn at a sign that read, BEAUFORT HIGH SCHOOL – *Home of the Eagles,* Nick drove down a paved two lane drive and following Shelby's directions, pulled into one of six *VISITORS* parking spots. Picking up the briefcase, Shelby gave Nick a thumbs up and stated with excitement, "Let's get in there and see what we can find!"

Stopping at an information desk, Shelby inquired, "Excuse me, but could you direct us to the library. It's been ten years since I graduated from here. Is the library still in the same spot it always has been?"

A woman looked up from a brochure she was reading and responded. "No, the library is now in the new section. Walk down the hall on the right, until you pass through a set of large doors then continue until you come to another set of doors. Pass through, then make a left and then an immediate right. That's the library." They were about to walk away from the desk but were stopped as the woman asked, "Is there something I can help you with?"

Shelby waved the woman's offer of help off, "No, we just need to do some local research on some past students."

Three minutes later they entered the school library: a large room lined with rows of tall, walnut stained, eight foot high bookcases. In front of the numerous cases there were a number of long, twelve-foot tables flanked by neat rows of wooden chairs. Every three feet on the tables there were reading lights. Centered in the room was a circular desk manned by a middle-aged woman who smiled when they approached. "What can I do for you today?"

Shelby did all of the talking. "My Name is Shelby Lee Pickett. You're Mrs. Stavely…right!"

The woman smiled. "That's correct."

Shelby continued to explain, "I graduated from Beaufort ten years ago, I spent quite a bit of time in the library, but that was before they moved it. I don't suppose you remember me?"

"I'm afraid not," answered the woman politely. "I've only been full-time here at the school library for the past four years. I may have seen you before but there are so many students in and out of here. I'm sorry."

"No need for an apology. Could you please lead us to the past yearbooks?"

"Why, of course. The bookshelf along the far wall on the right, about halfway down. Every yearbook since the school had been open is arranged by year. Maybe there is a question I could answer for you?"

"No, that's fine. We're just doing some research for a possible book my friend here and I might consider writing."

Trying to keep a straight face, Nick simply nodded at the woman.

The woman smiled back at Nick and offered, "If there is anything you need to know while conducting your research, please feel free to stop by the desk."

Following close behind Shelby, Nick Joked, "You've got to be kidding me! A book…we're writing a book?"

"Trust me," said Shelby. "You can go almost anywhere and get anyone's attention and help if you tell them you're writing a book."

Arriving at the last row of shelves, Shelby spotted the yearbook section half way down the wall. "Here we are. Here is the 40's, 50's, 60's…" Skipping a number of years she went on, "The 70's and the 80's…1986, 87, 88 and here we go…1989." Pulling the book down from the shelf, she asked, "Where do you think we should sit?"

Checking to see if anyone was watching, Nick suggested, "As far as possible from the main desk…maybe a table close to a corner. We have to make absolutely sure no one and I mean…no one sees what's on those three enlarged photos from folder number 3."

Seating themselves at the end of the farthest table in the room, Nick checked the room. There was only one student present at the moment. "I think this should be a good spot. But, before we start we have to come up with a system. We don't want to spend too much time looking at the yearbook and writing stuff down or we may bring attention to ourselves. We need to act normal, get the information we need and then skedaddle! While one of us is writing down what we find the other has to keep an eye out for anyone approaching. If anyone sees what's on those pictures, we're going to have some explaining to do."

Shelby corrected him. "We don't have to write anything down. We just have to make it look like we're writing information down."

Nick gave Shelby an odd look. "What do you mean? We don't have to write anything down. How else are we supposed to remember the information? We can't just memorize everything we see!"

Giving Nick a look of amazement, Shelby spoke and pulled out her cell phone, "We take pictures of anything we think is important."

Confused, Nick responded, "But we don't have a camera with us. Besides, if we did, that would be too obvious."

"What am I going to do with you?" said Shelby in a comical, but sarcastic tone. "We take pictures with my phone."

"Oh, I didn't even think of that. But still, how does that help us. We'll have to look at your phone each time we want to compare the enlarged photos and the pictures taken by the phone."

"We can make pictures from the photos taken."

"We can? How does that work?"

"It's simple. Later on, after we take pictures of what we want I then connect my phone to my computer and upload the information on my phone to the computer. The computer will create a full size photo on the screen and then if we want an actual hold in your hands picture, we can print it from the computer. We can actually make photographs up to 8 X 10."

"That's amazing," commented Nick. "We look up what we want, take a picture, then later, create an actual picture."

Looking over at the desk at the librarian who was busy talking with a student who had entered, Shelby suggested, "Let's get started. I think the first thing we should do is look up Abigail James' senior picture." Removing the three enlargement pictures from the folder she laid them facedown. "I brought along a magnifying glass so we can get a close look at the girl in the picture who we assume is dead."

Picking up the yearbook, Nick flipped to a section where the students were listed alphabetically by name and photograph. Locating the students with last names beginning with the letter J, he had to turn the next page where at the very top was a stunning picture of Abigail James.

Bending over slightly, Shelby took a phone shot of the picture while Nick read what the yearbook had to say about her. "Dean's list, four years running, and that's about it for extra curricular activities. It also states she was going to attend Cornell University. There is also one of those italicized remarks that identifies what the person pictured was remembered as, her caption reads: *Face of an angel!*" Looking closely at the senior picture Nick remarked, "I can see what the caption means. She really was a very attractive girl." Looking back at the desk, he whispered, "Hand me those enlargements we brought along."

Placing all three pictures above the yearbook he looked at the photos and then at the yearbook picture. "Is it her?" asked Shelby impatiently.

"It's hard to tell for sure. The picture in the yearbook shows Abigail as having long blond, flowing hair. The girl in our photograph does have long hair that appears to be blond, but because of where she is, it looks matted. Hand me the magnifying glass." Placing the glass directly over the section of the photo where the girl appeared from just below the shoulders up, he closely examined the facial features and then looked at the yearbook picture. "Once again, it's hard to say without any doubt that it is one and the same girl. The features look the same but then again there is nothing unusual about her face that stands out. No wait…wait a sec. It looks like the girl in our photo is wearing some sort of chain, a circular medallion." Inspecting the yearbook shot, he spoke softly, "Well, I'll be. In this yearbook photograph Abigail James is sporting a chain with a medallion. It could be the same piece of jewelry." Looking through the glass at the medallion in the yearbook, Nick could just barely make out the outline of the jeweled name *Abigail.* Going back to the enlargement, he could not see any inscription. Leaning back, he asked, "Is it possible to make these photos any larger?"

Shelby checked the desk again and answered, "These enlargements are 8 x 10. I can enlarge them to 12 x 14 but if we need them any larger than that we have to go to a professional film developer, but then we take the risk of whoever enlarges the pictures questioning what they see. I don't think we want to put ourselves in that position." Looking at the medallion hanging from the James girl's neck, Shelby asked, "So what do you think? Could the girl in the enlargement be Abigail James?"

"It could be, but I can't say it's definitely her. I feel there's a 60-40 percent chance it's her…maybe even 70-30, but we have to be 100 percent sure. Let's move on to the other victim…Chester Finch."

Flipping back to the F section, there were only four students with last names beginning in F. Chester was third. Shelby snapped off a picture and remarked, "Chester is the exact opposite of the James girl. She was nothing short of beautiful and Chester here appears to be the typical nerd: thick glasses, not that attractive, pock marked face. I mean, for crying out loud. Look at his sport coat. He has one of those stupid penholders in his breast pocket. That is really nerdy. Let's see what it says about Mr. Finch."

Nick commented before he read what was written. "Once again the exact opposite of the James girl. She wasn't that involved in school activities whereas Chester Finch seems to have been involved in everything. Dean's list four years running, student council all four years, his senior year the vice president, senior editor, school newspaper, he won the science fair two years in a row. Then there's chess club, young entrepreneurs and business club, photography club. This kid appears to be very intelligent. Down here at the bottom it states he is going to attend Harvard University. Not just anyone goes to Harvard."

Looking closely at the caption at the bottom of his photo, Shelby read, "*Say cheese!*" What on earth could that mean? This kid is recognized a genius and he is remembered by a goofy saying like that."

Nick snapped his fingers. "It has to be about taking pictures. Ya know, like when you're posing and someone says, `Say cheese!"

Shelby cleared her throat to get Nick's attention as two female students were walking in their direction. Nick quickly turned over the enlargements and smiled at the two when they walked past. Watching the two girls disappear around a corner of book shelves, Nick turned one of the photos back over and looked at the numbers on the backs of the three football jerseys. "Okay, let's see if we can figure out who these three players are numbers 17, 6 and 23." Flipping through the pages he remarked, "All we have to do is locate the sports section which should be quite large if Beaufort High is like most high schools."

Three-quarters through the thick book, they came upon a page entitled: BEAUFORT HIGH SCHOOL SPORTS - *Home of the Eagles.*

"Here it is." announced Nick. Flipping the page, he came across a number of pages of team photographs: track team, basketball team, baseball team and then the football team. Above the team photo there it was in bold lettering 1989 STATE HIGH SCHOOL FOOTBALL CHAMPIONS. Nick tapped the photo with his finger. "Get a shot of this team photo. We might have to get an enlarged picture of this." The names of the players were listed beneath the photographs and the numbers on most of the players could not be completely seen. Then, at the bottom of the page, the players were listed again with their uniform numbers. Running his finger down the numbers he stopped at number 23 and read the name, "Tim Durham, tight end. That's one of the names your father mentioned when I was at your house. This is one of the boys who was a person of interest in the murders."

Checking the large room once again, Shelby commented, "This is getting more interesting by the minute. What's the next number?"

Looking at the enlarged photo, Nick spoke up, "That would be number 6 which I just found. Brad Schulte, quarterback. And here's the last number. 17…Miles Gaston…running back. These three boys are the ones your father talked about; the boys he claimed got away with murder and walked off Scott free. Get a shot of this list also."

Getting the picture, Shelby asked, "What's next?"

"Next," suggested Nick, "is we go back to the graduating senior pictures and see who and what these boys were all about."

A voice from behind, surprised them, "Are you finding what you were looking for?" Both Nick and Shelby looked up and noticed Mrs. Stavley hovering over them."

Shelby quickly scooped up the three enlargements and placed them in the folder and responded, "Yes, we are. We should be finished in a few minutes."

Interested, Mrs. Stavley inquired, "What is the book you're thinking of writing going to be about?"

Caught off-guard, Shelby stammered, "Ah…it's a book about football here in the Lowcountry. Did you know that in 1989 Beaufort won the state championship?"

"Vaguely. I was still in college when that happened. Well, if there is anything else I can do for you, just let me know."

When Mrs. Stavely walked off, Shelby breathed deeply. "I hope she didn't see our photos."

"I don't think she had enough time," said Nick. "That being said, I think we need to finish up and be on our way."

Flipping through the book, he came to the senior picture of Tim Durham. "Okay here's Durham. Take a shot of him. We can read what it says about these three boys later."

A minute later, Shelby had snapped off pictures of Brad Schulte and Miles Gaston and was about to put her cell phone back in her pocket when Nick, still flipping pages, came across something of great interest. "Look at this. In the front of the book they have a dedication page for Abigail James and Chester Finch. Get a shot of this. We can review it later."

Getting the shot, Shelby asked, "Do you think we got everything there is?"

"No, I'm not sure. There could be other pictures of Abigail or Chester engaged in various school functions. I think we have enough for now. We can always come back if we need to. Let's get out of here, grab some lunch and look at what we have so far."

Just before they walked out the door of the library, Mrs. Stavely spoke to them, "Good luck on your book!"

Parking downtown at the waterfront park, they walked to the Common Ground restaurant where they took a corner table and ordered coffee and sandwiches. Looking out the window at the Beaufort River, Shelby cupped her coffee in her hands and remarked, "This is the coldest winter I can remember in years. When the wind blows it feels like it's freezing out there."

"We can sit here all afternoon and drink coffee," said Nick. "We don't have to meet Mrs. Yeats for five hours. That gives us plenty of time to go over what we've discovered. Get your phone out so we can see what these three football players were all about."

Pushing her coffee to the side, Shelby got her phone out and following some fancy finger work, she laid the phone on the table where they could both see who was pictured. "Here we have the Durham kid. Says he was in the school choir for all four years and he lettered in football four years. He was a member of the 1989 Championship Football Team and he is going to be attending college at Texas A&M. His caption reads: *"Stand together!"*

Moving right along, she pulled up the next picture while she continued to speak, "Next we have Brad Schulte. Dean's list, four years running, lettered four years in football and is also a member of the '89 State Football Champs. It also says he was a member of the student council his junior year and he sang in the choir. He was going to Penn State. His caption reads, *"The Three Musketeers!"*

"That makes sense," said Nick. "When your father and I were talking about football when he was in high school, he talked about these three boys and told me they were known as The Three Musketeers. He said they lived just up the street from where he was raised and the three boys were tight. If you tangled with one you had to contend with all three." Moving his hand for her to proceed, he went on, "Let's pull the last player up. What was his name, Milo?"

"No, it was Miles and here is his photo. Lettered four years in football and was a member of the '89 Championship Team as well. He was going to attend South Carolina University. His caption is no surprise. *"One for all and all for one!"* Giving Nick a look, Shelby asked, "Isn't that what The Three Musketeers always said?"

"Yeah, I think you're right. What about the last picture you took? The dedication page to the James' girl and the Finch kid."

Running her fingers across the screen, Shelby spoke to herself, "No, no, no, yes, here it is!" Clearing her throat, she began to read, "The year of 1989 will always be remembered by its graduating seniors as each year is always remembered by those graduating that particular year, but 1989 will always hold a special place in our hearts for the loss of two of our best friends and students. Abigail James and Chester Finch will always be remembered as brilliant students with bright futures ahead of them. The world is less of a place now that they are gone and Heaven is a far better place. Abigail and Chester. We here at Beaufort High will never forget you."

Sitting back, Shelby looked out the window and spoke softly, "It's apparent the school took the loss of these two students quite seriously."

"I can see why the school would feel that way," said Nick. "The loss of two eighteen year old students just like that! One day they are here, the next day…gone! For the school, the teachers and the community that's hitting pretty close to home, especially when you consider they didn't just die. They were murdered!"

Propping her feet up on a nearby empty chair, Shelby sipped at her coffee and then added, "So, let's see what we have so far. Two students who we know were killed at the end of Fripp Island at a school football celebration. The James girl and the Finch kid from what I can tell had nothing in common. She was exceptionally good looking while he was not exactly what you would call eye candy, and yet they were found on the same beach…dead! I suppose the first thing people thought was they were having an affair, but I can't buy into that. The only thing they seem to have had in common was that they were both quite smart. They were both on the dean's list for four straight years. She was going to Cornell and he was going to Harvard. These were some intelligent students. I can see why the police may have been confused. These two students were the most unlikely to be together on that beach."

"Okay," said Nick. "Let's go in another direction. We now know from the pictures Schulte, Durham and the Gaston kid were at the scene of the crime, at least at some point. What we don't know is if the James girl was killed before they arrived, *or,* did they kill her and maybe even Chester Finch. What sort of connection could there have possibly been between the three football players and two students who have nothing in common. Was one of the football players having an affair with the James girl?"

Opening her briefcase, she removed the three enlargements. Spreading them out on the table, she pointed out, "Look at number 17, Miles Gaston. In all three photos he has a section of lumber, maybe a short 2 x 4 in his right hand. In the third picture where they are just starting to turn around he is lowering the wood. That piece of lumber may be the murder weapon. At this point we don't even know if the police discovered the wood. Look at the end of the wood where it is darker in color. It's the same shade or discolor that's on the girl's face and upper body. It could be blood."

Nick agreed, but also stated, "There are a lot of things we don't know. I'm sure the police back then had a lot more to go on than we do, and still they didn't take these three boys down for the murder. If they would have had these photographs I think it would have made a big difference." Standing, he finished his coffee. "Look, I've had enough for the moment. We can sit here all day and try to figure out what happened on that beach twenty-seven years ago and still wind up with a big fat zero. I say we call it a day until we meet with Mrs. Yeats tonight and we discuss the camera with her." Holding up his cup, he smiled. "I'm getting a refill. How about you?"

"Yes, a refill sounds good and I agree with you. I think we should take it easy and let what we've discovered sink in. So what do we do for the next four hours?"

"Well, I was going to head back over to Fripp and get at least one room painted, but all of a sudden, I'm not in a working mood. One thing I need to get done is move the golf cart Mrs. Yeats gave me over to my house. By the time we get back out to Fripp and get the cart moved that could chew up an hour or so. If we have some time left we could drive over to the boathouse and have a couple of beers and just chill? When it gets to be, let's say around three-thirty we can head back over here for our dinner with Gretchen."

Nick stepped down onto the dirt parking lot of Dockside and scanned the surrounding area. Pointing at the maroon Corvette three spaces down from where he had parked the Lexus, he laughed. "Gretchen Yeats is already here!"

Shelby, walking at his side, inquired, "She is?"

Walking past the Corvette he touched the rear on the sports car and explained, "This is her car."

Shelby stopped in her tracks. "This…this is *her car?"*

"Yes, it turns out Mrs. Yeats is Beaufort County's little ol' lady from Pasadena! Go granny go!"

"I thought we were going to be meeting an older lady…a grandmother type."

"She's eighty-three years young. I think you'll like her."

Walking up the wooden incline leading to the main dining area, Nick stopped at the reservation desk and asked, "We're meeting a Mrs. Yeats for dinner this evening. Can you please tell us where she is seated?"

The young girl smiled and pointed at a window table overlooking the bay. "I believe that's her by the window. I'll send your waitress right over."

Approaching the table, Nick waved at Gretchen who stood when she saw the couple. "Mrs. Gretchen Yeats, I'd like you to meet Shelby Lee Pickett. Shelby, this is Gretchen."

Shaking Gretchen's hand, Shelby nodded politely, "Nice to meet you. Nick speaks highly of you."

Not giving the compliment any attention, Gretchen sat and gestured at two chairs on the other side of the table. "What a nice looking couple you make."

Nick gave Shelby a funny look that caused Gretchen to apologize. "I'm sorry, I just thought you two were a couple. You know, boyfriend-girlfriend, that sort of thing."

Shelby sat and answered, "Let's just say Nick and I hang out quite a bit together." Tapping Nick on his shoulder, she winked. "I think we get along rather well!"

The waitress approached and took their drink orders. After she left, Gretchen gazed out the window while three boats passed by. "I just love coming here. The food is always good and the view is very relaxing. Have you been here before?"

"I never have," said Nick. "I usually go to the Dockside over in Port Royal."

Shelby spoke up, "I've been here once with my folks. I really enjoyed it."

Surprisingly, Gretchen opened up the conversation in regard to why they were meeting. "You said you found something that may be of value to me. I, for one can't imagine what it could be. I went over everything in the house three times."

Nick nodded at Shelby, who reached into her purse and withdrew the camera. "We found this camera up in the attic space. It looks really old, and we thought maybe it had some special meaning to you."

Gretchen hesitated and stared at the camera, then spoke up, "I assume you found it in that old trunk."

Shelby laid the camera down in the middle of the table. "That's exactly where I found it. It appears to be nearly thirty years old."

Picking up the camera she smiled sadly. "This camera does have a special meaning to me, but it's not a meaning I like to think about. I put the camera up there in the attic almost twenty-five years ago along with the rest of the stuff my grandson left behind. That camera has a unique story attached to it. My grandson and one of his classmates were killed out on Fripp Island. I guess now, it's been close to twenty-six or twenty-seven years ago when they found Chester and Miss James on a beach down near the end of the Tarpon turnaround. Those who murdered my grandson and the girl were never caught and the case was never solved and still to this day remains cold."

Shelby gave Nick a subdued look of amazement as Nick stared back at her in disbelief. Trying to act like what Gretchen had said was news to them, Nick fabricated his next statement. "I haven't lived down here that long. Actually, I just moved to Fripp last summer. I can't remember where, but sometime over the past few months I overheard someone speaking about those two murders. You say Chester was your grandson and he was one of the two students that were murdered?"

"Yes. Chester was my grandson. He and his parents were involved in a bad automobile accident over on Rt. 95 back when Chester was seven years old. His parents were killed, but Chester survived. It was a miracle. He was thrown from the car and landed in some thick brush off the side of the road. There wasn't a scratch on the kid. Anyway, Clark, that's my former husband, and I raised Chester right here on Fripp. Clark died back in 1985 and I continued to raise Chester. Of course by that time he was a freshman in high school, he was the nicest kid you'd ever want to meet. He had his own photography business and believe me, he was smart as they come. Made the honor list four straight years at Beaufort High. He was accepted at Harvard which made me so proud."

The waitress returned with their drinks and asked if they were ready to order. Nick told her they needed a few more minutes. Looking over the menu, Nick casually asked, "So what's this unique story you mentioned that comes with the camera?"

"The camera," explained Gretchen, "was found two years after the murders by two youngsters who were down on Fripp with their parents on vacation. These two boys were apparently hiking out in the salt marsh area down at the end of Tarpon past the turnaround when they were snooping around some rocks. They discovered the camera down in between the rocks." Picking up the camera she inspected the underside. "At one time there was a metal I.D. tag here on the bottom. It must have fallen off. It's probably lying in the bottom of the truck in the attic. These boys, seeing the I.D. take the camera to their parents who, in turn, drive them over to the house on Deer Lake so they can give me the camera. I told them it belonged to my grandson and they went on their way. From the description of the area where they had found it, it sounded like it was really close to where they found Chester's abandoned car the night of the murders. I thought that was rather strange, but I never turned the camera over to the police." She placed the camera back down on the table and started to read the menu.

Shelby rolled her eyes at Nick, wondering where the story was going to lead.

Nick, not wanting to make a big deal out of what Gretchen had just told them laid his menu down and announced, "I'm going with the seafood platter."

Shelby, who hadn't even looked at the menu agreed, "That sounds good to me. I'll go with that too."

Nick casually probed, "This might not be any of our business, but I'm wondering since the camera was found so close to the murder scene why you didn't report it to the police?"

"I had my fill of the police," said Gretchen. "I did back then and always have felt they dropped the ball. There were three boys, actually friends of Chester and the James girl, who, though never mentioned as suspects were considered persons of great interest. They were questioned a number of times. It was quite obvious they were involved somehow, but they walked. They were never arrested, brought to trial or convicted for killing my grandson and the girl. During the investigation the police questioned me a number of times and had the audacity to suggest that Chester, my squeaky-clean grandson, was somehow involved in a sexual encounter with the girl and he might have killed her. It got to the point where I didn't want anything to do with the police. When the camera showed up, it brought back a lot of bad memories. I wasn't about to supply the police with anything that would give them a reason to bring Chester down. My grandson at that time had been in the ground for nearly two years. I wanted him to rest in peace. I don't want anything to do with the police. My grandson, who had his entire life ahead of him, has been dead now for going on twenty-eight years while the men who killed him are still out there walking around. There was *and is* no justice."

Pointing at the camera she explained once again, "So, when that family brought me the camera I tossed it in Chester's trunk and went on with my life as best I could. I have no need for that camera. As far as I'm concerned you can destroy the thing."

Shelby looked across the table at Gretchen and spoke, "I'm sorry for the death of your grandson. It's sound to me like he was a great kid."

Nick chimed in, "Are there a lot of people around these parts that feel the same way as you in regard to the three boys who were persons of interest?"

"Oh yes! Back then everyone thought they were guilty. I suppose the police even thought they were guilty but they just didn't have enough proof. That's the problem with our judicial system. Now, I agree wholeheartedly with our legal philosophy that an individual is innocent until proven guilty, but those three lads were guilty and everyone knew it. The end result is the system worked for them, but not so for my grandson and Abigail James. They did not receive justice."

Probing even farther, Nick asked, "What about the girl's family…the James family. How did they feel about the investigation?"

"That's another story all together. Abigail James father, Bernard P. James, was and still is the wealthiest man in these parts, maybe the state. Abigail was his only daughter…his pride and joy. She was spoiled rotten, but she certainly didn't deserve to die at such a young age. Mr. James and his wife were absolutely livid when the police finally gave up on the case. Mrs. James, so it has been said, was never able to get past her daughter's death. It ate away at her day and night until it got to the point where she became sick. Four years after the death of Abigail, Mrs. James went into a deep depression and died. This inflamed Mr. James' hatred of the police even more. He had not only lost his daughter but his wife as well. Still to this day, he blames the police for his daughter's death going unsolved and the subsequent death of his wife. He even tried to sue the Beaufort Police, but you know what they say, you can't sue city hall! After all these years he is still bitter. I ran into him about two years ago at a function down at the community center on Fripp. He had gotten quite ill himself and was confined to a wheelchair. We got to talking about the deaths of Chester and Abigail; and he told me as long as he lived he would continue to search for a way to bring down the boys, who are now grown men. As far as he is concerned, they killed his daughter. The truth be told, I think in the end we'll all go to our graves and we'll never know the truth about what went on that night on Fripp Island." Realizing she was rambling, she waved off what she had been saying. "Enough of this doom and gloom. I think I'm ready to order. Let's just have a nice dinner."

It was just after seven o'clock when Nick and Shelby sat in the Lexus and watched Gretchen pull out of Dockside's lot in her Corvette. Turning sideways in the seat, Nick yawned and stated, "Well, you can't say it hasn't been an interesting day."

Shelby scratched her head as if she were in deep thought. Removing the camera from her purse she held it up. "We started out this day anticipating what we might find out by going to the high school." Holding up her cell phone in the other hand, she compared the two. "We got some interesting photos from the yearbook, but the information about this camera makes things more complicated now. This camera and the film I developed might be what could break these unsolved murders wide open. Think about it." She laid the cell phone and the camera down, picked up the folder and removed the three enlargements. "We know someone took these three pictures of Tim, Brad and this Miles boy while they were killing the girl or right after they killed her. Or, *maybe* the pictures were taken of them after they found the girl on the beach. When you consider we now know the camera belonged to Chester Finch, it's obvious he may have taken the shots. Maybe that's why he was killed."

Nick nodded toward the camera. "And here's another thing. Why was the camera tossed or maybe even hidden in the rocks, not at the crime scene, but near it? It just doesn't make sense. We're still missing something."

"You're right, and I think the thing we're missing is what the connection was between the three football stars, Chester and the James girl. If we could figure that out, then we might be able to figure out what happened."

Nick started the car. "We came away today with a lot more information than what we thought we'd collect. I think we should both go home and let what we discovered sink in. Right now, I'm confused. This thing…these murders could wind up going in any number of directions. I say we sleep on what we have so far. Maybe tomorrow after we've had a chance to digest all this information, maybe something will fall into place."

"I agree. Why don't you drop me off at my parents? I can get the pictures from my phone transferred to some 8 x 10's and besides that I need to enlarge these three beach shots up to 12 x 14. Then, maybe we'll be able to identify the medallion as the one Abigail James wore in her senior picture. I still have tomorrow off. I can drive out to Fripp tomorrow morning with all the pictures and then we might be able to make some sense of this."

"It's been a long day," said Nick. "Your plan sounds good. After I drop you off I'm going to head home and just relax and think about what we accomplished. I think we made some headway. I'm not sure where any of this will take us, but it sure is getting interesting."

As Nick pulled out onto the road and made a right headed for Beaufort, Shelby stuffed the camera down into her purse and laid the folder on the dash. "Just when we thought things were calming down after last summer it appears things are heating up again on Fripp Island. What with this stolen golf cart business, Chic Brumly and this Maria Sparks tailing you and now some twenty-seven year old, unsolved double murder on our plates, this could wind up being as interesting as last summer."

Nick looked at Shelby and smiled sarcastically. "God…I hope not!"

CHAPTER FIFTEEN

"MORNIN' SUNSHINE!"

"Good morning. Are you on the way out to Fripp?"

"That I am. I hope you haven't eaten breakfast yet. I have bacon, egg and cheese on toasted wheat and hot chocolate fresh from the Publix deli."

"Bring it on. How far out are you?"

"I'm crossing the Harbor Island Bridge right now. I should be there in less than ten minutes. Be waiting out front for me. I've got a little island excursion planned for this morning. I'll tell you all about it when I arrive."

"See you in five," said Nick. He stuffed his cell phone in his pants pocket and grabbed his windbreaker from the back of one of the kitchen chairs.

Leaving by the front door, he locked the house and descended the stairs into the front yard. Three birds that had been drinking in the bottom of the three-tier fountain flew off to a nearby tree when Nick approached. The fountain had been there in the front yard for as long as he could remember. Amelia never complained that the local birds used the decorative water display for a watering hole and he wasn't about to either. The bright South Carolina sun had, over the years, faded the brilliant white paint. The concrete fountain needed a good cleaning and paint job. The water in the actual fountain base was low. He'd been meaning to fill it up for the past week but just hadn't gotten around to it. He thought about getting it done while he was waiting for Shelby to arrive but didn't think he'd have enough time.

Walking out the driveway he noticed the grass needed cut again! That was one of the things he couldn't quite grasp. When he lived in Cincinnati, grass cutting normally started for most folks around Mid-April and ran up to the end of October, depending on the weather. He always enjoyed the first few cuttings at the beginning of spring, but soon the week after week cutting of the grass became a task. From November until the following spring people put their push and riding mowers up for the winter. Not so in the south. Cutting grass on Fripp Island was a year round chore. *This weekend,* he thought. *This coming weekend I'll not only cut the grass but I'll get the fountain filled up and painted.*

At the end of the driveway, he bent down and pulled a number of small weeds from the edge of the pavement, when he was interrupted by a voice he didn't relish hearing. "Good Morning, Mr. Falco."

Looking up, there was Chic Brumly, sitting behind the wheel of his Lincoln, Maria in the passenger seat. Brumly did not wait for a response but drove on up Tarpon as if Nick were of no concern. Nick shook his head in amazement and thought about what an ass Brumly really was. Walking out to the edge of the road he watched when the Lincoln turned onto Bonito and crossed the canal bridge.

The Lincoln no sooner disappeared than Shelby's red Jeep crossed the intersection of Bonito and Tarpon and stopped in front the house. Rolling down the window, she signaled, "C'mon, get in. We're going up to the turnaround."

Inside the Jeep Nick was presented with a small sack. "Here, hold this. We can eat when we get there."

Looking inside the sack, Nick asked, "Why are we going up to the end of Tarpon. There's nothing there."

"Oh, you'd be surprised what's there." Changing the topic, Shelby asked, "Wasn't that Brumly's Lincoln I saw going over the canal bridge?"

"Yeah, and he had Maria Sparks with him."

"Don't tell me they were already bothering you this morning?"

"I really didn't talk with either of them. They just pulled up, said 'Good morning', and then they were on their way. Brumly's an idiot! It's just his way of letting me know he's still watching me."

The drive up to the end of Tarpon was short and soon Shelby was guiding the Jeep from the pavement to the dirt turnaround. Pulling up to the edge of the dirt, she stopped just short of one of the log barriers that separated the lot from the grassy and stone embankment bordering the salt marsh. Turning the Jeep off, she sat back and displayed the marsh. "Well, what do you think?"

Nick shot her an odd look and repeated her statement, "What do I think? What do I think about what?"

"Hand me one of those breakfast sandwiches," said Shelby. Unwrapping the foil, she took a bite and explained, "I was up until 1:30 last night." Reaching down, she held up a folder. "I pulled the data from my phone and created photographs of everything we took pictures of at the high school. I also enlarged the three pictures from our third folder to 12 x 14. I brought along the magnifying glass. Hopefully we may be able to identify the medallion in Abigail's senior picture as the same one on the beach photos. But, before we get into that I discovered something else last night while reviewing all the pictures I developed. We happen to be sitting in the approximate place where Chester's car was found abandoned the night he was murdered!"

Nick looked at her like she was crazy. "How in the hell could you possibly know that?"

"Remember when I told you my father did some plumbing work for Mr. James."

"Yes, I do remember when we talked about that."

"Well, the word got around my father was a pretty good plumber and before long he was getting jobs left and right here on Fripp. Still, today he gets calls. Back when I was in high school, during the summer if he had a job out here, he'd always bring me along and drop me off at the beach. I'd sunbathe and when he was finished he'd pick me up and we'd go back to Beaufort. Well, on one occasion just before my freshman year came to an end I heard some of the girls at school talking about when Abigail James was killed on Fripp Island. That very week my father had some work over here so he brought me along. When he picked me up later that afternoon, I mentioned what I had overheard earlier in the week. I asked him if he knew anything about the past murders. He told me from talking with a lot of folks on Fripp over the years about the murders that he actually knew where Chester Finch's car had been found and where he and the James girl were murdered. I asked him if he would show me…and he did. We are sitting in the very spot or at least very close to the area where they found Chester's car." Finished with her sandwich she got out of the car and signaled for Nick to do likewise.

Standing in front of the Jeep, she placed the camera and the three folders on the hood and took a drink of her hot chocolate. "I was up late last night thinking about what Mrs. Yeats told us about the camera…Chester's camera." Picking up the camera she walked over and looked down the side of the embankment covered with large rocks. "Gretchen said the boys who found the camera claimed they found it down in between some rocks and she said the area they described where the camera was discovered was close to where they found the car, so that means the camera…this one right here, was tossed or maybe, *even hidden* right down there in those rocks somewhere."

Leaning on the Jeep, she picked up the original three folders and remarked. "I developed nineteen pictures taken the night of the murders." Holding up the first folder, she went on, "The first nine pictures we identified as being at the celebration party in 1989, the night of the murders." Picking up the third folder, she explained, "The last folder contains the three disturbing photos. We know those were taken some time after the first nine were taken at the party. What we don't know is when or where the seven pictures in the second folder were taken. What we do know is they had to be taken before the last three were snapped off."

Opening the second folder she removed the two enlargements and handed them to Nick. "All seven of the pictures in the second folder were taken in some remote, out of the way area. Even though the pictures were taken at night you can see they are in a salt marsh type environment. The two enlargements show a long string of lights in the background. Where else on the island is there a long string of lights other than right over there on the other side of this marsh. I feel the lights on these photos are from the Cabana Club. In other words; Chester Finch took the second group of pictures right down in there."

Nick took one of the photos, looked at it, and then looked across the marsh where the Cabana Club stood in the morning sun. "It's hard to tell right now with it being light out, but let's just suppose for the moment you're right. Gretchen said her grandson was into photography and he had his own photo business. I think it's safe to assume the Finch kid was at the party and took the first nine shots. It doesn't make any sense someone else would have used his camera. With all the lights there must have been at the party it's hard to tell from the pictures if it was dark out or not. We do know from the second set of pictures that it was dark. Chester Finch, at some point left the party, drove down here to the turnaround, and parked his car, according to you, right about here. Now, did he come up to this end of Tarpon by himself or was someone with him? This we do not know. All we know is he, more than likely, took the second group of pictures. We also don't know how much time elapsed before he took the three final shots on the beach. All we know is it was dark; I guess sometime later that evening."

Placing the camera and the folders in her briefcase, Shelby started up the dirt next to the embankment, "C'mon, let's walk over to where the bodies were found."

It was only thirty yards when Nick found himself staring out across Skull Inlet. He stopped and looked across the water at the island on the other side. Shelby, realizing he had stopped, asked, "Is something wrong?"

"No, it's just I haven't been this far up Tarpon since last summer." Nodding at Pritchards Island, he explained, "I guess there are a lot of bad memories over there on Pritchards. The afternoon when I found Susan Dunn's hand and then there was my narrow escape from the Carnahans after I was nearly drowned by Derek Simons." Shaking off his negative thoughts, he started south along the edge of the steep embankment that led down to the water.

Shelby took the lead while they walked down a sand and rock covered path that ended after fifteen yards. Stopping, she pointed at a high wall of gigantic rocks. "This is about as far as tourists venture when they come to the end of the island. On the other side of this rock barrier is where the James girl and the Finch kid were murdered."

Handing the briefcase to Nick, she started the climb up. "When I get about halfway up, toss me the case, then follow me."

At the top of the rocks, Shelby stood and shouted back down to Nick, "Toss me the case!"

Nick was getting the strange feeling he knew where he was going. Finally, standing next to Shelby at the top they both looked down at the small beach, three sides protected by high rocks, the western edge open to the Inlet and then the ocean beyond. Breathing heavily, Shelby pointed down at the sand. "Right down there is where they found the bodies." Sitting down on a large rock she opened the case, removed folder number 3, and extracted the three photos. "Chester must have taken the three shots from up here. Look at the first two pictures. It appears that whoever took the photos was standing above those on the beach. And look at the third and final picture. All three boys have turned their heads in this direction like they were surprised."

Nick agreed. "It looks like they were not expecting someone to snap off some pictures."

"That's precisely right and I think that might be the reason Chester was killed. This is just an educated guess, but Chester Finch may have shown up at the wrong time at the wrong place...*and* it may have cost him *his life!"*

Before Shelby realized it, Nick was climbing down to the beach. Standing in the warm sand, he yelled, "Toss me the case and come down. I think I may have been here before, actually...earlier this week!"

Standing next to Nick, Shelby took a deep breath and remarked, "I think climbing down the rocks is harder than climbing up, and what do you mean you think you've been here before?"

Looking up at the wall on the opposite side of the tiny beach, he walked across the sand and stated, "Give me a minute."

Scaling the rocks, he stood at the top and looked out at the Atlantic two hundred yards to the South. "Yep, I was here. If you're up to it, come on up."

Laying the case down, she remarked and stepped up onto the first rock. "When I told you we were going on an island excursion I didn't expect a workout."

Following yet another few moments of physical exertion, Shelby joined Nick at the top of the rocks. Out of breath, she sighed and looked out at the vast ocean and spoke, "Okay, so what am I looking at other than the ocean?"

Pointing, Nick described the landscape. What you're looking at is the Southwest edge of Fripp Island. Out there to the right of where the beach ends is where the ocean meets with Skull Inlet. Notice how the beach curves around and runs parallel to the inlet. That low stone barrier, in all the years I've been coming to Fripp is the farthest I've ever ventured, and for good reason. I always knew if I kept going eventually I'd come out at the turnaround. Last week when I walked up this way from the house, I ventured across that wall and climbed these rocks." Turning, he gestured down at the tiny beach and continued with his explanation, "Do you see that large rock next to the edge of the water?"

Shelby, not quite sure where Nick was headed, answered, "Yes."

"There was a man sitting on that very rock. He just sat there staring out at the inlet. He never even noticed me until I was down the wall and standing in the sand. We greeted each other with a 'Good morning', and had a very pleasant conversation. We talked about how hardly anyone comes down the beach this far, meaning over this wall. He told me he grew up in Beaufort and used to come to this part of the beach a lot as a kid. After graduating from high school, he went away to college and only returned to Beaufort on occasion. One thing led to another and soon we were talking about the RPS Killer. Here's something really weird. Remember the first night after we met on the beach and we met at the Dockside in Port Royal? Turns out this man was there eating that night and witnessed the altercation between myself and Ike Miller. We talked about some other things. I told him I inherited my grandmother's house and he told me he owned a chain of restaurants across the country. Just before we parted ways he mentioned that he wondered if they ever found out who killed that monster…meaning Harold. He was talking about you and didn't even know it. I felt awkward. Just as I was turning to climb back up the wall and be on my way, the man said the strangest thing. He said he was glad the RPS killings were over. Then, he hesitated and said, the one thing we all seem to forget is there is always a reason why a man kills and no one but that man really understands his motive!"

Finished, Nick stared at Shelby, waiting for her reaction. She held her hands out in confusion. "I know you told me that story for a reason, but I don't have a clue what it means."

"I have one more thing to share with you about this strange man, but to get the full impact we have to climb back down to where I met him. Then, you'll understand."

Shelby started back down the rocks. "I sure hope so, because right now I'm clueless!"

Nick jumped the last two feet and landed solidly in the soft sand.

Walking over to the rock near the edge of the water, he motioned for her to follow and offered her a seat on the rock.

Seated, she placed her elbows on her knees and commented, "This sounds like one of those moments when you're about to hear something unpleasant and someone tells you that you better sit down."

Walking to the water's edge Nick looked across the inlet and then back to Shelby. "Well, that's not my intention. I just wanted you to sit on that rock because that's where the man was sitting when we talked." Walking back to the rock wall, Nick pointed up the rocks. "After the man made the odd statement about a man knowing his own motive, I was about halfway up the wall and I yelled back down and told him my first name. And that's when he told me his name. It was Miles!"

Shelby, reacting like the rock were a hot seat, jumped up. "Do you mean to tell me you met Miles Gaston right here on this beach where Abigail and Chester were killed?"

"Take it easy," said Nick. "I'm not saying the man I met was, in fact Miles Gaston, but it just seems odd."

Shelby walked to the briefcase, opened it and removed the high school pictures she had created. She sorted through them until she came to Miles' graduation photograph. Handing the picture to Nick, she asked, "Did this Miles character look like our Miles Gaston?"

Nick looked at the picture and tried his best to recall the man's facial features. "I can't say for sure. It might be. This picture was taken nearly thirty years ago. People change. Without having a recent picture to compare this one to, it's difficult, but I will say this. I think there is a very good chance it may have been Miles Gaston."

Shelby took back the photo, walked to the water, and looked down at the rock. "Okay...let's assume for the moment the man you met was actually Miles Gaston. Why would he come back here to the very spot where he and his two high school football pals may have murdered two of their fellow students?"

"Look," pointed out Nick. "There are a lot more intelligent people in the world than you and me. There are people who have over the years studied human behavior. I think it's safe to say they have concluded that we as people are the most intelligent creatures on the face of the earth. We are also the most unpredictable. You can't tell from one day to the next what we'll think...or even do. So, to answer your question as to why this man, if he is Miles Gaston, would return to the spot where he may have taken part in killing Abigail James and possibly Chester Finch is hard to figure. Maybe he comes here and sits on that rock and prays God will forgive him. Maybe he comes back here because it's the only way he can deal with the day-in day-out memories of what happened right here on this small beach twenty-seven years ago."

Shelby thought about what Nick said and then asked, "Aside from his facial features what did this man, this Miles, look like. How was he dressed?"

Nick thought back to the short time he spent with the man. "If I recall he was dressed rather expensively, at least for the beach. He was dressed in mostly white: white ball hat, powder blue shirt, white sweater, white pants and expensive looking light tan deck shoes. He reminded me of someone who just stepped off a tennis court. He had salt and pepper hair, a small mustache; he was slender. He didn't look anything like someone who at one time played football. He looked...successful."

"You said he mentioned he owned a chain of restaurants. Did he mention the name?"

"He did. I think it was something like Peterson's or Patterson's...no, it was Patterson's...I remember. It was definitely Patterson's." Snapping his fingers, he reached into his pocket and took out his wallet, opened it and began to search for something. "I forgot all about it, but he gave me one of his business cards and told me if I presented this at one of his restaurants it would entitle me to a free drink and complimentary dessert. Here it is. Patterson's Restaurants Inc. He told me he had locations in both Savannah and Charleston, but they were under a different name. I think he said he had forty-three Patterson locations, the closest in Atlanta."

Reaching for the card, Shelby examined it. "Yes, here are the names in Savannah and Charleston. The Savannah and the Upper Deck." Flipping the card over, she discovered the back was blank. Handing the card back, she asked, "Do you remember anything else about this Miles?"

"No, not really. He seemed like a nice person. He offered to drop me off back at my house, but I told him I wanted to take another swim. He told me he was packing later that day for a flight out to the west coast and then down to Florida. He also mentioned he had homes out in Sacramento and down in Palm Beach."

Shelby walked over and picked up the case. "Things certainly turned out differently than what I thought they would this morning. I thought the information I had discovered was going to be, well...big news compared to what we already knew." Turning, she pointed toward the rock, "But this...the fact you may have met one of the three boys who may have killed the James girl and the Finch kid is mind blowing!"

Looking around the small beach, Nick asked, "Is there anything else we need to discuss before we head back to the Jeep?"

Walking over to the rock wall she sat down and opened the case. "Yes there is something else. We need to examine the new 12 x 14 photos I created and see if the medallion in the three beach photos matches the one Abigail is wearing in her graduation picture."

Placing the three enlargements on top of the rock, she grabbed the magnifying glass and examined the picture closely. Removing the photograph of Abigail's graduation picture, she remarked, "I don't know if these larger photos will make a difference or not. It looks like the medallion is the same size as the one in the graduation picture but I still can't see an inscription on the enlargement." Handing Nick the glass, she suggested, "Here, you take a look."

Nick leaned over and squinted though the glass. "You're right. The medallion itself does appear to be the same size, but you still can't see the inscription, that is if there even is one. Myself, I'm leaning toward the fact they're the same. The girl in the enlargement in my opinion is Abigail James. I mean, who else could it be?"

Putting everything back inside the case, Shelby walked to the base of the rock wall and looked up. "I guess we've done just about everything we can here today. Let's head back up."

Halfway up, she stopped and looked back down at Nick who was just beginning to climb. "Ya know what, Nick? I think maybe we should just turn over the photos and the camera to the police and let them figure this whole thing out."

Three rocks up the side, Nick stopped and shrugged. "I suppose we could do that, but what fun would that be? Besides, if we turn over the camera and the developed pictures to the authorities, that doesn't mean all of a sudden after all these years they are going to solve the case. The only thing the pictures prove is Brad Schulte, Tim Durham and Miles Gaston were on a beach somewhere with a dead girl that may or may not be Abigail James. There is still no proof they, in fact, did kill Abigail and Chester. I do agree with you about going to the police, but we don't hand over the camera or even mention the film we developed."

"If we are not going to turn everything we've discovered over to them, then why would we even go to them?"

"To find out what they knew…back then."

"We can do that without going to the police," pointed out Shelby. "We could go to the Beaufort Public Library and look up all the newspaper articles from back in 1989 and find out what they knew."

"Maybe…maybe not! Do you think the police always give the press every shred of evidence they have. There may still be someone around on the force who remembers the case and would be willing to talk with us."

"But why would they talk to us?"

"Simple," said Nick as he stepped up over the last rock. "We utilize your idea of writing a book just like we did at the high school. Once that woman was convinced we were actually doing research on a book we were going to write she couldn't have been move helpful. I say we just walk into police headquarters and tell them we are considering writing a book on past unsolved murders here in Beaufort County. All they can do is tell us the information is not available and even if they do, then we can still go to the library. We don't have anything to lose. I think it'll be fun. Whadda ya say?"

Starting down the path, Shelby held up the case, "I don't know how much fun it'll be walking into police headquarters, all the while with information we really should turn over to them, which according to you, we are not going to do just yet. Let's just say I agree with this. When would we go?"

"Today…why wait? If we get down there and it turns out they are not going to reveal to us what happened…then, if we want we can turn over what we have. I'm sure we'll have to answer some questions, but eventually we'll be on our merry way. I think it's worth a shot."

Shelby stopped, turned and looked back at Nick. "All right…I'm game! We've come this far. I guess I'm not really ready to throw the towel in just yet."

"It's a go then," said Nick. "Let's drive back to my place first. We can get cleaned up from our trip up here to the beach. Then, we'll head over to Beaufort."

Nick parked the Lexus on the street just down from police headquarters. Getting out, Shelby held up the briefcase and asked, "Do I look like a writer?"

Holding up the legal pad and pen he was carrying, Nick responded, "Yeah, ya do. And even if we don't, remember what you said. We can get in anywhere and talk with anyone as long as they are convinced we are writing a book. Let's go on in and see what happens."

Pausing on the front steps, they looked up at the bold address on the front of the building. BEAUFORT POLICE DEPARTMENT – 911 BOUNDARY STREET. Nick joked while they walked up the steps. "I've never been in a police station before. How about you?"

"Just once," said Shelby. "Back when I was in grade school we came down here on a field trip. Aside from that…no."

Entering the main doors they walked down a short hallway and stopped at a reception desk. Seated behind the cluttered desk sat a younger, uniformed female officer. Smiling at Nick and Shelby, she pleasantly greeted them, "Good afternoon. What can we do for you?"

Nick held up his notepad and attached pen. "We were wondering if someone here in the department could give us some information on a double murder that occurred back in 1989?"

The officer gave them a funny look and then doing some quick math in her head responded, "So, you're interested in some murders that took place…twenty-seven years ago?"

Shelby, stepped forward, held up the briefcase, and nodded at Nick. "Mr. Falco and myself are collaborating on a book we are considering writing. The book is about past unsolved murders here in Beaufort County."

Again, Nick raised his notepad and pen for effect and added, "Yes, and we are quite interested in that particular murder…back in 1989."

The officer shook her head like she understood but then commented, "I've only been with the force for three years. I wasn't even born when these murders you speak of were committed. Just let me call Lieutenant Pierce. He's been on the force for a quite a long time. He might be able to help you." Turning to a phone, she excused herself and in a muffled tone spoke to someone. Facing them once again, she spoke, "Lieutenant Pierce said he'd be right out if you would care to have a seat over there on that bench."

Sitting on the uncomfortable bench, Shelby leaned over and whispered, "So far so good!"

Within seconds an older man dressed in an impeccable uniform stepped out into the hallway and introduced himself, "My name is Lieutenant Pierce. I understand you're interested in some past murders in, I believe if I was told correctly…1989, to be specific."

Shelby was the first to speak. "That is correct. We are doing research for a book we're going to write."

Pierce looked at Nick and then back to Shelby and explained, "You do understand those two murders have never been solved. After all these years it still remains a cold case."

Shelby confirmed his statement. "Yes, we are aware of that fact. Is there some sort of problem with us having interest in the murders?"

"No, it's just most of the force employed here may not be aware of those particular murders. They happened nearly three decades ago. I remember those murders. I was just a rookie that year. The truth is there is probably no one here you could sit down with and talk to about the murders. You have two options. The first is you could look at and examine all the documentation we have filed away on those murders. That is not something, especially with a case that in all actuality is still on the books, which can easily be done. No one is just going to drop a lot of pictures and folders filled with information down in front of you and say, 'Go for it!' You may have to answer some questions, get official approval. A cold case is something the department, or any police department for that matter is not proud of. We are in the business of not only preventing crime but also solving crimes that are committed. This crime was never solved. The department may not be enthused about two people, in this case, you folks digging into information we for some reason could not figure out."

Nick spoke up. "Doesn't sound very promising. Maybe we should just forget this."

Sitting on the bench, Pierce reminded them, "Remember, I said there were two options. The second is you could talk with someone who is no longer on the force, but who worked on the case. The two detectives who worked that case are now both retired. One lives right here in Beaufort County and I think the other one moved down to Florida somewhere. I don't know if either one of them would be willing to sit down with the two of you or not."

Shelby politely asked, "And who are these detectives?"

"The two detectives who worked that case are Jim Silk and Melvin Barrett. Barrett is the one who still lives here in the area. I think he has a home out on Dataw Island."

Nick inquired, "Could you supply us with his phone number. I mean do you have it?"

"I'm sure we do, but department policy dictates we are not permitted to give out personal information. I think if you take the time you'll find Melvin's phone number is listed in the phone book. You could give the former detective a call and see how it goes. Like I said, there is no guarantee he'll talk to you, but It's worth a try." Pierce stood, a silent message their brief meeting had come to an end.

Nick stood and extended his hand. "Thank you very much. You've been most kind and quite helpful."

Shelby shook his hand as well, but remained silent when Pierce spoke up, "Good luck with your book!"

Outside, at the bottom of the steps, Shelby let out a long breath. "I didn't, until this very moment realize how nervous I was in there."

"I know what you mean," said Nick. "It's almost like we're keeping something from them; something that's not ours *to keep!* The more I think about this the more I'm thinking we should have just turned over the camera and the film to the police."

"Well, maybe we will, but not just yet. I am of the opinion we still have a ways to go and until that point arrives I'm not willing to give up. Do you agree, because if you don't, then we need to just forget about all this and let the police handle it?"

"I'm not ready to give up either. At least for right now. Let's give this Detective Barrett a call and see if he'll talk with us. I think you should make the call. A female voice may come off as being more convincing over the phone. Let's get a phone book and see if we can locate his number."

Using a phone book at a small gift shop up the street, Shelby ran her fingers down over the residents with the last names starting with the letter B. Much to her surprise there it was. Melvin Barrett, his address and phone number. Pointing at the small lettering, she spoke to Nick, "Here, write this down so we can give him a call."

Seated once again in the Lexus, Shelby punched in the number and waited as she looked across the seat at Nick. On the fifth ring, a female voice answered, "This is the Barrett's."

Assuming the voice was that of the wife, Shelby inquired, "Is this Mrs. Barrett?"

"Yes …it is. Who may I ask is calling?"

Shelby cleared her voice and then answered, "My name is Shelby Lee Pickett. I live in Beaufort. A Lieutenant Pierce from the Beaufort Police Department suggested I give your husband, Melvin a call in regard to some research my partner and I are doing for a book on some past unsolved murders in Beaufort County. It was suggested Detective Barrett might be willing to talk with us."

"Ah….he is outside at the moment. If you'll hold on I'll get him."

"Thank you," said Shelby to no one, since Mrs. Barrett had already laid the phone down.

Looking again at Nick, Shelby flashed him a smile of hope and stated, "That was Mrs. Barrett. She's getting him to the phone."

Nick was about to say something but was cut off when Shelby held up her hand for silence when a voice on the other end, spoke, "This is Melvin Barrett. My wife informs me you would like to talk to me about some past Beaufort County murders; that you're doing research for a book?"

"That's correct, sir. My friend and I would like very much to sit down with you for a few minutes and ask you some questions, that is, if you have the time."

Barrett laughed, "Now that I'm retired I have nothing but time. When would you like to get together?"

"Today if it's not too inconvenient."

"Today would be fine. I don't have anything on my calendar. Do you know where I live?"

"Not really. I got your address from the phone book but I'm not familiar with the street."

"I live out on Dataw Island. What time today would you like to drop by?"

"We're in Beaufort right now. We could be over to Dataw in twenty minutes. Would that be all right?"

"That would be fine. I need a break anyway. My wife has me doing yard work today, which I hate. Dataw is a gated community. I'll call down and let them know to be expecting you. If you ask at the gate they can give you directions to our home. See you soon."

Shelby spoke while she placed the phone back into her purse. "Barrett said he would meet with us. He's expecting us within the next twenty minutes or so."

Nick couldn't believe how easy it had been. "This book writing ruse really works! Let's drive out to Dataw and meet this Melvin Barrett."

"Shelby fastened her seatbelt. "And on the way we need to discuss what we want to ask him."

Pulling up to the Dataw Island gate, Nick rolled down his window and spoke to the man behind a window in a guard shack. "My name is Mr. Falco and this is Shelby Pickett. We have an appointment to see a Mr. Melvin Barrett."

"The guard looked at a clipboard hanging in the small office and then stated, "Yes, he just called. Do you know where the house is? He informed us you might need directions."

Looking across the seat, Shelby spoke up, "Yes that would be very helpful."

Stepping out of the shack, the guard pointed up the long paved road and explained, "Follow this road until you come to the first right. Take that; it runs right next to the golf course. Barrett lives in the fourth house on the left. It's a green ranch with a red tile roof. Welcome to Dataw. Have a nice day."

Driving up the paved road flanked on either side with professionally manicured green grass and dotted with a number of ponds, Nick commented, "I've never been over here to Dataw before. My grandmother always used to say this community is designed around the golf course and most of the people who live here enjoy playing golf."

"I was here once when I was younger with my parents," said Shelby. "My family had to attend an event following a wedding. I think the restaurant we went to was called Sweetgrass. The food and the atmosphere were nice. I remember I enjoyed myself." Pointing to the right, she continued, "I think this is the turn the guard was referring to."

Making the turn, Nick commented when they passed the first few houses. "The lots are really big. It's really nice here but I think I prefer Fripp better. Fripp just seems to be a more natural setting."

"There's the house," said Shelby. "Green ranch with red tiled roof."

Pulling into a circular driveway, Nick looked out the front windshield at the far end of the house where there was a large attached glassed-in room that housed a swimming pool. "Detectives must make pretty good money."

They no sooner stepped out of the car than a slender man with a crew cut appeared at the front door and waved. "Hello," he shouted. "I hope you didn't have any problems finding the place."

Shelby followed Nick as they walked across some red and gray staggered pavers that led to the six-foot wide, oak, double entry doors. The man stuck out his hand. "Melvin Barrett...welcome to my home. Please come in. My wife is in the process of making some iced tea." Guiding them through a hallway with cherry hardwood flooring and expensive beige stucco walls, Melvin led them out to a screened-in porch overlooking the golf course. They were just seated when Mrs. Barrett entered the room with a glass container of tea and four tall glasses. Mr. Barrett introduced his wife," This is my wife, Nel, and this young lady is surely the one we talked with on the phone, Shelby Lee Pickett. Actually, I know your father. He has done some plumbing work for us in the past at our marina. I'm on the repair committee. Your father came highly recommended."

Nick introduced himself, "Nick Falco...nice to meet you both."

Pouring tea in all four glasses, Nel looked at Nick and smiled broadly. "Don't tell me you're Amelia's grandson?"

"That I am," said Nick proudly.

Placing a glass in front of Shelby, she continued to speak, "Your grandmother was the nicest lady I think I've ever met. We worked together on a number of fundraisers here in the county. I was so sorry to hear about her death. I heard you inherited her home over on Fripp."

Nick humbly answered, "Yes, I did."

Once everyone had tea, Nel excused herself, but Melvin insisted she stay. "My wife is an avid reader. I believe you said you were doing research for a book you are writing. I wouldn't think of having her leave. Besides that, there is nothing about my past work as a detective she is not aware of. I guess you could say I always had a bad habit of bringing my work home."

Nel took a seat and sweetened her tea while Melvin focused on Shelby, "I'm to understand the book you're working on is about past unsolved murders here in Beaufort County."

"That's correct, Mr. Barrett," said Shelby.

Melvin held up his large calloused hands. "Please refer to me as Melvin. I had enough of that Mr. Barrett business when I was employed by the Beaufort Police Department." Taking a sip of tea, he stated, "The number of unsolved murders in Beaufort County are and always have been at a minimum. There are only three I can recall. Back in '92 there was a killing at a small trailer court on Lady's Island and a shooting along the Sea Island Parkway the year before that. The most frustrating unsolved murders we've had here in the county happened back in 1989 when two students were found murdered on Fripp Island."

Shelby opened her briefcase for effect and removed a small pad and pen. "That's the case we have questions about. It seems since it happened such a long time ago a lot of folks have forgotten all about those murders."

"I haven't forgotten them. Jim Silk, that's the other detective who worked on the case. Jim and I worked that case for a solid year after it happened. Here it is twenty-seven years gone by and there isn't a week that goes by I don't think about that case. As a detective, what happens one day is eventually replaced with a new set of circumstances on another case, which tends to take your mind off what happened in the past. But the case of those two students found out there on Fripp will always haunt me." Realizing he was rambling, he apologized, "I'm sorry, but when it comes to that particular case I think I could discuss it for days. There are so many questions that were not answered. So, what is it you would like to know about the case?"

Nick spoke up, "Now you've thrown us for a loop with your statement about how you could discuss this case for days. Maybe we've bitten off more than we can chew here."

"Why don't we do this," suggested Melvin. "You ask me questions and I'll try to answer them the best I can. Sound fair?"

"That's sounds more than fair," chimed in Shelby. "Let's start off with when the bodies were actually discovered. How did that go down?"

"According to the three men who found the bodies it was early Sunday morning around seven o'clock just after the sun came up. These men were out on Skull Inlet trying to get an early start to their day of fishing, when one of them spots what appears to be two bodies lying on the beach. They motor on over there and discover the bodies of Abigail James and Chester Finch. They contacted Fripp Island Security, who contacted us and we were on the scene thirty-five minutes later."

Nick asked the next question. "What did you find when you arrived?"

"The bodies had not been touched by anyone. We found the James girl clad in her undergarments and the Finch kid was fully clothed. We also found on the beach back against the rocks, a purse and female clothing belonging to the James girl. There was three hundred and fifteen dollars lying in the sand and floating around just off the beach. Later in the week another ninety dollars was found further up Skull Inlet. The medical examiner showed up about an hour after we got there and hauled the bodies back to Beaufort for examination."

Shelby, writing down short notes asked, "What were the results of the medical examination?"

"The M.E. squashed what we thought actually happened. With the James girl being practically naked we thought it was a crime of passion, a sexual assault of some sort. This was ruled out because there was not a shred of evidence indicating sexual activity. There was no semen on or inside the girl's vagina. There was no DNA from either body on the other body. So, that led us to believe there was no sexual contact between the two victims."

"How did they actually die? What was the cause of death?"

"That was something else that threw us for a loop. The James girl died from being beaten to death with a wooden object. The M.E. claimed fragments of wood were found imbedded in the girl's skull. At first we thought maybe a piece of driftwood had been used, but we were quickly corrected. The fragments indicated the wood used was white pine; maybe something like a two by four anyone could purchase at a lumber store. But this white pine was weird. It was waterlogged, like it had been in the ocean for some time. The girl was hit a number of times until she breathed her last. Now, the Finch kid was also beaten with the same section of wood, but only hit a few times. He did not die because of a beating, but he was drowned. There were bruises around the back of his neck area indicating someone held him under while he struggled to free himself."

"I'm confused," said Shelby. "When you consider the tide probably came in during the time the two bodies laid on the beach, wouldn't they both have their lungs filled with water?"

"That's what we thought too, but the M.E. explained when the tide rises, if a body is on the beach, by the time the water gets high enough to enter a person's mouth or nose, the body floats. There was some seawater in the girl's lungs but the Finch boy was filled to capacity. He was drown, she was not!"

"What about the victims' cars," asked Nick as he clicked his ink pen?

"Melvin sipped at his tea. "That's when things really started to get confusing. We located Chester Finch's car at the first parking space up on the turnaround at the end of Tarpon Blvd. It had been backed in, but for some reason was up over top of a log barrier. I can't imagine Finch parking his car like that. We considered maybe he was trying to leave quickly and accidentally backed over the log. We dusted the car for prints and found nothing. We felt we would find Chester's prints all over the car since he owned it. There wasn't a single print anywhere on that car. Someone wiped the interior and the exterior completely down."

"Who would have done that…and why?" asked Shelby.

"Someone who didn't want us to find out they were in or near Chester's car…probably the killers."

Nick spoke up, "You said killers…not killer, like you feel there was more than one person who committed this crime."

Melvin smiled. "You should consider becoming a detective, Mr. Falco. I'm surprised you noticed that. That being said, we're getting a little ahead in the story here. I'll explain why we think there may have been multiple killers in a minute or so." Moving on, Barrett explained, "Later that morning we found the James' girl's car…a little sports car parked on the side of the Sea Island Parkway on Lady's Island. It was sitting on the side of the road with the hood up. The keys to the car were found in her purse on the beach. We tried to start the car but it was dead. We figured with the hood up, she probably had car troubles. We dusted her car for prints and found her fingerprints all over the interior, which made sense. When we dusted the engine, the driver's side door and the hood, we found two more sets of prints. At the time we didn't know who they belonged to, but soon we found out."

Nick, his pen poised in his right hand, asked, "Whose prints were they?"

"Now hold on," said Melvin. "You're getting a little ahead of the way things panned out. The following Monday, just two days after the murders we decided to interview every student at Beaufort High: freshman, sophomores, juniors and seniors. It didn't make any difference. We even interviewed the teachers. We talked with everyone at the school, whether they attended the party on Fripp Island the night of the murders or not. We figured someone had to know something or heard something. It was still early in the investigation, but still, we had no murder weapon, no motive and no witnesses. We didn't have anything to go on accept those prints on the girl's car. I'll get back to those in a minute."

Nick spoke up again, "It must have taken a long time to interview everyone at the school."

"It took Jim and me a solid week to talk with everyone. The interviews per student only lasted about ten minutes or so, but we did glean some valuable information that changed our initial theories. We found out the *only thing* the James girl and the Finch kid had in common was they were both brilliant. She was going to be attending school at

Cornell University and he had been accepted at Harvard. The victims, as it turned out, were the smartest in the school…by far. The James girl came from money and was, according to most of the students, spoiled rotten. She liked to sleep around and had quite the reputation. Most of the female students did not like her and most of the male students *did like her!* Thirty-seven male students admitted to having a sexual encounter with Abigail James over the years at school. Turns out she slept with every player on the football team…except for three. When asked about the probability of Abigail and Chester hooking up sexually, the students ruled that out since Chester was a known virgin and the only thing he was in love with was his camera. He was always taking photographs around the school. The thought of he and the James girl hooking up was ridiculous and would never happen!"

Shelby tapped her pen on top of the table and asked, "So you came away from the school interviews and still had no suspects?"

"That's right," said Melvin, "but we did have some persons of interest. The three football players Abigail never had sex with, Brad Schulte, Tim Durham and…"

Shelby cut the former detective off, "Miles Gaston!"

Surprised, Melvin smiled. "I see you two have been doing your homework."

"We have," said Shelby. "This morning we were over at Fripp Island at the previous murder scene where Chester's car was found. It's no secret those three boys were, and today still are thought to be the killers by many people in the area. It's not talked about that much but when someone brings the subject up, people point their finger right at those boys and claim they got away with murder."

"I know a lot of folks feel that way," remarked Melvin. "But the law is the law and those three boys were never even arrested, convicted or served time. Then again, there are many people around these parts who feel there is no way those three lads could have committed those murders. These kids were squeaky clean. They all came from fairly religious families, they were good students, never got into any trouble, in or out of school. They were looked upon as heroes…football heroes…state high school champions. They all went off to college and I've heard they are all quite successful."

Nick inquired, "Why were these three particular boys singled out as persons of interest?"

"During the school interviews, two out of the three boys acted quite nervous. Schulte, who I initially interviewed, was nervous, but overall, cool as a cucumber but the other two didn't fare as well. Jim interviewed the Durham kid and the Gaston boy. They all claimed on their way out to Fripp they had run into the James girl and she had car problems. They tried to get her car started, failed and wound up giving her a lift out to Fripp. They said they dropped her off at the pool, parked their car and then never saw her again that night. None of the students or faculty members at the party ever saw her anywhere near the festivities. We verified the boys had taken her to Fripp. The gate guard on Fripp said he saw three boys in a red Mustang with Abigail when they passed through security.

"Days passed and we were getting nowhere when we discovered a glass bottle neck at the murder scene. It turned out to be a Bourbon bottle. The bottle had been smashed and the only part of the bottle we found was the upper part of the bottle. We found saliva DNA that indicated Abigail James had drunk from the bottle. There was DNA from another person on the bottle who we could not identify. I can tell you this, it wasn't that of Chester Finch. We interviewed those three boys four times; even took samples of their DNA. That's when we discovered the other person who had been drinking from the bottle was none other than Miles Gaston. This was odd because we asked the boys if they had been drinking that night and they all said, *'No.'*

"So you caught them in a lie," said Shelby.

"Indeed, we did! We decided to put some pressure on the Gaston kid. He broke down and told us that Brad and Tim and he had been drinking. According to him, Brad took a bottle from his father's liquor cabinet and brought it along to celebrate the fact that they were state champions. They lied about drinking because they didn't want to get in trouble with their parents. We then asked the Gaston kid how his DNA showed up on the broken bottle down on the beach. He told us when they dropped Abigail off at the pool that she took the bottle with her. He said they both had been in the backseat drinking on the way to Fripp."

"Let me get this straight," said Nick. "That bottle was the only proof linking the boys to the beach and now even that wasn't panning out."

"No, we had some other clues that loomed as suspicious. When the James girl pulled over to the side of the road earlier in the evening with car troubles there was a Hunting Island Park Ranger up the street getting gas at a station. He saw the James girl and was about to go and see if she needed help but then this red Mustang; Brad Schulte's car pulled up. Now, here's the thing. All three boys said they had tried to get her car started. The state park officer said he only saw two boys looking under the hood. The fingerprints we found on the engine of her car were that of Brad Schulte and the Durham kid. So, where was Miles Gaston while all this was going on? Later, in an interview Miles admitted he was in the back of the Mustang passed out. Nothing was discovered when we dusted Brad's car for prints of the girl. The car had been completely cleaned. What was strange was there were traces of bleach in the trunk. Bleach is commonly used to eradicate traces of blood. All in all things were starting to stack up against these boys. They were the last ones to see her alive and the Gaston kid was a bundle of nerves. Still, we didn't have enough to arrest them. The investigation went on for weeks. Before we knew it, it was June and the boys all graduated. The investigation continued on through the summer and by the time the boys went off to college we were left holding the bag. We still had an unsolved double murder on the books. No murder weapon, no motive…nothing. It still stands as unsolved today."

Shelby frowned. "Is the case officially closed? I mean, let's just say these boys did kill Abigail James and Chester Finch. Can they never be brought to justice?"

"A cold case is never closed, especially when murder, or in this case, two murders are involved. There is no statute of limitations on murder. If someone were to come forward or something suddenly surfaced that proved these boys are guilty, they could still be brought to justice. To tell you the truth, I think that ship has long sailed. I don't think we'll ever know the truth about what happened out there on Fripp twenty-seven years ago. I think for the most part, people have moved on with their lives and have forgotten about Abigail James and Chester Finch. It's sad, but that's life."

Shaking his head in wonder, Melvin finished his tea and then stated, "Let me rephrase that last comment. Not everyone has forgotten. Bernard P. James, Abigail's father will no doubt take his daughter's death to his grave. During the investigation he was down at headquarters every day demanding we tell him what we were doing and what we had discovered. Finally, we had to tell him to back off. He was becoming a real pain in our ass! He wanted those boys arrested, convicted and sentenced to the death penalty. When he found out the case had gone cold, he decided to hire a local attorney, Khelen Ridley."

Nick immediately spoke up, "Khelen Ridley! I know him well. He was my grandparents' attorney for years. He just helped me to purchase a house down on Fripp. Actually, you're not going to believe this, but the house I purchased belonged to Chester Finch's grandmother."

Mrs. Barrett laughed, "You know what they say about it being a small world!"

Melvin picked up where he had left off. "Khelen refused to represent Mr. James, telling him it was a case he could not win. As far as Khelen was concerned the police had done everything in their power to solve those murders but they just didn't have the proof to bring those three boys down. Bernard P. James has more money than there are grains of sand on the beach. He wasn't about to give up. He hired another local attorney by the name of Charles Brumly."

Nick interrupted, "You mean Chic Brumly!"

Melvin surprised, finished his tea and asked, "You sound like you know ol' Chic."

"I don't know the man personally, but I have had some dealings with him. In my opinion he can't hold a candle to Khelen Ridley."

Melvin stood. "Well, that about sums everything up. I've got to get back to my yard work. I hope I've been of some help to you."

"One last question," said Shelby. "And this is off the record. In your opinion do you feel these three boys committed those murders?"

"Yes, yes I do. But until someone comes up with better proof than what we had things will remain as they are. I think bringing those three boys in for murder…well, I don't think we'll see that day"

Getting up and closing her briefcase, Shelby pushed for another question, "Do you know what happened to the boys. Where they are today or what they do for a living?"

"No, but I can tell you who does know. Lu Ann Dawson. She was Tim Durham's girlfriend back when the murders happened. I believe they dated all through high school. She wound up marrying a police officer up in Beaufort. I know she lives in Beaufort. She heads up the 1989 reunion class so she has to keep tabs on all the previous students. If anyone could tell you what those three boys are up to these days, she'd be the one."

Mrs. Barrett jumped up and offered, "Just let me look in our phone book. Maybe I can get her number and address for you."

Seated at the bar at Steamers, Nick downed a shot of Wild Turkey, followed by a swig of draft beer. Shelby nursed her mixed drink and commented, "Well, now that we have Tim Durham's ex-girlfriend's number, do you think we should give her a call?"

"Yes, I do, but not today. Maybe tomorrow. I've had enough today. We've learned a lot. I think we need to take the rest of this evening and figure out what we've found out before we decide on our next move. Nick held up his empty beer glass and spoke to the bartender, "Can we get another round here?"

CHAPTER SIXTEEN

THE GRANDFATHER CLOCK CHIMED THE TIME AT THREE IN the morning. Nick opened his eyes and they slowly adjusted them to the dim light coming from the kitchen. Sitting up on the couch, his head in his hands, he had a throbbing headache. His neck and shoulders were stiff from sleeping on the couch. He was still wearing the clothes he had worn the previous day. He felt like his head was going to explode.

Standing slowly, he braced himself with the arm of the couch and once he had his bearings made his way down the hall to the downstairs bathroom, where he opened the medicine cabinet, took down a plastic bottle of aspirin, threw two of the tiny pink tablets inside his mouth and downed them with a glass of tap water. He stared at his haggard reflection in the vanity mirror. The face that stared back at him was not a pretty picture. Splashing cold water across his face, he soaked a washcloth with the cool water, wrapped it around his neck and walked into the kitchen. Removing a bottle of cold water from the fridge, he went back into the living room, plopped down in an easy chair, and stared at the clock, 3:15.

Holding the cold bottle against his forehead he thought about how he and Shelby had stayed far too long at Steamers, sitting at the bar, drinking and discussing everything they had discovered about the murders of Abigail James and Chester Finch. He hadn't gotten home until just after ten o'clock. He remembered standing at the bottom of the staircase and looking up the steps. His alcohol soaked brain erased any thoughts of climbing the stairs so he had opted for the couch. That was five hours ago. He needed more sleep, but at the moment, just wanted some fresh air to clear his head.

Walking out the backdoor, he crossed the yard and dirt road, climbed the steps on the small deck and sat, staring out at the dark Atlantic. The breeze from the ocean felt invigorating. Far out at sea, he saw an orange and red glow in the distance. A storm was on the way.

The last thing Shelby had said to him when they parted ways was she was not going to call him until after lunch. She had to go to work in Savannah and was going to call LuAnn Dawson to see if they could set up a meeting with her later in the evening. He thought about some of the things Melvin Barrett had shared with he and Shelby. He could see why people thought Brad, Tim and Miles were guilty. The broken bottle found at the murder scene with not only Abigail James DNA prevalent, but Miles' as well, meant he was probably there on the beach. He *knew* he was on the beach. He and Shelby had photos proving that. Barrett explained that Miles said they had given the bottle to Abigail when they dropped her off near the pool on Fripp. That, now, appeared to be a lie. And what about traces of bleach found in the trunk of Schulte's car. Both Chester's car and Brad's car had been cleaned of prints before the police got to them. It sounded like someone was trying to cover their tracks. One of the last things Barrett said was he felt those three boys committed the murders, but it would never be proven. Did he and Shelby have the proof that the three boys were involved? Would the twenty-seven year old pictures be enough to bring the three to justice? Who was he kidding? These three former high school football stars were no longer boys. They were now grown men, maybe with families of their own.

At 4:15 he decided to take a swim. Stepping down into the sand he stripped naked and walked toward the cold Atlantic water. He had never swum in the ocean in the buff before. He looked up and down the beach realizing he was breaking the law, but who in their right mind would be on the beach this early.

The tide was still out so it was a long walk before he was standing on wet sand. As the first cold wave of ocean water swept up and over his toes, he realized that once in the water he wasn't going to spend too much time swimming. Besides the icy water, the wind was also discomforting. Looking up at the sky there was not a star to be seen. The rapidly moving cloud cover occasionally broke up allowing the moonlight to filter down on the beach. Standing there he was having second thoughts about venturing out into the dark, murky water as he was beginning to shiver. *It's now or never!* He thought. Taking the first step into the ankle deep water, he noticed a set of headlights suddenly flash on when a vehicle entered the beach access road fifty yards to his left. The vehicle was coming in his direction. He had no time to run back across the beach. Running for deeper water, the lights engulfed him. Diving under a wave he swam underwater until he could no longer hold his breath. He slowly surfaced and saw a floodlight scanning back and forth across the water. When the light swung back in his direction, he took a deep breath and went back under.

Beneath the freezing water, he thought, *Who could it be? Surely it wasn't Brumly this early in the morning.* Then it came to him. *Fripp Island Security.* It was probably nothing more than a routine beach check, except for the fact they had seen a naked man dash into the ocean. If he were caught he would most likely be arrested. Swimsuits were a must on the beach, even in the middle of the night.

Slowly he resurfaced and noticed the beam of light farther down the beach. Swimming back toward land, he noticed the headlights when they swung around and headed back down the beach in his direction. Not having enough time to run across the flat sand to his house, he dove back into the water and swam back out, going under. If it were security, eventually they would have to give up and move on up the beach. *The sooner the better!* He thought. *I'm freezing!*

Surfacing again, the lights were back up the beach going away from where he was. Swimming as fast as his arms and legs would propel him, he was soon standing in knee deep water at which point he awkwardly ran to the beach and then across the sand, the brisk wind tearing at his wet body. By the time he got to the deck he was shivering. Grabbing his clothes, he ran across the deck, across his yard and into the house. Going into the living room he wrapped himself in a large handmade afghan his grandmother had knitted and curled up on the couch and watched a flash of lightning streak across the dark sky, followed by raindrops beating against the picture window. Between the warmth of the afghan and the sound of the rain, he soon drifted off to sleep, his headache no longer an issue.

The grandfather clock once again woke him, but this time it was seven o'clock. Wrapped in the afghan, he walked to the large window and stared out at the pouring rain. He was wide awake now. There was no need for a shower. The frigid dip in the Atlantic had cleansed his body. Tossing the afghan on the couch, he went up the stairs and threw on his painting clothes. He had five hours before Shelby said she was going to call. He could be at the rental on Deer Lake in thirty minutes. He could probably knock out at least two rooms before noon. Grabbing a couple of waters and a stale donut from the counter, he walked out to the garage and loaded up the trunk of the Lexus. Normally he would have taken the golf cart, but since it was still pouring out, the car made more sense. Placing three one gallon cans of eggshell white paint, two large drop clothes, can opener, paint tray, stir stick, paint thinner, 3-pack of medium nap rollers, extension pole and three brushes in the trunk, he opened the garage door and backed out, only to find two garbage men standing at the side of the driveway as they peered into the garage. "Sorry!" said one of the overall-clad men. "We didn't see any cans set out today."

Nick apologized, "I forgot today was garbage pickup. I'll just wait and set them out next week." Both men nodded and walked to the end of the drive where their truck was parked. Nick followed them up Tarpon and turned off at Deer Lake.

Pulling into 311 he parked under the house and after two trips up the front steps, finally had everything unloaded on the front porch. The guttering at the far end of the porch was overflowing. That was something he was going to have repaired. Reaching for the keys to the house he noticed Carson when he pulled up in his car. Hopping out, he raced up the steps with two steaming cups of coffee in his hands. Handing a cup to Nick he set the other on the porch railing and wiped his face with a handkerchief he removed from his coat pocket. “Man, it’s really coming down out there!”

Gesturing with the coffee, Nick probed, “I’m sure you just didn’t drop by to deliver a hot coffee to me.”

“You’re right…I decided to drop by and see if you’d be over here and since I was up at the marina store I picked us up some coffee.” Lifting the lid from his cup, he pulled the collar of his jacket up around his neck and looked back out at the intense rain. “It’s kind of a coffee day out right now.” Turning back to Nick, Carson took a seat on a wicker chair and kept right on talking, “I tried to call you three times yesterday, but you didn’t answer.”

Nick apologized, “I’m sorry, I didn’t even check to see if I had any messages. So, what’s up?”

“Two things: one is important, the other not so important. I called a close friend of mine who is on the up and up on who knows who in New York. He found out Charley Sparks does indeed have a sister. She’s pretty well off as far as money goes, but other than that doesn’t seem to be much of a threat to anyone. The other thing he found out is in regard to the phone number you found in her purse. It happens to be a direct line to our ol’ nemesis, Joseph Carnahan.”

Nick sat on a porch swing and pumped his fist. “Just like I thought. She is working for the Carnahans. She was sent here by them to see if what we told them about Charley and Derek is the truth.”

“We can’t be absolutely sure of that. She may know of him through her brother, but I’m leaning toward the fact she’s a plant. So far, you’ve managed to stick to our original story. She’s probably in contact with the Carnahans on a daily basis. As long as we don’t change our story, she’ll just reinforce what they already know; that Charley and Derek took off with their millions. The fact she is here in the Lowcountry keeping an eye on you could really bolster you and I as being truthful with the Carnahans. I realize Chic Brumly and the Sparks woman have really been a pain in the ass, but if we remain patient and go on with our lives as if nothing other than what we told Carnahan is going on, eventually, this will all go away. I have no doubt the Carnahans, after this blows over, will finally close the books on their lost money. I called your grandmother this morning and updated her on Brumly and the woman. She is concerned, but I assured her, that for now she has nothing to worry about."

Swallowing some of the hot coffee, Carson explained further, "That was the important topic I wanted to discuss with you. The unimportant issue is about these missing golf carts. Brumly, the bastard he is, has gone not only to Fripp Island Security but the Beaufort police as well and has strongly suggested Grady Phillips is responsible for the thefts."

Nick almost choked on his drink. "You've...got to...be...kidding me!"

"That's what Chief Lysinger said too. It doesn't make any sense Grady would be involved in something as petty as stealing golf carts."

"Why would Brumly accuse Mr. Phillips of something like that? Does he have any proof?"

"To answer your first question why? I have no doubt it's just his way of trying to make trouble for Grady, especially since Grady just recently popped him on the nose. Secondly, Lysinger said when Brumly came and reported what he thought was happening, the Chief asked him what proof he had. Brumly's answer was Grady Phillips was not only an ex-con, but it was just too strange the theft of the carts started just after he moved back here to Fripp. Needless to say, Grady is pretty steamed about the whole thing. He'd be the first to admit, that at one time he had been a thief; a driver for a professional group of thieves, but in the eyes of the law, still a thief. As an ex-con, if he does or is suspected of doing anything outside the law, based on his past record, it's the responsibility of the police to check it out. Brumly is like a tick that gets underneath your skin you just can't dig out! What with this nasty and untrue rumor he has started here on the island, he's got some folks believing it to be the truth, or at the very least looking at Grady as someone who could have stolen those carts."

"But how can Brumly get away with saying something that's not true about someone else?"

"I warned you about the type of man Chic Brumly is. When it comes to the law, that is, what is right and what is wrong, he'll run right on the edge, doing just enough to create havoc, but still avoid getting in any trouble himself. A good example would be how some lawyers operate in a courtroom. They will ask someone on the witness stand a question that is not appropriate, which the opposing lawyer will instantly object to. If the judge agrees with the objection he will inform the jury to disregard what the lawyer said. But, you see the damage has already been done. Which one of those jury members will forget what they heard? The answer is *none of them!* Once something is said it can never be unsaid.

In this case, once some of the people here on the island hear Grady Phillips may be guilty of stealing those golf carts, even if it is not true, they will never look at him the same way and Chic Brumly knows how this type of nasty tactic works. He didn't have to file charges to make things difficult for Grady. All he had to do was start an untrue rumor. The news that Grady Phillips may still be a criminal will spread across this island rapidly. It really pisses me off!"

Getting up, Carson walked to the far end of the porch, took a drink of coffee, stared out at the rain and turned back to Nick. "I've got an idea on how, if we need to, we can shut down Maria Sparks and eventually, Chic as well. Remember the information you gave me from Maria's purse?"

Before Nick could respond, Carson smiled and continued, "I told you the information might come in handy. This person I know in New York owes me a favor. We not only have Maria's home address, but her driver's license and credit card numbers. In the wrong hands, or in this case, the right hands, we could make Maria Sparks' life a nightmare. Her bank accounts could be frozen, her electric and phone could be cut off, her car could actually be impounded. The information we have about her could be used against her. We could make her life quite miserable."

"I don't know," said Nick. "That sounds so underhanded, unethical...illegal! We could get in trouble."

Carson laughed. "There is so much about the world you don't know, Nick. If, and I say if, we decide to let's say pry into Maria Sparks' financial life in order to get her off your back, it can be done without our involvement whatsoever. Remember, as long as she is paying Brumly, he'll continue to dig into your life. He'll do whatever it takes to get to the truth *and we,* at some point may have to do whatever it takes to prevent it from happening. If it comes to that, don't worry. I'll handle everything. All it takes is a phone call to New York." Downing the last of his coffee, he gestured at the painting supplies next to the front door. "Listen, I'm going to get out of here so you can get to work. I've got to run into Beaufort on a few errands. Keep me up to date on Brumly and this Maria Sparks. Talk to you later."

Watching Carson pull away in the rain, Nick unlocked the house and placed his painting supplies in the hallway. He walked the downstairs making sure everything was in order. Checking the upstairs rooms he folded the stepladder they had left below the attic entrance where they had found the camera. Starting for the stairs he then thought, *Wait a minute!* Remembering something Gretchen Yeats said during their dinner engagement, he returned to the bedroom and unfolded the ladder.

Climbing up the ladder he reached up, opened the attic door, and crawled up into the confined space. Pulling the string for the light bulb he first looked for his friend the raccoon. Satisfied he was alone he moved three feet to his right and opened the dusty trunk where Shelby found the old camera. Piling the old clothing: jeans, shirts, socks and two pair of old high top sneakers on the broken rocker, he then began to look at some of the pictures that were held together with rubber bands. There were photos of students, the front of Beaufort High School, a number of ocean shots, flowers and old oak trees. He examined the student photos closely to see if there were any pictures of the James girl or of Brad Schulte, Tim Durham and Miles Gaston. None of the students looked familiar. Next, he flipped through two photo albums of photographs, but it was just more of the same. The trunk completely empty, Nick searched the bottom and saw what he was looking for, a small, one inch square section of flat metal. Flipping the piece over there is was, just like Gretchen said.

Chester Finch
311 Deer Lake Drive
Fripp Island, SC

Mrs. Yeats was right. The camera Shelby found did indeed belong to Gretchen's grandson, Chester. Placing the metal square in his shirt pocket he threw everything back into the trunk, closed the lid, turned off the light and climbed back down to the bedroom. Looking at the inscription once again, he tossed the I.D. plate into the air and caught it as he thought, *Shelby will be excited when she sees this!*

Back down on the main floor he placed the ladder in the kitchen. He was going to need it later while trimming out the molding. Going down on one knee he opened the first can of paint and using the stir stick he began to prepare the thick white substance for application on the bedroom wall. Seconds later, satisfied the paint was ready, he walked into the bedroom and spread the paint-stained drop cloth across the floor.

Looking out the bedroom window, his shoulders slumped in hopelessness when he noticed Brumly's car parked in the street directly in front of the house. *This is ridiculous,* thought Nick. The day was just beginning and he was staring at the blue Lincoln. Brumly, holding an umbrella over his head stepped out, opened Nick's mailbox, found nothing and stared at the house. The rear passenger side window slowly rolled down and there was Maria framed in the opening while she took some pictures of the house. Even though the concept of she and Brumly constantly interfering with his life was becoming commonplace, he still wished there would be just one day where they were not following him and prying into his life. Smiling to himself, he was going to take Carson's advice and just go on acting like nothing unusual was happening, but if Charley's sister and her scumbag lawyer continued to push his buttons, he just might give Carson the go ahead to start the ball roiling on using Maria's personal information against her. *No!* If they went ahead and did that it just might make Carnahan even more suspicious. Brumly closed the umbrella, climbed back in the car and the Lincoln slowly pulled away.

Walking out to the hallway to grab a roller and the extension pole, he realized simply acting like nothing out of the ordinary was happening wasn't going to erase the fact something out of the ordinary *was happening* in his life. The events of the past summer were now nothing but bad memories that had slowly faded from his everyday thoughts. Ike Miller was gone and the RPS Killer was no longer a menace to society. Now, the situation with the Carnahan's still lingered in his life with the sudden appearance of Maria Sparks in Beaufort County. In three weeks it would be Christmas and it appeared a new set of unusual circumstances was on the rise for he and Shelby. A twenty-seven year old unsolved double murder case, a sleazy local attorney-private detective on their trail, and even though he knew nothing about the recent stolen golf carts, it was yet another unpleasant event happening right in his own backyard, Fripp Island."

Pouring an appropriate portion of paint into the flat paint tray, he moved the roller back and forth, and then began to roll it professionally up and down the bedroom wall. Miraculously, a wave of peacefulness seemed to come over his mind. He had always viewed painting as therapeutic. He loved the smell of new paint and the sticky sound of the roller when it covered the old paint, giving the wall a new, fresh look. Running the roller through the paint tray again he was confident he would be able to get two rooms done before Shelby's call.

Standing at the kitchen sink he checked a clock on the wall, 11:45. Within the next fifteen to twenty minutes Shelby would be calling. Rinsing the paint tray out with hot water he watched while the milky-white, watered deluded paint, swirled around the drain. Satisfied the tray was clean, he ran the first of two rollers he had used under the water, the yellow nap cover slowly showing when the paint dissolved away. He had completed painting two rooms. *It was amazing!* During the past three hours he hadn't given Maria Sparks, Chic Brumly, Joseph Carnahan, Abigail James or Chester Finch a single thought. Painting really was good for him. It took his mind off any problems he had.

Instead, he had thoughts about his relationship with Shelby Lee, and how well he got along with her daughter, Kirby. He really liked meeting her parents on Thanksgiving. He thought about his past visit to Amelia's place up in Canada. He was glad she was safe. Cleaning the first of three brushes, he smiled and thought about how blessed he was. Six months ago he had been living a lonely life in Cincinnati, broke, driving a van that was on its last legs; a dismal future ahead. Now, here he was living on a private island, in what he considered to be a tropical paradise. He owned a lavish home right off the beach, owned two vehicles and a motorcycle, had more money than he would probably ever need, was surrounded by great friends and now, he even had a rental property. Turning off the water, he thought, *Things aren't that bad!*

Placing all of his painting tools on the side of the sink to dry, he then walked down the hall to move the drop cloth to the next room he was going to paint later in the week, when his cell phone sounded. Looking at the clock, he answered the phone, "Right on time! How is work going?"

"Work's work," said Shelby sarcastically. "The question of the day is, how's your head?"

"Better than it was earlier this morning. Those last two shots of Wild Turkey really took its toll. I had a brisk swim in the ocean. The freezing water really brought me around."

"What are you doing right now?"

"I just finished up some painting at the rental. I'm cleaning up. I knew you'd be calling soon. Did you manage to get in touch with this LuAnn, what was it…Dawson?"

"Yes, I did. She was very pleasant over the phone. I used our old book writing routine on her and she agreed to meet with us this afternoon at her home at four o'clock. She only lives three blocks from where my parents live. I thought maybe we could meet at three in downtown Beaufort and grab an early dinner so we can discuss what we want to ask her. We need to have our ducks in a row."

"Sounds good," said Nick, "How does the Plum on Bay Street sound?"

"I'll be there about three. See you then."

Nick put his cell back in his pocket and looked out the window. It was still raining. It looked like one of those all day rains. He had two and a half hours before he needed to head up to Beaufort. He had time to knock out another room, but since he had just cleaned everything up, he decided to go back to the house and relax.

Shelby was already seated at a window table at Plums when Nick arrived. Pulling out a chair, he remarked, "I'm starving. I haven't had anything to eat yet today."

Shelby glanced at a menu and added, "It's been raining all day. I'm in the mood for soup. Maybe I'll get a sandwich to go with it."

Nick agreed. "Bowl of hot soup and a sandwich. I might go with that too. Maybe a side salad."

Looking at her watch, Shelby commented, "We need to come on and order. It's almost three now. We'll have to leave in forty-five minutes for LuAnn's." She signaled at a passing waitress. "We're pressed for time. Do you think we could order?"

Ten minutes later, Shelby sipped at her mug of hot chocolate while Nick looked out at the Beaufort River. Pointing his coffee cup at Shelby, he asked, "How do you think we should approach this LuAnn?"

Picking up her sandwich, Shelby answered, "I think we should just play it by ear."

A voice from behind them got their attention. "Good afternoon folks. I hope you're enjoying your meal." Nick frowned when he looked up and saw Chic and Maria standing next to their table. Brumly was wearing one of his obnoxious bright sports coats, a blue and grey checked design; light blue shirt, two-tone striped gray tie, grey slacks and white shoes. Maria was once again overdressed for the area. Sequin covered Stetson, bright pink blouse, expensive pearl necklace, short, white leather jacket trimmed in some sort of animal fur, white leather pants and spiked snakeskin heels."

Nick's patience was running out. "Look Brumly. I'm getting a little tired of you following me everywhere I go. *And you,* Ms. Sparks are wasting your time. Why don't you go back to New York and save yourself some money, because the truth is there is nothing other than what I already told about your brother for you to discover. In short, there is nothing *to find out!*"

Chic grinned. "Whatever do you mean…following you? Is there a law against a lawyer and his client having a late lunch?"

"Cut the crap, Brumly. I saw you and your little friend here in front of the house over on Deer Lake this morning. You've really got nerve! Looking in *my mailbox* and taking pictures of *my property.* The people I talked to about you were right. You are a slime bag!"

Maria took a step toward Shelby. "You must be Shelby Lee Pickett. I noticed you the other day over on Deer Lake. With everything that happened we did not get an opportunity to speak. Chic here tells me you're a local girl, a Lowcountry girl…raised right here in Beaufort." Reaching over she touched the edge of Shelby's blouse. "You're an attractive young girl. Perhaps if you learned to dress a little better, you could actually be beautiful."

Shelby never said a word and looked across the table at Nick, who could tell she was upset at Maria's comment. Following a few moments of silent awkwardness, Chic gently took Maria by her arm and suggested, "Why don't we get a table and then order."

Smiling smartly at Shelby, Maria backed away and stated, "Whatever you say, Chic."

Shelby watched every step Maria took until they arrived at a table on the other side of the room near the exit. Maria turned and gave Shelby a look of defiance and slowly seated herself.

Shelby leaned across the table and whispered to Nick, "I'm really pissed!"

Nick responded, "I can tell."

Nodding at his sandwich and soup, she softly suggested, "Eat up, because you've only got about ten minutes or so to get your fill."

Confused, Nick asked, "What are you talking about? We don't have to leave for another thirty minutes."

Shelby emphasized, "In the next few minutes, believe me…you'll want to get out of here." Standing, she reached for her purse. Be right back, I'm going to go pay our bill. When I get back, be ready to leave."

Nick, still confused, uttered, "But…

Shelby walked to the counter and signaled she was ready to settle up.

Chic and Maria had just ordered when Shelby returned, sat down and took a drink. "When their food comes out I want you to head over to the door and wait. Don't ask me any questions…just do what I ask…please. Now, finish your sandwich."

Shelby went about eating her soup and never gave Brumly or Maria another look. Finally, minutes later, their food was delivered to Chic's table; bowls of tomato basil soup, iced teas and salads.

Shelby picked up her purse and whispered, "All right, go to the door and wait. Don't get too relaxed."

Nick stood and walked to the door while Shelby approached Chic's table. He and Maria were seated side by side against a wall, reviewing some paperwork. "Excuse me," said Shelby. "Your lunch looks good. I was thinking about ordering the tomato basil myself, but then again that wouldn't have been a very good idea with me being a good ol' Lowcountry girl. I'd probably wind up just spilling it on myself and ruining this blouse, that you, Maria do not seem to approve of." Shelby suddenly dropped her purse to the floor. "Oh, how clumsy of me!" Bending down she picked up the purse and nodded at Nick, for what reason he wasn't sure. In the next seconds she stood up and raised the edge of the table off the floor by two feet, causing the drinks, the salads and the red soup to tip and spill down over Chic and Maria.

Chic jumped up and yelled, "What the hell!"

Maria screamed and looked down over her soaked clothing as Shelby apologized, "I'm so sorry! We Lowcountry gals are rather clumsy. Enjoy your lunch!"

She then calmly turned and walked out the door Nick was holding open. When she got down to the bottom porch step she turned and ordered, "Nick, run!"

Running behind Shelby up the brick pathway Nick yelled, "What the hell was that all about?"

Without looking back, Shelby yelled back, "She just really pissed me off! When we get to the parking lot follow me to LuAnn's house!"

Chic ran out onto the porch, but it was too late. He considered himself too dignified to chase someone down the walk in the rain. Standing next to the table, Maria was fuming. A waitress approached and asked, "Can I help you? Can I get you anything?"

Maria yelled at the young girl. "Don't touch me. Just get away!"

Nick backed out of his parking spot and followed Shelby's red Jeep, but they had to stop for a red light at the Bay Street intersection. Nick kept looking in his rearview mirror, half expecting Brumly to come sprinting around the corner in hot pursuit. Looking at the circular red light, he spoke to himself, "Come on…come on…change!"

The light changed and Nick breathed a sigh of relief. It appeared they had made good their escape. Turning left on Bay he followed Shelby through town, where they made a right, went two blocks, made another right, then drove three more blocks when they pulled over.

Shelby grabbed her briefcase, got out of the Jeep, ran back and climbed in the passenger side of the Lexus. Pumping her fist, she smiled. "God…that felt good! That little New York hussy got what she deserved." Without waiting for a response from Nick, she looked at her watch. "We're about ten minutes early." Turning and looking out the rear window, she went on, "You don't think they'll follow us…do you?"

Nick laughed and joked, "I've think you've pretty much eliminated that possibility with your *Lowcountry girl clumsiness!"*

Nick turned off the Lexus and sat back in the seat. "When we finish up with this LuAnn, I think I'm just going to head back to Fripp. By the way, Carson found out the number I found in Maria's purse is none other than Joseph Carnahans'. So, we can be pretty sure the Carnahans sent her here. Carson assured me we have nothing to worry about. He already has a plan to shut down Brumly and the woman if need be."

Interested, Shelby asked, "What's he have in mind?"

Minutes later, Nick completed his explanation of what Carson had suggested. Shelby looked at her watch and opened the car door. "It's time. Let's go see LuAnn Dawson."

Running up the walk through the rain, they stood on the front porch of a typical Beaufort home: white, two story, front porch with four white columns, the windows covered with black hurricane shutters. Shelby checked herself to make sure she was presentable, then rang the doorbell. Within seconds, a short, spunky looking woman with a pixie style hairdo opened the door and with a greeting that could only be described as enthusiastic, extended her small right hand. "You must be Shelby Lee and Nick. I'm LuAnn! Please…step in out of the rain."

Once inside they stood in a dark rosewood paneled foyer, a large antique chandelier suspended above their heads. LuAnn gestured to a room on the left. "Why don't we just relax in the sitting room?"

The room had a twelve-foot high dazzling white ceiling, light lavender painted walls and custom designed borders near the ceiling. Sitting on a lavender and green flowered couch, trimmed in oak, Shelby complimented LuAnn, "What a lovely home you have. It feels so comfortable."

LuAnn smiled and walked toward an adjoining room separated by two large French doors. "If you'll just give me a minute I have a pot of coffee on."

After LuAnn left the room, Shelby whispered to Nick. "It looks like LuAnn has done well for herself. Didn't Barrett say she married a Beaufort police officer?"

"Yes, I believe that's what he said."

Reaching down, Shelby ran her fingers across the edge of a 12 x 16 foot Oriental rug. "I bet this rug cost a pretty penny. They must pay the police rather well here in Beaufort."

LuAnn entered the room carrying a tray containing a silver coffee urn, three china coffee cups, small cream and sugar pitchers and a plate of cookies. Setting the tray on a cherry coffee table, she offered, "I thought with the rain coffee might be nice." Bending down she held up the urn, "Anyone?"

Grabbing a cup, Shelby responded, "I would love a cup of hot coffee right about now. I've been chilled all day what with this rain."

Nick joined in, picked up one of the cups and smiled, "Please."

Pouring three cups, LuAnn placed the urn back on the tray and added two cubes of sugar to her cup and spoke, "We have cream and real sugar. Please help yourself."

After everyone prepared their coffee, LuAnn sat in a light green chair across from the couch and pointed at the cookies. "Please try some of my homemade cookies." Rolling her eyes, she confessed, "We don't get many visitors here at our house, but when we do, people always ask me how can we afford this type of home on a policeman's salary." Getting up she walked over, scooped up a chocolate chip cookie, and returned to her seat. Taking a small bite she went on to explain, "These little devils right here are the reason we can afford this home. I started baking cookies about ten years ago. People really seemed to like them and told me I should start a business. I thought it was a crazy idea but I wasn't working at the time so I started baking at home and got myself a Facebook page and a website and before long I'm shipping cookies all over the country. We now have a bakery over in Walterboro and a warehouse we ship from. Our cookie business brings in ten times the money my husband could ever make on the force." Changing the subject, she sipped at her coffee, "I believe you told me, Shelby, you and Nick are thinking about writing a book?"

"Yes, and that's why we're here," said Shelby. "We talked earlier this week with a former Beaufort detective by the name of Melvin Barrett. We asked him quite a few questions about a twenty-seven year old double murder that happened out on Fripp Island. Nick and I are to understand those murders have never been solved and the three suspects or people of interest that were thought to somehow be involved were never arrested or convicted of the crime. We've done a lot of research on the murders and about the only thing we are unclear on is what happened to the three suspects. Melvin told us if anyone knew what these three men were doing today, since you head up the '89 reunion committee you would know."

LuAnn set her unfinished cookie and cup of coffee down on an end table. Folding her hands she rested them on her legs. "The three men you are referring to are Brad Schulte, Tim Durham and Miles Gaston. I graduated with all three back in 1989. I haven't talked about those murders for let's see, it's been a little over two years now. Detective Barrett is correct. I do head up the '89 reunion committee. Our first reunion was back in 1990, and then we try to have one every year. They are pretty well attended. A lot of the former students still live here in the state, while others make the annual trip to Beaufort. I'd say we've had better than average attendance at our reunions, but that's only because I keep after everyone to attend. Now speaking of those three boys, who by the way were never officially mentioned as suspects, but persons of interest, they never attended one reunion until two years ago when we had our twenty-fifth. It was well attended. Former students came from all over the country, including Brad, Tim and Miles. Why they finally chose to attend is beyond me...but they did."

"I was told you and Tim dated throughout high school," said Shelby as she opened her briefcase. "I hope you don't mind if we take some notes."

"No, go right ahead. I don't mind at all. Tim and I were sweethearts in high school…all four years, and then some. We met when we were freshmen. It was so strange. Neither one of us had ever dated before. Looking back, I can say as young as we were that we were truly in love. Before long everyone knew we were an item. It's the story you always seem to hear about: football hero dating a cheerleader. By the time we were sophomores we had already agreed and planned on getting engaged after we graduated and then when we were finished college we would tie the knot."

Nick scooted forward on the couch while he held his pad and pen. "If we could, I'd like to back up and start with the year you guys graduated; the year when Abigail James and Chester Finch were murdered. What can you tell us about how all that went down or the way the students felt when they found out two of their friends and fellow students had been murdered?"

"That year; 1989, was supposed to be special. It was the year we all would be graduating and moving on with our lives. But then when we became the state high school football champs, it went to another level. I'll never forget that year and the way we all felt; how proud we were. If you've done your research then you already know about the celebration party held out on Fripp. Everyone from school was supposed to be there. I was so mad. I had a severe cold and according to our family doctor not allowed outside the house. I needed bed rest. Tim was upset because, at the last minute, I couldn't go. I told him it was all right and to go ahead with his pals."

Shaking her head as if she were remembering, she held up her hands, "Pals…hell those three were more than just pals. Everyone called them The Three Musketeers. All for one and one for all. That was what they were all about. If Tim wasn't with me, I guarantee, he was with Brad and Miles. They went everywhere together, did most things together. But, ya know I never got jealous of Tim's close and personal relationship with those boys. They were the best friends he could have had. They never drank, ran with the wrong crowd or got in trouble of any sort. The truth was; I was dating one of the best young men at Beaufort High in 1989."

Sitting back and looking up at the high ceiling she took a deep breath. "I didn't hear about the murders until the next morning. It was…well…its kind of hard to explain the way I felt. Abby and Chester were by far the smartest kids in our school. This really hit close to home. Abby was in two of my classes and Chester was in science with me. I really wasn't that close to Abby. I mean, she was a nice kid. She just went in a different direction than what I chose to go. Hell, she went in a different direction than any of the girls at Beaufort High. Abby liked, for lack of a better phrase, her sex. She slept around and didn't care who knew it. Tim and I talked about her a number of times. He told me she had slept with every player on the football team except he, Brad and Miles. She never dated anyone for any great length of time. It's like she was never satisfied."

Shelby asked the next question, "And what about Chester Finch? What kind of a kid was he?"

"Chester was as pure as driven snow. A nicer kid you couldn't meet. I was friends with Chester. We served on student council together and we were both on the school newspaper. He was such a nice person. He never had an unkind word to say about anyone, despite the fact a lot of kids in school considered him a nerd and wouldn't give him the time of day. The fact he was not all that popular never bothered Chester." Holding up a finger to make a point, LuAnn went on, "I remember about two weeks before the murders Chester and I were assigned to a school newspaper project about education beyond high school. One evening after school we stayed late to wrap things up and we got to talking about our futures. I was going to be attending college over in Charleston to study nursing and Chester, well, he was going to be off to Harvard University. He was aware Tim and I planned to be married and Chester said he envied Tim and I for looking ahead and planning our futures. He said we were so far ahead of the other students. I remember asking Chester if he ever planned on getting married. He told me for now he didn't have time for things like dating and the like. After he graduated from college, he knew there was a girl out there in the world for him somewhere."

LuAnn laughed. "Chester was such a hoot! We talked about Abby and her reputation and he said he'd never be caught dead with someone like her…with no moral values. He just couldn't imagine how she could be sexually involved with one boy this week and then the next…another. He claimed it had to be some sort of sexual insanity!"

"So what was the feeling like around school the next week following the murders?" asked Nick.

"I recall it as one of the most awkward and horrible weeks I've ever experienced. The following Monday, just two days after the murders the police came to the school and informed us we all would be interviewed whether we had attended the party on Fripp or not. At that point the police were looking for answers. They had no murder weapon, no motive, no witnesses…nothing! Needless to say, not only I but every student at Beaufort High was nervous. Tim was especially nervous and that was unusual for his personality because very few things, if any, seemed to bother him. I figured he was reacting like the rest of us. I mean, here we were, sixteen, seventeen and eighteen year old kids being questioned about two of our fellow students who had been murdered."

LuAnn hesitated and Nick was quick with yet another question. "How did the interviews go?"

"Surprisingly, they were not that hard to sit through. Most of the kids agreed their individual interviews lasted no more than ten to fifteen minutes."

Nick pressed his next question, "What, if anything, did the police discover?"

"During the first round of interviews about the only thing they discovered was Abby and Chester couldn't have possibly been on that beach together, at least for a sexual encounter."

Shelby picked up on something LuAnn had said. "You said the first round of interviews. Were there more interviews? Were all of the students talked to a second time?"

"There was a second round of interviews but the only students interviewed a second time were Brad, Tim and Miles. I've got to tell you, this raised some eyebrows around the school, but we were assured by the teachers from what they had been told, the three boys were interviewed a second time because they were the last ones to see Abby alive. They had run into her on the way out to Fripp, she had car troubles, they tried to get her car running, could not, and wound up giving her a lift to Fripp. The boys claimed they dropped her off at the pool on Fripp and never saw her again. No one at the party ever saw her that night."

"So was that it then?" asked Shelby.

"No, they interviewed the boys a third time, but this time the police had discovered something that pointed the finger of fate right at The Three Musketeers. They were caught in a lie."

Shelby guessed and confirmed what LuAnn said. "This lie they were caught in. Was it about the broken bottle top they found in the rocks at the murder scene?"

"Precisely. All three boys admitted there was alcohol at the party students had smuggled in. They said they did not partake before, during or after the party. The broken bottle had not only Abby's DNA, but also that of Miles Gaston. Miles broke down and finally admitted they had been drinking bourbon prior to the party. Miles said the reason they didn't reveal they had been drinking is because Brad had taken the bottle from his father's liquor cabinet and they didn't want to get into trouble with their parents. This led to yet another fabrication. The three boys said they all tried to help Abby get her car started. An eyewitness claimed he only saw two boys trying to assist Abby with her car. Miles fessed up and told the police he was passed out in the back of Brad's car. The police knew the three boys had been involved in the murders somehow, but they still couldn't put it together. Then the boys were interviewed a fourth time after the police discovered traces of bleach in the trunk of Brad's Mustang. I was mad as hell with Tim. In the four years I had known him he never took so much as a single drink. I asked him why he had been drinking and he said the three of them were celebrating the state championship. Students at school were starting to talk. It wasn't looking good for our three football stars. But then the investigation came to a grinding halt. Months dragged on and eventually we all graduated. That first summer before we all went off to college, the police kept close tabs on the boys. Those of us who knew them well were convinced it couldn't have been possible for them to murder Abby and Chester. Those who didn't know the boys well were convinced that they did commit the murders. Even after we all went off to college that fall, back here in Beaufort the investigation continued, but without the murder weapon, motive or any witnesses to the actual crime, those three boys walked. After all these years those murders are still unsolved."

Nick wrote something on his pad and then asked, "What happened to the boys? I assume you and Tim were still dating? Was the engagement and future marriage still on the table?"

"We didn't talk about the future like we had in the past. There was just something missing between us. It was almost like a piece of the puzzle we had put together had dropped out and we couldn't seem to get it snapped back in place. I remember those days as very awkward. I wasn't sure what to do. I thought I knew Tim well, but with the way everything seemed to point, I wasn't sure. I guess I was just biding my time, waiting to see what would happen. With Tim and I off to college it was easier for me to deal with the situation. Tim was down in Texas playing ball for the Texas Aggies and I was attending school in Charleston. We continued to write and call each other, but it was now different. During high school we had been with each other every day. Now, it was weekly when we talked. It was like we knew the relationship was coming to an end. Then it happened. Tim wrote me a letter. I've got it around here somewhere. In short, he told me after playing football for two years he was leaving college and going into the priesthood. I couldn't believe it. Tim had always been a good Catholic boy and I was Catholic as well. I can't tell you how many times we attended Mass together while in high school. I mean, I just couldn't believe it…a priest! He wrote he was sorry things hadn't worked out the way we planned. I couldn't understand his way of thinking. He could have been a professional football player; he was that good. But there it was in black and white. Tim, my high school sweetheart was going to become a priest."

"Is Tim still a Catholic priest?"

"As far as I know…yes. After our twenty-fifth reunion the word got around he was in line to become the next Archbishop in a Catholic Diocese in St. Louis."

"And what about the other two?" inquired Shelby, "What became of Brad and Miles?"

As far as college goes, Brad fared slightly better than the other two. At the end of his third season as starting quarterback for Penn State, he just walked off campus and then completed his senior year at Duquesne University in Pittsburgh. After graduating, he got involved in politics in Pittsburgh, married a woman, slightly older than he and worked his way up through the political ranks and is now, it is said not only the Mayor of Pittsburgh, but being groomed for the next Governor of Pennsylvania. I hear he is a powerful man. It is to my understanding that over the years he has accumulated vast wealth, and is very connected in political circles."

"That leaves Miles Gaston," said Nick. "What's his story?"

"Ol' Miles according to what I've been told only made it one season playing for the Gamecocks right here in South Carolina. He left school before even completing his freshman year. He had a little money saved up which he used to buy a small restaurant over in Charleston. I think it may still be there today. I'm not sure. Eventually, he opened a second eating establishment in Savannah and then I guess it was a few years later, purchased a chain of restaurants, and today has eating locations throughout the country."

Picking up her coffee, she thought back and stated, "Between the three boys, Miles possessed the weakest personality. On the football field, he was dominant at his position, but off the field, not so much. In the four years I attended school with him I never saw him once with a girl. It was thought around school that he was gay, but Tim assured me a number of times this was not the case. Miles was simply bashful, especially around members of the opposite sex. As of two years ago when he was at the reunion he hadn't married. Brad Schulte was the only one out of the three who took a wife."

Shelby munched on a cookie and asked, "Tell us, if you would, about this twenty-fifth class reunion. That had to be awkward. No one had seen these three former football heroes for two and a half decades and suddenly they show up. What was that like?"

LuAnn hesitated when her eyes began to fill with tears. Wiping her damp eyes with a napkin, she apologized, "I'm so sorry. I'm sure you didn't come here to see me get upset." Dabbing at her cheeks, she explained, "I can only pass on to you what I was told...because, you see I didn't attend. It's the only class reunion I haven't been to since graduating from Beaufort High. When I found out Tim was going to be there, I just couldn't bare to face him. I didn't think I'd be able to handle it. I told my husband I wasn't feeling well and was not going. I called my assistant and she handled everything at the banquet. My husband is as good a man as you'd want to marry, but here's the thing. Tim Durham was my first love and I've always heard people say there is nothing quite like your first love. When I was in high school I truly loved Tim and I know he loved me. We thought we had it all figured out. I wanted so much to see him, but then again, I didn't want to see him. It would do nothing but bring up bad memories."

"So, since you were not there you can't tell us what happened at this banquet."

"Oh, I can tell you everything that went on. My friend, Caroline, the assistant I told you about was there and witnessed everything that happened that night. Brad showed up with his wife. They sat at a table with Tim and Miles. They never danced or for that matter even got up from their table to go talk with anyone. They were approached by some of their former football buddies and students, but most of those in attendance avoided them. I guess the thought that they *may have* murdered Abby and Chester was on everyone's mind. Every year at the reunion we always have a toast for classmates who have passed on. Caroline said when the toast was given for Abby and Chester, Miles got up and left the room. Maybe he was just using the restroom, but Caroline said it was an awkward moment."

Seeing LuAnn was still upset, Shelby suggested, "We didn't come here LuAnn to upset you. Perhaps we should call it a day."

"I think you're right," chimed in Nick. "I do have one last question though, but because you were not there, you may not be able to answer it."

LuAnn looked at Nick but remained silent while he asked, "Do you have any idea what these boys, or I guess now, men, look like?"

"Only from the way Caroline described them. Better than that...I have pictures from the banquet. We always go around and get shots of people dancing or those seated at tables. I keep them in albums by each year."

When LuAnn got up and left the room, Shelby gave Nick a concerned look. "I can't believe this. She must have really loved this Tim. I'm feeling a tad bit guilty about coming here. As soon as we see the pictures, I think we should leave."

Nick smiled somberly, "I couldn't agree more."

LuAnn returned carrying a large blue photography album. Placing the album on the coffee table she pointed at the cover that read: Beaufort High School - Class of 1989. Reunion years — 2009-2013. Opening the album, LuAnn went on to explain, "I can usually get five years in an album. Let's flip toward the back for the 2013 reunion pictures. Ah, here we go!" Flipping through three pages she finally stopped and said, "Here they are. Brad, Tim and Miles sitting at their table." She turned the book around and pushed it across the table, while pointing at three photos. "All three of the pictures are pretty much the same. That's Brad and his wife on the left, then there's Tim in the middle and Miles on the right. When I first saw the pictures of the boys I was shocked. Normally, I see most of the former '89 graduating class each year at the reunion. So, as they age you really don't notice it that much. But these three boys I hadn't seen them in twenty-five years. I knew they were the same age as I, but I guess I wanted to remember them the way I last saw them, especially Tim. They no longer looked like The Three Musketeers from my high school days. They looked like old men. I realized they were only forty-three, but the last time I saw Tim, he was twenty. Even now when I look at these photographs, I can't believe how time has passed so quickly." Reaching for the album, she spun it around, removed one of the photos, and handed it to Shelby. "Here, I want you to have one of these. Maybe it will help with your research."

Shelby was amazed. "Oh, I wouldn't think of taking one of your pictures."

LuAnn closed the album. "It's all right…I have two others."

Nick stood and announced, "Well I think we've gotten more information than we planned on this afternoon. Thank you so much, LuAnn. You've been very helpful."

Placing the photo in her briefcase, Shelby stood and shook LuAnn's hand. "Once again, thank you!"

Walking them to the foyer, LuAnn opened the front door only to find the rain coming down harder than it had all day. "Perhaps you would like to stay and wait for the rain to slow down."

"We'll be fine," said Nick. "A little rain never hurt anyone!" With that he grabbed Shelby's arm and shouted, "Let's go!"

Sitting in the Lexes, Nick turned on the wipers while Shelby dug out the photographs from LuAnn. Pointing at the man seated on the right, LuAnn identified as Miles Gaston, she asked, "Is that the same Miles you met on the beach where the murders were committed?"

CHAPTER SEVENTEEN

DIPPING HIS TWO-INCH BRUSH INTO A CAN OF WHITE TRIM paint, Nick ran the brush down the side of the wooden casing of the front door. Looking at his watch, he thought, *Where does the time go?*

He had been working on the Deer Lake property since seven o'clock that morning. It was now close to three-thirty and he needed a break. According to Shelby's phone call at noon, she was going to drive over to Fripp around four after she was finished at work and help him do some painting.

Grabbing an ice water out of the fridge, he walked out onto the front porch and seated himself on the suspended wooden swing. After two days the rain had finally stopped sometime in the middle of the night. It had been two days since he and Shelby had talked with LuAnn Dawson. There was no doubt about what they had discovered. The 2013 reunion photograph LuAnn had given them identified the man known as Miles Gaston in the photo as the same man he had met recently on the beach; the very beach where the murders had been committed.

Taking a drink, he thought about how amazing it was. He had come face to face with one of the three boys, whom he was convinced more than ever killed Abigail James and Chester Finch. All those years, the proof of the boys' presence on the beach that night laid dormant inside an old camera in the tiny attic of the house he had just recently purchased.

His line of thinking suddenly switched to that of Chic Brumly and Maria Sparks. Since the table incident at Plums he hadn't seen the couple for the last two days. That didn't mean they were not around. He just hadn't noticed them. They had to be pissed! Especially Maria, her designer clothing possibly ruined. He couldn't imagine why she was still paying Brumly, when after all this time he couldn't come up with anything that proved something fatal had happened to her brother on Fripp. He hoped their lack of presence in his life the last two days meant she was finally giving up. But then again, if she had been sent by the Carnahans, that was not her decision to make. Until they were convinced Charley took off with their millions they would continue to utilize Charley's sister or whatever other means they could to find out what really happened.

A neighbor drove by on a golf cart and gave him a wave. Returning the wave, Nick remembered hearing on the late night news last evening that two more carts had disappeared on Fripp. Grady Phillips had to be upset, with a lot of people now looking at him as the potential golf cart thief. That just couldn't be true. What was it Carson had said? Four million dollars in diamonds from the last heist Grady had been involved in that were never recovered? It was thought the diamonds might be buried somewhere on the island. He agreed with what Carson had said; stealing golf carts would be considered petty to someone like Grady, who at one time had been probably considered *Big time!* But that was all in the past. Grady, according to the law, had served his time and was now a free man. He liked Grady. He had the nerve to do what he himself wanted to do. He smiled when he thought about the look on Brumly's face when Grady punched him.

Getting up, he walked back inside the house, grabbed the brush and bucket and proceeded into the downstairs bedroom where he needed to paint not only the ceiling trim, but the baseboards and window trim.

He no sooner dipped the brush into the can than he heard Shelby's voice from the hallway, "Hello! Reinforcements have arrived!"

Nick smiled and walked back out into the hall. Holding up the brush, he joked, "Do you know how to use one of these, Rebel?"

"Sort of. I figure you can show me what to do. I pick things up fast." Walking into the kitchen she admired the freshly painted walls. "This really looks good. What's left to be done?"

Sitting on a kitchen chair, Nick explained, "The only thing left is trim work and then we have to paint the ceilings. I may texture them. I haven't decided yet."

"Well, let's get this show on the road. I'm going to be starving a few hours from now. My services are going to cost you a dinner. Where do you want me to start?"

Handing her the can and brush, he got up and walked her into the bedroom. "All the faded trim in this room needs a good coat. I'm going to start on the hallway ceiling. I think we'll knock off at six and then head for a bite."

Bending down she placed the can on the drop cloth and dipped the brush into the bright white paint. Painting the sill of the bedroom window she giggled, "I wonder what happened after we left the Plum the other day."

"Well, one thing is for sure," said Nick. "They didn't have a chance to follow us. I was thinking earlier today about how I haven't seen either one of those two since we left them in Beaufort."

"Maybe it's over."

"I doubt it. If anything, Maria will probably press Brumly even harder to get to the truth."

Pointing at the surrounding walls, Shelby silently reminded Nick of the possibility that the house could be bugged and then spoke, "Well, she and Chic can look until the cows come home and there is nothing for them to discover. You told them everything you know about Charley Sparks. Her brother took off with the Carnahan's money and that's all there is to it!"

Running the brush up the side trim of the window, Shelby spoke with compassion, "I really feel sorry for LuAnn Dawson. Based on what she told us, I can understand why she didn't want to go to that reunion and face Tim Durham. I think what she said is true. No matter what happens in your life you'll never feel the way you did following your first love."

Pointing the extension pole at Shelby, Nick inquired, "So if that is true, then Harold T. Benjamin was your first love?"

"No way! That was nothing more than infatuation and stupidity on my part."

"Then surely it must have been Ike Miller who stole your heart, at least in the beginning."

"No, it wasn't Ike either. To tell you the truth, I'm not sure I have ever experienced true love. I mean hell, I've had two previous relationships that both turned out to be nightmares when you take a good hard look at Harold and Ike."

Placing a roller on the end of the pole, Nick probed, "I guess you could say that now, I am the third man in your young life. How's that working out for you?"

Pointing the brush directly at Nick, Shelby laughed. "You're really putting me on the spot with that question. I will admit this. You're a damn site better than Harold or Ike Miller. I guess my choice of men has improved. What about you? Will you always remember your first love?"

"There was a time, and not too long ago when I thought I would never forget the pain of that girl in college I told you about the night we met for dinner the first time. At the time, I thought I was in love with her, and when she just up and ended the relationship, I thought I'd never get over the way I felt. So, yeah, I guess in a way I can see where LuAnn is coming from. But there is good news! Since the day I met you down on the beach, those feelings of never wanting to get involved with someone ever again have slowly faded. I have you to thank for that."

"Does this mean we are in a serious relationship?"

"Now it's you putting *me* on the spot! I entered this relationship with my parking brake on. I never want to get hurt again. Over the past few months I've reminded myself a number of times to just take it slow and see what happens. Is that all right?"

Shelby laughed and dipped the brush back into the can. "This conversation is getting way too serious. I think we should just get back to work. Nick breathed a sigh of relief. "Yes, I agree… back to work!"

Standing at the sink, Nick cleaned the roller and the brushes and announced to Shelby, "its quarter to six now. I say we finish up around here, drive over to my place, get cleaned up and then head up to the Bonito Boathouse for drinks and dinner."

Wiping some trim paint off the wall, Shelby agreed, "That sounds good. I'm looking forward to a nice meal and some pleasant conversation."

It was close to seven o'clock when they pulled into the marina parking lot down from the Boathouse. Walking across the lot, Shelby looked around at all the cars and golf carts. "Looks like it's really busy tonight."

Stopping at the reservation desk just inside the main entrance, Nick signaled the hostess by holding up two fingers. Grabbing two menus, the young girl smiled and recited her canned welcome, "Right this way…please!"

The main dining room was packed, every table crammed with locals and a few tourists. Guiding them toward the back of the restaurant, the girl motioned with the menus, "I hope the bar will be all right?"

Nick looked at Shelby and shrugged, "The bar will be fine."

Seated at one of the only two tables not occupied, Shelby gazed out the window at the lights from the dock that jutted out into the river. Beyond the lights there was total darkness.

Nick noticed the prolonged stare and asked, "Something interesting out there?"

Turning her attention back to Nick, she responded, "No, I was just thinking about all those girls Harold dumped out there in the marsh. I don't think I'll ever view the marsh again without thinking about last summer."

"You and me both," commented Nick, "but we agreed to come here and enjoy not only dinner but some pleasant conversation. Talking about last summer does not in my estimation qualify as pleasant conversation."

A waitress was suddenly standing next to the table. "Good evening…what would you like to drink?"

Nick looked across the table at Shelby and asked, "Pitcher of beer sound okay?"

"Long as it comes with two frosted glasses…I'm fine!"

After the girl left, Shelby folded her hands on top of the table and looked directly at Nick. "So what shall we talk about tonight?"

Nick nonchalantly reached into his pocket and removed the small I.D. plate he had found in the attic. Tossing it on the table he suggested, "Well, we could talk about this."

Shelby stared at the object, picked it up, flipped it over and silently read the name, *Chester Finch.* Holding up the plate she asked, "Where did you find this?"

Nick smiled. Right where Mrs. Yeats said it would be. I climbed up in the attic and found it at the bottom of that old trunk."

Shaking her head in amazement, Shelby couldn't believe what she was looking at. "This proves beyond any doubt the camera we found belonged to the Finch kid. Another piece of the puzzle falls into place."

Looking at the menu, Nick suggested, "When it comes to what we should talk about this evening, I don't think we have any choice. I think we have to discuss what our next move is in regard to what we've discovered about the three boys, *The Three Musketeers!"* Laying the menu to the side, he explained, "I don't think talking about what we've been involved in lately is unpleasant…do you?"

"No, I think it is something we need to discuss. Actually, I've been thinking about that very thing quite a bit ever since we left LuAnn's house. We have collected information from not only Mrs. Yeats, but the high school library, the ex-detective, Melvin Barrett and finally LuAnn Dawson. I don't know where else we could go or what else we can do at this point."

Nick signaled by running his thumb across his throat when the waitress returned with the pitcher. Shelby, getting his meaning stopped talking and smiled when the girl approached. After placing the pitcher and two cold glasses on the table, the girl inquired, "Have we decided yet or do you need some time?"

Nick reached for the pitcher and stated, "I'm going with the special they had posted out front."

"Me too," chimed in Shelby.

The waitress wrote on her order pad and told them their food would be out in about ten minutes.

Picking up where they left off, Nick poured two glasses of beer. "Look, if you want to throw in the towel on these twenty-seven year old unsolved murders, that's okay with me. Like you said, what else is there for us to do at this point?"

"All right," said Shelby. "Let's just say we do go to the police. We take the camera and the pictures we developed along with all the photos from the school library and hand it all over to them. I'm sure they are not just going to simply say thank you and then we're on our way. There are going to be questions about where we found the camera and possibly why we waited to come forward with the beach pictures." Setting down her glass she got a strange look on her face. "You don't think we'll get in trouble for not coming forward right after we found the camera and the film…do you?"

"No, why would we? Here's an idea. Maybe we could go to Barrett and show him the pictures. Maybe he could go with us to the police. Even though he's not on the force, he was one of the two main detectives who worked the case twenty-seven years ago. I'm sure the police would welcome any input he has. I mean, he was right there in the middle of the investigation. He actually talked with the three boys. You heard one of the last things he said when we left his home about how he felt those boys did commit the murders; it would just never be proven. If we took the camera and the developed photographs to him, it might just turn out he would be chomping at the bit to have evidence that could finally, after all these years, bring the three killers to justice. Can you imagine what big news it would be if the three former football stars were arrested and then convicted?"

"It would be big news, but not for everyone. There are probably more people living here in the area who are not aware of those murders than those who are. In today's world something that happens can very easily be replaced a day, week or month later by something else. Abigail James and Chester Finch were killed over two and a half decades ago. If Miles Gaston and his two former high school pals were brought to justice for the murders, because it is such an old case, most folks probably wouldn't think much about it. That being said, I know of one person who would take great notice and consider it *very big news!*"

Nick hesitated in taking a drink and looked at Shelby in confusion. Shelby cleared up her statement and revealed the name, "Bernard P. James! Remember what Barrett said? Mr. James would take his daughter's death with him to the grave. The more we sit here talking about what we should do, the more I think we should go see Mr. James first. He deserves to know the truth about who killed his daughter."

"But he already knows the truth," pointed out Nick.

"That's right… he does, he just couldn't prove it and neither could the police. We now, have in our possession the photographs that *could* prove it. I have no problem with taking everything we've collected to the police. I just think we owe it to Mr. James to allow him to see what we've discovered first. After all, he's the one who lost the most…his only daughter. I think he should have a say in how all this is handled."

"What about Mrs. Yeats. She lost her grandson, Chester."

"Yes she did, but she has moved on. Remember what she told us when we questioned her about why she didn't take the camera to the police. She told us she was done dealing with them. No, I think Mr. James on the other hand would be quite interested in what we have discovered."

The waitress interrupted their conversation when she and another young lady returned with their dinners. Shelby quickly blessed the meal then proceeded to dump ranch dressing on her salad and continued with their previous conversation. "So, if we do decide to go to Mr. James first, how do we handle it? I can't imagine just walking up to his house, knocking on the door and when he answers we say, 'Hey, we know who killed your daughter!'"

Picking up his knife, Nick began cutting into his cod. "Didn't someone mention he still lives here on Fripp?"

"Yes, I think it was Mrs. Yeats who told us she ran into Mr. James a couple of years ago at the community center. She said after all these years he was still bitter and blamed those three boys not only for the death of his daughter but also his wife. She also said he would never stop looking for the proof that would convict those boys. I think that now, we have the proof he's been looking for. Maybe we could give him a phone call first and explain we have something of great importance to show him in regard to his daughter's death."

"Do you think he'll believe us? Do you think he'd even agree to see us?"

Stabbing a bite of coleslaw, Shelby answered, "I don't know. This is the one of the wealthiest men in the state. When my father did work for him at his home here on Fripp, he said Mr. James was a very private man. You just don't knock on the man's door or simply give him a jingle. This is not the typical Fripp Island resident we're talking about, so it might not be easy to get to see him."

Washing down a bite of fish with a swig of beer, Nick leaned forward and smiled, "I know who could get us into see him…Carson Pike!"

"Really…does Carson know him?"

"Probably, he knows everyone who lives on the island. Besides that, I think we should confide in Carson before we make our next move. We can tell him everything we've learned so far and trust him not to say a word to anyone. He's a good man to have on your team. Who knows what would have happened to us if we had had to deal with the Carnahans without Carson's assistance. If it weren't for him we might not even be sitting here right now. I know I wouldn't. He saved my skin. I trust him impeccably."

Shelby smiled. "If that's what you want to do, I'm fine with it. I don't know Carson as well as you, but what I do know of him, I think he might be able to give us some good advice on what we should do at this point."

"Good then, it's settled," said Nick. Reaching for his cell phone he announced, "I'm going to give him a call right now and see if he's available to come by the house tonight so we can lay it all out."

Nick no sooner held the phone in his hand when he noticed Brumly and Maria being escorted into the bar where they were seated at the remaining empty table. Laying down the phone, Nick nodded in their direction and warned Shelby, "Trouble! I think our evening of a quiet dinner and pleasant conversation may have just taken a turn for the worse!"

Shelby turned and watched the infamous couple sit down. Chic wasn't paying them any attention but Maria was staring dead at them. Frustrated, Shelby turned back and gulped down her beer in four long swallows. Holding up her empty glass, she stated, "Fill me up! This could be interesting!"

Picking up the pitcher, Nick shook his head in disbelief. "It never fails. It seems like you and I can never have a pleasant dinner. The first night we went to the Dockside, Charley and Derek came over to our table and then I got into that scrapple with Ike Miller. The night after we had dinner last summer at Johnson's Creek, I get kidnapped by Carnahan's goons and then just the other day at Plums, Maria insults you and winds up with soup on her lap *and now*...tonight, it appears our dinner is once again going to be scrutinized by Charley's pain in the ass sister and her crooked lawyer, Brumly."

Drinking half the beer, Shelby sat back and stated firmly, "Why don't we just ignore them?"

Nick took a drink and watched Maria stand as Brumly grabbed her arm and said something. Maria, jerking her arm away from Chic turned and marched across the room in their direction. "Ignoring them is going to be a hard thing to do," warned Nick, "especially when you take into account Charley's sister, at this moment is homing in on our table like a heat seeking missile!"

Shelby shrugged, "Just stay calm. She's all bark and no bite. I am not going to get ticked off like I did at Plums...believe me!"

Calmly, Shelby cut into her cod, dipped the piece of fish in tartar sauce and took a small bite. Acting like the approaching monster of a woman was not an issue, she commented, "This cod is really quite good."

Nick looked past Maria at Brumly who had a look of disapproval plastered across his face that clearly stated he didn't want her to come to their table. *Too late,* thought Nick when Maria pulled out a chair and sat between he and Shelby. Sarcastically, she remarked, "My, my…we have to quit meeting this way. People will talk." Looking Shelby up and down, she went on, "I see you've haven't taken my advice about dressing a little better. You continue to dress like a cute little South Carolina, backwoods country bumpkin! I guess it's true what they say. 'You can lead a horse to water but you can't make them drink!'" Displaying her expensive white and lavender pants suit, she explained, "This little number I'm wearing tonight only cost me around eight-hundred. The outfit I was wearing at the Plum the other day ran me close to a thousand dollars. I'll have you know I've taken it to one of your local dry cleaners and was told they may not be able to get the soup stains completely out. You, miss backwoods, cost me a grand!"

Shelby pointed her fork at Maria and retorted, "No…your mouth cost you a grand. If you would have kept your trap shut that littler incident at Plums would have never occurred."

"Mind your manners, missy!" snapped Maria. "You're no match for me. I'm not some sweet, small town local gal you can just push around." Proudly, Maria sat up straight and in a queenly fashion, stated, "I'm a city girl…a New York City girl. I was raised in a rough neighborhood in Brooklyn in the Big Apple, so don't sit there and try to go toe to toe with me. I'll chew you up and spit you out!"

Shelby calmly buttered a roll while Nick sat and watched the bantering. Shelby laid down the butter knife and pointed the roll at Maria. "The only thing you're going to be spitting out is your teeth if you don't back off."

Before Nick realized what was happening Maria stood, reached over and dumped Shelby's meal down over the front of her. Shelby never even flinched when she looked across the table at Nick and smiled.

Maria, standing next to the table nodded in approval of what she had done. "Well I guess that makes us even. Earlier this week I got to wear my lunch and now you get to wear your dinner!" Correcting herself, she raised a finger and pointed out, "I say we're even, but really we're not. The value of the clothing I was wearing you ruined was a thousand dollars." Giving Shelby a look of disgust she went on, "I gather those rags you're wearing are probably valued at what…maybe fifty bucks. The truth is I still owe you nine hundred and fifty dollars' worth of payback, but for now, I'm satisfied. I can now return to my table and enjoy some good seafood,"

Turning, Maria began to walk away. Shelby stood, picked up the three-quarter full pitcher of beer, walked up behind Maria, and yelled, "Hey!"

Maria no sooner turned around than Shelby threw the contents of the pitcher into Maria's face, beer splattering down the front of her clothing. Shelby smiled and commented, "There, now you can add another eight hundred to my tab!"

Maria was livid. Raising her large purse she slammed it into Shelby's right arm knocking her back against the table. Shelby quickly recovered and started to lunge at Maria but was held back by Nick, who whispered into her ear, "This is not the time or place for this!"

Maria was about to swing her bag a second time, but was restrained by Chic who ordered her, "Maria, let's go back to our table!"

A manager, who had been summoned, was now on the scene. "Is there some sort of problem?"

Nick spoke up first, "No, it was nothing more than a slight disagreement…that's all."

Chic, trying his best to calm down Maria, agreed, "Yes, that's right…just a disagreement."

A man who had been seated at a nearby table stood and spoke to the manager. "I saw the entire incident, sir." Motioning at Maria, the man explained, "This woman here came over to this couple's table and dumped this woman's meal in her lap, who in turn, defended herself by dumping a pitcher of beer on this lady. Then, this lady hits the other woman with her purse." Looking at Shelby the man shrugged, "It was a clear matter of self-defense!"

"Look," said the manager. "I really don't care who said what to who. If both couples can just return to your tables and calm down I think everything will be fine. If that cannot be done then I may be forced to ask you both to leave the restaurant."

"That won't be necessary," said Chic. "We're going to be leaving." Nodding at the manager, he apologized to the surrounding dinner guests and backed Maria out of the bar, "Sorry for any inconvenience we may have caused."

The manager turned to Nick and Shelby and asked, "Will you be staying?"

Shelby looked down over her food-stained sweatshirt and remarked, "Let me just step into the restroom and get cleaned up a bit."

The manager signaled at two employees and ordered them, "Clean the floor and the table, bring another Cod special and a pitcher of beer to this table." Turning in a circle, he spoke to those in the bar. "I think everything is back to normal. Enjoy the evening."

At the bottom of the steps outside the Boathouse, Chic grabbed Maria by both shoulders and backed her against the side of the building, pointing a finger in her face. "Look! You hired me to find out what happened to your brother. *You* hired *me!* I certainly don't need you interfering with the process I have planned for Falco and his girlfriend. I know you're interested in finding out what happened to Charley, but you must let me do my job. I happen to be quite good at what I do. So, from here on out you're along for the ride…nothing else. Understand?"

Maria didn't like being put in her place, but realized if she didn't back off she could lose Brumly's services.

"Okay Chic…I get it. It's just so frustrating we haven't found anything out other than what Falco told us."

Chic walked to the side of the building and stared out at the black marsh. "Did you ever stop to consider that maybe what he told the Carnahans is the truth? Maybe your brother did abscond with all that money."

Maria stomped her foot. "That couldn't have possibly happened! You need to keep digging. I know that Falco, along with Carson Pike and the girl are hiding something from us. I'll keep writing the checks and you keep on Falco's ass! Now, what's our next move?"

Shelby returned to the table only to find a complete cod dinner and a fresh pitcher of ice-cold beer in front of her. Seating herself she looked around at the other dinner guests, who had returned to their own conversations and dinner. Pouring herself a beer, she took a long drink, sat back and smiled at Nick.

Nick, still in a state of amazement leaned across the table and whispered, "I thought you said you were going to stay calm."

Winking at Nick, she shrugged her shoulders and remarked, "That was calm!"

Picking up a roll, Shelby asked, "Now, where were we before our brief interruption?"

Reaching for his phone once again, Nick chewed a bite of his dinner and answered, "I was just about to give Carson a call. You're still good with us filling him in on what we've discovered…right?"

Salting her dinner, Shelby nodded, "Yep, sounds like the right thing to do at this point."

Punching in Carson's number, Nick waited patiently while Carson's phone buzzed on the other end. Finally, after what seemed like enough time had passed without Carson answering, Nick laid the phone down next to his plate. "He's not answering. Let's finish our dinner then I'll try again before we leave."

"That won't be necessary," said Shelby, nodding toward the bar. "Look who just walked in."

Carson walked up to the bar, looked in their direction, and then ordered a drink from the bartender. Drink in hand, he approached the table and took a seat, grabbed a roll, took a bite and then spoke, "You don't have to say a word. I already heard about it from the girls at the front desk. The word is that you, Shelby baptized some fancy dressed woman with a pitcher of beer. When I walked in I noticed Brumly outside giving Ms. Sparks the *what for!* He didn't look that pleased with her. She looked like a drown rat. After I got inside and heard about the fiasco back here in the bar, I put two and two together and figured the two combatants were you and Maria Sparks. Care to fill me in?"

"She got what she deserved," stated Shelby. "It all started earlier this week when Nick and I were having lunch in Beaufort…"

Minutes later, Shelby wound up her explanation, "She and Chic decided to leave and we opted to finish our dinner."

Nick took his last bite and asked, "Did you drop by tonight for dinner or just a cold one?"

"Just a couple of beers. I've been working on one of my boats at the marina since early this morning."

"We were thinking about heading back to my place after dinner. We would like you to join us, if possible."

"Sure, why not. It must be something important because I'm sure you two would rather spend the evening alone rather than with an old fart like me!"

"It is important," said Shelby. "Do you recall last summer when we told you we were close to figuring out who the PRS Killer was?"

"Yeah, I do recall that conversation and if I remember correctly I told you that was for the police to figure out."

Shelby didn't respond but looked at Nick who picked up on the conversation, "Well, it would seem Shelby and I have gotten ourselves involved in another set of murders…unsolved murders. We have discovered something that might bring the killers to justice and we wanted you to take a look at what we have found, but we can't do it here. It involves some very revealing photographs."

Signaling for another beer, Carson asked, "Before I commit myself to this new adventure you two are off on, could you be a tad bit more specific…like photographs about what murders?"

Nick answered the question, "Do you remember back twenty-seven years ago when two high school students were murdered right here on Fripp and the murders were never solved?"

"Yes, I do remember when that happened. God, has it been that many years? I had only been a resident on the island for a few years when those murders occurred. I can't recall the names of the students but I remember there was quite an investigation. And you're right…those murders were never solved." Snapping his fingers, he suddenly remembered, "I believe one of the victims was none other than Bernard P. James' daughter. Is that what you're asking me about?"

"Yes," said Shelby. "And I have to say it's rather ironic you would mention Bernard P. James. We need to talk with him and we were wondering if you knew him personally."

"Bernard…of course I know Bernard James. Now to be honest with you, I haven't seen him that much since his daughter was killed. Before she was killed, Bernard and I were quite good friends. I took him out on fishing trips and we played poker up at the community center every Saturday night. He had lavish parties at his home here on Fripp where he still lives. Your grandparents always attended his parties. They were good friends with him. As I recall he was quite involved in the investigation and pissed off beyond belief when, I believe, three football players who were suspects got off Scott free. He was never the same after that. His wife died a few years later and then I guess it was back about ten years ago, his legs gave out on him and now he is confined to a wheelchair. He very rarely comes out of his house. I bet I haven't seen ol' Bernard in four maybe five years. The last time I saw him was at a Fripp Owner's meeting at the community center. He had become and still is to my knowledge today, a bitter old man who has more money than there are stars in the sky. I suppose I could give him a call on your behalf. But, first things first. I need to see what it is you have that he may be interested in."

"Great!" said Nick. "Finish up your beer and meet us at my place. We'll go over everything with you."

CHAPTER EIGHTEEN

"RIGHT HERE IT IS," SAID CARSON. MAKING A RIGHT HAND turn from Tarpon onto River Club Drive, Nick slowly drove up the palm tree and Palmetto lined paved street while he and Shelby stared at the large, southern antebellum homes.

Carson, from the backseat gave instructions, "Head on up the street to the fourth house. That's where Mr. James resides."

Admiring the houses Nick remarked, "I've never been back in here before. It appears very exclusive."

"Exclusive it is," said Carson. "This is the most prestigious street, or I guess you could say neighborhood on the island. These are the most expensive homes on Fripp, except for the one Grady Phillips owns over by the Ocean Point Golf Course and then there's another 'Out of everyone's price range home' further back up Tarpon. Most people who visit the island normally don't drive down this short street. The street itself leads to nowhere so there is no reason other than living here for people to come in this neighborhood. Some of the wealthiest people on the island live back in here.

"How long has Mr. James lived out here?"

"For as far back as I can remember. Now, he purchased the house we're going to probably close to forty years ago. Before that, he had a place he rented further down Tarpon. Like I said he's sort of a recluse. He has no living family members. He has a full time cook and cleaning maid and a live-in butler." Arriving at the palatial home, a two-story dark chocolate stucco mansion trimmed in beige, Nick pulled into a circular driveway and stopped.

Climbing out of the back of the Lexus, Carson looked at his watch. "Nine fifty-five. Our appointment is at ten. If I remember correctly Bernard is a very punctual man."

Standing by the car, Nick admired the stately home. "You say Mr. James lives here by himself?"

"That's right," said Carson. "When his wife was living she was quite the gardener. The James' home was always known as the best-landscaped property on the island. The front porch was always tastefully decorated with bright hanging baskets and large ferns. This circular drive was lined with bedding plants and at the base of the house there was the most exotic collection of hosta plants that could be found in the state. But, as you can see there are no longer any plants on the porch, driveway or around the house. Now, rather than a botanical showcase it's simply a large home of a wealthy recluse." Starting up the right side of the Savannah style steps, Carson motioned, "C'mon, Bernard awaits us. We don't want to keep him waiting."

On the elevated porch, fronted by four large white pillars, Carson rang the doorbell and waited. Shelby commented, "This is the first time I've had a dress on in, well, I can't remember."

Nick agreed and lifted up the only necktie he owned. "I don't think I've been dressed this nice since we had our first date."

A large man wearing casual grey slacks and a bright red turtleneck sweater opened the large oak door. Smiling at the trio standing on the porch, he inquired, "Mr. Pike, Mr. Falco and Ms. Pickett, I assume."

"That we are," answered Carson.

Opening the door widely, the man offered, "Please step in." After everyone was standing in a large foyer beneath a gigantic chandelier, the man motioned toward a hallway next to a massive walnut staircase. "This way please. Mr. James will receive you in the library."

Passing a set of large glass French doors, Shelby noticed a woman wearing an apron. She was dusting the mantle of a stone fireplace in what looked like a living room. The home was immaculate. Large framed pictures hung on the walls, expensive looking artifacts were centered on walnut or dark cherry antique end tables and bookcases, lamps covered with ornate lampshades. The house was on the dark side which normally would have exuded a gloomy sensation, but instead bespoke of a great deal of money. It was as if one could smell the wealth.

Walking past another open door of what appeared to be a vast kitchen surrounded by stunning deep cherry cabinetry, the counters were black and white marble and the appliances were a jet black. Passing through a circular oak-topped doorway, they were led to a large room where all four walls were crammed with books from the floor to the ceiling. They no sooner stepped into the room of apparent vast knowledge, than they saw a man seated in a wheelchair next to a large walnut desk.

The man was dressed in a three-piece, pinstriped black suit, starched white shirt, blue and grey paisley tie and deeply shined dress shoes. Placing a set of chain-suspended eyeglasses on the bridge of his nose, he smiled when they walked across the room and were offered seats on a long, dark green velvet couch. Once seated, the large man made the introductions. "Mr. James, this is Carson Pike, Nick Falco and Shelby Lee Pickett."

Mr. James nodded at the man and spoke, "Thank you, Conner. Would you please bring us an assortment of beverages? Coffee, hot chocolate, maybe some fresh brewed iced tea? And I would also like a tray of some of those cookies Mae baked last evening."

Backing out of the room, the man humbly replied, "As you wish, Mr. James."

Watching the man walk from the room, Mr. James ran his hand over a well-trimmed white beard and commented, "Conner has been my live-in butler ever since my wife passed on. As you can see I am confined to this wheeled contraption. If it were not for he and Mae; my cook and cleaning lady, I don't know how I would survive." Moving the chair out slightly from the desk, he held out his hands and spoke genuinely, "Welcome to my home. I hope this room will be suitable for our conversation." Reaching out for Carson's hand, Bernard continued, "Carson, what a delight to see you again. It's been what...quite a few years since we've talked."

Carson responded and shook Bernard's feeble looking hand. "I miss our poker games. Do you still play?"

"Yes, I do. Occasionally, Conner and I have a go at it. He's very good. He would never admit to it but I think from time to time he allows me to win."

Extending his hand he focused on Nick. "Mr. Falco, am I to understand you are the grandson of the Fripp Island Falco's."

Shaking Bernard's hand, Nick responded politely, "Yes sir, that is correct."

Fidgeting with a gold cufflink on his right hand, he explained, "Normally I don't receive guests at my home but when Carson explained to me you were related to Edward and Amelia, I could hardly refuse. When your grandfather died it saddened me deeply. He was a good friend and when it came to handling money, a smarter man one could not find. When Amelia died, what was it, earlier this year I believe, I attended the funeral at the community center here on the island. I'm not much for being around a lot of people these days but I wanted to pay my respects to your grandmother. I must have left before you arrived. This island will not be the same without Amelia Falco living here. I also understand you inherited her home?"

"Yes, I did. As a young boy I used to come down here for a week during the summer to visit she and Edward. I always dreamed of living here, but figured I'd never be able to afford it. Sometimes when I walk out the back porch and look at the ocean I still can't quite believe I live here."

"Your grandparents had a lovely home. I was only in it on two occasions for holiday parties. I especially enjoyed the large three-tier fountain in your front yard. I offered Amelia a small fortune for it, but she said there was no amount of money she would take for it. When you have accumulated as much money as I have over the years, there doesn't seem to be anything you cannot purchase. What I'm saying is everything and everybody has a price, except that is for your grandmother and her fountain." Smiling, he shook his head, "She was a hoot to say the least. I miss having her around this ol' island."

Looking at Shelby, the smile continued as he spoke, "And as for you, Ms. Pickett. Your father is by far the best plumber in Beaufort County. He did some work for me many years ago. I found he does quality work at a reasonable price and besides that, he seems to be a good man."

Taking on a serious tone, Bernard folded his hands on his lap and looked at the briefcase setting next to Shelby. "Carson tells me you two young folks have discovered some proof verifying the three boys who were suspected of killing my Abby, did *in fact* take my daughter's life. Carson explained to me over the phone, he has seen this information and that I need to take a look at what you have discovered."

Shelby held up the case and expounded, "Yes, we have brought what we feel after extensive research is proof placing those three boys at the murder scene." Looking around the room, she asked, "Is there some sort of a table we can use? There are a number of photographs you need to see that will tie all this together."

Pushing the wheelchair backwards, Bernard pressed a small button on a desk intercom. A voice answered instantly, "Yes sir, what do you require?"

"Conner, we will need a card table brought in from the front room and set up between the couch and my desk here in the library."

"Yes sir…right away."

Pushing himself back away from the desk, Bernard looked again at the case and explained, "There has not been a day since my Abigail's death I have not prayed someone, somehow would come up with the proof in regard to what happened that night here on Fripp. As the days, weeks and months passed during the initial investigation, it became evident with the minimal proof the police did come up with that Brad Schulte, Tim Durham and Miles Gaston killed not only my daughter but Chester Finch as well. That next fall when they, all three of them, went off to college on football scholarships, I just couldn't believe they had not been arrested. My daughter never got to go to Cornell and the Finch lad never got to Harvard. It was without a doubt a miscarriage of justice. Those three boys, who are now grown men are still out there living their lives while Abigail and Chester have been gone from our lives for nearly three decades."

Conner entered the room and excused himself, "Where exactly would you like this table set up, sir?"

Motioning with his right hand, Bernard ordered gently, "A few feet out from the couch will be fine."

After unfolding the legs and positioning the table, Conner nodded at the three guests and walked out of the room, closing the large oak double doors. There was a moment of silence that Shelby broke when she opened the case and removed the camera. "Well then, let's get started." Standing, she walked around the table to Bernard and handed him the old camera and explained, "This camera, which is about thirty years old was found by some tourists down in some rocks on the side of the turnaround at the end of Tarpon, not far from the murder scene. It was not found until two years after the murders. At one time, apparently there had been an I.D. marking on the bottom that is no longer there. But at the time when the camera was found the identity of the owner and their address was on the camera."

Turning the camera over in his hands, Bernard asked, "And who did the camera belong to?"

"The camera belonged to none other than one of the victims, Chester Finch, of 311 Deer Lake Drive."

Turning the camera over in his hand, Bernard raised his bushy grey eyebrows. "You haven't even been speaking for a minute and I find this already quite interesting. How did you come across this camera?"

Nick cleared his throat and explained, "Just recently I purchased a home here on the island from Gretchen Yeats, Chester's grandmother. I don't know if you are aware of this or not, but Chester was living with her at the time of his death."

"Yes, I am aware of that, however, I never realized it until after his death."

"Well, anyway, Mrs. Yeats left most of the furnishings at the home. The other day while I was preparing the house for a good painting, Shelby here was up in a small attic snooping around where she found an old trunk, which contained the camera. She brought it to me and explained it was quite old and according to the film indicator box on the top there were still five pictures that hadn't been taken. Being familiar with cameras she explained this particular camera took twenty-four pictures and that meant there were nineteen undeveloped photos on the film. Just for the fun of it Shelby took the camera home and developed the film. What we discovered was very disturbing. We decided to go visit Mrs. Yeats and try to get some information on the camera, but we did not tell her about the developed film because when we examined the photos we were not sure what we were looking at. She told us the camera belonged to her grandson Chester, who was quite the camera buff. He had his own photography business and was always taking pictures wherever he went. She told us about how her grandson and your daughter had been murdered and the crime was never solved. She was not pleased with the way the police handled the entire investigation and when the camera was brought to her, rather than turning it over to the police she just pitched it in Chester's trunk along with a lot of old pictures he had taken."

Laying the camera down on the table, Bernard remarked, "Mrs. Yeats was correct when she told you the police had not handled the investigation very well. I agree with her wholeheartedly. The police dropped the ball on those three boys." Displaying his feeble, frail body with his hands he went on, "I'm not much of a physical specimen these days, but my mind is still sharp as a tack. I remember everything that was done and said during the investigation." Tapping the camera, he continued, "One of the things that came out during the student interviews the police held was that Chester was, in fact, a camera nut. He did have his own small photography business and was known to constantly take pictures. The students all agreed that Chester, wherever he went always carried two cameras with him. A great number of students who had attended the Fripp Island celebration the night of the murders verified that Chester was indeed at the party taking pictures and that he did have two cameras. When they discovered Chester's car at the turnaround near the murder scene there was not one camera to be found, let alone two. The police concluded both cameras were probably destroyed or taken. The fact this camera was found years later near the murder scene can only mean it was either hidden or dropped in the rocks."

Shelby held up the I.D. tag and explained, "And here we have the plate that at one time was attached to the camera. It was found at the bottom of the trunk where we discovered the camera." Handing the plate to Bernard, she commented, "I think you'll find this to be quite interesting."

Looking at the plate closely, Bernard read the name aloud, "Chester Finch." Laying the plate on his desk, he gestured at the briefcase. "Please continue."

"And now for the pictures we developed," said Shelby. Removing the three folders from the case, she laid two of the folders on the couch and opened folder #1. Laying the pictures in order so they were facing Bernard, she added, "There are nine photos here that were taken, we believe at the celebration party that night." Handing Bernard the two photographs she had enlarged she pointed out. "You can tell from the partial signs and banners in the pictures where the party was held. We feel Chester was at the party and did take these pictures."

Examining the photos closely Bernard picked up the enlargements and confirmed, "I agree. These look like they were taken at the large swimming pool area just down from the John Fripp Condos." Looking closely at the photos again, he stated, "There are a great number of students in these pictures, but not one indicates that Abby, Brad Schulte, Tim Durham or Miles Gaston were in attendance. Another thing that came out of the student interviews was that Chester was at the party and was taking pictures early in the evening, but then disappeared. The boys claimed when they were interviewed, that after trying to help Abby get her car started they drove her over here to Fripp and dropped her at the pool. My daughter was never seen by anyone who attended the party. The only person on the island who reported her as being seen was the guard at the security shack. He reported she was in a red Mustang with three football players. So, the question remains, where did my daughter go after they dropped her off?"

"We," commented Shelby, "figure Abby went with the boys since no one saw her at the party. One thing we know for sure is that they wound up on the same beach where she and Chester were murdered. But, before we get to that there is a second set of photos you need to see." Moving the first set to the side, she opened the second folder and lined up the seven photos of the nighttime salt marsh shots. "As you can see these were taken at a later time, probably later that night. After examining these photos, especially these two enlargements we think these were taken down at the turnaround at the end of Tarpon." Pointing at the pictures, she added, "These strings of lights look like they may be from The Cabana Club on the other side of the marsh."

Looking closely at the two enlargements, Bernard commented, "I tend to agree. And that makes sense since Chester's car was found at the turnaround. These first two sets of pictures allow us to track or have a pretty good idea where Chester was during the evening. What we still do not know is where my daughter went."

Opening the third folder, Shelby hesitated. "These next group of photos, of which there are three, are quite disturbing, so you might want to prepare yourself."

"If these photos reveal what really happened, well I'm ready. I've been waiting years for the truth."

As Shelby laid the photos on the table in front of Bernard, she explained, "We enlarged the photos so we could get a better look at those on the beach. You'll notice the three boys are turned and looking up as if whoever took the pictures was standing above them. From the looks on their faces I'd say they were not expecting to have their pictures taken *and* we are convinced Chester was the one who took the pictures."

Picking up one of the pictures, Bernard stared down at the images. Holding the picture to his chest, he got a tear in his eye. "The girl in this picture is my Abigail." Composing himself he looked at the photo again and asked. "What proof do we have these three boys in the picture are Schulte, Durham and Gaston?"

"That's easily proven!" Removing yet another folder from the case, she explained, "We have some pictures we got from the 1989 Beaufort High yearbook." Laying a team photo in front of Bernard, she went on to explain, "This is a picture of the '89 Beaufort football team." Pointing at three different players in the picture she stated, "That's Brad Schulte right there, then to his left you have Tim Durham and on his left, Miles Gaston. You cannot make out their uniform numbers completely but we also have another photo of the team players listed by name and their number. The numbers on this photo match the numbers on the back of the team jerseys Chester took at the murder scene. From right to left Shelby identified each boy; Brad Schulte, number 6; Tim Durham, number 23; and last but not least, Miles Gaston, number 17. It couldn't be more obvious."

Bernard picked up all three photographs and matched them. "This is incredible! These old photographs place the three football players at the scene of the crime." Putting his forefinger on the photo, Bernard remarked in amazement, "This boy right here, number 17, Miles Gaston, is holding what could very well be the missing murder weapon which was never found. The medical examiner reported Abby was beaten to death with a wooden object, possibly a two by four, which appears to be in the hands of the Gaston kid. These last three photos are very incriminating. They place the three boys not only on the beach but show one of the three wielding the murder weapon. If they would have had this type of proof back twenty-seven years ago those three boys would have never walked."

"There's more," added Nick as he sorted through a stack of yearbook pictures picking out one of the enlargements. Handing the photograph to Bernard he explained, "This is the picture they took of your daughter for her graduation. We happened to notice she is wearing a medallion that appears to be similar to the medallion on the beach pictures." Taking the magnifying glass from the case he handed both to Bernard and asked, "Is that medallion one and the same?"

Holding the glass over the picture, he smiled sadly. "Yes...it is. I purchased that medallion for Abby for her seventeenth birthday when we were in France on vacation. It was quite expensive as I recall, around seven thousand dollars. It was diamond studded in her first name. She loved the medallion and wore it everywhere."

"Well that does it then," exclaimed Shelby. "We were not sure if it was the same as the one in the graduation photo. So therefore, we couldn't be sure the girl in the three last pictures was actually your daughter."

A knock on the door was followed by Conner who opened the door and entered with a roll-around cart, which held glasses, cups, three pitchers and a plate of cookies. "Ah…refreshments have arrived," stated Bernard.

Placing the cart at the end of the card table, Conner stood back and asked, "Do you want me to remain and serve, sir?"

Bernard waved Conner's question off as he smiled at his three guests. "No I think we'll be fine. When you leave please close the door and do not disturb us. Thank you, Conner."

When the large oak door was shut, Bernard gestured at the cart and spoke, "Please, help yourselves."

Shelby stood and offered, "I'll serve if that's all right?"

Holding up a cup and a glass she spoke to Bernard, "What's your pleasure, Mr. James?"

Bernard nodded his head in approval and stated, "I believe I'll just have a cup of the hot chocolate. I used to be strictly a coffee drinker, but as of late I seem to have grown fond of the warm chocolate. I would also like one cookie."

Pouring chocolate into the cup, Shelby asked, "If I could be so bold as to ask, would you mind telling us about your lovely daughter. I'm afraid with all the research we have done we still don't know much about her."

Taking the cup and the baked treat, Bernard set them on the edge of the table. "Of course. Abigail was always a brilliant child, even when she was younger. We had plans of raising her with qualities of sophistication, grace and charm, but our little Abby had plans of her own. It didn't take us long to figure out our daughter was going to march to the beat of a different drummer. We gave her dance lessons, but about the only thing she managed to accomplish was flirting with the little boys who attended. We would, on a regular basis, take her to the country club as she grew older. She was not interested in golf, tennis or horseback riding, the things my wife and I were involved with. When we did attend club activities she was always hanging with boys around her age…not the girls. By the time she got to high school, there was no changing our little girl into what we had planned on. We didn't smoke, she did. We didn't drink, she did. We didn't cuss, she did. Looking back I think the only attribute we may have passed onto her was brilliance. My wife, Margaret was extremely brilliant and well, myself, I have always been reasonably intelligent. Abby was brilliant to say the least. I can't ever remember during her school years when she ever got a grade in any subject other than an A. And here's the thing. She didn't have to try hard to get good grades. It just came natural to her."

Sipping at the chocolate, Bernard went on to explain, "Following her freshman year in high school, the word got around that our precious Abigail liked to sleep around. We sat her down and had a frank discussion with her, but she had already made her mind up that she liked the entire sexual process. Finally, after months of talks and counseling, it became evident she had no immediate intensions of changing. The one thing we did demand from her was she not get pregnant out of wedlock and if she did we would completely disown her. My wife gave her a weekly allowance of five hundred dollars. Abby always told me she saved most of the money she was given, because the boys she dated always gave her whatever she desired. To tell you the truth I think my wife gave her the money so if Abby ever did get pregnant, she would have the funds to get the child aborted. I never discussed this with my wife because it was rather awkward."

Shelby, dumping a spoonful of sugar into a coffee she was preparing, thought about asking her next question, but decided against it. Bernard caught her look of doubt and stated comically, "Young lady, if there is anything I've learned over decades of being a businessman it's that I can read people rather well. It's easy to see you want to ask me a question but are hesitant. I have the distinct feeling you want to ask me if Abigail ever did get pregnant *and* the answer is no. Her death was, is and may always be puzzling to me. When she was first discovered on the beach in nothing more than her underclothing it was first thought her death was a crime of passion but that was ruled out when the M.E. reported there were no traces of sexual activity. The fact her medallion, which we know was quite valuable and a few hundred dollars were still at the scene of the crime ruled out robbery. Those three boys killed my little girl and as it stands now, even with this new proof we may never know the truth."

Nick sipped his coffee and politely stated, "Mr. James, we apologize if by bringing by this new evidence today has caused you any grief. You've probably already been through enough."

Bernard took a long deep breath and looked up at the wooden beam and planked ceiling. Looking back at his three guests, he spoke softly, "You would think after all this time the pain of my daughter's death would have passed, but the wound is still open, and very real." Placing his hand over his heart, he expressed, "The pain is still here. There is no need for any apology. Depending on how all this turns out, I may still get my revenge. It's more than just my daughter's death. You see,

Margaret really struggled with Abby's death and it got to the point where she got ill, never recovered and eventually died herself four years after Abby was gone. Those three boys took not only my daughter from me, but as far as I'm concerned, my wife as well. My present physical condition I can only attribute to old age setting in. My daughter and my wife were my life. After they were both gone, the only thing I had left was this large house and more money than I could ever spend. In order to keep from going insane I dove into my work and unfortunately didn't take the best care of myself. So, to be honest with you, if this new evidence has brought any grief to me today, the answer is most definitely no! As the years have passed I have resigned myself to the grim prospect the murder of my daughter would never be solved. If anything, the information you have presented to me today is a glimmer of hope in a long list of what seems now like unending days with no hope whatsoever of ever knowing the truth." Picking up one of the last three photographs, he smiled, "But, with this new information you have brought to my attention, I think there may be an opportunity to bring these boys to justice. Thank you…thank you, so much!"

Nick, feeling better about the decision they had made to come to Bernard, held up his coffee cup and stated, "There's something else…something that happened to me a few days back. I actually ran into Miles Gaston while walking on the beach right here on Fripp." Bernard's eyes grew wide with interest while Nick continued, "I didn't realize it at the time but I wound up on the small beach where your daughter and Chester were murdered. There was a man sitting there staring out at Skull Inlet. We had a short conversation about how, as a young boy, he had come to that very spot quite a bit as a kid. The man, who at the time I did not know was Gaston, went on to tell me he just recently moved back to Beaufort County, actually here on Fripp in one of those tree houses on the island. He also told me he had homes in Sacramento and Palm Beach. He told me he travelled a lot and he owned a chain of restaurants called Pattersons. He owns two eating establishments that are local; one in Charleston, the other in Savannah. When we parted ways he introduced himself as Miles. I never realized it was Miles Gaston until we got a look at the boys' yearbook pictures."

Holding up a photo of a number of graduating students Nick placed his finger next to Miles Gaston's senior picture. "Even though it's been twenty-seven years since this picture was taken I could tell the man on the beach was the same boy in this photo…Miles Gaston." Remembering, Nick produced his wallet and withdrew the card Gaston had given him on the beach. "He gave me one of his business cards."

Bernard took the card and stated, "This just keeps getting better by the minute. Would it be all right if I kept this card?"

"Actually," shrugged Nick, "if it's okay with Shelby, I'm okay with you keeping everything we've brought to you today."

Shelby agreed, "Most definitely! You were our last stop before taking what we have found to the police. If you would rather approach the authorities with what we have found, I have no problem with that. We will even go with you, if you'd like."

"If you're okay with turning over this information to me, I will accept it, but with a condition."

Carson, who had remained quiet throughout the presentation finally spoke up, "Since Nick and Shelby have confided in me, I must ask; what condition?"

"I'm glad you asked that question, Carson. The condition I'll require includes you as well. I'm about to tell you what I intend to do with this new information. The problem is after I tell you what my intensions are you may not agree to my conditions."

"We cannot disagree unless we know what your wishes are, so give it to us straight."

Munching on his cookie, he smiled deviously, "I have no intentions of taking this information to the police…at least not right off the bat. I don't know if you're aware of it or not, but when these three boys walked away Scott free, I decided to sue the Beaufort Police Department. I contacted Khelen Ridley, but he told me it was a case I could not win. I went with another local attorney and just like Ridley had informed me, I lost. So, in all actuality, the police got off as well. I have no trust in the local police. I'm sure all the men and woman who worked the case of Abby and Chester's deaths are no longer on the force, but still, after all these years I don't feel they would react with much vigor about bringing in these three men. It would take too long and the process would be quite complicated. I have another plan in mind for our three former high school football stars."

Putting the remains of the cookie down on his lap, he explained, "I want these three men to suffer, and I mean suffer to great lengths. I want to ruin their lives, their businesses, their reputations, their marriages, if they are indeed married, their status in the communities where they live, and their bank accounts. In other words I want to strip them down to their very bones. The local police will eventually figure out what's going on anyway. I'll fill them in when I think it's time. Not in the best physical condition, I can only mastermind and fund the plan I have in mind. I am going to need a small team of people I can trust to pull this off." Pointing at his three guests, Bernard smiled, "You three are to be on my team, if you so desire."

Carson was about to speak but Shelby beat him to the punch, "What would we be required to do *and* would it be dangerous?"

Bernard folded his hands on his lap and answered the question immediately, "First of all, I know Carson has a talent for getting things done. Plus, I know he has connections who can get things done as well. As far as you and Nick are concerned I admire the way you followed up with the simple discovery of this camera that has brought you to this point. You two seem to be quite good at gathering information, which is going to be the first phase of my plan. Depending on what we discover will determine how the reminder of the plan will work. Your second question as to if this will be dangerous, I really can't answer. I would think it would not involve any danger. But, then again, we will be digging into the lives of three men who have killed and gotten away with their crime for twenty-seven years. Once we begin to expose them it's hard to predict how they will react. We have an advantage no one else has." Holding up one of the three photos of the beach, Bernard explained, "We know these boys killed Abby and Chester. We have the proof. Once we begin to bring the truth to the surface and the general public starts to become aware of who these men might *really be,* they will have to be careful how and what they do and say. They have been skating for almost three decades with nothing or no one to fear. Now, all of a sudden when we bring their past life into the public eye who knows how they'll react. I can't imagine any of this being dangerous but then there are always the unknown, unforeseen things that can happen in life. So, that being said I cannot guarantee it will not be dangerous. I will say this; I will make it worth your while. I will fund any expenses incurred, whether it be, travel, meals, lodging…whatever it takes. I have unlimited financial resources. If we bring these three men to justice, there will be a substantial monetary reward for each of you…let's say one hundred thousand each!"

Shelby almost choked as she responded, "One hundred thousand dollars…each? That's a lot of money!"

"To most folks that is indeed quite a bit of money. To me it is a pittance in comparison to what I have accumulated."

Nick objected, "We did not come here today to gain financially from what we have discovered, nor did we come here to sell you this information."

"I am not buying the information from you. I am merely suggesting I am willing to reward you for your assistance in bringing down the boys who killed my daughter. I could actually end the nightmare I have been experiencing for years by simply picking up the phone and calling someone. Who that someone is I do not know, but it would be easy enough to find out. I could pay far less than three hundred thousand dollars I am willing to dole out to you plus the added expense of my plan. There are people is this world who would pull the trigger on another person for as little as a hundred dollars. I can't tell you how many mornings I have awoken with that very thought in mind. The reason why I have not gone that route is because I am a businessman, not a killer. I have always been, let's say ninety-nine percent sure those boys killed my Abby. That one percent chance I could be wrong keeps me from making that call. That one percent has now been erased with the photos you have brought to me. I want these three men to be brought down and down hard, but I want to stay if at all possible within the parameters of the law."

Nick turned to Carson and asked, "What do you think Carson?"

"It's not my decision to make. You and Shelby did all the legwork that brought you to this point. It's your decision. If you want to go along with Bernard's plan, then I'm in. If you just want to turn the info over to Bernard and walk away then I can walk away also. Like I said…it's your choice."

Nick looked at Shelby who started to laugh. "Ya know, ever since I met you last summer it has been a constant rollercoaster ride of excitement. I thought after last summer the ride was over but now it looks like we are at it again. I'm in…but only if you agree, Nick."

Nick popped a cookie in his mouth and smiled." What the hell…let's do this!"

Carson rubbed his hands together and spoke, "Looks like you've got yourself a team, Bernard! When do we start?"

Bernard took a final drink of chocolate and stated, "Not until the entire team has been assembled. There are to be two more members of the team. First, my butler, Conner. I trust him implicitly. He is aware of everything that goes on in this house and in my life. I will require him at my side throughout our endeavor. I will fill him in after you have departed for the day. He is all too well aware of the grief I have suffered due to the deaths of Abigail and Margaret. The final member of our team has to have special skills; skills that will be required to deal with the type of men we will be pursuing. The fifth member of the team must be able to do what others do not want or desire to do. A man who is not afraid to get his hands extremely dirty. A man who has no scruples, a man who'll do whatever it takes to acquire the final results of our plan. The man I speak of is Charles Brumly, a local Beaufort attorney and private detective."

Carson, Nick and Shelby were at a loss for words as they stared across the room at Bernard who, noticing the odd looks, asked, "I take it I have said something wrong or off-color."

Nick was the first to respond, "Charles Brumly, or Chic, as I have come to know him is indeed everything you have said and probably more. That man would sell out his mother for the right price. He is nothing more than a pain in the ass!"

Bernard pursed his lips, "I take it you know Chic?"

"Not all that well. Let's put it this way. He has been hired by a woman from New York who believes that I, and well Shelby and Carson had something to do with the disappearance of her brother. Brumly for the past week or so has been everywhere we go. A friend of mine punched him in the mouth, soup and beer tossed on his employer in his presence, and yet he refuses to give up the chase. In my opinion he is nothing more than a nightmare in a cheap suit."

Holding up his right hand, Bernard asked, "Are the accusations of his employer true?"

Lying, Nick confirmed, "No, they are not true. I have no idea what happened to this woman's brother."

Smiling, Bernard said, "You underestimate me and the power of money. If you decide to become members of my team perhaps I can do you all a favor. All it will take is a phone call from me and Chic will drop this New York woman like a hot skillet."

Shelby asked, "Why would he do that. I understand she is paying him quite well for his underhanded services!"

Opening a drawer of the desk he removed a checkbook and held it up high. "This is why! Remember what I said earlier; everyone has their price. I'll buy Brumly off. I'll pay him far more than this New York client of his. I'll admit Chic Brumly is a pain in the ass until he's on your side and then he suddenly becomes a necessary and valuable asset. If Chic decides to come over to our side, do you think you can work with him?"

"I can't imagine that," said Nick, "but I suppose so. I can tell you this from my recent experience in dealing with the man, Brad Schulte, Tim Durham and Miles Gaston are about to experience having their lives pried into in a way they could probably never have imagined. I've been on the crap end of the stick Brumly wields. He reminds me of water in a leaky basement. You plug up one hole and he'll find another way to seep in. He's relentless."

"So, let me get this straight," confirmed Bernard. "If Mr. Brumly backs off on you and comes over to our team you'll be able to deal with it?"

Looking at both Shelby and Carson, Nick nodded, "Yes, I believe I can. How about you guys?"

Shelby was in agreement. "If that's part of what it's going to take to bring down the three men who killed your daughter, then I'm in."

Carson walked to the table, grabbed a cookie and stuffed it in his mouth. "Whatever you two kids decide, that's the way I'll go."

Bernard clapped his hands softly. "Very good then. Unless there is anything else to discuss then I say we adjourn for the day. I want to spend some time going over all the information you have brought me and I have to give Chic a call. Let's say we meet right here at my house tomorrow morning at nine. Come hungry. I'll have Mae whip us up a healthy breakfast. If everything works out the way I feel, by the following morning we can begin."

CHAPTER NINETEEN

RAISING THE GARAGE DOOR, NICK LOOKED OUT AT THE front yard. The bright, early morning sun was just beginning to penetrate the row of palm trees separating his property from the neighboring house. Aside from three different sets of vacationers over the summer the house had stood empty. He had never met the owners. A cleaning lady came every Wednesday and cleaned the place, a lawn service kept the grass and the landscaping in good order. He recalled many years ago on one of his summer visits to Amelia and Edward's, his grandmother told him the home was owned by a wealthy family from Atlanta, who only came once a year to spend a week on the beach. The remainder of the time the home was simply a rental.

Pushing a wheelbarrow loaded with cleaning items down the drive he cut across the grass and stopped just short of the large fountain. A variety of birds that had been bathing and drinking in the concrete oasis flew into the safety of the nearby trees. Taking a small bucket from the wheelbarrow, he began the process of removing water from the top tier. He had never cleaned out the fountain before but figured it would be easier to start at the top and work his way down to the lower tier.

Dumping his fourth bucket of water onto the lawn he was startled by a voice, "Good morning, Nick!"

Looking over his shoulder, there stood Genevieve and her pup. Smiling, she walked over and touched the side of the fountain and commented, "Amelia was quite fond of this fountain. Your grandmother gave it a good cleaning every spring, summer, fall and winter. She was very particular about keeping it clean for her feathered friends."

Nick turned and emptied yet another bucket down into the grass and remarked, "I guess you and Ruth just finished your morning walk. Except for the rain we had earlier in the week the weather has been pretty nice." Dipping the bucket into the water of the second tier, he asked, "I don't suppose you've heard anything about your missing golf cart, have you?"

"No, I haven't. And I probably never will. I guess I'll have to purchase a new one. My insurance man told me the policy I have covers theft so I'm not out any money. Speaking of carts, there was another one stolen yesterday over on Harbor Island."

Changing the subject, Genevieve asked, “I haven’t seen that pesky lawyer and his girlfriend around for the past few days.”

Correcting her, Nick confirmed, “Oh they’re still around…believe me! They’ve been over at my new rental and then Shelby and I ran into them at the Boathouse recently.” Dipping out another bucket of water, Nick laughed, “It’s almost like we’re getting used to them being everywhere we go. I think that’s all about to end though. I have a feeling Mr. Brumly is going to turn over a new leaf. I should know later this morning.”

“I certainly hope so,” said Genevieve in an exasperated tone. “I don’t like those two hanging around the neighborhood all the time. If Amelia were here why she’d chase the two of them off with a broom!”

Stopping for a moment, Nick reached out to pet Ruth. “I can only assume she still enjoys her walks on the beach?”

“Yes, indeed,” she does. “She always sleeps with me, and then around five o’clock in the morning she starts to paw at me, letting me know it’s almost time for her walk.” Running her fingers through the water in the lower tier, Genevieve inquired, “Are you considering giving this thing a new coat of paint?”

“Yep, that’s why I’m cleaning it first. I don’t think I’ll have enough time to get it painted this morning. I’ll probably have about enough time to get it cleaned out and then I have a nine o’clock meeting to attend. I might not get to painting until later this afternoon or maybe even tomorrow.”

Genevieve looked at her wristwatch and surprised at the time, spoke up, “Oh my, we spent more time on the beach than I thought. I’ve got to run. Today is grocery day for me and I have to get to Publix for the senior citizen early bird special. It only runs from eight to ten. I better get a move on. It’s almost eight right now. Do you need anything from the store?”

Picking up the bucket, Nick responded, “Not that I can think of, but thanks anyway.”

Crossing the driveway, she started for her own front yard and yelled back, “I’m going to make a pineapple upside down cake this afternoon. I’ll make sure I bring you and Shelby each a piece over to the house.”

Waving at Genevieve he turned his attention back to the fountain when he noticed a small green compact car pull into the drive and stop. Not recognizing the car, he thought maybe it was a tourist seeking directions. The car door opened and one of the last two people on earth he wanted to talk to stepped out.

Maria Sparks, dressed in an all-black, silver studded leather getup crossed the grass in knee-high black spiked boots and stopped on the opposite side of the fountain. Before she could utter a word, Nick sarcastically stated, "It must be my lucky day! If you've come to insult Shelby, I'm afraid she's not here."

Giving Nick an awkward smirk, Maria looked at the house and then back to Nick. "I've come to see you, not your beer throwing girlfriend. I have a bone to pick with you."

"Well, if it's about the disappearance of your no count, lowlife brother, I've already told you and Brumly everything I know. That bone has been picked clean."

"Chic is no longer representing me. What in the hell did you say to him?"

Nick smiled and in his mind figured Bernard P. James' phone call to Brumly must have been successful. "Like I said, this must be my lucky day. It might not be good news for you since Brumly is no longer in your corner, but for me, well that's the best news I've heard lately. And, while we're on the subject, I didn't say a word to your former lawyer. What could I have said that would possibly cause him to no longer represent you? Maybe he finally figured out I told you and he the truth when I was at his office."

"That's bullshit and you know it! There is no way my brother could have run off with the Carnahans' money. You know what happened to him. You might even be responsible. This is far from over. Brumly is not the only private detective in the world. This is just a minor setback. If I have to, I'll bring in someone from New York. *I will* get to the bottom of this!" Flipping her long black hair she turned and left abruptly, got back in the car, backed out and sped up the street.

Dipping the bucket into the fountain, Nick stopped when he saw Shelby's red Jeep pull in the driveway. Getting out she stared back up Tarpon and placed her hands on her slender hips. "Did you see that car? Whoever was driving it nearly ran me off the road!"

Joining her at the edge of the driveway, Nick filled her in, "That was none other than our ol' friend Maria Sparks. She just stopped by to let me know Chic Brumly is no longer her lawyer. I guess Bernard's phone call did the trick! She was quite pissed and told me this was far from over." Looking up at the bright sun, he asked, "What time is it?"

Shelby checked her watch. "Eight fifteen. We have to be at Mr. James' house in forty-five minutes."

Walking over, he tossed the bucket back in the wheelbarrow. "I better wrap this little project up. Carson will be here before long. I need to grab a quick shower and get dressed. This should really be an interesting meeting."

Descending the stairs in a pair of khakis in his bare feet, Nick dried his wet hair with a towel when he noticed Carson and Shelby seated in the kitchen. Carson, noticing Nick, held up a coffee cup. Coffee's on…want a cup?"

"No thanks. Didn't Mr. James say something about breakfast at his house when we arrive?"

Shelby drank the last of her coffee and stated, "That's right, and we are supposed to be there in twenty minutes, so you better come on and finish getting dressed."

Sitting on the couch, Nick slipped into a pair of socks and then his loafers. Donning a green and grey Hawaiian shirt he buttoned up the front, stood and comically displayed himself. "I'm ready…let's go!"

Producing his car keys, Carson suggested, "I'll drive."

Leading the way out the back door, Carson spoke to Nick, "Shelby tells me you had an unhappy visitor this morning."

"Yep…Ms. Sparks, and she was pissed to say the least. She is not happy Brumly dropped her as a client. She told me she might bring in someone from New York."

Shelby jumped in on the conversation. "You don't think the Carnahans will send someone…do you?"

Carson, unlocking his car, responded, "I doubt it. Maria, when she originally hired Chic, probably informed Joseph Carnahan who she was using as a private detective. With the resources the Carnahans have, I'm sure they checked Brumly out. With Chic's reputation of being a bulldog, they were probably pleased with her choice of attorneys here in this area. When they find out Brumly is no longer representing her, they may finally give up on the mystery of Charley Sparks. At some point Joseph and his brother Emil will decide to move on to other business."

Inside the car, Shelby inquired, "What if Maria decides to pursue the issue on her own…without the Carnahans?"

Backing out of the driveway, Carson smiled. "Don't worry about Maria Sparks. If she continues to ruffle her feathers in our faces, we can deal with her. All I have to do is make a few phone calls and suddenly she'll have other problems that will supersede her interest in the three of us.

Five minutes later they pulled into the circular drive at the James mansion. Conner met them at the front door and ushered them down the hall to the library where Bernard sat in his wheelchair, impeccably dressed in a grey suit, white shirt, bright red tie, his feet encased in black wingtips. Seated in a grey leather chair next to the couch, sat Chic Brumly.

Brumly, as usual looked the part of a used car salesmen: green leisure suit, lime green shirt and white shoes. Nick so sooner stepped into the library when Chic jumped to his feet and approached the trio. Extending his hand to Nick, he spoke as if he knew them for years. "I understand we are to now be on the *same team!"* Reaching for Shelby's hand he went on, "I must apologize to you for the actions of my previous client, Ms. Sparks. I don't think she likes to be told what to do. Bernard and I met yesterday after he phoned me and filled me in on his plan. I represented Bernard twenty-seven years ago when we attempted to sue the Beaufort Police Department, but that was to no avail. Those three boys walked. In my estimation they were guilty as hell, but they got off. Last night, after I agreed to be on Bernard's team, he showed me the photographs you folks came across. If there was ever any doubt in my mind those three boys were not guilty, that ship has sailed. Those photographs completely implicate those boys." Shaking Carson's hand he continued speaking to all three, "I sincerely hope we'll be able to work together to bring down these former high school football studs!"

Conner waited until Brumly was done rambling and then politely asked, "When do you want Mae to serve breakfast, Mr. James?"

"Let's go for ten o'clock. We'll just have coffee and hot chocolate for now." Gesturing at the couch and chairs in the library, Bernard suggested, "If everyone would please have a seat, we can get started."

Chic returned to his chair, while Carson, Nick and Shelby seated themselves on the expensive couch. Conner took a seat next to a large stone fireplace."

Waiting until everyone was comfortable, Bernard folded his hands and spoke firmly, "Before we begin, let me make sure everyone is comfortable with everyone else on the team, because if we cannot get along and function as a team my plan will never work. That being said, I assume you, Nick, along with Carson and Shelby accept Chic here as a team member."

Carson and Nick nodded in approval, while Shelby spoke up, "As long as I don't have to deal with Maria Sparks, I think we'll be fine. She already paid Nick an early morning visit at his house and read him the riot act about how this was far from over."

Chic grinned and explained, "She may try to hold on, but without me she'll get nowhere. The truth is there may be nowhere for her to go. When you first came to my office Nick, and explained your side of the story I have to say you were quite convincing. Maria was not convinced and she demanded I continue to press for the truth. I did a little checking of my own and it turns out her brother Charley was not what one would call an upstanding citizen. She may cause a few ripples, but in the end just like the tide goes back out to sea, she'll go back to New York. I believe she has more money than she does sense. She offered me twice the fee she was paying me if I would continue to press you folks. Bernard here made me a very attractive offer I could not turn down."

Looking back and forth at the group sitting in front of him, Bernard inquired, "Then I can assume we're all good?"

Everyone in the room nodded an affirmative yes.

Turning to Conner he instructed him, "Would you please set up the easel and corkboard in front of the desk."

While Conner was busy setting up the easel there was a knock on the door followed by a short, chunky woman pushing a cart of beverages and condiments.

Noticing everyone went to complete silence, Bernard assured the group, "Mae is from Mexico and has worked for me for nearly ten years. She does not speak or understand a word of English, so there is no need for silence in regard to our plan while she is present. Conner here speaks fluent Spanish." Spreading his hands, displaying the house, he went on, "This house is safe. Here we can speak freely without fear of our plan leaking out."

Conner muttered something in Spanish to Mae who set up the cart at the opposite end of the desk, smiled at the group and backed out of the room humbly.

The easel set up, Bernard nodded at Conner to begin. The loyal butler stood and opened one of the folders and removed three photographs that had been enlarged from the yearbook pictures. Pinning the three photographs to the corkboard, Conner, by means of an erasable red magic marker, circled the photos of Brad Schulte, Tim Durham and Miles Gaston. Standing off to the side of the easel, Conner picked up a pointer and waited patiently for his employer to speak.

Gesturing toward the easel, Bernard explained, "As we proceed Conner will direct your attention to whatever person, place or thing we are discussing." Looking at the easel, Bernard went on, "Here we have the three men who are our targets; the three boys who twenty-seven years ago killed not only my daughter Abigail but a fellow student, Chester Finch. The first step in my plan is to establish who these three men are today. When they committed the murders, they were, back then, high school football stars. Three teenage boys who, according to the police, had never been involved in criminal activity. Upstanding student athletes, who had high grade averages and were all awarded scholarships to well-known institutions of higher learning. These were boys with bright futures ahead of them. The two students they killed, my daughter and Chester were brilliant students, also with bright futures. My daughter was to attend Cornell University and Chester was accepted at

Harvard. Our first topic of conversation this morning will be to familiarize ourselves with the three killers. Let's begin with Mr. Schulte."

Conner rested the tip of the pointer on Brad's picture while Bernard spoke directly to Nick and Shelby. "I believe you told me you talked with a LuAnn Dawson, a former high school sweetheart of the Durham kid. Bring us up to speed on what you learned about Brad."

Shelby looked at Nick who nodded at her to begin. Sitting forward on the couch, she explained, "We know every little about Brad, or for that matter, the other two as well. LuAnn told us Brad completed only three years at Penn State. He was their starting quarterback. He just simply quit playing football, which I think is rather strange when you consider he was being considered for the pros. He transferred to Duquesne University in Pittsburgh for his senior year, but never played football again. We know he graduated from college and wound up getting involved in politics. How, and to what level, LuAnn did not say. He must have been rather successful at his political aspirations when you consider he is currently the Mayor of Pittsburgh and it is thought he may be the next Governor of Pennsylvania. He is married to a woman who is older than him. She is currently a United States Senator. He is known as a powerful man, who has accumulated great wealth and is very connected in political circles. We also know that as a youth, he was always the leader of the three boy friendship, The Three Musketeers, as they were known. We don't know where he actually lives, what his interests are or even if he has children."

Smiling in approval of her rundown of Brad, Bernard added, "If I recall, the police told me the same thing after interviewing the three boys, about how Brad seemed to be their leader. The police felt he was the most intelligent of the three. He may have masterminded the murders. This we do not know." Motioning at Conner, he ordered, "Let's move on to the Durham kid."

Conner tapped the edge of Tim's picture with the pointer when Shelby began to reveal what she and Nick had discovered about the second member of the high school football trio. "LuAnn spoke more about Tim than she did the other two. I imagine this was because she had a much closer relationship with him than the others. She and Tim dated all four years during high school. She claimed he was the only boy she had ever been sexually involved with at that time in her young life. As far as she knew Tim had never been with another girl. He was known as one of the nicest kids in school and she had always been so proud because he had picked her. They had plans of being engaged when they graduated and after their college years came to an end they were going to get married.

LuAnn said after Abigail and Chester were murdered and the police came to the high school to interview everyone, Tim was extremely nervous. This was unusual for him because, as a general rule he never got upset about anything. She said a lot of the students were nervous about being questioned so she attributed Tim's odd behavior as normal when you consider two of their fellow students and friends had been murdered. She also explained that Tim and the other two boys were interviewed, I think it was, three or four more times. She questioned Tim when she found he had lied about drinking that night. As the days, weeks and months passed it looked like the police might place them under arrest, but they never did. They had no murder weapon, no eyewitness, no motive...nothing! Finally, they all graduated from high school and that fall they all went off to college. LuAnn said after that it was so different. Previously, they had seen and been with each other practically on a daily basis for four years and now they were apart for months before they would get together. They continued to write back and forth and call, but LuAnn knew things were coming to an end. She didn't know why. Their awkward relationship continued for two more years, but it was never the same. Then, she gets this letter from Tim. In the letter he explained that after attending two years of school he was dropping out and was going to become a Catholic priest. He wrote he was sorry things hadn't worked out. LuAnn told me she was confused. She couldn't understand what Tim could have been thinking. He was such a talented football player. He could have been a professional. She didn't see her high school sweetheart again for, let's see I guess it was about twenty-three years, when all three of the boys returned for a high school reunion. LuAnn told us when she found out Tim was going to be attending she faked an illness and did not go. She said she just couldn't face him."

Realizing she had been talking a mile a minute, she hesitated and took a breath.

Chic, quite interested, asked a question, "Is this Durham still a priest?"

"Yes he is. He is not only a priest but I think he may be the Archbishop of St. Louis."

Pleased with the information Shelby shared with the team, Bernard shifted in his wheelchair, crossed his legs and loosened his necktie. Looking at Conner he asked, "Could we please have the heat turned down a notch or so? It seems awfully warm in the house this morning."

Conner stood, crossed the room and adjusted a thermostat, then returned to his chair.

Bernard took a sip of chocolate and smiled graciously at Shelby. "That leaves just Miles Gaston. What do we know of him other than what Nick learned when he recently met him here on the island?"

Shelby once again took the reins. "LuAnn told us Miles was the weakest personality of the three boys. During his high school years many students were of the opinion Miles was gay. She told us Tim assured her this was not the case. Miles was extremely shy around members of the opposite sex. Even though he was a member of The Three Musketeers, he was not as close as Brad and Tim were, who had been friends for the first six years of their life before Miles moved to Beaufort at the age of six. As far as his after high school life is concerned the only thing LuAnn could tell us was he barely finished his freshman year at The University of South Carolina. He just walked off campus and never returned. He purchased a restaurant in Savannah and years later purchased a small chain of restaurants called Pattersons. Over the years he has become quite successful and has to date, forty some locations around the country. As of two years ago when he attended the reunion he still had not married. Like Nick said, Miles just recently moved back to Beaufort County. I suppose it might be easier to find out where he resides here on the island. Let's face it. Pittsburgh and St. Louis are a damn sight larger than Fripp. We do know he has homes in both Sacramento and Palm Beach."

Bernard turned, faced Chic and asked, "Well, based on what you just heard, do we have enough information on these three men to start digging into their lives?"

Chic raised his eyebrows and presented the group with somewhat of an evil grin. "The information is sparse, but it's a start. In my business it doesn't take much. Look at it this way. Water can find its way into the smallest crack; a mouse can fit into a tiny opening where you may think it's impossible to go. Shelby here has supplied us with some small cracks and tiny openings. Once the water or the mouse gets inside, havoc can begin. I assume, Bernard, that you want to raise havoc in these men's lives."

"The worst kind," agreed Bernard. "How easy will it be to become a menace in their everyday lives and eventually expose them for who they are?"

"Now, there's the sixty-four thousand dollar question. These three men are not what I would consider normal, everyday citizens. Mr. Schulte is the mayor of a major city, Durham is a high ranking religious figure in the largest religion in our country, maybe the world, and Gaston is a successful restaurant entrepreneur. What I'm saying is not many people become or even desire to become a politician, the mayor of a major city and definitely not a potential governor of a state. Not many people become a Catholic priest, let alone an archbishop, and out of all the folks across the country that own a restaurant, not many own multiple locations like Gaston. The power these men hold because of their station in life may make it difficult to touch them, but that very power makes them vulnerable, susceptible to attack or damage. They have, whether they realize it or not, placed themselves on the pedestal of success. A place where most folks would like to be but are not willing to do what it takes to get there. It's the same today, always has been and always will be. When someone who is highly successful falls or gets a chink in their armor, the rest of us tend to stand up and cheer."

"I could not agree more," said Bernard. "When I was just a young buck, just out of high school which was sixty some years ago, I was full of piss and vinegar. Everyone said I was crazy for not going to college. I purchased a six unit apartment complex and then started to build a small strip mall. I invested everything I had in those two projects and wound up going belly-up, bankrupt. People didn't exactly line up to sympathize with my plight. My friends told me I had bit off more than I could chew. No one was willing to help me. I think people were glad because I had failed. People will always react to success in this manner. If you attempt to do something they cannot do, if you fail, they'll always be around to say, 'I told you so!' The average Joe on the street in Pittsburgh, even though they may be supportive of their mayor, will not display the slightest bit of compassion when Brad Schulte takes the fall I have in mind for him. Tim Durham is no doubt viewed by thousands upon thousands of Catholics in Saint Louis as a great leader in their faith. When it comes out that he murdered my daughter twenty-seven years ago, well, for lack of a better phrase, they'll crucify him! And then there is Miles Gaston, who supplies people all over this country with a nice place to go and have a great meal. How many of those people do you think will continue to eat at his restaurants after we expose the man?"

Carson, who had remained silent, spoke up and pressed the question, "So, who do we go after first?"

Chic was quick with the answer. "Gaston will be the easiest to knock off his pedestal. The reason I say this is that, unlike the other two, he answers to no one. If he is the sole owner of his restaurants, we only need to concentrate on him and him alone. His little empire will begin to crumble under the pressure we are going to apply at a faster pace than that of the mayor and the archbishop."

Standing to make his point, Chic walked to the easel and tapped Schulte's picture. "Now, ol' Brad here is a different story. Whatever political party he belongs to, Democrat or Republican, means he will have everyone in that party across the State of Pennsylvania in his corner, not to mention the connections his state senator wife probably has. When we begin to try and expose him as a past murderer, people on his staff and people who surround him will claim it is nothing more than a smear campaign. There is not a politician alive who, at one time or another, has had to fight off political mudslinging. What we have to do is get the information we have in the right hands…the opposing party. Who better to get bad news out about a potential candidate than another politician?"

Placing his hand on Tim's photograph, he went on to explain, "The priest here will be the most difficult to bring down. There probably is not a month, week or possibly a day when a Catholic priest somewhere in the world has broken a law of the church. Modern day religion has become a business and the Catholic religion is probably one of the largest businesses in the world with millions of followers. You would think in a case like this we could simply send off the incriminating evidence we have to the Vatican…to the Pope. If that were even possible, the information would never reach the Pope's desk. If we go that route the information could be buried in the bureaucracy and the red tape of their religious system. It would be better to go to St. Louis and deal with him on a more local basis."

Walking back to his chair, Chic hesitated and inquired, "Do we have any idea of what these three men look like today. Right now all we have are high school graduation photos that are twenty-seven years old. I'm sure these men look somewhat different today."

Jumping up, Shelby exclaimed, "We do have one! I just remembered. LuAnn Dawson gave Nick and I a photograph taken at the reunion two years ago. According to her it was the only reunion the three boys ever attended." Walking to the table, she picked up one of the folders. "It should be right here with the yearbook pictures." Dumping the pictures onto the table she sorted through them until she found what she was looking for. "Here it is. All three of them seated at the same table. You can clearly see their faces as they posed for the pictures." Standing next to Bernard, she leaned over and explained the picture, "That's Brad and his wife on the left. Tim is seated in the middle and Miles is on the right." Walking to the easel she pointed at the yearbook pictures. "This is what they looked like back in 1989." Holding up the picture she stated, "And this is what they look like today."

Chic got up and walked to the easel and taking the photo from Shelby compared it to those pinned on the easel. "Well, it appears Brad has put on quite a few pounds. Tim, the archbishop, is now sporting glasses and still appears to be in good physical condition. Milles looks the most youthful. He still has a baby face and now has a fashionable mustache." Handing the photo to Bernard, Chic remarked, "This picture will come in quite handy. We now know what these men look like. My next question is, are we going to actually approach these men, because if we do then we can see their reaction to the 1989 murders."

Bernard looked at the photo again and then laid it on the table. "That's the one part of the plan I have not quite figured out yet. How do we approach them without tipping them to our intentions?"

Nick spoke up, "That's easy. We can use the same system Shelby and I have been using in order to collect information. We tell them we are in the midst of writing a book. It's amazing how people are willing to spill their guts to an author. I suppose they feel, or hope something they may say might be used in the book."

"That's very interesting," said Chic. "What type of book have you told these folks you're writing?"

"We've been telling them we're writing a book on past unsolved murders in the Lowcountry."

Shaking his finger, Chic offered, "That may have worked with everyone you've talked to so far, but that will never fly with the three men we're after. Once they hear you're writing about unsolved murders in the Lowcountry, they will have no interest in talking with you. It's just too close to home. Remember, they've been sidestepping these murders for twenty-seven years. They, no doubt have long since put all this business to rest and have moved on with their lives. They will not want to be involved in anything that rekindles interest in Abigail or Chester's deaths. If they get the slightest inclination we are investigating the past murders they'll clam up and avoid us like the plague."

Shelby walked back to the couch in deep thought and sat down. Snapping her fingers, she suggested, "How about this approach? We can still go with the 'We're writing a book' routine, but come at it from a different angle. What if we tell them we are writing a book about past Beaufort High School students who have reached high levels of success? Maybe we could tell them the book is going to be entitled, Beaufort alumni…where are they now?"

"That is an excellent idea," said Carson. "When you approach it from that aspect why wouldn't these three men want to talk with us? A former high school football quarterback who became a state champion and goes on in life to become the mayor of a major city and has the potential to become the governor of the state. A high school football star who becomes an archbishop in the Catholic religion, and last but not least, Miles Gaston who starts out with a single restaurant and now owns a chain of forty plus eating establishments. If they agree to talk with us they will no doubt think we are simply interested in their careers."

"Perfect!" announced Bernard. "In the course of *interviewing* these three men, at some point we could interject that they graduated in '89 and then casually ask them if they recall when two of their fellow students were murdered, how they felt, did they know Abigail or Chester. We could catch them completely off-guard. It would be interesting to see their initial reaction to those questions. They'll have to give us some sort of an answer, because if they do not answer or if they cut the interview short at that point, they may think it's too obvious. I think this is an excellent approach."

Carson spoke up again, "So how do we approach these men…and when?"

Bernard held out his hands to the group and stated firmly, "I would like to get started on this tomorrow. Why wait? I've been waiting twenty-seven years for just this sort of opportunity. The way I see this is we will break up into four different operating units." Looking at the group, he stated, "I assume everyone here will be able to do some travelling?"

Shelby raised her hand. "I have a job in Savannah. I do have a week of vacation coming. I'm sure my boss will give me the time off. Another option I have is I could just call in sick. Either way, I can get this week off in order to travel. If this thing goes longer than that, then I may not be able to travel."

"I think a week for starters will be fine," remarked Bernard. "Now, back to what I said about four different units. Chic, since you feel the priest will be the most difficult to bring down, I'm going to send you to St. Louis. Carson, you will be assigned to Miles Gaston. I did a little checking last night and found that Pattersons' home office is in Atlanta. That may be a good place to start. You may have to go out to Sacramento or down to Palm Beach or whatever restaurant location he may be at. Nick and Shelby will be sent to Pittsburgh to try to get into see Mayor Schulte. I am footing the bill for all traveling expenses; flights, lodging, meals and whatever else in required. I will spare no expense in bringing these three men down. Conner and I will arrange for all your flights from the house here. This will be our operation headquarters. Before you leave the house later on this afternoon, I will supply you with ample cash. Once this thing kicks off I will expect daily updates on how we're doing. If there are any questions do not hesitate to give me a call."

A gentle knock on the door interrupted the conversation when Mae entered pushing a cart filled with silver trays of bacon, scrambled eggs, sausage, pancakes, bagels and an assortment of donuts, plates, silverware and cloth napkins.

Conner walked over to assist Mae and announced, "Breakfast is now served."

"I don't know about everyone else, but I'm famished!" Said Bernard. "After we eat we can further discuss how we want to approach these men and what we are going to ask them." Removing a black and gold whiskey flask from his suit coat, he opened the container and held it up. "Here's to justice! Anyone care to join me!"

CHAPTER TWENTY

NICK MADE HIS WAY DOWN THE CROWDED AISLE AND checked his boarding pass, stopping at B17-B19. "This is us. Do you want to sit by the window?"

Shelby brushed by him and answered, "Yes, I like sitting by the window." Plopping down in her seat, she reached up and adjusted the air nozzle. "I love flying."

Sitting next to her, Nick frowned and glanced out the small window. "I don't mind the flying part. It's the takeoff and the landing that turns my stomach." Looking down at his ticket, he asked, "This is supposed to be a direct flight into Pittsburgh…right?"

"Yep. Once this baby takes off, the next time our feet touch ground we'll be in the Steel City."

Motioning to a passing flight attendant, Nick inquired, "Please tell me they're serving drinks on this flight?"

The attendant leaned over and smiled pleasantly, "We will be serving a variety of drinks, including alcoholic beverages, but not until we're in the air and settled in at 29,000 feet. I'd say about twenty minutes or so from now, you'll be able to order."

Nick fastened his seat belt and kicked off his shoes. "Might as well be comfortable as I can. What time do we get into Pittsburgh?"

Shelby put her boarding pass in her purse and settled back. "It's about an hour and a half flight. I think we're supposed to get in just before noon. Then, we pick up our rental car and head for downtown Pittsburgh to the mayor's office. We have reservations for the night at the Downtown Hilton. If we're lucky and get right in to see Schulte, we might not have to stay the night."

"I wouldn't count on that if I were you. This is a major city and I'm sure the mayor has a full plate on a daily basis. We may have to try and get an appointment with him."

The last few passengers were seated and the plane began to back out. Nick checked his seat belt and took a deep breath. "I'll be okay when we get to 29,000 feet. It's just between where I am now and getting up there that bothers me."

Shelby clicked her seatbelt and looked out the window at a passing row of carts attached to a tractor. "Do you really think Bernard's plan will work? I mean, a lot of things have to fall in place if we're going to bring these three men down."

"This is true, but for the moment all we have to be concerned about is making sure our part of the plan falls in place. I sort of feel strange. If and when we get to see this Brad Schulte, I already feel like I know him. To think we might, later today or in the next few days be sitting across from a killer is somewhat unnerving. This isn't any ol' person we'll be talking with. I'm sure he didn't get to be the Mayor of Pittsburgh just because he may be popular. I imagine we'll find him to be quite intelligent. He has no doubt, over the course of his political career, talked with tons of people. I hope he doesn't see through us. I hope we can pull this off."

"We must stick to our plan. We're just a couple of Lowcountry folks who happen to be writing a book. We have to do our best and try to relax when we get in front of him. The only reason he'll be suspicious is if we give him a reason to think that way. Now, try to relax. We'll be in the air in the next few minutes and you'll be enjoying a cold beer."

The businessman seated next to Nick removed a flight magazine from the holder in the back of the seat in front of him and started to flip through the pages. The man, following a few moments returned the magazine into the cloth holder and spoke to Nick. "Do they really think anyone is going to buy all the crap they put in these magazines?"

Nick was about to respond when the huge aircraft started down the long Charleston runway. "Excuse me," said Nick. "Right now I've got to concentrate on *not* throwing up!"

The man nodded as if he understood and pulled out another magazine.

Nick chanced a look out the window at the rapidly passing buildings when suddenly the plane lifted off the tarmac. He was getting that ol' dizzy feeling he dreaded when flying. Closing his eyes he sat back and breathed deeply. *Relax,* he thought. *You'll be at 29,000 feet before you know it.* He felt Shelby's hand on his left shoulder. He wanted to turn and give her a smile, but for the moment his stomach seemed calm. He didn't want to move a fraction of an inch and upset his insides.

It seemed like an eternity passed when Shelby tapped him on his shoulder. "We're leveling off." Laughing, she continued, "I think you're going to be okay now."

Opening his eyes, he chanced a look out the window. Nothing but blue skies dotted with large puffy white clouds. Letting out a long breath, Nick looked at the ceiling of the plane and muttered, "Next stop Pittsburgh."

The man seated next to him, offered his hand, "Hello there…my name is Richard. I'm actually from Pittsburgh. I'm heading back home after a week on the road. You from Pittsburgh?"

Nick returned the handshake, "No, I'm from down around Beaufort, South Carolina. My name is Nick and my traveling partner over here is Shelby." Shelby nodded at the friendly man and then went back to looking at the clouds.

The man continued the conversation, "Are you getting off at Pittsburgh or going on up to Montreal?"

"As much as I'd like to head up to Canada, we're getting off at Pittsburgh. We have some business there."

"If I could ask, what type of business are you two in?"

Not prepared to answer the question, Nick did some quick thinking. "We're authors! We are in the process of writing a book about successful people from the Lowcountry, which just happens to be a part of Beaufort. We are going to be interviewing Pittsburgh's Mayor…Brad Schulte."

"Ah," responded the man. "A nicer man you could not meet."

Surprised, Nick asked, "Do you know Mr. Schulte?"

"Not personally. I've seen him on the news many times discussing situations or projects in the Pittsburgh area. I did meet him once. It was last year at a fundraiser downtown at the Riverpoint to raise money for a new homeless shelter the city was putting up. I was working in one of the booths and the mayor and his entourage walked up. He shook my hand and told me he appreciated my being there. His wife was with him. You do know she is a United States Senator?"

"Yes, we are aware of that. So, you say the mayor is really a nice man?"

"Best mayor I think Pittsburgh has ever had in office. They say he's in line to be the next Pennsylvania Governor. This is his third term in office. He has done so much for the city, from building ball fields for intercity kids, to working at the soup kitchen downtown. He is very active in keeping the city clean and has been instrumental in attracting many businesses to the Steel City. To tell you the truth, I'm going to hate to see him leave the mayor's office. I can't imagine getting anyone who has been more effective than Brad Schulte."

Shelby, who had been listening gave Nick an odd look.

Nick thought that maybe via some casual discussion he could learn more about Schulte. "Does the Mayor live in some sort of a mansion provided by the city or does he have his own residence?"

"The only time Brad Schulte will live in a mansion supplied by the State of Pennsylvania is if he is elected the governor. For now, as the mayor, he actually does live in a mansion, but he owns it. He lives in Squirrel Hill, which is the wealthiest part of Pittsburgh. Anybody considered important normally lives in the Squirrel Hill area. I've driven by his house but have never actually seen it. It sets right on the outskirts of Squirrel Hill on a forty acre, wooded, fenced-in estate. Between he and his senator wife, they are quite well off."

Nick probed, "Do the Schulte's have any children?"

"Yes, they have two daughters, both in college. I think their oldest is a junior and the younger one is a freshman. They both attend an exclusive girl's school in upstate New York somewhere."

Asking the next question in a roundabout way, Nick pressed his luck, "With as busy a man as you say he is, he probably doesn't have that much leisure time."

"You're probably right there, but I do know he enjoys golf and horseback riding. It's been said he and his wife own a number of horses stabled on their property. He and the senator are members of Pittsburgh's finest country club. If I recall, I think he enjoys fishing. I know he has taken a few fishing trips up into Canada and has done some deep-sea fishing off the Delaware coast. Like I said, most of his time is devoted to improving the city and supporting various projects."

"Sounds like it might be hard to get in touch with him."

"Oh, I don't know. He seems to me to be the sort of man that's easy to approach. I don't think you'll just be able to walk into his office. More likely than not, you'll have to go through the chain of command and set up an appointment. But, I think since you're writing a book and it sounds like there is a possibility he might be in it, I would think he would be interested in giving you an interview."

Interrupted by the flight attendant, the young woman handed a packet of peanuts to each Nick, Shelby and Richard and then asked, "Would anyone care for a beverage?"

Nick spoke up instantly, "I'll have a cold beer. I don't care what brand it is, just make it cold."

Shelby agreed, "Me too!"

Richard held up his right hand. "Let's make it three…I'm buying!"

Please fasten your safety belts. We are beginning our descent into the Pittsburgh International Airport. Nick fastened his belt and commented, "I should have had two beers rather than just the one. I think landing for me is worse than takeoffs."

Shelby checked her belt. "You'll be fine. We'll be down before you know it."

Looking over at Shelby, Nick asked, "Can you see anything down there yet?"

"Just the Pennsylvania countryside. Farms, roads, a few cars; there's a herd of cows…and it looks like snow."

The man sitting next to him tapped Nick on his shoulder. "Listen…good luck with the mayor. I think you'll find him quite pleasant to talk with."

Nick, for some reason, decided to say something he probably shouldn't have. "I wouldn't worry too much about losing Brad Schulte as governor. I have a feeling within the next few months, why he might not even be in politics any longer."

Shelby gave him a hard nudge in his side and gave him a look that indicated, *What the hell's wrong with you?*

The flight attendant came by and collected all the empty cans, plastic glasses and peanut wrappers while announcing, "We should be on the ground in about five minutes."

Nick turned to Shelby, "I'm going to close my eyes and hope for the best. I'm going to apologize to you right up front, so if I throw up all over the place…I'm sorry!"

Shelby looked out the window. They were now flying through low, dense cloud coverage. There was a sudden break in the clouds, which revealed the snow covered rolling hills outside the city limits of Pittsburgh. *Amazing,* she thought. An hour and a half ago they had left Charleston where snow was considered an aberration of weather. Here, in the north, it was an expected yearly winter event that occurred quite often.

The earth was coming up rapidly to meet the landing gear and Shelby looked over at Nick who had his arms wrapped around his mid-section, his eyes tightly shut, his face squinted, almost as if he were in pain. Seconds passed when the landing gear thumped onto the runway, followed by the engines being placed in reverse.

At first it seemed like the large plane would never come to a stop, but then suddenly it slowed and eventually came to a complete halt when the pilot turned the aircraft toward the main terminal. The flight attendant's voice announced over the intercom, *Please remain in your seats until the plane comes to a complete stop. Welcome to Pittsburgh.*

Shelby, looking out the window watched while large snowflakes blew by the glass. In an excited tone, she exclaimed, "It's snowing!"

Nick looked out the window and shrugged, "You almost sound like you're excited."

"I am excited. In case you haven't noticed Beaufort is not known for snow. In two weeks it'll be Christmas. What was it like living in Cincinnati, I mean with the snow during the winter."

"Just because I lived in Ohio doesn't mean we always got snow. Cincinnati is located in southern Ohio on the Kentucky border. Some folks consider Kentucky the beginning of the south. On average, I'd say we probably got eight to nine inches a year. Hell, up here in Pittsburgh they could get that in one afternoon." The plane came to a stop and Nick stood. "Let's go get our car and then see if we can meet Schulte."

Shelby unbuckled and stood. "Lead the way...I'll be right behind you!"

Inside the immense terminal they followed the directional signs that led them first to baggage claim and then to the rental agency where a friendly lady explained their car was paid for and waiting in the parking garage.

Walking through the terminal, Shelby looked down at their rental agreement. "Between Conner and Bernard, it appears they have taken care of everything. By the way, you're driving. I don't know how well I'd do driving in this stuff. Actually, I've never driven in snow."

They located their car, a white Ford Focus parked down the third row on the very end. Tossing their luggage in the backseat, Nick climbed in the driver's seat and gestured at Shelby. "You're navigating. Which way are we going?"

Opening her purse, she removed a printed list of information. Unfolding the paper, she spoke, "Let's see. According to Bernard, the address of the Pittsburgh Mayor's office is 414 Grant Street, #512. Sounds like the office might be on a fifth floor. We also have the phone number here if we need it."

Pulling out of the below ground parking garage, Nick asked, "Which way?"

Reading the printed directions from the airport to downtown Pittsburgh, Shelby pointed. "It says here it will take us about twenty-four minutes to get downtown. Make a right when you get out of the garage, then a quick left. Follow the road for two miles. That will put us on Rt. 79 South. We'll be on that for about seventeen miles, then we make a left onto Rt. 376 that takes us right in."

Looking at the surrounding countryside, Shelby estimated, "Looks like they have about two inches of snow on the ground and it's still coming down."

Getting onto Rt. 79, Nick turned on the wipers while Shelby reached over, turned on the heater and commented, "God, why do people live here. The snow is nice to look at but I don't think I could deal with it all winter long."

Nick passed a slow moving truck going up a slight incline and asked, "What was that strange look you gave me back there on the plane all about?"

"Oh that! I thought the comment you made about how the mayor might not be governor or for that matter even in politics in a few months was uncalled for. We have to be careful who we share things with. Brad Schulte might be the best mayor this city has ever had, but we know something about him no one in Pittsburgh knows or may even believe when it comes out. The leader of their city is a killer…a past killer, but nonetheless, a killer!"

Nick agreed, "I suppose you're right. I guess that was a foolish thing to say."

Looking out the passenger window at the falling snow, Shelby, with a lack of enthusiasm spoke, "I'm a little concerned about bringing Brad Schulte down. You heard what that man on the plane said about how he felt Schulte was the best mayor the city has ever had. If everyone, or the majority of people here in Pittsburgh feel that way, it may be hard to convince them he is indeed a killer."

"I know, I was thinking the same thing when we got off the plane. Chic said he felt Tim, the archbishop, would be the hardest to bring down, but after hearing about all the wonderful things Schulte has done for Pittsburgh, it might not be easy to dent his armor."

Travelling down an exceptionally long hill, they broke out of a cut in the mountain and down below them a mile or so away the tall downtown buildings of Pittsburgh loomed into sight. The snow had slowed to just a few flurries here and there. Coming to a bridge that led directly to the downtown section, Nick looked down at the muddy water and remarked, "According to that sign we just passed we are now crossing the Monongahela River. What do I do when we get on the other side of this bridge?"

Scanning the printed directions, Shelby read aloud, "Looks like we just keep going straight for three blocks when we'll come to the Downtown Hilton on the left where we'll be staying the night. Do you want to check in first or just head to the mayor's office?"

Nick looked at his watch. "It's twelve thirty right now. Where is the mayor's office in relation to where we are now?"

It looks like walking distance from the hotel. Maybe we should go ahead and check in. With it being lunchtime, Schulte may have stepped out of the office. I say we get our rooms, get settled in and then around one o'clock or so stroll down to Grant Street and make our entrance."

The snow was starting to pick up again when Nick stopped for a red light. Shelby stared out the front windshield while pedestrians bundled up in heavy warm coats, earmuffs and gloves crossed the street.

The light changed and Nick continued up the street, turned into the main entrance of the hotel and luckily located a parking spot on a side lot not too far from the entrance doors. Grabbing both pieces of luggage he started across the lot, Shelby close behind. Crossing the wet pavement, Nick commented, "I guess I should have worn a warmer jacket."

Shelby's lack of a response caused him to turn back to repeat what he had just said. He no sooner turned when a snowball glanced off his right shoulder. Shelby stood a few feet away advertising a wide grin on her face. "Not bad for a girl…huh? I always wanted to do that, but never had much of a chance living down south."

"You're lucky my hands are full," joked Nick. "In my day I was known in Cincinnati as a pretty fair snowball thrower."

Opening the front door for Nick, Shelby gestured, "After you, sir!"

Strolling up to the massive check-in area, Nick dropped the luggage to the floor while Shelby dug in her purse for the information Bernard had supplied them with. A younger girl walked down behind the long blacktopped walnut counter and smiled. "May I help you?"

Shelby, producing the paper, unfolded it and spoke, "Yes, we have reservations for two rooms. The reservations were called in from Beaufort, South Carolina, I believe yesterday. Here, I have our confirmation number if that will help."

Taking the paper from Shelby the girl punched in the number and stated, "Yes, here it is. We have a Mr. Falco and a Ms. Pickett. The reservations are for a full week, if needed. The rooms have been prepaid and include our morning breakfast buffet. The rooms are adjoining and are on the second floor. Here are your keys. Do you require any assistance with your luggage?"

"No," said Shelby, "I think we'll be fine!"

Turning to walk away from the counter they were stopped when the girl spoke again, "Wait a second…please! According to our computer you folks are the one thousandth reservation we've had this month. It's our ten year anniversary of being at this location and we are celebrating. When you get up to your rooms we will be delivering a basket of some of Pittsburgh's finest wine, fruit and cheeses." Handing Shelby an envelope, the girl went on to explain, "In here you will find a free dinner for two at the Duquesne Incline; a four star restaurant here in Pittsburgh and a bunch of other money saving coupons of things to do around the city. On top of that your names will be placed out front on our jumbo sign welcoming you as special guests here at the Hilton. If I could just get a little information from you for our bulletin board and sign. I already know where you're from, I just need to know why you are visiting the Steel City this week?"

Nick was at loss for words, but Shelby spoke up instantly, "Why we're authors, here to do some research on a new book we're writing."

"How interesting," commented the girl. "I'll make sure to let the manager of the hotel know so the information can be put out front on our sign. Have a nice stay while in Pittsburgh."

Stopping at the elevator door, Nick pushed the UP button, looked back at the desk and whispered to Shelby, "Do you think it's wise to have our names plastered on their jumbo sign out front just a few blocks from the mayor's office?"

The doors opened and Shelby stepped into the Rosewood paneled interior and she responded, "Sure, why not. If nothing else, it might help us to get into see Mayor Schulte."

Three businessmen were walking out when one of the men stopped and addressed Shelby, "Did I hear my name mentioned?"

Shelby, taken off-guard, muttered, "Pardon?"

Sticking out his hand, the man spoke firmly, "I'm Mayor Schulte. You mentioned something about seeing me."

Nick stood just outside the elevator doors and froze as he stared at the man. Well over six foot in height, receding hairline, a pudgy face matched the rest of his out of shape body, which was covered by a tailored dark blue suit, white shirt, expensive two-tone gray tie and Italian loafers.

Shelby stared at the man for a second and then composing herself, answered, "How ironic! I mean meeting you here at the hotel. We were planning on checking in and then walking up the street to your office." The elevator door closed and everyone stepped out into the lobby.

Smiling broadly, the mayor offered, "Well it looks like I may have saved you a trip. What can I do for you?"

Shelby held up her briefcase. "My name is Shelby Pickett and this is Nick Falco. We are from Beaufort…your hometown. I believe you graduated from Beaufort High back in, I think it was, the late 1980's" Not giving the mayor an opportunity to speak she went on, "Nick and I are authors and we are currently working on a book about past Beaufort High School students who have become highly successful. We flew up here today in hopes of getting an interview with you."

The man who stood on the mayor's right leaned forward and suggested, "Brad, we really need to get moving if you're going to make your one o'clock meeting back at the office."

Looking at his watch the mayor informed his aide, "We've got fifteen minutes. I can surely give these nice folks a minute or so." Turning back to Shelby, he explained, "I am a very busy man, especially this week. I have meetings and appointments scheduled every day of the week. I'm full up. However, tomorrow I am going to be at the Pittsburgh Convention Center. It's just up the street a few blocks. The city is sponsoring our annual downtown Christmas Shopping

Extravaganza. There will be hundreds of vendors from around the area. It's free to the public. I am going to have a booth there. As you may well know I am running for the next governor of the state. Since there will be a lot of local folks in attendance, I'll be there shaking hands and kissing babies…all that political nonsense we as politicians go through." Laughing, he continued, "The only time I can give you is maybe about thirty minutes or so when I break for lunch tomorrow. I'm planning to have a chicken dinner at the show. If you would care to drop by the show tomorrow, late morning, let's say around eleven-thirty, I'll be glad to talk with you. Other than that, you're looking at maybe next week or even later."

Shelby didn't hesitate. "We'll be there Mayor, and thank you."

Reaching out, he shook Nick's hand and then Shelby's. "Then I'll see you both tomorrow at lunch. Enjoy your time in my city."

Watching the mayor walk away, Shelby asked, "Is he what you thought he'd look like?"

"Well, he certainly doesn't look anything like his high school photograph," said Nick, "but, he does look the same as he does in the reunion picture LuAnn gave us. He did strike me as very approachable, even a nice man, like Richard told us on the plane, but we know different. We know that within him there lies the heart of a killer…maybe not anymore, but still, he has hidden the dark secret of what happened back on Fripp from everyone all these years. It'll be interesting to see how he reacts when Bernard drops the bomb on him."

Looking down at the envelope in her hand, Shelby suggested, "I say we go up to our rooms, get settled in and then walk around downtown some. Then, later this evening we can have dinner at the Incline restaurant the counter girl mentioned."

"Sounds like a plan," remarked Nick. "That will give us an opportunity to discuss what we want to ask Schulte. And don't forget. We need to give Bernard a call sometime today and update him about our progress."

Chic stepped out of the long arrival corridor that led from his flight. Once inside the Lambert-St. Louis International Airport, the Lowcountry lawyer stood off to the side to get his bearings. The first thing he looked for was directions to baggage. Not locating any such directions he stopped a passing flight attendant and politely inquired, "Excuse me. Could you please direct me to baggage pick up?"

Smiling, the young lady nodded at a set of stairs. "Baggage is down on the lower floor. Just take those stairs, make a left and after a short five minute walk you'll be where you need to be."

Thanking the woman, Chic headed for the stairs and glanced at his watch. It was nine-fifteen in the morning. According to the information Bernard had supplied him with Archbishop Timothy Durham operated out of the Cathedral Basilica of St. Louis. During the weekdays daily Mass was held each day at seven in the morning and then at twelve-ten. His goal for the day was to attend the late service and see if he could get an appointment to see the archbishop. Arriving at baggage pickup he asked an airport employee where car rentals were. He wanted to be on the road no later than ten. That would give him a good two hours to drive into St. Louis to the old cathedral.

Waiting for his single piece of luggage, he reviewed the information Bernard had sent him off with. The cathedral was located on Lindell in the Central West End of the city. As a general rule he didn't enjoy driving in big city traffic. Sure, Savannah and Charleston were large cities, but nothing compared to St. Louis. He had flown to Boston years ago on business and found driving there quite frustrating compared to Beaufort where everything seemed to unfold at a slower pace. In Boston, everything was fast paced and he figured from the way people were scurrying around the airport that St. Louis might be the same. Spotting his bag, he scooped it up and headed for the rental section of the airport. Surprisingly there was no line at the agency where Bernard had arranged for his car and he soon found himself standing next to a black Chevrolet. He tipped the attendant who led him to the car, tossed the bag in the front seat and pulled out, following directional signs to Rt. 70.

Heading down Rt. 70 he found himself constantly turning on the wipers as a morning rain had dampened the road causing an aggravating wet mist to repeatedly coat his windshield. The winter here in St. Louis was drastic compared to Beaufort where the temperature when he had departed Charleston earlier in the morning was in the high forties. He looked down at a gauge on the dash that indicated the exterior temperature, which was hovering at twenty-seven degrees. Turning on the heater he adjusted the vents in his direction and then looked down at the directions Bernard had supplied him with. He was to take Rt. 70 toward the downtown section, then turn on Kings Highway, which would take him down to Lindell. After that it was a few short blocks to the cathedral. Shivering, he thought a cup of hot coffee sounded good. He should have purchased a cup while at the airport. If he had enough time maybe he'd stop somewhere in the city.

Ten minutes down the road he saw the tall buildings and the Arch of downtown St. Louis in the distance. He rolled over in his mind what he had found out about Archbishop Durham and the position he held in the Catholic Church. The St. Louis Archdiocese was huge to say the least.

Durham, as their archbishop, represented and probably controlled a number of bishops, hundreds of priests and hundreds of thousands of Catholic believers in the St. Louis area. He was definitely in the upper echelon of the Catholic hierarchy; a worldwide religion more organized than the United States Government. Durham was one of their own; a man who had moved up through the ranks of Catholicism, a man who was probably well-respected. Despite the fact Tim Durham swung some weight, still he was just a man; a man who, as a high school senior twenty-seven years in the past, had taken the lives of two of his classmates. As far as Chic was concerned being an archbishop did not give the man a pass. He and his two friends had to be brought down. They had to answer for what they had done and he was going to do everything in his power to make sure Durham, who he had been assigned to, got what was coming to him.

A large green exit sign read, KINGS HIGHWAY ONE MILE. Moving over to the far right hand lane he realized with the way things were moving along he was going to get to the church with over an hour to spare. One block off the exit, he pulled into a Quik-Stop, a local gas station - mini mart. Pulling up to the front of the building, he was going to get that coffee.

Three minutes later he was once again travelling down the highway that would eventually lead him to Lindell where the cathedral was located. Glancing down at his dark blue suit pants, Chic smiled. It had been at the request of Bernard he dress a little less flamboyant when going to see the archbishop. This was the first time in a long while he hadn't worn one of his bright colored sports jackets and white pants. The dark suit encasing his body was his funeral and wedding attire; hardly ever worn but most appropriate for meeting an important man in the Catholic religion.

The street sign for Lindell came up on him quickly and he almost missed the turn. Four blocks down the street he came to Newstand Avenue where the cathedral sat on the corner. Pulling into an empty parking spot on the street, Chic got out and stared up at the impressive church. Grey stone, large stained glass windows, and massive steps led up to arched oak double doors. Apparently he had stared too long at the massive structure when a passerby stopped and asked, "First time here?"

Startled, Chic answered, "Yes, it is. That's some church!"

The old man shifted his bag of groceries from his right arm to his left and pointed across the street at the church. "I live up the street. I've been walking by the cathedral for years now. Not too many people know it, but it's Byzantine Revival Architecture. You don't see many churches or for that matter many buildings designed in that fashion. Are you going inside?"

"Yes…I am. I thought I'd go to the late service."

Walking up the street the man went on, "Well you're in for a real treat. The interior is nothing short of jaw dropping. Enjoy!"

Chic checked the time, not quite eleven o'clock. He had over an hour to wait before the service began. He downed the last of his coffee, tossed the empty cup into a nearby trash container and walked across the street and up the steps. Surprisingly the church was open. Closing the large wooden door behind him, Chic took five steps down the wide aisle and took in the surroundings. The man on the street was right. It was jaw dropping! Dark cherry pews flanked either side of a wide, polished marble floor that ran the distance all the way up to the altar, which was unlike any he had ever seen before in his life: huge gold candle stands, three gold plated seats that reminded him of thrones, the walls covered with hundreds of colors of mosaic images.

Walking halfway into the massive church, he stopped and turned in a complete circle and stared in amazement at the tall arched entranceways into what appeared to be side chapels, once again covered in mosaics. Stepping into a pew on the left he was awestruck in regard to the detail of the mosaic walls that were depicted. He felt as if he were in the midst of power and wealth. This then, is where Tim Durham, a young high school lad who had killed two of his friends, now resided. Sitting back he relaxed and tried to review in his mind the things he wanted to ask the archbishop, that is if he even got in to see this man.

A voice behind him interrupted his thoughts, "Excuse me, but I've never seen you here at Mass before. Are you visiting town? Do you have relatives here in St. Louis?"

Turning, Chic noticed and older woman, probably in her eighties he estimated, sitting directly behind him. "No, I've never been here to Mass before. This is my first time here at the church, or for that matter, St. Louis."

The woman smiled and gazed up at the ceiling. "I've been coming here to the noon Mass for years. I always like to come early and just sit and look at the mosaics. It's amazing. I always see something I've never seen before." Pointing at the right side sanctuary wall, she explained, "That's the chapel of the saints over there and on the other wall we have out baptistery. The decorative millwork on the end of the pews is some of the best you'll find in any church…anywhere!" Pointing at different mosaic depictions on the ceiling, she continued to ramble on, "That one towards the front displays the life of St. Louis IX; the King of France. Just above us we see the Easter celebration and then there is the Pentecost. My favorite is the large mosaic behind the altar that displays American saints, Mother Cabrini, Elizabeth Seton, Rose Phillipine Duchesne and Isaac Jogues. Why you could sit here for hours on end in awe and wonder."

Appreciative of the woman's vast knowledge, Chic realized he needed to take over the conversation or he would be sitting there for the next hour while the woman went on and on. Casually, he inquired, "Have you ever met Archbishop Durham?"

Proudly, the woman answered, "Many times, practically every day. Archbishop Durham always says the noon Mass. I can't tell you how many times I have received the holy sacrament of communion from his hand. He'll be conducting today's service."

"Then you've never met him personally."

"Yes, I have met and talked with him personally. I have attended a number of church functions where he has been present."

"Did you find him easy to talk to?"

"Oh my…yes. He is a wonderful man and a credit to the Catholic faith. He is a very holy man and a man of great wisdom."

The woman began to explain another mosaic display on the ceiling when Chic stood and apologized, "I'd love to sit and talk with you, but I'm going to move further toward the front. I need some prayer time…excuse me."

Stepping out of the pew, Chic felt bad for lying to the friendly woman. He wasn't the least bit interested in praying. He just wanted to get away from her so he could concentrate on how he was going to conduct himself when he and Durham met. Walking up the wide aisle, he took a seat in the fourth row of pews from the front, settled back and closed his eyes. In forty-five minutes Mass would be starting.

Church was not the most comfortable place for Chic Brumly. The last time he could recall being in church had been three years ago when he had attended the wedding of a client's daughter. He hadn't known the young lady but her father was paying him a large fee for a case he was working on. He had been invited and felt obligated to go. Aside from a few funerals and weddings over the years he had no other reason to sit his butt in a church pew. He was not a man who believed. Well, he did believe; but in what he wasn't sure. He felt there probably was a God and if he was the sort of God most people described, he probably wasn't in all that good of a standing with the Almighty. But, for the moment, sitting in this absolutely amazing house of God, he felt for a change, maybe this God was on his side. After all, an archbishop of the largest religion in America, possibly the world, was a killer and right now it was his appointed job to bring Tim Durham down. Looking around at his surroundings he was beginning to get the feeling it was not going to be that easy.

Gazing back at the rear of the church a few parishioners were beginning to file in. Not wanting to look out of place he decided to move toward the back of the church so he could see what those in front of him were doing during the service. Picking out an empty row of pews he sat and waited for Mass to begin.

Just prior to twelve noon he looked at his watch. In ten minutes the service was to begin. The church was not overcrowded, maybe a hundred people at the most. The small congregation consisted of a combination of locals and visitors. Those visiting were easy to spot while they stared around the church in total awe. During the next ten minutes another twenty to thirty people drifted in and sat down.

At exactly twelve-ten, two altar assistants entered from either side of the massive altar carrying long golden candle lighters. First they lit two long candles at the foot of a large crucifix behind the altar then proceeded to light a number of other candles around the altar. During this process, the archbishop, followed by two priests walked reverently from the right and took seats at the altar. The archbishop took the seat in the center with the priests on either side. Chic had seated himself so far back he couldn't make out the faces of those on the altar. Getting up, he walked up a side aisle and took a seat in the second row. There, not twenty feet away sat Tim Durham, Archbishop. From where Chic sat the man looked holy, or at least what he thought a holy man should look like. Royal blue robe with a bright yellow shawl lined with black crosses, large bishop's ring on his left hand, pectoral cross and gold chain hanging around his neck and small violet colored skull cap. In his right hand, he held a golden staff. *God!* Thought Chic. *He looks like one of those ancient kings from one of those old religions films.*

Following two hymns one of the priests stood and welcomed everyone to the cathedral. After some announcements another hymn was sung and then the Mass went on and on; parishioners standing, kneeling and sitting which included three readings; two from the Epistles and one from the Gospel. Chic followed along kneeling and standing whenever everyone else did so. Finally it was time for the sermon at which point Archbishop Durham took center stage behind an elevated cherry pulpit and delivered his message. As Chic listened he thought Tim Durham was not only an excellent speaker but a man who was passionate about his faith. All eyes were glued on this man who spoke for a full twenty minutes.

The next part of the Mass was the celebration of Holy Communion, which the archbishop announced with great vigor, reciting the canned rhetoric he had no doubt repeated thousands of times over the years as a man of the cloth. Chic never in his life received Holy Communion and despite the fact he was not Catholic was not going to detour him from walking to the altar to receive one of the wafers. There were three stations set up for receiving the sacrament. Chic stood in line to receive the blessing from the archbishop. Finally, it was his turn and he stood face to face with Tim Durham. The archbishop picked up one of the wafers, placed it in Chic's outstretched hand, and spoke softly, "This is the Body of Christ."

Chic looked directly into the green eyes of Tim Durham and thought to himself, "If these people only knew who they were really dealing with! Tim looked directly at Chic and smiled genuinely. Chic hesitated too long and Tim nodded at him; a silent signal he needed to move on.

Chic took a large sip of what he thought was going to be grape juice but in all actually was wine. He didn't care for wine and almost choked when he walked back to his seat. A few more songs and the Mass ended as everyone filed out. Chic remained seated and after everyone had left, walked to the altar and approached one of the altar assistants. "Excuse me, sir. How would one go about getting to see the archbishop?"

The man smiled and answered, "In order to see the archbishop you must walk around to the back of the cathedral where you will see our business office. There will be a secretary there who can make an appointment for you."

Chic thanked the man and made the long walk back down the aisle to the front doors. Walking around to the rear of the church he noted a sign that read: CHURCH OFFICE.

Entering the small office he was greeted by an older woman. Chic went right to work and introduced himself as he turned on the charm, "Good afternoon. I was just at the Mass. The cathedral is amazing. I've never seen a church quite like it. It's my first time here in St. Louis. I flew up here this morning in hopes of getting to see Archbishop Durham."

Laying down an ink pen she had been holding, the woman smiled and asked, "And what is the reason for your request?"

Pulling up a chair next to the desk without being asked, Chic introduced himself, "My name is Charles Brumly. I'm from Beaufort, South Carolina. You may not be aware of this, but Archbishop Durham was born and raised in Beaufort. He was also a state high school football champion back in the late 1980's. That's why I've come to see him. You see, I'm an author and I am in the process of writing a new book about past Beaufort students who have achieved great success. I think we can both agree the Archbishop has come a long way since his high school days. If at all possible I would like to sit down with him for, well maybe twenty minutes or so. I'd like to have an opportunity to interview him for my book."

Raising her eyebrows the woman replied, "There are many reasons people want to talk with the archbishop, but your request is by far a new one. It just so happens I screen all his meetings. You can understand the archbishop does not have the time to talk with everyone who desires a meeting with him. Let me check his appointment book."

Opening the desk drawer she removed a binder, flipped it open and continued talking. "It looks like he is quite busy this week…no wait, here's a cancellation for tomorrow at three in the afternoon. You say you only requite about twenty minutes?"

"Yes, I think that would suffice."

"Very well then. I'm going to slot you in for tomorrow at three. How does that sound?"

Getting up, Chic reached out and gently shook her hand. "That sounds wonderful. Thank you so much for your assistance. You have been more than kind. Where do I come for the meeting?"

"Right here at the office. When you arrive you'll be escorted back to his private quarters."

Backing out of the office, he thanked the woman again.

Seated again in his airport rental, he opened a folder Conner had supplied him with. The hotel he was booked at was seven blocks back down Kings Highway. Turning out onto the street he thought to himself, *That was easier than I thought it would be.* Once on the highway he decided to give Conner a call and update Bernard on his progress.

Sitting in the sun at the back of his house, Bernard was interrupted by the voice of Conner. "Excuse me sir, but I just received a call from Mr. Brumly. He has garnered an appointment with Archbishop Durham tomorrow at three o'clock. He said he will call us after tomorrow's meeting."

"Very good, Conner. Things are going better than I planned. Shelby and Nick have a short luncheon with Mayor Schulte tomorrow and now this good news. Now, all we need is to hear from Mr. Pike."

CHAPTER TWENTY ONE

ON THE VERY TOP FLOOR OF THE PARKING GARAGE, CARSON Pike got out of his car and gazed out over the city, Atlanta, Georgia. He had been to The Big Peach many times in his lifetime. From time to time he had attended Falcons' games in the fall and Braves' games in the summer. He had driven down to Atlanta in the past on three different occasions with Nick's grandfather, Edward, on business. The largest city in the state of Georgia was not his most favorite when it came to big cities. He found the city hard to get around in and the traffic was horrendous. In general, he looked at folks in Georgia as friendly, but many of the people he ran across in Atlanta seemed to be rude and always in a hurry.

Sitting on a concrete abutment, he opened his wallet and removed the printed instructions Conner had supplied him with. Gaston Enterprises was located on the seventh floor of the Atlas Building in suite 704. Walking across the open-air lot, the wind ripped at his bare face. It was December in the south and normally Georgia held a routine winter temperature in the high forties to the mid-fifties. Carson did not care for colder temperatures and the brisk wind atop the tall building was uncomfortable.

Stepping into an elevator he pushed the seventh floor button and waited while the door slowly closed. According to the research Bernard had conducted, Miles Gaston, sole owner of Gaston Enterprises, was more than just a successful restaurant entrepreneur. He owned a 76-unit apartment complex in Palm Beach, Florida; a trucking company in Sacramento, California; and a great number of small businesses in and around Atlanta that included laundromats, convenient stores, two nightclubs, two apartment complexes and three car washes. Miles Gaston did not have the backing of a political party or of a powerful religion. He was a self-made, extremely wealthy individual who answered to no one other than himself. Unlike Brad Schulte and Tim Durham whose lives were constantly in the limelight, Miles kept somewhat of a low profile. His private life, away from the business world was far from an open book. He had never been married, had no children, and did not belong to any clubs or organizations. When not traveling around the country he was not seen on a golf course, a country club, or out in public much at all. Any information Carson was going to collect on this man was going to have to come from Miles himself.

Getting off on the seventh floor, he read a gold plated, lettered list of companies and offices posted on the beige stucco wall. The third listing down read, GASTON ENTERPRISES – SUITE 704.

Stepping into the hallway, Carson took a right and examined himself. He felt rather uncomfortable, dressed in a suit, tie and dress shoes. His dress attire caused him to feel out of his element. Back down on Fripp Island, his normal clothing consisted of shorts, flip-flops and T-shirts, or in many cases, soaked, muddy fishing gear. Approaching large glass double doors at the end of the hall topped by three-inch letters, GASTON ENTERPRISES, he thought to himself, *I hope I can pull off this author business!*

Stepping into the ultra-modern office, he quickly familiarized himself with the surroundings and instantly became at ease: the walls tastefully decorated with fishing boats and beach scenes. There were large tropical plants in gold basins and expensive nautical odds and ends placed around the reception area. Since he was a fisherman he felt at home and smiled when he approached a large desk centered in the middle of the room. An older woman looked up from a computer and spoke politely. "Good morning, sir. May I be of help to you?"

Trying to act casual, Carson leaned on the desk and looked around the office, hesitated for effect and then answered, "Yes, I believe you can. My name is Carson Pike. It just so happens I hail from the same town as your employer, Miles."

The use of the first name and not the last was a nice touch and caused the woman to inquire, "You are a friend of Mr. Gaston then?"

"No, we have never met. I'm from Beaufort, South Carolina where Miles grew up and graduated from high school. I am an author. Perhaps you've heard of me? I have written a number of books about the Lowcountry. I guess you could say I'm an expert on that part of the country."

The woman smiled. "I'm an avid reader, but I'm afraid I've never heard of you. Mostly, I read murder mysteries that are best sellers."

"Murder mysteries are not my genre. My expertise is strictly centered on the Lowcountry and things of interest in that part of the country. My current work is going to be about people from the Lowcountry who have become successful in life. Miles most definitely falls into that category. I was hoping to get an interview with him. I realize he is probably a very busy man and I may have to schedule an appointment."

Turning in a swivel chair the woman spoke to another unseen person through an open door office. "Alice, is Mr. Gaston scheduled in today?"

A young woman appeared in the doorway and answered, "No. I'm afraid not. He will not be here at his office for at least a week. Currently he is down in Palm Beach but I think he's scheduled to be in Tampa tomorrow at Pattersons and then he's flying over to another Pattersons' location in Dallas." Stepping out into the office, the woman looked at Carson and inquired, "Is there a problem?"

The receptionist answered, "No not at all. This is Mr. Pike. He's from the same town where Mr. Gaston grew up. Mr. Pike is an author and is writing a book about folks from that area. He just simply wanted to get an interview with Miles."

"Unless you go to Tampa or Dallas it'll be a week before he returns here to Atlanta."

Carson smiled. "Just suppose I decided to fly down to Tampa. Do you think I could catch him there?"

The younger woman spoke up, "That might be a possibility. Normally when he visits one of his restaurant locations he spends the better part of the day there. I'd say if you got there first thing in the morning you could probably catch him. Here, let me write down the address and phone number for you."

Taking the written information from the woman, Carson thanked both ladies as he backed out of the office. Walking down the hall, he took a seat on a couch and dialed Bernard's phone number.

Two rings passed when Bernard answered, "This is Mr. James."

"Bernard! It's Carson. I'm now just leaving Gaston's home office. If I can be in Tampa by tomorrow morning I think I've got a better than average chance of getting into see him at one of his restaurants."

"Very good!" said Bernard. "Here's what I want you to do. Drive your car over to the airport there in Atlanta, park your vehicle in long-term parking and then proceed to Southwest Airlines. By the time you get there I will have scheduled you a flight down to Tampa. Keep me posted."

Shelby stood in awe a few feet inside the Pittsburgh Convention Center. Looking at one of the show brochures Nick picked up at the entrance, he asked, "So where do you want to go first. It's ten thirty. We have an hour before we meet Schulte for lunch."

"I think the first thing we should do," suggested Shelby, "is to locate something hot to drink. That four block walk from the hotel in below freezing temperatures got the best of me. I'm a southern girl. I'm not used to all this cold weather and icicles."

"I could use a warm drink myself. There's a sign for the food court. It's to the left. What say we grab a hot drink and then locate the mayor's booth? Maybe he'll be there. We can find out where he's going to have that chicken dinner he told us about."

Walking past a number of craft booths, Shelby commented, "There is really a lot of nice stuff here: jewelry, handmade quilts, paintings. I might have to get my Christmas shopping done before we leave. There are less than two of weeks of shopping left before the big day. Have you done your shopping yet?"

"Me? No way! I always wait until one or two days before Christmas. I guess I should get on the stick though. This year is different. In the past, as a loner I really didn't have anyone to buy for. Now, why I have both you and Kirby and then there's Carson and probably Genevieve. I think I'll wait until I get back to Beaufort. There's still plenty of time."

"You say that now, but we don't know how involved this plan of Bernard's will get. We may be too busy with Schulte and the others."

Stopping in front of a small drink kiosk, Nick scanned the printed menu. "I'm going with a large hot chocolate."

"Let's make it two," agreed Shelby.

Walking down a center aisle they came to an information desk where Shelby inquired where Mayor Schulte's booth was located. Using a long pointer a young girl spoke while she pointed to a large framed printed layout of the show. "You're right here now. What you do is you go down to the end of this row, turn right and go down to Row P, make a right and you'll find the mayor's booth down three spots on the left. Have a nice day at the show."

Locating Row P, Shelby pointed down the aisle at a banner, which read, BRAD SCHULTE – PENNSYLVANIA'S NEXT GOVERNOR. Walking up to the sixteen-foot booth, there were four girls seated at blue-skirted tables stacked with brochures about the future candidate. There was a life size cardboard makeup of Schulte at the back of the booth. On the tables there were hundreds of ink pens and shopping bags advertising the mayor as the next governor.

Approaching one of the girls, Shelby inquired, "Is the mayor here today?"

"Yes, he is. Right now I believe he's out making the rounds visiting folks. Can I help you in any way? Would you like a free pen or shopping bag?"

Gesturing back at Nick, Shelby explained, "Actually we have an appointment today with the mayor. He told us we were to meet him at eleven thirty while he was having a chicken dinner."

"That would be over in row W by the Third Street Baptist Church tent where they have a lunch and dinner set-up. You can't miss it. I guarantee you, the mayor will be there at exactly eleven thirty. He is a very punctual man."

Grabbing a pen, Shelby plunked it into one of the shopping bags and thanked the girl. Walking away from the counter she held up the bag and remarked, "I love collecting free stuff. By the time we get out of here I might have this bag filled up."

The Third Street Baptist Church was advertised on the front of a large tent backed up against a wall fronted by a long food line and a number of tables and chairs on the right. Nick looked at his watch and commented, "It's eleven-fifteen now. We might as well grab a seat and wait for the mayor."

Seated at one of the tables, Shelby removed the pen from the bag and read the embossed writing on the side: *Brad Schulte for Governor.* "This is a pretty powerful man we plan on taking down. Do you think we could get into any trouble by slandering the next possible governor of the state?"

Pulling out a chair, Nick answered, "I hope not. I do know this. He won't go down without swinging. This is an accomplished politician we're talking about. He didn't get to the position he's at without knowing how to pull a few strings. When the truth comes out about how he murdered Abigail and Chester twenty-seven years ago, his political constituents may view it as slander, but we know it's the truth. He'll probably try to blow the accusations off and sidestep the issue. Power and money can change a lot of things. Don't forget. We have Bernard P. James behind us. He has deep pockets and has said he will spare no expense to bring Brad and his two old high school friends down. I'm not saying it won't get ugly."

Fidgeting with the ink pen, Shelby looked at the long line of hungry Christmas shoppers who had gathered and formed a long line for one of the chicken dinners. "I don't know about you but I'm feeling a little nervous. After we met the mayor at the hotel yesterday and we arranged to meet with him here today I was confident things were moving along well, but now that the moment will soon be upon us, I'm afraid we might mess this thing up."

"Don't go losing it on me now, Rebel," said Nick. "Yesterday it was me who was nervous and it was you who told me we just had to stick to the plan. I agree with what you said. If we don't give him a reason to get suspicious, then he won't! If things look like they are going the wrong way we can always excuse ourselves and leave, saying we feel we have enough information for our book."

Suddenly Shelby sat up and nodded when the mayor and one of his aides appeared from the crowded aisle. Standing, Shelby remarked with less than an enthusiastic tone, "Here goes. I'm going to approach him and tell them we already have a table." Before Nick could say a word she was on her feet and across the tent. He watched when she approached the two men.

Shelby boldly walked up to the mayor and extended her right hand. "Good morning, Mayor. I hope you haven't forgotten our luncheon appointment today."

Shaking her hand, Brad confirmed. "No, I have not forgotten. I was reminded of our appointment when I drove into work early this morning. I saw your names advertised as visiting authors on the Hilton marquee downtown. Actually, I'm looking forward to talking to you about your book. I can only give you about thirty minutes. I hope that will be enough time?"

"That will be fine," said Shelby. "Nick and I already have a table."

The mayor looked in the direction she pointed and asked, "Have you two ordered yet?"

"No, we haven't."

Turning to his aide, Brad ordered, "John, go around to the back and let them know to bring out four chicken dinners and lemonades for the mayor."

In an instant the aide answered, "Yes sir," and walked past the food line and around the back.

Following Shelby to the table, the mayor stuck out his hand when he saw Nick. "Mr. Falco…right?"

Reaching for his hand, Nick replied, "Yes, that's correct. Please, have a seat."

Shelby, trying to make herself comfortable, sat opposite the mayor and commented. "It looks like the line for lunch is really filling up fast."

The mayor, after he was seated, remarked, "My wife and I are Methodists but when it comes to chicken and waffles nobody in the Pittsburgh area comes close to what the Baptists at Third Street cook up. Have you ever had chicken and waffles before?"

"No," said Shelby. "I've never even heard of it."

Folding his hands, the mayor smiled. "Well, you're in for a real treat then. I already ordered for the four of us."

Shelby reached for her purse. "Then we owe you for two dinners."

Brad held up his hand and laughed. "You don't owe me a cent. Free meals happen to be one of the perks of being the mayor of the city. Now, since we don't have much time let's get into this book you two are writing. Tell me again what it's about?"

Nick spoke up, "It about former Beaufort High School students who have gone on to great success. You sir, happen to fall into that group."

"How many former students are you interviewing?"

This was a question Shelby and Nick had not planned on answering.

Nick thought quickly and answered, "At last count I think we have about twenty five so far. Professional athletes, doctors, successful business people."

"Anyone I would know of?"

"Well I'm not sure." Making up some names, Nick listed two people, "There's Jack Reynolds who played professional ball in the American League for a few years. He graduated before you were even born so you may not be familiar with him. Then there's Pamela Charles who became a rather famous concert pianist. She graduated from Beaufort around ten years after you did."

Shelby jumped in on the pack of lies and stated, "There is a Doctor Kaywood who also graduated long before you did. That's just a few of the folks we plan to sit down with. That being said there are two others we plan to talk with I know you are quite familiar with, Tim Durham and Miles Gaston. Correct me if I'm wrong but I believe you three were known as The Three Musketeers?"

"Yes, I do know Miles and Tim. We played football together long before we got to high school."

Opening a small notepad Nick clicked a pen and spoke, "Let's start at the beginning. I assume you were born and raised in Beaufort?"

"Yes, I was. Lived on the same street for eighteen years."

"Do your parents still live in Beaufort?"

"No, they moved a few years after I graduated from High school."

Writing on the pad, Nick continued, "We have talked with people at Beaufort High and have spent quite a bit of time in the school library. We are to understand you quarterbacked the school football team all four years during high school."

"That I did," said the mayor with a smile of pride.

"After you graduated it was off to college for you…right?"

"Yes, I got a full ride right here in Pennsylvania at Penn State."

"It was thought by most folks in Beaufort that after you finished up with your college years you would go pro."

"That was the plan, but as they say time can change things. I only played three years of ball at Penn State. I transferred to Duquesne University here in Pittsburgh for my senior year."

Nick already knew Brad didn't play football for Duquesne, but he didn't want to let on he knew that much about the mayor. "So then you only played the one year here in Pittsburgh?"

"No, that is incorrect. When I transferred to Duquesne I had already decided my football career was over."

Shelby jumped in on the conversation. "That seems unusual and I think it's something our readers would enjoy reading. It's kind of hard to understand how a young man with so much talent would throw away a professional football career, what with all the fame and fanfare, not to mention all the money you could have made."

The mayor tugged at his coat sleeve and commented, "I can see where most people would think that an unusual decision, but most folks are not aware of the wear and tear one has to experience as a football player. When I played Pop Warner ball and then middle school football, we were all so small and quite frankly not capable of hitting another player that hard. That all changed in high school. Players were bigger and faster and when I got to college it only got worse. I guess after playing for three years at Penn State I grew tired of being run over by three hundred and fifty pound linemen. It was rare a game went by where, as a quarterback, you didn't take a serious hit. Reality set in and I realized all the future money wasn't worth my health. I had always been interested in politics so I transferred here to Pittsburgh and finished up my schooling with a degree in political science."

John returned to the table trailed by two young men carrying two trays each. The aide politely suggested they place the trays on the table and then tipped them as they walked off. Taking a seat, John was all business as he stated, "Lunch is served."

Rubbing his hands together, the mayor tucked one of the napkins in the neck of his custom fit shirt, grabbed a plastic fork and remarked, "Let's dig in!"

Looking down at the meal set before her, Shelby remarked, "This is different. I've had waffles before and I've had chicken, but never the two combined."

Taking a bite, Brad wiped a spot of the rich thick chicken gravy from the side of his mouth and nodded in approval. "That's some good eatin'."

Nick took a bite and agreed. "You're right, this is good. I would have never dreamed chicken gravy over waffles could taste so good."

John spoke up, "Growing up in Pennsylvania, I was raised on this stuff. I think it's an old Pennsylvania Dutch concoction." Pointing with his fork, he added, "Try some of that coleslaw. It's the best I've ever had."

Tasting a bite of waffle and gravy, Shelby smiled and continued their previous conversation. "So we left off with you stating you graduated with a political science degree. Did you go directly into politics?"

"No, not right away. Real estate had always intrigued me as well as politics. I got my real estate license and started to work for a local relator. Turned out I was rather good at selling homes. I saved my commissions and soon I started to purchase and flip properties. A couple of years drifted by and I had accumulated over three million dollars in real estate. Then I met Arcadia; she's my wife. At the time she was deeply involved in politics and still is today. Currently she is a United States Senator and over the years has been instrumental in my own political career. She got me on the mayor's staff nineteen years ago, I just worked my way up through the ranks, *and* here I am today. The Mayor of Pittsburgh."

John pointed out. "And soon to be the new Governor of The Keystone State."

Shelby took another bite. "So then you got out of the real estate business and strictly into the political field?"

Wiping more gravy from the side of his mouth, Brad explained, "I gave up being an agent but I still dabble in properties. Today I have over seventy-five rentals in the city. It has been a great source of income over the years."

Shelby was on a roll. "Do you live in the city?"

"I live in Squirrel Hill, a community outside the city limits."

"Do you have any children?"

"I have two daughters. Presently they are both in college."

"Where do they attend school?"

"Wells College...it's very exclusive."

Nick was writing as fast as he could while Shelby continued to draw information from Schulte. "Do you belong to any clubs or organizations here in Pittsburgh?"

"Oh, yes indeed. I belong to the Young Men's Republican Party of Allegheny, The Elks, The Rotary Club and Pittsburgh Kiwanis, just to mention a few."

Shelby wanted to know what other organizations Brad belonged to but thought if she asked, the mayor might get suspicious. Changing the subject, she asked, "Where do you attend church?"

"Mary S. Brown – Ames United Methodist in Squirrel Hill. It's a few blocks from where my wife and I reside."

Shelby was rolling right along and pushed for even more information. "What charitable organizations are you involved with, if any?"

"Probably too many to name. My favorite charities are the Greater Pittsburgh Commission for Women, The Salvation Army, The American Red Cross and St. Jude."

Shelby was about to ask her next question when she was interrupted by the aide. "Brad, it's eleven twenty. We have to leave in ten minutes to get ready for your television spot at noon."

Stretching his arm so he could see his Rolex, Brad agreed, "I'm afraid

John is correct. Perhaps we should wrap this up."

Nick looked down at his notes and suggested, "Well then, let's sum things up. You graduated from Beaufort High back in the late 1980's, I think it was 1989…correct?"

"That's correct."

"You were the quarterback on the 1989 South Carolina State High School football team."

"That is also correct."

Here goes! Thought Nick. "Speaking of 1989, we spoke with some of the teachers at Beaufort about our book. They told us 1989 turned out to be a frustrating year for everyone, students and faculty as well. According to what we were told two students were murdered down on Fripp Island during a celebration for the football team. I think their names were Abigail…something and a kid named Finch."

The mayor did not verify the names but hesitated as he stared across the table briefly at Nick and then turned to his aide, "John, why don't you head on back to our booth and make sure everything is a go for my next interview. Tell them I'll be along soon."

John's timely interruption of the topic of Abigail and Chester's deaths seemed to have been pushed to the side as the mayor took another bite followed by a drink of lemonade.

Shelby, not wanting to let the man off the hook that easy, pushed, "The teachers at the high school said the murders made everyone really nervous and even still toady the crime is still on the books as unsolved. Do you recall how you felt back then?"

"Yes, I recall how I felt, but let me ask you this. What do those two murders have to do with the success I have had? What happened back in 1989 to those two students has nothing to do with my life." Wiping his mouth, both Shelby and Nick realized the interview had come to an abrupt end.

Nick quickly bounced back when he closed the notepad and casually remarked, "Those murders have absolutely nothing to do with this interview. We were just, both of us, intrigued with what they told us at the school. We don't plan to include any of that information in our book. We apologize if we have, in any way upset you in mentioning what happened back in your senior year. It just seems so strange the killer or killers were never brought to justice. The teachers told us both of the students killed were really quite brilliant and they would have no doubt gone onto greatness themselves in life. Who knows? If they wouldn't have been murdered we might be sitting here today interviewing them over their accomplishments, but someone killed them so I guess we'll never know their story."

The mayor didn't finish his last few bites but stood and announced politely, but curtly. "The interview is concluded."

Watching him walk away from their table, Shelby pushed her plate to the side. "Mayor Schulte is as guilty of those murders as the day is long. Did you see the way he dismissed his aide when the topic of the murders was brought up. It's all too apparent he doesn't want anyone he knows to associate him with those killings. I could see the guilt on his face and in his mannerisms. He was trying his best to be polite in ending the interview, but I could tell he was upset at the very end of our talk. Do you agree?"

"We already know he's guilty," said Nick. "His reaction at the mention of Abigail and Chester just bolsters the truth." Taking one last bite of his lunch, he looked across the table at Shelby. "You did a fabulous job of pulling information out of the mayor. If we would have mentioned the murders early on in the interview he would have clammed up."

"So what do we do now? What's our next move?"

"I think our job here in Pittsburgh is finished. I don't know what else we could accomplish. Maybe we should go over to his booth and watch his next interview. If he notices us there I think it would be interesting to see his reaction. On the other hand we could just walk around. You can do your Christmas shopping and then later on today we can catch a flight back to Charleston."

"Let's do both," said Shelby. "Let's head to the interview and hang around. Let's put some icing on this cake."

Standing in a group of twenty-some bystanders, Nick followed Shelby while she forced her way up to the front of the interested onlookers. Two of the four tables had been rearranged to accommodate a female interviewer, a cameraman and the mayor himself. As the mayor took his seat he did not look out at the small crowd, but busied himself getting comfortable in front of the camera.

Leaning sideways, Shelby whispered, "You don't think he suspects anything...do you?"

"I don't see how he could. He's kept the murders a secret for twenty-seven years. The possibility, at least in his mind, that someone figured out what he and his friends did nearly thirty years in the past is highly unlikely. I do know this. He doesn't want the past, at least 1989 and what happened on Fripp to be part of his life. He has too much at stake. It strikes me he is a very respected and well-liked individual here in Pittsburgh...maybe the entire State of Pennsylvania. This man, Brad Schulte, could very well be the next governor of the state. He'll do whatever is necessary to squash any inkling of his involvement in the murders of Abigail and Chester."

Nodding toward the mayor, Nick whispered, "I think they're about to begin."

The interviewer sat directly across from the mayor while the cameraman made some last minute adjustments to his tripod camera. Another woman stepped forward carrying a clipboard. The woman held up three fingers and counted down, "Three, two, one," and then pointed at the interviewer who instantly spoke up as she faced the camera.

"Good afternoon. This is Susan Rush of KDKA TV in Pittsburgh. We are here at the thirty-seventh annual Downtown Pittsburgh Christmas Show. I have with me today Pittsburgh's Mayor Brad Schulte." Turning to the mayor she asked her first question. "Mayor Schulte. It is thought by many in the Pittsburgh area and across the state that you are running for the next governor. Can we make this official today? Are you definitely in?"

Looking at the reporter, Brad smiled at the camera and announced. "Let's make my intentions official today. I am indeed running for the next Governor of Pennsylvania."

For the next ten minutes the reporter fired off one question after another, Brad answering each question with what seemed like deep knowledge and an air of confidence.

The female reporter turned to the audience and addressed the gathering crowd, "For the next few minutes I would like to field some questions from some of our local citizens."

The clipboard-carrying woman approached the crowd with a handheld microphone. A woman standing at the end of the group took the mic and spoke, "Mayor Schulte. My name is Carol and I live right here in Pittsburgh. My husband is an over the road truck driver. He travels the Pennsylvania Turnpike every week and tells me the highway is in need of great repair. If you get into the office of the governor what do you propose to do to fix this problem?"

"I myself over the years have travelled back and forth across our turnpike which connects one end of the Keystone State with the other," remarked Brad. "I would be the first to admit the state has not maintained the turnpike to the degree it needs to be. Not if, but *when* I am elected to the office of governor I will appropriate funds to get not only the turnpike but our state highway system to where our citizens feel safe while travelling our roads and highways."

A man next to the woman who had spoken up took the mic and asked, "What is your stand on gun control here in our state?"

The mayor shook his head in an affirmative manner and answered, "I am in support of the National Rifle Association and I believe every citizen in our state has the right to own and carry a weapon if they desire to do so. At the same time I am also in favor of stronger laws when it comes to purchasing firearms. We must take great efforts to keep guns out of the hands of criminals."

Shelby reached out, took the mic, and introduced herself. "Hello, my name is Shelby Pickett and I am from the town where Mayor Schulte was born and raised. I think it is important for the voters of Pennsylvania to know where Brad comes from and what he stands for. A lot of folks may not realize this but Mayor Schulte back in 1989 was the quarterback of the Beaufort, South Carolina High School football team and he led the team to the state championship that year. Would you care to elaborate on your senior year when you won the state championship?"

Brad gave Shelby an odd look but responded instantly. "This young lady is correct. I did quarterback the 1989 Beaufort team to the state championship. We defeated Charleston South by a score of 33-0. It still remains one of the best years of my life."

Shelby continued, "Folks down that way have told me it turned out to be a tragic year. Is it not true two of your fellow students were murdered the night of the celebration of your victory and those murders are still unsolved? How did you feel back then about those murders?"

Brad stared back at Shelby but recovered quickly with a wide smile when the reporter interrupted, "I think we need to keep our questions for the mayor centered on his upcoming bid for governor."

Brad held up his hand and responded, "Susan, I'll answer the question. In the past during my political career I have never refused to answer a question and I'll not start now."

Shelby got a cold feeling when Brad stared directly into her eyes and stated firmly, "I remember those murders all too well. As a fellow student of course I was upset. All of the students at Beaufort High were on edge as well as the faculty and the people living in town. The two students that were killed were Abigail James and Chester Finch and they were friends of mine. We grew up together in the same community. I recall times when I danced with Abby at school dances and how Chester was always going around taking photographs of everyone at school. I stated earlier that 1989 was one of the best years of my life. Well, it was also one of the saddest. To answer the other part of your question, young lady, I have no idea if the murders were ever solved. I've only gone back to Beaufort one time since I graduated high school and that was two years ago for a school reunion."

The mayor had recovered well from the awkward question and most of the people in the crowd were staring at Shelby like she had asked an inappropriate question. There was silence for a few brief seconds when the reporter cleared her throat and requested, "Next question, please."

Nick leaned over and whispered to Shelby, "I think it would be best if we leave!"

Shelby, backing out of the crowd answered with conviction, "I think you're right."

Brad looked over at his aide and gave a slight nod at which point John walked around the side of the crowd on the opposite side from where Nick and Shelby were standing.

A few feet out from the crowd Nick turned and looked back when he noticed many of the people in the crowd still staring at them. Taking her gently by the arm, he started up the aisle. "I think we pissed some folks off. It may not have been your intention but I think you may have insulted their precious mayor with your question."

Looking back, Shelby saw John and two other men wearing suits walking toward them. Picking up the pace she commented, "I think we're being followed. C'mon, let's get out of here."

Nick glanced back and saw the three men closing in. Pushing Shelby forward, he suggested strongly, "Run, we're not that far from the exit."

Running past three booths, they took a right at the next intersecting row as they moved in and out in between shoppers. Nick looked back and shouted, "They're still coming! They're gaining! We'll never make it!"

Pushing open an exit door they found themselves in a long hallway. Sprinting down the narrow passage they turned a corner when John appeared in the hall behind them.

Entering yet another doorway, Nick shouted and he pulled Shelby along. "We have to get back to where there are people. We cannot afford to get caught back here. There's no telling what they'll do."

Shelby at his side, yelled back in amazement, "This can't be happening! What's going on?"

'I'll tell you what's going on. We went and pissed off a very powerful and apparently dangerous man."

Shelby stumbled, twisted her ankle, and stopped. "This is crazy! Where are we going?"

"I have no idea. I only know this. I'm not interested in finding out what the mayor's goons want. Let's keep moving. We have to find a place to hide and let them pass."

Entering another passageway they took a right and ran through a large overhead door where there were a number of trucks parked. Shelby bent over, out of breath and rubbed her ankle. "I don't think I can run anymore."

"C'mon," said Nick. Climbing up the back of a dump truck, he ordered, "Get up here." He offered his hand and hoisted her up and over the side. Lying down in the bed of the truck covered with rank smelling garbage bags, he whispered, "Don't make a sound."

Peering over the side of the truck he watched when the three men, led by the man called John entered the large football size room. Ducking down, Nick placed his index finger over his lips and signaled Shelby for complete silence.

John looked at the line of trucks but then walked out into the large open room and turned in a circle. "Damn it! We may have lost them."

Nick chanced a quick look over the side of the truck while John ordered the other two men, "Robert, you need to run down to the other end and see if you can see any sign of them. Lew and I are going to have a look over around those trucks."

After Robert ran off across the vast expanse of concrete, John ordered Lew, "Start down there on the end and work your way toward me. I'll start at the other end. Check the cabs and the back of the trucks."

Shelby, who heard the conversation whispered, "What are we going to do?"

Moving one of the bags, Nick gave her an odd grin and stated, "Somehow we have to hide in this garbage. Get down here!" Pushing the bags gently to not make any noise, he covered Shelby first with four bags and then crawled down deep into the bags covering himself. Seconds passed when they could both hear John climb up the side of the truck. They listened when he moved two bags and then swore, "Damn if this crap doesn't stink." Moving around the rear of the truck John stepped on Nick's unseen arm and yelled down the line of trucks. "Anything Lew?"

"Not a thing. Do you want me to keep looking?"

Nick lay perfectly still until John moved further back in the truck. Disgusted, John answered, "No, I don't think they came in here. Go find Robert and tell him to watch the main entrance in case they circled around. Then I need you to go back and tell Brad I'm heading on over to the Hilton where're they're staying. Call me if Brad has further instructions."

Minutes passed when Nick slowly emerged from the trash bags and seeing the coast was clear, uncovered Shelby. Shelby sat up wiping rotten tomato from the side of her face and smiled in a glib fashion. "Like I've always said…you really know how to show a girl a great time!"

Helping her up, Nick started down over the side of the truck and then assisted Shelby to the ground. "How's the ankle?"

Testing it by moving her foot from side to side, Shelby answered, "I can walk okay, but running is definitely out. If we run into them again, we won't be able to get away."

Walking Shelby out into the hallway, Nick looked both ways and spotted a door that read Freight Elevator. "C'mon, let's see where that leads. If we can just find a way out of the convention center without going back to the main entrance, I think we can escape."

Limping along next to Nick, Shelby looked back down the hall and mentioned, "This is ridiculous. Do you realize we are running from the Mayor of Pittsburgh? Why do you think he sent his goons after us?"

"I have no idea what he wants with us, but it can't be good. He may be of the opinion you exposed him in front of not only the crowd at the interview, but also on local television."

Stopping in front of the large screened-in elevator door, Nick pushed the button and heard the sound of the elevator above them when it kicked in. They no sooner stepped into the elevator than they heard a shout from up the hall. "Stop…right there!"

Looking down the hall they saw Robert running in their direction while talking on a hand-held two-way radio. Nick quickly pushed the down button and the elevator started to move painfully slow. Robert approached and yelled at them as they disappeared, "Get back here. The mayor would like a word with you two!"

Nick, looking up at the man could hear him speaking into his radio. "Lew, they're in the freight elevator heading for the below ground parking area. I'll take the stairs down if you can head them off at the parking garage exit!"

Nick let out a long breath and commented, "Well, at least we know where we're headed. I just hope this thing gets down there before they do."

After what seemed like an eternity the cumbersome elevator touched down. Shelby looked out through the wire mesh and stated, "Looks clear."

Opening the large wire door, they stepped out. Shelby checked her ankle again. Nick walked forward a few steps and announced, "I think we've found a way out of here. There's a sign over there by those parked cars that says Street Exit. If we can get out to the street, I think we'll be all right.

Suddenly, Robert appeared at the bottom of a stairwell and seeing them, shouted, "Stop!"

Pulling Shelby back inside the elevator, Nick closed the door and hit the button for the second floor. As Robert raced across the paved lot, Shelby yelled at the elevator out of frustration, "C'mon, c'mon…move!"

Just when Robert arrived at the wire gate the elevator began to move upward. Robert stared at them through the mesh and spoke into the radio, "Lew! They're going back up in the freight elevator. I'm not sure what floor they're going to. I'm going back up to the first floor. You might want to go to the second. Call John and let him know what's going on."

"We're going to the second floor," said Nick. "From there I don't have any idea where we'll go. We'll just have to wait until we get up there."

As the elevator passed the first floor they could see Robert when he exited the stairs and seeing they were still going up, returned to the stairwell. "Damn it!" said Nick. "As slow as this thing moves he'll be up top waiting for us."

Shelby reached over and hit the STOP button. "There's no sense in going up then." Hitting the FIRST FLOOR button, they heard the elevator mechanism reverse itself as it began to make its slow descent. "I think we'll have a better shot at losing them if we go back to the show and get lost in the crowd. That character who has been running up and down the stairs has to be getting tired. I'm guessing he'll run all the way back down to the parking garage. By the time he gets down there it'll be too late. He will have lost us."

Nick shrugged. "That's if he goes all the way down."

"What other choice do we have? We can't just keep going up and down in this damn thing. Eventually they'll have every floor covered and then we'll be screwed. We have to do the unexpected. They think we're trying to leave the building. We'll just hang around the show for an hour or so and then when they figure we slipped by them we'll leave. I know it sounds risky, but what other choice do we have."

"I guess you're right. We need to lose them and go somewhere inside this building where you can rest your ankle. I've got an idea. We should almost be at the first floor."

Within seconds the first floor hallway appeared and there stood Robert waiting for them, his hands on his hips while he glared at the couple. The elevator continued on, not stopping. Cursing, Robert ran toward the stairwell. When he turned the corner, Nick hit the STOP button and then hit FIRST FLOOR. The elevator momentarily stopped and then began to go back up. Before Robert was down the stairs they were back on the first floor. Nick flung open the wire door and stepped out and motioned to Shelby, "I know it's hard for you to go that fast but if we don't get out of the hallway before he gets back up here our goose is cooked."

Shelby stepped out and half ran, half limped down the hall with Nick's help. When they turned the corner, Nick looked back and seeing no one, pulled Shelby along. "I think we made it…at least for now. We should be back on the show floor in a few seconds."

Robert emerged from the stairwell and waited for the elevator that never came down. Cursing again, he called Lew. "It's Robert. They never came down. They must be going back up."

"Get back up to the first floor…now!" shouted Lew.

Robert was exhausted from running up and down the stairs. He frowned and started back up again, but this time he was walking.

Nick pushed open the door and examined the crowded aisle of shoppers. Holding out his hand for Shelby, he encouraged her. "C'mon, once we get lost in this crowd we'll be able to relax."

Staying close to Nick, Shelby constantly looked back through the crowd while she limped along. Ten minutes passed and they found themselves standing just down the aisle from the three entrance doors that led to the lobby and the main entrance. "Wait here," said Nick.

Walking out the closest door, he stayed near the wall and scanned the large lobby. People were filing in and out of the show. Then he saw them. Robert and Lew were stationed on either side of the three exits checking everyone who was leaving.

Going back into the show, Nick pulled Shelby to the side. "They're watching all the exit doors. Unless we can find another way out we seem to be trapped. We could be here for quite some time."

"I can't do that. I have to get off this ankle." Looking around, she snapped her fingers. "Wait here."

Limping down the aisle she stopped at a rental booth that offered wheelchairs and baby strollers for customers. Touching one of the wheelchairs, Shelby inquired, "What is the rental on a chair for let's say an hour?"

A baldheaded, overweight man smiled and answered, "Ten dollars per hour. Fifty dollars for the entire day."

Opening her purse, she handed the man a ten and said, "I'll just take this one for an hour."

Hopping in the chair she backed up into the aisle and signaled for Nick.

"Good idea for your ankle," remarked Nick, "Now all we have to do is figure out how to get out of this place."

Tapping the wheel of the chair, Shelby nodded. "This is the answer for both my ankle and the means of getting out of here. This chair will hopefully kill two birds with one stone. Push me down that first aisle. We've got some shopping to do."

An hour later, sitting off to the side next to some benches, Shelby asked, "Well, what do you think?"

Stepping back, Nick looked her and the chair over and remarked confidently, "This just might work. With that new winter coat and hat you just purchased and those large shopping bags shielding your face, they'll never recognize you."

Shelby nodded in approval and looked back at Nick bundled up in a heavy winter coat and Pittsburgh Pirates baseball hat. "We're going to walk right past them. They won't even give us a second look. The wheelchair and these winter clothes are the perfect disguise. Let's go. There's no sense in sitting here wondering if this is going to work. Let's just do it! We can walk right past these clowns."

Out in the lobby, Robert and Lew were still positioned so they could observe every customer exiting the show. Pushing Shelby toward the middle door, Nick leaned over and whispered, "I hope this works!"

Shelby reached up and touched his arm. "We've faced tougher characters than these two goons. Don't' forget, you took out Ike Miller and the RPS Killer met his demise when he tried to eliminate me from the face of the earth. Onward!"

Nick pulled the collar of his jacket up around his neck while Shelby positioned two large shopping bags on her chest, partially covering her face. When they got to the middle door there was a jam up of people and they had to stop. Nick chanced a look over at Robert who started to walk toward the group of shoppers. Shelby reached out and tugged on a woman's dress. "Please excuse us."

The woman, seeing Shelby was wheelchair confined immediately stepped to the side allowing Nick to push the chair through the door and out to the lot. "Don't even look back," said Shelby. "Just keep going!"

Crossing the paved lot they stopped next to the street. Nick looked back at the convention center. "I think we're in the clear."

Shelby bent forward and rubbed her ankle. "If I can get off this ankle for a few hours I think I'll be all right."

Light snowflakes began to fall when a voice from behind them caught their attention, "Hey you, hold up!"

Nick gave Shelby a look indicating that they hadn't made it. They both turned and saw the large wheelchair vendor running toward them. Out of breath the man stopped just short of the chair and explained, "I'm sorry but you can't take the chair off the lot."

Relieved, Shelby slowly got up and handed her two bags to Nick. "I'm so sorry. It's just that my ankle is really sore."

Reaching for the wheelchair the man suggested, "Maybe you could call a cab. Where are you headed from here?"

Nick looked up the street. "We're staying at the Hilton."

The man turned the chair around and pointed up the street. "The Hilton is only three blocks. Have a nice holiday."

The snow was now falling with more intensity and the flakes were larger. Turning in a circle, Nick joked, "Welcome to Pittsburgh."

Stepping out into the street, Shelby smiled. "Three blocks isn't that far, but we need to get away from here. If the mayor's goons spot us out here we'll never be able to elude them."

Crossing the street, Shelby struggled when she stepped up on to the curb. "This is really going to be slow going. Looking up at the sky the snow was now a miniature blizzard, blowing sideways, stinging their faces.

Nick pulled her forward and suggested, "There's a coffee shop two doors up. Why don't we go in there where you can sit down and get off that ankle? We'll have a cup of coffee and warm up."

The quaint coffee shop was crowded with people, all six tables filled. After they ordered their coffee they managed to get a window table when two businessmen left and ventured out into the cold Pennsylvania air. Shelby held her cup in her hands while Nick dumped cream and sugar in his cup. Sipping at the hot liquid, Shelby asked, "Well, what's our next move?"

"We need to get out of Pittsburgh…pronto," said Nick. "First we need to get back to the Hilton and check out. Out flight tickets back to Charleston are open ended which means whenever there is a flight down to Charleston we can board it, provided we call ahead and get a seat. The problem is right now we don't know when the next flight to Charleston leaves. It might have already left. So, we might be stuck here until tomorrow. That'll never fly because Schulte knows we're staying at the Hilton. Hell, he might have someone watching the Hilton right now."

Shelby looked out the front window at the passing traffic. "Schulte doesn't know what kind of a rental car we have…does he?"

"I don't see how he could."

"Why don't we do this? With the way my ankle is acting up, maybe I should just stay here while you go back to the Hilton, check out, grab our bags and drive back here and pick me up. In the meantime while you're gone I can call the airlines and see when the next flight to Charleston leaves. If the flight has already left for the day, then we can check into another hotel and wait."

Nick smiled. "You're just full of ideas today. Why didn't I think of that? I'm going to get a coffee to go. I should be back in less than a half hour. Why don't you give Bernard a call and let him know what's going on. Remember all of this is on his dime. He might have another suggestion for us."

"Be careful," warned Shelby. "When you get back to the Hilton if they have someone watching the front desk or the main entrance, you might have to forget our bags. In that case just get the car and come get me."

Outside, on the street Nick checked to see if he was being watched. He didn't notice anything out of the ordinary so he waved at Shelby and started up the avenue. The snow had slowed down and was now a light sleet. He hoped Shelby would be all right by herself. With any luck, he'd be back to pick her up in no time at all.

Shelby sat and looked out at the street and drank her coffee. Now that she had met Mayor Schulte face to face and had talked with the man she began to realize what they were trying to accomplish could wind up being dangerous. The mayor had already ordered men, who obviously worked for him, to stop them from leaving the convention center. What would they have done if they had caught them? Sipping at her coffee again, she thought about how glad she would be once they were out of the city and on their way back to Charleston.

Nick entered the large gold, glass double doors of the Hilton and slowly walked into the massive lobby. There were a number of people walking around but none that seemed out of the ordinary. There were three men in suits seated around the lobby; one on a couch and the other two in individual chairs. He didn't recognize any of the three as the men who had been running after them. Taking a chance he started to walk across the expanse of carpeting. None of the three men so much as gave him a look. Arriving at the elevator he waited patiently for the car to come to the lobby level.

It arrived and a couple got off when Nick stepped in. Pushing the second floor button, he breathed a sigh of relief. It looked like he was going to make it to the room. All he had to do was grab their bags and back down the elevator he'd go. He'd check out at the main desk, walk to their rental car and pick up Shelby just up the street three blocks.

Stepping out of the elevator on the second, he turned a corner to walk down the long hall that led to their room toward the end of the building when he saw a man seated on a loveseat a few yards away. Their eyes met at the same time. John jumped up and ordered, "Falco…you have to come with me!"

Nick instantly turned and raced back to the elevator and realizing he would not have time to wait, opened the stairwell door and ran down the first flight of stairs. On the second flight he could hear John behind him yelling, "Falco…you can't get away."

On the lobby floor, Nick sprinted across the carpet and out the front door. He knew John would not be far behind. Outside, he made a left and ran beneath the large marquee that boldly displayed he and Shelby as visiting authors. Running into the parking garage he ran up to the second level where he had parked their car. He looked back and saw John running up the ramp. He was almost to the car but figured he had no time to unlock it, climb in, start the car and drive off before John would be on him. Instinctively, he walked in behind a van and hid next to a concrete wall. It wasn't but a few seconds when John ran by, but then stopped and looked in every direction. Taking out his radio, he made a call. Nick listened intently, John's voice amplified due to the closed quarters, "Brad, it's John. I just chased Falco into the parking garage to the second floor. I'm not sure where he went. I think I'll go back down and watch the exit gate. He can't get out of here without passing by me. We've got him now."

Looking around the edge of the van Nick watched John walk around the corner. There was no way he could get past John. That is, unless he acted now! Running to the rental he unlocked the door, hopped in and turned the ignition. He figured John, now on the lower level, may have heard the car start up. Backing out, he turned toward the exit ramp down to the first level. When he turned the corner there stood John in the middle of the ramp. Without the slightest hesitation, Nick floored the accelerator, the car lurching forward. John had little time to react as Nick guided the car directly at him

John jumped to the side and rolled on the hard concrete when Nick blasted past and smashed through the self-pay wood gate out to the street. Making an immediate right hand turn he sped up the street but had to stop for a red light at the next block. Looking in the rearview mirror he saw John running up the sidewalk. The light changed green just when John reached out and touched the trunk of the car. Nick glanced back and saw John standing in the middle of the street, out of breath, his hands on his hips in frustration.

The next two lights were green and he found himself pulling up in front of the coffee shop. Shelby saw him and got up slowly. Nick jumped out and signaled for her to hurry. She no sooner jumped in the car than Nick hit the gas and turned at the next intersection. Out of breath, he gasped, "We have to get out of Pittsburgh…now!"

CHAPTER TWENTY TWO

CHIC SAT IN HIS CAR DIRECTLY ACROSS THE STREET FROM the rear entrance to the church office. He checked his watch, 2:57 in the afternoon. Wanting to be exactly on time he got out of the car and started across the street, briefcase in hand. Stopping at the door to the office, he examined himself one last time. He thought he looked appropriate for meeting a high-ranking member of the Catholic religion. Stepping into the office the same woman he had conversed with the previous day sat at her desk. Looking at a clock on the wall, she commented, "Right on time, Mr. Brumly."

Putting on an act, something Chic was quite good at, he remarked, "I have to say I'm a bit nervous. I've never had an opportunity to interview a priest before; let alone an archbishop."

The woman got up and motioned for Chic to follow her down a long hallway. "I think you'll find Archbishop Durham quite easy to converse with. His office is just down the hall."

Following close behind, Chic asked, "If I could ask, how do I address an archbishop?"

The woman turned back and answered, "In Catholic circles archbishops are normally referred to as The Most Reverend or Your Grace. Most people when talking with the archbishop address him as Your Excellency. Now, before we go in. The archbishop has set aside forty-five minutes for this interview. He is a very busy man and has a number of people he is meeting with this evening. So, that being said Mr. Brumly, make the best use of the time His Excellency has granted you."

Knocking on a large oak door, a voice from inside the room responded, "Enter."

The woman opened the door and gestured for Chic to enter at which point she closed the door without another word. The archbishop, or as Chic thought of him, Tim Durham, stood behind a large desk and extended his hand. "You must be the author from Beaufort I was informed of. Welcome to my office. Please have a seat."

Reaching across the desk, Chic shook the archbishop's hand and commented, "You look quite different than you did yesterday during the late service."

"I take it Mr. Brumly you are not that familiar with the vestments of the Catholic Faith."

"No, I'm not, and to be honest with you I am not Catholic. I hope this will not keep me from our interview."

Holding up his hand, Tim offered, "Don't concern yourself. There are many who are not of the faith I practice. The vestments you saw me wearing yesterday at the Mass are referred to as liturgical vestments. The vestments I am presently wearing are for everyday casual wear. The black hat is called a zucchetto and the black robe is referred to as a cassock." Sitting down, Tim waved off what he had just said and continued, "I know you didn't come here to see me this day to gain information on Catholic vestments. What do you wish to ask me?"

Opening his briefcase, Chic removed a legal pad and a pen and making himself comfortable, crossed his legs. "As you are aware, I am an author. I am currently conducting research for my latest book which is going to be about past students from Beaufort High School who went on later in life to become famous, well-known or successful."

Humbly, Tim folded his hands on top of the desk and replied, "Perhaps you have made a mistake by choosing me as one of the subjects for your new book. I say this because I am far from famous. I am only well-known by those in the Catholic religion and, at that, the Catholic population in St. Louis."

"Well nonetheless," spoke up Chic. "People in the Lowcountry will want to read about your life as an archbishop." Wanting to move things along, Chic commented, "I have conducted quite a bit of research on your past life in Beaufort. If I am to understand correctly, during your senior year in high school, which I believe was 1989, you were a member of the Beaufort High football team and you were very instrumental in leading the team, not only to an undefeated season but the state championship as well?"

Folding his hands on his chest and sitting back, Tim answered, "I was a tight end on the team and I recall that particular game as one of my best. I caught three touchdown passes and intercepted our opponent once. It was one of the best games I ever participated in."

Chic nodded in agreement and then went on, "One of the people I interviewed back in Beaufort was your old high school girlfriend...LuAnn Dawson. She told me you and she dated all through high school and into college."

"That's correct. But that was back in a part of my life that has been replaced with my new life of serving the Lord. I will say this. LuAnn was the only female I have ever been with as a man, if you get my meaning."

"You mean sexually?"

"Yes, but that subject is not part of my life anymore. Back then when I was a young buck…a high school football player, I met LuAnn my freshman year. She was a cheerleader and as I recall, cute as a button. She was the first girl I ever dated…and the last. I never dated another and as far as I know, she was always faithful to me during our years as a couple."

"LuAnn said you were going to be engaged to be married, but then after your second year at college you wrote her a letter stating you were leaving school and you were going into the priesthood. She told me it came as a complete shock."

"I suppose it was a shock." Shifting in the chair, Tim went on to explain, "Mr. Brumly, have you ever met a young person who seems to have their entire future planned out?"

"I guess I'd have to answer that question with a no. Take me, for instance. When I was growing up I wanted to be a railroad engineer, but as it turns out, I'm an author. I think there are very few people who figure out what they want to do for the rest of their life as a young man or woman. Practically everyone winds up doing something other than what they planned on or making a living doing something they could never have imagined themselves doing."

"Precisely," remarked Tim. "I had my sights set on being a professional football player since I was six years old. I carried that dream with me all the way through my second year at college before I made the change in my life that leads me to where I sit today. Especially in high school. LuAnn and I had our entire future mapped out. We talked about it all the time. I was going to be a professional football player, LuAnn the wife of a star in the NFL. We talked about where we would live, what our home would look like, even how many children we would have. We even picked out names for our future children. Back then if someone would have told me I was going to go in a completely different direction and join the priesthood, I would have told them they were nuts." Displaying himself, Tim smiled. "But…here I sit; an archbishop in the Catholic faith."

"Here's a strange question," stated Chic. "Over the years have you ever regretted not following your high school plans of marrying and having a family? I mean, let's face it. Your life would have been drastically different than it is now. You could have made big money and lived anywhere you desired with your wife and children. What would make a person, in this case you, decide to go the route of religion? A priest no less. I find that fascinating and I think my readers would as well."

"Most people who go into the faith business, whether it be Catholicism, Methodists, Baptists or what have you do so because they get the call. By that I mean they receive a message from God that they are to serve as a priest, minister, preacher or some other sort of religious leader in their community, or some just follow in the footsteps of a parent who may have been a man or women of great faith. For me, well, I didn't receive a call from God. My life was just so frustrating. As a young man I wasn't pleased with what I had done with my life and I didn't like the direction it was going. I wanted a change…a dramatic change! To be honest with you, over the years from time to time I wonder if I made the right decision. After all, I've missed out on so many normal things people experience in life. I'll never have a wife or children or even own a home of my own. I have dedicated my life to the Catholic faith and by doing so I have long since come to the conclusion I did make the correct decision in becoming a priest. When you think about it, I do have a family, a very large one. During my years as a priest, bishop and now an archbishop I have baptized over one thousand children, married hundreds of couples and have given the last rights to many people who have gone on to the next life. So, to answer your question, I have no regrets about my decision years ago of going into the priesthood."

"Based on what you have told me," said Chic, "being an archbishop is more than an occupation; it's a way of life, a way few choose to go. You have revealed to me many of the joys associated with being an archbishop, but surly there must be something, some aspect of being a priest-archbishop that bothers you from time to time. Something you are obligated to perform but don't particularly enjoy."

"That's easy to answer. Hearing confessions. I have been ordained for almost twenty years now and every Saturday between four and six o'clock I have been hearing confessions. It has always been, and still is today, the most frustrating part of being a priest and now an archbishop. In the old days people would come to the confessional and confess their sins to me. That practice is still in effect but today an individual can actually come to me face to face and confess their sins. This face-to-face business has always made me just a wee bit uncomfortable. I prefer the confessional myself. But even then, it seems so personal. People from all walks of life come to see me, sometimes weekly in confession and reveal to me their deepest sins.

It has always amazed me I have been granted the power by the Catholic Church to absolve people of their sins. I am always so humbled people would confide in me to speak to God Almighty on their behalf. I have to say that hearing confessions can get old very quickly. After a period of time I begin to recognize certain people's voices and week after week they confess the same sins. I often think to myself; what good am I doing for them…or even myself? At times, I think I've heard just about every sin there is in the world, and then someone drops a bomb on me with their sin."

Chic looked at a clock on the wall and realized he had been talking to Durham for twenty minutes. He only had twenty-five minutes left. At some point he was going to have to interject the murders of the James girl and the Finch kid. This subject about confession might just be the *in* he required. "I am not all that familiar with how the Catholic religion is structured, but I have always heard a priest is not allowed to share with anyone what is confessed to him. Is this true?"

"Most definitely," declared Tim. "Priests take the vow of the seal of confession which means we are not allowed to reveal what is confessed to us."

Amazed, Chic asked, "Is this true in every case…for every sin?"

"Yes, there is not a situation that would require us to reveal what we are told in confidence."

Chic saw his opportunity and casually asked, "Even murder!"

"Yes, Mr. Brumly…even the sin of murder."

Acting as if he wasn't sure of what he was saying, Chic grabbed his opportunity to work the murders of Abigail James and Chester Finch into the conversation. "I just happened to think of something; something by the way that has absolutely nothing to do with our interview. When I interviewed LuAnn and some of the folks over at the high school they told me 1989 was not only a wonderful year because they had been crowned the state football champions, but was shadowed by the tragic deaths of two students that same year. Apparently they had been murdered down on Fripp Island during the celebration for the football team. I can't recall the names of the two students…the victims, but I do remember LuAnn told me the murders still today were unsolved. That means somewhere out there in this world a person or a number of people are walking around Scott-free. I find that amazing! To think those responsible for the deaths of those two kids could come forward and confess their sin, in this case, murder, to a priest and not be reported is unbelievable. Do you remember those murders when they happened and how you felt at the time?"

"I do remember when that happened. It was indeed a tragedy. The names of the students were Abigail James and Chester Finch. I knew both of them. They were not what I would call close friends, but still friends. I'd see them in the hallway at school and they were in a couple of classes I attended. I have no idea where the case stands today. But, like I said my high school days were a part of my past life I have erased from my daily living. These days I concentrate on my daily duties as the Archbishop of St. Louis."

In Chic's estimation, Tim had talked about those he had murdered without showing the least bit of emotion. The only other thing Chic wanted to do was to collect information Bernard could use in the near future to bring the archbishop down. "So, tell me Your Excellency, as an archbishop what are you allowed to do, let's say in the outside world from the church?"

"Surprisingly, I lead an interesting life," stated Tim. "I jog five miles a day Monday through Friday and I swim Tuesdays and Thursdays up the street at the YMCA. Probably the most interesting thing about me most people are not aware of is I own a 1959 Corvette Stingray. I've had it ever since my freshman year at college. In a conversation with one of my professors I learned she had a vintage Corvette parked in her garage she had no need for. Her grandson had passed on and the car was just sitting there wasting away. I asked her if she would be willing to sell it and she said yes. I've had it ever since 1991. It's parked in the rectory garage right outside. It's a beauty…an antique...bright red and white exterior, red leather seats, four speed. Everything on the car is original. During the winter I never drive it unless the roads are clear of snow or road salt. Come next spring I'll pull her out on the weekends or on a hot summer night and drive out into the countryside. Occasionally, I like getting away from everything and everybody and cruising the back roads. Actually, I am a member of the St. Louis Corvette Club. That car is the only thing, aside from some clothes, I kept from my past life. Let's face it, a man, even an archbishop, has to have some sort of hobby."

Chic kept digging while he wrote on his pad. "How about local charities. Do you participate?"

"Yes, I am very active in local Catholic charities. I do not give financially, because I do not have much of an income. The church itself does earmark a certain amount of funds for charities. My involvement is strictly from an administrative position. I sit on the board of directors for Catholic Family Services and Cardinal Ritter Senior Services. I am also very active with the Queen of Peace Center."

Chic continued to ask questions for the next ten minutes, but it seemed there was not much more to learn about this man. Looking at the wall-mounted clock again, Chic placed the pad and pen back inside the briefcase and smiled across the room at Tim. "I think that about wraps things up. I see my allotted time is almost at hand. I want to thank you for your time and your openness about your life. I'll make sure you get a copy of the book when I get my hands on the finished product."

Tim stood and offered his hand. "Autographed, of course."

"Of course," said Chic as he stood to leave. "Thank you once again for your time."

About to open the door, Tim stopped him and asked, "Maybe you could do me a favor when you return to Beaufort."

"If it is in my power, I'll see it's done. What do you wish?"

"Well, if by some chance you just happen to run into LuAnn would you please tell her I think of her often. She is the only part of my past life that had any real meaning. Tell her I am glad she is happy."

Chic reached for the doorknob. "Consider it done. Good day to you, Your Excellency."

"Have a blessed day, Mr. Brumly."

At the same time Chic was walking across the street to his car in St. Louis, Carson was walking across the street to Pattersons Restaurant in Tampa. It was 3:45 in the afternoon and he hoped he wasn't too late to catch Miles. His flight from Atlanta had left Georgia late in the evening but had been delayed in Dallas due to horrible weather. He then flew over to Jacksonville where he had to stay the night, until the next afternoon when he could catch a commuter fight over to Tampa. It seemed like he had gone through Hell to get to his destination and if he missed Miles Gaston, he was going to be disappointed.

Pattersons had attractive curb appeal. A one story, all glass front structure fronted by large palm trees and colorful plants. Pleasant piano music drifted from the building and across the street. Pushing open a full view glass door, Carson entered and was instantly welcomed by a young hostess. "Good afternoon, sir. Will there be the one for dinner?"

Carson approached the small hostess desk and replied, "Yes, I'm afraid it's just me, but I am not here for dinner. I am here to see a Mr. Gaston, who I believe is the owner. His home office told me he might be spending the day here. I do not have an appointment with Mr. Gaston but I would like to talk with him if at all possible."

The girl smiled and confirmed, "Yes, Miles is still here. I believe he is just about to have dinner. Let me send someone back to his office and see if he is available. What is the name and what reason can I give for your visit?"

"My name is Carson Pike and I'm an author. I'm from the same town he was born and raised in. I'm writing a book and may include Miles in it as a successful South Carolinian. I was just trying to get a short interview with him."

"The girl smiled again and stated, "Please wait right here. I'll go check with Mr. Gaston."

Looking around the establishment Carson noted Pattersons was an upscale restaurant. With white linen tablecloths draped over candle lit tables, fine crystal drinking glasses, china plates and expensive looking utensils. The pleasant music he had heard when approaching the building came from an elevated piano where a man in a tuxedo ran his fingers over the keyboard. Waiters adorned in crisp black and white uniforms walked here and there carrying silver trays of food and bottles of wine. It was the type of restaurant Carson hated. The food was generally quite good but the tab at the end of dinner usually set one back seventy-five to a hundred dollars. Carson enjoyed a good meal, but nobody's food was that good!

The girl returned and motioned to Carson. "Mr. Gaston will see you now. Please follow me."

Walking through the dining area to a back room, Carson was led to a corner, candlelit table where Miles was seated. The girl made the introductions, "Mr. Gaston, this is Carson Pike. Mr. Pike this is Miles Gaston."

The girl left when Miles stood politely and offered Carson a seat. "Please…sit."

Remembering what the girl had said about Miles sitting down for dinner, Carson humbly refused, "I wouldn't think of interrupting your dinner."

"If you'll have dinner with me then it will not be considered an interruption."

Carson probed, "Are you sure?"

"Quite sure, Mr. Pike. Pull up a chair. What would you prefer to drink? I'm having a dry wine from southern France."

"I'm not much on wine," admitted Carson. "That being said, I do enjoy a cold glass of beer now and then."

Snapping his fingers, Miles got the attention of a passing waiter. "Charles, would you please bring me a bottle of my favorite wine and a tall glass of cold beer for my friend here."

The waiter nodded politely and replied, "Right away, sir."

The hostess tells me you're a writer…an author from Beaufort? Actually, I got a call from my home office yesterday. They informed me you had dropped by to see me. They also told me you might be flying down here to Tampa for an interview. That being said, if you do not mind interviewing me over dinner then it's a go."

"I wasn't expecting dinner," joked Carson, "but I think I can eat and talk at the same time."

The waiter returned with the wine and glass of beer and asked if they were ready to order. Miles smiled and spoke up, "I've already decided on the special. Would you care to look at a menu, Mr. Pike?"

"I don't want to complicate things. I'll have the special as well."

"Very well," said the waiter. "I'll be right back with some hot yeast rolls."

The waiter nodded at Carson and walked off as Miles asked, "Have you ever dined at one of my restaurants before?"

"No, I never have. As a general rule of thumb I stick rather close to Beaufort. I get over to Savannah and Charleston on occasion. I'm familiar with most of the restaurants in the Lowcountry."

"Actually, I own a restaurant in each one of those cities."

Sipping his beer, Carson remarked, "That's odd. I've never heard of Pattersons before."

Pouring himself a half glass of wine, Miles interjected, "That's because they are under different names. They were the first two eating establishments I purchased. I own the Savannah *in Savannah* and the Upper Deck in Charleston."

Acting like he was amazed, Carson lied, "I have eaten at the Upper Deck…was a couple of years ago."

Miles smiled and took another short swallow of white wine and asked, "So about this book you're writing. Why is an interview with me important?"

"Because you're one of the people I want to include in the book. You see, the book is going to be all about folks who graduated from Beaufort High that became successful." Pointing his glass of beer at Miles, Carson explained, "You graduated from Beaufort and you're quite successful!"

"Well, I have to tell you right up front, my life is hardly one of interest. I'm what's more commonly referred to as a workaholic. I've never been married, I have no kids or hobbies. I spend the better part of the year travelling around to my restaurants or various business interests."

"In other words," suggested Carson, "you have over the years been willing to do what most folks are not. You have worked hard at building up your restaurant business and now all that hard work and dedication is paying off."

Miles agreed, "I guess that more or less hits the nail on the head."

"You don't mind if I take some notes, do you?"

"No, go right ahead."

Laying his briefcase on one of the empty chairs around the table, Carson opened the case and removed a writing pad and ink pen. Holding up the pen, he remarked, "One of the tools of the trade." Sitting back,

Carson relaxed and began the interview. "What say we start out when you were back at Beaufort High? I do know you played on the high school football team all four years while at school."

"Yes, I was a running back."

"According to research I did at the school, you were on the 1989 championship team. I believe you beat Charleston South 33-0."

"That is precisely correct."

It was also explained to me you were part of a dynamic trio, referred to as The Three Musketeers."

"Also correct."

"I believe the other two members of the musketeers are Brad Schulte and Tim Durham."

"Correct."

"Have you remained in touch with your high school pals over the years?"

"If you are referring to Brad and Tim, I'd have to say…not really. After the three of us graduated we went our separate ways…to different colleges, actually in different states. I attended school down in South Carolina, Brad in Pennsylvania and Tim in Texas."

"Did you all receive athletic scholarships?"

"Yes, we all got a full ride to college."

Writing for effect, Carson probed, "Folks back home say you three could have gone on to be professional football players, but as it turns out, none of you made it to the pros. Tell me about your years at college and what made you change your mind about playing football professionally?"

Nodding at the waiter who placed a basket of hot rolls on the table, Miles continued, "I only played just the one year, my freshman year, for the Gamecocks. I left school two months before my freshman year was over. I knew I could stay at school and wind up getting drafted by a professional team, but I realized I could make just as much money, if not more than a professional football player, by utilizing my brain and not so much my body. I had done a rather good job of saving any money that I managed to earn up through high school, so after I left college, I worked for a year at the Upper Deck and I continued to save the bulk of what I earned. The next year when I found out the owner of the Upper Deck was selling out, I took out a loan and bought the place. Two years later I purchased the Savannah and then three years after that I purchased Pattersons that at the time had ten locations. Today, I have forty-three locations across the country."

It seemed to Carson, Miles Gaston liked to talk about what he had accomplished and as long as he was opening up, why not press for more information. Carson, still writing, probed, "Do you have other business interests or are you strictly involved in the restaurant business?"

"My business interests are varied. I have learned it is not wise to place all your eggs in one basket. I have diversified over the years expanding my interests in some apartment units, some laundromats, car washes and even two nightclubs. Actually, most of those businesses are in the Atlanta area."

Ten minutes passed while Carson casually grilled Miles about his life that was centered on work. When their dinner arrived Carson decided he would engage Miles in some rhetoric about the Lowcountry and some of his favorite eating places in Beaufort County, then a few minutes into their meal he'd pop the question about the 1989 murders. He complimented Miles on their meal: fresh tilapia with a special clam sauce, bacon wrapped asparagus, baked potato topped with melted brie cheese, chunky applesauce topped with cinnamon and key lime pie for dessert.

Halfway through the meal, Carson swallowed a bite of fish and sprang the question. "Folks still talk about you, Brad and Tim and say the team would have never won the 1989 state championship if it hadn't been for you three. After you three left for college, Beaufort High has never again even gone to the state playoffs, let alone won the state championship. That year, 1989 will always be remembered and revered as one of the best years the school has ever had, at least when it comes to football."

Buttering one of the rolls, Carson pointed the circular portion of bread at Miles and continued, "That being said, it's funny though. Most folks, especially those who attended Beaufort High in that era, claim 1989 was a tragic year. When I start talking about how the high school won the state championship they always interject the fact that two Beaufort students were murdered that year, and at that, during the celebration for the football team. I believe the murders occurred down on Fripp Island. Do you recall any of that?"

Miles openness suddenly seemed to disappear. He stared across the table at Carson, hesitated and then answered in a defensive manner, "Two things, Mr. Carson. I do recall when that happened and I really don't care to discuss it. Up until I turned seventeen years of age, I led a pretty normal life, a life minus a lot of tragedy. When those two students were murdered, everything changed and as far as I know it has never been proven who actually killed them. It still remains an unsolved case. Abigail James was the name of one of the victims and I have always been convinced she died because she was a promiscuous young lady. She slept around like nobody's business. She was heartless and cruel and had no compassion for anyone but herself. I believe she died due to her loose moral code. And the other victim, Chester Finch? I think he was just in the wrong place at the wrong time. Over the years I've tried to put that year out of my mind, which is yet another reason why I never wanted to play football again following my first year at college. It's just a bad reminder of what happened that night! We were all celebrating our victory while Abigail and Chester were being murdered. I've moved on with my life since 1989 and I do not enjoy going back and reviewing that time." Miles sat back in the chair he was sitting in and gave Carson a long hard stare, then laid down his fork and stated firmly, "Our interview is concluded. Furthermore, Mr. Carson, if you intend on using any of the information about my life I shared with you today, you'll need my written permission and right now, at this point, I'm not inclined to give that privilege to you! You are excused from my table. You can take your dessert with you." Standing, Miles gestured at the waiter, "Charles, please bring Mr. Carson a go box for his pie."

Tossing his napkin back on the table Miles gave Carson an unfriendly look and stated, "I'm going back to my office now." Walking across the room, he stopped, turned back and spoke in earnest, "Mr. Pike, I would strongly suggest you brush up on your interview skills. You started rather strong but you failed when you opened up this murder business. You say you came here to interview me about my career and what I have accomplished in life but you got way off track. There was no reason for you to question me about those murders. I do not now, and never had anything to do with what happened that night. Good day! Mr. Pike!"

If it were any other circumstance Carson would have agreed he had been put in his place, but what had really happened was Miles' true color came out. The mention of the two murders had a definite effect on his demeanor. As Carson placed his pie in the small container Charles brought him, he smiled at the waiter, got up and excused himself. "Thank you Charles. The meal was quite good." Handing the waiter a five-dollar bill, he gestured, "That's for the good service you provided me."

Outside, seated in his rental car, he dialed Bernard's number in order to find out what he was to do next."

Thirty miles outside of Columbus, Ohio, Nick waited in their car while Shelby ran into a truck stop to use the ladies' room. Sitting back in the seat he looked out at the surrounding snow covered landscape and realized he was less than three hours from Cincinnati where he had been born and raised. He wondered what his mother was up to these days. Sooner or later, despite the fact they no longer seemed to get along he was going to have to give her a call and make sure she was okay.

Shelby walked across the lot holding a cardboard tray. Approaching the car she signaled for him to roll down the driver's side window. Handing him a hot coffee and a hotdog she stated, "Thought you might be getting hungry. I know I am."

Inside the car, she sipped at her coffee and waved a map of Ohio in the air. "I thought I'd pick up a map. There should be an enlarged section of Columbus in here that will help us get to the airport."

Nick sat his meager dinner and coffee on the console and backed out of the lot. Shelby bit into her hotdog and unfolded the map. "When you get to the end of this feeder road take a left and get back on I-70 West. We should hit I-270 North in less than a half hour. Then we take 270 North until we come to Exit 35. According to the map that should take us right to the airport."

Back on I-70, Nick drank his coffee. "Tell me again what Bernard said when you called him right after we left Pittsburgh."

Picking up her coffee, Shelby explained, "He said for us to head over to Columbus where he would have a flight lined up for us. When he called back he said our flight leaves out of Columbus at 7:15 this evening. It's 5:45 right now. It's gonna be tight. We might not get to the airport until round 6:30. That leaves us forty-five minutes to locate the airlines and get checked in. If we miss the flight this evening, we'll have to stay the night in Columbus. If that happens we'll be altering Bernard's plans. He said Chic and Carson are flying back to Charleston tonight. Bernard plans to have a meeting at midnight so we can put everything we've learned together. If we miss the flight then the meeting will have to be put off until tomorrow."

Pressing the accelerator, Nick watched the speedometer register 80 mph. "We're gonna make that flight. If it's all the same to you I want to get back down to Beaufort where there is some level of warmness. This winter crap doesn't suit me at all."

Thirty minutes later, Nick pointed at the road sign for Exit 35, which also read Port Columbus International Airport - One Mile. "I think we're going to make that flight. What time is it?"

Shelby held up her wrist and answered, "Six-twelve. That gives us a little over an hour to get checked in. I'll feel a lot better when we're in the air. The fact Mayor Schulte's goons were after us back there in Pittsburgh still bothers me."

Brad Schulte sat at an upscale Italian restaurant in downtown Pittsburgh with Lew and Robert when John entered the eating establishment. Seating himself at their table, John explained, "I'm sorry,

Brad. It looks like they may have slipped town. I checked all the airlines and they were not booked on any flights leaving anytime today. The last time I saw them they were in a white compact Ford with Pennsylvania tags speeding down Penn Street."

Brad finished his mixed drink and remarked with confidence. "It was probably a rental. They said they were from South Carolina. If they had driven up here from the south, the car would have had Carolina tags. First thing in the morning, I want all three of you over at the airport. They may try to fly out tomorrow. I also want you to check the rental agencies to see if they rented a car here in Pittsburgh and if it has been turned in."

John held up his arm displaying his torn suit coat. "Falco practically ran me over when he pulled out of the parking garage at the Hilton. Let me ask you something, Brad? Why are we after these folks?"

Brad gave John and the others a stern look. "I pay you all quite well to protect me and that's all you need to know. I will say this. Those two young people, I feel, are trying to implicate me in something I had absolutely nothing to do with. That's all you need to know for now. Your futures with me can be even brighter than they are now when I am elected the governor of the state. If anyone, and I mean *anyone* slanders my good name and keeps me from the office of the governor, it will affect your careers as well."

John interjected, "But they said they were simply authors."

"People say a lot of things," said Brad, "but that doesn't mean it's the truth."

CHAPTER TWENTY THREE

SHELBY LOOKED AT THE GLOWING GREEN FACE OF HER wristwatch when Nick stopped at the red light on Bay Street. Glancing up the deserted street, she commented, "It's good to be back in Beaufort. I'm just now beginning to feel safe. I was so nervous back in Columbus while we were waiting for our flight to arrive. I expected to see one or two of Mayor Schulte's men pop up out of nowhere. Then, when we landed in Charleston I had the same feeling; that somehow they had followed us."

"I know what you mean," said Nick. "I'll feel better once we're back on Fripp."

Checking the time again, Shelby watched the light turn green as Nick started to cross the bridge to Lady's Island. "We're either going to be right on time for Bernard's midnight gathering or just a couple of minutes late. I wonder how Chic and Carson made out. If Durham and Gaston acted anything like Brad Schulte this could get real ugly, real fast."

Adjusting the seat, Shelby kicked off her shoes and propped her feet on the dash. "Speaking of Schulte. He seemed fine until we started to talk about the murders. Do you still think he believes we're authors?"

"I'm not sure. It's hard to say what he was thinking when he sent those men after us. We can only assume after twenty-seven years, he has put what happened that night on Fripp behind him. It's probably like a wound that has healed. Then we show up and reopen the wound by discussing something he doesn't want to discuss, something he'd rather forget. Whether he still believes we're authors is highly unlikely. We ran from his men. In his mind he may be thinking we ran because we have something to fear; like we're hiding something, something to do with the twenty-seven year old murders. Those murders are something he has buried deep in his brain and are no longer a part of his life. The look he gave you when you brought up the murders at his television interview indicated to me the memories of that night were suddenly transferred from the recesses of his brain to the forefront of his thoughts. I don't know about Durham and Gaston, but Brad Schulte strikes me as a dangerous man. He has a lot to lose and anyone or anything that gets in his way or interferes with his run for the Governor of Pennsylvania may have to be eliminated in his eyes. Right now, we may have a target on our backs. The sooner we get this thing wrapped up the better. Hell, he may already be planning to send someone down here to track us down…to check us out. We have to make sure we let Bernard know about our concern. The sooner Bernard brings these three men to justice, the better. These men have killed before and when they are exposed I'm sure they're not just going to say, 'Okay, you finally got me!' They are going to be scrambling for a way out. When that happens we don't want to be anywhere near them."

Bernard, dressed in an expensive green and black smoking jacket, lit his pipe and took a seat behind his desk. Conner threw another log in the blazing stone fireplace. Chic sat on the couch drinking a brandy while Carson scanned the rows of shelved books lining the walls of the library. Bernard looked at a grandfather clock in the corner and suggested to Conner. "Shelby called me from Charleston when they landed. She told me they would try to get here by midnight but they may be a few minutes late. Would you please walk out front and wait for their arrival. They should be here in the next ten to fifteen minutes."

Obediently, Conner nodded to Bernard. "I'll see to it, right away sir."

When Conner left the room Chic got up, poured himself another full measure of brandy, and commented, "Conner seems like a very competent man."

Puffing on his pipe, Bernard answered, "Conner is quite competent. He is a former marine, a highly decorated sniper he tells me. These days and for many years now he has been a high paid butler who doubles as my personal bodyguard. To most folks he comes off as very polite and laid back. Myself, well I wouldn't want to get on the wrong side of the man. I can't begin to tell you how many documented kills he had while serving our country. He really doesn't like to talk about it and I never press him for information about his past. Depending on how this business with Schulte, Durham and Gaston goes down, the talent Conner has may become invaluable to us."

Chic gave Carson and odd look and then asked Bernard, "You almost sound like you're saying if it becomes necessary you'll have Conner take out the three men we're after. I mean...would you really have them killed?"

Without the slightest hint of remorse, Bernard laid down his pipe and smiled, "Yes, if it becomes necessary. However, killing these three men will be my last resort. First, I want to destroy their very lives. They must experience the pain I have felt all these years due to my daughter's death at their hands." Holding up one of the photographs of the three boys on the beach standing over Abigail, he explained, "With the proof I now possess and the pressure I plan to put on these three men, they will fold, their lives will crumble, any respect people have for them will deteriorate and they will be destroyed. When everything I plan on doing comes to light, the police themselves will catch wind and become involved."

"Correct me if I'm wrong," said Carson, "but the first time around the police here in Beaufort, according to you, dropped the ball and that's why these men are free today. What makes you think it will be any different this time?"

Bernard, with the end of his pipe, pointed at a large map of the United States and elaborated, "The Beaufort Police, who screwed this case up way back when, will at some point be contacted by the Pittsburgh Police, not to mention the police in St. Louis and Atlanta, Tampa and anyplace else these three men are known or have business. We are going to bring the case back to life. We are going to rejuvenate interest in the deaths of my daughter and Chester Finch. The crime these men committed twenty-seven years ago is soon going to return to haunt them."

Bernard's statement of payback was interrupted when Shelby walked in the room, trailed by Nick and Conner. Bernard, pleased everyone on the team was present held up his hand to the two new arrivals. "Ah, the first part of our puzzle is complete. Everyone has returned from their assignment. If everyone would please be seated we can begin."

Addressing Conner, he went on, "Would you please notify Mae everyone has arrived and she can bring in the food she has prepared for us."

Conner bowed slightly and backed out of the room, "Of course, sir."

Back behind the desk, Bernard blew a long stream of aromatic tobacco smoke into the air. "I am glad that all of you have returned safely here to the island. I promise you I will not keep you long tonight. We should have tonight's proceedings wrapped up in about an hour or so. What I want to accomplish tonight is to have each member of the group give the rest of the team a rundown on how things went during their particular assignment. I am going to record our conversations tonight so that, after you leave, Conner and I can piece together the information you supply us with."

Conner entered the room and excusing himself, announced, "Our late night snacks will be here in a few minutes."

Turning to Chic, Bernard suggested, "Chic. Why don't you start us off with how your meeting with Tim Durham, the Archbishop went."

Chic carried his drink with him and stood in front of the fireplace.

Emphasizing Durham's title sarcastically, he stated, "Mr. Durham...*the Archbishop*, as I anticipated lives a rather simple life. He resides right there at the church and seems quite dedicated to his profession as a high-ranking member of the Catholic Faith. Aside from his daily duties as the Archbishop of St. Louis, his outside interests are very limited. He jogs five miles a day, swims twice a week and is a member of the local Corvette Club." Chic capsulized his forty-five minute meeting with Tim Durham over the next ten minutes explaining that Durham sat on the board of directors of a number of local charities in St. Louis and how they had discussed his short college career and his entrance into the priesthood. Chic fielded a number of questions Bernard had when he mentioned that Tim remained unnerved when they discussed the past murders of Abigail and Chester.

Chic summed up his short dissertation by stating, "Tim Durham, despite the fact he seems to be a man of great faith strikes me as an extremely cool character. I'm pretty good at reading people, but Durham gave me no indication he is the slightest bit worried about ever being implicated in the murders of your daughter or Chester Finch. Myself, well I believe he has been, and still is, hiding behind the iron wall the Catholic religion constructs to protect the members of their clergy. Remember, this is the largest organized religion in our country...by far. It won't be easy to dent their armor, but it can be done."

"I agree," said Bernard. "When the word gets out one of their members, in this case an archbishop, did in fact take part in murdering two people twenty-seven years ago, the news will spread through the ranks of the Catholic Church quickly."

Chic was seating himself when a knock sounded at the closed door. Getting up, Conner smiled. "That will be our food." Walking to the door he opened it and ushered in Mae who was pushing a three-tier stainless steel cart loaded with covered china bowls and trays. The top shelf contained plates, silverware, coffee cups and crystal glassware.

Bernard motioned toward a cherry table next to the fireplace and ordered Conner, "Have Mae set up the food on the table and then she can be excused."

Mae quickly and efficiently set up the late evening display of food, nodded pleasantly at everyone and exited the room. Looking at Conner, Bernard asked, "And what do we have this evening?"

Conner, removing lids from the various trays and bowls announced. "Let's see. First of all we have shrimp and also some scallops. We have a cheese tray and crackers and what appears to be some sort of dip along with a vegetable tray and some chicken wings. The beverages include coffee, iced tea and a bottle of white wine."

Acting the good host, with the aid of the desk, Bernard stood and gestured at the table. “It’s every man for himself. If you would care to grab a plate and a beverage we can then proceed sharing information.”

Popping a shrimp inside her mouth, Shelby leaned over and whispered to Nick, “I’ve never had shrimp this late at night.”

“Neither have I,“ remarked Nick. “I imagine it tastes just as good as it does any other time of the day.” Placing two wings, five shrimp and a glob of cocktail sauce on a plate he poured himself a glass of tea. “I’m really hungry. That hotdog I had in Ohio didn’t quite fill me up.”

Seated on the couch next to Carson, Shelby asked him, “How did things go with Miles Gaston?”

Bernard, overhearing her question, spoke while he seated himself behind the desk once again. “That is something I’m sure we are all interested in hearing about. Mr. Pike? Why don’t you share what you found out about our restaurant entrepreneur?”

Swallowing a bite of chicken, followed by a drink of tea, Carson smiled at the group. “Of course, I’d be glad to.” Sitting back, he crossed his legs, made himself comfortable and then began. “The first thing I did was drive down to Atlanta where Gaston is headquartered…” For the next fifteen minutes, Carson gave a detailed report of his encounter with Gaston. Finished, he stood and walked to the table for a refill of tea as if he were giving his final statement. “Miles Gaston, initially was nothing less than a gentleman who was interested in cooperating with me as an author, but then when I brought up the murders, I found myself in the middle of a Jekyll and Hyde situation. It was obvious I had struck a nerve. He all but threw me out of his restaurant. I doubt that would have actually happened. Miles Gaston is not what I would call a physical specimen.”

Looking at Chic, Carson went on, “Unlike Durham, the Archbishop, who seems to have varied interests other than what he does for a living, Gaston appears to have no outside of work interests. It seems to me he is a very private man. He has no wife or children, no hobbies we know of. He spends most of his time travelling around to his varied business interests. From what Chic told us about the archbishop being a cool character, Miles Gaston, toward the end of the interview was anything but unnerved. He may be a lot easier to get to than the others.”

Bernard took a sip of wine and spoke up, “Based on what we have heard so far about the reaction to the past murders of my daughter and Chester Finch, Tim Durham and Miles Gaston possess the same demeanor they had when they were back in high school. Gaston was known as the weakest or I guess one could say the mildest of the three. Durham was easy going and always listened to what Brad Schulte said.

In other words, Brad was always the leader of the three. It will be interesting to hear what Nick and Shelby have to share with us."

Nick, who had a mouthful of chicken placed his hand over his mouth in a gesture of apology since he couldn't respond at the moment. Shelby stood, and carrying her glass of wine with her, walked to the front of the group. Leaning against the stone wall of the fireplace, she began, "On the way back here from Pittsburgh, Nick and I had a discussion in regard to how Carson and Chic made out. After listening to what has been said so far this evening, Brad Schulte, by far, had the most physical reaction to the past murders. We ran into Mayor Schulte by accident when we checked into the hotel where we were staying the night..."

It took nearly thirty minutes for Shelby to relate in detail the events of what transpired in Pittsburgh. Finishing up, she explained, "Not wanting to remain in Pittsburgh, Nick and I drove over to Columbus, Ohio and caught a flight back to Charleston *and* here we are!"

Shelby returned to the couch when Bernard asked Nick, "Do you have anything to add to what Shelby shared with us?"

Nick thought for a moment and then spoke, "I think Shelby pretty much summed everything up. The only thing I would add is after hearing about the reactions of the other two, Brad Schulte seems to be the most dangerous. I do have a concern though. What if these three men decide to communicate with one another and they discover they were all interviewed by different individuals all claiming to be authors. If nothing else, that will send up a definite red flag and therefore place them on guard."

Bernard smiled at the group and with confidence stated, "I knew going into this plan there may be some problems that would pop up. If these three men do discover they have been duped, they may indeed become guarded. But, here's the beauty of our plan. The very lives they have surrounded themselves with are a form of captivity. When *and if* they realize we are on to them, they will find themselves trapped with nowhere to turn. Take Tim Durham for instance. He is not just going to be able to drop off the face of the earth. If he does decide to run it would be national news. An archbishop from St. Louis *suddenly disappears!* He is a person, who, whether he realizes it or not, has placed himself in the limelight. People look to him daily or at least weekly for leadership in their faith. Brad Schulte falls into the same category. The mayor of a major city just can't up and run off. He knows too many people; he's involved in too many things. I mean...think about it. The future Governor of Pennsylvania just up and disappears? If either Durham or Schulte run, the news media will be all over it, shedding even more light on their lives."

Carson spoke up. "That leaves Miles Gaston, who, believe it or not, could take an extended vacation for however long and no one would think the worse, at least until the news of his involvement comes out. He may be the weakest or the mildest like you say, but he is the one who would have the best opportunity to slip away without raising a lot of suspicion."

"That's why we can't lollygag on our plan," pointed out Bernard. "Right now we have the element of uncertainty leaning in our favor. Schulte, based on his actions, revealed to us he suspects something. Gaston, according to what Carson explained to us, is most definitely upset with the mention of the past murders. It is obvious he is upset. To what degree we can't be sure, but like the mayor, he is aware something is going on. The archbishop, at this point, doesn't seem to have the slightest clue what we are up to."

Bernard dumped his pipe ashes in an empty glass ashtray, reached for the tape recorder and turned it off. "I am going to excuse you for the remainder of the night. I would strongly suggest you all get a good night's rest and relax tomorrow. We will not meet again until two days from now on Thursday. Let's make it ten in the morning. At that time I will have everything laid out for the next step in our operation. Conner and I need to listen to the information we have taped tonight. When you come back here on Thursday bring your bags. You'll all be flying out to various cities where these three men do business. Shortly after that, *the you know what* should hit the fan."

Nick stood and asked a question, "I have a concern, actually Shelby and I have some concerns. Mayor Schulte may send some of his goons down here to Beaufort and try to find out what we are up to. Should we, or do we need to take any precautions?"

"Excellent point," remarked Bernard. "Brad Schulte, even though no longer residing in the Lowcountry, grew up here and is very familiar with not only Beaufort but Fripp Island as well. I don't think he'll come down here to investigate you and Shelby. He probably still knows people in the area. He may make some phone calls in order to find out who you two really are or he may send some men down this way. Depending on how serious he took your presence in Pittsburgh, his men may already be here. It may not be wise to return to your home here on the island or for Shelby to go back to her parents' home or her apartment."

"That's all well and fine," said Nick. "But what do Shelby and I do for the next two days?"

Bernard held up a finger to make a point and went on, "Perhaps a short local getaway for you two is in order. Of course, I'll pay for everything since this may be inconvenient for you both. Perhaps you could spend a couple of days over in Charleston or maybe even Savannah. That way, if Schulte has someone watching your homes, they'll come away empty handed."

Shelby smiled, "I like the way you think, Bernard. After what we went through in Pittsburgh, a couple of days down on Tybee Island sounds like the ticket. I'll just have to phone my parents and let my daughter know I'm all right."

"Good," emphasized Bernard. "It's settled." Turning to Conner, he ordered, "See to it Shelby and Nick get one of my credit cards and a couple of hundred dollars in cash for their two days of relaxation on Tybee Island. Everything they need will be supplied by me: lodging, food...whatever." Addressing Shelby, he offered, "If you two are too tired to head over to Savannah tonight you are more than welcome to spend the night here."

Shelby looked at Nick and inquired, "What do you think?"

Nick shrugged, "If we leave now we can be at Tybee in less than two hours. I say we head on over that way."

Bernard smiled. "All right then, I'll see you back here at the house on Thursday at ten in the morning. In the meantime I am going to have Chic and Carson keep an eye on your homes just in case Schulte's men show up. If they do, well they do. Mayor Schulte may be a powerful man in Pennsylvania, but the truth is he does not know who he is dealing with." Shaking Nick's hand and patting Shelby on her shoulder, he stated, "You two best be on your way. Give me a call when you get settled in. I know this may seem rather inconvenient but this will all be over in a matter of days. Once again, I thank all of you from the bottom of my heart for your assistance in bringing these three men to justice. I'll see you all back here Thursday morning."

Mayor Schulte closed the door to his downtown Pittsburgh office, walked to the large window that overlooked the Allegheny River and spoke to the two men who were seated across from his large desk. "Robert, John, there on the desk you will find airline tickets departing for Charleston, South Carolina later this afternoon. Upon landing in Charleston, you will pick up a rental car and drive over to a town called Beaufort, which will take a little over an hour. When you get to Beaufort give me a call and I'll give you further instructions."

Without the slightest hesitation, John scooped up the tickets and motioned to Robert, "We better get moving if we want to catch our flight." Exiting the office, he confirmed with Brad, "We'll call when we get to Beaufort."

The two men no sooner left the office than the phone on his desk buzzed and lit up. Picking up the phone, Brad spoke to his secretary, "What is it, Grace?"

The answer was professional and to the point. "Mayor, you have a call from a Miles Gaston. He says he is a close friend of yours."

Smiling, Brad responded, "Put him through!"

Sitting on the edge of his desk, Brad spoke with a tone of happiness, "Miles…it's good to talk with you. We haven't talked since, let's see, over two years ago when we were at our high school reunion. Have you talked with Tim Lately?"

Answering in frustration, Miles snapped, "No, I haven't seen or talked with him since our school reunion. And, depending on how this conversation goes, I may give him a call!"

Sitting down, Brad's face twisted in confusion, he tried to calm his old friend. "Miles, take it easy. What the hell's wrong with you? We don't talk in nearly two years and you're practically screaming in my ear. Calm down. What's the problem?"

"I'll tell you what the problem is. I think someone is on to us…that's what! A man by the name of Carson Pike came to see me at one of my restaurants yesterday. He told me he was an author from Beaufort and he was writing a book about past Beaufort High students who had become successful. He seemed on the up and up so I sat down with him for an interview. Toward the end of our conversation he brings up the subject of the deaths of Abigail James and Chester Finch. He caught me totally off guard. I should have kept my cool, but I blew up and kicked him out of the restaurant, telling him the interview was over. I'm not so sure this man even is an author. There was just something about the way he asked me about the murders. Somebody out there knows something and *I don't like it!*"

"Calm down, Miles. First of all, we agreed a long time ago not to discuss what happened that night on Fripp. That happened nearly three decades in the past. Don't you think if someone knew something they would have come forward long before all this time?"

"I suppose so, but it was just so strange. Maybe I'm getting upset over nothing."

Brad got up and looked out the large window at the city below. "Look Miles, I'm glad you called me. You did the right thing. I too was interviewed by an author, actually two people, who claimed to be authors from Beaufort. They asked me about the murders as well and despite the fact they tried to cover it over by saying it had nothing to do with why they were interviewing me, I saw right through it. They managed to get out of Pittsburgh before I could question what they were up to. I am sending two men who work for me later today down to Beaufort to see if we can find out anything about these people. The fact someone claiming to be an author interviewed you confirms my suspicions. Here's what we're going to do. As soon as I hang up I'm going to give Tim a call and see if he knows anything about this. I'll call you back after Tim and I talk. Don't do anything stupid. As a matter of fact, don't do anything until I call you back. I'm sure we're making more out of this than there is. We need to stay calm. Don't worry. Everything will work out. It always has. Trust me! I never let you down when we were growing up and I won't now. I'll get us through this. I'll call you when I finish talking with Tim."

Miles seemed to be somewhat relieved. "All right, I'll wait for your call."

Brad hung up the phone and slumped in his chair and thought, *Someone does know something! What...I'm not sure. It's too coincidental someone would interview Miles and myself. The fact the so-called authors are different people makes it clear someone is up to something. I've got to find out what this is all about and eliminate it. I've got too much at stake!*

Reaching for his cell phone he dialed Tim's private number and waited patiently for his friend to answer. On the tenth ring tone he was about to hang up when the familiar voice answered, "Archbishop Durham."

Joking, Brad spoke up, "Cut the religious crap, Tim. It's Brad calling from Pittsburgh."

Tim lit up with an enthusiastic response, "Brad, I was just thinking about you the other day. An author from our old hometown came to see me here in St. Louis. He's writing a book about famous or successful people from Beaufort High. We talked about how I was a member of the 1989 South Carolina State Football Championship Team from Beaufort and how I left school after just one year at college and went into the priesthood. The author never really mentioned you or Miles or even what we were called back then, The Three Musketeers. The conversation brought back a lot of great high school memories of the three of us and what great friends we were...and despite the fact we have gone our separate ways, we are all still friends. After the interview was concluded and the author left I thought about you and Miles and what great companions you guys were when we lived in Beaufort. God, we were close for twelve years before we all went off to college..."

Realizing Tim would ramble on for the next ten minutes, Brad interrupted the archbishop, "Tim...stop talking. The man who interviewed you was not an author. He may have been from Beaufort, but he is not an author."

Tim, surprised at Brad's tone, asked, "What on earth are you talking about? Of course he was an author. He was so nice…and polite. Why would you say something like that? You weren't here. You didn't talk with this man."

"True, I didn't meet or talk with the man who interviewed you, but I did talk with two people who said they were from Beaufort and fed me the same line of crap about being authors. Another man, also claiming to be an author, talked with Miles about this so called book he's writing. I could be way off base here, but I think these individuals are working together and I think it may have to do with Abigail James and Chester Finch."

There was silence on the St. Louis end of the conversation when Brad spoke again, "Tim, are you still there?"

"Yes, I'm still here. I'm just sitting here dumbfounded. Come to think of it, the man who interviewed me did ask about when Abigail and Chester were killed. He brought up the murders as if it were not even part of the reason why he had come to interview me."

"And how did you respond when he mentioned the murders?"

"I told him I recalled when Abigail and Chester had been murdered. I said I didn't know them that well, but when in high school I considered them friends. I also informed him the incident was part of my past life and I had moved on dedicating my life to the Catholic Faith. He then bid me goodbye and left. I didn't think there was anything suspicious about the interview."

"What was this man's name?"

"Brumly…Chic Brumly. Is he the same man who interviewed Miles?"

"I really don't know. Miles told me the man who talked with him was a Carson Pike. It could have been the same man. Maybe he was using different names."

"Look, Brad, I'm sorry if I did anything wrong. How could I have possibly known this Brumly was not an author or that he might know something about Abigail or Chester?"

"You couldn't have. The truth is we've all been had. You have no reason to apologize to me, or for that matter Miles. Of the three of us you were the only one who didn't react to the mention of the murders. When the murders were brought up during a television interview I was at it was rather uncomfortable. I had some people who work for me try to question these *authors,* but they managed to get out of Pittsburgh before I could find out who they really are. Miles, on the other hand totally lost it when asked about the murders. I just got off the phone with him.

When I realized not only he, but I as well had been duped, I decided to give you a jingle and see if you had been interviewed by these people."

"Is this anything we need to be concerned about?"

"It could be. I'm not sure yet. We have to get more information on these people. My people should be in Beaufort this evening. I should know something by tomorrow. I'll be in touch. Do not mention what we have discussed with anyone."

"Brad," said Tim softly. "Please tell me after all these years that night out on Fripp is not going to come back on us."

"Look, we've made it all these years without any problems, and I will do whatever it takes to ensure it remains that way. Don't worry about this. I'll call you when I have more to go on. It may me be nothing."

"I hope so," muttered Tim.

Laying down his cell phone, Brad walked to a glass fronted liquor cabinet, opened it and removed a bottle of scotch and poured himself a drink. Sitting on a black leather couch he looked out at the falling snow and thought to himself, *This can't be happening. Not after all these years. Who are these people and what do they know? I've got to figure this out. Ever since I've known Tim and Miles I've been the leader. They have always depended on me whenever there was a problem. They always looked to me. I can't afford to have the murders come back on me now. I've got too much to lose. We all do.*

Picking up his phone he dialed Miles number. Miles answered almost instantly, "Brad, what did you find out?"

Brad finished off his drink and explained, "Tim was also interviewed. He was fed the same line of crap we were. Some man claiming to be from Beaufort talked with him and asked him about the murders."

"Was it the same man who interviewed me?"

"At this point we don't know. The man who talked with you identified himself as a Carson Pike…right?"

"That's right, his last name was Pike."

"The man who talked with Tim called himself Chic Brumly. Do either one of those names ring a bell? Did we graduate with someone by those name?"

"I don't recall anyone by those names when we attended Beaufort. Who are these people?"

"I don't know, but I intend to find out. Like I told you. I have two men on their way to Beaufort. When I find something out I'll give you a call just like I told Tim. Stay calm and don't do anything stupid. These people, whoever they are, may just be grasping at straws. You should be hearing from me in the next day or so. And, don't worry. Whatever this is, I'll take care of it."

Pouring himself another small shot of scotch, Brad loosened his necktie and flopped down on the couch. *The one thing I can't do is panic,* he thought. *I've come too far in life to let that night on Fripp ruin everything I've worked for. I've got to find out who these people are.* Opening a drawer on a side table he removed a legal pan and a pen. He wrote down the names of the four people who had posed as authors as he spoke each name out loud, "Nick Falco and Shelby Pickett. Carson Pike and Chic Brumly." He stared at the written names and repeated them once again but hesitated when he came to Brumly. "Wait a minute! Brumly, Brumly? That name sounds familiar. Where have I heard that name before?"

CHAPTER TWENTY FOUR

SHELBY, SITTING ON AN OLD LOG STRETCHED HER LEGS and gazed out at the ocean. Standing, she motioned toward the water and remarked, "The last time we were here at Tybee was the afternoon after Ike Miller had my apartment ransacked."

"I remember that," said Nick. "Later that evening we stopped at a bar, what was it called…"

Shelby remembered, "Chester's."

Snapping his fingers, Nick agreed, "That's right and we got to talking with the owner."

Interjecting, Shelby added, "And that was the evening we got our first clues, which eventually led us to the discovery of the RPS Killer. What a summer that turned out to be."

"I remember Chester as being a nice fellow. Maybe we should drop by his place later tonight for a drink."

Shelby smiled. "That sounds great, but going back there might not be a good idea. We'll have to be careful what we mention to Chester. There are only three people who know I was apprehended in Chester's parking lot by the RPS Killer: you, me and of course, Harold. I am the unknown individual who wound up killing the RPS Killer and that has to remain a secret."

Nick apologized for suggesting the idea, "You're right. I wasn't thinking clearly. Maybe we shouldn't go there tonight."

"No, we can go there, we just have to be careful what we say. I thought it was a nice little place. A bar burger, some fries and a couple of stiff drinks sounds good right about now. I mean, we might as well enjoy ourselves while we can. When we go back to Bernard's place he said we'd be travelling again. I wonder what he has in mind for the next part of his plan."

"I don't know, but I hope it's quick…and effective. We're already faced with the possibility of Mayor Schulte sending men down here."

"And that's not all," said Shelby. "If the three men we're after put two and two together and they figure out something's up, it could get dangerous."

"I agree," said Nick, "but I don't think ol' Bernard will allow that to happen. Out of the three men, Schulte seems to be the only one who could be a threat to us. Besides, we have some pretty tough characters on our side. Let's not forget how Carson handled the Carnahans and then we also have Conner in our corner. If Bernard turns him loose on these three men, it'll be curtains for them. I hope that doesn't happen and all of this can be resolved without violence, but I guess that depends on how Schulte and his old high school pals react."

Brushing loose sand from his bare feet, Nick slipped into flip flops and suggested, "I say we head back to our hotel, get freshened up and head over to Chester's. I don't think we have anything to worry about. Hell, he might not even be working this evening."

Parking in the dirt lot, Nick looked at the bar and commented, "Looks the same as I recall." Scanning the six cars parked in front of the building, he shrugged. "Doesn't look busy at the moment."

Getting out of the car, Shelby reminded him, "Remember when we were here before, Chester told us he never got busy until after ten o'clock. That's four hours from now."

Feeling a rumbling in his stomach, Nick started across the lot. "Let's get those burgers, I'm starving!"

Chester's Bar and Grill hadn't changed one bit. Three customers sat at the far end of the bar smoking and drinking, two other customers were playing darts and another man stood at the jukebox, looking over the selections."

Shelby pointed at the long bar when she noticed Chester washing some beer glasses. Looking up, he saw the two faces he instantly recognized. Waving at the couple, he grinned and spoke up, "I was wondering what happened to you two and if I'd ever get to see you again. Belly up to my bar. What can I get for ya!"

Pulling out a barstool, Nick climbed on and answered, "We're feeling kind of hungry. Thought maybe we'd order a couple of burgers."

"And!" added Shelby, "in the meantime while our burgers are on the grill I'll go for a seven and seven."

"Tall glass of whatever's on draft for me," said Nick.

Snapping his fingers, Chester got the attention of a waitress who was coming out of what appeared to be a kitchen door. "Hey Barb…these folks would like to order some grub."

The waitress squeezed in between Nick and Shelby and produced an order pad, taking a pen from behind her ear. "What can I get you folks?"

By the time Chester returned with their drinks the waitress was off to the kitchen with the food order. Setting the drinks on the bar, Chester leaned forward and asked, "So what have you two young detectives been up to since the RPS Killer bit the dust? When the news came on the television last summer he had been found dead floating out in the marsh, I thought about you two right away. Let's see, if I remember it turned out to be some character from over Charleston way, a rich fella…right? His name was Harold something or other. They really didn't put a photo of him on TV so I couldn't tell if the man they found dead was the same as the man who came in here…the one you were following. Was it the same man?"

"Yeah, it was him," said Shelby, taking a short sip of her mixed drink.

Nick chimed in, "Looks like somebody else got to him before we could expose him. All the same he's dead and gone and no longer a threat to anyone around these parts."

"There was a lot of talk around here," said Chester. "I mean in the Savannah area, seeing as how all the girls found murdered were from over here. Folks were saying this Harold got what he deserved. I guess they never did find out who took his life…did they?"

Shelby gave Nick a casual look of caution and answered, "No, they never did. They say whoever it was did the right thing."

"I agree with that," said Nick. "Remember, I found Susan Dunn's hand and then Shelby and I discovered one of the girls who managed to escape. It was horrible what the killer did to the girls he killed and the ones who got away could be scarred for life. I, for one, am glad the RPS Killer is no longer walking the face of this earth."

Loud laughter came from the three men seated at the far end of the bar and Chester shook his head and smiled. "Don't mind those boys. They're always in here. They normally drop in after work for a few beers and some laughs. Listen, I'll be right back. I'm going to check on those burgers."

Looking down the bar at the loud threesome of men, Shelby commented, "That man on the end looks so familiar to me. I know I've seen him somewhere around Savannah before." Thinking for a moment and not coming up with an answer, she waved off what she had said and went back to her drink. "I guess we need to get a good nights' rest tonight."

Stuffing two pretzels from a small bowl of snacks from the bar into his mouth, Nick responded, "Yeah, I wonder if Bernard is going to require us to go back to Pittsburgh? If he does we're going to have to be careful. We left Mayor Schulte with a rather bad taste in his mouth. I really don't want to confront him again. I hope Bernard understands that. I hope he understands how dangerous Schulte can be."

"Boy, you can say that again," said Shelby. "We barely slipped through his fingers on our first trip to *his city!* If Bernard sends us back to Pittsburgh we'll once again be on Schulte's turf. I sincerely hope Bernard knows what he's doing. I want these three men brought to justice as much as anyone else on the team but in the process I don't want to suffer or be injured in any way."

"Me either," remarked Nick, "but like I said before, I don't think Bernard will allow it to get to that point."

Downing the last of her drink, Shelby smiled sarcastically, "I sure hope so."

The waitress pushed her way through the swinging café kitchen doors carrying two plates that contained a burger each and a pile of hot fries. Placing the plates in front of Nick and Shelby she reached beneath the bar and set bottles of ketchup, mustard and relish next to their food. Sliding a set of salt and pepper shakers down the bar she walked away and commented, "Enjoy! If you need anything else let Chester or me know."

Admiring her burger, Shelby flipped the warm bun from the top and reached for the ketchup when Chester returned from the kitchen and asked, "How do those burgers look?"

Squirting a circular blob of the red liquid on her cheese covered burger, she remarked, "If this tastes as good as it looks I'll spread the word."

Nick was removing two pickles from his burger when one of the men from the end of the bar approached, holding up three fingers and gestured at Chester. "We'll have three more, Chet!"

Smiling, Chester bent down and removed three beers from a refrigerated cabinet. "Comin' right up, Lester!"

Removing the twist off tops he slid the bottles toward the man and inquired, "You still working over at Miller's Auto Mart?"

The mention of Shelby's previous boyfriend caused her to hesitate in taking her first bite. Staring at the man, she listened while the conversation continued, "Yep! Been there now for seven years. Probably the best mechanic Miller's got!"

Running a damp rag across a section of the bar, Chester asked, "Speaking of Miller, is Ike still down in Florida?"

The man frowned and answered, "Yeah, he is. Ever since he took that beating last summer, he said he just couldn't live in Savannah anymore. He told me some girl he had been dating had someone she knows put a whuppin' on him."

"Really!" said Chester. "I never heard anything about that."

Shelby laid down her burger and gave Nick an *uh-oh* look that went unnoticed by Lester or Chet.

Lester went on to explain, "Yeah, this girl Ike was dating was a real piece of work. Before he met her he was a player...always had a good looking woman on his arm. He fell head over heels in love with this broad; even got her an engagement ring that ran him ten grand. Ain't no woman worth that much money up front."

Nick looked into Shelby's face and could tell she was seething. Gently he reached down and squeezed her knee; a silent signal for her to *cool it!*

Lester rolled his eyes and continued with the story. "I guess they had a falling out and this woman broke it off with Ike. That broad was crazy. She kept the ring. Can you even imagine that? And then, on top of that she has the hell beat out of the poor guy. If you ask me, I say a diamond ring stealing wench like that deserves a slap up the side of her face. I mean, hell. She walks away with a ring worth ten grand and Ike gets the crap beat out of him and can no longer live here in Savannah."

"Now, wait a minute," said Chester. "I guess it was a few weeks back someone who I go to church with said they saw Ike downtown."

"That was temporary. Since he still owns the dealership he drops by town on occasion for a brief meeting and then back to Florida he goes. He has a lot of friends here in Savannah and apparently some enemies. Makes a man think twice about who he decides to date…ya know."

Interested, Chester inquired, "Have you ever seen this woman. Does she live here in the area?"

"No, I've never seen her. From what I've been told she's pretty good looking, but mean as a snake!"

Shelby jumped up. "That's it! I'm not going to sit here and listen to any more of this bullshit! I know where I've seen you before. You're one of the two men Miller sent to trash my apartment over on Liberty Street."

Chester stared in wonder, while Nick's head sank when he realized trouble was brewing. Lester looked at Shelby and gave her an ugly smirk. "What on earth are you talking about lady?"

One of the other two men who had been at the end of the bar joined the group when he noticed something was wrong. "Lester…is there a problem?"

Lester held up his hand. "Go back and sit down, Lopez. This young lady here has got her dander up for some reason."

Moving around Nick, Shelby stood eye to eye with Lester and pointed at Lopez. "When I came in here I thought I recognized you from someplace and now I know exactly where I saw you two idiots! You were the two dumb asses Ike sent to find that ring and when you didn't find it you tore up my apartment."

Lopez gave Lester an odd look as Lester refuted her statement,

"Lady…you're nuts! We don't know anything about any apartment."

Lopez stepped forward, pointed a bony finger at Shelby, and raised his voice. "If someone trashed your apartment that's no concern of ours and besides that if what you say is true how would you know who tore your place up? Did you actually see them?"

Shelby placed her hands on her hips and looked directly into Lopez's eyes. "Yes, I did see them. I saw both of you from when you entered my place up until you left. I heard every word you said and witnessed everything you did." Looking Lester up and down she went on, "I remember everything about that afternoon. You were wearing brown khakis, a black sweatshirt and sandals." Pointing at Lopez, she explained, "Your partner in crime here was wearing cargo shorts, a see through mesh shirt and deck shoes."

Lester, trying his best to defuse the truth of her statement looked at Chester and raised his hands in a gesture of hopelessness. "I gotta tell you Chester, you've got to start letting a better breed of customer in this place. This lady is crazy! What she says doesn't make sense. If someone trashed her apartment like she says how could she have seen them?"

"You're more stupid that you appear," snapped Shelby. "Nick and I were in the apartment when you and Lopez entered. We hid in the closet you searched before you left. You were two feet from where we were and didn't even realize it. We heard everything that was said and witnessed all the damage you did. You tipped over my hutch and ruined my collection of cups and saucers, went through all my personal stuff and smashed a picture of me and my daughter."

Chester looked at Lester and asked, "Is what she's saying the truth?"

Nick, who had remained silent through the exchange between Shelby and the two men stood and stepped in between Lester and Shelby. "Yeah, every word Shelby said is the truth. I was right there in the closet next to her. She was scared to death. There was nothing we could do at the time but wait until these two left. It was then Shelby decided she was going to keep the ring to cover the cost of the damage they caused."

"Bullshit!" yelled Lester. He shoved Nick roughly who was slammed back against the side of the bar. Before Nick could regain his balance, Shelby picked up one of the barstools and swung it hitting Lester in his chest. Lopez pushed Shelby to the side and stumbled over Lester who was falling to the floor in pain. Nick had just enough time to react and body slam Lopez, both being catapulted across the room, knocking over a table and three chairs. Lopez got to his feet first and kicked Nick in his ribs when Shelby jumped on his back, pulling his hair and scratching his face. Swinging around wildly, Lopez flung Shelby to the wooden floor.

Nick picked up one of the chairs and smashed it over Lopez's shoulders, the man collapsing to the floor next to Shelby. Lester was on his feet again. Spinning Nick around, he hit him a glancing blow on his right jaw. Nick fell back against the jukebox as Lester advanced for another punch, but was prevented from doing so when Chester brought an old baseball bat down over the man's left shoulder, sending Lester to the floor.

Standing in the middle of the four bar patrons scattered around the floor, Chester held up the bat and shouted, "That's it! This stops now!"

Nick helped Shelby to her feet as he rubbed his sore jaw. Lester was on his knees, staring with anger at Shelby. Lopez tried to get up but sat on the floor while he rubbed his shoulder. The waitress joined Chester and whispered, "I called the police. They said they'd be here in five minutes."

Pointing the bat at Nick and Shelby, Chester suggested, "You two better get the hell out of here before the cops show up. They don't cut much slack around here when it comes to this sort of stuff."

Nick started to pull Shelby toward the door but Shelby walked to the bar, picked up her burger, and smiled at Lester, still sitting on the floor. "Not leaving here without my burger." Looking at Nick, she motioned, "Pay Chester for our food and we're out of here."

Chester objected, "Don't worry…it's on the house. You two need to get moving." Pointing the bat at Lester, he explained, "We'll give these kids a couple of minutes to clear out and then you two assholes can exit my bar. You're not welcome here any longer."

Shelby hesitated at the door when Chester spoke to her, "Don't worry about the police. I'll handle everything. I'll explain to them what happened here. Now, get the hell out of here!"

Sitting in the passenger side of Shelby's Jeep, Nick continued to rub his sore jaw. Shelby hopped in and started the Jeep and backed out, stating, "Lately, it would seem there is nowhere we can go without getting into some sort of trouble." Just as she was guiding the Jeep across the lot, a police cruiser pulled in, blocking them from leaving. Shelby patiently waited for the cruiser to pull up in front of the building, and then she pulled out onto the highway. Nick looked back at the two officers who were entering the building and commented, "That was close!"

As they pulled out onto the road Shelby looked back at the two officers who were entering the bar. "I thought this Ike Miller business was a dead issue, but it looks like it has resurfaced. I have no doubt those two will give Ike a call and tell him what went on here today. Now, whether he instructs them to follow up with further action we don't know."

"That's right," said Nick. "Those two men still know where you live here in Savannah. Maybe it's time for you to move."

"I've been thinking about that ever since last summer. I could move in with my folks until I find a place in Beaufort. That would mean I'd have to drive over here to work, but I think that's a small price to pay when you consider the safety of not only myself but Kirby. She would have to change schools. If I do decide to move she'll be upset. She really loves the school she's attending."

Rubbing his jaw again, Nick laughed, "Seems like we're a magnet for trouble...doesn't it? I've had enough activity for the night. Let's head back to the hotel. We've got a big day on Thursday at Bernard's. One more thing. I don't think we should mention any of this Ike Miller business to Bernard. He's got enough on his plate at the moment."

Stopping for a red light, Shelby looked across the street at a man decorating a Christmas tree if front of a business. "It sure doesn't seem like the holiday season, does it?"

Miles placed his carry-on luggage in the overhead storage compartment, settled in his seat and looked out the window at the activity at the Palm Beach International Airport. Reaching up, he adjusted the air nozzle so the thin stream of cool air caressed his sweating face. He had cut his stay in Florida short, following the interview with the man who had identified himself as Carson Pike. Catching the attention of a passing flight attendant, Miles inquired, "How long is the flight to Charleston today?"

The young woman smiled and answered pleasantly, "One hour and twenty minutes."

Loosening his necktie he unbuttoned the top button of his tailored shirt, took a deep breath and asked, "Do you think I could get something cold to drink. It seems really hot in here."

The attendant leaned over and asked, "Are you not feeling well sir?"

"No, I'm fine, I'm just so hot. A cool drink will do the trick."

"We'll be in the air in about ten minutes. Unless it's an emergency I'm afraid you'll have to wait until we're up for that drink."

Patting the girl on her hand, Miles responded, "I can wait. I'll be fine, thank you."

Miles sat back and watched while a long row of passengers filed by. An extremely large man squeezed down in the seat next to him, buckled himself in, flipped open a laptop and scanned the bright screen that popped up. The man, who seemed to be engrossed in the screen didn't utter a word to Miles. The lack of an exchange between he and the man sitting so very close to him didn't bother Miles in the least. Normally he was cordial and talkative while flying but at the moment just wanted to sit in silence. He had a lot to think about. The so-called author, Carson Pike, the fact that Brad had been interviewed as well by two people claiming to be authors, the phone call Brad made to Tim and the follow-up call from Brad. Miles had always fashioned himself as someone whose gut feeling was normally right on target. There was something about Pike that bothered him. The way he went about mentioning the twenty-seven year old murders. It had been very casual, almost like it wasn't part of the interview, but yet it had been quite nerve racking. He was totally caught off-guard. Maybe he had overreacted. Maybe he shouldn't have kicked Pike out of his restaurant. Pike had to have noted the drastic attitude change he displayed at the end of the interview. Is that why he had come in the first place or was he just imagining the worst? Maybe, later on in the day when Brad called, his mind would be put to ease. Brad had a way and ever since he knew him, he could take a problem and come up with a solution. The last passenger boarded the plane and took their seat while the flight attendant went through the standard safety precaution routine Miles never paid any attention to.

A minute or so passed and the plane began to back out. Miles shut his eyes and tried his best to relax, but the thought of the past murders lingered in his mind. Trying to reassure himself, he thought when the plane landed in Charleston, he'd get his car from long-term parking and he'd be on his way to his secluded home on Fripp Island.

The plane completed its taxi procedures and waited at the end of the long runway for the go ahead to take off. The flight attendant stopped by Miles' seat and nodded at him. "As soon as we get up and leveled off I'll get with you on that drink."

The large man seated next to him closed his laptop and checked his belt to make sure he was fastened in. Turning slightly he spoke to Miles and extended his chubby left hand, "Hello there. My name is Clark Gunther. You getting off in Charleston?"

Miles shook the man's hand and answered, "Miles Gaston, and yes, I am getting off in Charleston. Do you live in Charleston?"

"Yes, I do," said the man proudly. "Born and raised there. I'm an author by trade. I just finished a three-state book tour and now I'm heading home. What do you do for a living?"

Miles, more interested in the fact the man was an author, answered the question quickly but then asked a question of his own, "I own a chain of restaurants, but let me ask you something. Do you know most of the local authors in the Lowcountry, I mean let's say from Charleston to Savannah?"

"Most definitely," answered the man with confidence. "I've been writing and living in the Charleston area all my life to date. There isn't an author worth their salt in the Lowcountry I haven't heard of or probably met."

"How about Beaufort. Are you familiar with authors from that area?"

"Yes, I am. Just before I started my book tour I attended a seminar in Beaufort for local authors. If there is an author in Beaufort they were in attendance."

"Was an author named Carson Pike there?"

The man looked up at the ceiling of the plane and thought. "The name doesn't sound familiar as far as local authors are concerned, but I have met a Carson Pike from Beaufort. My brother is quite the fisherman. He drives over to Beaufort a couple of times a month and does some fishing with a Carson Pike. Let's see, I guess it was a few months back I went along with him. We drove over to the marina in downtown Beaufort and went out on this Carson Pike's boat. I remember him as quite the character. If I recall I think he lives out on Fripp Island. We drank beer, caught a lot of fish and listened to quite a few stories Carson shared with us about fishing in the area. He never mentioned anything about being an author, although with all the stories he had, I suppose he could be one. We authors are quite the story tellers."

His interest peaked, Miles probed, "What does this Pike look like?"

Rubbing his pudgy chin the man responded, "Well, let's see. He's a big man. I'd say about six-two, maybe six-three; probably goes two-thirty or so." Patting his bulging stomach the man smiled. "Unlike me, he appeared to be in rather good physical condition for his age which I'd say has to be up in his late fifties-early sixties. Muscular, ruddy features; a man's man, whatever that means."

Miles looked directly at Mr. Gunther and smiled. "Yep, that's him."

Clark put his laptop to the side. "Sounds like you know this Pike."

"Not really…I just met him a couple of days ago down in Tampa. He told me he was an author."

"Well, maybe he is and he just never mentioned it in my presence. What kind of stuff does he write?"

"I'm not really sure. We didn't get into that. He did say he was writing a book about former Beaufort High School students who had become successful in life. Actually, he was interviewing me for his book."

"And how did that go for you? I ask because I always enjoy it when I have to interview someone while doing research for a book. I always wonder what they think after I leave their presence."

Hesitating, Miles wondered if he should explain any further, then spoke up, "The interview didn't end well. For some reason I still haven't been able to figure out, this Pike goes off on some tangent about two kids who were murdered on Fripp Island almost thirty years ago. It just didn't feel right and it pissed me off so I ended the interview right then and there."

"I take it from your tone you do not approve of this Carson Pike."

"It's not so much that, but I do question if he is really an author."

"Then why would this man interview you?"

"I don't know. It almost seemed to me this so-called interview was nothing more than a means to gather information on the murders he asked me about."

"Maybe that's what he *was really* writing about. Seems to me I remember when that happened. That was the year I was a junior at Charleston South and we played Beaufort for the state championship. They beat us hands down. Really whupped us a good one! If I recall it was later in the week or maybe even that night when those two kids were killed during a celebration party out on Fripp. I remember there was a big investigation and after months of questioning folks the police came up empty-handed: no suspects, no murder weapon, no motive. There were three football players they thought might have been involved somehow but that never panned out and they were never arrested. I could be wrong, but I don't think the case was ever solved."

Resting his foot on the side of the moving conveyor belt that would soon deliver their luggage John looked around at the interior of the Charleston Airport and spoke to Robert. "I really don't like it down south, especially here in the Lowcountry: gators, snakes, insects all year long. I hope when we get to this Beaufort we don't have to spend more than a day or so down here."

Motioning at the conveyor, Robert smiled, "We should have our bags in a few minutes then we can pick up a rental car. By the way, did Brad give you any further instructions on what we are to do, when and if we find out who the people are we chased back in Pittsburgh?"

"No, but he did say we are to contact him when we get to Beaufort. I took it from his tone he is not all that happy with these people."

Maria Sparks dialed a number on her cell and then patiently waited. On the fourth ring tone, a voice answered, "Joseph Carnahan."

Maria, with a serious tone, responded, "Joseph…I've come to a dead end down here in Beaufort. That attorney, Brumly jumped ship on me and said he was no longer interested in representing me. I offered him more money but he said he had gotten a much better offer from here in the area. I'm thinking on getting another local attorney or maybe you could send someone down here. This can't be over just like that. I know Falco and Pike know something. I think they know more about what happened to Charley than they're letting on."

"Look, Maria, I know Charley was your brother and you two were really close, but I think you may be barking up the wrong tree. Your brother and Derek have been missing, off the charts since last summer. Charley was one of my most loyal employees. I for one, find it hard to believe he would take off with my millions. Derek, well that's another story. But still, I don't think Derek would have done anything without Charley's say so. I have spent countless man hours and a small fortune trying to locate he and Charley. After all these months we've come up with a big fat goose egg. I know you are concerned about what happened to your brother, but I have bigger fish to fry...like what happened to 5.8 million dollars that belongs to me! It was your idea to go down to Beaufort and see what you could find out. I went along with your request, but to be honest with you I think that ship has sailed. This Chic Brumly, who I thoroughly checked out after you went and hired him, happens to be quite good at what he does. You say he hasn't uncovered anything that would lead me to believe your brother and Derek were killed by Falco or Pike. I'm not saying they didn't, but their story was rather convincing. Once Charley had the money in his possession he called me and told me he and Derek were on their way to Charleston. That's the last I ever heard from them. If you want my advice, I say you should come back to New York and forget this business. Let me handle things. To tell you the truth, all you have done is mucked up the works. Your presence in Beaufort has done nothing but put Falco and Pike on the alert. I've made the decision to back off for a period of time. As long as they know they are being observed they'll be careful not to make any mistakes, saying or doing the wrong thing. Now, if you want to pursue this yourself, there is little I can do about that, but hear this. If you mess this up for me I am not going to be a happy camper. If the Falco kid or Carson Pike did take out your brother and Derek, I'll eventually find out. Don't make things difficult for me by being a pain in the ass! I would strongly suggest you just fly back to New York and let me handle this business as I see fit. Do you understand what I'm saying?"

Reluctantly, Maria answered, "Yes, I understand, but I'm not sure if I agree with backing down for a while as a good idea."

"It doesn't make any difference what you think. You are not in command of what needs to be done. You are simply Charley's sister. If

I need you to assist me in any way I'll contact you. Until then, you need to back off. I'll be expecting a phone call from you when you return to New York."

Maria was about to respond but then Joseph ended the conversation as he pushed the off button on his cell. Maria didn't like being told what to do, but she knew Joseph Carnahan well. Charley had worked for this man for over twenty years and some of the things Charley told her Carnahan had done or ordered done were appalling and therefore she had always feared the man. She really didn't have much of a choice. She had been ordered to return to New York. She didn't work for Carnahan, but knew if she didn't do what he had strongly suggested, she might wind up on the wrong end of the stick. For now, she'd go back to New York, wait for a few months, but then return once again to continue her own private investigation in regard to her brother's disappearance. She knew Falco and Pike were hiding something and she was determined to get to the bottom of whatever it was.

CHAPTER TWENTY FIVE

NINE O'CLOCK ON THE BUTTON. SHELBY AND NICK WERE seated on the couch. Carson warmed his hands by the fireplace while Chic pulled back a large floor to ceiling, crushed velvet green curtain and gazed out at the ocean. Turning back to Bernard who was seated behind his large desk, the lawyer commented, "Nice view."

Bernard nodded in agreement, pushed up the sleeve of his suit coat, looked at his Rolex, puffed on his pipe and addressed Conner who was standing obediently by the large oak library doors. "Conner, would you please inform Mae we'll be having our breakfast here in the library at nine-thirty."

Conner bowed slightly and responded, "Yes sir, I'll see to it."

Speaking to the other *team members,* as he referred to the four people in the room, Bernard apologized, "I'm sorry I've had to put breakfast off. I was planning on having it served at nine, but the truth is, we're expecting a new member of our team. I talked with this individual last evening at great lengths. I am convinced he will be an asset to our efforts in bringing in Schulte, Durham and Gaston." Looking at Shelby and Nick, Bernard further explained, "You two have met this person and I think you'll be surprised when he arrives. He was planning to arrive here at nine, but gave me a call around seven-thirty this morning explaining he had an electrical problem he had to take care of at his home. He told me he wasn't sure if he could make it at nine and he might be a few minutes late for our meeting." Looking at his watch again, Bernard smiled, "So...we'll wait."

Shelby gave Nick an odd look and then spoke to Bernard. "You say we have met this person?"

"Yes, and just recently." Changing the subject, Bernard went on, "I hope everyone had two good day's rest and managed to stay out of trouble."

Shelby, remembering the events at Chester's, gave Nick a bump on his arm, "Things over on Tybee Island couldn't have been more pleasant."

Chic, still at the large window, asked Nick, "Have you heard any more from the Sparks woman?"

"No, we haven't heard a peep out of her. Perhaps she has returned to New York."

"She's still here on the island," confirmed Chic. "I took the liberty this morning to check up on her whereabouts. She's still staying at one of the condos at John Fripp. Her rental car is still parked in the lot and I actually saw her walking back from the beach. I think her days here are numbered. She is not capable of conducting an investigation by herself and if she does take on another attorney, as far as I'm concerned, there is nothing for her to discover. As we all know, I've been down that road with her and I am convinced her brother, Charley, did indeed take off for parts unknown with Carnahan's millions — case closed!"

Nick chanced a look over at Carson who smiled, indicating the Carnahan con was still, in fact, working.

Conner opened the large doors and entered, followed by none other than Melvin Barrett. In amazement, Shelby stood and exclaimed, "If this is the new member of the team, you're right, it is a surprise!"

Melvin shook Carson's hand and spoke, "Mr. Pike, we have never officially met. I've heard you are one of the best fisherman in Beaufort County." Walking to Chic he extended his hand. "Chic, it's been quite some time since our paths have crossed." Approaching Nick and Shelby, he shook both their hands and commented, "We meet again."

Pointing at a chair by the fireplace, Bernard offered, "Please have a seat, detective."

Melvin seated himself and responded, "It's not necessary to address me as detective. I was at one time a detective on the Beaufort police force but now I am just an ordinary Lowcountry citizen."

"I beg to differ," said Bernard. "If an individual was at one time in their past a doctor or a professor they are still referred to as such. So, if it's all the same I would rather refer to you as Detective Barrett."

Gesturing at the group, Melvin agreed, "Then so be it, Detective Barrett it is."

Nodding at Conner, Bernard spoke, "Would you please see our breakfast is brought in."

Backing out of the large room, Conner smiled. "Right away, sir."

Shelby, once again seated, inquired, "I'm a bit confused here. How did it come to be that Detective Barrett is now on the team? Not that I have any objections. I'm just wondering how this happened."

Bernard looked at Melvin and answered, "It's really quite simple. When you and Nick first approached me with the new evidence you discovered, one of the things you explained to me was you went to see Detective Barrett in an effort to collect information on the case. As you are well aware I expressed my dissatisfaction with the way the case was handled by the Beaufort Police during the investigation. Seeing as how Detective Barrett was one of the two detectives assigned to the case I was not overly enthused in the way he and Detective Silk handled the murders of my daughter and Chester Finch. I have always been of the opinion, even after all these years, with the clues they had they should have not only arrested but convicted those three boys. As we all know, they walked and have been free now for twenty-seven years. When you mentioned some of the things the detective here said during your interview with him it got me to thinking. Then, you said a week did not go by in all the years since the murders that Detective Barrett did not think about what happened back then and the fact he said if he ever came across any proof that would connect these boys to the crime he'd be on board. You told me that he still feels they are guilty. Melvin, as one of the two investigating detectives back then, probably knows more about the past case than anyone. I decided to bury the hatchet; mend the fences as they say. I gave the detective a call and told him I had something I wanted him to take a look at. He drove over here to the house and I showed him everything you gave me. Amazed, after looking at the photos, he said if they would have had these photos back then, those three lads would have gone to jail. After I explained to him what I had in mind he asked me if there was any way he could be involved. It was at that point I invited him to join the team…and here he is!"

Bernard hesitated, which gave Barrett an opportunity to speak up. "That's right…and here I am! When Bernard showed me the photographs of the three boys on the beach standing over Abigail…well, let's just say, those photos are quite incriminating. We can now place them at the murder scene. The section of wood the Gaston boy has in his hand may be the murder weapon we never found. After twenty-seven years these three boys have been caught in another lie; a lie they cannot dispute. Originally, they claimed when they arrived on Fripp they dropped Abigail off at the pool and then parked the car and attended the party. At that point we really don't know what went on but now we have proof beyond any doubt they were on the beach; the same beach where Abby was killed. Now, the fact we discovered DNA from both Abby and the Gaston kid on the bottleneck of a broken bourbon bottle found at the crime scene is rather strong proof Gaston was on the beach with Abby and was no doubt drinking with her. When these photos are distributed these three men are now going to have to do a lot of explaining."

Jumping in on the conversation, Bernard elaborated, "Which brings us to the next step in our plan." Opening a folder on his desk, he held up two of the three beach photographs. I have duplicated the first and the third photos I received from Nick and Shelby. The first photo shows the three boys on the beach next to my daughter. From that photo we can assume Abigail was already dead or near death. The second photo on the beach is simply a repeat of the first, but the third shows the three boys as they have turned and are looking up, no doubt, at the individual who took the photos. The first photo displays the numbers on the back of their football jerseys, but not their faces. The third photo clearly shows their faces. We also, in both photos, have the Gaston kid raising what we assume is the murder weapon. I have had a few hundred of these photos made up along with a matching number of duplicated photos of the Beaufort High football team yearbook picture and the listing of the team members and their jersey numbers. Anyone who looks at these photos can easily identify who the boys on the beach are."

Nick raised his hand in confusion, "Wait a minute. How could you possibly have these pictures duplicated without whoever processed the photos getting suspicious, especially when you consider what the pictures indicate?"

"Easy," said Bernard. "I just happen to own a printing and duplicating company over in Charleston. I pay my people well to do what I ask. Believe me, not a word of this will leak out." Holding up his checkbook, he smiled, "It's amazing what money can accomplish in life."

Pitching the checkbook on the desk, Bernard went on, "These photos will be included in a package along with duplicated numerous newspaper articles I saved in regard to the murder and investigation of my daughter. Between the articles and the photos I think we're going to raise some eyebrows."

Carson, who had been listening, held up his hand for attention. "What do you mean when you say package?"

"I'm glad you asked that question," said Bernard. He pulled a draw cord that drew back a large curtain behind the desk, which revealed a long credenza stacked high with manila folders. Wheeling around in the wheelchair, he picked up one of the folders and explained, "Each one of these folders, or packages, contains the photos and the newspaper articles I talked about. Along with me, Conner and Detective Barrett, we will be mailing packages with said information to every newspaper office, radio and television station in Pittsburgh, St. Louis, Atlanta and every location where Gaston now has a restaurant. While we are accomplishing that part of the plan the rest of you will once again be on the road distributing packages to other locations I will shortly reveal to all of you. Carson will be returning to Atlanta, Chic will be going up to Pittsburgh and Nick and Shelby will fly to St. Louis."

Shelby frowned and asked, "Why are Nick and myself going to St. Louis rather than Pittsburgh?"

"Have you forgotten the close call you two experienced with Schulte in Pittsburgh? I'm sure you do not relish the thought of running into the Mayor of Pittsburgh or his people again."

"Most definitely," said Nick. "It would be better if Chic goes to Pittsburgh. Schulte won't know who he is. So, let me ask. When we get to our assigned locations, who and where are we going to be delivering these packages to?"

"Good question." Picking up three printed 8 x 11 lists, he gave them to Conner to hand out. "Each one of you will have on your list locations where you will drop off packages. For instance, Carson, while visiting Atlanta, will drop copies off at Gaston's home office, the manager's office at the two different apartment complexes he owns, his two nightclubs and a number of other small businesses Gaston has. The only business he has that Carson will not visit will be Gaston Trucking which is located in Sacramento. We will be mailing a copy to his trucking company from here."

Chic, walking across the room reviewed his list. "Well, it looks like I'm going to be visiting Mayor Schulte's office, the Democratic Party of Pittsburgh, Brad Schulte's church and a number of charities and organizations the good mayor supports or belongs to."

Bernard smiled and added, "We, from here at the house, will be mailing a copy off to the Governor of Pennsylvania's office and to Wells College, the private school Schulte's daughters are attending." Gesturing at Nick and Shelby, he explained, "Another reason why I'm sending both Nick and Shelby to St. Louis is because they have the most extensive list. Aside from the St. Louis Corvette Club, the YMCA where Durham swims and the organizations he belongs to, there are a number of Catholic churches that you must visit; actually, there are approximately 3,777 churches in St. Louis."

Looking at Bernard in amazement, Shelby stated, "Surely, you don't expect us to deliver a package to each one of these churches?"

"No," said Bernard, "just the Catholic Churches of which there happens to be around 215. But, sitting here thinking about the amount of churches you will have to visit, I think what I'm going to do is after Chic and Carson finish up in Atlanta and Pittsburgh, is to fly them to St. Louis and join you there. It's imperative we get all of the packages delivered in two to three days. When people start reading what we are sending or giving to them, things will start to heat up…and fast!"

"All right," said Shelby. "I kind of have an idea what is going to happen, but what is it you, Bernard, *want to happen?"*

Pointing his pipe at Melvin, Bernard explained, "Aside from knowing more about this case than anyone else alive, Detective Barrett also has vast knowledge of how not only people in general, but the media, will respond to our information. Detective…if you will!"

Melvin crossed his legs and sat back comfortably. "Well, as you put it, *people in general,* depending on who they are, will react to this information in a number of differing ways. People who are close to these three men, and people who work for them, are more likely to start asking questions while those who are not familiar with who they are may not take the info to heart. Now the media…that's different! In my experience with the media during my police career I have found them to be some of the nicest people you would want to meet, until it comes to the latest bad news that seems to flood our everyday lives. Somewhere in the Bible it states quite clearly that wherever there is a carcass, it is there the vultures will gather. In this case the carcass will be our three targets and the vultures will be the media. They thrive on stuff like what we are about to unleash on the public. As far as the media is concerned, receiving this information will be like unearthing buried treasure, a fortune that was thought to be long lost…but now, discovered. Every media contact we make will be scrambling to be the first to bring this news to the public. They will not hesitate when hearing this information. They'll go for the throat. The very idea the Mayor of Pittsburgh, an Archbishop in St Louis and a highly successful businessman are all connected to a murder case, in this case a twenty-seven year old cold case, would be similar to winning the Lotto. It'll be big news! Like vultures in real life, the media won't dally too long after receiving this information. More than likely they will call the Beaufort Police to verify any truth to the articles and that's why it's important someone on our local police force has one of these packages. I just happen to have an old friend who is still on the force. I will be meeting with him, going over what we plan on doing and warn him to expect calls from around the country about these past murders. Believe me, he'll keep a lid on this until the proper moment. Once the media defines the past story and the photos as legit, Schulte's office, Gaston's headquarters and Durham's home base church will be flooded with calls and visits by local reporters. These men may try to avoid or sidestep the media, but that will only make things worse. The media has a way of getting to the truth or what they may think the truth actually is. After we deliver all the packages we sit back and watch while the puzzle slowly comes together…an unsolved puzzle where the missing pieces finally fall into place. Schulte's successful political life, Durham's, what I assume must be a rather peaceful life and Gaston's many successful endeavors will be flooded with phone calls and questions that will seemingly come at them from every angle."

Nick raised his hand. "I have a question. One can only assume we are going to be delivering these packages in person. Do we identify ourselves, wait around until the packages are opened to see the reaction of people…what?"

"That's an excellent question," said Bernard. "At each location you visit, you will simply ask for the person in charge, be it a manager, secretary or what have you. You hand over the package while explaining who is to receive it and at the same time point out it is of the utmost importance. Then, you leave and move on to the next location. You do not answer any questions. Eventually you will all be described as male, female, tall, short…what have you. It is important you get the packages delivered and then return here to Fripp; stepping out of the picture would be a good way to put it."

Conner opened the large door and followed Mae into the library as she pushed a cart stacked with breakfast foods. "Ah!" exclaimed Bernard. "Breakfast is served."

John pulled the rental car into a parking spot at the Beaufort Marina. Robert, looking out at the boats, remarked, "Seems like a nice little town…this Beaufort."

Stepping out, John answered, "From what Brad tells me, it is. He grew up here. He was the quite the football star around these parts to hear him talk."

Looking at the parking meter, Robert reached into his pants pocket for some change. "Should we feed this thing or are we not going to be here that long?"

Taking his cell from his suitcoat, John shook his head, "No, let's give Brad a call first and see what he wants us to do."

"All right, I'm just going to walk over to the docks and check out the river."

John hit speed dial on his cell and waited, at the same time nodding to Robert.

Robert crossed the paved lot, walked past a restroom, and then down a walkway that ran adjacent to the river, then stepped out onto the wooden dock. Passing a number of various sized boats, he walked to the very end of the wooden walkway and sat on a small bench, where he lit up a cigarette. It had been many times while living in Pittsburgh he had walked down to the Monongahela, Allegheny and Ohio Rivers for a moment of relaxation. The Beaufort River, which he was now staring at, seemed rather clear compared to the constant muddy water that flowed through Pittsburgh. Looking to his left he saw a bridge spanning the wide river and then to the right in the distance he could see yet another bridge, a more modern bridge he thought. Watching a speedboat make its way rapidly past the docks, his thoughts were interrupted by a female voice, "Good afternoon."

Looking back, Robert noticed a well-dressed woman strolling to the end of the dock. Robert no sooner responded with a greeting of his own, when the woman continued, "I'd ask you how they're biting, but sitting there in that three piece suit you really don't appear to be a man who is interested in catching fish."

Robert politely stood and spoke when the woman stepped closer. "Never been fishing in my life, or for that matter hunting. If I want fish or meat of some kind I just go to the local supermarket." Looking the woman up and down, he surmised, "Just as I do not appear to be a fisherman, likewise, you do not appear to be someone who is from a small seaside town like Beaufort."

Extended her well-manicured right hand, the woman smiled and answered, "My name is Maria Sparks and you're right. I'm not from this area. I'm from New York; the city, and I'm here on some personal business. You don't appear to be from this area yourself."

"I was actually born in New York State, up around Ithaca. Ever been to that part of the state?"

"Yes, I have been to the western part of the state. It's beautiful over that way, especially in the fall. What brings you this far south?"

"I work for the Mayor of Pittsburgh and I, like yourself, am down here on business. How long have you been here?"

"Just a couple of weeks. I'm staying on an island down here called Fripp."

Fripp Island had not only been mentioned by John but Brad over the past couple of days as an area where they might get some information on the two people they were seeking. Taking a shot, Robert probed, "This Fripp. Is it a large island?"

"Oh my…no! It's the last island down the Sea Island Parkway." Pointing across the river she went on, "Over there, that's Lady's Island, then there's St. Helena, Harbor and Hunting Islands and then finally Fripp. It's a private island. I've been told there are about 1400 homes on the island, but most of those are rental properties. I've been renting a small condo on the island, but today will be my last down here. I'll be flying back to New York later this afternoon."

Robert asked his next question. "I imagine with Fripp being mostly rentals this time of year there must not be many people on the island?"

"Well, I have never been here during the tourist season. The island itself is very nice and I imagine during the summer there are a lot more people there than now."

Robert couldn't see any harm in his next question, so he pressed,

"During your stay down there on this Fripp, I don't suppose you ran into a person by the name of Falco…Nick Falco?"

Maria's jaw dropped. She looked directly into Robert's eyes. "How on earth do you know Nick Falco?"

"I don't know the man. I saw him in Pittsburgh a few days back. Actually I chased him through the Pittsburgh Convention Center. I believe he was with a girl; a Shelby Lee Pickett."

"What on earth would those two be doing in Pittsburgh?"

"I'm afraid I can't answer that. It sounds to me like you know these people better than me."

Maria sat on a bench opposite Robert and asked, "Your business down here. Does it have to do with Falco and this Pickett woman?"

"Yes is does. Our boss, the mayor, sent me and another man to see what we could find out about them. We were kind of hoping we'd find out where they live and go from there."

Maria smiled broadly. "I can tell you exactly where this Nick Falco lives. I've actually been to his house. Now, the Pickett woman? I am not familiar where she lives. I do know it's somewhere here in Beaufort. She works in Savannah and has a young daughter. She also has an apartment in Savannah. It would seem we have a lot more in common than just the fact neither one of us is from the area. You claim you have business with Nick Falco; well, so do I."

"So, you've met these two people then?"

"Yes indeed, I have. I sat no more than a few feet across from Falco in a meeting with my attorney shortly after I arrived here in Beaufort. Since then, I've had quite a few run-ins with not only Falco but this Pickett woman as well."

Robert stood, "Tell you what. I think you should meet my associate. Maybe we could have lunch together. If you could lead us to this Falco's house, my employer in Pittsburgh would be most appreciative."

Maria stood and responded with great interest. "That sounds like a splendid idea. I'd really be interested in hearing about why Falco and his girlfriend were in Pittsburgh and why you were chasing them. Let's go meet your friend."

John had a strange look on his face when Robert walked side by side with Maria Sparks across the lot. Approaching, Robert made the introductions, "John, this is Maria Sparks from New York. Maria, this is John from Pittsburgh. It just so happens Maria here knows our Mr. Falco and the girl as well. She knows where Falco lives and has talked with both he and the girl. She can get us onto Fripp Island and take us to Falco's residence. I thought maybe we could have some lunch and talk about going out to this Fripp."

Amazed, John smiled in agreement. "That fits right into our plans. I just got off the phone with Brad. He said the first thing we need to do is find out where Falco lives. This is almost too good to be true."

Maria spoke up, "There's a nice little place called Plums just up the street. We can grab a bite there and talk."

Seated at a window table near the back of Plums, Maria spoke to John, "Your friend here tells me you chased Falco and the girl through the Pittsburgh Convention Center. How could this possibly be? I was under the impression Falco was still here in the Beaufort area. Why were you chasing him?"

"As odd as it may sound," answered John, "we're not sure. This Falco character and his gal pal posed as authors writing a book about some of Beaufort's past high school students. They managed to get an interview with Brad Schulte, the current Mayor of Pittsburgh and a highly successful past student of Beaufort High. During the interview Falco and this girl all but accuse the mayor of being involved in an old murder case that happened some twenty years ago. The mayor was quite upset and informed us he wanted to talk with these people privately. When we approached them, well, they took off. They escaped and got out of Pittsburgh, so the mayor sent us down here to find out what we could about them. That's our story…what's your interest in these people?"

"My interest in these people has to do with the disappearance of my brother, Charley Sparks. Charley was employed by a man named Carnahan from New York. From what I'm to understand Nick Falco's grandfather worked for Carnahan also and wound up embezzling around seven million dollars from the company. The money supposedly was hidden in the house or on the property of ol' man Falco. He wound up dying, which left the grandmother living in the house, which just happens to be on Fripp. The grandmother, last year passes away and leaves the house to her grandson, Nick Falco. Charley and another man were assigned to come here and negotiate with Falco about searching the house for the money. Nick refuses, saying he doesn't know anything about any such money. The Carnahans, not satisfied with his answer, put the pressure on Falco and eventually he and another man named Carson Pike arrange to meet with my brother and his associate at the house to hand over the money."

John, at the name of Carson Pike, gave her a strange look but did not interrupt while she continued, "It turned out they only had around 5.8 million which they say they turned over to Charley. Upon receiving the money, Charley contacts Carnahan, who happened to be in Charleston at the time and tells him he'll have the money to him within the next few hours. Charley never showed up in Charleston and neither did his associate. I feel Nick Falco and this Pike character had something to do with their mysterious disappearance. That's why I'm down here. My brother and I were very close. If he had taken that money he would have told me. He just plain dropped off the face of the earth. Falco and Pike claim that possibly Charley took off for parts unknown with the 5.8 million. I don't believe this for a second. They know what happened to my brother and the money. There's just something suspicious about Pike and Falco and now you tell me Falco is questioning your boss about some past murder. I've met this Carson Pike. He's sly as a fox. I know he and Falco are responsible for my brother's disappearance. I just can't prove it."

Pouring coffee from an urn into his mug, John smiled and remarked, "I think Robert here is correct when he says we share interests in this Falco. What's surprising to me is we also have something in common when it comes to Carson Pike. According to Mayor Schulte, one of his high school friends he grew up with was also interviewed for this fictitious book Falco and the Pickett girl claim to be writing. A man who claimed to be an author interviewed the mayor's friend down in Florida. The so-called author's name was none other than Carson Pike. Doesn't it seem strange that the three people you suspect who may be responsible for your brother' disappearance are the same people who are posing as authors. If you ask me there's a fly in the ointment."

"I agree," said Marie. "Something does smell fishy. Now, I have already said I would take you gentlemen to Falco's house. I can place you right in his driveway. That being said, how will you be able to help me with my own personal dilemma with Falco and Pike?"

"That's easy," stated John. "Mayor Schulte is a very powerful man. He still has a lot of friends in this area. If necessary, Schulte could make things quite unpleasant for Falco and Pike."

"I don't mean to insult you or your boss, but when I first came down here I thought I could ruffle some feathers. After nearly two weeks of intense investigation, I find that I have accomplished nothing. I happen to be from New York, the largest city in the country, but down here that doesn't mean a tinker's damn! This Mayor Schulte may be quite powerful, but his power may only be effective in Pittsburgh. This is the Lowcountry and things down here move at a much slower pace. So, when you say the mayor can make things difficult, I have my doubts because I thought I could apply pressure in order to get to the bottom of my situation, and I have gotten nowhere."

John pointed at Robert and then thumped his own chest. "Robert and

I, along with some other men who are employed by the mayor, can *and have* made things at times difficult for those who are not in favor of the mayor."

"That sounds on the heavy-handed side."

"Call it what you will, but the more powerful you get in life the more people there are who want to steal your power. Over the years Mayor Schulte has had more than his share of adversaries who will stop at nothing to gain the power and control he holds. Those of us who are in his employ are there to ensure he retains his power. In short, we do whatever's necessary to keep the peace. Especially, these days. Mayor Schulte is going to be running for the Governor of Pennsylvania. He cannot afford to have anything stand in his way. Like I said; if we find Falco and Pike or even this Pickett girl are out to besmirch the mayor? Well, things could get nasty. But I think for the moment what we need to do is have you guide us to Falco's home and we'll go from there."

Robert spoke up, "I have a question. I've heard Fripp is private and you just can't drive onto the island unless you own a property or are a guest. How do you propose to get us on the island?"

"This is not an issue. I've been renting a Condo down there for the past couple of weeks. Even though I was planning on flying back to New York today, I still have two days rental left. We'll park your car and you can ride out there with me as guests. When we decide to head that way it'll only be about a twenty minute drive and you'll be sitting in Falco's driveway."

"This sounds good," said John. "Just let me call the mayor first and see if that's what he wants us to do."

Maria got up from the table, excused herself, and then walked to the restroom. Once inside the small drab green cubicle, she dialed Chic's number and waited.

Chic, just about to spoon some gravy on homemade biscuits, held up his hand and apologized when he reached for his cell. "Who on earth could that be?"

Getting up he walked over by the fireplace and answered, "Chic Brumly!"

The voice on the other end startled Chic while he listened in amazement, "Chic, it's Maria. Just like you said, if we were patient and waited long enough sooner or later Falco and the girl would mess up and the truth would be revealed. I was just about to leave Beaufort and fly back to New York when I ran into two very interesting characters by the downtown marina…"

For the next few minutes Chic listened as Maria went on about what she had recently learned, all the while Chic responding with an occasional, "I see, really?" or "uh…right."

Finally Maria finished. "I thought with this new information maybe you would be interested in getting back on my payroll. I think with what we now know we may be one step closer to solving the mystery of my brother's disappearance."

Chic responded by telling her he was in the middle of something and he would call her back in a few minutes. Holding up his cell, he stared at the others in Bernard's library in disbelief and explained, "You'll never guess in a million years who just called me."

Everyone in the room looked at each other and shrugged and then finally Chic spoke up again, "Maria Sparks…of all people! Remember when I said earlier she would soon return to New York. She just informed me she was in Beaufort ready to drive over to Charleston to head back to The Big Apple. She walks down to the marina in downtown Beaufort for a last look at the river and she runs into two men. They get to talking and it turns out they are employed by none other than Brad Schulte, the Mayor of Pittsburgh."

Shelby hesitated in drinking a glass of juice and responded in amazement, "You've got to be kidding!"

Ignoring her comment, Chic continued, "And that's not all! One thing leads to another and she finds out these men are down here looking for Nick Falco, Shelby Lee Pickett and Carson Pike. She goes on to explain to these men she also has interest in the same people." Looking at Carson, Nick and Shelby, he went on, "In short, they said they were prepared to make things quite difficult for you three. Maria agreed to lead them out here to Fripp…right to your driveway, Nick. They're on their way right now." Turning to Bernard, Chic asked, "How do you want me to handle this?"

Bernard didn't seem phased by the latest news. He rubbed his hands together, then addressed the group, "Nick and Shelby were correct in saying they felt Schulte would send men down here. We have to assume they are the same men who chased you in Pittsburgh. They have seen you and can identify you. We can also assume since Maria told Chic a Carson Pike interviewed a friend of Mayor Schulte, this friend has to be Miles Gaston. Apparently, Schulte and Gaston have communicated. They realize someone is on to them; to what extent they may not be sure, but nonetheless, we have their attention. Here's what I think we should do. First of all, we have to prevent them from coming onto the island or get them escorted off, if they do get on. I'm going to give Chief Lysinger a call."

Shelby, still amazed at what was happening, asked, "Can you actually make that happen?"

Picking up his checkbook, Bernard remarked, "I've mentioned this before and I'll say it again. Money equals power. Money is very influential and can be quite effective when it comes to getting things done…getting things done fast. I, currently, am the longest residing resident of Fripp. Over the years I have invested more than you can imagine on this island. I have donated or funded every single project that has been proposed by the homeowners association. I funded the building of our bridge, was instrumental in giving funds for the construction of our security office and have been very active financially in supporting repairs to our beach and the marsh areas. All it takes is one call to Lysinger with a complaint from me about these people who are coming to Fripp and they will be stopped dead in their tracks." Gesturing at Conner, he ordered, "Would you please get island security on the phone for me. I would like to speak to the chief."

Conner stepped out of the room. "I'm on it, sir."

Chic, now seated turned his attention to Bernard. "What do you want me to do as far as calling back Maria Sparks?"

"Well, let's think about it. She already knows you are currently working for someone else. The thing is she doesn't know who that someone is. I find it quite ironic the very men she is now working with are employed by one of the three men we are going to bring down. Here's the way I want you to handle her. After this Sparks woman and her two cronies are kicked off the island, I want you to give her a call and set a meeting at your office in Port Royal. You need to indicate at this meeting that you are interested in taking Maria back up on her offer to continue the investigation into her brother's disappearance. This is the perfect way to remain one step ahead of what Schulte will do. Another thing we must be mindful of is that Maria is going to spill her guts to these men. Before the day is out they will know everything she knows not only about Nick, but Shelby and Carson. This makes it even more vital we get the packages delivered pronto!"

Conner walked back in the room with a somber look on his face. "Lysinger is on vacation down in Florida. Travis, one of his deputies is running the show this week."

Extending his hand, Bernard snapped, "Give me the phone!" Speaking into the cell, he asked, "With whom am I speaking?"

A female voice replied, "This is Alice, the office dispatcher and secretary."

"Could I please speak with Travis? This is Bernard James. Travis knows who I am."

"I'm afraid Travis and the only other officer on duty are down at the marina right now out on the river. It seems like they've got a boat out there that sank and they took out the rescue boat to pick up two fishermen."

Bernard frowned and then spoke again, "Listen, Alice, I need you to contact Travis immediately and tell him there are three individuals that are going to be coming on to the island. They are going to Nick Falco's residence. These people are nothing but trouble. There probably isn't enough time to head them off at the gate so Travis needs to go to Falco's house as soon as he can. As a resident, I am placing a complaint on these people. I do not want them on the island. In the meantime I'm going to send over a couple of people to deal with these undesirables so you better let Travis know he needs to get cracking. Good Day!"

Handing the phone back to his trusted employee, he asked, "Conner, are you armed today?"

Pulling up his cardigan sweater Conner revealed a pearl handled revolver snuggled comfortably in a hidden shoulder strap. "Always, sir!"

"Good! I'm sending you and Carson down to Nick's home to await the arrival of our unwelcome visitors. They may know of your name Carson, but these men probably are not aware of what you look like."

Melvin stood and approached Bernard. "If it's all right I'd kind of like to tag along. My expertise may be required on the scene. If we confront these people before Travis gets there, that means there will be no authority to take control. Even though I'm now retired I know how to handle these types of situations. Besides that..." He pulled his jacket away from his body exposing a revolver. "I'm still licensed to carry. Two guns are better than one."

Chic stood. "Do you think I should go also?"

Bernard objected, "No way. At this point Maria does not know who you are working for. She doesn't need to know you are on the island. Within the next hour, you can give her that call back you promised and set up a meeting with her tomorrow. I'm quite sure after we give them the boot, she'll be even more interested in getting together with you, especially if she feels you're back on her team."

Nick shrugged his shoulders. "What about myself and Shelby? What do we do?"

"You, my dear friends are going to stay here and enjoy breakfast with me. Motioning at Conner, he ordered, "You better get moving. Take the Land Rover."

Carson, from the backseat, gave Conner directions when they approached the Bonito Road Bridge on the right. "Go past the bridge, then the second house on the left, the big white one with the fountain in the yard. Park in front of the house in the driveway across the street. According to Nick the owners are only there during the summer months. We'll walk across the street to his house. Bernard suggested we raise the garage door so they think Nick is home. We want them to park in the drive and get out so we can confront them. Bernard wants Conner to sit on the front porch while Detective Barrett and I hide in the garage. After Conner confronts these people, we'll come out at just the right moment. Of course, all of this could change if Travis shows up before they do. If that happens then we'll let him handle the situation."

Conner bounded up the stairs and positioned himself on a wicker rocker and propped his feet up on the porch railing while Carson and Barrett walked inside the garage after Carson punched in the code.

Removing his revolver from its holster, Conner admired the weapon. Flipping open the chamber he checked: *a full load.* He tucked the revolver back into his waistline as if would be easier to get to if necessary. Cracking his knuckles he thought about the fact that in all the years of being employed by Bernard he never had cause to use his gun. He took great pride in the weapon; cleaning it weekly, driving into Beaufort every Wednesday morning to practice at the local firing range. He hoped it would not be necessary to use the weapon, but Bernard had asked him if he was armed. If these people showed up he would try to talk with them first. If that didn't work then he would resort to pull his firearm. His thoughts were interrupted when a light green car turned from Tarpon and pulled in the driveway.

A woman, who was driving, stepped out followed by a man who had been seated in the passenger seat and then another man who crawled out of the back. Both men were dressed in expensive business suits and the woman was over-dressed for a day at the beach. The woman looked at the open garage door and said something to one of the men when they approached the stairs. When the woman stepped up, Conner arose and stood at the top of the stairway and announced with an air of authority, "Can I help you folks?"

Maria stopped and looked up the stairs at Conner who gave an impression of a man in great physical condition. Muscular arms folded across his chest, feet planted firmly, an unfriendly face displaying cold blue eyes and a firm chin. Looking over at the open garage door, she asked, "My name is Maria Sparks. I'm here to see a Mr. Nick Falco. I know he lives here. I've been here before." Gesturing at her two companions, she explained, "We have business with Mr. Falco."

Conner gave the threesome a confident smile and answered, "Not today you don't!"

Maria took the first step and asked, "And who may I ask are you?"

"Someone who you don't want to mess with."

Confused, Maria inquired, "Now why would you find it necessary to say something like that? For all you know we may be friends of Nick's."

Conner aggressively took one step down and responded, "I doubt that. If you were friends of Mr. Falco, I'm sure he'd be here to greet you. Let's not beat around the bush. You and I both know you're not on Falco's Christmas card list."

John moved around Maria and pushed back his suitcoat revealing a revolver. "You're right! We are not on friendly terms with Mr. Falco. That being said, we are here on business *and you* are preventing us from doing so."

Robert stepped to the side and displayed a holstered gun beneath his jacket. He placed his hand on the revolver and repeated John's statement. "Like the man said…we have business with Falco. Now, why don't you just step to the side or mosey on into the house and tell Mr. Falco he has visitors."

Conner calmly walked down the stairs, gently pushed Maria Sparks to the side and stood nose to nose with John. "I strongly suggest you and your friend here take this lady with you, climb back in your car and leave the island." Stepping even closer, Conner continued, "If you elect to remain here it could be, let's say, unhealthy for all three of you."

Robert reached for his revolver, but was interrupted by a voice from behind him. "I wouldn't do that, sir!" Carson, trailed by Detective Barrett joined the group, Barrett's gun drawn."

John smirked at the two new arrivals. He was about to say something when one of Fripp Island's security Jeeps turned wildly into the driveway. Travis and another deputy stepped out. Barrett placed his gun back in his shoulder holster and backed off when the two officers approached. Travis immediately walked up and shook Barrett's hand. "Detective, what was it…two weeks ago when we last saw each other over at the gun range in Beaufort?"

Next, Travis nodded at both Carson and Conner when John spoke, "Officer, I'm so glad you arrived. It seems we have a problem here. My associate and I along with Ms. Sparks have business with Nick Falco. These three gentlemen have refused to let us even go on the porch. We haven't broken any laws. We would just like to talk with Nick."

"Well, before we get into any of that I need to ask some questions," said Travis. "I know Detective Barrett here as well as Conner are licensed to carry a firearm here in the state of South Carolina. Are any or all three of you packing today?"

Maria raised her hands. "Not me…I don't care for guns."

John answered and produced his wallet. "Robert and I are employed by the Mayor of Pittsburgh. We are members of his staff and we are required to carry firearms for the mayor's protection."

Travis smiled and professionally demanded, "I'll need to see some I.D. and your permit to carry."

Opening his wallet, John confirmed, "I was just getting to that."

Maria spoke up and pointed at Conner. "This man here shoved me when I started up the stairs. I'd like to press charges!"

Travis placed his right foot on the bottom step and asked, "Any truth to that, Conner?"

"Yes, but I would hardly call it being shoved. I was coming down the stairs and she was blocking my way so, I brushed her to the side."

Looking Maria over from head to toe, Travis asked, "Are you injured in any way *from this shove?"*

"No, I don't have any cuts or bruises if that's what you're asking. But, I am hurt!"

"If I could ask…in what way?"

"He hurt my feelings!"

"I can arrest an individual for harming someone physically. I cannot arrest this man because you say he hurt your feelings."

Taking both John and Robert's gun permits and identification, he read them and handed them back while he addressed Maria. "I'll need to see some I.D. from you also."

"I told you…I don't like guns. What do you need with my identification?"

"Two reasons. First, it is my duty to ask for I.D. and it is your obligation to produce it for me."

Reaching inside her purse, she handed Travis her license and asked, "You said you had two reasons. You only supplied me with one."

Scanning the license, he handed it back to her and answered, "The second reason is our security department had a complaint lodged against the three of you by one of our residents."

"Who is this person *and what* did they complain about?"

"I am not at liberty to divulge the individual who lodged the complaint. I can only inform you they feel you have no business here on the island. This is a private island and the people who live and visit it like it that way. Unless you are employed here on Fripp or are a current resident or a guest of a resident you really have no business being here. You say you have business with Mr. Falco. What business is that?"

"Since you feel strongly about not revealing who it is that complained about me and my friends, I have no desire to inform you about *my business!"*

"If there is a complaint about anyone on this island, then what that person does becomes my business. So, if you or your friends here are not residents or guests then I will have to ask you to leave the island."

"It just so happens I am a resident, not a permanent resident, but still a resident. I have been renting a condo up the street at Captain John Fripp's."

Travis signaled at his deputy, "Nelson, would you please bring me the list of current renters?"

As Nelson walked back to the Jeep, Maria gave Conner a hard, long stare. Conner, not the least bit disturbed by her stern look, spoke up, "If looks could kill, Ms. Sparks. Perhaps you're trying to hurt *my* feelings. Don't waste your time."

Nelson, returning with the printed list handed it to Travis, who flipped to the third page. Let's see…here we go P, Q, R, S. Here it is, Maria Sparks, 338 Captain John Fripp North. You have two days left on your rental. Handing the list back to Nelson he placed his hands on his hips and asked, "Ms. Sparks, are you planning on staying here on the island for the next two days?"

"I'm planning to stay until I have an opportunity to speak with Mr. Falco. Is that a crime?"

"No, it's not a crime. But, if you or your two friends here step out of line, I will have you escorted off the island. Now, here's what we're going to do. Fripp is a place where people come to relax and get away from everyday life. It's peaceful here and we like to keep it that way. The people who live here also like it that way. If I receive another complaint on you, I will be paying you a visit. We don't have many confrontations like this down this way. I mean…think about it. I'm summoned to Mr. Falco's home and what do I find? Six people, none of whom happen to be Falco, standing around in front of his house. And to add to that, four of the six are carrying firearms. Why you'd think we're in Downtown New York or Atlanta." Looking squarely at John and Robert he emphasized, "This isn't Pittsburgh, gentlemen. Now, I would strongly suggest everyone be on their merry way…and I mean now!"

As Travis and Officer Nelson walked back to their Jeep, Conner followed and spoke, "Travis! Mr. James is not going to be happy when he finds out the Sparks woman and her two friends were not kicked off the island. What would you suggest I tell him?"

Travis popped a stick of gum in his mouth and answered while he climbed in the driver's side. "These people have done nothing wrong that would warrant them being kicked off the island. If your boss has a problem with that, have him give me a call."

Back at Maria's car, John asked, "You say you still have a rental here on Fripp? I know you said you were leaving today. Do you still have access to the keys?"

"Yes, I can still get into the place. I placed the key in a lockbox. I know the code."

"Good. I think in lieu of what just transpired, we need to sit down and discuss what our next move is going to be. I need to call Mayor Schulte and update him on how things are going."

Maria agreed. "That sounds like a good idea. I need to make a call as well. I'm going to call Brumly back and see if we can get a meeting set with him. He knows how to work around this stuff. Let's go. The condo is less than five minutes from here."

Conner walked back and joined Barret and Carson. "Let's go give Mr. James the bad news!"

CHAPTER TWENTY SIX

BERNARD, DRESSED IN SILK PAJAMAS AND A MATCHING GOLD trimmed smoke jacket, relaxed in his luxurious front parlor. Sipping on a morning mimosa, he scanned the front page of the Beaufort Tribune. Conner entered the spacious room, carrying a silver tray with Bernard's breakfast; poached egg, two slices of rye toast and a small bowl of peaches. "Good Morning, Sir. It looks like it's going to be a dreary day. We've got a line of thunderstorms coming out of the west. It's going to be an all day rain."

Bernard maneuvered his wheelchair next to the ten-foot arched window and drew back the massive curtain. "It would seem you are correct, but the inclement weather will not alter our plans for the day." Wheeling around, facing his trusted butler, he explained, "A little rain will not deter us from forging ahead with our plan, but I want to run a few things by you. I value your advice. Please sit and have a mimosa with me."

Conner sat on an imported leather, Italian chair next to the window and poured a portion of the orange juice and champagne concoction into a tall glass. Holding up his own drink, Bernard proposed, "Here's to success over the next few days."

Hoisting his glass, Conner inquired, "And what is it you wish to discuss, Sir?"

"I received a call last evening while you and Mae were in town getting groceries. Shelby Lee Pickett will not be able to go with Nick to St. Louis. She got a call from her employer yesterday. She has to return to work in Savannah. I was thinking about sending Melvin with Nick to St. Louis. It's imperative we get all the packages distributed to the churches in the next two to three days. If I send Barrett with Nick that will put us short here at the house organizing and mailing out packages to not only the other locations I mentioned in St. Louis, but Pittsburgh and Atlanta also. If this plan is going to work everything has to fall in place at approximately the same timeframe."

Conner smiled at his employer. "Perhaps Ms. Pickett could come to the house here after she finishes up her day at work in Savannah. She could assist you and I in compiling and mailing off the packages. Your plans will not be the slightest bit altered. You're just simply swapping out team assignments with Barrett and the Pickett girl. When Chic and Carson finish in Pittsburgh and Atlanta they can still fly to St. Louis and assist with the distribution process as planned. I really don't see any problem here."

"Excellent!" said Bernard. "The other thing I want to discuss with you is this staged meeting Chic has set up with the Sparks woman. When Nick and Shelby first told me about their problems with her, it really didn't seem like this Ms. Sparks was going to interfere with our plans, but it would seem she has tossed the proverbial monkey wrench in the works when one considers she has joined forces with Mayor Schulte's men. If she knew or finds out Brumly is in fact working for me, this could wind up setting our plan back; however, Chic has stated she's not that sharp. Depending on how Chic's meeting goes with the Sparks woman and Schulte's men, if we stick to our plan and get the packages delivered in the next couple days, it'll be too late for her to interfere. My question for you Conner…is... do you think we should wait and find out how the meeting goes before we send Carson, Nick and Melvin off to their assigned destinations?"

Conner looked at the massive Grandfather oak clock in the corner and remarked, "It's just after seven right now. Chic's meeting with the Sparks woman and Schulte's men is not scheduled until ten. Everyone else will be here by eight. According to what you said last night everyone will be driving to Charleston for their flights out by the time the meeting is in full swing. I guess we could wait until Chic phones us with the results of the meeting before we send the team off, but that could be as late as early afternoon. We'd be losing valuable time if your goal is to get all the packages delivered in the next few days. I think you should consider going ahead with your plan. You can always contact Carson, Nick and Melvin if you want to change things up based on the outcome of the meeting."

"I think you're correct, Conner. When everyone gets here at eight I'll give them their last minute instructions and their packages and send them on their way, informing them we may have to change boats, as it is said, in the middle of the stream."

Enjoying another drink of morning champagne, Conner smiled and reminisced, "This situation of possibly having to change our plans reminds me of my high school football days in West Virginia."

Surprised, Bernard responded, "I never knew you played football."

"I did. For four years I was the quarterback for our local high school."

"What do our plans and the fact they may be changed have to do with your high school football days?"

Leaning forward, Conner held out his hands in explanation. "As the quarterback of the team you call all the plays. Who goes where, who does what. When the team lines up, the quarterback always scans the defensive setup of the opposing team. If they are set up in a fashion that could prevent or at least make it difficult for the team to succeed, at the last second the quarterback yells out a signal changing the play. He must be able to make a split second decision, regardless of the pervious play. Now, let's take a look at our situation. Depending on how the Sparks woman and her two cronies react to Chic's meeting, you may have to make a change, *and* you can't wait too long to do it. Remember this. Brad Schulte was a quarterback, and quite good from what I've heard. He was headed for a professional football career. That means he was better than average. During a football game, the team with the ball always has the advantage until the other team gets their hands on the pigskin. When you control the ball you are the offence and when you do not have the ball you have to be on the defense. Right now, we're holding the ball and when we deliver these packages it will resemble throwing a long forward pass. The second the ball leaves your hand it then becomes anybody's guess what the outcome will be. Will the ball be caught or intercepted? Believe me, Brad Schulte will scramble at the last second and change his plan when these packages start to surface. That's why it's important if you are going to make a change it must be done quickly."

Firing up his pipe, Bernard shook his head in amazement. "I have never been a fan of sports...especially football. But I have to admit sitting here listening to you explain the game it sounds quite intricate and even complicated."

Conner agreed, "Football is an excellent example of life. We all want to score a touchdown in life; that touchdown being, success, money...what have you. In football each and every play is designed for success. And if every member of the team does exactly what they are called upon to do, then the team succeeds. What often happens is someone on the defensive side of the ball screws up the offensive team's plans. If everyone on our team does exactly what they are supposed to do, then we'll succeed. But, I say again. As a former quarterback, Schulte will not hesitate once he figures out what we are doing. Now, the other two, Gaston and Durham. For four years playing on the Beaufort High team they took orders and direction from Schulte. When this thing comes down, they'll be scrambling. They may contact Schulte for advise...they may not. Personally, I feel we have the upper hand. If we play our cards right *we will succeed!"*

The sound of the doorbell interrupted the conversation. Conner stood and finished his drink. "I think our team members are starting to arrive."

Walking toward a set of French doors, Conner stopped and asked, "One more thing, Sir. Can we trust Mr. Brumly? You know he doesn't have the best reputation in these parts as an attorney. His services always go to the highest bidder. What if, during this upcoming meeting, the Carnahans or this Mayor Schulte offer him more money than you have. Can you be sure he won't jump ship?"

"I can assure you our Mr. Brumly will not jump ship."

"What assurance are you basing your statement on?"

"You!"

"Me!"

"Yes…you. I have informed Mr. Brumly if he in any way double crosses me, then he'll have to deal with you. I informed him this was something he did not want to experience."

"Very good, Sir. I'll just be getting the front door."

It was pouring rain when Chic pulled into his office. Parking directly in front of the door, he unlocked the office and stepped inside. He checked the time, 8:37. He had well over an hour to prepare for the meeting. Throwing his coat over the back of his chair, he looked around the two-room affair. He hadn't spent much time in the office for the past two weeks. The banana plant needed water and it wouldn't hurt to run the vacuum across the well-traveled carpet. Pulling up the Venetian blinds he noticed the rain had suddenly stopped. *Good,* he thought, *just enough time to run across the street to Parker's and grab a hot coffee…maybe a donut.*

Throwing his coat back on, he placed the banana plant outside by the door. It looked like the rain could start up again at any moment. He ran across the street where he had to wait in line while numerous customers stood in line paying for gas, breakfast sandwiches, drinks and snacks. Five minutes later he stood under the overhang of the combination gas station-convenient store and sipped at the coffee. Outside, the rain returned and didn't appear like it was going to let up any time soon. Bolting across the lot, he waited for a truck and two cars to pass by and then ran across the street, picked up the now waterlogged plant and sat it inside the door. Draping his coat over the coat rack in the outer office, he walked into the tiny restroom and dried his face off with some paper towels. Finally seated at his desk, he took a long drink of the wonderful coffee and unwrapped his cream-filled donut. Reclining in the chair he placed his feet on the desk and reviewed how he was going to handle Maria and her two new friends.

He was well aware of Maria's strengths and weaknesses. Her strength was centered on her dogged determination to simply never give up...seemingly no matter what. Her weakness was her lack of patience and the ability to keep her mouth shut. He imagined he wouldn't have any problems dealing with her, especially if he gave her the opinion he was going to take up her case again. Now, the men Schulte had sent to Beaufort; that was a different matter. It would only take him a few minutes after talking with them to size these men up. It was what he did. He was an expert at reading people. Bernard had given him instructions to keep the meeting short but not to hurry things along. It was important to find out what the men as well as Maria had in mind. If he could find out what their next move was they could stay one step ahead of Schulte.

Getting up, he realized sitting around going over what he would say was a waste of time. He was never at a loss for words and he knew how to manipulate a conversation. Walking to a small closet he grabbed the ancient vacuum, plugged it in a nearby socket and started to run the machine back and forth across the carpet. His visitors would be showing up in about an hour.

"Shelby, it's Nick. Melvin and I are just about to board for St. Louis. Carson just took off for Atlanta. I'm sorry you're not coming along. I was all set to buy you a great dinner in St. Louie!"

"Don't worry about me. Bernard called me and it turns out I'm going out to Fripp to his house after work to help put together the packages. Conner and I are going to see they get mailed tomorrow morning. Have you heard how Chic's meeting with Maria went?"

"It's quarter of ten now. They'll be getting started soon. We'll all hear something later today. Listen! Be careful. With two of Schulte's men running around down there you never know what might happen. I'll talk with you later. We're just about to board. Give Kirby a big hug for me."

Carson settled back in his seat when the plane leveled off and beverages were served. Nursing a cold glass of apple juice he opened a briefcase containing ten packages he planned to deliver before the day was out. Bernard told him if he didn't get them all delivered, then he was to stay the night in Atlanta and finish up the next morning, then fly to St. Louis and assist Nick and Melvin with their deliveries. With any luck he'd be back on Fripp in two to three days. He thought about how Miles Gaston had gone off on him when he mentioned the murders. The other boot was about to fall.

Straightening the top of his desk to the point where he thought it looked presentable, Chic checked his watch, 10:01. His visitors were running late, no doubt because of the rain. He no sooner walked to the front doors when he noticed Maria, an umbrella held in her hands, trailed by two men in suits running across the wet lot. Being polite, *a nice touch,* he thought, he opened the door for them. Maria stepped through and commented, "Thank you so much, Chic."

Inside the door, one of the men, the tallest, reached for Chic's hand. "Mornin'! My name is John Lord. I'm from Pittsburgh." Gesturing at the other man, he continued the introductions, "This is Robert Peller, also from Pittsburgh. We are both employed by the Mayor of Pittsburgh."

John had an exceptionally strong handshake that sent out a clear message to the recipient of his grasp, he was in control. Chic wasn't about to be intimidated by this man. He returned a solid grip with a cutting comment delivered in a comical way. "That's quite a grip you've got there, John. I wouldn't have expected that from someone up north." Without giving John an opportunity to respond, Chic reached for Robert's hand. "Nice to meet you, Mr. Peller." Moving the conversation along Chic began the process of gaining control of the upcoming meeting. "Please, hang your coats over there on the rack and then we can go into my office and talk. I understand Maria here has discovered something new about Mr. Falco."

Hanging her coat up, Maria answered the question, "Yes, it would seem a twist of fate has occurred that I hope will bring you and I back together in pursuit of the truth about my brother." Removing a slim cigarette from a thin gold container, she sat in a chair next to the desk, flipped her lighter open, and proceeded to light up. Crossing her legs, she clicked the long nails on her right hand together and explained, "Yesterday morning I had every intention of flying back to New York to reevaluate my position here in Beaufort. With you no longer in my corner Chic, I found myself at a dead end. On my way in from Fripp to the airport in Charleston, I decided to take a walk down by the downtown marina. I think it's one of the more pleasant places I like about this area. Looking back I'm glad I decided to take a stroll down by the river, because it was there I accidentally ran into Robert. We got to talking and when he found out I had been staying on Fripp he asked me if I knew of a Nick Falco. You can imagine how shocked I was when he mentioned the name of one of the three people you and I pursued for the past two weeks. Robert introduced me to John and we had lunch together where I discovered they were not only seeking information on Falco, but Shelby Lee Pickett and Carson Pike as well."

"I see," said Chic. "It does seem rather ironic the three individuals we were questioning about your brother's disappearance are the same three people John and Robert are seeking." Directing his next comment to John, Chic inquired, "Why are you interested in Falco and his two companions? If I am going to get involved in this situation I have to know all the facts."

Feeling he was still in control of the conversation, Chic removed an ink pen from his shirt pocket, clicked it and moved a legal pad on the side of the desk to the center as if he were prepared to take notes. John cleared his throat and began to answer the question, "As employees of Mayor Schulte, Robert and I are obligated to do what the mayor asks. I am not completely sure why the mayor wants information on Falco, Pickett and Pike. I can only tell you what I experienced when Falco and the Picket woman were in Pittsburgh. I was there and I witnessed first-hand what went on.

Adjusting his suit coat he went on, "The mayor and I first ran into the couple at the downtown Hilton. We were just coming off the elevator when they mentioned the mayor's name. Being a politician, the mayor introduced himself and asked if he could help them. Following a short conversation we discovered Falco and his female companion were authors from Beaufort, the town where the mayor was born and raised. They simply wanted an interview with the mayor. He agreed to meet them the next day for a half hour lunch at the convention center.

"They showed up as planned. I sat in on the interview. Turns out they were writing a book about past highly successful students from the high school Mayor Schulte attended. The interview went along just fine until they mentioned something about some murders back in 1989 of some fellow students that occurred during his senior year. They asked how he felt at the time and if he knew the victims. The mayor answered their questions but I could tell he was upset. It wasn't but a minute or so later when he ended the interview. Falco and the woman thanked the mayor and off they went.

"We had another interview lined up for twelve noon with a television station at one of the kiosks there at the center. Wouldn't you know it, Falco and Pickett show up and are standing in the audience. During a question and answer period which was being filmed this Pickett woman asked Mayor Schulte about the murders again. The mayor, once again, answered her questions. I thought it was quite the awkward moment. The questions were so out of line with what the mayor was talking about. Everyone was staring at Falco and Pickett like they were nuts for asking such questions. Toward the end of the interview Falco and the girl walk off into the surrounding crowd. The mayor signals Robert and I to follow them and find out what the hell is going on.

"The convention center was packed and before we could get close to them they noticed us. We couldn't believe it. They started to run! We took off after them. My job, on the mayor's staff, had up to that point never involved chasing someone, but there we were, running after two people and when and if we caught up to them, I had no idea what to say other than the mayor would like to speak with them. We chased them through the convention center down to the parking garage, where they somehow managed to escape. Needless to say, the mayor was not pleased. We already knew they were staying at the Hilton so we went over there immediately hoping we would find them. We never did see the girl again, but I did run into Falco who ran off before I could speak to him. He nearly ran me down with his car in the parking garage, crashed through the gate and disappeared up the street. We haven't seen either one of them since. We assume they returned here to Beaufort."

Chic pointed his pen at John and asked, "And what makes you, or the mayor think they came back here to Beaufort?"

"Look," said John. "Brad Schulte didn't get to be the mayor of a large city like Pittsburgh by not knowing people. His political position as mayor allows him the flexibility of getting information normal people may not have access to. He sent us to the airport where we discovered when Falco and Pickett flew into the city. We also found out they were not booked on a departing flight. Then, we checked the rental car agencies and found out they had rented a car. Turns out the car was returned in Columbus, Ohio. The mayor's powers were not as effective in Ohio so we were unable to determine if they flew back to Beaufort or rented another car and drove back."

Robert jumped in on the explanation and added, "The manner in which they returned here hardly seems important. *We know*...they are here. Maria drove us out to Fripp to Falco's house. We stood in his driveway."

Sitting back in confidence, Chic asked the threesome. "And while you were there did you talk to or see Mr. Falco or Ms. Pickett?"

Maria answered the question, "No, we did not. We were confronted by three men who prevented us from even knocking on the front door. The police came by and told us all to disperse."

"Did you recognize these men?"

"Only Carson Pike. The other two I've never seen before."

"Then, at this point we do not know if Falco and Pickett are here in Beaufort, down on Fripp or even back in Pittsburgh...do we?" Directing his next comment at John and Robert, he emphasized, "Gentlemen. If you have the opportunity to work with me you will rapidly discover I deal in facts, not speculation. It is what it is! Anything other than that is a waste of time." Speaking to Maria, he smiled, "I am interested in getting back on the case of your missing brother. I assume the fee I was charging you before will resume?"

Maria patted the purse. "Most definitely!"

John spoke up. "I'm sure the mayor will be more than happy to also pay for your services."

"Good!" said Chic as he stood and looked out the window. "Here's what we're going to do. First of all it's going to take me a good two days to physically finish up with my current client, then I'll be yours full-time. Over the next two days I will be mentally putting together a plan of attack. Don't do anything until I call you."

John, taken aback, subtly objected, "So, we're just supposed to sit back and do nothing for the next forty-eight hours. I don't think Mayor Schulte will approve of that tactic. He is running for the next Governor of Pennsylvania. He is not a man who likes to just sit around. He wants to get to the bottom of this Nick Falco business. Time is money and sitting around for the next two days is not something he is going to approve of. He wants action…he wants answers."

Chic sat back down at the desk and pushed the legal pad to the side. "Your Mayor Schulte doesn't sound like he's all that patient. This area, Beaufort County, Fripp Island, the Lowcountry is not Pittsburgh. Things move at a much slower pace down here. If we try to move on this situation at a faster pace than what people travel we will not be successful. So, what's it going to be gentlemen? My way, which I guarantee, will work, or your way, which at this point in the game has…not worked."

Maria, sensing the opportunity to work with Chic was slipping away, spoke up, "John, listen to me. Mr. Brumly is very good at what he does. He knows the people in this area; what they do, how they react. If we forge ahead without his assistance we will run into a brick wall. I have no problem holding back for the next couple of days while Chic comes up with a plan. You need to call this mayor of yours and explain to him the way things are down here. He needs to be patient while we figure this out."

John held up his hand. "Look, I have no problem going along with your lawyer's plan of waiting two days. It doesn't make a tinker's damn to me. But you have to understand that I'm obligated to follow through on Mayor Schulte's orders. I'll call him and do my best to convince him to hold off, but I can't guarantee you anything."

"Fair enough!" said Chic. Wanting to end the meeting, he stood, walked to the coatrack and started to put on his jacket. "I can only assume, Maria, you will not be going back to New York as planned. Are you planning on remaining out on Fripp?"

"That's precisely what I plan on doing. I have one day left on my current contract at the condo on Fripp. The owner told me when I originally rented the place I could stay there until May." Turning to John, she inquired, "And what about you and Robert? Will you be returning to Pittsburgh while we wait to hear from Chic?"

John, getting up to retrieve his coat, shook his head. "I'm not sure. We'll have to call Mayor Schulte and see what he wants us to do. I have a strong feeling he will require us to remain here until we have some solid answers."

Snapping her fingers, Maria remarked, "I've got an idea. My place on Fripp sleeps up to eight. There's more than enough room for the three of us. We'd be no more than five minutes from Falco's house. We could keep an eye on him for the next two days until we hear from Chic."

"Now that sounds like something the mayor would approve of," said Robert.

John slipped his right arm into his coat and asked Chic. "Do you have a problem with us staying on Fripp right down from Falco's house?"

Chic didn't like the idea, but realized he didn't have a choice but to agree. He had pushed hard enough. He had to make it appear as if he were on their side. "I don't foresee any problems with that providing you don't contact or approach Falco if you run into him. This has to be done right. If you forge ahead without my assistance our plan will not work."

John reached out to shake Chic's hand. "That sounds reasonable. I think I can sell the mayor on waiting for two days, especially since we now know where this Falco lives. But let me just say this. Depending on how your plan works or does not work, Mayor Schulte will only wait for so long and then he'll take action."

"Good," said Chic as he shook John's hand. "Later this week we'll get to the bottom of why Falco and his friends interviewed your mayor and we may be one step closer to finding out what happened to your brother, Maria. Now, I've got to get to work on this. I'll give you a call in two days."

Casually ushering his three visitors to the door, he watched while they ran across the lot in the downpour. The umbrella Maria was holding unfolded awkwardly in the stiff wind and blew across the pavement. Maria flipped the tumbling umbrella the bird. Chic watched until they pulled out of the lot. Satisfied with how the meeting had gone he walked back into his office and dialed Bernard to update him on how things had gone. Minutes later, he climbed in his car, grabbed yet another coffee at Parkers and began to drive to Charleston where he would board a flight to Pittsburgh. Driving down Ribaut Road, he looked at the briefcase on the passenger seat that contained the packages he was to deliver in The

Steel City.

After parking his car in the lot at the Atlas Building in Atlanta, Carson took the elevator to the floor where Gaston Enterprises home office was located. Straightening his tie he checked his appearance in a large mirror at the end of the hall, then entered the large double-glass doors. Approaching the reception desk, he reminded himself, *Keep it short and simple!*

Fortunately, a different woman was at the desk than when he had been at the office before which would eliminate the possibility of him being remembered as having been there just recently. Smiling pleasantly, he removed the 8 x 10 folder from beneath his arm and handed it to the woman. “Good afternoon. Would you please see Mr. Miles Gaston gets this folder? It is very important.” Before the woman could utter a word, Carson smiled, thanked her, turned and walked out of the office. Once in the elevator he thought to himself, *That was easy! Next stop. The Four Seasons Apartment Complex.* According to the printed directions Bernard had supplied him with, he should be arriving there in about forty minutes.

Nick pulled the rental from the St. Louis Airport to the curb directly across the street from the cathedral. Melvin opened one of two suitcases in the backseat and placed one of the folders on the dash. “You’re up! All you have to do is walk in there, hand the folder to the receptionist or secretary, tell them to make sure the archbishop gets it and then get back out here.”

Nick grabbed the folder and took a deep breath. “Here goes! I should be back in a few minutes.” Getting out, he stared up at the back of the towering stone steeple and stained glass windows. Taking three stone steps in stride he crossed a cobblestone walk and opened an old looking oak door with a sign above it that read, CHURCH OFFICE.

Inside the office he walked through a small vestibule where there was a bulletin board housing pinned up brochures and advertisements; parish craft show, canned food drive, services offered by various church members. Stepping into the main office there was a picture of the Pope centered behind a simplistic wood desk, a crucifix on the left and an embroidered framed message of scripture on the right, *Fear not for Lord is with thee!*

Two younger women stood at the desk talking with what appeared to be a secretary. He wanted to walk up to the desk, politely interrupt and explain he had something for the archbishop, but thought that would be rude, so he waited patiently next to a magazine rack containing Catholic literature. The secretary held up a finger indicating she would be right with him. Nodding back, he thought to himself, *I'll be out of here in just a few moments.*

Suddenly, emerging from a hallway on the right a man dressed in a black robe entered the small office. Nick, not being that familiar with the Catholic religion figured the man was a priest or a deacon. The man, noting Nick standing there smiled and greeted him, "Good afternoon to you young man."

Nick responded nervously, "Good afternoon." Things were not working out the way he planned. He should have delivered the folder and have left by now, but he was still standing there. The longer he remained inside the church office the more noticeable he was becoming.

The two women at the desk turned, one of them addressing the man in black, "Hello…Your Excellency! How are you?"

Approaching the women, he extended his hand. "I'm doing just fine. How is the fundraiser going for our scout troupe?"

The woman closest to the man, answered, "We just exceeded our goal last evening and we have another week to go."

The man in black responded, "Very good," then turned and walked across the room to a row of filing cabinets. Just about to open one of the sliding drawers, he turned and spoke to Nick. "Can we be of some help to you? Are you waiting to speak with someone?"

Nick found himself in an awkward moment. Stepping forward he handed the folder to the man and explained, "I have some very important information for the archbishop. Would you please see he receives this?"

The man took the folder, reached out and shook Nick's hand. "I am the archbishop…Archbishop Durham. And you are?"

Nick thought quickly. Lying, he blurted out a name, "Harold…Harold Ward."

"What kind of information is it?"

Continuing the lie, Nick went on, "Just some charity stuff. But, it is important."

Starting to lift the tab on the backside of the folder, the archbishop smiled, "Well, let's just take a gander at what you have."

Nick was at a loss for what his next move was. He wanted desperately to run out of the building, but that would raise a red flag. He certainly couldn't stand there and watch while Durham looked at the damning evidence inside the folder. Durham was just about to reach inside the folder and withdraw the documents when the secretary interrupted him. "Excuse me, Your Excellency, but you have a call on line two."

Without looking at the documents, Durham shoved them back down in the folder, walked over to the desk and handed it to the secretary.

"Would you please place this in my in box? I'll get to it later."

Turning back to Nick, he spoke, "It was nice to meet you, Mr. Ward. If you'll kindly excuse me, I have a call. Good day!"

Nick backed casually out of the office and once in the vestibule pushed open the door and ran down the steps and across the street, jumped in the car, turned the ignition key and started to pull out, nearly colliding with a delivery truck coming down the street. Melvin, noticing Nick's odd behavior reached over and touched his shoulder, "Take it easy son. Don't kill us just yet. We've got a lot more deliveries to make."

The delivery truck passed and Nick pulled out and sped up the street as he looked in the rearview mirror at the church. "Things didn't go well in there. I had to give the folder to Durham himself! I really didn't have a choice. The secretary was busy talking with some parishioners. He almost opened it right in front of me. When he does get around to seeing what's in that folder he's going to remember me!"

"You didn't give him your name...did you?"

"No, I gave him a false name, but still he knows what I look like." Making a left hand turn, going a short block and then making a right he finally slowed the car down and in a frustrating tone, remarked, "I don't even know where I'm going! What's our next stop?"

Looking at the list held in his hand, Melvin angled his thumb back over his shoulder. "The YMCA where Durham swims. It's on this street but in the other direction. You'll have to turn around. You're really upset over running into this Durham character. It's not that big of a deal. You got the folder delivered and I'm sure later today or tomorrow he'll discover what's inside."

Turning around at a gas station, Nick drove back up the street. "I'm the only one on our team who has come face to face with all three of our targets. I sat right across the table from Brad Schulte during our interview in Pittsburgh, I met Miles Gaston on the beach at Fripp, no less, at the scene of the murders and now I was no more than a few inches from Tim Durham. I shook the man's hand. To think that these three men murdered Abigail James and Chester Finch is hard to imagine. They all seem...so normal."

"If it's any consolation, that's what I thought too. Remember, twenty-seven years ago my partner, Detective Silk and I sat with these three boys four times and discussed those murders. Even though we thought we had the goods on them, we just didn't have enough to nail the coffin shut. As you know...they walked and have now been free for close to three decades. When Silky and I interviewed those boys it was hard for us to imagine them as the killers of Abigail and Chester. They were just high school kids: high grade averages, well liked by their teachers and fellow students, active in school activities, members of the football team. They all came from good families, went to church regularly, and as far as I know never got into any sort of trouble. They were all college bound and destined to become professional football players. So, you see things haven't changed. Now, we have the mayor of a major city, an archbishop and a highly successful businessman. Even as grown men, it's still hard to fathom the idea they killed two of their friends." Holding up one of the folders, Melvin stated firmly, "I know how the wheels of the law turn and when the information in these folders gets out these three men will finally be brought to justice." Checking a passing address, he pointed out, "According to Bernard's directions, the Y should be in the next block. When we get there I'll deliver the next folder." Examining the list on his lap, he looked at his watch. "It's gonna be dark in about an hour or so. We'll only be able to make a few more deliveries today. There are five churches on the list within a ten-mile radius. I think we should try to knock those out and then call it a day. We'll get a good night's rest and hit it hard tomorrow. Chic and Carson will probably join us sometime tomorrow and then things will speed up. There's the Y. Pull over."

Bernard poured himself a glass of expensive sherry as Conner entered the front parlor and announced. "It's still raining, sir. I just finished helping Shelby load up her Jeep with the remainder of the folders. She is going to mail them from Savannah tomorrow morning. Have you heard anything from Nick and Detective Barrett?"

"No not yet, but it's only seven o'clock." Pulling back the drapes, Bernard looked out at the falling rain. "I am quite satisfied with the way things are going so far. Carson will be finished in Atlanta tomorrow and then fly to St. Louis. Chic called and said he got into Pittsburgh too late to deliver any of his packages. He said he was confident he could knock them out tomorrow and be in St Louis the next evening. The other thing we have going for us is Chic bought us two days with the Sparks woman and Schulte's men. I figure in the next two days all the packages will have been delivered. I feel we have a recipe for success. The ingredients for this cake we are about to bake has been well planned. Now, all we have to do is turn up the oven."

CHAPTER TWENTY SEVEN

NICK SWALLOWED HIS LAST BITE OF SCRAMBLED EGGS AND washed it down with orange juice when his cell phone buzzed. Scooping up the phone, he answered, "Hello!"

Shelby, her usual enthusiastic self, replied, "Hello yourself! How are things up there in St. Louis?"

"Great! Melvin and I are just finishing our breakfast and then we're off for a day of visiting Catholic churches in the city. I told Bernard last night when we called in we're considering renting a second car so we can split up and cover more ground. Even with Carson and Chic flying in later today or tomorrow, it's a big task to get all the deliveries completed. Bernard informed me you took the rest of the packages with you last evening."

"I did and I just mailed them at the post office here in Savannah."

"Anything new with Maria and her two henchmen?"

"Nope. Haven't seen or heard from them."

"Well, just the same. Don't let your guard down. Schulte is already upset with us. When he receives his package it's hard to say what he'll do. Listen! We have to get moving on these folders. I'll give you a call this evening when we finish up the day." Looking out the restaurant window, Nick frowned. "It's starting to snow. I miss the Lowcountry."

"You'll be back down here before you know it. Maybe we'll have Frogmore Stew later this week."

Nick smiled at the thought. "I'll talk with you tonight."

Melvin picked up the check and examined it carefully. "Looks like breakfast is on Bernard."

"That's right," said Nick. "He's financing everything on this trip."

"Well, nonetheless, I'm still leaving a tip." Melvin extracted three one-dollar bills from his wallet and tossed them on the table. "One more cup of coffee and I'm good until lunch." Looking at the printed list next to his plate, Melvin took out an ink pen and circled four churches. "Our first four stops for the day are not that far away. We've got St. Johns at Plaza Square, St. Pius V on Grand Boulevard, St. Mary Victories on South Third and then St. Nicholas on North Eighteen Street. I'll deliver St. Johns and then we'll keep switching off. It'd be great if we could knock thirty or so of the churches on the list off today."

Carson's breakfast consisted of chocolate milk, a banana and a package of cupcakes he purchased at a convenient store down the street from the Westside Apartments. It was a huge complex with what looked like more than a hundred units. He looked at the clock on the dashboard of his rental car, 8:57 in the morning. He'd wait for another five minutes, then drive through the complex, locate the rental office and deliver the package. The way things looked, after he dropped off the folder at Westside, he only had two laundromats to visit. He figured, if everything went smoothly he'd be at the airport no later than noon. He was planning on being in St. Louis late afternoon. *Time to go!*

It only took him a few minutes before he located the office. Parking in one of four empty spots he got out and walked to the door where a maintenance men was hanging a Christmas wreath. "Mornin'," said Carson. "Is this the rental office?"

"Indeed it is," answered the man. Politely, he opened the door and offered, "Step right in. We have five units available I know of right now."

Stepping through the doorway, Carson held up the folder. "I'm not interested in renting. I'm just dropping off some information."

The man gestured at the inside of the office. "Just give it to Gina. She's one of our rental agents."

"So, the manager is not in yet?"

"That'd be Thelma. She usually doesn't get in until about ten thereabouts. You give what you've got there to Gina. She'll see ol' Thelma gets it."

An attractive young woman stood at a window while she watered a plant. Carson approached and asked, "Gina?"

The woman, hearing her first name turned and smiled, thinking someone had entered the office that knew her. Instead, she was staring at a stranger who was holding a manila folder. Carson didn't waste any time. Stepping forward he presented the package. "I have some information for Thelma, the complex manager. I know she's not in yet, but would you please see she gets this. It's very important."

Taking the folder, Gina responded, "Of course."

Not giving the woman an opportunity to speak further, Carson thanked her and left the office.

Gina tossed the folder face up on the desk, sat down and finished her coffee. Looking down at the folder she noticed it was not addressed to Thelma, but Westside Apartments. There wasn't even a return address. *Odd,* she thought. Normally when any type of mail came into the office, unless it was addressed to a specific person, it could be opened by any of the agents. Turning the folder over, she unclasped the flap and dumped the contents on the desk. There were a total of seven 8 x 11 sheets of paper, all face down. She flipped the pile right side up and what she first saw caused her to pause in confusion. A black and white photograph of what appeared to be three men wearing some sort of athletic jerseys, each numbered on the back. The person on the end held a piece of thick wood high in the air. On the ground in front of the three she could see the top portion of what looked like a girl who was dead or at least unconscious. *What an odd picture for someone to take. What the hell was she looking at?*

The next sheet of paper was a second photo, but this one pictured the three individuals turned so they were facing the camera. The female was still lying on the ground in the same position. The three men, who now appeared to be young boys were not smiling for the picture. Their facial features clearly displayed they were upset or taken by surprise. The third and fourth papers were of a team football photograph and a list of players and their team numbers. The next two sheets contained a number of photocopies of newspaper articles. TWO BEAUFORT HIGH STUDENTS FOUND DEAD ON FRIPP ISLAND - MURDER SUSPECTED OF STUDENTS FOUND ON FRIPP – NO MURDER WEAPON, SUSPECTS OR MOTIVE ON RECENT FRIPP ISLAND MURDERS. The Last sheet of paper was simply typewritten in italics. *There is no statute of limitations on murder! Brad Schulte, Tim Durham and Miles Gaston. I know what you did!*

*Miles Gaston, s*he thought! Gaston Enterprises owned Westside. She knew of Miles Gaston. He owned Gaston Enterprises. She had been employed at the complex for the past three years but had only met Gaston on two occasions. Two years back when two six-unit buildings were added on the north side of the complex and last year when Gaston had briefly attended a small Christmas party at the complex community center. He had shaken her hand and wished her a Merry Christmas. All the agents received a bonus check and then he left. He seemed like a good man. Picking up the second photo again, she looked at the picture closely. If the girl in the photo was dead, why was the picture taken?

Her concentration was interrupted by a familiar voice when Thelma entered the office, "Good morning! Sorry I'm late. A semi broke down on the bypass and totally screwed up traffic." Gina didn't respond but continued to stare at the photograph.

Thelma threw her coat over a chair and comically objected to Gina's lack of enthusiasm of returning her a good morning. "Did we get up on the wrong side of the bed today?"

Gina laid the photo down and apologized, "I'm sorry. I was in a great mood until just a few minutes ago some man delivered a folder here to the office. He said it was for you, but it was not addressed to you, so I went ahead and opened it." Gesturing at the sheets of paper, she explained, "I've been sitting here looking at what the folder contained and I don't know what to make of it."

Stacking the seven papers in order, Gina slid them across the desk. "If you can explain what these mean I'll be absolutely amazed."

Staring at the first photo, Thelma raise her eyebrows, pursed her bright red lips and flipped to the second photo. She compared the two pictures and moved onto the other papers without saying a word. Following a few seconds she looked across the desk at Gina and asked, "Would you consider me a reasonably intelligent individual?"

Instantly, Gina answered, "Yes!"

"After looking at these documents and photos I can't make heads or tails of what they mean. The only thing that makes any sense to me is the name, Miles Gaston. We work for the man."

Gina thought for a moment and then suggested, "Maybe that's why the man said I was to give it to you."

"But, why me?"

"Because you're the manager of this place. He told me it was important and I was to make sure you received it."

"Okay, I'll buy that. But what does all this mean?"

"Look, I had a little more time to spend looking at these photos than you have. If you want my two cents, this is what I'm thinking. After reading the newspaper articles and identifying the three youths in the photos as the same three football players the police interviewed who were persons of interest and, the fact one of the boys just happens to be Miles Gaston, I think someone is trying to tell you Gaston was involved in the murders mentioned."

"But why now?" probed Thelma. "Look at the date on one of these articles, 1989. That was twenty-seven years ago. Why now and *why me?"*

"I think the man who delivered the folder wants you to know or figure something out about Miles Gaston. I mean, that makes sense. You work for Miles, he owns the complex."

"If what you're suggesting is in fact true, then what am I supposed to do with this information? This stuff could be incriminating."

Gina picked up one of the photos and examined it again. "Maybe we should take the folder and its contents downtown to Gaston's headquarters and hand it over to someone who will make sure Gaston receives it. We could place all the documents back inside and clasp it shut. They, or I guess, Mr. Gaston will never know we are aware of the contents. Then, we'll be done with it?"

Getting up, Thelma walked over and fiddled with one of the ornaments on the office Christmas tree. "Gina, you are by far my best agent. You're aggressive and innovative. Where is your sense of adventure? If we turn this information over to Gaston Enterprises, depending on who gets their hands on it, that could be the end of this…whatever that means. I'm interested in seeing where this goes. I'm going to give my brother, Dale a call. He's a detective with the Atlanta Police. I'm going to ask him to drop by and take a gander at this stuff and see what he thinks. This could turn out to be quite interesting."

Getting off the crowded elevator of the third floor of the Allegheny Building, Chic stepped to the side to get his bearings. During the two block walk and even on the elevator he had gotten quite a few odd looks. He hadn't considered the Pittsburgh weather in mid-December might be just a tad bit colder than Beaufort. Walking down the street dressed in a sports coat and casual slacks made him stick out like a sore thumb. Everywhere he looked people were bundled up in warm overcoats, gloves and earmuffs. He had taken notice of the time and temperature on a large downtown bank clock during his walk from the Hilton, twenty-eight degrees. He couldn't recall the last time the temperature had dipped that low in Beaufort. Looking down a long hallway he spotted what he was looking for, The Office of the Mayor of Pittsburgh was presented in gold leaf lettering on a glass wall. When he approached he could see a large reception desk on the opposite side. He'd walk in, deliver the package and be on his way in no time.

Opening the large glass door, he entered the spacious office and crossed the carpeted floor. On the right hand side of the room there was a large cardboard image that displayed a man with a printed message: **BRAD SCHULTE - THE NEXT GOVERNOR OF PENNSYLVANIA.** Schulte's image gave a very distinct impression of someone who appeared to be tough; a Teddy Roosevelt character. Looking down at the folder in his hand, Chic thought, *We'll see how tough you are, Mr. Schulte. Your strength is about to be tested.*

Stopping at a desk centered toward the back of the room, he waited patiently while a receptionist took a phone call. Behind the desk, out the large plate glass window he could not only see PNC Park where the Pirates played but the Monongahela River. The receptionist hung up the phone and asked professionally, "Can I help you, sir?"

Chic held up the folder. "Yes, you can. I have some very important information for the mayor. If you would be so kind and see he receives it."

The woman took the folder, placed it in an in-box and responded, "I'll see Mayor Schulte gets the information. Thank you."

Picking up a campaign button from a basket on the side of the desk, Chic looked at the circular metal disc and smiled. "The next Governor of Pennsylvania!"

"That's right," agreed the woman. "Our own mayor from right here in Pittsburgh will be governing our state. It's so exciting!"

Placing the button inside his coat pocket, Chic nodded, turned and started across the office, smiled and had a thought. *Amazing! Everyone on the mayor's staff is on board with Schulte. They see a light at the end of the tunnel. Little do they know it's a speeding train!*

Standing on the street in front of the building, Chic looked up at the foreboding sky as snow flurries raced by in the stiff downtown Pittsburgh wind. Pulling the collar of his sports coat up around his neck he started back up the street to the Hilton where he would return to his room and pick up his next folder he was going to deliver two blocks beyond the Hilton to Pittsburgh Democratic Headquarters. After that, he was going to drive to Squirrel Hill, the community where Schulte and his wife resided. After giving a copy of the devastating info to the minister of the church Schulte attended, he would be visiting a number of local charities the mayor was involved with. By late afternoon, he'd be on a flight to St. Louis.

Pastor Richard Martin of the Ames United Methodist Church nodded at the church secretary when he entered the reception office. "Good morning, Susan. Looks like we're going to get some snow today."

Smiling, the woman responded, "This is my first winter here in Pittsburgh. Growing up in California, snow was only something we heard of or saw on the weather channel." Nodding toward the window, she pointed out, "They say we might get five inches today. I can't wait. I told my husband and two children maybe later on tonight we might build a snowman in our front yard."

Walking over to the window, Martin looked out at the street. "I grew up down in Myrtle Beach, where, just like California, snow is rarely experienced, if ever. When I first moved to Pennsylvania, I remember my first year at the seminary. I really enjoyed the snow, but as the years went by I grew tired of the wonderful white flakes that eventually turn to a greyish-black slush." Motioning at the large flakes floating gently past the window, he admitted, "But still, you have to agree the snow can be quite beautiful." Hoisting his briefcase, he informed his secretary, "I'll be in my office working on Sunday's sermon."

Susan snapped her fingers. "That reminds me. A man dropped off a folder for you this morning. He said it was very important. I put it on your desk. I'll be leaving for lunch in about fifteen minutes. If you want me to pick you up something let me know."

Opening the door to his office, the pastor patted his large stomach. "I think I'll take a rain check. I could stand to miss a few meals these days."

Walking into his neat as a pin office he immediately spotted the manila folder centered on the desk. Taking off his overcoat, he hung it on a wooden clothes tree and sat in his comfortable, cushioned swivel chair. The folder in front of him simply read, *Pastor Richard Martin.* Normally, the preparation of his weekly sermon took priority over everything else, but because the folder was the only object on the desk, rather than pitching it into a things to do later basket on the top of his file cabinet, he flipped the folder over and opened it. Pulling the small stack of papers from inside, he stared at the first photograph, and then moved on to the second. Next, he scanned the football team photo and quickly recognized the name, Brad Schulte. According to the jersey numbers in the photographs and the team picture, his old friend and beloved parishioner was indeed one of the youths in the photos. He read the other boys' names; he had no clue who they were. Slowly, he read one of the newspaper articles and once again the name of Brad Schulte along with the other two mentioned boys came up; *persons of interest!*

Persons of interest to what, he thought? The students who had been murdered back in 1989 were an Abigail James and Chester Finch. He answered his own question while he read on and discovered Brad and his two companions had been questioned a number of times during an investigation into the murders. The last article explained the boys were never actually arrested or convicted. The case remained unsolved.

Getting up, he walked to the large window in his office and looked out at the falling snow, wondering if Brad knew about the information he had received. Turning, he looked back at the papers spread out on the desktop. *Why on earth would someone send me this type of information?* He considered that someone wanted him to know about what happened twenty-seven years ago. The last sheet of paper stated there was no statue of imitations on murder and then listed the three boys' names and ended with a chilling message, *I know what you did!* Who knew what these boys did…or what, at one time they were thought to have done? It had to be the man who delivered the folder to the church.

Walking back out to the reception desk, he was going to ask Susan about the man who dropped off the folder, but she had left for lunch. What was he supposed to do with the information? He had some thinking to do and he always did his best thinking in the sanctuary.

Walking across the carpeted hallway he opened the sanctuary door, the aroma of old wood penetrating his sense of smell. He seated himself in the cushioned first pew and looked at the large stained glass portrait of The Last Supper behind the altar. Normally, this time of day the sun shining through the multi-colored glass cast a combination of red, blue, green and purple over the altar, but the overcast snow-filled sky made the interior of the church seem gloomy.

It was obvious what the photographs, newspaper articles and the final note meant. Someone, possibly the man who delivered the folder to the church, was trying to expose Brad Schulte and his two friends as the murderers of the James girl and this Chester Finch. One of the articles read that it had become a cold case. Richard figured that now, someone was trying to heat things up.

Brad and his wife, Arcadia, had been members of the church for eleven years. They were active in the church and extremely generous when it came to tithing. Brad and his wife had donated a large portion of the needed funds for construction of the new gym. He, as the minister, considered them more than just great parishioners; he considered them dear friends. Now that he had read the information what was he to do with it? The way he looked at it, he had three choices: place the information back in the folder, pitch it in his desk and forget about it, turn the folder over to the police or give the mayor a call. He felt it was only fair to contact his friend, Brad and get an explanation from him. Getting up, Richard went to the altar and kneeled on the padded kneeler for a few moments of prayer before he made the call.

Brad Schulte sat in his plush downtown Pittsburgh office and gazed out the window at the now intense snowfall. Firing up an expensive Havana cigar he thought about the call he had received earlier in the morning from John who was still down in Beaufort with Robert. He wasn't keen on bringing in two other people in regard to Nick Falco and the Pickett woman, but if this Maria Sparks and her lawyer friend could get him closer to what Falco and Pickett were up to, he would wait for a couple of days while this lawyer worked things out. He hadn't asked what the lawyer's name was. He needed to call John and get that information. He didn't like dealing with people he didn't know anything about.

Just about to dial John's cell number, he was politely interrupted by his secretary who knocked on his door and peered into the office. "Mayor Schulte, I've got three pieces of mail that came for you early this morning. It looks like junk mail." Holding up the folder, she went on, "This was delivered by a man who said it was very important and to make sure you received it."

Brad smiled and gestured at a tray on his desk. "Pitch them in my incoming mail. I'll get to the mail later. Right now, I've got a couple of calls to make."

The secretary placed the folder along with two white envelopes in the tray and exited the office without another word. Dumping the ashes from the tip of the cigar into a Pittsburgh Pirates ashtray, Brad reached for his cell phone in order to call John when his desk intercom sounded with the secretary's voice, "Sir, you have a call on line one. It's Dickie Lee Peterson. Do you want me to put him through?"

Smiling, Brad answered, "Dickie Lee! Sure, put him through."

Pushing the blinking white light on the intercom system he picked up the receiver and spoke, "Dickie Lee, the only good Democrat in the city. How could I be so lucky to receive a call from my old friend today?"

The voice on the other end answered, "Brad…how have you been? We haven't talked since the last time we played golf at the country club. That was about two months back."

"I can only assume you're calling to cash in on the lunch you won by beating my tail off me on the links."

"No, this is business."

"You sound quite serious. Is there something wrong? Maybe I should ask how you are."

"I'm fine, but there does seem to be something wrong. I'm not sure. That's why I'm calling."

Sitting back in his chair, Brad blew a long stream of cigar smoke toward the ceiling. "Dickie, if there is a problem we need to discuss just spit it out."

"There is a problem and I'm asking you to keep an open mind. We've been close friends since our college days at Duquesne when we first met."

"That's right and despite the fact you chose to go the Democratic route, I chose the Republican forum, we have never, in all the years we've known each other allowed our political differences to interfere with our friendship. So, what's this all about?"

"What I am about to share with you, well, you didn't hear it from me. If word got out that I tipped you to certain information I could lose my job here at the Democratic Headquarters. In short, I have received some information that could prove to be devastating to your run for governor of the state."

Brad sat forward in his chair and asked, "What on God's green earth are you talking about?"

"Here it is," said Dickie. "I'm sitting down here at the office like I normally do every morning enjoying a cup of coffee when in walks this man. I could tell right off he wasn't from this part of the country by the way he was dressed when you consider our current weather. He wasn't wearing an overcoat, gloves, earmuffs…nothing that would combat a Pittsburgh winter. He strolls in the office wearing a sports coat, slacks and loafers. He was only here for maybe thirty seconds. He handed me a plain manila folder and told me the information inside should be considered very important in regard to Mayor Schulte running for governor. He told me to read everything inside the folder and then left before I could ask any questions."

Without skipping a beat, Dickie Lee went on to explain, "The folder was simply addressed to the Pittsburgh Democratic Headquarters with no return address. I opened the folder and found seven different documents, four of which were photographs, two crammed with newspaper articles and a final typewritten note. Before I could really get into the information in walks my boss…Mike Brown."

"I know Mike Brown well," said Brad. "He and I have never been what you'd call the best of friends. As a matter of fact, I think it's safe to say we're political enemies."

"I'm aware of the bitterness between you and Mike and I also know he would do anything to prevent you from becoming Pennsylvania's next governor. For the past few months and the upcoming months that will be his entire focus. He is adamant, to say the least, in retaining our current Democratic Governor. Anyway, he asks me what I'm reading and since I really wasn't sure what I was looking at, I said I had just opened the information. When he saw the first two photographs from the folder lying on the desk he pulls up a chair and starts to go through the material. It didn't take us long to figure out what the information was about. It was about you and two of your high school friends…football players I believe."

No longer relaxed, Brad stubbed out his cigar in the ashtray and asked, "What was pictured in these photos?"

"The photos clearly displayed you and your two friends standing over a girl that appears to be dead. I can only assume from the articles enclosed in the folder that the name of the girl was Abigail James. There are two different photos. The first shows the team numbers on the backs of the jerseys and the second photo shows the three of you turning to face the camera. It doesn't make much sense for someone to take this type of photograph. The third and fourth documents are a football team photo from the 1989 Beaufort High yearbook and a list of players and their team number that indicates you and your two friends, a Miles Gaston and a Tim Durham are clearly identified as the boys on the beach. The next two papers are newspaper articles that cover everything from when the murders were committed up through the investigation. The articles go on to state you and your two friends were considered persons of interest. That being said, another article says you were never arrested or convicted of the murders. You, Gaston and Durham graduated and went off to college and the case still remains unsolved after all these years. The most disturbing document is the last sheet of paper which is typewritten and states there is no statute of limitations on murder and someone knows what you, Gaston and Durham did. Needless to say, Mike, who has been looking for a way to discredit you in the eyes of the public, has not been able to dig up any dirt on your past life. His eyes lit up like a Christmas tree when he read and finally understood the meaning of the entire contents of the folder."

Brad got up, walked to the window and looked down at the busy street far below and asked, "The man who delivered this information...what did he look like?"

"Like I told you, I don't think he was from the area. He was close to six foot in height, and I guess one hundred and fifty pounds or so, neatly trimmed hair. There wasn't anything special about his appearance that would make him stand out except for the lack of what I call winter dress attire."

Brad quickly reviewed in his mind what Nick Falco had looked like and the man who delivered the folder to Dickie Lee didn't sound like the same person. Maybe it was Carson Pike, the man who had paid Miles a visit. The one thing he was sure of was the visits by the so-called authors had something to do with the information Dickie Lee received. "Can you get this information over to my office or can I meet you later this afternoon so I can see the contents of this folder?"

Dickie Lee's answer was not what Brad wanted to hear. "I'm afraid that will not be possible. When Mike discovered what the folder suggested, he decided to call Beaufort, South Carolina, the town where you grew up and went to high school. He talked with the Beaufort Police and they verified the information as true. That was all Mike needed to hear. He plans to use this stuff to muddy up the political waters for the governor's race. He stepped out for coffee not five minutes ago. He'll be back here at the office any minute. I don't even have the time to copy the info. Besides that, I can't afford for Mike to even think I'm leaking this information to you. I only called because I consider you a good friend. Look, I have to go! Mike's back. Remember, you didn't hear any of this from me!"

Brad sat back down in his chair, the lonely sound of the dial tone buzzing in his ear. Hanging up the phone, he reached for his cell. He had to get in touch with John. He needed to find out the name of Maria Spark's lawyer. He had to find out what was going on and squash it before it got out of hand. The phone on his desk blinked again and the secretary voice sounded, "Mayor, you have another call on line two. The caller says he's a Richard Martin."

"I'll take the call," said Brad as he pushed the flashing button. "Pastor Martin, how are you?"

"Fine Brad, just fine. Do you have a few moments to speak with me about something?"

"Of course. Actually, I've been having a rather rough morning." Joking, he went on, "I can only hope what you want to discuss has nothing to do with politics."

"This is probably going to sound crazy, but I'm not sure what this is all about. My church secretary placed a folder on my desk delivered by some strange man this morning. My name was written on the front. I just, a half hour ago, finished reading what was in this folder."

Brad got a sinking feeling in his stomach as he responded, "Let me guess. There were two photographs of myself and two other young men on a beach with what appears to be a girl who is dead. There is also a team photograph from a 1989 high school yearbook and some newspaper articles about two Beaufort High School students who were murdered on Fripp Island, which is south of Beaufort. The articles mention that I and the other two boys were persons of interest, but we had not been arrested or convicted. There is also an attached typewritten note stating something about the statute of limitations on murder and how someone knows what we had done. I know all about this mysterious folder. I just got off the phone with a close political friend of mine who works for the Democratic Party here in Pittsburgh. He also received one of these folders. It contained the same exact information as the folder you have. Am I right?"

Surprised, Pastor Martin answered, "It sounds to me like the folder your friend received is identical to the one on my desk. What's going on Brad? Are these photographs authentic? Did you have anything to do with these mentioned murders?"

"Come on, Richard! Do you really think I'm the type of person who could kill someone? You know me better than that. You know me better than most of the people I associate with. You married Arcadia and I right there at the church. My daughters were baptized at the church. I certainly hope you don't believe any of this nonsense!"

"I don't want to believe what I've read, but I do feel I deserve an explanation."

"It's simple," pointed out Brad. "This is nothing more than a political ploy meant to disrupt my upcoming run for governor. Be glad you chose a career in the field of religion rather than politics. This folder is what we refer to as political mudslinging."

There was a moment of silence, then the pastor asked, "Then none of this *mudslinging* as you put it, is true?"

Brad hesitated, then answered, "Martin, let me explain how political mudslinging works. Politicians, or those who work for them, at times, come across information that may or may not be true. This information can make or break a political career. If the information is true it can be twisted around to sound untrue and if it is not actually true it can be reworded to sound like the truth. It's a very vicious way to conduct business, but nonetheless is widely accepted in political circles as part of the game. In order to be a politician one must have thick skin. In the case of the information you received in that folder, the information is true, but someone is using it to defame me as the next governor of the state."

Martin, trying his best to understand came back with another question, "Look, I understand people can be dishonest, especially if a twisting of the truth will benefit them or their cause. You state the information in the folder is true. I find this quite disturbing. Whoever is behind sending out this information, I feel is indicating you and your two high school friends were actually involved in the murders of those two students. I mean, how can you possibly explain away the two photos of you and your companions standing on the beach next to a girl who appears to be dead? When you consider all the information included along with the photographs, a very strong message is being sent."

"I realize that," said Brad. "The only reason my two friends and I were even considered persons of interest was because we were the last to see that girl alive. We were questioned along with everyone else who attended the party that night." Lying, Brad continued, "We just happened to come across her body after she was killed."

Interjecting, Martin emphasized, "But that doesn't make any sense. Who took those horrible photographs and how can you explain what appears to be blood on the piece of wood one of your friends is holding? This appears to be incriminating. I don't see how you're going to be able to explain any of this."

"I can explain it all, but right now I don't have the time. You're just going to have to trust me. Have you ever known me to be dishonest, in any way?" Not waiting for a response, from Martin, Brad decided to end the call. "I promise you I will get together with you later this week and clear this up. But for now I need you to do me a favor. Place all the information back inside the folder and put it away somewhere. If you share this information with anyone without knowing the entire story you'll be reacting exactly the way those who sent this information desire. This is the very thing we must prevent. Listen…I have to run. We'll talk later."

Hanging up the phone, Brad walked back to his desk when he noticed the manila folder on the top of his in-box. The front of the folder read, Mayor Brad Schulte. *It can't be!* He thought. *It just can't be!* Opening the folder his thoughts of *It can't be,* suddenly became *It can be!* As he shuffled though the seven documents, he sank down in his chair. Looking at the first two photographs he swore. "Damn it all to hell! This is really pissing me off!" He had to get out of the office and go somewhere so he could think without being interrupted. He jammed the papers back inside the folder and tucked it inside his briefcase. Aside from trying to figure his way out of what was rapidly becoming a hurdle that was going to be difficult to jump, he needed a stiff drink, maybe two or three. Walking out to the reception room he addressed his secretary, "I'm going to be out of the office for a couple of hours and will not be able to be contacted unless it's an absolute emergency."

Dale Sessions walked in the front door of the Westside Apartments main office and waved at his sister. "Hey Thel! What's this mysterious folder you want me to take a look at?"

Thelma, looking in a file cabinet motioned at Gina. "Gina, this is my brother, the detective I told you about. Give him the folder. I'll be right with you two."

Tossing the folder on a circular table, Gina offered, "Coffee?"

Dale, taking a seat responded, "Coffee does sound good. I take mine with cream and a small pinch of sugar."

Joining them at the table, Thelma pointed at the folder and explained, "Gina and I have been sitting here for the past two hours trying our best to figure out what the information in there means. We think we may have it figured out but what we have come up with is just too unbelievable. It's about our boss, Miles Gaston, who owns the complex. We don't know whether to forget about what we read or take it down to Gaston's headquarters and give it to him. We also considered giving it to the police and that's why I decided to give you a call and have you look things over."

Opening the folder, Dale looked at the first photo and gave both women an odd stare. Looking at the second photo, he asked, "Is the girl in the photos dead?"

Thelma sipped at her coffee. "This we do not know. She sure appears dead!" Placing her finger on the first photograph, she added, "That boy on the end…number 17…that's our boss, Miles Gaston. So, what do you think?"

"I don't think anything yet. I haven't gone through all the information. In my business it's important to collect all the information available before one jumps to a conclusion. Give me a few minutes to look everything over."

Two blocks down form the Allegheny Building, Brad, braving the downtown gusty wind stepped inside Winston's Bar and Grill, an upscale drinking establishment. He had only been to the tavern once before and that was when he had been in college. The interior was on the dark side with a row of booths running next to the large front windows. There was a polished bar with padded barstools and a few tables in the back, a lit candle centered on each table and booth. *Cozy,* he thought as he sat at a corner booth. Placing his briefcase on the seat next to him, he waited patiently for the waitress who slowly approached, order pad in hand. The woman was older and despite the fact she was dressed in a tuxedo affair, she looked like she'd been around the block a few times. In a somewhat friendly voice, she politely asked, "What can I get for you today, sir?"

Brad answered instantly, "Scotch…straight up. I'd also like to run a tab. I might be here for some time."

The waitress backed away and replied, "Very good, sir."

If the woman recognized him as the city's current mayor she certainly didn't let on. Brad found it hard to believe she didn't know who he was. It was just as well. He really didn't want any special attention at the moment. He wanted to sit, have a couple of drinks and review the information the folder held. Waiting for his drink he decided not to open the folder until after the drink arrived. Looking around the establishment he noticed three businessmen seated at the bar and two people at one of the tables.

The information in the folder could not have come at a worse time. The infiltration of the information into his very life was disturbing. He was confident he was going to be able to sidestep this attempt at slurring his life, but first he had to get his head around who was behind the assault. It was too ironic Nick Falco and Shelby Lee Pickett had paid him a visit a few days prior to the folders hitting Pittsburgh. He needed later on in the day to call Miles and Tim and see if they too had received folders. Falco, Pickett, Pike and Brumly were up to something. He wondered if anyone else was involved. Did these people know who they were dealing with? He was a powerful man with a ton of money and connections. His concentration was interrupted when the waitress returned with his drink and informed him she'd check on him in ten minutes.

Taking a long gulp of his drink, Brad removed the first photo from the folder. There was no doubt about what it revealed. He, Tim and Miles standing over the body of Abigail James. For the first few years following that horrid night on Fripp Brad thought he would never get over what had happened; what he and his two close friends had done. But, with time, he had put the events of that night behind him and had moved on with his life. He often thought about how he had dodged the bullet of being implicated in the murders of Abigail and Chester; about how his life had turned out just fine. Better than fine. He had a wonderful wife who was a United States Senator, two beautiful daughters who were now in college, a massive home, plenty of money and a great political future in front of him. He was going to be the next Governor of Pennsylvania. The photo laying on the table in front of him brought back all the bad memories of that night twenty-seven years ago. Suddenly, he remembered the look on Miles' face as Abigail lay there in the sand, dead! He recalled the blood on her face and how he just couldn't believe what happened. The worse part was when he made the decision Chester had to be killed as well. Looking back, he wondered what would have happened if they had told the truth. There was no wondering about it. He, Tim and Miles would have spent the last twenty some years behind bars.

He was just about to look at the second photo when he was interrupted, "Excuse me…Mayor Schulte!"

Looking up from the photograph, Brad instinctively covered the two photos with the folder. The man standing next to the table was dressed in an older trench coat and a derby hat. In his hand he held a worn briefcase. Not recognizing the man, Brad answered, "Yes."

The man stuck out his right hand while introducing himself, "Name's Horace Franks, reporter for the Pittsburgh Gazette. We met briefly last summer when you spoke at the Rotary Club." Gesturing toward the bar, Horace added, "It's surprising the best coffee in town can be purchased at a local tavern. I don't believe I've ever seen you in here before. I'm in here nearly every day to get my daily dose of caffeine."

Returning a strong handshake, Brad commented, "I've only been in here once and that was a long time ago." Picking up his Scotch, he took a swallow and held up the glass. "I decided I needed a drink and I'm not talking about caffeine."

Horace, acting like a typical reporter, took a seat on the opposite side of the table without being invited and kept right on talking, "I hope I'm not interrupting you in any way, but running into you is ironic. I was on my way uptown to your office to see if I could get in to see you."

Finishing off the reminder of his drink, Brad responded, "I guess my timely visit here has saved you a trip then. So what would a reporter from the Gazette want to see me about?"

"My editor, Gil Farmer suggested I pay you a short visit. I believe you know Gil quite well."

"That I do. Gil and the Gazette have always supported the Republican Party here in Pittsburgh."

"That's correct, and he and the paper support you in your run for the governorship and that is precisely why I was coming to seek you out. I received a folder mailed from Savannah, Georgia earlier this morning." Placing the briefcase on the table, he flipped it open and removed a folder identical to the one in Brad's possession while he kept talking, "I get a lot of junk mail…every day. It's never ending. You wouldn't believe all the crap mailed to the paper. Normally, I scan through this crap and wind up tossing it in the trash." Tapping the edge of the folder with his index finger he went on to explain, "This folder was mixed in with my daily pile of incoming garbage, but when I opened it I found the contents to be anything but junk. It was quite interesting."

Brad reached across the table, took the folder from Horace's hand, and compared the handwriting on the folder he had received. "Look at this," said Brad. "The writing on the front of both these folders is identical. I too received one of these folders along with the church I attend, and the Democratic Headquarters here in Pittsburgh." Picking up the two photos, he slid them across the table. "I can guarantee you these two photos are included with other various documents that are in the folder you received. The information suggests quite strongly that I and two of my classmates were somehow involved in the murders of two students twenty-seven years ago. Correct?"

The conversation was interrupted when the waitress approached and spoke to the reporter, "Good morning, Horace…coffee as usual?"

Turning the photos facedown, Horace replied, "Yes please, and if you would be so kind bring whatever the honorable mayor is drinking."

After the waitress walked away from their table, Horace opened his folder and compared both sets of photos. "Spot on! I've got to tell you, mayor. I had intentions of bringing something you were not aware of to your attention, but you have gone and burst my bubble."

"Bursting your bubble is the least of my problems. Someone has decided to dig up some dirt on me and they're well on their way to succeeding. I have an idea who these people are. Some of my people, at this very moment, are down in Beaufort, South Carolina snooping around. They've contacted a lawyer down there and I think soon we'll be able to put a lid on this nasty business."

"Speaking of Beaufort," said Horace. "Gil is about as honest as the day is long. As editor of the Gazette he will not allow anything, good or bad, to be printed unless he verifies it as the actual truth. He took the liberty of calling the Beaufort Police Department. Turns out, they verified the folder information as the truth. They also received a folder. They did emphasize you and the other two boys were never bona fide suspects and the case was never solved and to this day remains a cold case. What I'm trying to tell you mayor is Gil intends on running an article on the information in tomorrow's Gazette. It's our obligation as the major paper in town to inform the public about the latest news. That being said…the information in the folder is news! You, the Mayor of Pittsburgh, are news. Being the mayor of the city places you in the limelight, elevates you on a pedestal. I'm sure you are aware of the fact wherever you go and whatever you do will always be scrutinized. I am going to suggest to Gil, that along with printing the article we also mention we interviewed you and you stated there were two students killed your senior year in high school, but you had nothing whatsoever to do with the murders. We'll try and sugarcoat this as much as possible. You're well liked here in Pittsburgh. I'm sure this will pass and then you can move on to the governor's mansion after the upcoming election."

The waitress returned with Horace's coffee and Brad's drink. Horace picked up the folder and placed it back inside his briefcase, and remarked, "I've got to get back to the office. It was nice to see you again, mayor." Gesturing at the waitress, he requested, "I'll need this coffee to go."

Brad waited a few minutes after the reporter left the tavern before he took the last swallow of his drink. The folder back in his briefcase, he laid a twenty on the table, got up and left the bar.

Outside, it was a typical week before Christmas in downtown Pittsburgh. Making his way slowly up the street he noticed a Salvation Army volunteer standing on the corner ringing his bell and wishing people a Merry Christmas. Dropping a ten-dollar bill into the suspended bright red bucket, Brad smiled at the man and moved on up the street, his next destination a walk down by the river in the crisp winter air. He needed to clear his head, get his hands around what was happening. Stopping at an intersection, he decided to call his office and explain to his secretary he was taking the rest of the day off, when his cell phone buzzed. Digging it out of his coat pocket, he answered, "Hello."

The familiar voice of his oldest daughter on the other end responded, "Daddy, it's Mercedes."

Looking at his watch, Brad made a strange face. "Is there something wrong, honey? Shouldn't you be in class?"

"I'm in between classes right now. I'm considering grabbing sis and heading home to meet with you and Mom."

"Why, is there some sort of problem at school?"

"Yes, there is a problem, but it has nothing to do with school. Olivia and I both received some very disturbing mail about you and we are very concerned."

Crossing the street, Brad took a wild stab, "Let me guess. Both of you received folders containing pictures of myself and two of my high school buddies standing over a girl by the name of Abigail James. The girl in the photos is dead…am I right?"

"Yes, but how did you know we received these horrible folders?"

"I know because I received one along with a lot of other people here in Pittsburgh. This information could make things difficult for me…especially since I'm running for governor. Did you read everything in the folders?"

"Yes, Olivia and I read every word….a number of times. We just can't believe any of this?"

"Look, I have never lied to you or your sister. In regard to the folders there were indeed two students who were killed. I can assure you I had nothing to do with their deaths. This is nothing more than a ploy by some very nasty and detestable folks to dethrone me as the next governor of the state. Here's what I want you and Olivia to do. Place the folders somewhere where they will not be discovered by anyone until I can get this matter cleared up. There is no reason for either of you to come home. I have not talked with your mother about any of this yet. I will be discussing these folders with her this evening. I'm sure after talking with her, she'll give you and your sister a call. Don't worry about any of this. We've talked about politics and both you and your sister know how vicious things can get at times. Hide the folders and forget about this crap, because that's all it is…crap!"

Detective Sessions gathered all seven documents and photos together, tapped them on the table and then placed them back inside the folder. Thelma stared at Gina and then turned to her brother. "Well what do you think, Dale? Is there anything to this information?"

"After going over everything it's evident that someone wants whoever reads this stuff to think somehow Miles Gaston and the two other boys pictured had something to do with the murders of Abigail James and Chester Finch. When you look at the entire package it seems pretty convincing. Let me do this. I'm going to give the Beaufort Police a call and see if I can get this information verified. Let's wait and see what they say before we decide on what we want to do."

Brad wiped the snow off a park bench next to the river, sat and stared at the large sections of ice flowing slowly passed the city. For twenty-seven years he had managed to keep the horrible night on Fripp Island away from his life. But now, he was being slammed from every angle. Someone had done their homework. But who? Nick Falco, Shelby Lee Pickett. He was sure they were somehow connected. He had to keep his cool. First, he needed to call his wife before she found out what was happening. He wanted the information to come from him, not by means of one of the folders or by word of mouth. He was going to have to lie to his wife. He had already been untruthful with his pastor and his two daughters, not to mention his good friend, Dickie Lee. Gazing across the river he decided to give John a call down in Beaufort and find out what this lawyer they had met had figured out, if anything. He also needed to give Tim and Miles a call to see if they had received folders to see if this attack was leveled at just him. Lowering his head in dismay he recalled something his father had told him when he was a small boy growing up back in Beaufort. *Make intelligent decisions during your life because you have to answer for everything you do...good or bad. You will always be rewarded for the good things you accomplish in life. The bad things you initiate or create will eventually bite you right on your backside.* A tear came to Brad's eye and he realized more than ever before just how true his father's wisdom was.

CHAPTER TWENTY EIGHT

CONNER WAS JUST PUTTING THE FINAL TOUCHES ON A twelve-foot Christmas tree in the library when the phone rang. Laying down a package of ornament hooks he picked up the receiver and spoke, "James residence…who may I ask is calling?"

Melvin, seated at a table in the restaurant of the downtown St. Louis Hilton, sipped his coffee and then answered, "It's Melvin Barrett, Conner. Is Bernard available? I'd like to give him an update on our progress."

"He is available. Just a second please." Holding up the phone, he addressed his employer. "Mr. James, we have Melvin Barrett on the phone with a current update."

Bernard smiled and moved his wheelchair across the room. Phone in hand, he spoke, "Melvin, I'm so glad you called this morning. Conner and I were just wondering how things are going. So, exactly where are we?"

"Chic got into St. Louis yesterday, mid-afternoon and checked in at the hotel. Carson was late getting here. He had a flight delay of two hours. Nick and I had dinner with them last evening. We are just finishing breakfast before we hit the road to make the remainder of the deliveries. Our plan is to rent three more vehicles so we can knock out the rest of the churches today. We should return to Beaufort tomorrow sometime. Chic and Carson made all the deliveries in Pittsburgh and Atlanta. Nick and I knocked out twenty-seven churches yesterday and despite the fact we have not contacted all the churches on our list here in St. Louis, the results of the deliveries we have made are starting to pay off. I have been in contact with my friend on the Beaufort Police. He told me the phone calls are starting to come in hot and heavy with inquiries. So far they have received two calls from Pittsburgh. The Democratic Party Headquarters and the Pittsburgh Post-Gazette. They also received calls from the Atlanta Journal - Constitution and the St. Louis Post Dispatch. We also got calls from the Denver Post and the Austin Chronicle, two cities where Miles Gaston has restaurants. We got one call from a church in St. Louis and that was just after the first day. By tomorrow, more calls will no doubt come in. My friend on the Beaufort Police said he is going to the chief this morning with the folder.

He feels very strongly with this new evidence and the commotion it has caused around the country that Schulte, Durham and Gaston will be brought in for questioning. The cold case of the deaths of your daughter and Chester Finch are heating up. That's about all we have for now. We'll call you when we have a better idea when we will arrive back in Beaufort. Is there anything else…Bernard?"

"No, I don't think there is anything else we need to do aside from getting the rest of the folders delivered. Now, all we need to do is sit back and let justice take its course. When you return we'll have a meeting at my house to discuss further action. Thank you for the call."

Nick was just returning to their table when Melvin laid his cell down. Finishing his coffee, he asked, "Is everything with Shelby all right?"

"Yeah, everything is fine with her." Looking around the table Nick gestured, "If everyone is done eating what say we pick up those three rentals so we can finish up here in St. Louis."

Getting up from the table, Chic's phone buzzed. Picking it up, he spoke to the others. "Bet ya I can tell you who that is!"

Grabbing the phone, he answered, "Chic Brumly."

Maria's caustic voice sounded on the other end of the connection, "Chic…where are we on figuring out what we're going to do about Falco and the girl? John and Robert are getting a bit antsy!"

"I told you I needed two days. I'm out of town right now for another client. I should be back in town tomorrow. Tell Schulte's men I've had a lot of time to think this out. I've got a few ideas I will discuss with you when I return. Just tell Schulte's men to hold on. They can assure their boss I'm all over the situation. I'll call you when I get back and then we'll meet." Not giving Maria an opportunity to talk any further, he said good-bye and turned off the phone. Slipping on his jacket he addressed his three companions, "The Sparks woman and Schulte's two goons are yet another problem we're going to have to deal with when we get back but we'll cross that bridge when we come to it. I have no doubt I can handle Maria but as far as Schulte's men are concerned we may need the assistance of some of Conner's skills. John Lord and Robert Peeler strike me as quite loyal to Brad Schulte and seem like the type of men who will stop at nothing to prevent Schulte from being brought down. We're going to have to handle them with kid gloves. For now, let's go give some St. Louis Catholics the bad news about their archbishop." On the way out of the restaurant, Chic hesitated and informed the others, "I have to use the restroom. Give me a couple of minutes and I'll meet you at the car in the lot."

Brad Schulte added a shot of whiskey to his morning coffee. Standing at a large plate glass window he looked down at the Mississippi River flowing past downtown St. Louis. Sitting in a luxurious chair positioned next to the large window, he reviewed the past twenty-four hours and the decisions he had made. After leaving the park in Pittsburgh he had gone home, contacted his wife and explained to her about the devastating folders. He assured her he was in the process of getting to the bottom of who was responsible for flooding his life with accusations he was somehow involved in the murder of two of his high school friends in the past. He told her to contact their two daughters as they too had received the horrid folders. Brad also informed his wife he was flying to St. Louis to meet with two of his closest friends who had also suffered at the hands of someone who wanted to destroy their lives with the so-called information. After calling Miles and Tim he made arrangements for them to meet in a private suite at the top of the Hilton in St. Louis where they could discuss how they were going to handle the current situation. Looking at his watch, he noted the time at 7:50 in the morning. Miles and Tim were to meet with him at eight o'clock. They should be arriving any minute.

A knock on the door was followed by the entrance of his close friend, Miles. Miles closed the door and looked around the suite. "First class, all the way…I like it."

Getting up, Brad crossed the room covered with deep, plush beige carpet and extended his right hand in welcome. "Miles, it's good to see you. I wish it could be under more pleasant circumstances." Motioning at a stainless steel cart, Brad offered, "We have three kinds of Danish and some assorted fruit, coffee and ice water. Please…help yourself."

"No thank you, I had breakfast at the airport earlier." Holding up a briefcase, he stated in disgust, "I brought one of the folders with me that was distributed around Atlanta."

"We'll discuss all that when Tim arrives," said Brad. "He should be here soon."

"Actually, I ran into Tim downstairs in the lobby. He had to use the restroom, saying he couldn't wait until he got up here. He told me he'd be right along. Is that a bottle of whiskey I see sitting over there?"

Holding up his cup, Brad remarked, "Gives a whole new meaning to morning coffee."

Walking to the table, Miles smiled, "Considering our reason for today's meeting, alcohol infused coffee does sound good. By the way, how long do you think we'll be here?"

"That depends on how serious this turns out to be. At first, I thought these folders were aimed exclusively at me, but it turns out it involves all three of us. We need to figure out what we're going to do and that could take some time. I've already ordered a lunch buffet sent up later around noon."

Pouring a small portion of whiskey into a mug, Miles added coffee, took a sip and then added, "Alcohol always seems to make things better."

Holding his cup up in a toasting fashion, Brad commented jokingly. "You've come a long way since that time you, Tim and I parked at the downtown marina in Beaufort and shared a bottle of my father's bourbon. I remember your reaction to how you coughed and gagged and said you couldn't believe people drank."

"I recall that day. I got tanked *and well,* we know what happened later that evening. Abby lost her life. After her death I swore I'd never drink again, but after a few years I changed my tune and I do find myself taking a nip here and there. I've never allowed myself to get drunk. I guess that would bring back to many horrible memories of what happened on the beach that night so long ago. I've never really gotten over what we did. I guess I've just tried to move on and forget about it. It hasn't been easy all these years to live with what happened and now the events of that night out on Fripp have raised their ugly head and are once again a part of our lives."

Walking to the window and looking down at the river, Brad spoke back over his shoulder. "That's why we're here today. I'm confident if the three of us put our heads together we can figure a way out of this mess."

Chic walked across the brightly polished tile floor of the Hilton's men's room and stopped at a long row of impeccably clean sinks imbedded in marble and topped with stainless steel state of the art faucets. Splashing hot water on his hands he then reached for a shot of hand soap and began to rub his hands together. Chic was extremely germ conscious when it came to public restrooms. Rinsing his hands he noticed out of the corner of his eye a man dressed completely in black who stepped up to one of the porcelain urinals. Applying a second glob of soap on his hand Chic repeated the hand washing process. Satisfied his hands were now free of any germs, he placed them beneath a wall mounted blower and rubbed his wet palms together. His hands partially dry, he reached for a paper towel, dried his hands again, pitched the towel in a disposal area cut out of the marble, then turned to leave and ran directly into the man in black. Raising his eyes to the man's face, Chic began to apologize, but then hesitated, finding himself face to face with Tim Durham. The archbishop stared back at Chic in utter amazement, his face quickly turning from one of friendliness to one of confusion. Durham spoke with reservation, "Chic...Chic Brumly!"

Chic, normally quick to adapt to awkward or embarrassing moments, stumbled for the correct response, "Ah…I'm sorry, but you seem…to have…me confused with…someone else." Stepping around the archbishop, Chic continued with his feeble attempt to escape the moment, "Have a good day, sir."

Tim turned and watched Chic make his way to the exit. Following Chic out of the men's room he called to him, "Brumly…hold on there. I need to ask you some questions."

Acting as if he hadn't heard the archbishop's request, Chic continued across the lobby for the main exit doors. Durham was not about to be put off. He crossed the lobby and exited the doors a few yards behind Chic and called out, "Brumly…wait, I need to talk with you."

Chic had no desire to speak with the archbishop. It would not be comfortable like before when they had met at the church. Chic couldn't be sure what Durham wanted to speak to him about, but if it had anything to do with the folders it would be too awkward. It would be best to avoid the conversation. Picking up the pace, Chic considered running, but to where? Nick and the others would be waiting at the rental car. By the time he climbed in Durham would catch up. *The hell with it!* Thought Chic. *When I get around the corner I'll take off running and lose him in the parked cars.*

Chic's plan was blown out of the water when Nick pulled up and stuck his head out the driver's side window, gesturing, "We decided to pick you up."

Chic, realizing it was too late to make good his escape turned, ready to face Archbishop Durham. Tim, who had been running stopped just short of the car. "Mr. Brumly, I need a word with you. When we ran into one another back there in the restroom why did you blow me off?" Before Chic could think of an answer, Durham went on, "This has something to do with the information being unleashed here in St. Louis. I recall when you first interviewed me we discussed the murders of two students when I was a senior back in high school. I thought it was odd you would mention something like that. It seemed so out of line with what we had been discussing during the interview."

Chic found himself at a loss for the correct response. "I'm afraid I don't know what you're talking about. Like I said before, you must have me confused with someone else. I'm sorry, but I've got an appointment I cannot afford to miss. Good day to you, sir." Opening the rear door he climbed in the car and suggested to Nick. "C'mon, let's go!"

Nick, who at the moment was shocked Archbishop Tim Durham was standing not two feet away, was slow to react when Chic ordered again, "C'mon…let's go!"

Durham leaned down and looked directly into Nick's eyes and then across the seat at Melvin as Nick pulled out of the lot. Carson looked out the rear window at the archbishop who was watching the car pull away. "Was that really the archbishop…one of the men we're after?"

Chic slammed his fist down on the vinyl seat. "Damn it all! Of all the people to run into."

Carson turned in the seat and addressed Chic, "What the hell is the Archbishop of St. Louis doing at the Hilton? Do you really think he noticed you?"

"Of course, he recognized me. You heard what he said about our interview."

Nick chimed in, "And that's not the worst of it. Did you see the way he looked in the car at me? He now knows what we look like. Remember, I gave Durham his own package at the church. It won't take him long to put two and two together. Hell, for all we know some of the churches we contacted with the folders may have given Durham our descriptions. This changes things here in St. Louis. I think we should give Bernard a call and see what he wants to do. He may want to change things up."

"Look, let's not panic," said Melvin. "Pull the car over and let's discuss this. I think we need to go back and find out why Durham is at the Hilton. It's a strange place for an archbishop to hang out."

Nick pulled the car over at the first street after they left the lot while Melvin kept right on talking, "Before we call Bernard we need to make sure we have all the information available. For all we know he might be meeting Schulte and Gaston back there at the Hilton. If that's not the case, we haven't lost anything, but I think it's worth checking out. Drop me off back at Hilton's parking lot and I'll go in and see what I can find out."

Nick objected, "What could you possibly find out?"

Melvin smiled. "You'd be surprised. Remember, I was a detective for over thirty years. I've got a nose for this sort of thing."

Nick looked in the rearview mirror at Carson and asked, "What do you think?"

"It makes perfect sense to me," said Carson. "If it turns out to be nothing, then what have we lost? I say we let Melvin check things out and then we give Bernard a call."

Nick made a U-turn in the middle of the street. "Okay, what's our plan?"

"It's not complicated," remarked Melvin. "You just drop me off in front of the Hilton, drive back out here and park and then wait for my call. It's simple."

As Nick drove back onto the lot, Chic was beside himself. "I'm sorry I lost my cool with the archbishop but frankly I don't know what else I could have done."

"It's not your fault," said Carson. "How could we have possibly known the very man we're after here in St. Louis would show up at the Hilton…of all places!"

Stopping three rows out from the entrance, Nick waited while Melvin hopped out. "I'll call you in around ten minutes or so. And don't worry. If the archbishop is here for a particular reason I'll find out what it is."

Nick watched Melvin walk in between the rows of cars. "Well, today sure got off to a rough start." He pulled back out of the lot when Melvin entered the massive front doors of the Hilton.

Inside, Melvin got his bearings, then made his way across the lobby to a large check-in area where he saw three employees standing behind the long curved walnut desk. Approaching a young girl who he assumed would be the easiest to extract information from, he introduced himself and flipped open his wallet, then closed it quickly. "Excuse me young lady. You appear like someone who knows what's going on here at the Hilton. I'm Detective Melvin Barrett of the St. Louis Police. I noticed Archbishop Durham was here in the lobby a few minutes ago. Did you happen to see him?"

The girl looked confused and answered, "I have no idea who Archbishop Durham is. I'm afraid I can't help you."

A tall man standing just a few feet down the counter overheard the conversation and jumped in, "Yes, the archbishop was in the lobby a few minutes ago. I thought it was quite strange. First off, he came in and asked directions to room number 901, which is one of our luxury suites on the top floor. He said something about a meeting he had to attend. Then, he went to the restrooms after talking with another man in the lobby. A few minutes pass when out the restroom comes the archbishop yelling at some man who was heading for the front doors. It seemed so odd."

"Did the archbishop come back inside?"

"Yes, he did, a couple of minutes later, at which point he got on the elevator and I can only assume went up to the ninth floor for his meeting."

Melvin, acting concerned, leaned forward and spoke softly, "I don't suppose you can tell me who procured the suite to begin with…can you?"

"That's doable," said the man. He ran his long fingers over a computer keyboard. "Let's see…yes right here it is. The room was paid for by a Brad Schulte from Pittsburgh."

"Melvin smiled at the man and the girl and thanked them. "You have been quite helpful. Have a great day." Stepping off to the side of the lobby next to a large fountain he dialed Bernard's number.

Minutes later, he waited by the front door when Nick pulled up. Jumping in the back seat, he related Bernard's orders. "Bernard wants us to pack up and head back home."

"But why," said Chic. "We still have folders to deliver here in St. Louis."

"The way things appear to be standing right now Bernard feels it may not be necessary to distribute any more folders. The damage may have already been done when you consider Schulte is meeting with Durham right here at the Hilton. For all we know Miles Gaston may also be involved in the meeting. Bernard feels it's dangerous to be too close to them, especially when Schulte knows we're in town, which he will when Durham informs him he ran into none other than Chic and the rest of us. Bernard said for us to pack up and catch the next flight back to Charleston. He said we'd meet later tonight on Fripp. He thinks things are really starting to come together."

Following a knock, Miles opened the suite door, discovering Tim standing in the hallway. Miles held up his spiked coffee. "It's about time. What the hell took you so long?"

Tim stormed inside the vast room and pointed at Brad. "I hope to hell you've got some alcohol in this place."

Brad gave Miles an odd look, shrugged, walked over and picked up the bottle of whiskey. "You surprise me, Tim. I wouldn't have thought an archbishop would curse, let alone partake of the evils of alcohol."

Walking over and picking up a glass, Tim pulled himself a full measure and took a long swig, then looked directly at Brad. "The reason it took me so long to get up here is I ran into Chic Brumly, the so-called author who recently interviewed me. When I called him by name, he awkwardly told me I had him confused with someone else."

Miles took a seat on a long couch and commented, "Well, maybe you were mistaken. Maybe it wasn't him."

"No there was no mistake about it. It was most definitely Brumly. I could tell from the shoes he was wearing. They were the same off the wall, two tone grey and blue ones he wore when he interviewed me. Besides, I stood face to face with him. No, it was Brumly all right. I told him I needed to talk with him but he just walked out of the men's room through the lobby to the lot. I followed him and caught up to him just when a car pulled up. There were three men in the car. The driver is the same man who delivered the folder to me at the church. He had blond hair and was in his mid-thirties and the one in the passenger seat was on the thin side and wore glasses. I'm not sure of the third man in the back. He was quite muscular and had a crew cut."

Miles jumped in on the conversation as he swore, "Damn, that sounds like it could be Carson Pike, the man who interviewed me. He was muscular and had a crew cut."

Brad poured himself another coffee and shook his head in confidence. "This whole thing seems to be getting clearer by the moment. You say the driver had blond hair and was in his mid-thirties. That sounds like it might be Nick Falco, one of the two individuals who interviewed me."

Taking another drink, Tim explained, "Brumly referred to the driver of the car as Nick and yet this Nick character introduced himself to me as a Harold Webb when he gave me the folder."

"The only one who seems to be missing," said Brad, "is the Pickett girl. It's just too ironic three of the men in the car match the description of those who posed as authors. I think that was the beginning of a plan being set in motion."

Tim sat on a chair by the window and asked, "But the question is, who is actually pulling the strings. Who's the brains of this operation? It has to be someone who was around during the timeframe the murders happened. That just makes sense."

Walking across the room, Brad held up his finger and made a point. "When we were exonerated and never convicted there were a lot of people in Beaufort who were pissed to say the least, but there's one person who stood to lose the most and that's *Bernard James!* Remember what he said? He'd get even with us if it was the last thing he did."

"What about Chester Finch's grandmother," asked Tim? "If I recall she was just as unhappy with the way the police handled the investigation."

"No, it couldn't be her. She doesn't have the power and the money to pull something like this off. I'm not saying Bernard James is behind this but it's a possibility we should consider. Let's face it. The man hates us. He feels we killed his only daughter…and we did!"

"Now, just hold on," said Tim. "There's no we to this. Miles killed Abigail James. That was all his doing!"

Miles gave Tim a disgusting look. "After all these years and you still blame me for Abby's death. It never would have happened if you two wouldn't have convinced her to seduce me. We're all in this together and the fact twenty-seven years have passed nothing has changed."

Brad stood and walked between his two friends. "Look, there's no sense in arguing about what happened nearly three decades in the past. Miles is right. We, all three of us, are guilty. And let's not forget

Chester. We all played a part in his drowning. We all had our hands on him."

Still upset, Tim objected, stood and pointed at Brad. "Killing Chester was all your idea. I wanted to go to the police, but I was outvoted and forced to go along with killing Chester."

Brad, trying is best to remain calm took a step toward Tim and pointed out, "You went along with what we agreed on. We agreed it would be easier to make the entire situation go away rather than face possible prison for the rest of our lives. Now look! It's been twenty-seven years since that night. We managed to walk away from what we did just like I told you we would if you listened to me. You did listen to me and we got away with the deaths of Abby and Chester resulting in a cold case. We can't afford to argue amongst ourselves. We have to try and figure out what's going on and come up with a plan that will allow us, to once again, walk away from this. They couldn't convict us twenty-seven years ago because they had no witnesses, no motive and no murder weapon. Things haven't changed one bit. Whoever these people are, there is still no absolute proof we murdered Abby and Chester. They couldn't prove anything back then and if we remain as calm as we did before they will not be able to prove anything now either. Now, I say we calm down and get our heads together and come up with a way out of this. The clock is ticking and rather than arguing amongst ourselves, this time spent together would be better utilized coming up with a plan to combat the information being passed around."

Tim laid down his drink and calmed himself. "You're right, Brad. I guess with everything that seems to be happening all of a sudden and seeing those photos of us standing over Abby on the beach just brought everything back to me...I mean the way I felt that night. You're right. Let's see if we can figure this out. Where do we start?"

Brad took a deep breath of relief and reached for his briefcase. I think we should start with the contents of the folders." Taking the folder that had been mailed to his office, he dumped the contents onto a small table and asked Tim, "I noticed when you came in you had nothing with you. Did you not bring your folder along?"

Tim shrugged. "I had every intension of bringing the folder that was delivered to the church. My secretary actually opened the folder and took quite a few calls from other churches that had received them as well. She saw the contents of the folder before I had a chance to review what was inside. I informed her it was untrue I was involved in any murders and told her to put the folder in her desk until I could get to the bottom of the information. I left for the Hilton before she got in this morning. I searched her desk but could not locate the folder. She must have hid it well."

"It's not a big deal," said Brad. "Miles brought one of the folders from Atlanta with him."

Miles got up and placed his folder on the table, then sat back down and asked, "Just how wide spread do these folders reach. Every business I own in Atlanta received one as well as my trucking company on the west coast, not to mention every restaurant I own across the country. Whoever is responsible for this did their homework. They've covered all the bases when it comes to my life; the people I know, the folks who work for me."

"It's the same here in St. Louis," remarked Tim. "A number of churches have called my office wondering what's going on. Folders were also delivered to the Y where I swim, the various charities I'm involved with and the local newspaper gave our office a call. Looking back, now I can see how whoever is behind this got all the information they needed via those bogus interviews."

Brad picked up the empty folder and explained his situation. "In Pittsburgh, whoever is behind this has really done a job on me. Aside from having one delivered to my office, which no one other than myself has seen, copies have been mailed to my political adversaries at the Democratic Headquarters in Pittsburgh, the local newspaper who happens to be running an article this morning on the information they received, the church I attend, even my two daughters who are away at school. So far, I have had the luxury of blowing this off as a political move on my opponent's part to disrupt my run for governor. But, depending on how all this pans out I still might wind up being the most attractive horse in the glue factory. This thing can only get worse before it goes away and that's if it does. I was informed by two organizations in Pittsburgh that they contacted the police department down in Beaufort to verify the information. I feel it's just a matter of time before we are called in for questioning and that's why we are meeting today. We must prepare ourselves before this occurs. Just like before we have to stay one step ahead of the police. I would strongly suggest before we leave here today we have a plan in line we all agree on. Are we all in agreement on what we have to accomplish today?"

Miles answered, "Yes" while Tim nodded in silent approval.

"Good then," said Brad. He pinned the two photos taken on the beach up on a corkboard tripod. "These two photographs are the most incriminating documents in the folders. Ever since I received my folder and looked at the contents I've been racking my brain trying to figure out where these pictures came from."

"We know where they came from," remarked Tim. "Chester took

those pictures."

"That's right...he did," pointed out Brad, "but there's something missing. I remember the sequence of events of that night like it just happened yesterday. There were three camera flashes, which means there were three photos taken. We didn't turn and face Chester until after the second shot was taken. Why are there not three photographs?"

Miles suggested, "Perhaps one of the photos was bad, maybe it couldn't be developed or maybe it was out of line and didn't show us on the beach."

"That could be some of the possibilities," said Tim, "but the fact one is missing really doesn't take away from what the other two indicate. It appears we murdered Abigail James. The third photo is not necessary. The first two are enough to get us convicted."

"I agree," said Brad. "And here's something else. Where in the hell did the photos come from? We know Chester not only took the shots but he ran to his car to get away from us. We destroyed his camera and the film inside. During the investigation it came out Chester always had two cameras on his person. We only found the one, even after searching his car. So, my question is. Where did this camera come from and why did it take whoever developed the film to wait until now to expose the three of us?"

Tim got up, walked over and looked at the photographs and suggested, "Maybe Chester dumped the real camera before we caught up to him, and hence, we destroyed the wrong camera. Remember how scared he was when we questioned him."

Brad finished his coffee and remarked, "Okay, I can buy that theory. But that means someone later on found the camera, maybe down in the salt marsh or in the rocks next to the parking area. The question still remains why did they wait to develop the film? If the police would have discovered it they would have developed it immediately, plus if someone who lives on Fripp found it within a relatively short time after the murders they would have turned it over to the police. It doesn't make sense."

Miles joined them at the corkboard. "Maybe some tourist who didn't know anything about the murders found the camera months or even years later. Maybe they didn't know what they had. But still, it seems strange the photos are just now being brought to light."

Brad pinned the next two sections of paper onto the board. "We can sit here all day and speculate on who's behind this or where the photographs came from and still not be any further ahead of the game than where we are right now. What we need to be discussing is how we are going to talk our way out of this. I have an idea how that can be done, but first we need to go over the other documents that were in the folders."

Gesturing at the team football picture and page listing player names and team numbers, Brad explained, "It has to be someone who knew we were on the Beaufort football team. Otherwise how would they know to go to the school and take copies of these pages? Anyone who compares the photos with the team listing and photograph can easily tell we are the boys on the beach." Moving onto the two papers filled with newspaper articles, he further explained, "These articles tell the story of how the investigation went. The bad part of this is we are mentioned as persons of interest. That, combined with the photos of us on the beach, will raise some eyebrows. The final piece of paper, suggesting after naming the three of us, that they knew what we did means someone, somewhere is on to us. That person, whoever it may be, is pulling the strings. It could be one of the people who came to interview us or they may be working with someone else. These things seem important, but once again, we need to concentrate on what our story is going to be when we are questioned."

Miles seemed doubtful as he walked to the window and looked down over the city. "What type of story could we possibly come up with that would bail us out? Back twenty-seven years ago, we told the police the last time we saw Abby was when we dropped her off at the pool. One of the reasons we got off is because the police could not put us at the murder scene. The two photographs in the folder indicate we lied...we were in fact on the beach. The photos clearly show Abby is dead with the three of us standing over her. And let's not forget me standing there with that section of bloodstained two by four raised above my head. It appears that I just clubbed her to death. How on earth are we going to talk our way out of what seems obvious?"

"Simple!" exclaimed Brad. "We explain to the police we are actually victims ourselves."

Turning from the window in astonishment, Miles spoke in a tone of disbelief, "Victims...you've got to be kidding me! How are we going to prove something that farfetched?"

"Hear me out," said Brad. "Do you remember the center on our championship team...Rick Hemsly?"

Tim answered, "Yeah, but what's he have to do with any of this?"

"Don't forget, he was at the party with everyone who was on the team."

"So?"

"And let's not forget that ol' Abigail slept with every member of the team aside from the three of us. We are going to strongly suggest Ricky

Hemsly killed Abigail and Chester."

Miles walked back to the corkboard. "You've got to be out of your cotton-pickin' mind! Why would Ricky kill Abigail? For crying out loud, he was in love with the girl."

"And that is precisely why he killed her," said Brad. "He was one of the last boys to date Abby prior to her death. When we are questioned by the police we tell the same story we told them before, except for the part we left out because we didn't have a choice."

Tim looked at Miles and stated, "I don't know about you, but I'm lost!"

Brad walked to the middle of the room and held out his hands. "Let me paint the picture of what we are going to convince the police and everyone else of exactly what happened that night on Fripp."

Hesitating to gather his thoughts, be began, "The first part of our original story will not change. On our way to the party on Fripp we ran across Abigail who was having car troubles. We stopped to see if we could give her a hand and we couldn't get the car started so we agreed to run her out to the party. Now, here's where our story changes. We told the police that was the last time we saw her that night. But now, after all these years we've decided to reveal what really happened. While at the party we decided to take a walk down on the beach, which a lot of the kids were doing. We cut through John Fripp Condos and who do we see engaged in a three-way argument in the tree line on the opposite side of where the party was? Ricky Hemsly, Abigail James and Chester Finch. Taken by surprise we hid in the bushes and listened. The following is what we witnessed and heard."

Miles poured himself a cup of coffee and grabbed a Danish and comically remarked, "Come on, Brad, this doesn't even make sense!"

Brad smirked and gave Miles a sarcastic look. "Why don't you just wait until you've heard the entire story before you judge it…or me!"

"All right…go ahead. Tell us the rest of this unbelievable story. I'll not utter another word until you've finished."

Giving Tim a look that questioned if he should continue, Brad held out his hands.

Tim spoke softly, "Sure go on, finish your story."

"Like I said," pointed out Brad, "We accidentally came on the three while they were engaged in an argument of some sort. Ricky shoved Chester and called him a worthless, little pain in the ass nerd and tells him to get the hell out of there. Chester stands his ground and comes back with a statement about how he is now with Abby and that Ricky had his opportunity with her but blew it. Ricky then shoves Chester again and tries to explain to Chester that he loves Abby. Abby reaches over and slaps Ricky hard on his face and tells him he was a lousy lay anyway and he's the one that needs to leave. She is tired of hanging with athletic jocks and now prefers a man of intelligence. Ricky is now fuming. He gets right in Chester and Abby's faces and tells them he'll get even with both of them. At that point Ricky storms off across the lot and sees us behind the bushes before we could leave. With tears in his eyes he asked us how long we had been there. We told him we had just arrived and were heading for the beach. He gives us a look like he doesn't believe us and stomps off while Abby and Chester head for the beach…hand in hand." Looking at both Miles and Tim for approval of what he had said so far, he asked, "What do you think, so far?"

Both Tim and Miles remained silent which signaled Brad to continue. "Well, our new story about what happened gets even better. Later on. Let's say two hours later, we decide to drive up to the turnaround on Tarpon and go to a special beach we have been going to for years. When we get to the turnaround we see Chester and Ricky's cars parked there. We think it's odd but we park our car and walk along Skull Inlet, crawl over the rock wall and what are we confronted with? The dead bodies of Abigail James and Chester Finch. We were scared as hell. We didn't touch either body. We tried our best to figure out what happened, but quite frankly just wanted to get the hell out of there and report the murders to the police. We were just getting ready to leave when Miles here picks up the two by four and says let's go when, all of a sudden, someone behind us, up on the top of the rock wall took our photographs. We turned but couldn't see who it was. Now, we were really scared. We clamored up the wall and across the lot to our car where we discovered Ricky's car was no longer parked there. We started to put two and two together and figured since Ricky's car was gone maybe…just maybe he kept his promise about getting even and killed them both. We hashed it over and decided since someone took our pictures on the beach with the dead bodies that if they were turned in we'd be implicated. We decided to just go home without going to the police and see how things turned out."

Tim shook his head in approval and stated, "I think I see where you're going with this. Ricky, in a jealous rage followed Abby and Chester to the beach and kills both of them. It all makes sense the way you explain it, but I see a problem and that's Ricky Hemsly himself. He's going to have a completely different story. He'll say there never was a confrontation between he, Abby and Chester. It'll be his word against ours."

"Ah," said Brad, holding up a finger, "I've saved the best for last. Ol' Ricky isn't going to be able to refute anything we say because he died two weeks ago in an automobile accident out in California. He's the perfect patsy…the perfect scapegoat."

Miles couldn't believe what he had heard. "Ricky's dead?"

"As they come," said Brad. "It's perfect. All three; Abigail, Chester and now Ricky are dead. There is no one left to dispute our story about their confrontation the night of the murders. Ricky takes the fall and we walk."

"Wait a minute," said Miles. "There's something you have overlooked and that's the photos. Who took them and why are they spreading them around now, after all these years?"

"That's easily explained. We tell the police Ricky approached us a few days after the entire school was interviewed and shows us copies of these very pictures and says if we ever tell anyone, especially the police, about the argument he had with Abby and Chester or the fact his car was at the turnaround the night of the murders, he'll turn the photos over to the police as evidence that we, in fact, killed Abby and Chester. We then proceed to tell the authorities Ricky suggested we all just forget about what happened that night and move on with our lives…that we can all walk away from what happened. Looking at the pictures we knew we wouldn't stand a chance and more than likely we'd be implicated in the murders, so we just stuck to our story about the last time we saw her when we dropped her off at the pool. And, after all these years we always figured Ricky killed Abigail and Chester and we also knew if we ever accused him he'd produce the incriminating photos of us on the beach with Abby's dead body."

Addressing Tim, Brad asked, "So, what do you think?"

Tim walked over and placed his hands on Miles shoulders and answered the question, "At first, I thought your new version of what happened that night sounded crazy, but after hearing the complete story, I think it sounds believable. I mean when you think about it the main reason they couldn't pin anything on us twenty-seven years ago was due to the fact they had no motive, murder weapon or witnesses. This new story supplies them with all three and points the finger directly at Ricky Hemsly who is conveniently dead. The motive they never had now becomes evident: a crime of passion. Ricky, who happened to be in love with the promiscuous Abigail James, is jealous as hell because she dumps him and starts to date the nerd of the high school. When we explain to the police about the confrontation between the three of them and that Ricky said he'd get even with them. Well, he did get even. He killed both of them in a jealous rage. The murder weapon they never found, which was thought to be a section of two by four is pictured right there in the photos. The fact Miles is holding it up high can simply be explained away as a gesture for us to leave the beach. Ricky actually used the two by four to kill Abby. The witnesses they never had now become the three of us who not only witnessed the intense confrontation of the three but we saw Abby and Chester walk off together plus we heard everything that was said. We saw Ricky's car when we first arrived at the turnaround and when we got around to leaving, Chester's car was still there but Ricky's was gone. The only problem I see is the camera itself. That could wind up screwing up our new story. When the person who actually found the camera and developed the film finds out what we are claiming, depending on when they found the camera, they could poke a serious hole in our version of what happened. Maybe we should tone things down some and just say after we left Abby off by the pool, that later on we went to our special beach and found Abby and Chester already dead. Just when we were about to leave someone took our picture. We never found out who it was and we decided to protect ourselves and just let the whole thing go."

Miles brushed away Tim's hands on his shoulders. "I'll tell you what I think. I think both of you have lost your marbles. I don't believe the police are going to buy either of those stories. You both seem to think simply by throwing Ricky Hemsly into the mix and making things even more complicated than they already were back when the murders actually occurred, somehow that's going to get us off. There has to be another way out of this…a more simple straight forward way."

Brad took a deep breath and suggested, "Well we could get a good lawyer to represent the three of us. I know quite a few in Pittsburgh that owe me a favor or two. I feel any lawyer worth their salt could get us off. The photos in the folders only suggest we were on the beach, not that we killed Abby and Chester. They still to this day do not have a motive, murder weapon or any witness."

"Listen to yourself," snapped Miles. "First you say, Ricky Hemsly's make believe jealous rage is the motive and he killed Abby with the murder weapon that I, in fact used and then you state the three of us were witnesses to all of this. Now you're back to saying the police still have no motive, murder weapon or witness. We just can't make up some pie in the sky story and expect the police and everyone else to buy it."

Brad's cell phone buzzed. He held up his hand interrupting Miles, "I have to take this call. It's either my wife, my office or some men I have working for me down in Beaufort. Excuse me." Walking to the window, he spoke into the small black devise, "Good morning, this is Brad."

Tim and Miles waited when Brad got a strange look of disbelief on his face as he listened to the caller while making occasional statements during the conversation, "Really! Are you sure? This is not good.

You're meeting with them tomorrow? Here's what I want you to do. Go to this meeting and play along. The one advantage we have is that they do not know what we do. Keep me posted on what happens at the meeting. Maybe we can turn this around to our advantage."

The conversation over, Brad pocketed his phone and stared out the window for a few seconds before turning back to Miles and Tim."

Tim was the first to speak. "Bad news?"

Brad walked to the table and poured a glass of whiskey, took a swallow and then answered, "Most definitely. Gentlemen…we've been duped! That was John on the phone. He is one of two men I sent down to Beaufort to check out Falco and Pickett, the two so-called authors who interviewed me in Pittsburgh. My men in Beaufort hooked up with a woman who, as it turns out has an axe to grind with Falco and his girlfriend. She agreed to introduce them to a lawyer who she had been working with. The lawyer turns out to be none other than Chic Brumly, the man who staged himself as an author and interviewed you Tim right here in St. Louis; the same man you ran into earlier downstairs. Brumly, we know is on the opposing team, but this is a curve I didn't or couldn't have possibly expected. With this new turn of events if we are not careful, whoever is behind this folder business could be aware of our every move because of Brumly's association with my men. But, we could turn this around. We could have John feed Brumly false information which would give us the advantage."

Miles stood, and was clearly upset, "Whoa, whoa, whoa…listen to yourself! We are accomplishing nothing but going in circles. It's like we're standing at the bottom of a huge damn with a crack it in that's getting larger by the minute. The water is seeping out and getting more intense as the days pass. Now, it seems like the damn is going to break…and I feel soon. I do not want to be in the path of the deluge of water that is coming. I'm going to do something about this situation and that's just this. I'm going to fly back home, go to my home on Fripp, and think about all this. I'm leaning very strongly toward going to the police and telling them exactly what happened the night when Abby and Chester died. I think I'll have a better chance throwing myself on the mercy of the court. I think I can prove my killing of Abby was an accident…even self-defense. Everyone knew how loose Abby was and about her tainted life-style and reputation. I was clean as they come, a kid who had never been in any sort of trouble. Rather than making things worse by inventing a new set of lies, I'm going to tell the truth…something we should have done from the very beginning. You two can do what you please, but myself, well, I can't go on like this any longer. I need some sort of closure on what happened twenty-seven years ago. By not revealing the truth from the very beginning, we've only made things worse." Getting up, Miles started for the door. "I'm leaving. I'll have no part of this any longer."

Tim stood and grabbed Miles by the arm. "Do you realize what you're saying? You can't simply go to the police and turn yourself in. You'd not only be signing your own death warrant, but giving Brad and myself to them on a silver platter."

Brad intervened, "You've got to calm down, Miles. You're not thinking rationally. Tim is correct. You'd be taking the two of us down with you. I say we stand together and figure out what we're going to do. We can go with my plan of Ricky Hemsly or Tim's plan or we can just get a good lawyer, but to turn yourself in and tell the truth is not an option that makes any sense!"

"I'll tell you what doesn't make any sense," said Miles. "After all these years Tim and I are still listening to you. This is not 1989 and you're not the quarterback on the team any longer. I'm my own man and so is Tim. We've gotten along just fine for the past twenty-seven years without your guidance. Regardless of what new story you contrive here today will only make things worse than they are. I'm making my decision and I suggest you two do the same." Miles walked to the door and before opening it turned and spoke to his two friends. "You two are the best friends I have, but I have to do what's right." With that he opened the door and left, leaving Tim and Brad speechless.

Tim went to the table and poured a half-glass of whiskey, downed it in three swallows, took a deep breath and then spoke to Brad. "What in the hell are we going to do now? If Miles goes to the police...that's it, it's over! The story we told the police years ago would fall to pieces. We'll be implicated, the investigation will be reopened, we'll be found guilty of murder on two counts, convicted and sent to prison for the remainder of our lives."

Brad sat in an easy chair and placed his right hand on his forehead as if he were in deep thought.

Tim took another drink and remarked sarcastically, "Well, what's it going to be Mr. quarterback of the team, Mr. Mayor of Pittsburgh, Mr. future Governor of Pennsylvania? What say you now? How do we stop our best friend Miles from going to the police and ruining our present lives?"

Brad smiled at Tim and answered, "Miles is just upset...that's all. When he comes to his senses he'll realize what he is proposing is ridiculous."

"But how can we be sure. He sounded rather convinced to me he's going to follow through with going to the police."

"Here's what we're going to do. In the next half hour or so we're going to leave here. You are going to return to your office and continue with your archbishop duties. If questioned, and you will be by church members or anyone else that approaches you, you deny any involvement in the murders. Meanwhile I'm going to fly down to Charleston, drive over to Beaufort and meet with Miles. I'm sure I'll be able to convince him to reconsider going to the police. Miles has always been the weakest of our threesome. He'll listen to reason. After I get him back on track then we can continue with our plan. While I'm in Beaufort I'm also going to meet with my men and discuss how we want to deal with Brumly. Don't worry. I'll handle everything. Everything will work out. I didn't get to where I am today without learning how to sidestep a few problems."

CHAPTER TWENTY NINE

SHELBY LOOKED AT THE LARGE CHRISTMAS TREE IN THE corner and accepted a glass of wine from Conner. Checking the time on the grandfather clock in the opposite corner of the library, she noted the time, 4:07 p.m. "Nick called me from Charleston when they landed which was about an hour ago. They should be arriving here on Fripp soon. It'll be interesting to hear about everything that went on during their trip. The last couple of days I feel like I've been out of circulation; like when Nick and I went up to Pittsburgh to interview Schulte. I felt like I was right in the middle of things. It'll be good to get back in the swing."

Bernard, opening a Christmas card, read the name of the sender, smiled and tossed the card on his desk. "You've done plenty to support the team. Don't forget about all the folders you mailed from Savannah. Some of those folders may have resulted in phone calls to the Beaufort Police from newspapers or radio stations around the country. Let me ask you? Could you have ever imagined when you found Chester's camera in his grandmother's attic, that it would lead to the eventual truth about my daughter's killers?"

"No, I couldn't have. After I developed the photographs and Nick I looked them over we had no idea they would lead us to the point where we now are. It's hard to believe we are on the verge of solving a twenty-seven year old cold case. What I can imagine and what seems to be turning out to be very real is the way Schulte, Durham and Gaston must be feeling at this moment. Three boys, now grown men who got away with murder. Three boys, who for the most part, everyone here in the Lowcountry forgot about. Three boys who grew up. One the governor of a major city, another an archbishop and the third a successful businessman. I guess it's true what people say; things you do wrong in your life will always come back and bite you right in the backside. And then there's you Bernard. A man, a father, who never accepted the fact those three young football players were innocent. I'm glad Nick and I were able to bring the photos to you."

Walking to the tree, she fingered a bright red ornament with a golden handwritten inscription: *Abigail — Christmas 1973.* Noticing she was admiring the decoration, Bernard explained, "My Abby was only two years old when we got that ornament. Every year my wife would always drive into Beaufort and have a customized ornament made for our daughter. If you'll look closely you'll find an ornament dated all the way from 1971 when Abby was born up until she was seventeen. She never made it to her eighteenth Christmas. Abby loved Christmas. We bought that tree her first year. After she was killed my wife and I, especially at Christmas, just couldn't seem to get in the holiday mood so we didn't put the tree up for years. After my wife passed on, I decided to start decorating the house once again. In four days it will be Christmas day and to be quite honest with you, I'm really looking forward to the festive holiday this year. I realize the demise of those three boys who killed my daughter is not keeping with the Christmas spirit, but to think they'll finally get what's coming to them gives me a feeling of great joy."

Looking at another dated ornament, Shelby stated, "Speaking of the holidays, I've still got a lot of shopping to do. I've been so involved with what we've been trying to accomplish that gift buying sort of slipped my mind."

"Not to worry," said Bernard. "When the rest of the team shows up I only plan on keeping you here for about an hour or so. At this point there is little else we can do except sit back and see how this plays out. Over the next few days you should have plenty of time to get your shopping completed."

Miles Gaston pulled his car over and parked it at the far end of the Tarpon Blvd. turnaround. Getting out, he looked across the marsh at the Cabana Club and then farther out to the left at the edge of Skull Inlet and Wardle's Landing. Turning, he looked to the right where Chester's car had been parked that fateful evening so many years ago. Walking down to where the car had been parked, he looked down into the low rock wall and then down into the dry section of the marsh. It had to have been down in there somewhere where Chester had ditched one of his two cameras the night they chased him. *Poor Chester,* he thought. An innocent kid who had shown up at the wrong place at the wrong time. Sitting on a log next to the low wall, he relived those horrible moments when they made the decision to take Chester back down to the beach and explain Abby's death to him, knowing all along he, Brad and Tim were going to kill him. The decision to go along with Brad's plan of eliminating any eyewitness had been easy for him to go along with. After all, it was by his hands Abby had died. Tim had been the one who objected to killing Chester. If he could go back and do things over, would he have done anything different? If he would have voted to spare Chester's life and went along with Tim's suggestion of them just going to the police and explaining what happened Chester would probably be alive today. But, as always, The Three Musketeers voted like they had done many times over their years of friendship as youths. Getting up, he frowned. Brad was a fool if he thought twenty-seven years later that he could still be the most influential of the threesome.

Walking across the sand-covered parking lot he made a left and walked to the large stone wall that led to the secret beach where he and his two friends had spent many an hour, especially during the summer months. Climbing the wall was more difficult than when he had been younger.

Standing on the small walled-in section of sand he stared out across Skull Inlet and then back to the area where Abby had tried her best to seduce him. He recalled how he had felt that night; about how he was finally going to become a man. When he failed, Abby had been so cruel in her slanderous remarks. Why did she have to go and hit him and then threaten to spread it around the school he was queer? For years, following that night he could recall with great detail every movement he had made, hitting Abby over and over with that piece of wood. *How could he have done such a thing?* He had always been so mild mannered and even today, he considered himself a meek individual, a man who detested violence. The very idea of going to the police rather than going along with Brad's newest pack of lies seemed like the only thing left to do.

He sat on one of the large rocks at the base of the wall next to where Abby's life ended. He looked down at the smooth sand where she had taken her last breath. Twenty-seven years of tides had erased any trace of that night. The tide, twice daily, week after week, month after month and year after year had long since washed away any trace of what happened. If he would have just refused her sexual approaches that evening, he wouldn't be in the situation he found himself in. Standing, he walked out to the edge of the inlet and sat on the rock where Brad had sat and no doubt convinced Abby to seduce *his best friend!*

There was no way he was going to go along with Brad and Tim and their new story. If they thought the police were going to buy that pack of lies they were crazy. He was confident he could go to the police and plead self-defense. Abby had attacked him; she had hit and kicked him, not to mention the verbal abuse. He was sure with the money he had he could gain the services of a good attorney who would be able to get him off. Abby was known as a young lady who enjoyed sleeping around while he was a virgin. He considered himself the victim, but would he be able to convince the police or an attorney of his lack of intent to take her life? Looking down at the lapping edge of the inlet at the spot where

Tim and Brad held Chester beneath the water until his last breath, he wasn't sure how he was going to explain that. He'd let whatever attorney he hired decide how to handle Chester's death. Lowering his head, he wept. *How, after all these years could things get so out of control?* Getting to his feet, he decided to go back home to relax and try to reason things out. By the morning he would have to come up with a decision. Go with Brad's plan or go to the police?

Nick was the first to enter Bernard's library, followed by Melvin, Chic and Carson. Upon seeing Nick, Shelby wanted to jump up and give him a hug, but considering the reason for the meeting she felt it was inappropriate. Instead, she nodded and smiled at him while she welcomed he and the others back, holding up her glass of wine in a toasting fashion.

Bernard moved his wheelchair out from behind his desk and welcomed the four team members. "I am so glad you have all returned safely. If everyone would please have a seat we can then proceed by making sure we are all on the same page."

Nick walked to the large window overlooking the Atlantic. "It's so good to see the ocean. I've quickly grown tired of airports, Catholic churches and rental cars. It's good to be back on Fripp."

Chic walked to a small table where he spotted three bottles of liquor. Reaching for a glass, he inquired, "I hope you don't mind but I could use a good drink."

Bernard rolled his chair over next to the fireplace. "Help yourself." Reaching down he lifted a two-foot log and placed it over the low burning flames. "As I was telling Shelby before you arrived we'll only be meeting for about an hour. I want you all to go to your homes and relax. You've all done an excellent job of delivering the folders. As of yesterday, Melvin informed us the Beaufort Police have received a number of calls from newspapers, radio and television stations from not only Pittsburgh, Atlanta and St. Louis but some other major cities as well." Addressing Melvin, who was seated on a chair next to the couch, he asked, "Have you been in touch today with your contact at the Beaufort Police?"

"Yes I have. I gave him a call just after we landed in Charleston. The calls continue to roll in. Early this morning, my contact took the folder and went to the chief. As it stands right now Schulte, Durham and Gaston could be called in for questioning within the next twenty-four to forty-eight hours."

Carson spoke up, "Then, at this point there is little for us to do except wait and see what happens."

"That's precisely right," stated Bernard. "We are now and have been involved in a cat and mouse game. Has anyone in this room ever observed a cat while chasing a mouse?" Following a response from no one, Bernard continued, "My wife and I many years ago had a cat. He was what I would call a great mouser! He would chase a mouse until he had it cornered beneath a couch or maybe in a cabinet. Then the game would begin. That cat had great patience and would sit for hours on end waiting for the mouse to make good its escape. The cat always won the waiting game. When the mouse made its move the cat pounced. In our current situation we are the cats and Schulte, Durham and Gaston are the mice. We, the cats, are on the offensive and the mice are on the defensive. Whether they realize it or not they are being cornered. Now, we have to remain patient and wait until they make their move. The only difference is we won't be doing the pouncing! That will be up to the police, who after being contacted by a number of concerned businesses and organizations, will be forced to take action. The photos Nick and Shelby supplied us with are incriminating to say the least. They show quite clearly those three boys were on that beach in the presence of my daughter who at the time was dead. They are going to have a difficult time explaining why they lied back then."

Chic swirled the alcohol in his glass and apologetically added, "And I really didn't help matters any by running into Tim Durham at the Hilton…did I?"

"No, that little unexpected matter didn't help us," said Bernard, "It really didn't hurt us either, but it is a loose end we have to take care of. As I stated earlier I want everyone after this meeting to go home and relax. Unfortunately, that does not apply to Chic. He, according to his previous meeting and recent phone call with Maria Sparks, has a meeting with her and Schulte's men he must attend sometime today. And here folks, is where the cat and mouse game really gets iffy! When Chic ran into Durham at the Hilton, you can rest well assured Durham informed Schulte about the confrontation and how Chic reacted. What we do not know is if Schulte is aware the lawyer Maria has hooked Schulte's men up with is Chic. He may or may not know this. If he has discovered this, then he is aware a member of our team is actually on *his team!* If he is aware of your identity and that you may wind up representing him here in Beaufort in his efforts to gain information about Nick and Shelby he may feed his men false data about his next move, which could throw us off our game. On the other hand, if he is not aware of who you actually are, then when you meet with his men and Maria depending on what he tells them, we then can keep ahead of him. The thing is, we don't know what he may know. So, it's up to you Chic. Do you want to continue and meet with the Sparks woman and Schulte's men or do you want to cancel? This could be dangerous for you and that is something…the one thing I wanted to avoid any of you getting involved with. The decision is yours. Do you meet with them or not?"

Chic finished off his drink then wiped his mouth with the back of his hand. "I realize I'm the one who is scheduled to meet with these people but as a member of this team I don't think the decision should end with my say. When I joined up with you folks I agreed to go along with what the team thought was best. So, I guess what I'm asking for is some input from you. What do you think about meeting with Maria Sparks and Schulte's men?"

Shelby was the first to answer. "Nick and I are the only ones who have had what I would call a somewhat dangerous experience with these men. They chased us in Pittsburgh at the command of Schulte. We have no idea what they would have done if they would have caught us and that's when Schulte was not sure of our intentions. Now that he knows or has a rather good idea as to our goal of exposing him as one of three murderers of Bernard's daughter and Chester Finch it's hard to tell what he'll order them to do. We just don't know."

Carson stood up to address the group. "Maybe the meeting should just be cancelled. You already dumped the Sparks woman, unknown to her, so you could work for Bernard. She was ready to leave Beaufort when she accidentally bumps into Schulte's men. If Chic tells her he has decided not to take on her and Schulte's men as clients, she'll no doubt be disappointed, but what can she do? She may hang around for a few days but eventually she'll go back to New York. If Schulte is not aware of Chic's involvement as her lawyer, he may pull his men back. If he does know about Chic as the lawyer who may represent him down here, he may try something off the wall…maybe even retaliate. But, from what I've heard about Mayor Schulte he seems to be a man who only makes a move after he has calculated the risk. Besides that, this meeting may not be necessary any longer. If Schulte and his two high school pals are going to be questioned in the next day or so Schulte will have his hands too full to be concerned about any of us."

"Perhaps you're right," said Chic, "Here's what I'm going to do. When we leave here for the day I'm going to go to my office and hash this thing over. I'm still not exactly sure what I want to do, but cancelling the meeting makes the most sense. I'll call you this evening Bernard, and let you know what I've decided."

Bernard clapped his hands once and spoke, "If there are no other questions then I suggest you all go to your homes and relax, but be careful. Schulte's men are still in the area, so we can only assume. I am confident the police will question Schulte, Durham and Gaston soon."

"That could get a wee bit complicated and may not happen as soon as we may think," said Melvin. "They cannot be extradited back here to Beaufort because at this point they are still considered innocent of these murders. If they elect to come of their own accord...well, that's different, but I can't see them doing that. What the police here in Beaufort will most likely do is contact the authorities in Pittsburgh, Atlanta and St. Louis in regard to bringing these men in for questioning. The Beaufort police will send a representative from down here to each of the locations where the men will be questioned. That would be an easier route to take in order to question these men quickly. To try and get these three men to come down here is too complex. As it stands right now, if they desired to do so, they could actually leave the country, which would really complicate things. Here's the thing. We know they are guilty and the photographs pretty well substantiate that fact. But, it's not what we or the police know, it's what can be proved. I think we have the proof, but it could take some time before they can be questioned. Schulte is no doubt aware of this and he and his two friends may make it difficult, for at least a period of time before they can be questioned."

Shelby's shoulders dropped as she frowned. Bernard, noticing a moment of negativity in one of his team members, asked, "Ms. Pickett...you seem to be a bit discouraged after hearing Melvin's rundown on questioning our three targets."

"What I'm hearing is there is a chance we may not bring these three men down like we planned. Nick and I have been at this now since we found that old camera. I look at our operation here as a three phase plan. Phase one was when Nick and I first started to ask questions and do research after we discovered the photos that eventually led us to bringing what we think we discovered to Bernard. Phase two has been what we have been doing for the past few days and is now winding down to phase three which involves how the police will react to public interest in the unsolved murders that took place twenty-seven years ago. Melvin has outlined the questioning process and it sounds to me like the legal process is going to slow things down. It seems to me criminals have far too many rights. These three men we are trying to bring down got away with murder nearly three decades ago and now we have brought forth proof that could actually get them convicted. The police, according to you Bernard, screwed this up back when it happened and those three boys walked. So, I ask you Melvin, even though you are no longer on the force, could Schulte, Durham and Gaston once again dodge a bullet and walk away from this?"

"With the photos we have made available to the public and the police I really don't see how," said Melvin, "but stranger things have happened. Remember, these men are not criminals in the eyes of the law, not just yet. They are persons of interest just like they were before. The legal system must prove they killed Abby and Chester. Even though the photos display very clearly the three boys were at the scene of the murders, that still does not prove they killed those two students. I feel there's a better than average chance they will be proven guilty, but there is always a chance they could walk."

"If that happens, I'll lose all faith in our legal system," said Shelby.

"No offense," stated Bernard, "But I lost faith in the legal system, at least here in Beaufort, twenty-seven years ago when those three boys went off to college free as birds. The photos you brought to me motivated me to try once again to destroy the lives of these three men. Against my better judgement, I'm hoping the police will not only question these three, but convict them and send them off to prison possibly for the rest of their lives. If that does not happen, I too, like Shelby, will lose all faith in our legal system. But, let me state very strongly. If Brad Schulte, Tim Durham and Miles Gaston walk away from this again, it will only be temporary."

Chic with a confused look, asked, "What does that mean…only temporary?"

"What it means is, I will eventually, after waiting for a period of time take matters in my own hands. Of course, none of you will be involved in that, so I would prefer if you refrain from asking me any more questions about what may happen down the road." Wheeling his chair back to the desk, he raised his hands and with a smile said, "Off with you all! Enjoy the day."

Climbing into the passenger seat of Shelby's Jeep, Nick looked at three deer that were grazing in Bernard's neighbor's front yard and remarked, "I don't know about you, but I think the meeting kind of ended on a sour note. I never even considered that Schulte, Durham and Gaston would escape the proof of the photos and possibly walk away from this. And what on earth did Bernard mean about taking matters into his own hands?"

Shelby, backing out of the circular driveway, headed up Ocean Drive as she answered, "Do you remember one of the things Bernard said to us when we first met him?"

"He said quite a few things."

Turning left on Tarpon Blvd, Shelby looked across the seat at Nick and explained, "He made it very clear he could have taken measures into his own hands, but refrained from doing so because it wasn't the right thing to do. What he was telling us back there at the meeting is if those three walk again from being convicted of his daughter's murder, he'll take care of things himself. To be honest with you I think he was referring to having them killed. He trusted in the system almost three decades ago and as far as he is concerned, it failed him. If the system fails him again, I have no doubt Schulte, Durham and Gaston will suffer in the worse possible way; their very lives. He stated if that happened, none of us would be involved."

Nick stared straight up the road, not sure how to respond.

Shelby changed the subject. "Are we hungry?"

"Yes, I could eat. I'm surprised Bernard didn't have food at the meeting. I'm really too tired to go anywhere and I don't think I have much at the house in the way of what I would call a good meal."

"It's already been handled. Right now at this very moment, Genevieve is preparing a big pot of Frogmore stew, steamed shrimp, baked scallops and chocolate cake for dessert. Earlier today I dropped by your place to see if everything was okay at the house. I ran into your neighbor, who by the way is as sweet as they come. I told her we might be getting home between six and seven this evening. She said she'd have everything ready when we got there. So, when we get to your place we just relax, like Bernard suggested. We can have a great meal and forget about the Mayor of Pittsburgh, the Archbishop of St. Louis and the successful Atlanta businessman. I'm sure they are spending the evening thinking about us but we're not going to worry about them…agreed?"

"Hey, for a pot of Frogmore stew I could forget most anything!"

Chic pulled into the parking lot of his office in Port Royal. Grabbing his bag of cheeseburgers and fries he exited the car and started across the lot. Reaching for his office keys, he was startled by a voice. "Chic, it's me Maria!"

Turning, Chic noticed Maria sitting in a rental car close to the office door. "God Maria. You scared the hell outta me!"

Leaning across the seat she opened the passenger side door and ordered, "Get in the car. Schulte's men are across the street at the gas station. They're watching the office for your return. From where they are they can only see the lot, not your office. Get in. I'll drive around to the other side before they realize you're gone."

Confused, Chic hesitated and looked back at the lot.

Maria, more forceful, demanded, "Dammit Brumly…get in!"

Getting in, Chic shut the door as Maria pulled around the back to a side street and turned left. Chic, fumbling to fasten his seatbelt winced when Maria almost hit a parked car. "Geez…what the hell is wrong with you?"

"You could be in danger from those men we met with the other day at your office. I thought after talking with them they could be of some help in finding out what happened to my brother simply because they are also interested in talking with Falco and the Pickett girl. That's why I hooked them up with you."

Holding on for dear life while Maria whipped around another corner, Chic responded, "I already know all that. We discussed that at the meeting we had with those men. Why would I be in any danger?"

"I'm not saying you are…the whole situation is turning out to be kind of weird. It all started this morning after I called you and told you Schulte's men were getting antsy. I explained to them what you told me about meeting with us later today. That seemed to satisfy them. Then, later on in the morning I get this call from them saying they want to meet with me around two o'clock out on Fripp at the marina. They show up at two o'clock with an unannounced guest. Mr. Schulte…their boss from Pittsburgh. To make a long story short, Mr. Schulte informed me he was no longer going to need my services. He and his men could deal with you without my involvement. I objected and he strongly suggested I fly back to New York and forget that I ever met him. The whole thing seemed so strange. I felt I was getting involved in something dangerous and was getting an opportunity to get out before whatever was going to happen actually occurred. They left and I followed them at a distance. The men dropped Schulte off at the Marriott in Beaufort then they drove over to that gas station across from your office and parked at the edge of the lot. After observing them for about an hour I got the idea they were waiting for you. That's when I decided to pull around the back of your office lot where they couldn't see me. I thought you were never going to show up. What the hell have you got yourself involved in? Does any of this have to do with this new client of yours?"

Maria pulled into a small beach near Battery Creek used by local fisherman and parked on the sand. Answering her previous question, Chic explained, "Maybe it does and maybe it doesn't but that's not the point. Schulte was right when he suggested you go back to New York. I'm not saying you are in danger, but you might be getting involved in something that *could be dangerous.*"

Lighting a cigarette, Maria blew a stream of smoke out the open window. "But what about you. Those two men are waiting back there at your office. Do they mean you harm? Maybe I could stay on and help you in some way. I think we made a good team while we were trying to find out what happened to my brother."

"I appreciate your offer, but you need to get out of Beaufort. Brad

Schulte is not a man to mess with. He suggested you leave and if I were you I'd do exactly that."

"But what about you? Will you be okay? I know we've had our differences in the past, but if something happened to you I'd feel just terrible."

"Look, nothing is going to happen to me. It's going to be dark in about an hour. Drop me off a couple of blocks from my office and I'll wait until it gets dark. Then I should be able to get my car and get away from them before they realize what's happening. I know the streets around here like the back of my hand. If they follow me I'm pretty sure I can lose them. After you drop me off you need to get packed and get the hell out of here!"

Nick pushed his now empty plate to the center of the dining room table and patted his stomach. "Genevieve…dinner was exquisite. If I wouldn't have known better I'd swear we just dined at Johnson's Creek."

Genevieve, standing at the kitchen sink rinsed off her plate and smiled. "Considering the Creek has some of the best Frogmore stew in the county I'll accept that as a compliment." Walking back to the table, she held up a pot of coffee. "Refill, anyone?"

Shelby took her last bite of stew and replied, "Yes I'll have about a half cup please."

Nick got up, stretched and walked over to the couch where he seated himself. "I might have a cup later when we cut into that luscious chocolate cake you made."

Setting the pot on the table, Genevieve carried her own cup into the living room where she sat in a chair next to the fireplace. "Have you heard anymore from the lawyer and that woman who were looking for you?"

Nick, not wanting to get into a deep conversation about what was going on recently, waved his right hand. "No, I think that's over. Things should start to get normal around here again. I've got to get the garage cleaned out before spring and I also need to get the fountain in the front yard painted."

Changing the subject, Genevieve stated sadly, "Two more golf carts disappeared yesterday. I just can't figure out how whoever is stealing them is getting them off the island. The police are baffled."

"If that's the most violent crime we have here on Fripp," said Shelby, "well then I say we can consider ourselves lucky."

Changing the topic of conversation once again, Genevieve frowned. "Grady Phillips has decided to sell his place. He told me he is moving to Gatlinburg. Said he is going to build a log cabin out in the woods where no one will be able to bother him. The way I see it the Feds just won't let him be."

Nick yawned and stated, "Carson told me all about Grady and how he was involved in a diamond heist up in Boston. He said Grady was the only one to escape, but eventually did serve time and the diamonds were never recovered. Are they really hidden somewhere here on the island?"

Genevieve got a strange look on her face and was about to answer, but was interrupted by the buzzing of her cell phone. Reaching for the phone, she shook her head, "Who on earth could be calling me this time of day?"

Walking back into the kitchen out of courtesy, Genevieve answered her phone, "Hello."

At first, both Nick and Shelby didn't pay any attention to the call, but as Genevieve continued to respond to whoever had called, they looked at each other in wonder. "I'm at my neighbor's house right now…I guess I could drop by…What's wrong?...Seriously! When did this happen? Are you okay? I'll be there as soon as I can…Don't worry, I'm leaving right now."

The call complete, Genevieve put the phone in her pocket and stared blankly across the room. Shelby, sensing something odd had happened, asked softly, "Is there something wrong?"

Genevieve, composing herself plopped down at the kitchen table and explained, "That was my cleaning lady…Mrs. Betts. She cleans a lot of homes here on the island. A couple of hours ago she went to one of her customer's homes over on Fiddler's Ridge and found the owner shot to death on his back porch. She's very upset and wants me to drop by her place. She lives over on St. Helena Island."

Concerned, Shelby got up and went to Genevieve's side. "Did this Mrs. Betts call the police?"

"Yes, she did. She called island security, who in turn called the Beaufort Police. She told me she had never seen a dead body before and being in the house alone with the body while she was waiting for the police was unnerving. She's really upset. She has spent the last hour or so at the victim's home answering questions. It appears the man committed suicide. There was blood everywhere and a gun on the floor at his side. She did say she heard two of the officers speaking and even though it looks like the man took his life they are not ruling out foul play."

"Great!" said Nick. "Another murder on Fripp. I thought that all ended last summer. Did she mention who the victim was?"

"Yes, she did. She said his name was Gaston. I think she said Miles Gaston."

The look of shock on Shelby's face caused Genevieve to probe, "Do you know this man?"

Shelby stumbled in her answer and replied, "No…it's just that it's another murder here on Fripp…that's all."

Nick, desiring to tone things down so Genevieve would not get suspicious, commented, "We can't be sure it was a murder. It may have been suicide. Are you headed to this lady's house right now?"

"Yes…yes I am. She doesn't want to be alone, especially after discovering the body. I'm sorry I can't stay for cake but she is a dear friend and I need to be there for her. If I leave now, I can be at her place in twenty minutes." Getting up, she grabbed her coat and headed for the front door. "I'll talk with you both tomorrow."

Genevieve was no sooner out the door than Nick was on his cell. Shelby, still in a state of shock, asked, "Who are you calling?"

"Bernard James. I need to find out if he knows anything about this. If he doesn't, I guarantee he'll be interested."

Nick and Shelby were the first two to arrive at Bernard's house. They were no sooner seated in the library than Carson entered and announced, "Starting to rain out there. I was just about to hop into the sack when Bernard gave me the call about Gaston. Did anyone manage to get any more info on what happened?"

Bernard, poking at three logs in the burning fireplace answered the question, "No, nothing new, but Melvin said he was going to call the people he knows on the force to see if he could find out anything. He should be here in a few minutes."

Carson walked to the fireplace and extended his hands toward the flames. "The winter rain down here always puts a chill in the air." Turning, he faced the group and shaking his head in wonder, commented, "It's hard to believe one of the three men we have targeted is dead." Looking directly at Bernard, he asked, "Do you really think he'd take his own life?"

"I don't know," said Bernard. "We may never know. All we can do is wait for Melvin to get here. He may have more information for us. Either way, Miles Gaston is dead and gone. I can't say I feel bad for the man. To be truthful, I personally would have liked to see him humiliated in the public eye by having him questioned, convicted and sent off to prison, but it would appear Gaston has decided to sidestep the embarrassment of finally, after all these years, being caught and named as one of the three boys who murdered my daughter. I say he got off easy."

The library door opened and Conner announced the arrival of the final member of the team. "Mr. Barrett is here, sir."

Melvin entered the room and removed his sopping coat, which he handed to Conner. "It's really coming down out there."

Bernard gestured at the fire and spoke, "Please, warm yourself by the fire and tell us what you've learned about Gaston's death, if anything?"

Melvin backed up to the fireplace, his hands behind his back. "I called my contact on my way here. Here's what they have so far. The M.E states Miles took his last breath somewhere between eight and nine o'clock this evening. At first, it appeared to be a suicide. Gaston was discovered by his cleaning lady on his back porch shot to death. The weapon, a .45 caliber handgun, was on the floor next to Gaston's body. There are a few items that suggest Gaston's death was a murder. There were no powder burns on his hand or face, which there should be at close range. Another strange thing the police discovered was Miles Gaston was not a gun owner…at least a registered owner…thus they are not ruling out murder. That's about all they have at the moment…"

The rundown by Melvin was interrupted when Conner answered the phone in the nearby hallway. Walking back into the library, he walked over and whispered into Bernard's ear. Bernard thanked his faithful butler and then poured himself a tall drink. Following two long swigs he spoke, "More bad news. That call was from Chic who called from the hospital in Beaufort. He was attacked earlier this evening and the police are handling the attack as a robbery. Chic said he never saw their faces but there were two of them. He told Conner he recognized one of the voices as one of Schulte's men. He said these men kicked and beat the hell out of him, then took his wallet. He has a busted right arm, broken left kneecap and quite a few contusions and cuts. He's going be in their care for a week, maybe longer. This changes everything!"

Shelby looked at the other team members who remained silent when she asked Bernard, "What does that mean?"

"It's just too coincidental that Gaston is shot and Chic is attacked on the same day. Perhaps I should have said, this *could* change everything rather than it *does* change everything. What you don't know is something Chic shared with me earlier after our previous meeting ended. He told me when he got to his office he ran into Maria Sparks, who as it turned out, rescued him from Schulte's men who were watching his office. So, it just makes sense Schulte's men could have been his attackers. This changes things because maybe, just maybe Schulte is sending us a message that he can get to us. He may, through this beating, be suggesting strongly that we need to back off. As far as Gaston's death is concerned, if he was in fact murdered, who killed him? I know this must sound odd, even unbelievable, but Schulte and or Durham could have taken him out. What I'm saying is all pure speculation, but we can't rule out the fact that possibly Schulte killed or had Gaston killed."

"Committing suicide makes sense," said Nick. "The embarrassment of being convicted after all these years might have been too much for Gaston to stomach…so, he takes his own life. Maybe he thought death was a better path than spending the rest of his life in prison."

"True, very true," stated Bernard, "But we cannot rule out the possibility he was, in fact murdered. If Schulte or Durham are responsible for Gaston's death, that means we all have to be careful. Remember what I said when we first started this journey; that when the truth finally comes out these men will be scrambling."

Shelby sat back and crossed her arms across her chest. "Your idea of all of us relaxing and being careful for the next few days has suddenly changed to just being careful, because with the prospect of Schulte and or Durham being responsible for Gaston's death, not to mention Chic getting the hell beat out of him by Schulte's men, relaxing is not something one can easily do."

Melvin spoke up, "I'm going to visit the Beaufort Police and suggest they step things up in going after Schulte and Durham. If I can convince them Gaston's death and Chic's beating are somehow tied in with the folder information, maybe we can bring this thing to a head."

Bernard looked out the window at the driving rain. "I guess our meeting is over for now. Perhaps you would all like to stay and have coffee until this rains slows down."

Brad Schulte plopped down in a seat on the plane and looked out the window at the rain at the Charleston Airport. Turning to his two associates, he leaned toward the men and whispered, "Everything that went on in Beaufort is to remain between the three of us. The next few days or weeks could get rough for me. I pay you well and I need you to be ready to respond to my every request if necessary. I may have to call on you again, depending on what happens. Do you understand?"

CHAPTER THIRTY

ARCHBISHOP DURHAM CLOSED THE WOODEN DOOR OF THE church office and knocked the snow from the shoulders of his winter coat. Hanging the coat and his hat on a clothes tree, he addressed the secretary, "Good morning, Andrea. It appears we have another typical winter day on our hands here in St. Louis."

"Good morning, Your Excellency. Will you be having coffee this morning?"

"No, but I think I will have a hot chocolate if we have any."

"I think we have some. I'll bring it right in."

"Thank you and would you also bring me the folder I told you to keep for me. I looked for it yesterday, but I couldn't locate it."

"I'm sorry. I had it hidden at the bottom of one of the file cabinets. I'll bring it with your chocolate."

"Do I have anything on my schedule today other than saying Mass?"

"No, you're completely open today."

"Let's try and keep it that way. I'm feeling a little under the weather."

"I hope it's nothing serious."

"It's probably just a cold coming on."

"I'll get right on that hot beverage for you."

Going into his modest office, he bowed before the crucifix hanging on the wall and made the sign of the cross. He looked at the clock on the opposite wall, 7:55. He almost forgot. At exactly eight o'clock every Wednesday his mother would give him a call from Beaufort. Seating himself in his office chair he smiled. His mother had been calling him on Wednesday at precisely eight o'clock in the morning for years. *As sure as Jesus was coming back*, he knew the phone would be ringing in the next few minutes, his mother's pleasant voice on the other end. She would always update him on the latest goings on in and around Beaufort. She was always saying she wished he could be transferred down to Beaufort so she could spend more time with her only son. She held him in high esteem and always told him how proud of him she and his father were.

Following a soft knock on the office door, Andrea entered, a cup of hot chocolate in her right hand and the folder in her left. Laying both objects on the desk, she politely inquired, "Will there be anything else,

Your Excellency?"

"Yes. As usual my mother will be calling to speak with me in a few minutes. Would you please put her through to the office?"

"Certainly."

Taking a short sip of the chocolate he unclasped the folder and dumped out the contents. He looked at the two beach photos and thought, *The police will never believe the newly contrived story Brad had come up with, but what other choice did they have.* Next, he looked at the yearbook picture of the 1989 Beaufort football team. He looked closely at the photograph until he came to where he was seated right between Brad and Miles. He looked so innocent. Good 'ol number 23. He was smiling in the picture right along with Brad and Miles. Back then he didn't have a care in the world. He was a high school state football champion, a straight A student dating LuAnn Dawson, the spunky little cheerleader. He was going to be receiving a full ride at college down in Texas, then more than likely become a professional ballplayer. Sadly he looked at the beach photos again and thought about how that night so many years ago had erased all those dreams. Now, and for years, he had to live with what he and the others had done. Looking at the last page where his name was listed with his two friends and the message that there was no statute of limitations on murder and someone knew what they had done was unnerving. He could only hope if he, Brad and Miles were questioned the years that had passed had somehow lessoned the pain they had caused. Right now, his main concern was Miles had threatened he and Brad with the fact he was going to the police to confess he killed Abby. This could only lead to questions about how Chester was killed and why they were on the beach. One thing would lead to another and they would surely be convicted. His office phone rang. He looked at the clock. Eight o'clock on the dot. It was his mother.

Picking up his office phone, he spoke pleasantly, "Hello, mother, how are you?"

"Fine," replied Mrs. Durham, "just fine. How are things up north?"

"It's snowing right now. I think we're forecast to get maybe two inches. How's the weather in my old hometown?"

"We've got some light rain at the moment. It's supposed to be in the low fifties today. Pretty typical for the time of year down this way. Last Saturday it was colder than normal. When I went to confession it was about forty degrees. I had to wear a coat. I thought I would freeze to death. There weren't very many people at confession last week. When I was saying my penance I started thinking maybe we are getting less sinful down here in Beaufort."

"I wish I could say the same thing about St. Louis. It seems like this past year more and more folks are coming to confession." Smiling, Tim teased his mother, "Compared to Beaufort County, St. Louis is like Sodom and Gomorrah! There is not a day that passes where on the news someone is not killed, raped or some business broken into. In a large city like St. Louis it's a way of life. People up this way are used to bad news. In Beaufort County crimes are few and far between. Hearing confession down your way would probably be quite boring for me."

"Well, that's one of the things I wanted to tell you. Yesterday was horrible here in town. Do you remember one of your best friends, Miles Gaston? He played on the football team with you and Brad." Not giving her son an opportunity to reply, Mrs. Durham went on to explain, "I'm sorry to have to tell you this, but Miles was shot to death last evening at his home over on Fripp Island. The article in the paper said it appeared to be a suicide, but the word around town, and you know how fast news spreads down here, is that it might not be suicide at all and that Miles was actually murdered. There was a gun on the floor next to the body but it turns out Miles never owned a gun and there were some other suspicious things that didn't look right. I remember the day he moved here to the neighborhood and how the next day you came running home saying you and Brad had a new friend. I can't imagine why Miles would want to end his life. Worse than that, I can't even fathom why anyone would want to murder him. He was such a polite boy. I remember times when you had him over to the house for supper. Anyway, everyone in town is talking about the shooting. I thought maybe you'd like to know since you were childhood friends. They haven't said anything yet about a viewing or when the funeral might be. When I find out I'll let you know. I thought maybe you'd like to be here."

Tim remained silent, not believing what he had just heard. His lack of a response caused his mother to ask, "Tim, are you still on the line?"

Composing himself, Tim answered, "Yes, I'm still here. It's just...well, it's a shock to hear about Miles. When did you say this happened?"

"According to the paper he was shot somewhere between eight and nine o'clock last night. The paper said he was a businessman and lived by himself. I guess he never married. Just when I thought things were starting to get back to normal down here in Beaufort, someone gets murdered, or I guess maybe took their life. And that wasn't the only thing that happened last evening. Some lawyer by the name of Brumly was severely beaten outside of his office in Port Royal. What's the world coming to? The first half of this year was difficult in the county what with the RPS Killer still on the loose. That's another strange thing.

Come to think of it they never did find out who killed that monster."

"Listen Mom, I've got to get off the line. This news about Miles' death is disturbing. I need to give Brad a call and see if he has heard about this. Thank you for calling and letting me know. When you get information on the funeral, please give me a call. If I can get away I'd like to fly down for the service. We'll talk soon."

Tim hung up the phone then looked down at the Beaufort High football photo. Placing his index finger on Miles' image, he bowed his head and whispered to himself, *Miles, what have we done to you?*

Placing the documents and photos back inside the folder he opened his desk drawer, threw them in and locked it shut. Standing, he walked back and forth across his office four times and thought about his 'ol friend taking his life or worse than that, someone killing him in cold blood.

He needed to call Brad, but in order to do that he was going to require some privacy. Walking out into the reception area he spoke to the church secretary. "Andrea, I hate to ask you this but I need a favor. Could you please run out and pick me up some throat lozenges and cough medicine. I'm think I'm going downhill this morning. When you return could you please call Father George and tell him I'm under the weather and he'll have to say the noon Mass."

"I'll get right on it, Your Excellency. Is there anything else you'd like me to pick you up?"

"No, just what I asked for."

Grabbing her coat, Andrea spoke back over her shoulder as she reached for the door. "I should return in about thirty minutes."

Tim watched out the office window until she pulled out and drove up the street. He had to make sure he was not disturbed while calling Brad. Walking back into his office, he locked the door, sat at his desk, took a deep breath, and then dialed Brad's number in Pittsburgh. It wasn't even nine o'clock and he wasn't sure if the mayor would be at his office this early."

He waited and on the second ring, a female voice answered, "Mayor Schulte's office, may I help you?"

"Yes, you may," stated Tim. "I'm one of Mayor Schulte's close friends. If he is in I'd like to say hello."

"Yes, the mayor is in. Let me see if he is available at the moment to take your call."

Tim was put on hold while he listened to pleasant background music. Following a few seconds, Brad's voice sounded, "Tim, I was going to call you later this morning. I'm going to hang up and call you back on my cell. I think that would be better."

Tim never got to say a word when he found the phone buzzing in his ear. Hanging up, he assumed Brad would call back. Within seconds his phone rang. Tim picked up and answered, "Archbishop Durham."

"Cut the crap," said Brad. "It's just me. The reason I called you back on my cell is that what we have to discuss cannot be overheard by anyone. Are you alone?"

"Yes, I sent my secretary out on an errand. I've only got about thirty minutes before she gets back."

"When we last talked there in St. Louis, I told you I'd talk with Miles and try to convince him to change his mind about going to the police. After we broke up the meeting in St. Louis I flew down to Beaufort to meet with him. I gave him a call and he refused to see me, stating he had decided to go to the police. I did everything I could to change his mind but he wouldn't budge."

"When you say you did everything to change Miles' mind, what do you mean by *everything?"*

"I tried to talk some sense into him, but he was not open to anything other than going to the police. The last thing I said to him was he was making a grave mistake."

"That's sounds like a threat to me."

"It wasn't a threat…it's a fact! If he goes to the police, we all…all three of us go down the tubes."

"You don't have to worry about Miles going to the police…he's dead!"

"Well, that solves our problem then…doesn't it!"

"Brad, I've known you since we were little kids growing up in Beaufort. We were practically raised as brothers. I know you better than anyone on the face of this planet. Your reaction of 'Well, that solves our problem then…doesn't it', is not the reaction of the friend I grew up with. What did you do when you went down to Beaufort? What did you do?"

"Miles, you have to stop living in the past. We are no longer neighborhood kids in Beaufort. Whether you realize it or not the moment Miles decided to beat Abigail James to death our childhood days came to an end…abruptly. That night on Fripp Island the three of us stepped into the real world, which believe me is not fair. You know what Miles said when he stormed out of the meeting. He was going to go to the police. Eventually, even though he would have admitted he killed Abby, Chester's death still looms over us. He would have taken us all down and to be quite frank with you, I don't think he cared anymore. Miles was indeed our friend in high school, but you know it's true we all grew apart over the years. The only thing we really did share was the truth of that night on Fripp. When Miles told us he was going to the police he violated our agreement of never revealing the truth of that horrible night. He had to be stopped! I tried to reason with him, but he was set on going to the authorities. This may sound morbid but you should feel relieved because of his death. Even though tragic, his death has saved us from going to prison."

"You didn't answer my question, Brad. What did you do?"

"I did what I had to...for both of us. I knew you'd never have the stomach for it, so I stepped up to the plate and did what was necessary."

"Necessary! You found it necessary to kill our best friend! This is insane! Tell me Brad. Did you pull the trigger or did you have one of your people do it?"

"It doesn't make any difference...it's done and we're off the hook!"

"Off the hook! Have you heard what the Beaufort Police are now saying? They don't think it was suicide. Miles never owned a gun and the way everything was left it didn't look right to them. They suspect murder, and from what you're telling me...they're right! Off the hook! How are we off the hook?"

"If you'll just calm down for a couple of minutes, I'll explain."

"I'm listening, but I'm not sure I'll like what I hear."

"Okay, here it is. Remember when we talked about having Ricky Hemsly take the fall for the murders. We can accomplish the same thing but with Miles being the guilty party. Think about it? Miles is the one who really *did kill* Abby. Ricky Hemsly, because he is dead, would not be able to defend himself and likewise since Miles is no longer alive neither will he. Replacing Ricky with Miles makes all the sense in the world. Miles is a more believable story and it is backed up with proof. If you'll recall, they found Miles' DNA on the bottleneck of the broken bourbon bottle. Before, we talked our way out of that saying we had lied about drinking because we didn't want to get into trouble with our parents. When we finally did admit to drinking we told the police after we dropped Abby off at the pool she kept the bottle and probably took it with her to the beach. The reason for Miles' DNA being on the bottle is because he had been drinking with Abby in the backseat of my car and then on the beach. Another thing we now have going for us are the two beach photos that are the strongest documents contained in the folders. Even though we are all pictured on the beach, Miles is the only one who is holding the murder weapon...a bloody section of two by four. The M.E. discovered a section of wood, yellow pine, had been used to beat Abby to death. Now, they have a photo with Miles standing over her, the murder weapon raised high. It's perfect. It's our way out of this mess."

"That's only half of the mess. What about Chester's death? How can we possibly put that entirely on Miles?"

"To answer that let's start at the beginning of what we will tell the police, if questioned. We stick to the story we originally told them up until we dropped her off at the pool. But here is where we need to change our original story. We said we never saw Abby again that night. We tell the truth this time around and explain she wanted to go with us to our special beach. So, we took her along. When we get to the beach Abby and Miles, who had been drinking more than you and I, walked off to be by themselves. We didn't think anything of it. We knew Miles was a virgin and Abby had a reputation of sleeping around. We just figured…so be it. We walked off to give them some privacy but then later on we heard a scream. We ran back to the beach where we found Miles had beat Abby to death with that section of wood. We go on to explain about how Miles said he couldn't perform and Abby made fun of him; how she hit and kicked him. Miles said he just lost it. He didn't mean to kill her, but he did!"

Tim interrupted, "Everything you've said so far is the truth, but how does this tie Miles in with murdering Chester?"

"That's the beauty of all this. Miles is not around to dispute what we say. We explain that Chester, who we had already seen up on Tarpon earlier, took the pictures of us, which are verified by the photos that have now been brought to light. We tell the police we chased down Chester, knowing that the pictures, if developed, would not only incriminate Miles, but you and I. We say we tried to explain to Chester what happened after we took him back down to the beach and finally decided it would be best to go to the police and tell them the truth of what happened. We say Miles strongly objected to going to the police. The one thing we agreed upon was that the camera had to be destroyed. You and I climbed back over the wall to dispose of the camera while Miles stayed behind with Chester. We never in a million years expected Miles to kill Chester, but that's exactly what happened. When we got back we found Chester drowned in Skull Inlet. Miles said he had to die. He couldn't bear the thought of going to prison for killing Abby who had attacked him, which he said the police would never swallow. We decided to let things go and see how it went. As time went on, even though we were persons of interest, things just kind of worked out for us. Miles's death is our way out. Surely you can see what I'm saying."

"What about Chic Brumly being beaten the other night; the same night Miles was shot?"

"Brumly got what he deserved by sticking his nose in where it didn't belong. There is no way the police will be able to tie the shooting and the beating together. I think it's important we meet and get our ducks in a row on what we're going to say to the police. I think it's inevitable that we'll be questioned. They'll contact or come for us soon, within a matter of a few days. We must be prepared. When can we get together to discuss this further? I would say it should be soon, maybe tomorrow."

Tim hesitated in his response, "I need time to think this through. I'm not sure what I want to do. It's sounds to me like you're set on blaming Miles for everything. Besides that, we still don't know who mailed the folders. We don't know what they may know. I'm the Archbishop of St. Louis. Even if we get off the hook like you claim, I may still suffer. I may be excommunicated from the Church."

"I've considered things like that myself. Things like the fact this folder business may have ruined my shot at being the next governor. Who knows? I may even have the title of Mayor of Pittsburgh stripped from me, but at least I won't have to go to prison and *neither will you* if we blame everything on Miles."

"That's easy for you to say. Besides accumulating a vast amount of wealth over the years, you can simply retire from public life and live the rest of your life in luxury. That's not the case with me. I have nothing…I own nothing...I'm not qualified to do anything other than priestly duties in the Church. If I get excommunicated because of my involvement in these past murders, I will be left with nothing. I depend on the Church for everything. I receive no income. I have no insurance. The Church supplies me with food, lodging and even clothing. If I don't have the Church I have nothing. You're in a better position to just walk away from this than I am. I stand to lose everything I've worked for. If I'm going to lose everything, at least I'd like to keep my integrity. Maybe Miles was right. Maybe it's time to end this and go to the police and tell the truth…the real truth. We've dodged this bullet for a long time, but I think it might be over."

There was silence on the phone, but then Brad spoke up in a demanding tone, "Tim, do not bail on me now. We've been friends since we were kids. We knew each other six years before Miles entered our lives. You need to be with me on this. I was always there for you when we were growing up. You need to be there for me…for us…now. Don't let me down."

"There is nothing you can say at this point that makes any of this seem right," said Tim. "Why would I want to take advise from you; a man who killed his best friend to save his own hide. A man who orders another man he has never met beaten. You have changed from the boy I grew up with. I don't trust you, Brad. You scare the hell out of me. I don't know what I'm going to do, but I am not going to blame Miles for what we were all involved in. I have to do what I feel is right. At the beginning of this conversation when I answered the phone as the

Archbishop you informed me in a crass manner to 'cut the crap!' You hold no respect for the position I hold in the Catholic Church. Despite what you may think of me, I am a man of the cloth. I became a priest because I thought maybe I could do some good in this world, especially after what we had done to Abby and Chester. When we were young I used to think we were a lot alike. But that is no longer true. We are nothing alike. You killed our best friend. I've never even held a gun in my hand. You beat Chic Brumly. I have never raised a hand in anger toward anyone. I am a man who has grown accustomed to doing what's right."

"Don't go and get all self-righteous on me, " snapped Brad. "You are no better than me and don't try to make yourself out to be something you're not! Yours hands were on Chester when he drowned, just like mine were. You better think long and hard before you start preaching to me about what's right. You want some time to think about what you're going to do. That's fine. But, hear this. Just because you happen to be an archbishop does not exonerate you from what you did years ago on Fripp. I'll expect an answer from you by two o'clock this afternoon on when we can meet to discuss how we what to handle being questioned. Don't cross me Tim. I'm depending on you to do what's right for both of us…not just you. I'll call you at two."

Tim stared at the wall, the phone still at his ear. Seconds passed when he hung the phone up, placed his hands over his face and lowered his head. Things had gotten completely out of control. Miles was dead, Brumly had been beaten and now, he felt as if he had been threatened by his best friend, Brad. He sat up and thought about how horrible the whole situation seemed. The walls were closing in on him. He had to make a decision and soon. He looked at the clock on the wall, 9:15 in the morning. In less than five hours Brad would be calling him back for a decision. A knock at the office door grabbed his attention, followed by a voice. "Your Excellency…are you all right?"

Getting up, Tim unlocked the door and smiled at Andrea. "I'm fine. I locked the door because I was trying to take a nap. I'm so tired." Taking the cough medicine and the throat lozenges from her, he requested again, "Would you please notify Father George he'll have to say Mass at noon. I think I'm going to lie down on my couch and take a long nap. Please make sure I'm not disturbed."

Chic was gently brought out of a light sleep when the nurse nudged his arm. "Mr. Brumly…Mr. Brumly, you have some visitors." Chic slowly opened his eyes and turned his head toward the door of his hospital room. There, Bernard sat in his wheelchair, Conner standing directly behind him. Nick, Shelby and Carson stood against the wall.

Chic tried to smile but numerous cuts and abrasions on his chin, nose and cheeks prevented him from doing so. Shaking his head in non-belief he remarked in a joking fashion, "What a motley crew you are!"

The nurse patted Chic's good arm and stated. "I'll let you have some time with your friends."

Conner pushed Bernard over next to the bed while the others followed, Carson standing on the opposite side, Nick and Shelby seating themselves on a green vinyl couch. Bernard was the first to speak. "I'm so sorry this has happened to you. This is the one thing I did not want any of you to experience. We ran into your doctor on the way in. He informed us you'll be here for at least a week."

Nodding at the cast on his right arm and his covered left leg, Chic verified, "That's correct. Got me a busted arm and a broken kneecap and a list of other debilitating injuries."

Carson sat in a chair next to the bed and asked, "The police said your assailants lifted your wallet."

"That they did, but that was just to throw the authorities off. I know for a fact it was Schulte's men who attacked me. I never had a chance to see their faces. They came at me from behind. I recognized one of the men's voices. The one called Robert. He has a very distinctive New England accent."

"What did he say?" asked Shelby.

Chic gently shifted his body to gain some comfort and answered, "He said, 'Grab his wallet'. By that time I had been beaten badly. They kicked me in the ribs a few more times and once on the back of my head and then I assume they ran off. There is no doubt in my mind it was Schulte's men who attacked me. It makes sense. Remember when I called you Bernard, after Maria picked me up at my office? She said she had met with Schulte and his men and was told to go back to New York. Schulte told her he was going to deal with me and it wasn't necessary for her to be involved any longer. She followed Schulte's men who parked across the street from my office. She felt something was wrong. After we talked she dropped me off a few blocks from my office in the dark and I was sure I could get in my car and take off before they realized what was happening. They were waiting for me." Trying to raise his leg, he moaned, "Boy, they really nailed me!" Looking directly at Bernard, he continued, "With Schulte being down here now with his men this really is getting serious. Maybe it's time for us to back off. I'd hate to have anything like I went through happen to any of you."

Nick jumped in on the conversation. "It is getting serious. Have you been watching the news since you've been here?"

"No, I haven't. I've been so drugged up on pain medicine most of the time I've been sleeping. What's on the news?"

Nick hesitated but then answered, "Miles Gaston was found shot to death at his home on Fripp last evening within about an hour of when you were attacked. At first the police said it looked like a suicide but now they're leaning toward murder. So, yeah, I guess we would all agree things are getting serious."

In astonishment, Chic shook his head. "Sounds to me like they killed their best friend to protect themselves. Suicide makes more sense when you figure the pressure we placed on Gaston. But, why would they kill him?"

"That we do not know," said Bernard. "Gaston's death may have nothing to do with what we've been trying to prove. Someone may have just broken into his home and shot him."

Carson spoke again, "If you want my two cents, I say they shot him and then attacked Chic. I think this is Schulte's way of striking back and letting us know he is not a man to mess with. It would seem that now we are the mice and Schulte has become the cat."

"What about Archbishop Durham," asked Nick. "What, if any part do you think he may have played in any of this retaliation?"

"I don't know," said Bernard. "All I know is we need to be extremely careful for the next few days until these two men are questioned. I'm sure Schulte is no longer here in the area. His men might be, but he won't hang around. More than likely he'll head back to Pittsburgh. Hell, he might be there now."

Looking around the room, Chic observed, "Melvin, where is Melvin?"

Bernard smiled and answered, "Melvin, at this moment is down at police headquarters talking with the chief and his staff. I suggested he go see them and explain what it is we have been trying to accomplish in regard to Schulte, Durham and Gaston. Melvin is going to try to convince them to step up the process for questioning Schulte and Durham. He is going to express our concern over our safety in lieu of what has recently happened, what with Gaston's shooting and your beating, Chic. With any luck maybe we can have Schulte and Durham picked up for questioning within the next couple of days. We should hear news from Melvin later on today. In the meantime, I want everyone on the team to be extremely careful of where you go and what you do." Looking back at the door to ensure they could not be overheard, Bernard spoke in a low tone, "If anyone else on our team is injured in any way from the actions of Schulte and Durham I will, I repeat, I will take matters into my own hands. Mark my word!"

Archbishop Durham sat at his desk and looked at the clock on the wall of his office. It was 1:30 in the afternoon. He only had thirty minutes before the call from Brad would be patched through to his phone. He stared at the black phone on the corner of his desk. He dreaded the upcoming call. His three-hour nap had been restless as he tossed and turned on the couch. He rubbed his stiff neck and then went back to finishing his letter, which he signed, *Archbishop Timothy J. Durham.* Folding the letter, he placed it in an envelope and centered it on the top of his neat desk. Removing the crucifix he always wore around his neck he laid the solid silver depiction of Christ on the Cross on top of the envelope, bowed his head in prayer and wept.

CHAPTER THIRTY ONE

CONGREGATING JUST OUTSIDE THE MAIN ENTRANCE OF THE Beaufort County Memorial Hospital, Nick, Shelby and Carson listened while Bernard suggested, "The fact Miles Gaston lost his life last evening is indeed sad, but I've told you all before I hold no sympathy for the three men who killed my daughter. As far as I'm concerned the man got what was coming to him. If he did take his own life it was no doubt because of the pressure we placed on him. This was our objective from the beginning when we set out to destroy Gaston and the others. Perhaps you may view his death as tragic, which it is, however I feel his death has been justified. The problem as I see it is, if in fact Brad Schulte or his men took Gaston out that looms as a potential problem for all of us. More so you than I, which I apologize for. By now Schulte and Durham are aware of your identities, at least as far as what you look like. If all three of these men did meet in St. Louis they probably compared notes and described the people who interviewed them as authors. The only team members they may not be aware of are Conner and myself. That being said, after what happened to Chic, all of you must be careful until after Schulte and Durham have been questioned *and hopefully* brought to justice. I should be hearing about the results of Melvin's meeting with the chief of police in Beaufort later today. I'll update you when I hear something. In the meantime, rest assured *we will* bring the mayor and the archbishop down. Whatever you do over the course of the next few days…be careful. We can't be sure if Schulte's men are still in the area or not."

Carson responded, looking up at the overcast sky. "Looks like it could start raining again. I'm going to spend the next few hours at the Fripp Island Marina. I've got one of my boats dry-docked there. I need to do some minor engine repairs and some touch-up painting. After that, I'll probably relax at the Bonito Boathouse with a few beers and some seafood."

Shelby joined in and stated, "I'm going to go home and pick up my daughter Kirby after she gets out of school. Then we're going to hit the local stores and finally get our Christmas shopping done."

Nick shrugged his shoulders. "I too, have to buy a few Christmas gifts but that can wait until tomorrow. I'm going to go home, take a long relaxing shower then take an extended walk on the beach. I've had my fill of big cities. The snow and ice we encountered in Pittsburgh and St. Louis reminds me of the days when I lived I Cincinnati. I guess since I've moved down here I've grown partial to living at the beach."

Bernard motioned to Conner he was ready to leave. "Conner and I are heading back to Fripp. While waiting for Melvin's call we are going to be devising Plan B, just in case Schulte and Durham weasel their way out of the dilemma they find themselves in. Once again, if the police fail to question, prosecute, convict and send our remaining two targets off to prison for the rest of their lives, then they will have to deal with me, which believe me will not be pleasant."

Carson said good-bye to Nick and Shelby and offered to meet them later at the Boathouse for dinner, Shelby turning down the offer since her holiday shopping was going to take up most of the evening. Nick said he would think about it, but wasn't making any promises.

Walking across the lot Shelby asked Nick, "Do you really think there's a chance Durham and Schulte could walk away from the proof we have uncovered?"

"I don't know. I guess we'll have to wait and see what the Beaufort Police are willing to do."

Climbing in her Jeep she reminded Nick, "I hope you haven't forgotten with everything that's going on that you are expected for Christmas dinner at my parents' house which is in three days."

"I won't forget...and I'll bring your father's favorite spiked eggnog. Maybe we'll talk later tonight after Melvin calls Bernard."

Nick's mind was full of questions as he drove down the Sea Island Parkway to Fripp. *Did Miles Gaston commit suicide or did Schulte have him killed? Was Chic indeed attacked by Schulte's men? Would Durham and Schulte be brought in for questioning? Was Maria Sparks finally out of their lives for good? What was Bernard's Plan B?*

By the time he pulled into his driveway, his head was so full of unanswered questions he just wanted to take the rest of the day off and relax. A long casual stroll on the beach seemed like the ticket. Parking the Lexus in the garage, he was approached by his neighbor, Genevieve. "Nick, I've been trying to get in touch with you after our interrupted dinner last night, but you haven't been around. I spent the evening with my cleaning lady. She was a mess. She couldn't stop talking about all the blood and the way this Gaston individual was slumped over in a chair on his porch. I was reading the paper this morning and the police are saying it might not be suicide, but murder. I also read about where that lawyer who was bothering you, Chic Brumly, was attacked and robbed.

Oh, and one other thing I heard. I guess they caught the golf cart thieves. Early this morning someone noticed some garbage men acting odd around their garage. The next thing they know their cart is missing. Security stopped the garbage truck at the security gate and low and behold wouldn't you know it those garbage men had a hidden compartment in behind where the garbage is collected. That's how they were getting them off the island. It's a crazy world we live it…isn't it?"

Nick normally would have been amazed at the brazenness of the garbage men — golf cart thieves — but after what he had been through recently it seemed insignificant. Closing the garage door, he smiled at Genevieve. "Well I guess we don't need to worry any more about our carts being stolen. Look, Genevieve, I'd like to talk but I really have some things I need to get done." Walking toward his back porch he gestured, "One of the things I need to do is cut into that chocolate cake you baked the other night. I'll save you a slice…I promise."

Ten minutes later following a refreshing shower, Nick stood wrapped in a towel in the kitchen while he ate a slice of the cake, washing it down with a glass of cold milk. Looking out the living room window he noticed the rain had held off, but it was windy. Throwing the towel over one of the kitchen chairs he slipped on a sweatshirt, a pair of old painting pants, deck shoes and a windbreaker and headed for the back door.

Walking across the sand he looked up and down the long stretch of beach that disappeared in both directions. To his left, Ocean Point and to the right, Skull Inlet. Walking in either direction held memories of the past year. Ocean Point is where he had supposedly spread his grandmother's ashes just before he moved to the Lowcountry. The fact Amelia was alive and well and living in Canada was a pleasant thought. On the other hand, Skull Inlet held what he considered to be unpleasant thoughts. Beyond the inlet to the north is where he had discovered the dismembered, skeletal hand of the Dunn girl. Pritchards Island, on the other side of the inlet, is where he had barely escaped death at the hands of Derek Simons. Skull Inlet also butted up against the tiny recluse beach where Abigail James and Chester Finch had lost their lives so many years ago. The same beach where he had unknowingly met Miles Gaston, a man who was now dead, probably at the hands of Brad Schulte. Turning to the left, he thought, *Ocean Point, here I come!*

He zipped up his windbreaker. The wind was always more brisk when out on the beach. The ocean waves were up and the sky looked nasty; black, fast moving clouds against a backdrop of endless grey. The tide was going out and as usual fifty yards up the beach the all too familiar temporary small river of seawater was rushing back out to the Atlantic.

He waded through the ankle deep cold water and watched a White Crane standing at perfect attention, waiting for an unsuspecting fish near the large pond always prevalent near the back of the beach.

Further up the beach he passed some low dunes where there were three abandoned taped off turtle nests. The Loggerheads were long gone now, but would return in June for the beginning of turtle season. Angling towards the waters' edge he saw two sand dollars laying in the sand. Bending down, he scooped the thin circular objects up and placed them gently in his coat pocket.

Picking up the discarded sea treasures reminded him of his grandmother and the many walks they shared on the beach when he was a young lad. He had always viewed Amelia as a woman of vast knowledge. He recalled a moment when he was just six years of age, when on a week's vacation on Fripp. While walking with his grandmother on the beach at night he had gazed up into the sky at the vast number of stars. They had reminded him of sparkling diamonds imbedded in an immense black velvet sheet.

He had remarked to Amelia it was amazing the stars were millions of miles away and yet we could still see their light. He remembered how he had asked his grandmother how that could even be possible. Sitting on a log that had at one time washed up on the beach, she explained to him, that it was the hand of God and that man, despite all of their advanced technology and mathematical skills and knowledge could not create a light that bright. The conversation had switched quickly to the tide and he inquired how does the water know where to stop? Amelia explained it was due to the gravitational pull of the moon, but what a lot of folks did not understand was God is in control of all things, including the moon. Even though we as humans have the tide figured out as to when it will come in and go back out twice a day down to the minute, months ahead of when it actually occurs, it is the Hand of God who commands the water to only go so far and then stop. He tells the sun when to rise in the morning and commands it to go down in the evening. Back then, he didn't quite know what to make of this God business, but over the years Amelia had convinced him God did exist. Moving on up the beach even farther, he wondered what God thought about what he, Shelby and the others were doing to Brad Schulte, Tim Durham and Miles Gaston. Would God approve of their dismantling of their very lives? Amelia had told him God was just and merciful. How could God display any mercy to these three boys, now grown men, who had killed Abigail James and Chester Finch?

The beach began a long slow curve back to the right where the ocean flowed into a cove, the waves here much lower. The houses on this end of the island were set back from the water and were much older than the homes on the other end of the beach three miles away. Even when the tide was out there was only a six-foot strip of sand separating the water from the massive wall of rocks protecting the homes lining the beach. This was a part of the beach where no one sunbathed or swam. He always considered it the dirty portion of the three-mile stretch of sand because it was always littered with old broken shells and occasional bits of trash the ocean brought in.

Soon, he found himself climbing the rocks of Ocean Point and once on the top he looked across at Hunting Island and then out to the endless sea. At the end of the rock wall there were three fishermen standing patiently while they waited for a bite. He checked the time, 3:10 in the afternoon. He decided to sit down and relax for a few minutes. He had over three hours before the sun would set.

Only five minutes passed when the first heavy raindrops pecked at the back of his windbreaker. Climbing down the rocks he jumped the last two feet to the sand when his cell phone buzzed. Extracting his phone from his pants' pocket, he answered, "Nick here!"

The deep voice of Conner responded, "Mr. James would like to speak with you."

Before Nick could say a word, there was a moment of silence followed by Bernard's voice. "Nick, I hope I'm not interrupting your afternoon."

"No, not at all. I'm just spending some time on the beach. What's up?"

"Melvin called me about ten minutes ago."

"And what have our local police decided. Are they going to bring Schulte and Durham in for questioning?"

"Yes, they are, but something happened during the meeting that looks like it's going to speed things up. The news Melvin shared with me *is unexpected.* Archbishop Tim Durham was found hanged in his church office just before two o'clock. His door was locked and according to his secretary who discovered him, he was taking a nap. He used a chair and a sash from his robe. Found on his desk was a two page typewritten note in a sealed envelope signed by Durham himself. The information inside is the final blow we need to put Schulte away for good. The St. Louis Police had already received a number of calls about the folders distributed in the city so they were already aware something was going on. When they arrived at the scene and opened the envelope they decided to give the Beaufort Police a call. They faxed a copy of the letter down to Beaufort and it was read at the meeting. According to Melvin, it was quite eye opening."

Bernard hesitated which gave Nick an opportunity to ask, "Are you going to receive a copy of the letter?"

"No, it's considered evidence. I can only hand on to you what Melvin remembered about what the letter said. Basically, Durham admitted he, Schulte and Gaston were on the beach that night with my Abby. The letter states they had all been drinking but Gaston had passed out on their way out to Fripp. They did run into my daughter who was having car troubles. They offered to bring her out here, but when they arrived Abby decided to go with them to a secluded beach. Gaston continued to drink and Schulte convinced Abby to try and seduce Miles. Schulte and Durham left the beach to give them some privacy, but not long afterwards they heard a scream. Going back to the beach they found Abby dead, and Gaston kneeling in the sand with a bloody piece of wood in his hand. Gaston killed her because he had failed sexually. The letter goes on to say Gaston claimed Abby made fun of him and even hit him. He didn't mean to kill her...but he did! They tried to cover up what happened by staging what occurred as a robbery-murder, but then Chester Finch took their pictures. They chased him down and took him back to the beach to try and explain what happened. Finch did not agree with not going to the police. Durham states they had no choice. So they drowned Chester. He and Brad had their hands on Chester when he took his final breath."

Bernard took a breath which gave Nick another opportunity to ask a question. "So, your daughter's death was accidental, but Chester was killed to cover up Abby's death?"

"That's the way it appears, but there's more. Durham goes on to say in the letter Gaston's death was not a suicide, but Schulte either killed him or had him killed. According to the letter, Schulte ordered his men to attack Chic Brumly. Durham ended the letter with an apology to Chester's grandmother and myself and then stated he could no longer live with what he had done back in 1989. He also stated he feared for his life and if Schulte could kill one of his best friends, meaning Gaston, then he may come after him as well. The M.E. in St. Louis said the archbishop took his life somewhere between one and two o'clock."

Nick started walking back down the beach. "So where does that leave us now?"

"We'll continue to play the waiting game. Our part in this may have come to an end. It's now up to the police to go after Schulte."

"But, will they?"

"I don't see where they have any choice. Melvin said once the St. Louis Police found out two out of the three persons mentioned in the folders had lost their lives in the past two days they needed to act quickly. Melvin and two detectives from Beaufort are flying to

Pittsburgh where they will meet with a detective from St. Louis. They have contacted the Pittsburgh Police who will pick Schulte up after Melvin and the others arrive."

"Then it looks like our job is done. When you consider what the letter says, I don't see any way out for Schulte. Do we need to meet and discuss this latest development?"

"No, I don't think that's necessary. I just need to call Shelby, Carson and Chic and update them on what's going on. I'll call you later when I find out more, but you and the others still have to be careful. We can only assume Schulte and his men are not aware Durham took his own life. We are still not out of the woods just yet. Be careful."

The phone call over, Nick started to jog up the beach and tried to call Shelby. The connection was busy. She was probably on the line with Bernard. Deciding to give Carson a call, he dialed his number.

Carson answered almost instantly, "Hello."

"Carson, it's Nick. Listen...you're going to be getting a call from Bernard probably in the next few minutes. Tim Durham hung himself earlier today. He'll fill you in on all the details. Let's meet at the boathouse for dinner tonight."

"Whoa, whoa, whoa...what do you mean...hung himself?"

"It's starting to rain hard and the wind is blowing. I can hardly understand you. Meet me at the boathouse in two hours."

Carson laid down his paint brush. "See ya then."

The rain was coming down in sheets blowing sideways up the beach, Nick running straight into the downpour. He was blinded and running was impossible. He could hardly see where he was going. Walking up over the dunes into some brush he sat down behind a dune and hunkered down just like he and his grandmother had done during a storm the first full summer he spent on Fripp.

Brad Schulte called Tim's cell number, but there was no answer. Then, he called the church for the third time in three hours, his first two attempts no one even picked up. Just as he was about to hang up for the third time, the church secretary answered, "Archbishop Durham's Office. May I help you?"

"Yes, this is Mayor Brad Schulte from Pittsburgh calling for the archbishop. I talked with him earlier this morning. I had an appointment to talk with him again at two, but there was no answer. I called back at three and again...no answer. Is the archbishop in?"

As instructed by the police. Andrea answered, "Archbishop Durham is not in his office at the moment. Something unexpected came up and he can't be reached. Can I take a message?"

"No. I'll be in touch with him tomorrow."

Brad hung up the phone, sat back and looked out the window of his office at the surrounding tall office buildings. He didn't quite know what to make of Tim's reaction to Miles' death and Brumley's beating. The fact he was not in his church office for their two o'clock conversation, and then not even back by three and then four o'clock caused him to think Tim was avoiding him. Walking to the large window he lit up a cigar and looked at the vast number of framed plaques on the wall: Greater Pittsburgh Republican Party Member, Pittsburgh Chamber of Commerce, Rotary Club, Methodists' Men's Club. Walking to the wall he reached up and ran his fingers over his two most favorite plaques. The 1989 Beaufort High School State Football Champions and then a photograph of he, Tim and Miles when they were just fourteen years old. The printed message at the top of the photo read — The Three Musketeers – *One for all and all for one!* He frowned, walked back to his desk and sank in his office chair. The ever-present friendship he and his two childhood friends had shared was unequalled. Back then and all the way up through high school he could trust Tim and Miles with anything. They always confided in each other and helped one another to work out any problems they faced while growing up. That night on Fripp twenty-seven years ago was the beginning of the unraveling of the bond they had shared since they were six years old. He had thought after all these years the deaths of Abigail and Chester would fade away, allowing the three of them to live in peace for the rest of their lives. Sadly, he lowered his head. Miles, one of the Three Musketeers, was dead. Another, Tim, seemed to be wavering from the pact they had made that fateful night. If he could just talk with Tim and convince him Miles' death was their way out. He had to get in touch with him and he couldn't wait long. He had to fly back to St. Louis and talk with Tim face to face again. If he couldn't win Tim over to his way of thinking, then Tim would have to face the same consequences Miles did. It was a matter of survival and he would do what was necessary to avoid losing everything; his wife and daughters, the respect people in Pittsburgh had for him, becoming the next governor of the state and whatever a successful political future had in store for him. He stared at his cell phone, not wanting to make the call he had to make, but yet he knew he had to.

Finally, after a long minute he picked up the phone and dialed the number. On the second ring a voice answered, "John."

Brad hesitated, but then ordered, "John. I need you to get the next available flight to St. Louis for you, Robert and myself. I need to talk with someone there in town. If the conversation does not go the way it needs to I may need to call on you and Robert to solve a problem we have. Understood?"

"Yes sir. I'll schedule the flight, and call you when we are to arrive at the airport. Do we need to pick you up?"

"Yes, that would be fine."

The rain slowed down to the point where Nick could see where he was going. He made his way up the beach at a slow jog and tried to call Shelby again and found his phone was not charged any longer. By the time he got back to the house he was soaked to the skin and chilled to the bone. Shedding his wet clothes on the back porch he went up the stairs, plugged his phone in its charger, turned on the shower, waited until the water was warm and then jumped in. The hot water took the edge off the coldness he felt.

Ten minutes later, he stepped out of the shower and looked at an alarm clock by the bed. He had half an hour before he was to meet Carson at the Boathouse. After dressing, he ran down the stairs, out to the garage where he hopped in the Lexus, backed out of the garage, and headed for Bonito Drive. The rain had slowed down considerably, but by the time he pulled into the marina it picked up causing Nick to make a mad dash across the lot to the protection of the Boathouse's covered porch.

Inside, he removed his coat and smiled at the hostess. "Looks like I made it just under the wire. It's really starting to come down out there again. I'm supposed to meet Carson Pike here tonight. Do you know if he has arrived?"

A passing waitress answered the question, "Yes, he's in the bar seated at the second table by the window. If you follow me I'll take you back."

"That's okay...I know the way."

Making his way through the main dining room, he entered the bar and spotted Carson reviewing the menu. Seating himself, Nick asked, "What sounds good tonight?"

Lowering the menu, Carson responded, "I was thinking seriously about the shrimp and scallop platter." Grabbing a nearby waitress, Carson held up two fingers. "Two drafts please."

Looking across the table at Nick, Carson remarked while the rain beat against the window. "Looks like an all-night rain setting in."

Hanging his coat over a chair next to him, Nick asked, "Did Bernard get hold of you about the hanging?"

"Yeah, he did and it strikes me as quite strange. Two of the three men we're trying to take down have lost their lives over the past couple days." Leaning across the table, he spoke in a low tone. "While I was sitting here waiting for you I got the strangest feeling maybe, just maybe, Miles Gaston was not murdered by Brad Schulte and Archbishop Durham did not hang himself."

"What other possibility could there be?"

"I don't want to bring up the events of the past summer, but do you remember one of the things I pointed out to you while we were at your house waiting for Charley Sparks and Derek Simons?"

"You said a lot of things that night."

"If you'll recall I told you things may not work out the way we planned and are not always as they seem."

"I do remember that conversation and things indeed did not work out the way I thought they would. I never would have thought you would have shot and killed Simons and I certainly never would have expected that Amelia would show up and kill Sparks. I thought we would give them the money and that would be the end of it. Sparks and Simons were dumped out at sea and Amelia wound up with all the money and then on top of that the most shocking of all. I find out she is alive when I was led to believe she died. So, you're right. Things are not always as they seem. But what does any of that have to do with what we are facing now?"

"While I was sitting here waiting for you, I got to thinking about how much Bernard James hates Schulte, Durham and Gaston. When we first met him he informed us he had considered taking matters into his own hands many times but refrained from doing so. What if, and I'm just saying what if, Bernard has already put his Plan B into effect? What if what we've been doing as a team is just a front for what he intended to do from the outset? Destroy the three men who killed is daughter? What if he had Conner go over to Gaston's house, set up a sloppy suicide attempt and actually took out Miles? Maybe he even sent Conner to St. Louis and the hanging of Durham could have been staged."

"But what about the letter that was left. If what was written in the letter is the truth how could Bernard know these things?"

"I don't know, but I do know this. Bernard James has always held a reputation as a ruthless and conniving businessman. In his day he had no reservations about firing people or undercutting his competitors. He never, as far as I know, has done anything illegal, but he always runs right on the edge of the cliff."

Nick's mind was spinning. "If what you say is true, how could he have arranged to have Chic assaulted? Remember, Chic identified one of his attackers as one of Schulte's men."

"I'm not saying what I'm suggesting is true," said Carson. "It's just something to consider and if what I'm saying is true in the end it really doesn't make any difference. Between the photographs and Durham's letter of confession Schulte is left hanging out to dry. We, each one of us, will still receive our fee for helping Bernard to bring these men to justice and finally after all these years, Bernard James gets the justice he deserves."

"I can see what you're implying, and I realize Bernard would do almost anything to bring down the killers of his daughter, but I'm not buying your theory. I'm still of the opinion Schulte had Gaston shot and ordered his men to attack Chic. I also believe Durham hung himself because he feared for his own life. I mean, think about it. Brad Schulte orders his best friend killed to save his own hide. At this point, there is nothing Schulte will not resort to in order to escape his guilt."

The waitress returned with their drinks and asked if they were ready to order. Carson ordered the special and Nick followed by ordering the same. When the waitress left their table, Carson gazed out the window at the now driving rain as he changed the subject. "This rain reminds me of that day I found the body of that girl out there at the edge of the marsh. Finding her was so out of line with what goes on out there. Over the years, I've been up and down every nook and cranny where a boat can possibly go out there and it's always the same. The salt marsh never changes except for when the tide is in or out. Aside from the insects, snakes and gators it's rare, to say the least, that you'll ever see the footprint of a human being in the mud. It's not a place where one just gets out of a boat and walks around. In a way, I'm always at peace when I go out there. It's a different world than most folks are used to. Nobody cuts you off in traffic, nobody butts in line at the grocery store, it's not littered with beer cans and all the other trash people throw from their cars, there's no yelling or screaming. As dangerous as it is, it's actually quite peaceful." Drinking his beer he looked across the table at Nick. "I guess they never did discover who killed the RPS Killer…did they?"

Nick, desirous to change the topic, shrugged the question off, "That was last summer and I for one would just as soon forget all that. Right now I'm concerned with what's going to happen in the next couple days. I think we'll all be able to breathe easier when they put the cuffs on Schulte."

Buttering a roll, Carson remarked, "I've think we've seen the last of Maria Sparks. The Carnahans may question her but she'll have no new information to share with them. I think we're pretty much in the clear in regard to what happened last summer. They'll never find Charley or Derek, or their money. Have you talked with your grandmother lately?"

"The last time I spoke with her was just before Thanksgiving. I probably need to give her a call. What I'd really like to do is take Shelby and Kirby up there to meet her but that's just too complicated. The only way I would ever consider doing that is if Amelia approved and I don't see that happening."

The waitress arrived with their meals and asked them if there was anything else. Carson answered that everything looked fine. Stabbing a scallop, he pointed his fork at Nick and commented, "I reckon you haven't had the best of luck since you moved down here."

"You can say that again! After the crazy summer, what with Ike Miller, the RPS Killer and the Carnahans on my plate, not to mention Charley Sparks and Derek Simons, I was looking forward to a peaceful fall on the beach. But then Shelby had to go and find that old camera in the house I bought. Who would have thought the film in that camera would bring us to the point where we are today?"

Carson nodded in agreement, but then asked, "So what do you think about the letter this Archbishop Durham left behind?"

"I'm no expert on death bed confessions, but I believe people tend to tell the truth when they know they are dying or about to die. What could Durham gain by lying just prior to hanging himself? By telling the truth he really forces Schulte into a corner. I don't see how Schulte is going to wiggle his way out of this."

"You'd be surprised. A powerful man like Schulte will not go down without swinging. With the money he has he could hire a good attorney…even a group of attorneys. The photographs you and Shelby discovered only show that Schulte was on the beach. It doesn't prove he had a hand in killing Abigail James. The letter Durham wrote plainly stated it was Gaston who killed her."

"But the letter stated it was Schulte who convinced Abigail James to seduce Gaston. Doesn't that make Schulte an accessory?"

"I'm not sure. I'm not up on the law. Whoever prosecutes Schulte may have a rough time proving that. The one thing the letter does say is Tim and Brad had their hands on Chester Finch. They drowned him."

"So they could actually get Schulte for Finch's murder but maybe not Bernard's daughter."

"A good lawyer might be able to disprove Schulte's part in killing the Finch kid as well. Since Schulte is now the only person who was on the beach that is still alive he could have his lawyer state the archbishop or even Gaston killed Chester. There is no one to come forward and dispute what he tells the court."

"But he killed Gaston and had Chic Brumly attacked."

"That may be true, but there are no eye witnesses. All the prosecutor will have is a letter written by a man who took part in murdering Chester Finch. Even though Durham is dead, a good lawyer might be able to discredit him, thus making the letter insignificant."

Taking a drink of beer, Nick shook his head in disbelief. "You make it sound like Schulte might be able to walk away from this! I'm not happy because Miles Gaston lost his life and Archbishop Durham hung himself, but I guess in an odd sort of way justice was served. If, for some reason Schulte does walk away from being implicated in the deaths of Bernard's daughter and the Finch kid, not to mention Gaston being shot and Durham hanging himself, I'll feel like everything we tried to do was for nothing. In a way, we did get two of the three we set out to bring down, and despite what people say about two out of three not being all that bad, if Schulte does not go to prison for the rest of his life, then I say we have failed."

Taking another scallop in his mouth, Carson smiled. "You're forgetting something. Bernard James has a plan B in mind. If Brad Schulte walks away free as a bird, it will only be temporary. It could be months from now or maybe even years, but I have a very real feeling Brad Schulte will mysteriously die. I'm not sure how or when it will occur, but if the courts fail to convict the good Mayor of Pittsburgh, Bernard will arrange to have him eliminated from life and no one will ever know who was responsible. To tell you the truth. I'm glad I'm on Bernard's team. I'd hate to be on the wrong side of the man."

CHAPTER THIRTY TWO

BERNARD JAMES HUNG UP THE PHONE AND GAVE A LOOK of satisfaction to Conner and stated with confidence, "That was Melvin Barrett on the phone and he informed me he and two Beaufort detectives have just boarded a flight in Charleston to Pittsburgh. They should be getting in around ten this morning. According to Barrett the Pittsburgh Police masked a call yesterday to Schulte's office to make sure he was going to be in today. They're planning on going in and picking him up around two o'clock this afternoon. I wish I could be there to see the look on his face when they inform him he needs to accompany them down to headquarters for questioning."

Nodding in agreement, Conner asked, "Will they actually arrest him for suspicion of murder, read him his rights and place the cuffs on him?"

"That I cannot tell you. I think they'll have to tread lightly. Remember this is the Mayor of Pittsburgh, not just some common criminal. And because he is the mayor, the Police Commissioner of Pittsburgh is involved; whom I am told is not the best of friends with Schulte. The commissioner may extend the courtesy of not cuffing him, but if Schulte refuses to go along peacefully, then they may be more forceful. I'm really not familiar with police protocol. I know this. I'm sure they will not leave his office without him. Schulte can request to call his lawyer, but he'll still have to comply with the police. This will probably not be an easy task for the Pittsburgh Police as I'm sure Schulte is highly respected by the force. Even after they get him down to their headquarters Schulte may clam up until his lawyer is on the scene. If his lawyer is worth his keep he'll probably arrange bond and Schulte could be free within hours. Sadly, because of his respected political position as mayor, they'll cut him some slack. This could be a long process, but at least we've brought it to the attention of the public. Schulte's going to have a rough time squirming out of the proof that has surfaced. The two beach photographs are incriminating and let's not forget the letter the archbishop left behind. The letter ties right in with the photos. We've done all we can for now. We just have to be patient and see how things go."

Sitting at a window table, Nick looked out at Abercom Street as

Savannah shoppers went about their Christmas shopping. The temperature had climbed into the fifties and people were out in droves. The waitress had just delivered his sweet iced tea when Shelby approached the table. Hoisting his glass, Nick smiled broadly. "Merry Christmas!"

Shelby answered, "Right back at ya." Seating herself, she looked around the interior of the well-known restaurant. "I was really surprised when you called me this morning at work and invited me to lunch. This is only the third time I've been here to The Old Pink House. My boss has brought me and the other secretaries here for lunch on two occasions. I just love this place. They say it's an 18th century Georgian mansion and the place is haunted. I don't even have to look at their menu. I already know what I'm going to order, the BLT salad. I highly recommend it."

Tapping a picture of various meals the restaurant offered, Nick stated, "I think I'm going to go with this pork special they have today."

Pouring a glass of tea from a pitcher, Shelby inquired, "Whatever inspired you to invite me to lunch today?"

Holding up two colorful holiday shopping bags, Nick replied, "I got my Christmas shopping done this morning after I called you. I was going to shop in downtown Beaufort, but I thought it'd be nice to shop over here in Savannah's historic district and then meet you for lunch. So, I knocked out two birds with one stone."

"Today is a big and long awaited day for Bernard James," said Shelby. "All these years he has waited for an opportunity, for some sort of proof that would bring Schulte, Durham, and Gaston to justice and that moment, that day, has arrived. After he phoned me with the news about how the Pittsburgh Police are going to pick Schulte up later today I got to thinking on my way over here to work about what a chain reaction this whole thing is going to wind up being. According to the letter Archbishop Durham left behind, Schulte had Gaston killed because he was going to go to the police. Think about all the people who will be affected by Gaston's death. All the people who worked for him across the country, many of the customers who frequented his restaurants, the people in Beaufort County. And let's not forget all the Catholic parishioners who will be effected by their archbishop hanging himself right there at the church. It seems to me Schulte had his sights set on solving the problem we created for him, but actually wound up leaving himself holding the bag. With both Gaston and Durham dead and gone, now Mayor Schulte has to bare the blame for Abigail James and Chester Finch's deaths himself."

"I did a lot of thinking on the way over here myself," said Nick.

"Since Durham and Gaston are gone, now it is Schulte who stands alone with the most to lose. True, the other two men lost their lives, but they are no longer here to face the consequences of their actions years ago."

"And we can't forget the attack on Chic. He identified one of the voices of his assailants as one of two men he interviewed with Maria Sparks."

"Just thinking about the fact Schulte's men, the same men who chased us in Pittsburgh, could be the same men who attacked and beat the hell out of Chic gives me pause. I think we dodged a bullet in Pittsburgh when we escaped them."

"And I suppose that's why Bernard has warned us to be careful until Schulte is brought in."

"Yeah, that's another thing I've been hashing over in my head," remarked Nick. "Schulte may never even sit in a jail cell. Like we said, his lawyer will get him out on bail. What about the men who work for him? Are they going to be picked up as well? Because if they are not, we, Carson or even Melvin could be their next targets."

"Do you really think Schulte will retaliate when he's in custody? That would be a pretty stupid move to make."

"That seems logical, but I'm of the opinion that what seems logical is not what is happening to either of us. Since I moved to Fripp we have been pursued by a number of undesirable characters. First there was Charley Sparks and Derek Simons, then there was Ike Miller, and let's not forget how you had to tangle with Harold and then finally we had to deal with the Carnahans."

"And that was just last summer!" pointed out Shelby. "Look at what we've been faced with as of late: Maria Sparks and Chic Brumly. Well, Chic turned out to be okay, but he sure was a problem in the beginning. Now, we have to be concerned about Brad Schulte and the men who work for him. Kind of makes you wonder what the New Year will bring."

Nick was just about to take a drink when he looked across the room and then slumped in his chair in disbelief.

Shelby, realizing something was awry, asked, "Did I say something wrong?"

"No, I'm afraid I did! I've spoken Ike Miller into existence!"

"What on earth are you talking about?"

Gesturing, Nick responded in a low whisper, "Don't look now but Ike Miller is at this moment headed for our table."

"No way!" Shelby turned when Ike approached with a tall, well-dressed brunette, who he had his arm around.

Before Shelby could react, Ike and his lady friend stood at their table.

"Well, well," said Ike, "of all the people to run into here at the Old Pink House. Allow me to introduce my fiancée to you." Displaying the woman who could have passed for a professional model, Ike made the introductions, "Nick Falco and Shelby Lee Pickett, I'd like you to meet Olivia J. Hillard, of Hillard, Bateman and Ives Law Offices. Turns out Shelby, Olivia is a long-time friend with your boss, Franklin Schrock. Since I intend to marry Ms. Hillard and once again live in my hometown of Savannah, Olivia paid your boss a visit and explained our situation. Mr. Schrock has agreed, provided I no longer bother you in any way, that the pressure that was placed on me by certain people here has been lifted. I have a right to live in Savannah and I have a business here. Olivia has been informed of my previous relationship with you and we intend to keep things on a civil level, so you have nothing to fear from me. Have a great lunch."

The woman lingered behind when Ike walked off. Placing both hands on the table she leaned toward Shelby and whispered snidely, "See you at the office…honey!"

Nick overheard the comment and asked when she left, "Whatever did that mean?"

"I know exactly what it means. I was going to share some good news I received this morning with you, but as it turns out, it's not so good."

"I take it has something to do with that Olivia character."

"You're damn right it does and she's going to play it to the hilt!"

"I'm sorry, but I'm totally lost. What does that woman have to do with the news you were going to share with me?"

"I no sooner got to work this morning when Schrock calls me into his office. I never shared this with you, but even before we met I've been telling him eventually I wanted to work closer to Beaufort. Kirby is getting older and I need to spend more time with her. As it stands now, and has for some time, the only real time we get to talk is when we're driving back and forth to Savannah. This driving back and forth is really starting to get to me and I'd really prefer if Kirby went to school in Beaufort. Schrock sat me down and explained to me he is in the process of procuring another firm who has an office not only here in Savannah, but one in Charleston and Beaufort. They're an old firm that is quite reputable and does a lot of business. That firm just happens to be Hillard, Bateman and Ives. The story is ol' man Hillard and two of his college buddies started the firm years ago. As the years passed, Hillard's daughter, the one and only Olivia, becomes a lawyer herself and joins the firm. A few more years go by and Hillard dies leaving his portion of the company to Olivia, making her an active partner in the firm. More years drift by and just last year Batemen up and kicked the bucket and now

Ives has decided to retire. Olivia bought both of them out and is now the sole owner of the firm. But without Bateman and Ives being present she has found it difficult to handle all the business coming her way, so she approached Schrock about consolidating her firm with Wheller, James, Schrock and Levawitz. Franklin talked it over with his partners, and low and behold as of next March, Olivia Hillard will be named to the list of partners I work for."

Nick gave Shelby a look of confusion. "I'm sitting here listening to you explain all this to me and I've yet to figure out how this is good news for you. It sounds to me like it's good news for Schrock and his partners and this Olivia Hillard."

The good news is Franklin informed me as of March if I choose to do so I can work out of the new Beaufort office. If I make the move I'll receive a nice raise and won't have to drive back and forth to Savannah. Kirby will be able to attend school in Beaufort and therefore I'll get to spend more quality time with her."

"That does sound like good news. But you said it turned out to be bad news. How do you figure that?"

"It's bad because Olivia Hillard is going to be over the Beaufort office which means I'll be working directly for her. You saw the way she looked at me and that snippy attitude about seeing me at the office. If I go to work for her in Beaufort she'll slowly but surely make my life a living hell. I'm sure Ike has painted a false picture of what happened between us. He probably has her thinking I'm a no good, ring stealing woman, who had the hell beat out of him. It's a way for Ike Miller to get even with me without even being around. I was a fool to ever think he would just let bygones be bygones."

"This doesn't make any sense when you take time to think about it. You helped to save Schrock's daughter, Amanda. Has he forgotten that?"

"No he hasn't forgotten and we talked about that very thing. He said Olivia guaranteed Ike would never bother me again. I guess Franklin bought into her line. Besides that...it's business. Taking on Olivia Hillard and her firm as a partner could be worth millions in the long run to Franklin and his partners."

"Do you have to take the position in Beaufort?"

"No, I don't have to, but still, the fact Ike Miller's soon to be wife is someone I may have to answer to is just too unsettling."

"So, what do you think you'll do?"

"Up until Ike Miller and his her girlfriend walked over here to the table, I had no idea she was with or even knew Miller. It's only been in the last few minutes that I have realized what's happening. I can tell you this. There is no way in hell I would ever work for the woman!"

"That doesn't leave you with much of a choice. You don't want to work for her in Beaufort and you don't want to continue working for Schrock here in Savannah. "Are you just going to up and quit?"

"Actually I think I might. There's a friend of my father's in Beaufort who owns a small legal firm. He's been after me for years to come work for him. It's a much smaller operation and the pay would be less but with the money I'd save from not driving to Savannah five days a week, it would average out to be about the same as I'm making now. I don't have to make a decision right now. The change with Hillard won't be effective until March. That gives me a few months to think this thing through."

"If you want to make change, I think it sounds fine, but there is something you may not have considered. Despite the fact you helped save Schrock's daughter, once you are no longer in his employ, you might not be able to depend on him for protection from Miller like you have in the past."

"I realize that, but I can't live the rest of my life in fear. Listen, it's a couple of days before Christmas and here we sit talking about all the doom and gloom of last summer and the problems we are facing now. I say we forget all this crap, enjoy one another's company and have a great lunch."

"I agree," said Nick. Holding up his hand he signaled for a passing waitress. "I think we're ready to order."

Chic was just finishing his hospital lunch, which in his opinion wasn't one of the best meals he had ever had, when Maria stuck her head in his room and spoke pleasantly, "Chic."

Chic placed his empty tray on a bedside table and answered with a bit of surprise to his voice. "I thought you were going back to New York. The last time I saw you was when you dropped me off up the street from my office. I thought you would have been long gone by now."

Approaching his bed, Maria waved her manicured right hand in the air. "I had every intention of leaving, but decided to stay at the condo out on Fripp for another day. I really like it there. Once again, I was on my way to Charleston late this morning and I stopped in a coffee shop in downtown Beaufort to get a cup of coffee for the ride over when I heard two businessmen talking about how you had been attacked and beaten. They said what was written in the paper claimed it was a robbery. Based on the way we left things I knew that wasn't the truth. I got to thinking about the situation and decided to drive over here to the hospital and see if you were all right. Are you all right?"

Chic forced a smile while his bandaged right hand reached up and touched the side of his bandaged head. "I've had better days but I'll survive."

Pulling up a chair, Maria asked, "Do you mind?"

"No, go right ahead, but I have to say I'm confused because you're still here. Didn't you say after Schulte advised you to go back to New York and forget about him you felt you were getting involved in something dangerous?"

"That's exactly the way I felt, but I didn't think spending another day on the beach would do any harm. I'm glad I didn't leave right away. I would have never known you were attacked. I guess, in a way this is all my fault. If I wouldn't have met up with Ford and Peller and agreed to introduce them to you this would probably have never happened. I should never have let you return to your office by yourself. Speaking of meeting up with Schulte's men. The fact they were interested in Falco and Pickett now leads to me to believe they are somehow involved in this Schulte business. Are they?"

"Look, you need to stop asking so many questions and head to Charleston."

"I've worked with you and I know how good you are at what you do. I can't help feeling this *new client* you told me about has something to do with why you were attacked. And, somehow, this new client must be connected to Falco and the girl. Am I right?"

"Maybe you are and maybe you're not. I'm really not at liberty to discuss my current client's situation. But, while we're on the subject of Nick Falco and Shelby Lee Pickett the only thing I can say is they had nothing to do with the death and or disappearance of your brother, Charley. You and I went down that road. We turned over every stone possible and came up with no proof, so you just need to forget about them. They pose no threat to you, but Schulte and his men? Now that's another story. I'm sure Schulte has returned to Pittsburgh, but we can't be confident his men did. What I'm saying is they may still be down here in the area. We can't be sure yet, but Schulte's men may be capable of doing a lot more than just beating up on people. I don't know if you're aware of this or not, but a man by the name of Miles Gaston was shot and killed the same night I was attacked and the shooting took place out on Fripp. Fripp may be a tropical paradise of sorts but until Schulte and his men are brought to justice, it might not be so safe out there."

"So, I am right. You are involved in something dangerous!"

Holding up his bandaged arm, Chic gave her a stern look. "Do I look like a man who has avoided danger? You need to drive to Charleston today, right now and then get back to New York. If we were ever friends then please do what I ask…please."

Maria stood. "All right, I'll go back to New York but I don't feel good about it." Looking around the room she held out her hands and displayed the four walls. "When you consider the beating you've taken, I would have thought you'd as least receive some cards or even flowers to cheer you up. Do you have no friends?"

Chic laughed softly. "You knew when you first hired me I wasn't the most popular lawyer down this way. In many ways I guess you and I are alike; real pain in the asses! Don't worry about me. I have friends and they'll take care of me. Now, go on…get out of here!"

Walking to the bed, she leaned over and kissed him on his cheek. "All right, I'll do what you ask." Walking to the door she stopped and turned back. "You haven't heard the last of me, Chic Brumly! I'm going to call you in a few days to see how you are. You never know. I might even come back here next summer to visit you. And don't tell me no! You know what a pain I can be!"

She no sooner disappeared than Carson Pike walked in the door and stared back down the hall. "Wasn't that Maria Sparks I just saw leaving your room?"

"Indeed it was," said Chic. "She was just saying good-bye before she heads back to New York."

Carson entered the room and flipped back his coat revealing a handgun stuck in his trousers and then took a seat. "Mr. James has requested I keep an eye on you until after they pick up Schulte."

Melvin, trailed by Beaufort Detectives Mark Lewis and Nelson Webster, emerged from the long tunnel in Pittsburgh that led from their flight from Charleston. They no sooner stepped out into the large carpeted terminal than they saw the sign they were told to look for: Detective Fineburg. Fineburg introduced his partner, Detective Rodriquez, and suggested they grab some lunch right there at the airport while they waited for a Detective Gleeson who was flying in from St. Louis. It was just after twelve noon and Gleeson wasn't expected until one o'clock. They could eat lunch, discuss the plan for the day and then when Gleeson arrived it was only a thirty-minute drive into the city, which would place them in Pittsburgh at 1:30, a half hour before they picked Schulte up.

Entering a nearby restaurant, Melvin spoke to Detective Fineburg, "It isn't often the mayor of a major city is picked up for questioning…is it?"

Sitting at a table, Fineburg answered the question, "I've been on the force here in the city for nineteen years and I've had to pick up all sorts of criminals, or those thought to be criminals, but I have to agree this is by far the strangest assignment I've ever been given."

Rodriquez tucked his tie inside his shirt and remarked, "My wife just got me this tie for my birthday. If I get food stains on it she'll kill me!"

Fineburg opened a briefcase he was carrying and removed one of the folders that had been mailed to Pittsburgh. Laying the folder on the table, he placed his hand over it and stated, "Detective Rodriquez and I have looked over all the information included in this folder. Our Mayor, Brad Schulte, who I have always upheld with the highest respect, has done so many wonderful things for our city but the implications this folder brings forth are quite unsettling. I mean, I even attend the same church he and his family go to. To even think he was involved in the murders of two of his fellow students nearly thirty years ago is just plain unbelievable."

Rodriquez jumped in and commented, "And that's just the beginning of the incredible story that seems to be unfolding here in Pittsburgh. According to the Beaufort Police Department he may be responsible for the shooting death of one of his close friends. I believe his name was Miles Gaston. We were also informed he may have orchestrated the attack of a local lawyer there in Beaufort."

Detective Lewis confirmed the conversation as he nodded and then commented, "And his other friend, Archbishop Timothy Durham, after hanging himself in St. Louis leaves behind a letter naming Schulte responsible for Gaston's death. He stated he took his own life for fear of retaliation from Schulte. As much as you may like your mayor, the proof is right here in front of us. This will be awkward, but it appears to be justified."

Standing in the underground parking garage of the Allegheny Building, Detective Roy Gleeson asked no one in particular, "What floor is the mayor's office on?"

Walking toward an elevator, Fineburg held up five fingers. "Fifth floor. We called his office yesterday and were informed he would be in all day. We should be back down here and on our way to downtown headquarters in less than fifteen minutes."

Standing toward the rear of the elevator, Melvin pulled the collar of his coat up around his neck. "Is it always this cold here in the winter?"

Rodriquez hit the number five button and answered, "The winters here in Pittsburgh are normally on the rough side, what with all the snow, ice and cold temps, but after you've lived here for a few years you get used to it. Now, down where you're from they don't see much snow, do they?"

"I've lived there all my life to date, and in all that time I think it may have snowed two or three times. Now, freezing rain…that's different. It seems over the past ten or twelve years we have been the recipients of some severe ice storms. It hasn't happened that often but when it does occur it brings everything to a grinding halt."

The elevator began its ascend up into the tall building as Fineburg instructed the group. "When we go in Detective Rodriquez and I will do all the talking as the arresting officers. When we get back to headquarters you will all have an opportunity to question the mayor, that is except for Detective Barrett, who being retired and the lead detective at the time of the 1989 murders is here to observe. Are there any questions?"

No questions were asked as the elevator door opened on the fifth floor and the group filed out, Fineburg leading the way down the hall. At the rear of the small entourage, Detective Lewis nudged Barrett on his arm. "I've only been on the Beaufort force for eight years. Up until recently I wasn't even aware of the '89 murders. It must be of great comfort for you to be a part of this…to be on the cusp of solving a cold case of twenty seven years."

Melvin smiled and answered, "Justice will always prevail. Sometimes it just takes a few years."

Hesitating at the large glass doors to the mayor's office, Fineburg addressed the group. "Here goes gentlemen!"

The six men entered the spacious office and approached the main desk where a secretary looked up from her computer and asked, "May I help you gentlemen?"

Fineburg flipped open his wallet displaying his badge and professionally announced, "Detective Fineburg of the Pittsburg Police Department. We are here to see Mayor Schulte. We understand he is in today."

The secretary looked at the badge, and then replied, "I'm sorry but the mayor is not in today."

Rodriquez stepped up to the desk and leaned forward. "What do you mean…he's not in today? We called this office yesterday and were told he would be in."

"He was scheduled to be in today, but this morning, when he arrived here at the office, he informed me he and two of his aids are flying to St. Louis on some business. Would you care to leave a message for the mayor? I believe he is going to return tomorrow sometime."

Detective Lewis leaned toward Melvin and whispered, "Looks like your concept of justice always prevailing will have to wait a little while longer."

Detective Fineburg stared out the window in anger when Rodriquez inquired, "Do you happen to know what flight the mayor took out of Pittsburgh?"

"No, I do not have that information," the secretary answered, "Normally, I schedule all the mayor's flights, but he must have taken care of that himself."

Fineburg asked the next question, "Did Mayor Schulte say where he was going in St. Louis?"

"No, he did not. He just told me he would return to the office tomorrow."

Detective Glesson stepped forward and addressed Fineburg sternly, "What's going on here? You request I fly over here to Pittsburg so I can join in on *seeing the mayor,* and now we are informed that he is not here, but in St. Louis where I just flew out of. Something isn't right here. What's going on?"

Fineburg turned to the secretary and spoke, "Thank you for your time. We'll just try and get hold of him in St. Louis."

The secretary, trying her best to please the local police responded, "I can try and give him a call if you'd like."

Fineburg turned to Rodriquez and whispered for him to take the group back out into the hall. After they left the office, Fineburg politely asked the secretary if he could speak to her in private and gestured at a corner desk.

Shielding her from the others in the office who knew something strange was happening, Fineburg spoke to the woman in a low tone, "What is your name, Ma'am?"

The secretary answered skeptically, "Grace…Grace Adams."

"You and I have something in common, Grace. We are both employed by the same man…Mayor Brad Schulte. I am quite confident you are loyal to your boss. I have a feeling you always know where he is and what he's doing during the hours when he is in and out of the office, so don't you find it rather strange you do not know why the mayor is off to St. Louis?"

"I really didn't give it much thought until you mentioned it."

"The reason I brought you over here away from the other office employees is because of what you said about calling the mayor. We, the police, are in the middle of an investigation. The mayor is part of the investigation, so it is imperative, I repeat, imperative you do not notify the mayor we were in to see him. If you do notify him you may be in danger of obstructing justice. Understand?"

"I'm just the mayor's secretary. I don't want to get in any trouble."

"If you do what I tell you, you won't be in any sort of trouble. When I leave you need to go back to your desk and continue with whatever you were doing before we arrived. If any of the other office staff ask you what this was all about you just simply state we wanted to see the mayor…and that's all you know…all you know. Now, try and have a great day and forget we were here."

Back out in the hallway, Fineburg immediately took control. "There can only be one reason why Schulte and his two aids are going to St. Louis and that is to pay Archbishop Durham a visit. We know from the letter the archbishop left he feared for his life and he stated Schulte was responsible for the death of Gaston and the beating of Brumley. We're going to split into two different operating groups. Myself, Detectives Gleeson and Lewis will fly out for St. Louis while Rodriquez, Webster and Barrett will remain here in Pittsburgh in case Schulte gives us the slip and gets back here before we can contact him in Missouri. If we make contact with him in St. Louis then Glesson will be the arresting officer and he'll be questioned there. If we miss him and he returns here, then Detective Rodriquez will assume responsibility here in Pittsburg." Walking toward the elevator, Fineburg continued, "Gleeson, you need to give your office a call in St. Louis and get some men over to the church where Archbishop Durham served. If they run into Schulte and his aids at the church then they need to be detained until we arrive. If we cannot locate him in St. Louis and if he does not return here to Pittsburgh, then he's on the run!"

Hanging back from the rest of the group in the parking garage, Melvin dialed Bernard's number. As usual Conner answered the phone and within seconds Bernard was on the line. "Mr. Barrett, I can only assume you are calling me with the good news Brad Schulte is in police custody."

"I'm afraid not," apologized Melvin. "We were informed by his secretary he and two of his aids flew to St. Louis this morning. We have split up into two groups: one remaining here watching the office and the other flying to St. Louis. We have called ahead and have some men going to the archbishop's church."

"Keep me posted. This is of great concern because if our mayor is on the run and gets out of the country, it'll be next to impossible with all the international red tape there is to bring him back to the states. We can only hope they nab him in St Louis."

CHAPTER THIRTY THREE

BRAD SCHULTE, TRAILED BY JOHN FORD AND WILLIAM Peeler made their way down the long, wide corridor at the St. Louis Airport. Schulte looked at his watch and ordered, "John, I want you to pick up a rental car and meet William and I at the main entrance. It's now just after three. There is a Mass scheduled at five o'clock. That gives us two hours to get to the church. I'd like to get in and see the archbishop before the service. If I can reason with him then we should be back on a flight to Pittsburgh this evening."

William walked abreast of Schulte and asked, "And if you cannot reason with the archbishop...then what?"

"That's where you and John come in. If that's the case I'll fly back to Pittsburgh and you two will remain behind. When and only *when* I return to Pittsburgh and give you the go ahead will you proceed."

John, seeing the rental car signs veered to the left. "I'll see you out front in a few minutes."

Heading for the main entrance, William suggested, "Maybe you should try and call the archbishop before you drop by."

"I'd tried calling him four times yesterday. On the fourth call I got through only to be informed by his secretary something came up and he was not in. I think he may be trying to avoid me. He can refuse my calls, but he can't refuse to say Mass. Perhaps I should try to call him again. It can't hurt."

Stepping to the side of the aisle, Brad punched the number of the church in and waited. On the third ring, surprisingly a voice answered, "Archbishop Durham's office, Andrea speaking."

Perking up, Brad explained, "Yes, I'm a friend of the archbishop's…actually a childhood friend. I'm in St. Louis on business and decided to drop by and pay my old friend a visit. Is Tim in?"

The policeman standing next to Andrea pointed at a number of typewritten responses she was to give if Schulte called. "No, His Excellency is not in at the moment."

Brad pressed, "Will he be in later?"

"Yes, he should be back here to the church no later than four thirty for the five o'clock Mass."

"Well, maybe I'll attend Mass and drop by to see him after the service."

"That would be fine. Thank you for the call."

The officer immediately picked up his police radio and made a call to an unmarked car parked in front of the church. "Detective Springer…Officer Grey. This Schulte character took the bait. He just called. He is going to attend the five o'clock service. Afterwards he plans on paying the archbishop a visit."

Springer smiled and answered, "All right. That gives us around two hours to prepare for Schulte's arrival. I want you to send the church secretary home, but leave the office unlocked. I will be sending two other offices to remain with you at the office in case Schulte shows up there instead of going to the service. We'll keep you posted."

Turning to two other detectives in the car, Springer opened a folder and removed an 8 x 10 photo. "This is a photo of Pittsburgh Mayor Brad Schulte. We believe two other men will accompany him. About four o'clock I want each of you to station yourselves on either side of the steps to the church. Don't be too obvious. I'll remain in the car. We're either looking for the man in this picture, or three men together as it would be highly unlikely for three men to be attending a church service together. If they show we'll head them off before they enter the church. It will be easier to approach them before they go in."

Schulte and Peeler had to wait outside the airport entrance doors for only two minutes when John pulled up in a rental. The roads were wet from a recent, short snowfall and traffic was moving slowly. Turning on the wipers, John commented, "With this traffic slowdown we might not get to the church on time to see the archbishop before Mass."

Lighting up a cigar, Schulte responded confidently, "That does not pose a problem. We can see him after the service."

Detectives Gleeson, Lewis and Fineburg boarded their Pittsburgh flight to St. Louis at four-thirty. Checking the time, Glesson answered his phone after they seated themselves. The call concluded, he turned to the others and explained, "Schulte called the archbishop's office and informed the church secretary he is going to be attending five o'clock Mass and then would pay the archbishop a visit." Looking at his watch again, he stated with concern, "We're cutting it close. With the time change we're not going to be touching down until 4:15 St. Louis time. That's only going to give us around forty-five minutes to get to the church. Our men stationed there have been instructed to pick Schulte and his men up before they enter the church. We may have to meet them at headquarters. If that's the case, they will be held for questioning until we arrive. Legally we can hold Schulte for twenty four hours. The only thing that would alter that would be his lawyer getting him out on bail and that cannot take place until after he is arraigned." Seating themselves, Gleeson turned to Detective Fineburg and suggested, "You need to call Rodriquez, Webster and Barrett and update them on recent developments and tell them to grab the next possible flight to St. Louis."

John pulled the car over to the curb on a side street next to the church and checked the time: a few minutes past four. Light drizzle started to form on the windshield. John adjusted the heater and commented, "I think I'm going to let the car run. It's colder here than it was in Pittsburgh."

Gesturing up the street at a corner café, Schulte spoke, "There's no sense in going in the church yet. It's too early. The service won't get started for nearly an hour. William, why don't you go up the street and grab us three coffees."

Climbing out of the car, William walked the short block to the café, entered and stood in line at the busy counter. Minutes passed when Detective Springer, who was unknowingly in front of him, turned and ran smack dab into William. Springer apologized and walked off, not realizing he had come face to face with one of the three men they were to prevent from entering the church. William thought nothing of the confrontation and moved forward to order.

Back in the car William handed Schulte and John their coffee. Brad sipped at his and ordered John, "Since we have some time let's take a spin around the block and get the lay of the land."

Making a left hand turn they drove past Springer and the others unnoticed, then made a left at the next street, then another left at the rear of the huge church. At this point, Schulte ordered, "Pull over." Peering out the front window he pointed with the Styrofoam cup. "On the left we can see the church office and then on the right across the street it says church rectory on the front of that brick building. That is where the archbishop lives when he is not conducting his assigned church duties. After the service, I have no doubt I'll be able to talk with him, be it in his office or the rectory. You two will wait outside in the car until I return. When I return I'll either have good news or bad, the good news being the archbishop has agreed with my suggestion, the bad that he is in disagreement. If it turns out to be the latter, then that's where you will come in but not until after I return to Pittsburgh and call you. Understand?"

John looked across the street at the rectory and asked, "If this turns out to be bad news how do you want it handled? Do you want us to stage another suicide?"

"No, as we all know staging Miles' suicide didn't exactly turn out. The police suspect he was murdered. They can't prove it, but I am confident they realize Miles was murdered. If the archbishop does not agree with my terms, I want you to simply take him out. One shot in the head should suffice, but make absolutely sure the man is dead. Keep it simple. If he has to be shot, immediately after the deed, you two need to fly back to Pittsburgh. That should put an end to all this nonsense. Now, let's pull back around to where we were parked before. We still have about twenty minutes before we go in."

When their flight touched down in St. Louis Gleeson called Detective Springer. "Springer…its Gleeson. We just arrived at the airport. It's now four twenty and the service at church will probably begin before we can get there. What do things look like right now?"

"I have three officers inside the church office and two men at the main entrance of the church. So far we haven't seen anyone matching Schulte's description. A few people have shown up for Mass but it's still early."

"Don't wait for us. If Schulte and his men try to enter the church, they must be stopped. Take them down to headquarters and put them in three separate holding rooms until we arrive. Schulte will throw a hissy. He'll probably demand to call his lawyer right off the bat. You can stall this, but eventually he'll have to be allowed to make the call. We'll see you downtown."

Springer laid his cell on the seat, peered through a set of binoculars, and watched two different couples and an elderly lady climb the wide concrete steps to the church. He scanned the street. Everything seemed normal; no sign so far of Brad Schulte and his two aids.

Brad finished his last drink of coffee, held up his hand and gestured, "It's quarter till. Let's go on in. We'll sit near the back because we want to leave a few minutes before the service ends so we have time to get around to the back to the archbishop's office and the rectory. When we get back there wait in the car. I shouldn't be more than a half hour or so. If he agrees to what I'm going to suggest then we'll all head back to Pittsburgh, if not, then you'll run me to the airport, then return here and wait for my call. If that's how things pan out, then you know what must be done. Let's go."

Sleet was just beginning to fall when they crossed the street and started up the walk. Springer spotted them when they made the turn on the intersecting street. "Martin...Clay! I think our three men are coming up the street. Head them off when they get to the top of the first flight of steps. I'll join you and we'll take them off to the side. We don't want to make a spectacle of this. They should be at the top in less than a minute."

Detectives Martin and Clay casually looked at one another when the threesome approached the steps, Schulte leading the way. Climbing the steps, John asked, "How can we be sure who the archbishop is? There may be more than one priest attending the service."

"Don't worry, I'll point him out," assured Schulte.

They no sooner stepped up on the ten-foot flat level that separated the first flight of steps from the second when Martin and Clay closed in from two sides, Martin speaking first, "Excuse me…Brad Schulte!"

Not expecting to be addressed while going into the church Brad was taken off guard. His lack of a response caused Martin to repeat himself, "Are you Brad Schulte, Pittsburgh's Mayor?"

Brad answered confidently, "Yes, I am the Mayor of Pittsburgh. Have we met before?"

"No, I've never been to Pittsburgh." Flipping open his wallet, he displayed his badge and confirmed, "Detective Martin...St. Louis Police Department, and this is my partner Detective Clay. We need you and your two aids to step to the side."

Schulte looked Martin up and down and then gave Detective Clay a hard stare. "I'm afraid I don't understand. Is there some sort of problem?"

"Yes, there is a problem and we need to step away from the church entrance so we can discuss the matter."

John stepped forward and objected sternly, "Mr. Schulte is the Mayor of Pittsburgh. As one of his aids I strongly object to not being allowed to enter a house of worship."

Springer joined the group and spoke up, "Mr. Schulte! You and your aids will not be attending the service today. You need to come along quietly with us down to headquarters for questioning." Looking directly at William who he had run into at the café, Springer smiled, "Small world!"

Brad didn't understand what Springer meant but remained calm and apologized for John's actions. "You'll have to excuse my aids…but they are more than just aids; they are bodyguards. You may not be aware of this but I'm going to be running for the next Governor of Pennsylvania. I'm not that familiar with how politics work here in the State of Missouri, but I'm afraid that I, over the years have acquired a lot of political enemies. These men are simply doing what they are paid to do and that is to protect me."

Guiding Schulte and his men to a side courtyard, they stopped next to a large fountain when Springer suggested, "We'll need to see I.D, from not only you Mr. Schulte, but your aids as well."

Brad reached inside his coat for his wallet and gestured at John and William to do the same while he spoke, "I must say, the hospitality here in St. Louis is not what I thought it would have been. We were simply going to church."

Springer looked at Schulte's I.D. and handed it back. Detective Martin read the other two I.D.'s out loud, "John Ford...William Peeler." Handing back the I.D. cards, he politely asked, "Are either one of you gentlemen carrying?"

John gave Brad a look for approval, and Schulte replied, "Both of my men as body guards are indeed carrying weapons and are licensed to do so. They will be more than glad to show you their license."

Springer interrupted, "We'll not only need to see their license but they will have to surrender any weapons until after they are questioned."

"Well now," said Brad, "I don't necessarily agree with that but since I'm not in the State of Pennsylvania I guess we'll just have to abide by whatever you say. Hand over your weapons boys. We are guests here in Missouri and certainly wouldn't want to break any laws, but I feel I have a right to ask what it is we are to be questioned about."

"By all means," stated Springer. "We have received some information in regard to a set of murders that took place back when you were in high school...I believe it was in 1989. The investigation included not only you but also two of your close friends. We found it strange we would receive information on two murders committed in South Carolina here in Missouri so we contacted the police in Beaufort and they informed us they as well had received similar info. They requested we bring you in for questioning."

Brad waved off what Springer said and responded, "The information you received is not an accurate account of what happened back in 1989. I also received the same information you have. That information was mailed out not only here in St. Louis but Pittsburgh as well. It is nothing more than a political smear tactic to alter my attempt to run for governor."

"That may be, but nonetheless, you and your two companions must accompany us down to headquarters."

"Now wait a minute," said Brad. "What you said doesn't hold water, at least for my two aids. Neither one of them are from Beaufort and besides that, when those murders happened they were probably around ten years old. Why should they be questioned about something they have absolutely no connection to?"

"Since you asked," retorted Springer, "we are also going to be asking you some questions about another murder down in Beaufort...that of Miles Gaston. I believe he was a close friend of yours?"

"He was a close friend of mine...very close. I heard his death was a suicide. How could I or my aids here have anything to do with that?"

"We'll discuss all the details when we get to headquarters. For now, you need to come along."

Upset, John looked at Brad and then to Springer. "This is a pile of crap. Maybe I don't want to go along for this questioning."

Pulling back his suit coat, Springer displayed a set of handcuffs. "It's up to you. You can come along peacefully and cooperate with us or we can snap the cuffs on you. It's your choice."

Brad intervened and explained to his aids with a stern look. "We'll come along peacefully." Turning back to Springer, he warned, "It's only fair to inform you if things get too far out of hand I will notify my lawyer to fly out here."

"That's your right. Now, let's go back down the stairs and take about a twenty minute ride downtown."

Schulte was placed in Springer's car while Ford and Peeler were put in a second car with Martin and Clay. After Schulte was locked in the backseat, Springer stepped around to the back of the car and made a phone call.

Gleeson, driving down Route 70 toward downtown St. Louis, picked up his cell. "Detective Gleeson."

"Paul. This is Springer. We have Schulte and his two aids in hand. We are just about to transport them downtown. We should be at headquarters in about twenty minutes. What's your ETA?"

"Right now we're on Highway 70. Traffic is really bad at the moment and probably won't get any better when you consider the time of day. If things continue as they are now, I figure, maybe thirty, thirty-five minutes."

"Excellent!" said Springer. "We'll hold them until you arrive."

As the two car caravan pulled away from the church the bells in the tower sounded the time. Five o'clock.

From the backseat, Brad leaned up and spoke through the metal grating to Springer, "If you don't mind I'm going to give my lawyer a call in Pittsburgh. It'll probably take him a few hours to get here, but I can guarantee by tonight I'll be flying back to Pennsylvania. And another thing while we're at it. My wife happens to be a United States Senator. Between the pull she has and my lawyer you're probably not going to have much time to ask me many questions. You're department may have bitten off more than it can chew."

Springer looked in the rearview mirror. "You just go right ahead and make your calls, Mr. Schulte. Depending on how things go, by law we can detain you up to twenty-four hours. That's the law and no senator or fancy-assed lawyer from Pittsburgh can change that. Now why don't you sit back and enjoy the ride."

Detective Rodriquez, seated down the hallway from Schulte's Pittsburgh office, received the call when Barrett and Detective Webster were returning with coffees. Rodriquez said good bye to the caller, stood and informed his two current partners, "Might as well turn around and go right back down the elevator. Fineburg called me. Schulte and his men have been picked up and are presently being taken to St. Louis Police Headquarters. He, Gleeson and Lewis just touched down and are on their way to join them. We need to grab the next available flight to St. Louis. If we can get a flight in the next couple of hours, they'll hold off on the questioning until we arrive. It all depends on when Schulte's lawyer shows up."

Entering the rear of police headquarters, Schulte and his men were led down a long hall, Schulte placed in a room and his men taken further down the hall. Schulte looked around the drab room: a single table, four what appeared to be well-used chairs, a tinged yellowish-grey floor surrounded by off-beige walls. A large mirror, obviously one-way glass, centered on the right hand wall. Frowning, Schulte remarked, "Not the most accommodating room I've ever spent time in." Walking over and looking at the one-way glass he shook his head, turned back and asked Springer, "Mind if I smoke?"

"Personally," said Springer, "I could care less, but the State of Missouri prohibits smoking in public buildings, so why don't you have a seat. You may have to sit in here for a couple of hours before the questioning begins."

"Why wait?" asked Schulte. "Let's get right to it."

"No, I think we'll wait until all those involved have arrived."

"And who are *all those involved?*"

"You'll know soon enough. Would you care for a glass of water, soda…maybe a coffee?"

Seating himself in the uncomfortable chair, Schulte folded his hands on the table and responded, "Coffee will be fine…two sugars and some creamer."

Springer walked to the door. "Coming right up."

Minutes later, preparing his coffee, Schulte looked at the one-way glass and thought he was going to have to be careful about his facial expressions and body movements. Someone was no doubt, at that very moment, watching him and analyzing his every move. Standing, he removed his coat, draped it over the back of the chair, sat back down and took a sip of coffee. He wondered who *all those involved* were? He looked at his Rolex, 5:37. He hoped his lawyer would show up before the questioning began. He was going to need some time to speak with his lawyer beforehand, as the attorney was not going to be familiar with what Schulte was going to be asked. Stretching, he thought to himself it was going to be a long night, but it was early in the game and he was confident he'd be back in Pittsburgh before morning. In his mind he began to review and plan the false version he was going to tell his lawyer about what happened back in 1989.

Ten minutes passed when Gleeson, Fineburg and Lewis arrived at headquarters. Gleeson, after being informed by a desk sergeant, led his two companions down the hall, stopping at the room housing Schulte. Looking through the glass at the sole occupant inside the 10 x 12 room, Gleeson placed his hands on his hips, commenting, "So, there sits the Mayor of Pittsburgh."

Fineburg, standing next to him, shook his head in wonder. "Yep, that's Mayor Brad Schulte, the best Mayor Pittsburgh has ever had. He's more than just the mayor of our city to me; he's a personal friend. Like I said before, he and his family attend the same church as my family. I've known the man for years. I know his wife and his two daughters. I've been to outings at his home, been on fishing trips with him. Why, it was just two weeks ago he and I manned a grill at a church cookout. I find it hard to believe he would be involved in the murders of two of his high school friends not to mention the recent murder of what I'm told happens to be one of his best friends. His personality and the things he's done for the city of Pittsburgh; well it just doesn't add up. It doesn't make any sense."

Detective Lewis leaned on the glass and inquired, "When does the questioning start?"

Motioning down the hallway, Gleeson responded, "Let's go find Detective Springer and see what's in the works."

Springer was just coming out of an office when Glesson and the others approached. "Just in time gentlemen. I just got off the phone with Detective Rodriquez. They were not able to get a regular flight until later this evening, but they did manage to get a private plane to fly them up here. They should be here within an hour or so. We'll let Schulte and his men sit until then. Hopefully we'll have some time with them before Schulte's lawyer gets in. We've got coffee at a small lounge at the end of the hall. If you're hungry we can order in."

A half hour passed and Brad had grown tired of sitting in the drab room. Getting to his feet he paced back and forth. Not wanting anyone who was observing his actions to get the impression he was nervous he rotated his arms and stretched as if he were stiff from sitting. For the moment he was not in control; a feeling he did not like. He was always in control of any situation he was faced with. He would use this time to continue to plan ahead about what he was going to say. He had to stay a step ahead of the police. Even though the odds seemed to be quickly stacking up against him, he still had one thing in his favor and that was the burden of proving he did indeed kill Abigail James, Chester Finch and Miles Gaston. This loomed as still a problem for the authorities. Walking to the wall he tapped hard on the one-way glass. Within seconds an officer opened the door and inquired, "Yes, what is it?"

The immediate response answered his question whether he was being watched. Smiling at the female officer, he asked politely, "Would it be possible for me to get a glass of water?"

The woman smiled back. "I'll see what I can do."

At 7:10 p.m., Rodriquez, Webster and Barrett entered the downtown St. Louis Police Headquarters. The threesome was directed to a conference room where they met up with Detective Glesson and the others. Gleeson suggested they have a short ten-minute meeting to discuss how the questioning would proceed then finished up by dividing the group into three, three man interviewing teams. Gleeson, Fineburg and Barrett questioning Schulte, Springer and the remaining detectives split up between interviewing John Ford and William Peeler. Toward the end of the meeting Barrett excused himself to the Men's room where he called Bernard to update him on where they stood.

Gleeson, Fineburg and Barrett filed into the interrogation room where they found Schulte standing in the corner. Gleeson motioned at the seat and instructed the mayor, "Please have a seat. We are about to begin."

Barrett took a seat on a chair next to the wall while Gleeson and Fineburg seated themselves across the table from Schulte. Brad couldn't believe his eyes when they fell on his old friend. "Ralph...Ralph Fineburg. What on earth are you doing here in St. Louis?"

Fineburg smiled at Brad and spoke, "I suppose I could ask you the same thing. So, why exactly are you here?"

Looking at Gleeson, Brad explained calmly, "A Detective Springer decided to stop me from attending a religious service and hauled me down here for questioning."

"Look Brad," said Ralph. "You and I are both practicing Methodists. Don't tell me you flew all the way here to St. Louis to attend a Catholic Mass."

Brad smiled, "I have no intention of switching my beliefs. I came here to pay my close friend, Archbishop Durham a visit. You may not be aware of this but we grew up together down in Beaufort, South Carolina."

"I guess that brings us to this," added Gleeson. Holding up the folder, he then dumped the contents on the table. Holding up one of the beach photos he pointed out, "The boy in the middle of this photograph is Tim Durham; am I not correct?"

Brad saw his opportunity to control the meeting and answered, "Yes that's Tim and the other boy on the end with the section of wood raised in his hand is my other friend, Miles Gaston. We were, all three of us, the best of friends especially back in high school."

Gleeson coughed and then asked, "Are you still best friends with these men?"

"Well, you know how things go. After you graduate from high school and set out on your own, many of your childhood friends simply become pleasant memories of a time past. Over the years the three of us have stayed in touch from time to time, but not like when we were kids." Taking notice of Barrett who had remained quiet, Brad inquired, "You look sort of familiar to me. Have we met before?"

"That we have," stated Melvin. "Detective Silk and I were the lead detectives in 1989 when the Beaufort Police conducted an investigation into the murders of Abigail James and Chester Finch. Surely, you remember your two classmates who lost their lives that year out on Fripp Island?"

Snapping his fingers, Brad smiled. "That's right…now I remember you. I remember the day you interviewed me in Mrs. Trent's office at Beaufort High."

"I'm surprised you remember after all these years."

"How could I or any of the students forget that week when the police came to the school and interviewed everyone? I especially recall the day you interviewed me. You asked me a number of questions you already had the correct answer to. I felt like you were trying to throw me off."

"Indeed I did, and the reason was you seemed rather nervous, more nervous than the other students I interviewed. I knew just after a few minutes that you knew more than you were revealing. Your two pals, Miles and Tim, didn't fare any better than you. We knew you three were involved somehow; we just couldn't figure out how. If I recall we interviewed you three, what was it…three, four more times. I remember the story you three told us like it was yesterday. But, here's the thing that just didn't seem right. All three of you told the identical story down to the last detail, almost as if you had all rehearsed it. It was too perfect. I recall the entire story about how you, Miles and Tim were celebrating the fact you were state football champions. You told us after you drove around Beaufort you drove out to Fripp Island where there was to be a large party thrown in honor of the team. On the way to Fripp you ran across Abigail James, whose car was broken down. Not being able to repair her car you agreed to run her out to Fripp. All three of you claimed after you arrived on the island you dropped her off at the pool and you never saw her again that night. Later on during our investigation we discovered the broken bottleneck of a bourbon bottle with not only the James girl's DNA, but Miles Gaston's also. Previously, you told us the three of you had not been drinking. We caught you in a lie. The three of you agreed you had lied because you didn't want your parents to know you had been drinking. You then told us Miles and Abigail had been drinking all the way out to Fripp and after you dropped her off she kept the bottle, hence, Miles' DNA on the bottleneck. Try as we did, we could not tie the three of you in with the murders, so all three of you walked and we had a cold case on our hands that hasn't been solved in twenty-seven years."

Brad raised his hands. "Twenty-seven years has passed and nothing has changed, so why am I being questioned?"

"You're only half right, Mr. Schulte. It is true twenty-seven years has passed, but it is untrue that things haven't changed…because in fact…they have!" Getting up, Melvin walked to the table and held up the two photos from the folder and continued his explanation, "These two photographs clearly prove you *and your friends* were in fact on the beach the night Abigail James was killed." Leaning across the table he held both photos in front of Schulte. "Tell me, is that not Abigail James pictured in the photos and is that not Miles Gaston holding what very well could be the murder weapon?"

Brad remained in control. "I have no doubt the girl in the photo is Ms. James, but that does not prove *that I killed her*. The truth is…we did, all three of us lie to the police, but I had no choice."

Pulling the chair he had been sitting on next to the table, Melvin laid down the photos, "Well then, this should be interesting."

For effect, Brad reached over and picked up one of the photos. "There can be no doubt we were there, but I was not there when she was killed. The part of the story we left out was when we arrived on Fripp, Abigail refused to get out of the car. After finding out we planned on going to a private hidden beach we knew of since we were children, she demanded to go along. I objected, but Miles and Tim said it wasn't any big deal. So, she came with us. When we got to the beach Miles and Abby continued to drink. Now, Mr. Barrett, you as everyone else back then were well aware of the fact Abigail James would sleep with anything wearing pants. She suggested she and I have a go at it, but I refused. Then, she went for Tim who also refused, informing her he was soon to be engaged to LuAnn Dawson, a cheerleader he had been dating for going on four years. As we continued to talk Abigail found out Miles was a virgin. She said this was quite interesting. She had been with many a boy, but had never had a virgin and wanted to do so. Miles was half tanked and we thought this would be an opportunity for him to finally become a man. We left the beach so Abigail could have some alone time with Miles. I recall she still had the bottle of bourbon with her."

Picking up the other photo for effect, Brad went on, "Tim and I climbed over the stone wall to give them some privacy. I guess it was about twenty minutes or so later when we heard a loud scream. We clamored back over the wall only to discover Miles, stark naked on his knees in the sand, that bloody section of wood held in his right hand. Abby was sprawled out on the beach in front of him, her head and upper body covered in blood. I was shocked. When we asked Miles what happened he cried like a baby and explained he killed her, but he hadn't meant to. It was an accident, sort of like self-defense. He told us he could not perform…sexually...and Abigail had made fun of it and told him she was going to spread it around school he was queer. She just kept calling him names and said he was a little faggot. Miles said he couldn't stand being called names and he called her the Beaufort County whore at which point she slapped him hard across his face. He slapped her back and tried to leave but she kicked him in the groin and hit him in the face with her purse. He told us he lost it, picked up the piece of wood and just kept hitting her. He didn't mean to kill her, but that's the way things turned out."

Lowering his head, once again for affect, Brad placed his hand over his face and continued to lie. "That turned out to be the worse day of my life. Kneeling there in the sand holding that piece of wood, Miles asked me what we were going to do. I told him there was only one thing we could do and that was to go to the police and explain exactly what happened. Miles objected, saying the police would never buy into the self-defense story and besides, he didn't want it to get around school he was queer, nor did he want to spend the rest of his life in prison. He said we had to cover up what really happened. He told us we could make it appear like it had been a robbery-murder. I objected and told him there was no way I was going to be involved in a lie like that. Back then we were known as The Three Musketeers. Everyone knew that. We always were there for each other and always made decisions together regarding problems any of us faced. We would always take a vote and the majority of two always won out. Miles made it clear his vote was to cover up the murder. I, on the other hand strongly suggested we go to the police. It was a tie and the final decision was up to Tim. I pleaded with him to go along with my idea but surprisingly, he went against what I thought, saying Miles would not only be guilty of murder but he and I would go down the tubes as well. The vote was in: two to one in favor of protecting Miles. I know this must sound stupid, but we were only eighteen and we valued our friendship more than anything else. We went with Miles' idea of the robbery-murder concept. We threw Abby's clothes on the beach, scattered the money she had in her purse around, collected the broken bourbon bottle and were satisfied we had covered our tracks. The incoming tide would wash away any evidence we had ever been there with her."

Getting up to add more effect, that would hopefully display remorse, Brad walked to the corner shaking his head. "We checked and double checked to make sure we had left no incriminating clues behind and were just about to leave the scene when everything fell apart. Out of nowhere Chester Finch takes some photographs of us standing on the beach next to Abby. Chester was a nice kid, but kind of a nerd, always taking pictures at random and then making collages. We yelled at him and he took off. We ran him down at the Tarpon Blvd turnaround and after talking with him decided to take him back down to the beach and simply explain what happened. He agreed with us that Abigail didn't have the best morals but said he thought we should go to the police. Miles objected, saying he was not going to go along with that. During this conversation, Tim remained silent, which I thought was weird. We had forgotten Chester's camera and I volunteered to go back to his car and retrieve it. Tim finally began speaking, saying when I got back we had to destroy the camera, which Chester strongly objected to. Minutes later I returned only to find Miles had convinced Tim, Chester had to die. They claimed there wasn't any other way out of what we had gotten involved in. Miles and Tim drowned Chester in Skull Inlet. Once again I was outvoted. We left both bodies there on the beach, returned to the party, and well, you know the rest from there. We stuck to our story and walked away free as birds."

Returning to his chair, Brad looked at Barrett. "I say free as a bird, but there isn't a day that passes where I do not have to struggle with the fact

I did not do the right thing and went along with Miles and Tim. Who would have thought after all these years I would finally be faced with telling the truth about my two best friends and what they had done back in '89."

There was a moment of silence in the room, when Gleeson spoke up, "That's quite a story but it does not explain the death of Miles Gaston."

"That can be explained very easily, detective." Tapping the photos with his index finger, Brad continued, "When these photos recently emerged, at first I thought it was a political ploy to prevent my running for governor, but then I found out Miles and Tim received folders also. We decided to meet right here in St. Louis and try to figure out what was going on. We had no idea and I still don't know where these photos came from. Remember, we destroyed the camera. During this meeting, Miles loses his cool just like he did when he killed Abby. He storms out of the room we were at saying he was going to go to the police and confess he had killed both Abby and Chester. Tim was beside himself. He knew if Miles went to the police he would be dragged down also. He said he was an archbishop and could not afford to be involved in murders that took place years in the past. He told me I had nothing to fear. I had just simply gone along with what he and Miles had agreed to. I was at a loss for what should be done, but then Tim said he was going to go down to Beaufort and talk some sense into Miles. He told me not to worry and everything would be fine. The next thing I know, I find out Miles is dead; a suspected suicide that looked like murder. I decided to get in touch with Tim about Miles' death and that's why I came to St. Louis."

Fineburg spoke up, "Brad, you and I have known each other for a number of years. I, for one, can't believe you remained silent all these years, especially when you claim you didn't murder anyone. After listening to your story I believe you came here to see Tim Durham, but not for the reason you say. The story you have shared with us seems to have placed all the missing pieces of this twenty-seven year old puzzle right into place, except there is one piece that does not fit and that's just this. Archbishop Timothy Durham is dead as well. He hanged himself yesterday right in his office at the church."

Brad looked across the table at Gleeson, Barrett and Fineburg with genuine shock. "That cant' be! I talked with him on the phone yesterday. Why would he hang himself?"

"The answer to that," said Fineburg, "is noted in a typewritten letter Durham left behind." Holding up a copy of the letter, Ralph smiled. "According to what's written here, Archbishop Durham unveils a completely different story. It's quite compelling." Shoving the document across the desk, he stated, "Perhaps you would like to read what the archbishop typed?"

Inside Brad was a ball of nerves, but he couldn't show any emotion that would give the police an upper hand. Taking the letter he slowly read line after typewritten line. Finished, he handed the letter back to Fineburg and calmly stated, "This letter changes nothing. It in no way alters the truth, which I have already told you. I have admitted Miles killed Abigail James, which the letter verifies. I have no idea why Tim has named me as the one who suggested we kill Chester. I had nothing to do with that and as far as Tim fearing for his life from me doesn't make sense. The very fact that Archbishop Durham hung himself states very clearly of a man who was not thinking straight. I mean, let's fact the facts. When an individual takes their own life they cannot be considered to be in their right mind. I think Tim killed Miles and then later took his own life. And, even if Miles' death is in all actuality a suicide, that means both men; one who killed Abby and then both who took part in killing Chester, took their own lives. The truth is everyone who was on the beach that night is dead except for me. That letter is nothing more than the ramblings of a man who wound up taking his own life. I'm the only one out of the three who didn't kill anyone and yet you question me."

Gleeson spoke up, "There are quite a few unanswered questions we still have for you. Things like why were you down In Beaufort the night Miles took his last breath and then there is an attack on an attorney in Beaufort by two men. One of which is described as possibly one of your aids. And what about the fact your aids tried to waylay a man by the name of Nick Falco and a girl named Shelby Lee Pickett when they came to see you in Pittsburgh."

Brad held up both his hands. "I think I'm done answering questions. You gentlemen are a basket that I do not want to place all my eggs in. I think I'll wait for my attorney to get here if it's all the same."

CHAPTER THIRTY FOUR

NICK GUIDED HIS '39 BUICK DOWN NEWCASTLE STREET. *What a peaceful and quiet neighborhood,* he thought. Beaufort, South Carolina: *The smallest, friendly city in the South.* He looked at his watch, 8:07 in the morning. Smiling, he came up on a stop sign, two blocks from Shelby's house. It was Christmas Eve, well at least that's what people nowadays called the day before Christmas. Growing up in Cincinnati, Christmas Eve was always the night prior to Christmas, not the entire day. He waited while a man and woman walked their Irish Setter across the intersection. The woman waved at him, her broad smile indicating she was wishing him Merry Christmas. Waving back, he started again up the street.

The temperature was almost sixty-five degrees, the warmest day before Christmas he could ever remember experiencing. On the way into town he had listened to the weatherman who said for Beaufort County it was unseasonably warm; nearly fifteen degrees above normal for the time of year. Two children riding bikes on the sidewalk waved at a neighbor who was sweeping off her front porch. This was his first Christmas in the Lowcountry and it seemed odd: no snow, no ice, no cold temperatures. He thought about how strange the weather was in the South. In July and August the temperature could rise to the mid-nineties for weeks, at times topping the one hundred degree mark and people, even though used to the hot summer weather, would give anything for just one day where the temperature was only sixty-five. It was no different than folks up north during the winter months with below freezing temps. During those times he recalled as a young boy during the winter hoping for one ninety-degree day. He figured it was the same wherever people lived. They were never happy with the weather for very long. It was always too cold or too hot, there was too much rain or not enough and on and on. It didn't make a difference to him either way.

Pulling up in front of 714 he saw Shelby Lee and Kirby sitting on the porch swing. He no sooner pulled to the curb than Kirby came running out to greet him. Rolling down the passenger side window, he smiled at Shelby's daughter. "Well, good morning there Kirby. Are you ready for Christmas?'

Leaning in the open window, Kirby was all smiles. "You bet I am. I hear you're coming for Christmas dinner tomorrow."

"That's the word on the street," joked Nick. "I might even be bringing along a special gift just for you."

"Me and mom finished up our shopping yesterday. I picked out something special for you too." Before Nick could utter another word, Kirby rambled on, "We're having roast duck and glazed ham for dinner, with all the trimmin's. Grandma said I could help her with glazin' the ham. I'm going to make sugar cookies with red and green sprinkles on top."

"I can hardly wait. I'll be wantin' some of those cookies with a big glass of cold milk."

Shelby reached for the door handle and instructed her daughter. "Kirby, you need to get back in the house. There's a lot to do to get ready for tomorrow and Grandma needs your help."

Kirby politely responded, "Yes Ma'am," turned and ran back up the walk to the front door, turned and waved goodbye.

Pulling away from the curb, Nick remarked, "She really is a good kid."

"She is that," said Shelby, "and she thinks the world of you."

Making a left hand turn at the end of the block, Nick promised, "I'll have you back to the house in no time…maybe an hour or so. Bernard said he wants us to meet with him and the others on the team in Chic's room over at the hospital. I think he's gonna close the door on this Brad Schulte business."

"And not a day too soon," added Shelby. "I'd kind of like to spend the holiday without being concerned about Schulte and his goons."

Turning right on Carteret Street, Nick shook his head in amazement. "Who would have thought when you found the camera at Mrs. Yeats house that eventually the photos you developed would lead to the deaths of Miles Gaston and Archbishop Durham."

Shelby agreed. "And let's not forget Brad Schulte could be on the verge of spending a long time behind bars."

"That still remains to be seen. I guess that's one of the things Bernard wants to talk about today." Changing the subject, Nick inquired, "Are you still thinking about quitting your Savannah job?"

"I haven't thought too much about that since we talked. Actually, there isn't much to think about. I'm definitely going to quit. I have until March to inform Mr. Schrock. After the first of the year I'm going to meet with my father's long-time attorney friend and see if he's still interested in hiring me. If he says yes I'll probably go ahead and give my notice to Schrock. I haven't said anything about that situation to anyone in my family so I'd just as soon if the topic is not brought up tomorrow at dinner."

Running his thumb and index finger across his lips, Nick gestured, "Your secret is safe with me!"

Turning onto Ribaut Road, Nick continued talking, "I haven't even been living down here six months yet and we are hopefully coming to the end of a second adventure. Let me ask you this? That day we first met on the beach. Could you ever have imagined what we've been through?"

Looking out the window at a large Christmas sign along the side of the road, Shelby laughed, "Not hardly. I was all ready to spend another boring summer in Beaufort County, but then you strolled down the beach and everything changed. Hell, if I hadn't run into you that day, who knows what would have happened the last few months. I, believe it or not, might still be with Ike Miller and you and I would have never discovered who the RPS Killer was. You can't say our relationship hasn't been interesting!"

Nick made a right hand turn into the Beaufort Memorial Hospital parking lot, found a spot and parked. Getting out of the car, Shelby asked, "How long did they say Chic would have to stay here before he's released?"

"If I remember I think they said he had about a week before he gets to go home. Even then, he's going to be sore for quite a long time. Schulte's men really kicked the hell out of him."

Getting off at the third floor, they walked down a hallway, made a right and then a short distance later entered Chic's room. They were the last to arrive, Carson and Melvin standing by the window engaged in a conversation, Bernard sitting in his wheelchair next to the bed with Conner sitting off to the side, reading a newspaper. Upon seeing the newest arrivals, Bernard clapped his hands once and rubbed them together. "Now that everyone is here we can get started."

Chic, propped up in his bed, smiled and looked at those in his room. "I can't believe I'm going to be in the hospital over Christmas."

Bernard, reaching into his suit coat extracted an envelope and handed it to Chic. "Maybe this will make you feel better."

Chic took the envelope and noticed his name written very neatly across the front. *Chic Brumly.* Slowly opening the envelope, he stared in disbelief at the check as he removed it. Looking around the room, Chic announced. "I can't belief this! A check made out to me for one hundred thousand dollars!"

Bernard smiled and pulled out four more envelopes and gestured for Conner to hand them out to the other team members. "I told all of you from the beginning if you helped me to bring down the three men who killed my daughter you would be rewarded with one hundred thousand dollars each. You kept your end of the deal, so now it's time for me to pay up. It gives me great joy to hand out these checks. Since I no longer have my wife or my daughter when it comes to Christmas my gift giving is limited to Conner and Mae. This is the best five hundred thousand I've ever spent. It has been worth every penny to see the men who were responsible for my daughter's death to suffer the consequences for their past actions. Merry Christmas to you all!"

Shelby opened her envelope, stared at the check and then spoke, "I feel bad. I didn't think to get you anything for Christmas."

"That's where you're wrong Shelby," said Bernard. "You have, each of you, given me the greatest gift I have ever received; the knowledge that Miles Gaston, Tim Durham and Brad Schulte finally got what was coming to them. We set out at the beginning of this process with the idea in mind we would in the end make their lives a living hell and we have succeeded. Tragically, Gaston and Durham are no longer with us. I suppose it's just as well. They would have spent the remainder of their life behind bars."

Melvin held up his unopened envelope and pointed out, "I don't want to be the bearer of bad news but the outcome of our efforts as far as Brad Schulte is concerned still remains up in the air. I just got back from St. Louis earlier this morning. Schulte's lawyer showed up last evening and after meeting with his client, informed us the mayor would no longer be answering any further questions unless without legal counsel present. As it turns out Schulte was held overnight and is to be arraigned in St. Louis later this morning. Detective Gleeson, who is heading up the investigation in St. Louis, said following the arraignment Schulte would be assigned a court date, that would probably take place sometime this coming April. Oliver P. Cranston, Schulte's lawyer, is going to push for a change of venue for the future hearing. He'll no doubt want the proceedings to take place in Pittsburgh where the mayor has many important and political ties. There is already a rumor the State of South Carolina will push for the hearing to take place here in Beaufort. I think that may be a real possibility since the three murders involved took place in this county."

Carson folded his envelope and placed it in his coat. "If Schulte is not brought to court until April that means he and his lawyer will have nearly four months to prepare for his defense. That's quite a bit of time and a lot can happen between now and then."

Nick agreed. "That is a lot of time, and I for one still have a concern about Schulte's men coming down here. We're not out of the woods yet. According to the letter the archbishop left behind, Miles death was at the hands of Schulte or his men. We already know for a fact his men were the ones who attacked Chic. I don't want to walk around on pins and needles for the next few months while Schulte has an opportunity to wiggle out of the dilemma he finds himself in."

"To be honest, I don't think we'll have anything to worry about," said Melvin. "In my past experience once someone is arraigned, that places them directly under the microscope of the law. Schulte and his lawyer will be too busy trying to figure a way out of the mess he finds himself immersed in. Schulte won't want to do anything that will cast even more of a negative light on him. I have no doubt he'll make bail at the arraignment, which means he'll be on a flight later today back to Pittsburgh. Gleeson told me Detective Fineburg from Pittsburgh is going to push for Schulte's passport to be handed over and he not be allowed to leave the State of Pennsylvania. If that happens the same restrictions could very well be assigned to his men. I'm not saying we shouldn't be careful, but the pressure now is all on Schulte. His world is rapidly unraveling. Fineburg also informed me the word about Schulte's arraignment is spreading around Pittsburgh like wide fire. The Democratic Party in Pennsylvania is having a field day while the Republican Party is trying to figure out what they are going to do. Right now, the word is they are considering suspending Schulte as a candidate for the next governor. All in all I would suggest we try our best to enjoy what's left of the holiday season. And, if there is nothing else, I think I'll be on my way back out to Dataw. My wife has a rather large dinner planned for tomorrow. She has a lot of guests coming to our home and I've been told I've got a lot to do to help her get ready. By the way, if anyone here would like to drop by, do so, by all means."

Carson started for the door and announced. "I'd love to drop by your house but I have to drive over to Charleston and grab a flight to Canada. I'm going to be spending Christmas day with my sister Emily." Shaking Nick's hand, he winked. "My sister thinks quite a bit of you. You must pay her a visit again sometime…maybe in the spring."

Nick smiled and thought about his grandmother. Returning the handshake, he responded, "Tell Emily I said to have a Merry Christmas and I'll most definitely consider coming up next spring."

Turning to Shelby, Nick explained to Conner, "Well, I guess I'd better get Shelby back to her place, then I'll head back out to Fripp. I'll be having dinner with her family tomorrow."

Chic frowned. "Well, all I can say is I hope you all enjoy your delicious meals tomorrow, while I'll be here struggling through a hospital dinner, which if you have spent any time in the hospital, then you probably already know it's not like dinning at a four star restaurant."

"That's already been taken care of," promised Bernard. "Mae is an excellent cook and she is going to prepare a Christmas feast for Conner and myself. So, tomorrow around one 'o'clock Conner will be delivering a five course turkey dinner here to the hospital for you." Tapping Chic lightly on his bandaged arm, he remarked, "Enjoy yourself. And when they finally release you if there is anything you require don't hesitate to give me a call." Conner turned the wheelchair and started to move it toward the door when Bernard waved. "Merry Christmas to everyone!"

Outside, sitting in the Buick, Nick placed his envelope in behind the sun visor and asked, "So what plans do you have for your hundred thousand?"

Shelby removed the check again from the envelope and waved it in the air. "This is going right into the bank for Kirby's education."

Backing out of the parking spot, Nick reminded her, "Didn't you mention Harold's parents were interested in paying for Kirby's college education?"

"I haven't forgotten that and in the future I may consider allowing them to do so, but for now, I'd like to save up enough so if necessary, I can send her off to school myself. What about you? What with all the money your grandmother left you, why, you don't even need an extra one hundred thousand."

Turning onto Ribaut Road, Nick laughed, "One can never have too much money. I think what I'll do is open an account for my painting business. I'm going to have a lot of expenses getting the Yeats house up and running. Who knows, I may purchase a van or two, maybe hire some employees. There is a lot of painting work that always needs to be done on Fripp homes. I'll have to think about it, but right now I need to get you back home. Then I have to stop and grab a bottle of spiked eggnog for tomorrow. I think I'll just spend the rest of the day taking it easy."

After dropping off Shelby, Nick drove to Lady's Island, stopped at the liquor store and purchased his spiked eggnog, then headed down the Sea Island Parkway to Fripp. Driving along he thought about what Melvin said in regard to Brad Schulte and the fact the man might never serve a day behind bars. Maybe he would get off and for the second time in his life walk away from the murders of Abigail James and Chester Finch. If the letter Tim Durham left behind didn't hold up then Schulte might not be convicted of Miles Gaston's death either. If Schulte got off, it would only be temporary. Bernard had waited twenty-seven years to date and now it looked like those who murdered his daughter were getting their deserved punishment. Gaston and Durham were dead and gone while

Brad Schulte still walked the face of the earth. If Schulte did manage to get off, eventually somewhere down the line; be it months or possibly years Bernard would put into effect his Plan B. Brad Schulte didn't realize it, but if he was not sent off to prison, death awaited him; a death he'd never see coming. Crossing the Fripp Island Bridge Nick shook the thought of Bernard's Plan B off. He felt uncomfortable just thinking about how Schulte's number was up. Schulte just didn't realize it.

Parking the Buick in the garage, he didn't feel like sitting around and doing nothing. Then, he noticed the special can of white paint he had purchased for the fountain. Walking out of the garage he looked up into the clear blue sky. The sun felt good and he knew at that moment what he was going to do. He'd grab a couple of beers and enjoy the afternoon out in his front yard cleaning and painting the fountain.

Fifteen minutes later, dressed in an old painter's pants and a cut off sweatshirt he took a swig of beer and then started to scrape away the old chipped paint from the concrete fountain. He was only a few minutes into the job when he was interrupted by a voice, "Merry Christmas, neighbor!"

Turning, Nick saw Genevieve crossing the yard. Holding up the metal scraper, he responded, "Merry Christmas."

Placing her hands on her hips, she asked, "And this is the way you spend Christmas Eve…cleaning up that old fountain? I bet you haven't even put a tree up…have you?"

"No, I haven't. To be honest I haven't had the time. It's hard for me to get in the Christmas spirit. It's too warm and there isn't any snow."

"If your grandmother were still around, she'd have the house decorated, she'd be baking cookies and she'd always have a Christmas Eve gathering at the house. Are you even going to have Christmas dinner somewhere?"

"Yes, I'm not a complete scrooge. I'll be spending Christmas at Shelby Lee's house with her family."

Walking over, she touched the edge of the fountain. "I'm glad you're taking care of this monstrosity. Like I told you before. Amelia loved this fountain and always took great care of it. By the way, Grady Phillips sold his place for just over three million."

"That was quick," said Nick. "He just put the place on the market about a week ago. Houses down here on Fripp normally don't sell that fast."

"Grady told me a wealthy businessman from up Boston way bought the place without blinking an eye. I sure am going to miss that house."

Nick started to scrape away some paint but then stopped and asked, "You sound like you've been there before…I mean inside the house."

"Many times. You see, a lot of folks don't know this but Grady and I had a special relationship. I was much older than he but we just got along so well. Back in his racing days I used to keep an eye on the house for him."

Suddenly, it hit Nick. "Wait a minute…just wait a minute! When Carson first told me about Grady Phillips he told me Grady had a relationship with an older woman. Don't stand there and tell me it was you?"

Genevieve returned a wide grin while Nick shook his head and stated with doubt. "Ya know, that whole story about Grady and the fact there is four million dollars worth of stolen diamonds hidden here somewhere on the island is hard to believe."

Genevieve backed away from the fountain and gave Nick an evil smile. "Well, you just never know. I may or may not be the woman Grady was involved with and as far as those diamonds are concerned, they may be hidden here on the island and they might not be." Winking at Nick, she retreated back across the yard. "Merry Christmas Nick. Enjoy tomorrow in Beaufort."

Watching the old woman cross her yard and then disappear around the side of the house, Nick was left in a state of bewilderment. He didn't know whether to believe her or not. Finishing off his first beer, he went back to his scraping.

Two hours passed when Nick found he had the top left to clean before he could begin to apply paint. It was nearly three o'clock and the top tear was going to be the most difficult part to scrape. *Screw it,* he thought. He was done for the day. Placing the scraping tools and the unused paint and brushes back in the garage, he decided on a short walk on the beach, then maybe some TV time with a sandwich and then he'd hit the sack. Tomorrow was Christmas and it was going to be a long day.

Heading for the beach he thought about Amelia and how Carson was going to go up to Canada to spend the holiday with her. He smiled and continued to think about her; about how she probably had her Canadian A-frame decorated for Christmas and how she was probably baking cookies. He hated the thought Shelby Lee would never get to meet her, but that's the way it was.

He awoke Christmas morning just after six o'clock, took a refreshing shower, threw on a robe and went downstairs to make a pot of coffee. He didn't have to be at Shelby's until noon so he had almost five hours to kill before the drive into Beaufort. Following an hour of the local news, he threw on the same clothes he had worn while cleaning the fountain, grabbed a cup of coffee, went out to the garage and decided to fire up the golf cart. He hadn't been to his new rental property for quite a few days. He wanted to stop by and make sure everything was okay. Come Monday morning he had to get back to work on the place if he wanted to put the house up for rent by springtime.

Pulling out onto Tarpon Blvd. there was not a car or golf cart to be seen on the road. Minutes later, he made a right on Deer Lake Drive and seconds later pulled up in front of the house. Two deer grazed in the woods at the left of the house. The golf cart Mrs. Yeats had included with the sale of the house was still there beneath the elevated house. Walking up the steps he was glad his cart had survived the golf cart thieves. Following a quick walk-through and deciding everything was as it should be, he walked out the front door and locked up. Sitting on the porch swing he decided it was time to call his grandmother.

On the ninth ring Nick was just about to end the proposed call when Amelia picked up. "Hello."

"Emily…it's Nick. Merry Christmas!"

Amelia answered with her usual enthusiastic attitude. "Nick…I was wondering if I'd receive a call from you today."

"Well, since I can't be there with you for the holiday I thought I'd give you a ring. It seems odd to refer to you as Emily."

"I know, but that's just the way things are. How is my old friend Genevieve getting along?"

"She's doing fine. I think she's a little upset because Grady Phillips is moving up to the Smokies. Were you aware she has had a relationship with Grady for years?"

"Yes, and I was probably the only person on the island who knew anything about that. Promise me you'll keep an eye on her for me. She was always such a good friend to Edward and me. Are you going to be spending any time with that girl you've been seeing?"

"Yes, as a matter of fact later this morning I'll be heading into Beaufort to have dinner with she and her family."

"Sounds to me like this relationship is getting serious."

"It's not that serious. We seem to just get along well. I understand Carson will be rolling in there later today."

"Yes, actually he is scheduled to arrive here in about an hour. I'm having a large buffet Christmas dinner here at the house. I've invited some of the locals over. I'm looking forward to a wonderful day. I wish you were here."

"I was thinking of coming up next spring. Maybe we can hike around the lake behind your house."

"I'd like that. Listen…someone is at the door. Probably one of my neighbors. I've got to go. Enjoy your day in Beaufort."

Putting his cell phone back inside his pants' pocket he walked back down the steps to the golf cart. Since he had a couple hours to kill he decided to drive around the island. Passing his house he continued on to the turnaround at Skull Inlet. Parking, he climbed out and walked the short distance to the stone wall that shielded the beach where Abby and Chester had died. Climbing the wall he stared down at the small enclosed beach. The beach probably wasn't that much different back then; the same boulders, the same beach. Sitting at the top of the rock wall he stared out across the inlet. Everyone who had been on the beach that night twenty-seven years in the past was dead except for Brad Schulte *and* since Schulte was the only witness alive who knew exactly what actually happened, the possibility the truth would never be uncovered could wind up being a reality. There was no one left to dispute whatever story Schulte came up with. He watched as a lone fisherman slowly guided his small boat up the inlet. Thinking the man might see him, Nick waved. The man returned the wave when Nick got up to leave. Time to go back to the house and get ready to go to Beaufort.

At 11:15, the security guard waved a hello to Nick just before he crossed the Fripp Island Bridge. The Sea Island Parkway resembled a ghost town while he cruised along at fifty miles an hour. Nothing was open. There were no cars parked at Johnson's Creek, The Gay Fish Company, The Shrimp Shack or one of the many fruit and vegetable stands that lined the road. Frogmore was equally desolate, the only business open, a gas station. By the time he arrived at the Woods Memorial Bridge he hadn't passed ten cars during the twenty-minute drive. Downtown Beaufort was minus any of the numerous customers that flooded the café's and shops. All the restaurants were closed. Even his favorite candy store, The Chocolate Tree was closed.

Arriving at Shelby Lee's, he parked the car, grabbed his bag of gifts and the spiked eggnog, bounded across the walk and up the porch steps. He no sooner rang the doorbell when he heard Kirby's excited voice, "Nick…I betcha that's Nick!" Within seconds the front door was opened and there stood Kirby: Denver Broncos sweatshirt, embroidered jeans and high top, bright pink fashionable sneakers. "Nick…come in! The house smells so good. Grandma has four pies in the oven right now and one of them is blueberry…your favorite. Give me your bag and I'll put the gifts beneath the tree."

Shelby came to Nick's rescue. "I'm so sorry. All she has been talking about this morning is that you're coming to dinner."

"That's all right," said Nick, "There's nothing wrong with abundant Christmas spirit." Handing a brown paper bag to Shelby, he explained, "Here's your dad's spiked nog. I've kept in in the fridge over at my place but it may have warmed up on the drive in."

Handing the nog to Kirby, Shelby ordered, "Take this into the kitchen and put it the refrigerator." Leading Nick by the hand, Shelby led him into the living room where her father was watching a football game while he relaxed in his recliner. "Dad, Nick is here. I'm going to leave him here with you while we three girls put the finishing touches on dinner. "Turning to Nick, she offered, "How does a cold beer sound?"

Nick seated himself on the end of a couch and answered, "That sounds good."

Ralph raised his empty bottle. "I'll take another also."

Nick admired the Christmas tree and remarked, "The last and the first time I was here at your house I helped put that tree up and I see it's still standing."

Kirby, stepping into the room, carrying two beers overheard what was said and added, "I water the tree every day. If it was up to me we'd keep it up year round."

Handing out the drinks she retreated back toward the kitchen, commenting, "Gotta go. I have to peel some potatoes."

Mr. Pickett sat his beer on an end table and remarked, "Having a tree up year round is not as far-fetched as it may sound. There is a neighbor lady up the street, Mrs. Bland, who believe it or not, has an artificial tree in her front picture window 24-7. She not only decorates the tree at Christmas, but Easter, Presidents Day, St. Paddy's Day, July Fourth and a lot other of special occasions. Throughout the year Kirby is always walking up the street to see what concoction of decorations Mrs. Bland has placed on her ever-present tree of celebration." Picking up his beer he pointed the bottle at the tree. "That thing has been sitting here in my living room for almost a month. If it was up to me I'd take the dang thing down tomorrow, but Kirby insists I leave it up until after New Year's Day." Hoisting the beer, he toasted, "Here's to a Merry Christmas."

Nick raised his bottle. "Here, here!"

Turning his attention to the game on television, Nick asked, "Who's playing?"

Now that his favorite topic was brought up, Ralph responded with great interest. "South Carolina and Arkansas. The Gamecocks haven't had all that great a year what with all the injuries they have been plagued with but I think they'll give the Razorbacks a run for their money. The game just started before you got here." Snapping his fingers, he went on,

"Speaking of the South Carolina Gamecocks, me and three of my buddies were down at the cafe early this morning talking about football, namely the Gamecocks. I've been getting together for years with three of my friends for early morning coffee and gossip."

Joking, Nick responded, "I always thought that was a practice for older, retired individuals. There probably isn't a fast food restaurant or café in the country where on a daily basis you find small groups of elderly people who meet for morning coffee, and as you say…gossip."

"I suppose what you say is true but my three friends and I have been getting together in the morning for years and we are not retired. We all have a few years to go before we get to that juncture in our lives. I guess maybe we're just getting a jump on our future retirements. But, like I was saying, we got to talking about football but then the conversation changed quickly to the latest news here in Beaufort that seems to be spreading rapidly. If you'll recall one of the things we talked about when you were here for Thanksgiving were two Beaufort High students who were murdered down on Fripp Island. Even though those murders occurred twenty-some years ago, up until just recently those deaths were considered a cold case." Taking a sip of beer he continued, "You know what they say about bad news travelling fast."

Nick, realizing he was on the verge of getting into an awkward conversation couldn't change the subject without causing suspicion, so he went along. "I'm afraid I don't know what you're referring to."

"Sure you do," said Ralph. "You probably don't remember what we talked about when you were here before. Remember when I mentioned the names of the three Beaufort High football players, who happened to live up the street back in 1989 and were actually friends of mine? The police felt they were somehow involved with those murders and were considered persons of interest. Despite the fact those three lads were interviewed a number of times they were never convicted and walked away, many people here in the area of the opinion they got away with murder."

Leaning forward, Ralph lowered his voice like he was sharing some sort of secret. "Turns out someone discovered some old photographs showing those three boys were there that night, I mean on the beach where those two kids were killed. During the investigation years ago the boys claimed they never saw Abigail James again that night after they dropped her off on Fripp. These photos prove they were not telling the truth. Some folders were mailed out containing not only the photos but also some other information that ties everything together. Miles Gaston, one of the three boys, was found shot to death recently at his home out on Fripp. The police, at first, thought it was suicide but with the way everything was left it now appears he was murdered. Then, on top of that, another one of the boys who is actually an archbishop up in St. Louis goes and hangs himself right there at the church office. He leaves a note claiming the third youth, none other than Brad Schulte, the Mayor of Pittsburgh, is somehow responsible for not only the death of the James girl and the Finch kid, but Miles Gaston's as well. It seems Schulte was picked up for questioning in St. Louis, was held overnight but then released on bail. He was arraigned and has a future court appearance that might take place right here in Beaufort. Everything has come full circle. It may be that this cold case is on the verge of being solved."

Nick, trying his best to tread lightly, remarked, "You said this was bad news, but it sounds to me like it might be good news."

"Yeah, I guess you're right. It is good news, far too late, but still, it's always good news when an old case can be solved. I will say this. Whoever the person or persons are that sent out those folders deserve a pat on the back."

Shelby who had entered the room hesitated and listened to the conversation. Finally, interrupting she held out two chilled glasses of eggnog. When she handed a glass to Nick, she leaned forward and gave him a look that indicated he be careful of what he shared with her father.

Thanking Shelby for the holiday beverage, Nick changed the subject, "I really haven't followed college ball much this season. I don't even know who number one is this year."

Taking a drink of nog, Ralph answered, "Alabama. It seems like they are always in the top ten year after year."

Standing directly in front of the television, Shelby announced, "We'll be eating in about thirty minutes."

At precisely twelve noon dinner was served, then an hour later, followed by a gathering in the front room around the tree where Kirby went about systematically handing out gifts. She was beside herself when she opened the gift Nick had gotten her. A brand new Denver Broncos backpack complete with a calculator, three legal pads and a dozen Bronco number two pencils. Shelby, upon opening her gift from Nick, held up a dazzling sun catcher displaying a flock of brown pelicans against a background of azure blue sky. Nick smiled when he opened Kirby's gift, a new pair of white painter's pants. Kirby explaining Shelby had told her about the ripped and paint-stained pair he wore when painting his new rental property. Nick was equally surprised when he opened the gift Shelby got for him. A designer sand dollar clock he could place over top of the fireplace mantle at his house. Nick said it would go great with the current décor his grandmother had established in the house.

The afternoon passed quickly and before they realized it, it was four o'clock. Following generous slices of pie and large scoops of ice cream, Shelby stood and announced she and Nick were going to drive down to Fripp to deliver a gift to a friend of theirs. She said she'd be probably be back home in a couple of hours. Nick didn't know what she was talking about but remained quiet when she winked at him. Moments later, seated in Nick's car, she displayed a small colorful box. Pulling away from the curb, Nick asked, "Who is this mystery gift for?"

Looking up the street, Shelby smiled. "You'll know when we get there. Just keep driving south until you get to Bernard's place."

"Then the gift is for Bernard?"

"Yes it is. I had it custom made at a little shop in Beaufort. It's from both of us, so don't act surprised when he opens it."

Crossing over onto Lady's Island, Nick probed, "Are you sure Bernard is home today?"

"Yes, I called before I suggested we drive over. He's home and said we were more than welcome to drop by for a glass of Christmas cheer. He's expecting us."

At quarter to five, Conner opened the front door of Bernard's mini mansion, wished them Merry Christmas and ushered them to the library where they found Bernard seated in his wheelchair while he stared out at the Atlantic. Wheeling around, he welcomed his guests, "Merry Christmas! Conner and I just opened a vintage bottle of wine from my collection. Please join me for a drink."

Drinks in hand, Shelby walked over to Bernard and spoke, "We won't keep you long. We wanted to stop by and give you a gift from Nick and me."

Taking the box, Bernard smiled humbly. "This was not necessary. I wasn't expecting anything from you. Your participation in bringing my daughter's killers to justice is more than enough, nonetheless, since you have seen it to be so kind as to get me a gift I will receive it with great joy."

Opening the top of the box, he stared down at the circular object and then raised his face, tears streaming down his cheeks. "This is indeed the perfect gift. This means so much to me."

Curious, Conner asked, "What it is, sir?"

Removing the gift from the box, Bernard held up the bright red Christmas ornament with raised gold lettering that read: *Abigail 2016.*

The grandfather clock in the corner of his grandmother's Fripp Island house began the long chiming that occurred twice daily. It was midnight and Christmas had come to an end. Standing at the large picture window, Nick stared out at the black ocean. He couldn't see it but knew it was out there, not even fifty yards away. Switching off the living room light he climbed the stairs and hesitated at the top landing when the clock made its twelfth and final chime. Looking down into the living room he couldn't help but notice the gift from Shelby; the sand dollar clock illuminated by a nearby night light. He smiled to himself and thought, *Life is good!*

Not quite a mile away the incoming tide along Skull Inlet slowly and methodically made its way further and further across the sand at the secluded beach, countless particles of sand moved by the force of endless gallons of seawater. Twenty-seven years had passed since the night Abigail James and Chester Finch lost their lives on the very same beach, but any trace of that night had long since been washed away. Nick crawled beneath the cool sheets and stared up into the darkness of the bedroom. He had no idea what his future life on Fripp held, but for the moment everything seemed calm. He smiled, closed his eyes and thought about something Amelia had said to him when he was a young boy: *A rising tide lifts all boats!*

ABOUT THE AUTHOR

Gary Yeagle was born and raised in Williamsport, Pa., the birthplace of Little League Baseball. He grew up living just down the street from the site of the very first Little League game, played in 1939.

He currently resides in St Louis, Missouri, with his wife and three cats. He is the proud grandparent of three and is an active member of the non-denominational church The Bridge. Gary is a Civil War buff, and enjoys swimming, spending time at the beach, model railroading, reading and writing.

ALSO FROM GARY

Lowcountry Burn

Twenty-seven year old, Nick Falco considers himself a loser. He hasn't dated in five years, his painting business is failing, he only has a few hundred dollars to his name, his van is broken down, and he is being evicted from his apartment. On top of all of that, his grandmother, whom he dearly loves, has mysteriously passed away. Now, Nick must put the life he had planned for himself behind and prepare for the new life ahead.

Seasons of Death

In the fall of 1969 a backwoods farmer and his wife were murdered by four drunken hunters. The farmer's three dogs, a horse and two fawns were also killed. Two young sons managed to escape, but were unable to identify the killers. The murders were never solved.

Now, decades later, someone has decided to take revenge by killing one person every season in a manner that shocks even the most hardened law officer.

In the small town of Townsend, Tennessee, the four-man police force begins the daunting task of solving the murders.

With vivid characters and familiar Smoky Mountain settings, the reader will not be disappointed in this fast-paced thriller with an intriguing climax.

Echoes of Death

It's springtime and despite the four murders of the previous year, tourists from every corner of the country have made the journey to the Smoky Mountains. The hiking trails are packed, bumper-to-bumper traffic lead tourists to hiking trails, campsites and restaurants. Vacation season is in full swing on the peaceful side of the mountains, but then there is another murder.

Once again, there is an echo of death vibrating across the mountains...

Shadows of Death

After nearly two years and ten murders, the people of Townsend, Tennessee are still plagued with unanswered questions and hidden secrets in the shadows of the mountains.

Another dark cloud hovers over Townsend. It's the menacing Stroud clan whose actions create new problems for the police force.

Will peace and tranquility ever return to the Smokies?